"When was that written?"

Turning the page, Achier pointed to the set of small marks below the main body of text. "Eight days ago."

"This can't be," Ossgrym said. "Skar Magnol cannot have fallen so quickly. They could never have reached so far so soon."

"There were fewer ships here than we expected," Thera pointed out. "They must have gone somewhere." She took the documents from Achier, leafing through them until she found one she had noticed at first inspection, but failed to spot its import. It showed a crude drawing that she had initially taken for a map of some far-off Nihlvarian port. Now she saw a distinct familiarity in those poorly rendered lines. "This is a plan of the Verungyr," she said. "A long reach can become short if you have help. And we know our enemy is rich in spies."

"The Sister Queens," Ossgrym breathed, his gaze dark with unaccustomed fear. "Could they truly be under threat?"

"We have but one means of finding out," Thera said. Realising her statement had been spoken in a thin parody of her usual voice, she coughed and straightened. "As Vellihr of Justice, my course is clear. I must take the *Great Wolf* and sail for Skar Magnol, regardless of all hazards."

As Anthony Ryan

As A. J. Ryan

BORN

of an

IRON
STORM

AGE OF WRATH: BOOK TWO

ANTHONY RYAN

orbitbooks.net

Cover design by Ben Prior | LBBG
Map by Anthony Ryan
Author photograph by Ellie Grace Photography

Orbit
Hachette Book Group
1290 Avenue of the Americas
New York, NY 10104
orbitbooks.net

First Edition: August 2025
Simultaneously published in Great Britain by Orbit

Orbit is an imprint of Hachette Book Group.
The Orbit name and logo are registered trademarks of Little, Brown Book Group Limited.

The Hachette Speakers Bureau provides a wide range of authors for speaking events. To find out more, go to hachettespeakersbureau.com or email HachetteSpeakers@hbgusa.com.

Orbit books may be purchased in bulk for business, educational, or promotional use. For information, please contact your local bookseller or the Hachette Book Group Special Markets Department at special.markets@hbgusa.com.

Library of Congress Control Number: 2025935342

ISBNs: 9780316574624 (trade paperback), 9780316574631 (ebook)

Printed in the United States of America

LSC-C

Printing 1, 2025

For all the historians, too many to mention,
who continue to inspire these tales of mine

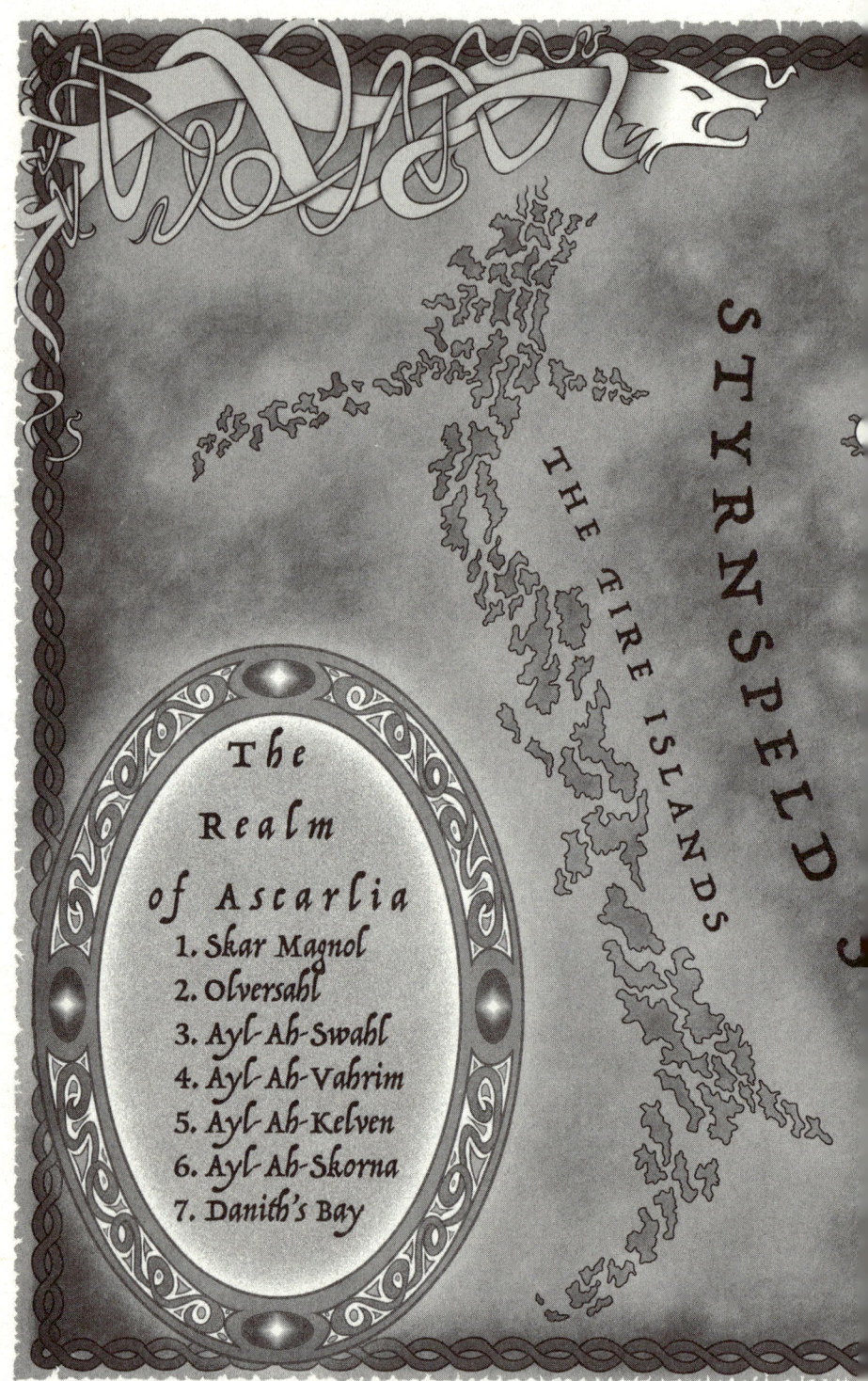

STYRNSPELD

THE TIRE ISLANDS

The
Realm
of Ascarlia
1. Skar Magnol
2. Olversahl
3. Ayl-Ah-Swahl
4. Ayl-Ah-Vahrim
5. Ayl-Ah-Kelven
6. Ayl-Ah-Skorna
7. Danith's Bay

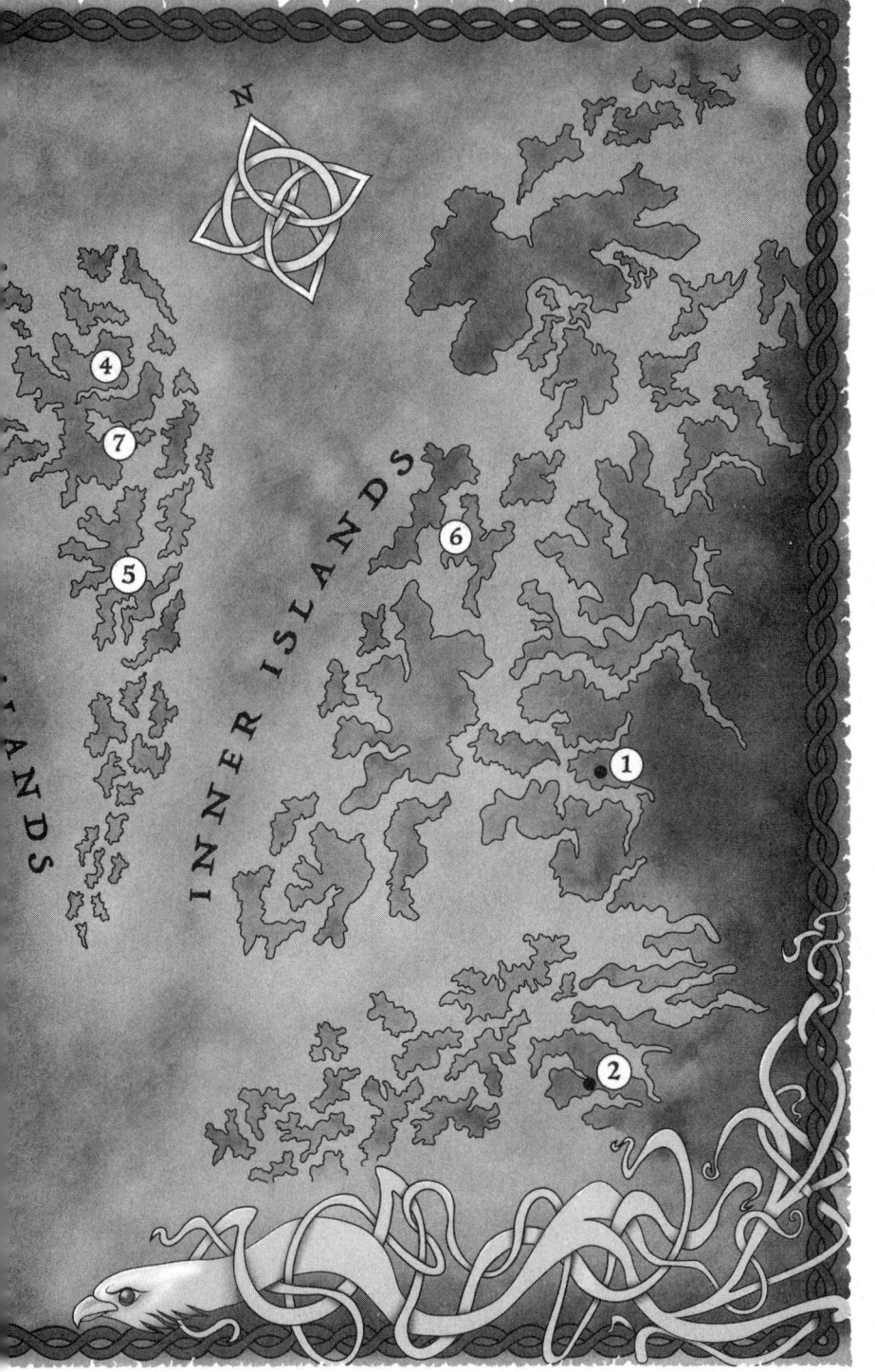

Niblvar

1. Turihmvek
2. Ossvek
3. Lyhs Skarta
4. Speltsaer
5. Lyhsmar
6. Tahrim Kyrn
7. The Ochra-Mah

TEYRACHA

VYRNKRAL MOUNTAINS

OSTAN SKARA MOUNTAINS

N

THE DEEP FJORD

The Realm
of Vorunvahl

1. Greencrest
2. Kahl Hardta
3. Raven's Nest
4. Hahl-Trova

THE SWATHE

THE CRAGGENS

THE RIVER BELT

SKYRN AGRYR

N

DRAMATIS PERSONAE

Felnir Skyrnrak Seafarer, warrior, great-grandson to the Tielwald Margnus Gruinskard, brother to Thera and Guthnyr

Thera Speldrenda Vellihr of Justice to the Sister Queens, captain of the longship *Great Wolf*, great-granddaughter to Margnus Gruinskard, sister to Felnir and Guthnyr

Lynnea Trahleyl Daughter to the slain Veilwald of the Skor Geld, Thera's ward

Achier Morvek and former slave, member of Thera's *menda*

Coelnyr Principal servant and spymaster to Margnus Gruinskard

Margnus Gruinskard Tielwald – Principal Advisor – to the Sister Queens

Ruhlin ehs Kestryg Fisherman of the Outer Isles

Berrine Jurest Renowned scholar and Skierwald at the Archive of the Sister Queens in Olversahl

Elvine Jurest Scholar in service to Sister Lore and daughter to Berrine

Hulnath Gaoler in the Verungyr

Aldunna Cook in the Verungyr kitchens, agent of the Tielwald

Guthnyr Warrior and brother to Thera and Felnir

Sygna Healer and archer, lover and trusted counsel to Felnir

Wohtin Ancient advisor to the legendary King Velgard

Colvyn Warrior and speaker of many tongues, half-brother to Elvine

Ragnalt Warrior in Thera's *menda*

Hemund The Chief Dockmaster of Olversahl, friend to Elvine

Mohlnir Ship's cat aboard the *Great Wolf*

Synghild Vyrnvest Veilwald of the Speldmeara Geld

Teylhar Master shipwright and son to Synghild

Aleida Daughter of the slain Aerling Eldryk, lover to Ruhlin

Ilvar Kastrahk Vellihr of Lore to the Sister Queens

Halkyr Warrior in Ilvar's *menda*

Hakkyn Rohnlank Veilwald of the Aiken Geld

Skahlvyr Estrynlud Renowned warrior and seafarer of the Aiken Geld, captain of the *Silver Hawk*, kinsman to Hakkyn

Obryn D'Shaine Albermaine-ish captain of the merchantman the *Northern Star*

Nahim Din Rabahs Southern seas captain of the merchantman the *Saffihr*

Tuhlan Caerith freed prisoner of the Nihlvarians, friend to Ruhlin

Julette Ahlpert Former Almerbmaine-ish pirate and freed prisoner of the Nihlvarians, friend to Ruhlin

Sygurn Freed Nihlvarian slave in Felnir's company

Iyaka Freed Morvek slave in Ruhlin's company

Behsla Freed slave and member of Ruhlin's band. Former sailing master and warrior aboard the *Sea Hawk*

Jolnyr Freed slave and member of Ruhlin's band. Former apprentice helmsman aboard the *Sea Hawk*

Ryma Orphaned Nihlvarian foundling, ward to Aleida and Ruhlin

Deyna Member of the Nihlvarian Tuhlvyr caste

Tirohk Morvek warrior, *Vakil-tuhk* (War Chief) to the *Vehlkasa* clan

Velkar Morvek elder, *Krisch-tuhk* (Chief of Wisdom) to the *Teyrak* clan

Olchar Morvek elder, *Krisch-tuhk* (Chief of Wisdom) to the *Vulksa* clan

Ossgrym Styrntorc Veilwald of the Kast Geld

Aldeyn Nephew to Ossgrym

Kahlvik Vahrimdorr Uhlwald of the Northern Shore of Ayl-Ah-Vahrim. Captain of the *Ohlira*. Renowned explorer and seafarer. Cousin to Ossgrym

Veltta Freed Nihlvarian slave in Thera's service, captain of the *Chainbreaker*

Alryhk Freed Nihlvarian slave in Thera's service, first mate aboard the *Chainbreaker*

Arnhilt Volksora Gyrwald of the Greencrest

Tulvik Warrior of the Greencrest, descendant of Arnhilt

Beyorn Warrior of the Greencrest

Ehdlur Orphan abducted by the *Ahrkun Krayl*, brother to Yuhlla

Yuhlla Orphan abducted by the *Ahrkun Krayl*, sister to Ehdlur

WHAT HAS GONE BEFORE . . .

To her most Royal Majesty, the Dowager Princess, Leannor Algathinet, from her most humble servant Edvard Baelforth, Senior Scholar, Royal Couravel Library.

Majesty, it is my pleasure to at last place in your hands the document you requested – to wit, an account of the curious and concerning events that overtook the realm of Ascarlia some years ago. Please, once again, accept my sincerest apologies for the delay in completing this task. The Ascarlians are, as you well know, a taciturn people at the best of times, especially when confronted by a foreigner seeking enlightenment regarding a subject many in that inclement land prefer not to discuss.

However, extensive travel and enquiry did eventually lead me to an individual willing to provide a fulsome account, albeit with two stipulations. The first being that his name would never be recorded and the second the provision of a large sum of silver coin. How this individual came to acquire such detailed knowledge of the events in question remains something of a mystery. He was highly disinclined towards any explanation, at times violently so. However, I have been able to corroborate enough of his testimony to regard it as at least worthy of interest, if patently incredible in places. I thought it best to present his tale in its unvarnished state and trust your majesty will forgive its occasional vulgarity and artless phrasing. The account reads as follows:

Where does this tale start, you ask? There are those who will claim it starts with the Volkrath, those heretic rebels driven from Ascarlia at the end of the Age of Discord. Some would delve deeper in time and tell you it began with the self-imposed exile of King Velgard, last man to sit the throne of Ascarlia who, weighed by guilt for slaying his brother, did take himself off across the Styrnspeld Sea to find the fabled Vaults of the Altvar. But it is a foolish tongue that speaks thus, for it begins not with fables and kings, but with a young fisherman of humble blood.

Ruhlin ehs Kestryg, his kin called him – that's 'Ruhlin the Quiet' to you, foreigner. He wasn't one for saying more than he had to, by all accounts. Given that the folk of the Outer Isles are hardly renowned as great talkers, he must have been a quiet soul indeed. There's those that claim Ruhlin as distant kin to Velgard, or some other hero of long ago, but that's all goat-shit. He was just a fisherman, orphaned and taken in by his grandmother, who raised him with the aid of Ihrkyn, her *mahkla* – one bonded to servitude by virtue of their misdeeds. Ruhlin grew to manhood in the settlement of Buhl Hardta upon the island of Ayl-Ah-Swahl, the Isle of Whales in your uncivilised tongue. A more remote and unimportant corner of Ascarlia is not to be found, yet it was here that the red-sailed ships first came with fire and blood.

What exactly occurred that day is all mixed up in wild tales and fanciful songs, but most agree that Ruhlin, seeing his best friend and grandmother slain by raiders, became . . . changed. Battle rage is well known among our people, of course, but this was different. It wasn't just Ruhlin's heart that changed, but his body. The wilder tales speak of a ravening monster possessed of strength beyond that of ten men. A monster that roared and rent and rampaged its way through the raiders, killing all he could lay his claws upon. That is, until one, a noblewoman of some kind, laid him low with a humble dart dipped in poison. But it didn't kill him. Something like him was too valuable for that. So he was gathered up and put on a ship back to their home-land, which, I suppose you know, was called Nihlvar, though no living Ascarlian at the time had ever heard of it. Would that we had remained so ignorant, but such is the will of the Altvar.

Chained and drugged to quell his inner beast, Ruhlin's only companion aboard the ship was a fellow islander, a girl about his own age named Mehlga. She was given to voicing many strange allusions to events that had not yet come to pass. Thinking her driven mad by her ordeal, Ruhlin gave her tales no credence until the day she told their captors she had something to tell their mistress. Conveyed to the deck, Ruhlin was amazed to find that the ship sailed through the heart of the Fire Islands, a barrier long thought impassable by the Ascarls. There, the air stinks of sulphur and the sundered mountains spew so much molten lava into the sea that it boils. The mistress of the ship was the same woman who had laid Ruhlin low with a poison dart. Her name was Angomar, and she held the Nihlvarian rank of Aerling, a person of property and influence. At this juncture, Mehlga paused to say this to Ruhlin: "You can trust the Aerling's daughter."

The words were meaningless to him and he watched in confusion as Mehlga approached Angomar, leaning close as if to impart a secret. Whatever words she spoke were lost to Ruhlin's ears, but they caused such a shock to Angomar that she failed to respond when Mehlga took hold of her and pitched them both over the side, there to perish in the boiling waters. Ruhlin was instantly set upon by the ship's vengeful crew, causing a return of his monstrous state, but only briefly before the drugs once again took hold and dragged him into sleep.

He awoke days later to find himself in a Nihlvarian port laid at the feet of Angomar's brother, Eldryk, another Aerling. Taken to Eldryk's underground holdfast deep in the Vyrnkral Mountains, Ruhlin found himself caged along with other captives. Some were Nihlvarian, but others hailed from more distant shores, including a Caerith warrior named Tuhlan, and an Albermaine-ish pirate named Julette Ahlpert. Ruhlin learned they were being trained to fight in the Meidvang, a spectacle of combat held in honour of the Altvar. Befriending Tuhlan and Julette, Ruhlin resolved to escape, despite the assiduous scrutiny and cruelty of Eldryk's giant overseer, Radylf. Ruhlin also gained the notice of a young maiden named Aleida who, he learned with considerable interest, was the Aerling's daughter.

There are others who stand tall in this tale, Thera Speldrenda for one, known as the Blackspear. As Vellihr of Justice, she was one of the most trusted servants of the Sister Queens, beholden most of all to Sister Iron, long our shield against enemies without and within. At the dawn of what became known as the Age of Wrath, Sister Iron dispatched Thera to the port of Skor Hardta, there to bring justice to Kolsyg Ehflud, the Saltskin, Veilwald of the Skor Geld. Having fallen to madness, Kolsyg had desecrated the barrow of Gythrum Fihrskard, the Dreadaxe, who sits highest in the annals of Ascarlian warriors. Not content with stealing Gythrum's fabled axe, Kolsyg had also slain a number of his kin. Answering only with ravings when Thera called him to account, her judgement was swift. Kolsyg died with her famed black-pointed spear, pinning him to his chair while all the kin arrayed in his hall looked on and raised neither blade nor word in his defence.

Temporarily appointing a man named Rolnar Tarhrimvest to undertake Kolsyg's duties, Thera took charge of the slain Veilwald's daughter,

Lynnea Trahleyl, known as the Silentsong on account of the fact that she never spoke. Thera stated her reason for taking Kolsyg's only child was to allow her to petition the Sister Queens to inherit his lands and titles. In truth, Thera took her in accordance with Sister Iron's order. Sailing away with Lynnea aboard her warship, the *Great Wolf*, Thera noticed the maiden's curious affinity for animals. First winning the affections of the ship's vicious cat, Mohlnir, she then seemed to commune with a pack of passing orcas, much to the disquiet of Thera's sailing master, Gelmyr.

Soon after, the *Great Wolf* weighed anchor at Ayl-Ah-Kayl, the Silver Isle, where lies the barrow of Gythrum Dreadaxe. There did Lynnea make recompense for her father's misdeeds by cutting her hand to spill blood upon that sacred soil. Thera wished to return the dreadaxe to Gythrum's kin, but they refused, making her a gift of the most prized weapon in Ascarlian lore. Sailing onto Skar Magnol, Thera was obliged, against her inclinations, to meet with her great-grandfather, the Tielwald Margnus Gruinskard, the Stone Axe. Tielwald, you must understand, foreigner, is a position of high importance in this realm. The Tielwald was both advisor and spymaster to the Sister Queens, set to work in the shadows and uncover any secret that might imperil the Ascarls. Ancient and steeped in blood, Margnus Gruinskard was never an easy man to like, and Thera's dislike of her great-grandfather was matched only by her disdain for her brother, also present at the meeting.

Here I must digress to pay proper attention to Thera's brother, Felnir Skyrnrak, the Redtooth, for his role in this tale is also of great import. Thera, Felnir, and their younger brother Guthnyr, had been orphaned when their parents fell in the retaking of Olversahl, the Ascarlian port seized by Albermaine-ish villainy in times past. It was through the guile of Margnus Gruinskard that the port was wrested from the clutches of the vile Evadyn Blackheart, that most fanatic and blood-soaked adherent of your absurd Covenant faith. Although still a callow maiden then, Thera had won great acclaim in the battle. Felnir and Guthnyr, both but boys, had suffered the disgrace of capture. This was the seed of resentment between Felnir and Thera, one that grew with the years.

Under his great-grandfather's tutelage, Felnir acquired the skills of a warrior and an education in the wider world. But for a renowned misdeed, he might have followed his sister on the Vellihr's path. Sent on an errand to the mining settlement of Turon Hardta, Felnir was obliged to rescue Guthnyr from a mob of boys taunting him for cowardice at Olversahl. This led him into a duel with Volund Stolntalv, the Strongback, the son of the local Uhlwald. Still young and not yet possessed of the skills that would make him so feared, Felnir found himself outmatched by a veteran opponent. His shield shattered, he lay at Volund's mercy. It is widely believed that Volund intended to spare Felnir, having administered a painful lesson in insulting one's hosts. Yet, before doing so, he made the grave error of laughing at Felnir's beaten state. Enraged beyond reason, Felnir flew at Volund and bit out his throat, thereafter earning the name Redtooth.

Despite his great-grandfather's status, this deed saw Felnir subjected to the punishment feared by all Ascarls, even more so than death: exile. Forced to forsake his homeland and leave his cherished brother Guthnyr behind, Felnir took ship to the arid eastern lands of Ishtakar. His adventures as a mercenary in service to the great Saluhtan are many and need no repetition here. Suffice to say that, ten years later, his renown was sufficient to enable Margnus Gruinskard to persuade the Sister Queens that his great-grandson would prove useful if permitted to return.

Enlisted as a spy by the Tielwald, Felnir sailed his warship, the *Sea Hawk*, to the southern coast of Albermaine. There he rescued a fugitive knight named Sir Aurent Vellinde, a worthless miscreant and famed torturer of inmates at the dreaded Pit Mines. Felnir forced Vellinde to hand over the intelligence he had been carrying, consisting of a scrap of parchment bearing an old runic design inscribed with coded Alberic script. Seeing no more use in Vellinde, Felnir pitched him into the sea and returned to Skar Magnol, there to find himself standing before his great-grandfather in reluctant company with his sister.

The fulsome list of causes for the enmity between these siblings has never been fully set down. But it did not arise entirely from Felnir's resentment of a more celebrated sister, for the acrimony flowed both ways. Thera's ire towards her brother was birthed not from hatred, but love. As children, they had not been the only orphans in their great-grandfather's house. Sygna, ward of Margnus Gruinskard, was as fair as she was fierce, with a heart that belied her fierceness. Her love for Felnir had blossomed early, and, in his absence, closeness had grown between her and Thera, but where Sygna saw friendship, Thera saw love. Sygna's love for Felnir had not been crushed by his departure, and so Thera's for Sygna was twisted into bitterness by his return.

Felnir's union with Sygna was swift, a true love despite Thera's suspicions that her brother's actions were driven by spite. In the aftermath, their shared grievance had only festered.

During their meeting in Olversahl, an event that held far more significance than Thera or Felnir could suspect, their great-grandfather made them each a gift: a silver trinket shaped like a knot. Describing these as tokens of great-grandfatherly affection, he enjoined brother and sister to wear them close to the skin. When Thera departed for her meeting with the Sister Queens, Gruinskard rebuked Felnir for failing to return with Vellinde. After examining the scrap of parchment with its strange design, the Tielwald ordered Felnir to proceed to Castle Granoire in the Cordwain Duchy of northern Albermaine. There he would orchestrate the escape of a prisoner held in the dungeons, a prisoner bearing this design upon his skin.

Many miles away in the realm of Nihlvar, an imprisoned Ruhlin began to understand that the population of this realm was divided between the Nihlvarians and the Morvek. The land had once belonged to the Morvek, but they were now laid low by the Nihlvarians who had come across the sea in great numbers with weapons of steel centuries before. To his surprise, Ruhlin discovered that Radylf was Morvek, as was Aleida's mother.

Attempting to rouse Ruhlin's monstrous state, her father pitted him against a Morvek captive, a spindly wretch reduced to bestial savagery. Although the Morvek's violence stirred the beast, Ruhlin was able to contain it and refused to fight. Seeing this, the Morvek also threw down his weapon, suffering Radylf's whip for his mercy. Enraged, the monster awoke in Ruhlin again and he lunged for Radylf, only to be brought down by a poison dart. With Radylf distracted, the Morvek captive leaped onto his back and succeeded in slicing off a portion of the giant's ear before being speared by a guard.

When Ruhlin awoke, he found the flesh around his collarbone had been pierced by an iron ring, a vile device of Morvek magic Aleida named as a *stagna*. Its purpose became clear when Eldryk appeared in company with an older Morvek woman named Achela. One glance at the *stagna* from this woman was enough to birth a freezing fire throughout Ruhlin's body, banishing the monster and leaving him helpless. He learned later that Achela was Aleida's aunt, like Radylf, an apparently willing and loyal servant to Eldryk. He also discovered that Aleida possessed her aunt's arcane command of metal but had kept it secret.

Later, Eldryk took Ruhlin beyond the confines of his underground prison to a high point in the Vyrnkral Mountains. There he was presented to Feydrik and Deyna, two members of the exalted Nihlvarian Tuhlvyr caste. Stoically bearing their caustic scrutiny, Ruhlin deduced from their conversation that there may be more significance to his upcoming role in the Meidvang than he realised. "Before long you will stand before the Vortigurn himself," Deyna told him, referring to the dread king of the Nihlvarians, who they appeared to regard with all the awe of the most servile dog for the cruellest master. "Such a terrible waste."

Soon, Ruhlin and his fellow captives were packed into wagons and taken to the northern Nihlvarian town of Lyhs Skarta, there to fight in the first Meidvang of the season. During the journey, Ruhlin succeeded in forming an alliance with a disgraced captive Nihlvarian named Sygurn. The Nihlvarian warned Ruhlin that their chance at escape would be fleeting and, to seize it, "that precious blood of yours will have to burn".

At this same time, Thera presented herself and Lynnea to the Sister Queens Lore, Iron and Silver in the great Hall of Nerlfeya beneath the mighty holdfast of the Verungyr. During their questioning of Lynnea, it became apparent that she had no desire to inherit her father's holdings and wished to be apprenticed to Thera. Given Thera's willingness to take the maiden under her guidance, the queens agreed. Later, during a private audience, Sister Iron revealed that she ordered Thera to bring Lynnea to her due to her affection for the maiden's mother, as well as the potential uses of her unusual gifts. She also explained the curious failure of the Kast Geld in the Outer Isles to provide its annual quota of stock-fish. Fearing rebellion, she commanded Thera to investigate.

Her forces strengthened by two ships, the *Swift Spear* and the *Wind Sword*, commanded by the Vellihrs Gynheld Volksora, the Waverider, and Alvyr Kahlsten, named the Silverlock, Thera sailed for the Outer Isles. First calling in at the port of Skyrn Hardta in the southern Outer Isles, Thera met with Hakkyn Rohnlank, the Greenhand, Veilwald of the Aiken Geld. He spoke of ships failing to return from northern waters and many ill rumours upon the wind. That night, as the crews of the three ships feasted, Thera and Lynnea were attacked by an archer. Missing his mark, the assassin was swiftly killed by Snaryk, a giant dog Lynnea had befriended. Unable to identify the man, Thera couldn't discern if she or her apprentice had been his intended target.

Sailing northward, Thera arrived at Ayl-Ah-Veyn and found the settlement there destroyed and its people slaughtered. Curiously, little appeared to have been stolen, the raiders intent on only murder and destruction. Further north, Thera's small fleet weighed anchor at the port of Buhl Hardta, finding baffling evidence of Ruhlin's rampage among the ruins. Thera's scouting party returned with a survivor named Annuk, who told the tale of the island's fall. He set the blame upon the shoulders of Ossgrym Styrntorc, the Ironbones, Veilwald of the Kast Geld. However, Thera was warned by Lynnea, using the uncanny wordless communication between them, that this man was lying. When questioned further, Annuk attempted to slay Thera, only to be quickly brought down and bound by her crew.

Subjecting Annuk to harsh questioning the following morning, Thera learned that he was a spy in service to the Volkrath, that malign, partly mythical band of rebels thought extinct long ago. She also discovered the name of the realm whence the raiders hailed: Nihlvar. Distracted by the sighting of a passing ship of unknown design, Thera returned to the shed where Annuk had been held captive to find him dead, having apparently bashed his own head in. She harshly chastised Eshilde, another of her apprentices, for leaving the prisoner unattended, then set off in pursuit of the unfamiliar ship. Following Gelmyr's advice, they made for the rocky islet of Iselda's Nail. Finding their quarry at anchor, her three ships swiftly boarded it after a vicious battle. Before she could properly scour the ship for information, a fire began to blaze in its hold. Pausing only to rescue Eshilde, who had, in an effort to recover her Vellihr's esteem, ventured below decks, Thera was forced to abandon the vessel. As they sailed away, Lynnea reported the appearance of a great many more red sails on the western horizon.

Far to the south in the Cordwain Duchy, Felnir had succeeded in gaining access to Castle Granoire by means of disguise, finding the prisoner he had been sent for to be a maddened wretch with a body entirely decorated in cryptic tattoos. The man's ravings obliged Felnir also to rescue an amiable youth named Colvyn with a knack for keeping his cellmate calm. Given the man's propensity for occasionally rambling in poetic Ascarlian, Colvyn had dubbed his cellmate Wohtin, the name of the author of the Altvar Rendi, most sacred book of the Ascarls.

Escaping the castle, they returned to Skar Magnol, where the Tielwald presented both Felnir and his prisoner to Sister Lore. Also present was a young scholar from Olversahl named Elvine Jurest, daughter of the respected archivist Berrine Jurest. Having been caught by Ilvar Kastrahk, the Vellihr of Lore, at a forbidden Covenanter gathering, Elvine had been obliged to submit to service in Sister Lore's tower for fear of recriminations against her mother.

Sister Lore revealed that the intent of Felnir's mission had been to discover a route to the fabled Vaults of the Altvar. Thanks to Elvine's interpretation of the tattoos upon Wohtin's skin, that route had now partially been revealed. According to Ascarlian legend, the Vaults had been constructed by the Uhltvar, the first most blessed race of mortals who shared the blood of the gods. Abandoned for centuries, they had reputedly been rediscovered by Velgard the Exiled King. Sister Lore then commanded Felnir and Elvine to find the Vaults and bring unto her its treasures.

Guided by Elvine's scholarship, Felnir sailed the *Sea Hawk* north to Ayl-Ah-Skorna, where the great monument to King Velgard lay in ruins. During the voyage, he noticed the closeness growing between Elvine and Colvyn and warned the young rogue against any amorous intent. Arriving at Ayl-Ah-Skorna, Elvine began her inspection of the ruined monument only to be interrupted when Felnir's company was attacked by a mercenary war band. However, even the bravest and most skilled warriors would be hard pressed to contend with the battle fury of both Felnir Redtooth and his brother. While Guthnyr slew the mercenary captain and Felnir carved a bloody path through the others, Elvine came close to being captured only for Colvyn to display considerable skill in cutting down those who sought to take her.

After the skirmish, Felnir's ungentle approach to questioning his captives extracted little save that this band had been hired from southern waters by persons unknown. Their instructions had been to slay Felnir's war band but take Elvine alive. Felnir, ever a man of harsh but fair inclinations, spared his prisoners after ordering the small finger be severed from their right hands. Returning to the task of inspecting the monument, Elvine revealed an inscription indicating they should follow Trieya's Quill, a constellation that rises in the eastern sky.

Felnir duly sailed the *Sea Hawk* east for weeks until the unwelcome sight of the Fire Isles rose on the horizon. Wary of the hazardous waters but guided by Elvine's interrogation of Wohtin's tattoos, Felnir weighed anchor at a point where he espied a lone tree growing upon the shore. Going ashore, Felnir's party soon discovered a hidden doorway behind a waterfall, working it open to reveal a steep descending staircase. Venturing into the bowels of the earth, they came upon an underground city. Beyond the city, they entered a huge chamber where each of the gods of the Altvar was commemorated in the form of a great statue. This, Elvine assured Felnir, could only be the Vaults of the Altvar.

Approaching the largest statue depicting Ulthnir the Worldsmith, they found a strange, misshapen concordance of rock at its base. Enmeshed in the rock were three weapons: a sword, a bow and a spear. Fearing Ulthnir's anger, Felnir hesitated before reaching for the sword, but his brother was ever a less cautious soul and swiftly took hold of the spear. As he did so, the malformed rock dissolved into dust and a great tremor shook the vast cavern. Kodryn, Felnir's steadfast comrade since his days in Ishtakar, was crushed by a stone fallen from the cavern roof. Felnir, Sygna, Wohtin and the crewman Falk, were imprisoned beneath the falling rubble while Elvine, Colvyn and Guthnyr made their escape with the spear as the great cavern tumbled into ruin around them.

Meanwhile, in Nihlvar, Ruhlin found himself forced into the arena alongside an unarmed Sygurn and Julette. Faced with no less than ten opponents, Ruhlin allowed his rage to blossom so that he might defend his friends. Made monstrous once again, he slaughtered the other fighters in bare moments, earning frenzied acclaim from the baying crowd. After another bloody spectacle in the city of Ossvek, they were taken to Turihmvek, capital of the Vyrnkral Veld and the largest city in northern Nihlvar. Here, Feydrik, the Tuhlvyr Ruhlin had met in the mountains, held sway as governor of the Vyrnkral Veld. Before his turn in the arena, Eldryk made Ruhlin an offer: if he would serve loyally, then he would be given his freedom and Aleida would be his wife. Ruhlin refused him, but saw truth in the Aerling's prediction that his taste for blood would grow the more he fought.

Arriving at the arena in Turihmvek, Ruhlin was briefly left alone with Achela. The Morvek woman revealed that, guided by ancient prophecy, she had been secretly plotting the demise of Nihlvar for many years. "Our roles in this story were written in ages long past, though to accept one's place in history is a hard burden to bear." She told Ruhlin that Aleida had a hidden knife and intended to kill her father in the arena. She cautioned him to await the right moment before acting. "What must happen will happen."

Entering the arena, Ruhlin found that this time he had been matched against a huge bear. The creature had been tormented and abused beyond the point of madness, but proved to be no match for his monster when unleashed. Maiming the beast, Ruhlin launched himself at the box where Eldryk and the luminaries of northern Nihlvar were gathered. All the while, he expected Achela to summon the power of the *stagna*, but she did not. Leaping into the box, he saw Eldryk holding a knife to Achela's throat, only for him to be struck down by his daughter. Ruhlin killed Feydrik and painted the marble red with the blood of many others before succumbing to the exhaustion that always followed his rampages.

Slapped awake by Aleida, he saw Achela kneeling by the near dead body of the bear. At Aleida's urging, the two of them escaped the arena to the vaults below, freeing the fighters held captive there. Their chains sundered, they fled through the tunnels until confronted by the giant Radylf. Finding himself crushed in the overseer's embrace, Ruhlin failed to summon the monster again and knew he faced the moment of his death. But then the bear, now healed of its wounds, appeared to slay Radylf in bloody and fitting fashion. Looking into the beast's eyes, Ruhlin understood that its mind was now occupied by Achela. Disguising themselves in the slain guards' armour, Ruhlin and his companions stole wagons and made their escape from the arena and the city, towards an uncertain fate, but at least knowing the taste of free air.

Elsewhere, upon the Styrnspeld Sea, Thera looked upon that vast fleet of red-sailed ships and realised that all Ascarlia was now under threat of invasion. Her duty therefore lay in avoiding battle and fleeing so that she might bring warning to the Sister Queens. Rather than sail directly east, Gelmyr advised they sail north since many of the approaching vessels were swifter than their three ships. Heading north with the enemy chasing hard, they encountered one of the fierce storms for which the Styrnspeld Sea is famed. It wrecked the *Swift Spear*, sending Vellihr and crew into the embrace of Ulfmaer, god of the sea. With the storm calmed, Thera found the Nihlvarians still in pursuit, albeit reduced in number. At this point, the Silverlock proved worthy of his renown by turning the *Wind Sword* about and sailing into the midst of the Nihlvarian ships. His valiant but doomed charge bought time for Thera. But still, their pursuers came on.

Entering the more placid but still treacherous waters of the far north, where bergs as tall as mountains are wont to crush ships like kindling, the *Great Wolf* was soon surrounded by a pack of the dreaded white whales. These beasts are very different from their peaceable and easily hunted southern cousins, displaying a ferocious hatred of ships and those that sail them. Although they did Thera the favour of utterly destroying the Nihlvarian ships, with the deed done, they turned their ire upon the *Great Wolf*. It was here that Lynnea Trahleyl proved her worth beyond question. Drawing from a previously unsuspected well of arcane power, the Silentsong did commune with the white whales and dissuade them from their ravening course, leaving the *Great Wolf* in peace. Afterwards, she fell into a deep sleep and could not be woken.

Keen to bring her warning to the Sister Queens, Thera immediately headed south. Happening upon the wreckage of the Nihlvarian ships, they discovered a man clinging to flotsam. Somehow he still lived even though the chill of the water should have killed him in moments. Taken aboard, he gave his name as Achier, a Morvek slave with no love for his former masters. Thera set him to watch over Lynnea's unresponsive person. She awoke shortly after, and Thera gained a sense of mutual recognition in the manner with which Lynnea and Achier regarded one another.

Sailing on, the ship was beset by a storm of the greatest fury, robbing the *Great Wolf* of her mainmast and leaving her to wallow in the calm that followed. Rowing south, and pushing her crew to the edge of exhaustion, Thera came to the upper reaches of the Outer Isles. They made for Ayl-Ah-Vahrim, the Grey Isle, where Ossgrym Ironbones held sway as Veilwald of the Kast Geld. Sailing close to the coast, Thera discovered that the Nihlvarians had already landed in numbers, establishing a stockade around the bay where the fleet had anchored. Realising there was no help to be had here, Thera resumed the southward course, intent on finding a way through the Outer Isles and onto Skar Magnol. Yet, that night, her fate was forever twisted, for her great-grandfather visited her in a dream, telling her she must turn north once again, and seek out the Endyr's Cut on the shore of Ayl-Ah-Vahrim.

Waking, Thera felt the heat of the trinket about her neck and suspected it had been the means by which Margnus had reached into her dreams. Yet, still unsure if the dream had been no more than the conjuration of a tired mind, she ordered Gelmyr to set course for Endyr's Cut, a place he knew thanks to his old days as a smuggler. Sailing into the narrow notch in the eastern coastline of Ayl-Ah-Vahrim, they found Ossgrym Ironbones and the remnants of his war band. Having suffered defeat in a sea battle with the Nihlvarians, Ossgrym had been forced into hiding. Hearing the Veilwald's intelligence regarding the Nihlvarian stockade, Thera conceived a stratagem that might secure victory.

Ordering Gelmyr to take the *Great Wolf* to sea with what few ships remained of Ossgrym's fleet, Thera marched out with her crew and the Ironbones' war band. Moving at night and gathering strength from the scattered, vengeful islanders, they approached the Nihlvarian anchorage. When Gelmyr's small fleet appeared off shore with all torches blazing, Thera used the distraction to launch an assault on the wooden wall of the stockade. The Nihlvarians had made an error in corralling stolen cattle alongside the wall, enabling Lynnea to make use of her gift to rouse the beasts to a fury and break the wall.

Storming into the breach, Thera wielded the dreadaxe to wreak slaughter among the Nihlvarians, cutting a path to the shoreline where she saw the *Great Wolf* battling the enemy ships. Clambering aboard, Thera found Eshilde weeping as she cradled the slain body of Gelmyr. As Thera knelt at Gelmyr's side, beset by grief, Eshilde drew a hidden knife and stabbed her in the chest.

"It's been a merry dance," Eshilde said with a smile. "But all revels must end."

She drew her knife back for a killing blow, but the great hound Snaryk fell upon her before she could drive the blade home. As the beast ravaged her assassin, Thera saw Achier reaching for her before she tumbled over the side, plunging into the sea with her life's blood staining the water.

Far away in the bowels of the Fire Isles, Felnir lay miraculously alive under the rubble of the fallen statue. He retrieved the Sword of the Altvar while Sygna took charge of the bow. Wohtin, now apparently restored to sanity, led them, and the lone surviving crewman Falk, into a passage beneath Ulthnir's statue which led to the western coast of the Fire Isles. They followed him to an abandoned city on the shoreline, where lay the barrow of the exiled king Velgard.

Carved upon the barrow were a number of faces, one of them unmistakably that of Wohtin. When challenged by Felnir, he revealed himself as Angmund, once Velgard's most trusted advisor and master of arcane lore. He related his tale to Felnir, how he had followed his king into exile and how Velgard had tasked him to find a means to commune directly with the Altvar. Journeying far throughout the known world, Angmund eventually found a youth named Moyirn, who appeared to possess an innate ability to command arcane forces. Returning to Skar Altvar with Moyirn, the two of them set about fulfilling Velgard's request, a task that required the work of years. The day finally came when Moyirn stood before the king and conjured a portal to what he claimed to be the realm of the gods. However, instead of the Altvar's blessing, Velgard was instantly driven mad and his people rendered senseless. When they woke, their king and Moyirn were gone.

In the aftermath, Angmund, also suffering repeated bouts of madness but blessed with unnaturally long life thanks to Moyirn's conjuration, embarked upon a search for his lost king. Gathering lore from all the lands he visited, he had it tattooed upon his skin so that it wouldn't be lost. Robbed of many years' worth of memory by his recurrent insanity, he awoke one day aboard Felnir's ship with scant understanding of how he had got there. Now, restored to reason, he told Felnir that a kingdom awaited him across the western sea. Despite grave misgivings, Felnir resolved to follow his course. Breaking open Velgard's barrow, they found a seaworthy ship. Launching the vessel, they set sail towards an unknown fate.

Meanwhile, Guthnyr, stricken by both guilt and grief for a brother he believed slain, reluctantly agreed to return to the *Sea Hawk*. Once aboard, he took command despite the evident misgivings of the crew, and set course for Skar Magnol. Yet barely a day later, with the ship bound by fog, they were attacked by two Nihlvarian warships. In the ensuing chaos of battle, Elvine and Colvyn contrived to escape in a rowboat with the Spear of the Altvar.

Adrift upon the Styrnspeld Sea and near to despair, Elvine heard the spear speak to her: *He is lying to you.* At first, she told herself the voice was a product of her distressed mind, but then it spoke again, warning that Colvyn was not what he appeared to be. Confronting Colvyn, she learned that the voice in the spear had spoken true: Colvyn was in fact her half-brother, guided to her side by arcane visions he had received since childhood. Further to Elvine's shock, he also revealed himself to be the son of Evadyn Blackheart, slain tyrant Queen of Albermaine. Colvyn had been fathered by the Blackheart's infamous consort, the scheming spymaster Alwyn Scribe, who, it transpired, was also Elvine's father.

Unwilling to believe him, but somehow knowing his words to be truth, Elvine kept the spear close in the hopes it would impart more knowledge, but it remained silent for the duration of their time at sea. Rescued by a passing fishing boat from the southern Outer Isles, they were taken to Skyrn Hardta. There, Elvine met with Veilwald Hakkyn, now busily engaged in gathering forces to meet the Nihlvarian threat. Hakkyn gave her leave to sail onto Skar Magnol, bearing his tidings and urgent request for reinforcement.

Arriving at Skar Magnol, Elvine and Colvyn were swiftly conveyed to the Sister Queens' presence. The audience was held in the Hall of Nerlfeya, and, before the eyes of the assembled servants of the Verungyr, Elvine duly presented the Spear of the Altvar to Sister Lore. Elvine also attempted to impart Veilwald Hakkyn's tidings, but Sister Lore bade her to wait as she inspected the fabled artefact. Turning to her sister queens, she asked them to look upon markings on the spear's blade, then, striking without warning, she slew both Sister Silver and Sister Iron. In the same instant, the war band of Vellihr Ilvar fell upon those present, slaying all save Elvine and Colvyn. Stained dark with the blood of her sisters, Sister Lore spoke thus unto Elvine: "Rejoice, my wonderful child, for you are privileged to witness the dawn of the Volkrath Empire!"

Archivist's note – Sealed under order of the Dowager Princess. Disclosure only permissible under Royal Warrant.

PART I

"Mistake not the sword as the wellspring of power. For, as with the sword, power is as nothing without the skill to wield it."

Ulthnir Horuhnklehr – the Worldsmith – from the
Altvar Rendi

CHAPTER ONE

Thera

I t was the cold that saved her. Drifting towards the seabed enveloped in a dark crimson cloud, the warmth in her body seeped away with the blood leaking from her wounds. The invasive chill sent jolts of pain through her chest and skull, shielding her from the lure of sleep from which she knew there would be no waking.

Fight! she commanded herself, red bubbles issuing from her mouth as she snarled in defiance. *Kick! Get to the surface!*

Her enraged determination produced only a feeble thrashing of limbs before the cold embrace of the water drew even tighter. Of all the many frustrations that beset her in that moment, she was irked to find that it was the image of Eshilde's face that loomed largest. The cruelty in it. The resentment Thera had always known to simmer beneath the surface now flaring in those eyes, twisting her apprentice's lips into a smile of malicious enjoyment. Thera had kissed those lips, and felt only passion when she did so. Now she felt hate. She knew Eshilde was dead, brought down and savaged by Snaryk, Lynnea's faithful hound. But still, the perverse need to kill the traitor raged within, keeping death at bay for another few seconds until her starved lungs made Thera convulse and gasp for air that couldn't be gasped. Salt water invaded her mouth and choked her throat, causing yet more convulsions. She had heard once that drowning was a peaceful way to die and found space in her frantic mind for an amused reflection on the ignorance of fools.

There is no such thing as a peaceful death . . .

The feeling of something beneath her summoned another reflexive jerk to her limbs. She assumed she had finally reached the seabed, then felt the object move. It was large and strong, pushing her upward with repeated shoves. *A seal?* she wondered. Perhaps an orca having a game with its prey. *Unusual to find one so close to a harbour though . . .*

She broke the surface gasping, this time rewarded with a lungful of blessedly sweet air. She felt the unknown beast shift beneath her and arms envelop her chest, legs kicking frantically against the back of her thighs. "Rope!" a voice called out in a loud sputter. "Throw the rope!" it shouted, heavily accented but familiar. *Achier.*

A wave of fatigue swept through Thera, causing her to sag in Achier's arms. "Hold on!" he hissed into her ear. "They're coming . . ."

But she could no longer find purchase on this world. Sensation leached from her body, taking even the cold with it to leave behind a dominating numbness and a desperate desire to sleep the un-waking sleep. This time she was saved by a bark, Snaryk's massive head poking from the water to deliver a loud, urgent rebuke directly into her ear. It pained her enough to keep the sleep at bay.

She was dimly aware of a splash nearby as another body plummeted into the water from the ship above, more arms encircling her limp form. A rope looped around her chest, drawing tight before Thera felt herself hauled from the water. More hands dragged her over the rail then came the hardness of the *Great Wolf*'s deck against her back.

"Two wounds," a voice said as her leather armour was quickly peeled away. "Deep. Not sure they can be stitched . . ."

"I can stitch them." Achier again, his voice imbued with a hard authority she hadn't heard before. "I was a healer," he added, Thera imagining him confronting an array of doubtful faces. She flapped a hand, trying to indicate that they should listen to the Morvek, but she was already being lifted. She felt a marginal increase in warmth, nose filling with the familiar scents of her shelter aboard the *Great Wolf.*

"Going to get blood all over my furs," she groaned, the words too faint to escape her lips.

"Out!" she heard Achier snap. "I need room and quiet to do this."

"She'd best not die, foreigner," another voice warned, Thera recognising the hard, gruff tones of Ossgrym Ironbones. "Or rest assured your life will be forfeit."

Didn't think he liked me that much, Thera thought, the chill returning as her sodden undershirt was cut away. She shuddered at the feel of deft fingers probing her wounds, then heard Achier's voice close to her ear, the words delivered in a soft, apologetic murmur: "This will hurt very much. I am sorry."

Hurt? Thera wanted to laugh. *You think I don't know hurt . . . ?*

All thought fled when Achier pressed a hand to each of her wounds and fire flooded into them. Thera would have screamed if her jaw hadn't clamped shut as every muscle and tendon in her body tightened. Her back arched, spine strained so much she felt sure it would shatter. She could feel the fire sealing the holes in her body, seared flesh puckering and melting into a seam, staunching the blood. Thera didn't know how long it took, the monstrous pain robbing her of any sense of time.

When finally the fire burned out, she slumped into her bloodstained furs, twitching in mingled shock and relief. Still, she couldn't move beyond a limp flexing of her hands. Her wounds still ached, but the agony had faded, leaving behind a dull persistent throb until, abruptly, it flared into a sharp pain. Finding to her surprise that she could see, Thera blinked and saw Achier working a needle and catgut through the edges of her uppermost injury. It was an unnecessary act since the wound, although livid and angry, was now completely sealed. The one Eshilde had delivered to the spot just below Thera's ribcage was also closed.

"Sorry," Achier apologised again. "For the sake of appearances, you understand."

She recalled then her first sight of this man, a small figure clinging to wreckage bobbing on the icy northern seas, suffering a weight of cold that should have killed him. "That's how . . . you survived . . ." she grunted, her voice annoying in its smallness. "Your fire . . ."

"Sleep now," he said, snipping off the last stitch to her upper wound and starting on the other. "You must rest."

She felt an urge to object, since the spectre of the endless sleep that had almost claimed her loomed large. But it seemed that the mere mention of rest was enough to summon her surrender.

"Could you . . . do the same . . . for Eshilde?" she muttered as she fell into the welcoming void. "I so much want . . . to kill her . . . myself . . ."

In her dream she was back on the *Great Wolf*'s deck, crouched alongside Eshilde as they regarded Gelmyr's corpse. The *Johten Apt*'s features were set in the same frown of incomprehension Thera remembered. At the time, it had been baffling. Now she knew the cause.

"I stabbed him in the back first," Eshilde told her. "He thought he'd been struck by an arrow until I stuck him in the chest. He was still trying to ask me a question when he died with that stupid look on his face." She laughed, the sound that of a child discovering the delights of cruelty. "Stupid old bastard. I do wonder what he was trying to ask, though."

"Why," Thera said. "He wanted to know why. As do I."

Eshilde laughed again, although this time it was different, coloured by a note of tired resignation. A stiff, icy wind gusted from the sea, tousling her braids as she shook her head. "You know why, Thera," she said. "You know why I pounded that weakling's skull to mush in Buhl Hardta. And why I killed the captain of that slave ship at Iselda's Nail. It was always there for you to see, but you chose not to. Despite years administering justice to the dregs of Ascarlia, at heart, you remain a trusting soul." She gave a tight, wincing smile, a friend imparting unwelcome advice. "It will be your death one day."

"Whereas yours comes now," Thera growled, readying her spear for a thrust. Yet her hands would not obey. The chill wind had grown fiercer, cutting through armour and skin with unnatural ease to birth a deep tremble in Thera's core. The spear slipped from her grasp, clattering to the deck. She sank to her knees, rendered helpless by the cold.

"You think you won something here?" Eshilde asked, jerking her head at the destroyed Nihlvarian stockade on shore. "All you've done is prolong the agony, like a condemned soul who continues to kick even as the noose draws ever tighter . . ."

Letting out a wordless grunt of rage, Thera lunged for the spear, intending to thrust it through this traitor's torso and enjoy her last few seconds of agonised life. But, when her hands closed on the haft, hard wood became soft wool and she awoke to find herself clutching a blanket.

Calm! A warm hand on hers, lowering the blanket to reveal Lynnea's face. Her brow was drawn in concern, sapphire-hued eyes wide as they roved Thera's face and body. The rapid thud of her heart slowed at the maiden's touch and she lay back on a bed of soft furs, the absence of matted hardness making it clear some kind soul had seen fit to replace the stained bear pelt. Thera's eyes flicked around the shelter, noting that they were alone. From outside, she could hear the chorus of hammer and saw that bespoke many hands at work. *Repairs*, she concluded.

"How many . . ." she began, her words ending in a parched rasp. Lynnea put a flask of water to her lips, and Thera drained the contents in a few gulps. "How many ships did we lose?"

Lynnea put the flask aside and shifted closer, Thera hearing the maiden's voice in her head after a pause for consideration. *A few boats only. We took more than we lost, but many need work before they'll sail again. Some were lost to the flames. A few managed to escape.* Lynnea shrugged her slender shoulders. *Such is war, I suppose. It turns out to be a good deal more random in nature than I thought.*

"War is a storm," Thera said, one of her great-grandfather's oft spoken nuggets of wisdom. "Once unleashed, it cannot be controlled, only survived if your hand is skilled enough."

A fresh bout of chills swept through her, the sensation made worse by the heat that came from her sealed wounds. They felt like two hot coals sizzling on a patch of ice.

Calm, Lynnea repeated, lying down next to her and pulling the blanket over them both. Her arms encircled Thera's shoulders, drawing her close. She wore only a loose shift and the warmth of her body soon banished the chills, the fiery heat of Thera's wounds abating. *Do they hurt?* Lynnea enquired, touching a tentative finger to the stitches on Thera's chest.

"They . . . burn a little. It's not too bad." Thera put an unsteady hand to Lynnea's chin, raising it so their eyes met. "You knew what he could do, didn't you? Back when we first found him, you sensed it."

Lynnea's lips curved a little in chagrin. *I didn't know the nature of his power. But yes, I felt it. As he felt mine. Sometimes that's how it is. Other times not. My mother said there were ways to hide it from others like us, but she never taught me how.*

Thera frowned in self-reproach as more memories of the night before crowded her head. "Your leg," she said, pulling back the blanket to reveal Lynnea's thigh. A bandage covered the wound, stained a soft shade of pink.

It's all right. Lynnea's hand closed on Thera's. She remembered the awful sight of the arrow that had pierced Lynnea's flesh, the blood welling around the wound. *Cleaned and stitched*, Lynnea assured her. *There's a woman in Uhlwald Kahlvik's menda skilled in healing. She said I was lucky. Just a hair to the left and the arrow would have cut a vein that would've seen me dead in seconds.* She gave a small grimace. *It's hard to walk, though.*

"Achier. He can heal you as he did me . . ."

No. A stern note coloured Lynnea's thoughts, blue eyes hardening. *He has risked much healing you. To do so again so soon would invite discovery. Besides, not all wounds can be sealed by his fire and he has no power over sickness.* Her face softened and she drew Thera close again. The feel of her aroused a curious mingling of intoxication and comfort, also a sense of connection she couldn't recall from such intimacy before now. *This is good. This is right.* She wanted to pull Lynnea closer, as close as her weakened muscles would allow, but questions still irked her.

"Eshilde," she began. "She lied. For years. You have the gift of hearing lies, yet you didn't hear hers."

It's not lies I hear, Lynnea replied, drawing back so that their noses barely touched. *It's truth. I heard the truth of Annuk's deceit in Buhl Hardta. And I heard the truth of Eshilde's anger and jealousy throughout our journey, and the hate she tried to hide. I thought it merely the resentment of spurned love and frustrated ambition. I didn't tell you because I knew you intended to send her away when our task was done.* She closed her eyes. *For which I am sorry.*

"From here on," Thera said, wincing with the effort of raising a hand to cup Lynnea's cheek, "keep nothing from me. Our road is long, and I shall need all the help you can give." Her voice dwindled as she spoke, eyelids growing heavy until Lynnea's face was a vague pale oval. Thera slipped into a dreamless slumber with the feel of Lynnea's lips upon her forehead.

"This is all we found." Ossgrym set the sheaf of parchment down on the table where Thera had seated herself. She would have preferred to stand at a meeting like this, but, despite three full days of healing, her legs retained a treacherous tendency to fold beneath her at inopportune moments.

She had gathered the captains of this small army in a large shed where the Nihlvarians had kept their slaves, the only building left intact after the Ascarlian assault. During the battle, these unfortunates had used what water they had to douse the wooden walls against the flames. Fortunately, they had been discovered by Uhlwald Kahlvik who smashed the chains securing the door and allowed them to escape. A less discerning and level-headed soul may well have left them to perish. With their masters slain or fled, the slaves had quickly formed themselves into two distinct groups. The smallest consisted of thirty or so Nihlvarians with their red-tattooed faces. These, Achier informed her, were a motley collection of thieves and otherwise disgraced outcasts condemned to servitude to atone for their misdeeds. The larger group, over a hundred strong, were all Morvek. The two factions clearly despised each other but were unified by fear of their new captors, despite Thera ordering their chains removed. Ossgrym wanted to put them to work cleaning up the stockade and gathering booty, but Thera forbade it. "Leave them be, for now. I will have words for them later."

Turning her attention to the pages, she found they bore an unfamiliar script. It resembled ancient Ascarlian but with a hard angularity and altered syntax that made it unreadable to all but Achier.

"This is a manifest of looted valuables," he said when she passed him the topmost document. "Gold, jewels and such."

"We found no such treasure," Ossgrym said with a regretful huff.

"Probably consigned to a chest aboard one of the ships," Kahlvik said. "Which means it's either sitting at the bottom of the bay or carried off."

"What else?" Thera prompted Achier, handing him the full sheaf of pages.

"A list of warriors slain in a battle on the sea," he said, leafing through the parchment. "This one appears to be a letter from the Tuhlvyr to the captain of a ship in his fleet."

"Tuhlvyr?" Thera asked.

"A person of high status," Achier explained. "It is the highest rank among the wealthy of Nihlvar. Only a Tuhlvyr would be appointed to command a force this large."

"Does this important man offer any insight as to our enemy's intentions?" Thera asked.

"He and the captain seem to be friends of old. Mostly he talks of voyages they shared and battles they fought. Also it speaks repeatedly of his love and loyalty for the Vortigurn. Probably, he was worried this letter would be read by spies before it reached the captain."

"Vortigurn?" Kahlvik enquired.

"The King of Nihlvar," Achier said, his eyes narrowing as he read on. "The Tuhlvyr also speaks of great bounty to be found in a place called . . ." he paused, hesitating at an unfamiliar name before pronouncing it with slow deliberation ". . . Skar Magnol."

The former slave blinked at the instant attention his words provoked in all present. Thera got to her feet, fists bunched on the table to prevent her swaying. "What exactly does he say about Skar Magnol?"

"It seems he expects it to have already fallen to Nihlvar." Achier blinked, disconcerted by the hard stares now fixed upon him. "He hopes to go there soon to present himself to . . ." The Morvek frowned, puzzled by the next few lines. "Someone he refers to as the Vortigurn's Ehlvyr. It's a rarely used word, meaning 'Chosen.'"

"When was that written?"

Turning the page, Achier pointed to the set of small marks below the main body of text. "Eight days ago."

"This can't be," Ossgrym said. "Skar Magnol cannot have fallen so quickly. They could never have reached so far so soon."

"There were fewer ships here than we expected," Thera pointed out. "They must have gone somewhere." She took the documents from Achier, leafing through them until she found one she had noticed at first inspection, but failed to spot its import. It showed a crude drawing that she had initially taken for a map of some far-off Nihlvarian port. Now she saw a distinct familiarity in those poorly rendered lines. "This is a plan of the Verungyr," she said. "A long reach can become short if you have help. And we know our enemy is rich in spies."

"The Sister Queens," Ossgrym breathed, his gaze dark with unaccustomed fear. "Could they truly be under threat?"

"We have but one means of finding out," Thera said. Realising her statement had been spoken in a thin parody of her usual voice, she coughed and straightened. "As Vellihr of Justice, my course is clear. I must take the *Great Wolf* and sail for Skar Magnol, regardless of all hazards."

CHAPTER TWO

Elvine

"Do all she says." Colvyn's whisper was a rapid flutter of air into her ear before Vellihr Ilvar's warriors clapped irons on his wrists and marched him away. "Take no risks on my account," he added, craning his neck to offer a parting smile she felt to be wholly inappropriate in its comforting surety.

Then he was gone, leaving her alone with Sister Lore and the warriors busily dragging corpses from Nerlfeya's Hall. Elvine tried not to look, but the sight of so many bodies trailing red streaks upon the polished floor of this sacred place was horribly magnetic. Sisters Iron and Silver were equally distracting, lying still and lifeless close to the fire so that the blood pooling around them appeared quite black.

"Never doubt the necessity of my actions, dear heart," Sister Lore said.

Elvine's gaze snapped back to the queen's gore-covered face, finding it moulded into a serious frown. She still held the Spear of the Altvar, wet from head to shaft with the lifeblood of her fellow queens. "We have much to do, you and I," Lore continued. "And no room for doubt. If you harbour any, now is the time to share, dearest one."

For a moment Elvine couldn't speak. Everything was so utterly wrong, so completely changed in the space of a few moments, that she feared the sound that would emerge from her lips might be the shrill giggle of a soul driven beyond reason. She searched Lore's face for some sign of madness, something to explain this horror. But saw only the brisk and purposeful countenance she knew so well from their days together in the tower library.

"No . . ." Elvine began, finding she had to swallow several times to complete the sentence. "No doubts, my queen. Though this is . . . unexpected."

"Yes." Lore sighed, a measure of regret passing over her besmirched features as she surveyed the surrounding slaughter. "I had hoped to fully enlighten you before sending you off on so perilous a mission, but time proved my enemy. Still—" she reached for Elvine's hand, her grip warm, that same bright smile lighting her face "—I knew from our first meeting that a mind so keen, not to say practical, would recognise a much-needed shift in perspective."

A small sputter came from the far end of the chamber, where one of the seemingly dead servants of the Verungyr began to spasm as he was dragged across the floor. The warrior holding his arms released them and crouched to drive a dagger into the man's throat. *A shift in perspective.*

Elvine's gaze shifted back to Lore's, still not seeing even a flicker of the insanity she expected. *She's mad,* Elvine insisted to herself. *She must be.*

"Might I enquire, my queen," she said, voice more steady than she imagined it could be, "as to my mother's whereabouts?"

"Hard at work translating a recent batch of foreign correspondence, I would hope. You'll see her soon." Lore squeezed her hand again and began to lead her from the chamber. "Ilvar," she called to the Vellihr of Lore as she made for the corridor leading to her tower, "be sure to search my sisters thoroughly before you burn the bodies. Then conduct a thorough inspection of their towers. Every document, regardless of how trivial, is to be brought to me."

"I'll see to it, my queen," he assured her with a grave bow. In his gaze at least, Elvine saw the gleam of a deranged mind. She had known him to be a fanatic since their first meeting, but now his fierce ardour for the Altvar shone forth as he surveyed the fallen queens. As they passed him, Elvine heard him mutter a phrase from the Altvar Rendi: "'Those who turn from the Altvar's gaze shall ever be cursed.'"

"Come on," Lore said, jerking Elvine's arm as she tugged her away. "I must hear the tale of your quest in all its glory. Then, of course, you will write an account for the archive."

Once in her tower rooms, Lore washed her face and hands in a bowl of steaming water provided by a burly woman named Lilda, a servant Elvine remembered from her days before joining Felnir's crew. She was quick to arrive at two salient realisations in recognising this woman. First, Lore must have told her to bring the bowl and washcloth before she went to Nerlfeya's Hall. The second was the fact that few of Lore's personal servants had been present for the massacre. *Planned,* Elvine thought, chastising herself for missing such an obvious conclusion. But then, her hands still shook and her mind remained a whirl of gruesome details and worry for both Berrine and Colvyn.

Upon entering the tower, Lore had set the Spear of the Altvar down upon the large oakwood table in the library. As in the chamber, Elvine found a dangerous distraction in the red beads dripping onto the polished surface from the iron head.

"Be so good as to clean that before you go," Lore told Lilda while towelling her hands dry.

"I shall, my queen."

"Although I am, of course, delighted with the fruits of your mission, dear heart," Lore said, coming to Elvine's side, "I confess myself a trifle disappointed in the treasure you brought me. I expected a gift of the Altvar to be more ornate, if not imbued with some form of blessed ability. Or am I, perhaps, missing something?" She arched an eyebrow at Elvine who spent a panicked moment wondering if it was suspicion she saw in the queen's gaze, or mere amusement.

Don't tell her! she instructed herself, the harsh certainty of it momentarily banishing Elvine's fears. *Tell her that thing spoke to me and she'll never let me or it out of her sight.*

"It appears to be just a spear, my queen," she agreed. "But I swear to its authenticity . . ."

"Of which I have not the slightest doubt." Lore laughed and began to offer a reassuring embrace, then paused to look down at the red spatter covering her robe. "I must change. Lilda brought refreshments. Feel free to partake." She waved a hand at the jug of lemon tea sitting on the table and made for her private chamber.

Elvine watched the servant wipe the gore from the spear with brisk efficiency, showing no sign that she might have felt anything more than old iron and wood. Her task done, she offered Elvine a wordless nod and departed with bowl in hand. Casting a furtive glance at the door to Lore's chamber, Elvine hurried to the spear, reaching out to grasp it, then stopping short. *What will it tell me to do?* The notion that whatever lived in this ancient thing might command her to use it on Lore caused her hand to hover over the dark wood of the haft. *It doesn't command*, she reminded herself. *It provides insight only. At least, it did before.*

Taking a breath, Elvine settled her hand on the spear. The familiar heat blossomed instantly, the heat that only she appeared to feel, and the same soft voice spoke in Elvine's mind, warm as before but now tinged with sorrow and a note of reproach. *You gave me unto dark hands*, it said.

"I had no choice," Elvine whispered back, eyes flicking to Lore's chamber door.

The absence of choice is always an illusion, child. A pause, Elvine feeling the heat against her palm fluctuate, a sensation that conveyed an impression of calculation. *She that wielded me is vile,* the spear said finally. *As poisonous a soul as I have ever encountered, made worse by her ignorance of her own vileness. She is also sharper of mind than most. But not you, child. Be wary. Be watchful. Be her trusted confidante, but trust nothing she says. Most of all, be her friend, for she has never known true friendship in all her life. It will be your weapon when the time comes. And it will come.*

Hearing the creak of hinges, Elvine removed her hand from the spear and hurried to the jug of tea. She surprised herself by not spilling any as she poured two cups.

"Now then," Lore said, striding into the library, her slender form clad in a clean white robe. "I believe it's time for your story." She accepted the cup Elvine proffered and gestured to the nearby couch. "Come. Leave nothing out. I'm especially interested in the Vaults of the Altvar. It occurs to me I should have sent an artist with you to capture them before they fell to ruin. Were they everything I imagined them to be, Elvine?"

Be her friend. "I believe they were, my queen." Elvine waited for Lore to sit, then settled herself on the couch, sipping her tea. It tasted so good she wondered if the recent sight of death had a tendency to sharpen the senses, perhaps force an appreciation for pleasures that can so easily be taken away. "They were wondrous to behold indeed."

She went on to relate the full tale of her time as part of Felnir's crew, beginning with the ambush at Velgard's monument on Ayl-Ah-Skorna. As she spoke, she studied Lore's reaction closely. Felnir hadn't been able to extract the identity of their paymaster from the mercenary prisoners, and it occurred to Elvine now that there may be more aspects to Lore's treachery than she realised. However, the queen reacted to this event with a seemingly genuine frown of surprise, and a modicum of anger, not that Elvine could trust her judgement of such things now. Less than an hour before, she had witnessed the starkest evidence of this woman's capacity for deceit. Continuing her tale, Elvine described the inscription she found on the ruined base of Velgard's statue.

"It depicted what I believed to be the constellation of Trieya's Quill. Setting our course to follow its rise led us to the southern Fire Isles. There beneath the mountains we discovered the underground city I believe to have been constructed by Velgard's followers, beyond which lay the Vaults of the Altvar. I have already told you what occurred there, and the destruction of the *Sea Hawk* shortly after."

Elvine saw the same frown of puzzled annoyance pass across the queen's face at this, accompanied by a soft mutter: "So, some things he is not content to leave in my hands."

"My queen?"

"Nothing of import." Lore smiled and waved a hand. "The *Sea Hawk*, you are sure she went down with all her crew?"

"That I cannot say for sure, my queen. The fog was thick, and battle, I have discovered, is as confusing as it is perilous."

"Yet you contrived to escape it with the aid of that handsome young Albermaine-ish mercenary." Lore's voice took on a coy note. "I assume the subsequent voyage was very . . . intimate." She evidently mistook Elvine lowering her eyes for embarrassment instead of fear. Laughing a little, she patted Elvine's hand. "It would be cruel of me to begrudge you some pleasurable distractions, dear heart. Worry not. I'll keep him safe for you. Perhaps, in time, he can be released into your very tender custody. We'll have to see."

Elvine fought down a lurch of nausea at the direness of Colvyn's predicament if Lore were to discover that, not only was he Elvine's half-brother, but also the son of Evadyn Blackheart.

"Now," Lore continued. "You mentioned earlier that you were also bearing a missive from Veilwald Hakkyn of the Aiken Geld. Please relate it in full." She listened with no indication of either surprise or dismay to Elvine's description of the Veilwald's plight. Lore merely pursed her lips upon hearing how Hakkyn's northern islands were beset by raiders, the Kast Geld appeared to have been completely overrun, and Veilwald Ossgrym slain.

"I know this must all seem very strange, even frightening," the queen said when Elvine finished. "But know this, my most cherished servant, all that has come to pass is necessary, if . . . regrettable in some aspects. I told you we stand witness to the birth of the Volkrath Empire, and birth was ever a bloody and painful business." Her face tightened into a serious intent as she met Elvine's gaze. "Soon there will be newcomers to the Verungyr, emissaries of a great people who come to aid us. You may find them fierce, uncouth perhaps, but know they are our allies, Elvine. That being said, it would be best when meeting them to make no mention of your prior allegiances. While I have always been of a more pragmatic mind when it comes to such things, our allies are different. What little they know of the Covenant of Martyrs leads them to believe it a disgusting affront to the Altvar. Within the sanctity of your own thoughts you are free to believe as you wish, but these—" she put a finger to Elvine's lips "—must henceforth speak only love for the Altvar whenever discussion turns to matters of belief. You understand?"

Elvine bobbed her head, wondering if she could really smell the blood on Lore's freshly washed hand or if it was just a product of her fear-ridden imagination. "I do, my queen."

"Excellent." Lore removed her finger and gestured to the door. "Now, you'd best go off and greet your mother. I know she's been worrying over you these past months. Be sure to pass on my regards. You'll find one of Ilvar's *menda* waiting outside to ensure your safety. We sail troubled waters these days, and you can't be too careful."

Her escort was a blunt-faced woman of muscular bearing and no inclination towards conversation, not that Elvine made any effort to speak during the long journey through the winding stairwells and hallways of the Verungyr. In her absence, her mother had been moved from her prior lodgings near the base of Lore's tower to a cell located in a damp corridor closer to the keep where Ilvar's *menda* resided. The warrior stopped at a door Elvine was surprised to find unlocked when she knocked and pushed it open. The action evidently unnerved Berrine, causing her to jerk upright from her small writing desk, scattering parchment onto the floor.

"Mother . . ." Elvine began, the words ending in a gasp when Berrine rushed to pull her into a tight embrace. All the horrors of the past few hours roiled in an instant, bursting through the dam of Elvine's reserve. She shuddered in her mother's arms, pressing her face into her shoulder to staunch the sobs. "She . . ." Elvine choked, blinded by tears. "She . . ."

"Hush." Berrine drew back, smoothing a hand through Elvine's hair, then glancing at the open doorway. "My thanks for escorting her," she told the unsmiling warrior and gently closed the door. "Speak softly," she said in a whisper, slipping into her lightly accented Alberic. She guided Elvine to the bed, holding her until her weeping subsided.

"I heard a commotion echoing in the halls," Berrine ventured, watching Elvine wipe her eyes. "What has happened?"

"Sister Lore has murdered her fellow queens," Elvine whispered in Alberic, her voice far more riven with emotion now than in Lore's company. "I gave her the spear, and she killed them both. Ilvar's *menda* slaughtered their servants. She said . . ." Elvine paused to swallow a fresh bout of tears. "She said we stand at the birth of the Volkrath Empire."

Elvine had rarely seen her mother surprised, let alone shocked. But she saw both now in her stark, unblinking stare. "Spear?" she repeated. "Volkrath Empire?"

Elvine glanced at the door, certain that the taciturn warrior would be straining to hear every word spoken. It was also possible, if unlikely, that the woman knew Alberic. "I must impart to you a long tale, honoured mother," Elvine said, switching to formal Ishtan. "But first, may I trouble you for a cup of water?"

She told her all of it, including those parts of the story she had kept from Sister Lore. This, of course, meant relating in full what Colvyn had told her during their time adrift on the Styrnspeld Sea. Berrine listened in silence as Elvine related how the spear had revealed Colvyn's duplicity, and his subsequent fulsome confession when challenged. Her mother's face took on a rigid passivity as the tale unfolded, betraying nothing when Elvine made it clear that she now knew the identity of her father. He had not, in fact, been an Albermaine-ish sea captain, but none other than Alwyn Scribe, once the most trusted servant of Evadyn Blackheart, and her ultimate betrayer.

"Colvyn said he came looking for me," Elvine told Berrine, her voice hardening a little, perturbed by the lack of a reaction. "Guided by visions he inherited from his dread mother, although he didn't know he would find a sister."

Berrine rose from the bed, moving to her writing desk. Elvine noted how her knuckles turned white as she gripped its edge. After what felt like an unduly extended pause, she muttered in Ascarlian: "I thought there was something familiar about that one when I saw him at the wharf."

"Why . . . ?" Elvine began, wincing at the angry hiss of her voice, then forcing a softer tone. "Why didn't you tell me?"

"Because," Berrine hissed back, "I knew my daughter. There are cats less riven with the curse of curiosity. If you had known, you would have tried to seek him out. And Alwyn Scribe, I believe, is a man best avoided. There are few souls in this world more gifted in attracting trouble."

Looking away, Elvine let out a long sigh. "An inherited trait, so it seems."

Berrine gave a muted laugh. "So it does." She resumed her seat on the bench, clasping Elvine's hands tight. "That wasn't the only reason," she said, leaning forward so their foreheads touched. "You were mine. All mine. The greatest gift I ever received, for which I thank the Altvar every day. Selfish, I know, but I didn't want to share you."

"I might have gone to find him," Elvine told her. "But I would always have come back. You know that."

"I do." Berrine's grasp tightened before she planted a kiss on Elvine's forehead and drew back, slipping into formal Ishtan once more. "Now, honoured daughter, tell me more about this spear you found. For I sense a great portent in its discovery."

CHAPTER THREE

Ruhlin

He was woken by the bear's growls, loud and angry. Blinking grit from his eyes, Ruhlin beheld the slatted boards of the carriage roof and enjoyed the briefest moment of calm before his body assailed him with a plethora of aches and pains. They spread from his neck to his ankles in angry progression, sharp enough to bring a groan to his lips but also banishing the dregs of sleep. Looking around, he found himself alone in the wagon, its door slightly open to permit an unwelcome stream of chill air, and the ongoing growls of the irritated beast beyond. It was counterpointed by a chorus of very human shouts, wordless exclamations of alarm for the most part, but followed by Sygurn's irate observation.

"Come on, you greedy fecker!" the Nihlvarian cried. "At least share a bit of it."

After several attempts, Ruhlin succeeded in gaining his feet. Taking up one of the furs littering the interior of the wagon, he wrapped it around himself and pushed the door fully open. The sight that greeted him provided a jarring reminder of just how altered, and strange, his circumstances had become in the space of a few months. Sygurn and a dozen or so freed slave fighters had formed a loose circle around the bear. The huge beast was hunched at the base of a tall pine, intermittently feasting on the carcass of a slain deer while casting warning growls at its human audience. Standing at the wagon's steps, Aleida and Julette watched the spectacle with an air of amused disparagement.

"Barely a scrap of food in this whole caravan," Sygurn called out to Ruhlin. "We're fecking hungry."

"So is the bear, I imagine," Ruhlin replied. He swallowed the croak in his voice and took a better look at their surroundings. It seemed the wagons had ascended a deeply rutted track to the crest of a forested hill, affording a good view of the valley below. The walled city of Turihmvek was a dim grey sprawl in the distance.

"Inside!" He stepped back as Aleida's stern, commanding visage loomed before him. "You still need to rest."

"I think I've slept enough," he protested, but allowed himself to be pushed into the comparative warmth of the carriage. He sat as she pressed a hand to his forehead, seeing her purse her lips in satisfaction. "No fever, at least. You were burning for most of the first day."

"Are we pursued?" he asked.

"If we are, there's no sign of it yet."

"How many are still with us?"

"All of them. Even the Morvek. All hungry. Tuhlan and Iyaka took bows and went to hunt, since the bear is so unwilling to share."

Seeing the troubled cast to her face at mention of the bear, Ruhlin ventured a question. "Has it . . . ?" He trailed off, unable to summon the right words. *How do you speak of the impossible?* he wondered.

"Spoken to me?" Aleida's frown shifted into a grin. "No. It disappears for hours, then comes back, usually dragging some unfortunate beast for supper."

"She did something to it," Ruhlin said, recalling the strangeness and horror of the *wuhltra*. Achela crouched at the bear's side, hands buried in its blood-matted fur as the beast gasped its last breath. Soon after, it had recovered enough strength to bite off Radylf's head with a single snap of its jaws. Then there was the awareness in its gaze, the sense of understanding that went far beyond the bestial. "You said there were old Morvek tales of those who could commune with animals."

"There are also Morvek tales of people sprouting wings and flying into the heart of the sun. Not every tale is to be believed." Aleida sank onto the couch opposite, tone softening as she gestured to his neck. "I can remove that, if you want. It'll leave a wound that needs stitching, though."

Ruhlin's hand went to the *stagna*, finding the metal cool to the touch. "Best leave it be," he said, the slaughter he had wrought among the luminaries of Turihmvek looming large in his mind.

She leaned forward to clasp his hand. "They stayed because of you," she said, inclining her head at the voices beyond the carriage door. "They believe in you. But they need a course. Not to mention something to eat."

He nodded, casting off the fur. "And I need some clothes."

Tuhlan and Iyaka returned near dusk with a brace of rabbits and a pair of wild fowl. Sygurn took charge of cooking the meal, skinning and gutting the catch with the skilful efficiency of ingrained habit. The rabbits were diced and consigned to a large stewpot he found in one of the carriages. The two fowl he spitted over the fire and seasoned with some thyme he foraged from the forest.

"Who needs your deer, you shaggy fecker?" he taunted the bear, now prowling the shadowed treeline. Its response consisted of a low growl shot through with an unmistakable note of irritation.

"I think it dislikes us lingering here," Iyaka said as they ate, gathered in a circle about the fire. In all, their company consisted of fifteen souls, all Morvek save for Ruhlin, Julette, Tuhlan and Sygurn. Of the Morvek that had been part of Aerling Eldryk's coterie of slave fighters, only Iyaka and four others remained. The rest had been liberated during their flight through the tunnels beneath the *wuhltra*. Judging by their wary, mystified frowns, and Iyaka's frequent pauses to translate the conversation, it was plain they had only a partial comprehension of their current circumstance. Yet they had chosen to stay rather than risk fleeing through the northern provinces of Nihlvar alone.

"As do I," Julette said around a mouthful of roasted fowl. "I do seem to recall talk of finding a ship when we were planning this little escapade. I, for one, have spent far too much time ashore."

"Need a port for that," Sygurn said, casting an admonishing glance at Ruhlin. "And since we've chosen to make our move so far north, it's a long trek to the nearest one."

Ruhlin thought about pointing out his lack of choice in the timing of their escape, but dismissed the notion. Like it or not, these people now looked to him for leadership, and leaders were rarely given to explaining themselves. "How long?" he asked.

"It's a good two weeks' march to Speltsaer," the Nihlvarian advised. "Probably longer, since we can expect to do a lot of hiding along the way. Roads get a good deal busier closer to the Deep Fjord."

"Deep Fjord?"

Sygurn's squint was rich in judgement of his foreign companions' ignorance. "The fjord around which the realm of Nihlvar was built. Runs all the way from the sea to the as yet unconquered Morvek lands to the west. As far as I know, no Nihlvarian has ever mapped it from end to end."

"Then a ship could carry us home," Iyaka put in, pausing to provide an explanation in her own tongue to her fellow Morvek.

Sygurn gave a grim laugh. "Going to be a lot easier sailing west than east, that's for fecking sure."

"My home does not lie to the west," Julette pointed out, jerking her head at Tuhlan. "Neither does his."

"Doesn't matter, anyway." Sygurn shrugged and spooned some more stew into his bowl. "Without a wayfinder, you'd never make it through the Smokes."

"Smokes?"

"He means the Fire Isles," Ruhlin said, recalling the bent-backed, crow-like man from the ship that had borne him to this land. "What exactly is a wayfinder?" he asked Sygurn.

"Part of an ancient guild that knows the sea like no other. They date back to the far olden days, when the Vortigurn ordered maps of his realm, but not set down on vellum." He tapped his head. "Only here, so that the secrets could be kept. Some say they carry the blessing of the Altvar since the courses they steer seem so impossible. But every one of them I ever met was a mummer and a miser. Fact remains, though, that they know their business and anyone who wants to sail distant waters must hire themselves a wayfinder, paying a hefty sum to the Vortigurn for the privilege. Only they know the routes through the most treacherous fjords and straits. And fewer still know the way through the Smokes. You lot want to go home, you'll need to find one that does."

"Such folk are likely to be found in a port, are they not?" Ruhlin said.

"Aye." Sygurn chewed stew, forehead crinkled. "But Speltsaer's likely to have only a few, and not one of the oldsters either. It's how it is with the Wayfinder's Guild, y'see. The older they get, the more secrets they learn, and the route through the Smokes is the biggest secret of all."

"Bugger these wayfinders, whatever they are," Julette stated, turning to Ruhlin. "I'll plot us a course home, dear boy. Even through the Fire Isles, if I must."

"Your home is not our home," Iyaka said, a measure of distrust creeping into her gaze.

"I promised freedom to all who joined their strength to this enterprise," Ruhlin said, attempting to imbue his voice with both decision and reassurance. "Come the morrow, we proceed to Speltsaer. There we take a ship and sail the Deep Fjord west so that our honoured friends can go home." He inclined his head at Iyaka as she related his words to the other Morvek. "Then Julette, in whose seafaring skills I have full confidence, will plot us a course to Ascarlia."

"Just four isn't much of a crew," Julette pointed out.

"Five," Aleida corrected, taking Ruhlin's hand.

"Even so." The sailor grimaced at the prospect ahead. "Navigating a fjord is tricky enough, but the open sea requires many hands working many ropes."

"Wouldn't worry about that." Sygurn sniffed. "Plenty of slaves in Speltsaer, most of 'em foreigners like you feckers. Reckon they'll be awful grateful to whoever breaks their chains. It's a decent enough plan, for want of any other." He favoured Ruhlin with a short nod. "Count me in."

"I can't force anyone else to follow me," Ruhlin said, surveying their faces. "You're free now and may go where you wish."

This heralded a short discussion among the Morvek, some of it fiercely spoken before Iyaka brought it to a close with a hard word accompanied by a fierce glower. "The seasons change," she said, turning back to Ruhlin. "To the north and west lie mountains, and the passes will soon be bound by snow and ice. To the east, the land is thick with *Rulchakin*. So we trust your word and go south to take a ship."

"Tuhlan?" Ruhlin asked, turning to the Caerith.

Tuhlan seemed reluctant to shift his gaze from the fire. Never verbose, he seemed especially reticent now. In truth, Ruhlin knew his friend's view of him had been fundamentally altered upon seeing the monster emerge. Its resemblance to a figure he referred to as the *Eithlisch* appeared to cause him deep unease, as if it offended his beliefs. Yet, like the others, he had stayed. When finally the Caerith spoke, it was in his own tongue, a question Ruhlin's minuscule understanding of the language didn't allow him to translate. But he heard the word "*Eithlisch*" among it.

Tuhlan paused, then spoke on in his broken Ascarlian: "There is great wrong in this land. Feels and smells worse even than her realm." He nodded at Julette, who replied with a mock offended pout. "I do not think," Tuhlan continued, "it will let us go easily. You are too . . ." he stared hard at Ruhlin, searching for the right word ". . . valuable."

"He's not wrong there," Sygurn said. "You are Amundyr made flesh, after all. Every Tuhlvyr in this kingdom will be vying with each other for the chance to present your captive arse to the Vortigurn."

"Why?" Ruhlin said. Although now fully aware of the power that lurked within him, the great importance the nobles of this land placed in him was still baffling.

"The blessed of the Altvar belong to the Vortigurn," Sygurn explained. "Tuhlvyr can earn his favour by finding them. I'd guess that was Eldryk's plan. Get you to do slaughter in every *wuhltra* between the Vyrnkral Veld and the capital, then bask in the Vortigurn's gratitude at the end of the journey. Might even have raised him to the ranks of Tuhlvyr, if you hadn't killed the fecker."

"I killed the fecker," Aleida said, more in satisfaction than pride.

"For which I'm sure we're all grateful, luv." Sygurn revealed yellow teeth in a smile that faded quickly. "Fact remains, we can't risk our mighty leader being recognised betwixt here and Speltsaer. There were more than a thousand eyes on him in Turihmvek, many of them who lived to tell the tale. Although . . ." He stroked greased fingers through his stubbly beard, brows crinkled in thought. "I may have a notion of what to do about that."

The bandages stank of dried blood and scraps of rotted meat. Sygurn said it was useful in discouraging prying eyes on the road south. Under his guidance, their company had taken on the guise of a merchant's caravan heading for Speltsaer. Sygurn, being the only one who could pass for a Nihlvarian of any status, donned some of Eldryk's clothes and played the role of a wealthy trader while Tuhlan and Julette became guards. Aleida and the Morvek, much to their evident disdain, were required to become servants. Ruhlin's role was that of Sygurn's brother, his face covered in bandages thanks to an unfortunate encounter with a wolf-dog some days back. Should any ask, he was being taken to Speltsaer in the hope a healer might be able to restore at least some of his features.

"People shy away from injury, specially when it stinks," Sygurn assured him. "Though, with that big bastard lumbering alongside, I reckon they'd shy away in any case."

Ruhlin peered at the bear through the gap in his mask of bandages. The beast sat at the edge of the rutted track, silently watching them prepare the carriages for the journey. Although he couldn't claim much skill in gauging the mood of such a creature, Ruhlin felt sure its slumped posture and narrowed eyes indicated disapproval.

At his urging, and much to her reluctance, Aleida had made a tentative attempt to communicate with the animal. "Aunt?" she ventured, crouching and peering into its gaze as she edged to within a few yards of where it sat. A brief baring of teeth accompanied by a loud huff had sufficed for her to beat a hasty retreat. Although the bear remained in sight of the carriages as they began their southward journey, it kept to the trees throughout the day, quelling the alarm of the oxen. On the rare occasions they met other travellers, it would fade into the deeper reaches of the forest, only reappearing come nightfall.

Most of the people they encountered were farmers taking produce to Turihmvek, all rich in lurid tales they had heard about the risen spirit of Amundyr himself running amok in the *wuhltra*. "Load of dog shit," Sygurn assured them cheerfully. "Just a Morvek slave that got loose and spilled some Tuhlvyr blood before they feathered him."

The farmers usually had food to purchase, and sacks of oats to sate the hunger of their oxen. Sygurn made a great show of bargaining down the asking price but still judged them inflated. Fortunately, Aleida had discovered a couple of fat purses her unlamented father had secreted in his carriage, so at least there was no more need to hunt for their supper.

To Ruhlin's surprise, they travelled for a week without encountering any Nihlvarian warriors. "You and that beast killed a fair few in the *wuhltra*," Sygurn explained. It was late evening, and the road stretched away into empty, lengthening shadows, allowing Ruhlin to escape the confines of the carriage. It had become a necessary habit for him to spend daylight hours inside, letting out plaintive groans when inquisitive travellers came too close. For the most part, it was a daily trial of tension and boredom, and he welcomed the chance to ride alongside Sygurn on the duckboard for a time.

"And Tuhlvyr Feydrik, don't forget," Sygurn added. "Which left the rest leaderless. Things get ugly when a Tuhlvyr dies before their time, especially when they were governor of a Veld. It's a sound wager the fecker's family will be squabbling over who gets to sit in the big chair. Such feuds can last for months. They might even start murdering each other until the Vortigurn sends a Ventra to sort it out."

"Ventra?"

"One of the Vortigurn's personal agents. Answerable only to him and bearing his authority to act in any manner that seems fit." Sygurn's face clouded. "Not folk you ever want to be within a mile of, if you can help it. In any case—" he straightened, snapping reins against the rump of an ox straying too close to the verge "—while they're all squabbling, and the poor folk raving about Amundyr's rampage, we find ourselves with a clear road. Just don't expect it to last when we get near Speltsaer."

His prediction proved accurate two days later when the forested track became both flatter and firmer, tracing a course through more open country. They saw the bear with less frequency, its shaggy bulk becoming just a vague shadow in the thinning trees, and its evening appearances became less regular. They also encountered more people, though none seemed to know anything of events in Turihmvek. It wasn't until Sygurn advised that Speltsaer now lay less than four days off that they came upon the first group of warriors. Half a dozen men and women with red-tattooed faces cantered by on horses, sparing the trader's caravan little more than a glance. Ensconced in the carriage, Ruhlin peered at them through a slat in the shuttered window, experiencing a worrying and familiar twinge at the sight of leather armour and weapons. His many aches had abated during the journey and he felt as hale and strong as ever, more so in fact.

Just six, he thought, mind crowding with visions of red ruin. His time as Eldryk's slave had instilled in him an abiding detestation of guards, and a fervent desire never again to suffer the twin curses of chains and whip. *It could kill them all in a heartbeat . . .* Feeling a very particular heat build in his core, he tore his gaze from the sight of the warriors, turning to extend a hand to Aleida. She took it, moving closer, eyes fixing on the *stagna*, her expression one of reluctant determination. Repeated discussion on this subject had extracted a promise from her that she would quell the monster should it choose to appear at an inopportune moment.

"Calm now," she murmured, soothing hands caressing his brow. "They're going, look." Turning back to the window, he saw the warriors exchange a few clipped words with a farmer further along the road before riding on.

"The richer you appear in this land, the less notice you draw from those set to keep order within it," Aleida said. She flattened her palm against his arm, tension slipping from her face as she felt the heat subside. He saw something else in her face then, something he had first seen through the bars of his cage and hadn't understood. He did now, though. "This does stink so," she said, voice heavy with regret as she leaned closer to pluck at the soiled bandages covering his face. "I look forward to the day it comes off."

"What a fleapit," Sygurn grunted. They were perched on a craggy hill rising from the coast a mile south of Speltsaer. Looking down at the walled port below, a close-packed cluster of grey houses and wharfs, Ruhlin could understand the Nihlvarian's distaste. The place had a decidedly unappealing air, the impression enhanced by the mingled odour of fish, dung and woodsmoke detectable even at this distance. Ruhlin had finally removed his bandages, and the cool air would have felt pleasant on his skin but for the taint on the wind.

"You know this place well, I hope," Ruhlin said, crouching at Sygurn's side.

"Well enough to get us to the docks without attracting notice," the Nihlvarian replied. "Once we get there . . ." He trailed off with a shrug.

"There's no quiet way to seize a ship," Julette agreed. She was crouched to Ruhlin's left, her gaze concentrated on the line of ships moored alongside the wharf. "All too big," she grunted, shaking her head. "Even if every one of us were a sailor."

"There's fishing craft." Sygurn pointed to the small boats dotting the water beyond the wharf.

"We've too few hands for a ship but too many for a boat," Julette said. "Besides, I'm not risking my neck sailing the open ocean in a wallowing tub that stinks of fish guts."

"So, we've come a long way for feck all, is what you're saying." Sygurn's shoulders slumped. "Could make our way along the shore, I s'pose. The port of Lyshsmar lies sixty miles or so to the east. Might find a smaller ship there." He began to rise. "Hope those fecking oxen haven't wandered too far . . ."

"Wait," Julette said, her gaze now shifted east. It was near dusk and a thin haze had settled over the broad, dark waters of the Deep Fjord, through which Ruhlin could make out a familiar sight. The red sail billowed sluggishly in the meagre wind, distorting the inverted crossed hammer and sword sigil he had first seen that terrible morning at Buhl Hardta. *A raiders' ship*, he concluded, watching it sweep closer to the port, oars leaving a line of white dots across the water. As it neared Speltsaer, the oars were raised and drawn in, and he was able to gauge the vessel's size in comparison to the others in harbour, judging it at most two-thirds their length and half their width.

"She's built for both speed and storm," Julette said with a clear note of admiration. Turning to Ruhlin, she grinned. "That's a beauty to bear us all the way home, dear boy."

"How long are they likely to stay in port?" Ruhlin asked Sygurn.

"Could be a day or a week," he replied. "Depends on their cargo."

"Slaves," Ruhlin said, grimacing at dire memories of his days chained below decks on Aerling Angomar's ship. "Their cargo is slaves."

"Even better." Julette clapped a hand to his shoulder. "Then we'll have us a willing crew into the bargain."

CHAPTER FOUR

Felnir

Speaking in his archaic Ascarlian, Wohtin named the sea west of the Fire Isles as the *Skyrn Agryr*, the Red Waves. The reason became obvious at twilight when the sky took on a shade of crimson far deeper than any Felnir could remember, and he had sailed many seas.

"Almost worth the trip just to see that," Sygna said as they stood at the prow, gazing at the fiery sky above the gently rocking hound that formed the figurehead of this fine but ancient ship. Felnir felt Sygna stiffen as he folded his arms around her, hearing a muttered addition, "Almost."

Trieya's Quill was already visible in the darkening heavens, beckoning them on to the reward Wohtin had promised. Felnir supposed he should regard himself a figure of future legend. An already celebrated warrior, albeit with a dire reputation in some quarters, bearing the Sword of the Altvar and sailing into uncharted seas to claim his kingdom. Yet, in truth, all he felt was abiding doubt, and the lingering grief of Guthnyr's loss. *Him and others*, he recalled, beset by the image of Kodryn's demise in the Vaults of the Altvar. Elvine's kind, smiling face. That young rogue Colvyn. All sacrificed so that he might ascend to the throne of a land unseen, despite ample evidence of his unworthiness.

"The smoke from the Fire Isles filters the light," Wohtin said, gesturing to the dimming red over the western horizon. "Something I noticed in my travels. Wherever there are fire mountains, the sunsets tend to be spectacular."

Sygna lowered her head and Felnir knew she was caging her tongue. Her suspicion of this absurdly old man had only deepened since their departure from the ruined city. Yet, as much as she yearned to turn south and seek passage through the Fire Isles, she voiced no complaints. Her place was always at Felnir's side, of that he had no doubt.

Hearing a triumphant shout, Felnir turned to see Falk hauling a large cod from the water. They had trimmed the sail and let the *Dehlgra* wallow so the Albermaine-ish outlaw could cast his lines and catch supper. The baited catgut dangled from a row of ebony-hafted spears they had found on a lower deck, part of a far larger collection of weapons that would have accompanied Velgard to the Halls of Aevnir. There were more than a score of swords, axes and spears, along with a number of helms and a shield. All were of remarkable craftsmanship and ornate appearance, decorated in ancient script. Upon first seeing it, Sygna had remarked that they had found treasure in the Fire Isles after all, for this was surely worth more silver than Felnir had expected to see in his lifetime. Yet, at this juncture, it was merely ballast, useless apart from providing Falk with makeshift fishing gear.

"Time to light a fire," Sygna said, disentangling herself from Felnir's arms. "He always overcooks it."

Left alone with Wohtin, Felnir watched him gaze towards the west, wondering if the frown he wore was one of calculation or uncertainty. "I need to know more about this kingdom you promised," Felnir said.

Wohtin lowered his gaze, the many lines of his face deepening. Although he appeared somewhere close to his sixtieth year, Felnir knew that much of the creasing and weathering to Wohtin's features came not from age. Countless miles travelled during an unnatural span of years had left their mark, as had his frequent bouts of madness. Although he tried not to, Felnir found himself constantly watching the old man's movements and expression. One day the twitchy confusion that marked his periods of insanity would return, but, for now, he appeared to have hold of his mind.

Noting a measure of reluctance in Wohtin's face, Felnir added, "If I'm to rule there, I should at least know its history."

As Wohtin turned to face him, Felnir saw a great weight of sadness in his eyes. He had seen it before when the old man talked of his great error, the calamitous attempt to reach between the worlds that had destroyed the underground city of Skar Altvar and led to the disappearance of his beloved king. But during the telling of that tale, there had been as much guilt as sorrow. The history of the land they sailed towards, it seemed, aroused only grief in his ancient heart.

"When Velgard disappeared and the inhabitants of Skar Altvar succumbed to madness," Wohtin began, "the subjects he left behind knew there was no longer a place for them in the Fire Isles. So they took ship to the west in search of a new home, and there did find a land of good soil, sprawling forests and tall mountains where there were many beasts to hunt. A land so rich but so empty of people must indeed be a gift from the Altvar, surely beseeched by our lost king so that we might prosper in his absence as we awaited his return. Thus was it named Vorunvahl, the King's Land. For a time we prospered there in peace. But, if there is one lesson I have learned in all my travels, it's that peace never lasts.

"Much of that time is lost to me, for the madness often returned. But there was a truth to be learned in the discord that followed: a King's Land must have a king, and we had none. And so, as those who had stood high in Velgard's court vied with each other for the mantle of leadership, did feud and grievance become the law of Vorunvahl. When I recovered my mind and resolved to leave, it was with disgust. Velgard had left us a mighty legacy, and we destroyed it."

"How long?" Felnir asked. "How long since you walked there?"

"Close to four centuries, as best as I can reckon."

"Four centuries?" Felnir laughed. "After so much time, surely a king has risen. As one generation fades and others blossom, the hatreds of past years are forgotten. It will be a transformed place. And you said my throne may well be secured without need of battle."

"That I did, but only if the Altvar bless our course. And they are fickle, as you know." Wohtin's features creased again, but this time in bitter amusement. "You are clever, my king. But, as you will discover, Vorunvahl is a land unlike any other. Velgard left us more than one legacy, and I have come to know it as a curse."

More questions rose to Felnir's lips, but the old man said no more. Moving to the mid-deck, he settled between the ship's arcing ribs and huddled into sleep. *Angmund*, Felnir reminded himself of Wohtin's true name. *Most sage and trusted advisor to Velgard, greatest king in Ascarlian history, and the author of his fall. Named both Eikralvyr and Sictalvyr, a tongue either wise or dire.* Felnir's hand went to the hilt of the sword at his belt, hoping the blessed weapon would afford him another vision, something that might guide him. It wasn't too late to turn south, seek passage back to Ascarlia, there to claim his reward from Sister Lore. But she had promised only restored reputation, whereas Wohtin promised kingship. Either way, the sword had no more guidance to offer.

What a fool I am to follow a man such as this, Felnir decided. Shaking his head at the absurdity of it all, he went to join Falk and Sygna as the tantalising aroma of roasted fish drifted across the deck.

Despite Felnir's doubts regarding Wohtin's counsel, the old man's promise of a shift in the wind after three days' sailing proved accurate. The breeze had been wayward and thin for much of their voyage, much to Sygna's annoyance. But, on the morning of the third day, the sail blossomed and a stiff westerly wind had the *Dehlgra* ploughing a steady course, albeit across a steeper sea. Although not as fractious as the Styrnspeld, the waves were tall and the weather markedly less clement. Rain lashed them in short but drenching bursts as both sky and water grew dark.

They sailed on for four more days of poor weather, Sygna correcting their course whenever the clouds thinned enough to allow a clear view of Trieya's Quill. So angry a sea prevented Falk from casting his lines and their stock of food diminished. They attempted to ration the brined goat meat Sygna had prepared before setting out, but by the time the waves calmed and the sky cleared, Felnir reckoned they had perhaps another two days' sustenance remaining. Falk cast his lines again, but the fish in these waters appeared less plentiful. The outlaw did manage to hook something big, both he and Felnir heaving the line in an effort to bring it to the surface. But the unseen beast proved too strong, breaking the line just as a vague, grey outline appeared below the rail. Given its bulk and ferocity, Felnir thought it best the creature had escaped.

Falk had better luck the next day, hauling up a couple of small pollock, which were gutted, roasted and eaten in short order. It was only a short reprieve, however, before the gnawing hunger returned to scrape at Felnir's belly. Moving to the prow, he eyed the horizon, seeing no sign of land. Repeated demands had elicited scant information from Wohtin as to how long this voyage would last. Felnir suspected mummery in the old man's apparent confusion over the issue. Aged by centuries he might be, and prone to madness, but until now his memory had shown no signs of dimming.

"Come, my love," Sygna said, embracing his arm. She had begun roasting the last portion of goat meat, the smoke casting a maddening scent across the ship. "You must eat."

"You and Falk have it," Felnir said, hoping she couldn't hear the growl of his stomach.

"Eat, or I'm throwing it over the side and we all starve." The clipped, angry insistence in her voice told him this was no empty threat.

Sighing in surrender, Felnir turned away from the prow, pausing when Sygna stayed put. Her eyes were fixed on the horizon, brow drawn in both surprise and hope. "Is that . . . ?" she began, raising a finger. Following it, Felnir saw a dim, hazy square rising above the distant waves: a sail. A few moments of hard staring confirmed that the shape was not a product of hungry optimism, but a true sail. Also, judging by its angle, it was heading straight towards the *Dehlgra*.

"Wonder if they'll have food to share," Sygna said.

"No," Wohtin said, appearing at Felnir's side. The old man's gaze was dark as he viewed the approaching ship. Evidence of his immunity to the depredations of age shone in the keenness of his vision, for he saw the sigil emblazoned on the sail before they did.

"They come for blood," he said. He cast an apologetic grimace at Felnir. "The Altvar's blessing is not bestowed, my king. You must fight."

"Fight who?" Felnir demanded. "Why?"

"The *Ahrkun Krayl* have taken wing." Wohtin nodded towards the oncoming vessel. Felnir could see the sigil now, a black bird, wings spread and claws raised, emblazoned on pale grey canvas. Wohtin's words were phrased in ancient Ascarlian and, although Felnir lacked the scholarship of poor, lost Elvine Jurest, he knew enough to translate.

"The Raven Hearts?" he said, looking again at Wohtin, finding impatience had replaced regret.

"It matters not who or why, in this moment," he said. "All you need know is that they come to kill you, Felnir Redtooth. And dawdling in expectation of another outcome will surely aid their task."

The certainty in the old man's bearing caused Felnir to subject the other ship to a more careful appraisal. It was less than four hundred paces off now, close enough for him to make out the sleek, familiar lines of a warship about the same draught as the *Sea Hawk*. He could also see her oars dipping in the choppy waves, heaved at fast stroke. With her sail full, there was only one reason a warship would be moving at such a clip.

"Take charge of the tiller," he told Sygna. "Put as much water betwixt us and them as you can."

"They'll still catch us," she warned. "With no hands for our own oars."

"I know. But in catching us they'll tire themselves, and a tired foe is easier to kill."

He and Falk set about hauling the sail while Sygna worked the tiller to bring them about. With the wind against them, there was no chance of a complete turn, so she opted to strike out towards the south. The *Dehlgra* quickly caught the wind, her narrow hull knifing through the swell with welcome speed. Still, whoever steered their pursuer possessed a skilled hand, matching the manoeuvre with nimble deftness. Moving aft, Felnir also noted that the stroke of her oars had slowed. It seemed her captain had refused to exhaust their crew, preferring to gradually close the distance at the expense of a quick kill. Felnir could see silhouettes on the pursuer's prow, marked as warriors by the sun glinting on their helms. Once again gauging the distance between the two ships, he estimated it at less than two hundred paces now, narrowing with every sweep of those oars.

"Hand the tiller to Falk," he called to Sygna. "And fetch your bow."

Joining him with bow in hand and quiver slung over her shoulder, she nocked a shaft to the string and stood up on the rail. Felnir didn't ask about her ability to hit the mark at this range. Even with her old bow, she could still have made the shot. And now she wielded the Bow of the Altvar.

Sygna's balance was peerless, riding the heave of the *Dehlgra's* deck with accustomed ease, her eyes fixed on the other ship. Felnir saw the silhouetted figures react to her appearance, catching sight of bows among them, but Sygna let fly before they could be put to use. Drawing the bow into a tight arc, she loosed her first shaft in a smooth, unhurried motion. Usually, Felnir's eyes were quick enough to track an arrow's course, even at short range. Not so today. The missile was but a dark flicker following the thrum of Sygna's bowstring, followed instantly by a shout from the other ship. He saw one of the warriors on the prow collapse and the others immediately fall into a crouch.

"Haul to port!" Felnir commanded Falk before glancing up at Sygna. "See if you can pick off some of their oarsmen."

He left her to her task and went forward to crouch beside the cooking fire. Drawing his dagger, he cut a length of rope from a nearby coil, then tied a thick knot at one end. Among the items found aboard the *Dehlgra* in a remarkable state of preservation had been a cask of pitch. It was hard to the touch at first but had softened when warmed. Tossing aside the lid, Felnir dipped the knotted end of the rope into the viscous contents before holding it over the fire. The instant it caught the flame, Felnir rushed to the port rail and hurled it at the other ship. It was a decent throw and the ship close enough now for the blazing projectile to land squarely on the mid-deck. Felnir had been hoping to hit the sail, but still took satisfaction from the sudden blossoming of grey smoke, accompanied by a chorus of alarmed shouts. A trio of rowers rose from their seats to combat the fire, two quickly falling victim to Sygna's arrows before the smoke concealed the third.

"I don't suppose," Felnir grunted at Wohtin as he cut and knotted more lengths of rope, "you have a blessed incantation or some such that might aid us?"

"No," the old man stated simply, stooping to take up one of the ropes Felnir had cut. "But I can tie a knot as well as any other. And my throwing arm is strong enough."

Together they doused, lit, and hurled another half-dozen makeshift torches, ducking the arrows cast at them by archers on the other ship. Thankfully, the increasing pall of smoke made for poor aim, at least among their enemies. Judging from the pain-filled yells of alarm echoing through the haze, Sygna was still finding targets. Felnir finally scored a hit on the other ship's sail when, thanks to a sudden effort by her oarsmen, she lurched close enough for the two hulls to touch. The flaming rope flew from Felnir's hand just as he was jarred from his feet by the impact. Flat on his back, he watched the missile leave curving loops of dark smoke through the air before landing on the upper portion of the grey canvas square. The flames spread with satisfying swiftness, obliterating the raven motif and leaving the sail in tatters. Although robbed of wind, and set alight in several places, the vessel's oarsmen were not easily daunted, continuing to sweep at fast stroke while her helmsman steered for the *Dehlgra*'s prow. Thus stalled, her sail sagged and the ship lost all forward motion. The thud of boots upon the deck sounded shortly after.

Surging upright, Felnir drew the Sword of the Altvar and instantly lashed at the first shape to loom out of the smoke. He was rewarded with a shriek of pain and a flash of blood before the figure spun away. Spying the dim shapes of more boarders directly ahead, Felnir charged. In his experience, there was room for neither restraint nor nuance in ship-to-ship fighting. It was ever a merciless affair that rewarded swift aggression above all else.

Hacking left and right, he felt the signature impact of a blade finding both armour and flesh, then jerked aside as a spear lanced at him through the grey swirl. The thrust was strong but clumsy, the spear wielder over-extending his arm, making it easy to hack off at the elbow. As shrill screams filled the air, a bearded face loomed at Felnir, a yelling, hateful visage of black ink tattoos and bared teeth. It divided into two as Felnir swept the sword in an upward stroke, the snarling warrior casting a fan of gore as he reeled away. Collision with the port rail brought the realisation that Felnir had hacked his way through the boarding party. Looking around, he saw another warrior leaping the gap between the two ships. Felnir moved to intercept him, but one of Sygna's arrows found him first, the skewered body tumbling into the sea with a tall splash.

Felnir stumbled again as the *Dehlgra*'s deck tilted, pushed into an oncoming wave by the larger bulk of their enemy. *Still rowing*, Felnir thought in puzzlement. Usually, when two warring ships came together, the struggle dissolved into a pell-mell race to get as many warriors onto the opposing deck as quickly as possible. Fortunately, a shift in the waves dislodged the *Dehlgra* from the other vessel's prow. She wallowed as the other ship swept by, the wind parting the smoke to allow Felnir a clear view of her deck.

Less than I thought, he judged, counting no more than ten figures. Six were still working the oars while the rest seemed fully occupied in fighting the fires Felnir had kindled on their deck and rigging. The lone exception was a tall, grey-bearded man perched on the mid-rail with a bow in hand, the arrow aimed straight at Felnir. Before the grey beard could loose, one of Sygna's shafts struck him in the chest. Felnir had known her an expert archer all his life, with the strength to draw even the thickest stave. Yet the power of the arrow that struck the enemy archer was beyond all prior experience. Propelling him off his feet, it bore him through the air to pin him to the mast of his ship. There he hung, coughing blood, while panic overtook his crew.

Bow of the Altvar indeed, Felnir thought.

"Nine to two, my lord," Falk said. He came to Felnir's side, hefting an axe, blade and haft smeared red. As ever in combat, the dullness faded from his eyes and he scanned the deck opposite with shrewd calculation. "Reckon we've faced worse odds. And," he added with a grin, "it's a fair bet they'll have some food aboard."

"Sygna!" Felnir called out. "Bring us closer."

He and Falk stood poised at the prow as Sygna steered the *Dehlgra* in a shallow turn, aiming her at the other ship's starboard flank. They had the wind's favour now, and the distance closed quickly, Felnir leaping across the moment the hulls collided. He cut down the first man to come for him with an overhead sweep of the sword. Evidence of this weapon's divine origins came when, instead of cutting into the warrior's helm, it shattered it and the skull beneath, suffering no damage in the process. Felnir kicked the dying man aside and charged on, parrying the sword thrust of another warrior and hacking at his shield. It didn't shatter this time, but the sword splintered its edge, Felnir's blow sending its owner stumbling back a pace. In doing so, he allowed Felnir to duck and slash the sword through his leg, leaving him writhing on the deck. He screamed and clutched at the stump, attempting vainly to stem the jet of red gore until Falk finished him with an axe blow to the neck.

The remaining foemen drew back, six in all, four to the front, crouched behind their shields, the other two bringing up the rear with spears. Felnir's instinct was to charge straight at them, but something gave him pause. *Fear*, he saw, seeing the bright, rapidly blinking eyes beneath their helms. It was not an uncommon sight when facing an enemy, but rare to find it shared among them all. *What manner of warriors are these?* he wondered.

Straightening from a fighting crouch, he twirled the Sword of the Altvar, casting a spatter of blood across their shields. "I am not unmerciful," he said. "Yield to me and earn your lives." In making this offer, he strove to keep the note of contempt from his voice. No Ascarlian would ever surrender their arms in such circumstances. Death was preferable to so great a shame. Yet, he saw them exchange questioning glances, the spearmen to the rear of the shield bearers edging back further. Whether their fear would have seen them cast their weapons upon the deck would forever remain an unanswered question, because at that moment the grey beard spoke.

"Craven dogs!" he cried out from the mast, the arrow pinning him to it shuddering as he vainly tried to wrest it free. A red mist accompanied his words as he grunted out an agonised rant, "Steel your hearts . . . and cleave to the creed of the *Ahrkun Krayl* . . . there is no king but Velgard!"

His exhortation had an immediate effect on the warriors, Felnir seeing their gazes harden and stances stiffen with fresh resolve. He didn't allow them any further leisure to gather their courage, feinting a slash to the right before launching himself at the two shield men to the left. His first blow succeeded in knocking one back a foot or two, the next forcing the other to raise his shield and sink to one knee. As Felnir had expected, the other two rounded on him, paying insufficient heed to Falk, who promptly side-stepped a sword thrust and hacked at their rear with his axe.

Felnir delivered a solid kick to the kneeling man's shield, sending him sprawling, then angled his body to avoid the unruly charge of his comrade. His roaring challenge was more impressive than his skills, the momentum of his attack making it easy for Felnir to hook an arm under his legs and pitch him over the side and into the sea. He didn't pause in turning to bring the sword down on the upper edge of the other man's shield as he attempted to rise. The blade bit through the wood and the shoulder beyond. As the warrior staggered, teeth gritted in pain, Felnir dragged the sword clear, used one hand to pull the shield aside and plunged it into the exposed flesh below the foeman's chin strap.

Flicking the sword to the right, he pulled it clear of the gurgling warrior's neck, half severing his head. Turning from the corpse, he saw Falk battling the sole remaining shield man, forcing him to retreat with fast, practised axe blows. His luck ran out when his foot tangled in a rope, sending him into an untidy fall. Never one to forsake an advantage, Falk leaped onto the prostrate man's shield, rendering him defenceless against the flurry of blows the outlaw delivered to his head. Within seconds his helm was a dented, rent mess, leaking blood and brains onto the boards.

Felnir moved to Falk's side, both readying themselves to face the spearmen, only to find them both lying dead. Each had been pierced through by one of Sygna's arrows. "Just as well," she said, hopping over the rail with a grappling rope in hand. "My quiver's empty."

Surveying the captured ship, Felnir regretted the fires he knew would soon consume her. This was a fine vessel, almost the equal in the elegance of her lines and solidity of her construction to his beloved *Sea Hawk*. But, with no hands to quell the flames or take charge of her, she would have to be left to her fate.

"Look for supplies, and be quick," he told Falk before striding towards the mainmast where the grey beard still hung upon Sygna's arrow. The blood drooling from his lips and the fading light of his eyes made it plain he would soon depart for the Halls of Aevnir. But a glimmer of defiance remained there, and it transpired he had breath enough to speak.

"Pretender!" It was more a cough than a word, Felnir grimacing in disgust at the feel of warm blood and spit upon his face. "We . . ." the grey beard gasped, "will never . . . bow to you!"

"I know not who you are," Felnir told him. "I sail a sea unknown to any map towards a land the name of which I've never heard. And yet you find me, with murder in your heart." He leaned closer, peering into the dying man's eyes. "How can that be?"

The grey beard's lips formed a sneer, eyes flicking towards Wohtin aboard the *Dehlgra*. The old man betrayed no reaction, his face like stone. "Ask him . . . the Diretongue," the grey beard rasped before faltering into a hacking cough that sent a dark red spatter onto Felnir's boots. Gasping, the grey beard spoke on, straining to meet Felnir's gaze. "What . . . lies did he . . . tell you, *Uhra Vorun?*"

Liar King, Felnir translated the curiously phrased archaic Ascarlian. Apparently, these Raven Hearts had a name for him.

"He said Vorunvahl is mine to claim," Felnir said, seeing little point in keeping secrets from a dying man. The response provoked a harsh, barking laugh from the grey beard, one that became a snarl when Felnir added, "He said your forebears sailed away from the Fire Isles when Velgard abandoned them."

"Our king never forsook us!" Blood welled around the arrow pinning the grey beard to the mast as he gripped it in two strong, scarred hands, trying to wrest it free. "He will . . . come to us! He will return . . . from his sojourn among . . . the Altvar . . ."

Letting out a despairing grunt, he gave up trying to free himself and slumped into glowering defiance. "Believe . . . nothing the Diretongue says," he told Felnir, voice laden with as much certainty as defeat. "And . . ." His head slumped, voice diminishing into a grating whisper so that Felnir had to lean closer to hear. "Know . . . that the *Sindra* himself . . . will cut your . . ." A final spasm of agony shook the grey beard before he sagged as all life fled his body, his last words forever unsaid.

"Some kind of pickled fish, my lord!" Falk's broad, besmirched features bore a cheerful grin as he appeared out of the smoke with a barrel under each arm. "Smells worse than my old da's britches after a visit to the outhouse, but I've never been picky." He cast a worried glance upward as a cascade of burning rigging descended to the deck, adding fuel to the spreading blaze. "If I might venture an opinion, my lord. I reckon it's time we got ourselves off this tub."

In addition to the pickled fish, Sygna also found a side of salt pork and several flasks filled with some form of sweet and potent liquor. Felnir twisted her arrows free of the bodies and gathered up what weapons he could before the fire grew so fierce he was forced to retreat. Dislodging the grappling rope, he leaped back onto the *Dehlgra* and joined Falk in angling the sail while Sygna steered them clear of the burning hulk. Fire soon covered her deck completely, a thick black column rising as it ate the hull. Wind and current soon bore the blazing wreck away until it was no more than a bright spot in the gathering gloom.

"The old one spoke a name before he died," Felnir told Wohtin, watching his face closely. "*Sindra*. A man intent upon my death. *Sindra* means 'messenger' in old Ascarlian, does it not?"

"In Velgard's time it usually meant 'herald,'" Wohtin replied, then adding in a soft, bitter sigh, "Of course, he would still be alive."

"So, you're not the only one. There are others in Vorunvahl just as ancient."

Wohtin replied only with a distracted nod, watching the last flicker of light from the distant blaze. It occurred to Felnir that this very old man had just witnessed the end of a soul he had known centuries before. Had they been comrades in Velgard's court? Perhaps even friends. Given the depth of hatred in the grey beard's eyes as he slipped towards death, Felnir doubted it.

When the bright spot finally dwindled to nothing, Wohtin went to his nook and lay down. Felnir resisted the urge to force more answers from him, for the old man's bearing told him it would be a difficult task and this had been a tiring day.

"I'll have it out of you," he said. Wohtin turned onto his side, his silence provoking Felnir into a laugh. "That's if I'm truly to sit your throne. Or is that just another lie?"

CHAPTER FIVE

Thera

"Sail to the south!" Ragnalt's shout interrupted Thera's survey of the eastern horizon. The apprentice Vellihr's face was grim as he turned to her, its lightly bearded handsomeness marred somewhat by the scars he had earned at the Nihlvarian stockade. One cut across his upper forehead, the other a vertical slash to his left cheek. Still pink and black from stitching, Thera felt they would, once healed, enhance rather than negate Ragnalt's charms. He had always been a capable, often formidable warrior, and now he had the marks to prove it. Yet, any justified pride he might have harboured remained absent from his gaze and Thera knew why: Eshilde's betrayal cut him as deep as it did her.

"Barely a mile out and we find battle," Ragnalt added, casting a doubtful squint over the *Great Wolf*'s crew. To make good their losses, Thera had been compelled to recruit from the warriors Ossgrym had been willing to spare, six in all, most north of their fortieth year. The sole exception was his nephew, Aldeyn, who Thera knew had been included principally because of his uncle's unwillingness to forgive the lad's service to her great-grandfather. Although she felt the Ironbones' judgement to be overly harsh, she hadn't thought it appropriate to intervene. Sister Iron had once told her that, within families, matters must be allowed to right themselves, or fester as the Altvar willed it.

In addition to Ossgrym's warriors, she had taken on four freed slaves, all Morvek, and carefully selected with Achier's assistance. Two women and two men of perennially suspicious bearing, they had consented to serve in Thera's *menda* on the promise that they would get to kill a great many Nihlvarians. Achier explained that, unlike most of the slaves liberated at the stockade, these four had been born free and had many scores to settle after long years under the whip.

Peering at the distant but growing sail, Thera saw no hint of red. That didn't necessarily mark the ship as friendly. The Nihlvarians had captured dozens of Ascarlian vessels and possessed a true gift for deceit. Feeling a flare of pain from her sealed wounds, Thera resisted the urge to put a hand to her chest and stiffened her back. She could shudder and bite down grunts of pain in the confines of her shelter, but not in front of her *menda*. Forcing her eyes to focus on the ship, she could see a stretch of its hull now, the bobbing prow pointed at the coast of Ayl-Ah-Vahrim. The ship was large, about two-thirds the draught of the *Great Wolf*, meaning it probably held a strong contingent of warriors. *Nihlvarian raiders?* she wondered. *Or have they come in search of their lost outpost?*

She could just sail on, her mission being so pressing. Taking her leave of Ossgrym had been a trial, given all the Veilwald faced. To his credit, he hadn't argued the point, but she still felt the sting of the rebuke she saw in his gaze as she bid him farewell with a nod and strode onto the *Great Wolf*. All she could offer had been encouragement to do everything he could to secure his island against invasion and the promise that she would return with all the forces Sister Iron saw fit to spare.

Save an island only to abandon it, she thought, watching the other ship continue to plough its course. *What manner of Vellihr am I?*

"Steer south!" she called out to Althsten, the veteran warrior who had taken charge of the tiller. He was a skilled hand at the helm, but no Gelmyr. *But then*, she reflected with a pang of grief, *few who ever trod the deck of a ship could make that claim*. "Put us in their path!" Turning to her *menda*, she raised her voice to a yet harder pitch of command. "Unship the oars, and keep your weapons close!"

Within moments, the oars swept the waves and the *Great Wolf* left a bright wake as she sped south. Sparing a moment to study her Morvek recruits, Thera was impressed by the skill and speed with which they wielded their oars. They easily kept pace with her veterans and the cadence of their pull was, if anything, more regular. The whip scars visible on their necks and arms made it plain how such skill had been instilled, and on each face she saw a grim, hungry desire for the coming confrontation.

As it transpired, their bloodlust would not be sated this day. Upon drawing closer to her target, Thera made out a familiar sigil on the sail: a tree flanked by a sword and a scythe. *A ship of the Aiken Geld*, she realised, squinting to make out the faces of her crew. They came into focus quickly thanks to the *Great Wolf*'s pace, and the fact that the other ship had turned to meet them. She could make out the archaic lettering on the hull now, proclaiming the ship as the *Silver Hawk*. Not a name she knew. Nor did she recognise the man who stood waving at the prow, but his face bore the blue ink of an Ascarlian, as did those of his crew.

"Slow stroke!" Thera called out to her crew. "These are friends. Althsten, put us on their starboard side."

As both ships drew alongside one another, trimmed sails, and shipped their oars, she beckoned Lynnea close. "Touch my hand if you hear any deceit," Thera told her. Although she saw no cause for suspicion when surveying the Aiken Gelders, her dire experience of Nihlvarian spies compelled a modicum of caution.

"Vellihr Thera Speldrenda!" the captain called to her, the same man who had hailed her from the prow. His head was covered in a mass of unruly copper-hued hair and he possessed a broad, muscular build with a booming voice to match. "Skahlvyr Estrynlud," he went on, patting his chest. Thera read a good deal of relief in his features, the expression that of a man completing a difficult mission. She knew his name if not his face. This was the Steelhide, another who had won fame in the retaking of Olversahl. Although, judging his age, Thera reckoned he couldn't have been much older than her at the time.

"You are kin to Veilwald Hakkyn, are you not?" she shouted back. "What tidings do you bring from the Aiken Geld?"

"I come on my Veilwald's orders, Vellihr. He bid me sail north and find you, and any other allies that could be sought to aid us." Skahlvyr grimaced in annoyance as a tall wave buffeted both vessels, nearly sending him into a sprawl. "Perhaps we could anchor closer to shore. Discuss matters properly."

"I have pressing business in Skar Magnol," Thera told him. "State your tidings so that I may report them to the Sister Queens."

"Battle, Vellihr. Those are my tidings. Our vile enemy has sent a great fleet into the Aiken Geld, spreading fire and slaughter. My Veilwald gathers all his strength to meet them, and will do so at the rising of the next full moon. But, without allies . . ." Another wave interrupted him, but Thera had already learned all she needed to. Turning to Lynnea with a raised eyebrow, she received a nod in response. *This is no liar.*

"Better if he was," Thera muttered. Looking back to the tree-covered shore of Ayl-Ah-Vahrim, she swallowed a sigh. *Save an island only to abandon it. If Hakkyn fails, the Nihlvarians will surely come to win back what they lost. What manner of Vellihr am I?*

"Sail for that bay!" she shouted to Skahlvyr, pointing to the shore. "You'll find a harbour." She spared the eastern horizon a final glance. *Forgive me, Sister Iron.*

* * *

"It would seem you were right, Vellihr," Uhlwald Kahlvik commented after hearing Skahlvyr's tidings. "Those we defeated were but the vanguard of a larger force."

She had called them all to the *Great Wolf*, the leaders of this small army gathered on the deck to regard the chart she had spread out on a tarpaulin. It was the map Sister Iron had gifted her before setting out from Skar Magnol, a copy of the most precise rendering of the Outer Isles ever set down. Most of those present viewed it with either scowling disapproval or grudging interest. By contrast, Achier exhibited unabashed fascination for the finely crafted chart, tracing a tentative finger over the various coastlines and islets, an almost childlike smile curving his lips. It appeared such things were a novelty to his people. Whereas, to Ascarlians, they were often regarded as an irrelevant, perhaps threatening, foreign contrivance. She resolved to indulge no tolerance for such prejudice now. Given their plight, all advantages must be seized, even those of outlander origin.

"You saw their fleet with your own eyes?" Thera asked Skahlvyr.

"I did, Vellihr. Counting over a hundred ships with more crowding the waves behind." He gave a small, discomfited cough. "I was forced to flee to bring word to Veilwald Hakkyn."

"And were right in doing so," Thera assured him. "Where exactly did you spy them?"

"Approaching the strait betwixt Ayl-Ah-Kelven and Ayl-Ah-Viehl. Given the recent raids, we knew more would be coming, but not there. It was pure chance that I spotted them. The waters are treacherous to those not familiar with local tides and currents. Yet, given all the havoc the red faces wreaked shortly after, it seems they had no trouble sailing through."

"More spies at work, no doubt," Ossgrym grunted, casting a short, baleful glance at his nephew.

"Spies?" Skahlvyr asked.

"They call themselves Volkrath," Thera explained. "Hidden servants of our enemy. Their plans have been years in the making." She folded her arms, studying the map. Ayl-Ah-Kelven and Ayl-Ah-Viehl formed the western arc of a circle of islands separated by a stretch of water that couldn't be more than ten miles across at its widest. "Still, it appears they've chosen constricted waters to start a full-scale invasion. The surrounding islands create a small sea of their own."

"With many avenues of egress and ingress," Kahlvik pointed out. "A sound choice if your object is to spread destruction ahead of conquest."

"Also, with many landing places for them to build more stockades,"

Ossgrym added. "If they can establish themselves there, digging them out will be a hard business."

"My Veilwald's thinking also," Skahlvyr said. "Which is why he gathers strength for an attack. Every craft that can float has been mustered and every hand that can wield a blade called to his *menda*. Yet, without allies, it still won't be enough."

"Allies you'll have," Thera promised. Catching Ossgrym's eye, she watched his brow crease in grim amusement.

"What of Skar Magnol?" he asked. "I thought your mission was clear."

"It is," she replied, inclining her head at the map. "Sister Iron sent me to quell trouble in the Outer Isles. That I intend to do, with the aid of all loyal bondsmen."

Ossgrym's lips thinned as he let out a sound that combined a sigh with a growl. "I lost many ships fighting this foreign filth," he said. "Although, those we captured here will make good some of the loss. There's more to be had in the outlying islands of this geld, and warriors too. But gathering them will take time."

"Battle dawns with the next full moon," Thera told him. "And we'll need seven clear days to sail south and join with Veilwald Hakkyn."

"Then, Vellihr," Ossgrym inclined his head, "we'd best not waste time staring at lines on paper and get about it, eh?"

Ossgrym and Kahlvik sailed with the following tide, the Veilwald heading north and his kinsman east. Ossgrym predicted they might be able to gather another fifty ships, and several more small craft, along with perhaps a thousand warriors. "With more time . . ." he said, trailing off into a helpless shrug.

"One more ship or one more sword is a boon at this point," Thera told him. "With your leave, I'll gather more warriors from Ayl-Ah-Vahrim. There are bound to be many who missed your summons to battle." She didn't require his permission for this task. In a time of war, even a Veilwald must cede authority to a Vellihr. But it was wise not to chafe the Ironbones' pride too much.

"Missed it or hid from it," Ossgrym said with a sour laugh. "When real war beckons, those who count themselves heroes will find excuses to be cowards. Feel free to flog any cravens, if you feel it necessary."

Before setting out, Thera paused to address the small number of freed slaves who had not made common cause with their liberators. They consisted of about twenty Nihlvarians and were a fairly wretched lot. Although uniformly possessed of a well-muscled wiriness thanks to their countless hours pulling oars at their masters' behest, they were also gaunt from poor food. Added to that was the permanent crouch and tense suspicion with which they regarded all around them, as if a whip stroke or execution might come at any moment.

"You don't seem to understand certain things," Thera told them, watching a few squint as they struggled to comprehend her accent, although most appeared to grasp her meaning. They were huddled in the corral where the Nihlvarians had gathered the herd of cattle that had been their undoing. Having been given materials to construct shelters, the freed slaves had assembled a ramshackle collection of hovels. In the days since their liberation, they rarely ventured from under these mean canvas roofs, nor had any opted to flee despite a minimal guard.

"You are free now," Thera told them. "Your chains are broken. Yet, while the Morvek among you have been quick to take up arms and join our cause, you squat here and eat food you haven't earned. My people can be generous to the destitute, but their patience grows thin towards the idle."

This heralded an exchange of glances from some but a lowering of heads among most. *Too cowed by the lash*, Thera concluded, smothering a sigh of disgust. *Beat a dog until it does nothing but piss itself, then what use is it?*

She was about to voice a parting warning that any further food would be provided only in return for labour, when a solitary figure rose from the huddle. Like the others, she was thin with a shaven head, but with a measure of defiance in the cautious gaze she offered Thera. The upper portion of her left ear was a ragged mess, indicating it had been chewed off at one point. There was no way to tell if it had been by human or beastly teeth. Her face was marked by a scar that traced from her right temple to her chin. Despite such disfigurement, and a patina of dirt, Thera could discern a certain youthful beauty to her features. Also, unlike most of her fellow Nihlvarians, she bore no red ink upon her skin. *Can't be much older than Lynnea*, Thera judged, voicing a curt, "What is it?"

"If we're free," the young woman said, her laboured tones conveying the impression that she was attempting to mimic Thera's accent in order to be understood. "Why can't we just leave?" She punctuated her question with a meaningful glance at the forest lying a few hundred paces away.

"Oh, but you can," Thera assured her. Gesturing to the trees, she went on, "Please, take yourselves off into the wilds of this island. There you will find only the empty ruins left by your captors' ravaging. If you don't starve, you may make it to a village that still stands, but don't expect succour from those you meet."

The freed slave's shoulders slumped as a discontented murmur spread through her companions. "No different," she said, shaking her head. "The whip-men forced us to work through pain. You make us work through hunger."

Thera began to snap out an angry reminder that, slave or not, this woman's people had not been invited to these lands, but fell silent at the feel of Lynnea's hand on her shoulder. She hobbled to Thera's side with the aid of the crutch she had fashioned from a sapling branch, since her leg was still far from healed. It pained her to walk, but when their thoughts touched, Thera saw that the plight of these people pained her more.

Another one who speaks truth. Lynnea's brow furrowed as she surveyed the beggared, ragged group, thoughts pulsing with sympathy. *You won't win their hearts with threats, or extra rations.*

"Then what?" Thera enquired.

Something they haven't known for a very long time. Lynnea's eyes settled on the young woman, still standing in expectation of Thera's word. *Dignity.*

Seeing the way the young woman strove to meet her eye, and her attempts to banish the slump from her shoulders, Thera felt a glimmer of admiration for her courage. *For all she knows, I could kill her and these others on a whim. Yet she dares to meet my eye.*

"What's your name?" she asked the young woman.

"Oar Number Six," she replied. "Or it has been these last three years. Before that, it was Veltta."

"Very well, Veltta. Know that, so long as you abide by our laws, you and these others will suffer no harm from me or any in my *menda*. As Vellihr of Justice in this realm, I have the power to make you subjects of the Sister Queens, with all rights that such honour entails. But honour, like silver, must be earned."

Without waiting for a reply, she turned to Ragnalt. "Go and fetch that pile of clothes and weapons we took from the Nihlvarian dead."

"You're going to arm them?"

"I am." Thera cast a small grin at Lynnea. "What affords more dignity to a humbled soul than a sword?"

The next day she headed west along the track that wound over the bluffs and cliffs of the island's southern shore. She left Ragnalt and Lynnea behind with instructions to transform the Nihlvarian freed folk into something resembling a war band. Ragnalt, despite clear but unspoken misgivings regarding his allotted task, had always been adept in training others, while Lynnea was in no condition to embark upon a journey of any length. Besides, Veltta and the rest of the Unchained, as they now preferred to be called, seemed to trust the silent apprentice most. Thera would miss her insights but counted on Aldeyn's local knowledge and status as Ossgrym's kin to aid what she suspected might be a trying chore.

"All the villages close by were raided early, Vellihr," he said as they guided their mounts along the track. Thera had been pleased to find Elkor alive and unwounded in the aftermath of the stockade's fall. Aldeyn and the half-dozen warriors from her *menda* rode horses captured from the Nihlvarians.

"We probably won't find any people until we reach the Wolf's Tongue," Aldeyn added.

"Wolf's Tongue?" Thera asked.

"A spit of land sticking out from the coast two days' ride from here. For reasons unknown, the Nihlvarians left it alone."

Thera nodded, her eye alighting on the chain about the young man's neck. She remembered him showing her the trinket it held, a small silver knot just like her own. "Have you . . . dreamed lately?" she ventured, unsure how to phrase this particular question. The fact that her great-grandfather appeared to have orchestrated his not inconsiderable network of spies by walking in their dreams was still a bizarre and uncomfortable notion. "Of *him*, I mean."

Aldeyn cast a cautious glance at the warriors following a short distance behind, then shook his head.

"Nor I." Thera frowned in consternation, remembering the night before. She had spent the moments prior to sleep willing her mind to conjure a dream, hoping, for one of the few times in her life, that the old man might appear. The captured Nihlvarian documents preyed on her, stirring an uncomfortable mix of guilt and doubt. Although she never relished conversing with her great-grandfather, he would at least be able to offer clarity on events in Skar Magnol. But her dreams had been an ugly melange of Gelmyr's death shot through with flashes of the *Great Wolf*'s encounter with white whales in the far north. Margnus Gruinskard had not consented to intrude upon any of it.

"Tell me," she said. "How did he happen to enlist you in his service? You might as well," she added with a small laugh when she noted Aldeyn's reluctance. "No point cleaving to a secret once it's been spilled for all to see."

"My father," Aldeyn said, voice clipped into a mutter.

"He was a spy too?"

"No. He was a mighty warrior my uncle loved dearly, and my mother despised. For he was also a drunkard and a gambler. Not content with owing silver to near every man with a set of dice upon this island, he had a habit of sailing away for months on end so that he might indebt himself to others. My uncle's protection spared him the worst of his creditors' ire within the Kast Geld, but not among those in Skar Magnol. Petitions were made to Sister Silver for reparations, or exile, since it was clear my father had no prospect of ever paying what he owed. The Tielwald was . . . kind enough to intervene."

"In return for your service, I assume?"

Aldeyn shifted in his saddle, avoiding her eye. "Because of my father's habits, and frequent absences, my uncle always made room for my mother and I in his hall. My cousins were more like siblings, and I was privy to many things. Reporting all I heard to the Tielwald disgraced me. I know this. But the disgrace of an exiled father was worse." He let out a short, bitter laugh. "All pointless, in any case, since he exiled himself. With his debts mysteriously settled, he took ship for southern waters and I have never set eyes upon him since. I think he knew what I had done. Before he left, I saw the shame in his eyes, and reproach. They were sentiments we shared."

"And yet, if not for that shame, your uncle would now be dead and his geld lost to our enemies."

"Perhaps. But such trust, once lost, cannot be regained. This war has cost my uncle his children, and many of his friends and bondsmen. I'll not begrudge him his anger, for I surely earned it."

After making their way past a procession of ruined, burned-out villages, the first settlement they encountered upon venturing onto the Wolf's Tongue proved to be surprisingly intact. The hundred or so crofters dwelling there were wary at the approach of an armed party, but less so upon catching sight of Thera's brooch. They professed themselves ignorant of the Nihlvarian incursion, but had glimpsed the villages burning along the coast.

"And you didn't think to investigate?" Thera asked the burly man who seemed to hold most authority here.

"The Uhlwald told us not to, Vellihr," he said, his weathered features tight with trepidation. "Or rather, the Uhlwald's son, Lohdur. Old Uhlwald Olnar died of a gut ailment some weeks back. We've been waiting to hear who'd be given charge of the Tongue ever since, but no word came from the Veilwald and we thought it best to follow Lohdur's judgement."

Looking to Aldeyn, Thera saw the same suspicion on his face that she knew must be on hers. "This Lohdur told you not to answer the Veilwald's call to arms?" she asked the villager.

"We received no such call from the Veilwald, Vellihr." A measure of shame showed in his eyes as he lowered his head. "Rest assured, had we heard it, our swords would have been his."

"Well, you've heard it now," Aldeyn told him. "I speak with the authority of Ossgrym Ironbones. He calls all able hands of fighting age to join his *menda*. Gather your arms and such provisions as you can carry and make for Danith's Bay." Aldeyn paused to nod at a collection of stone houses further up the hill. "And be sure your neighbours hear the call."

The villager offered a grave nod. "That I shall."

"As for this Lohdur," Thera said. "Where do I find him?"

"Rode off north a few days back, Vellihr. The morning after, we saw a big blaze towards the east. He said he was going to discover what had occurred. Hasn't come back, so I s'pose that leaves us without an Uhlwald at present."

"Veilwald Ossgrym will rectify that soon enough," Aldeyn assured him. "For now, you can win his favour by mustering all the strength you can. Battle comes swiftly. Be sure to spread word that the fate of this island rests upon victory."

They rode on, carrying the same instructions to several more villages before arriving at a small fishing port Aldeyn named as Ehf Hardta. Here they found the Uhlwald's hall empty save for a clutch of kinfolk to the recently expired Olnar. Like all others Thera had questioned, they professed ignorance of Lohdur's current whereabouts, although they related plentiful tales of his recent curious behaviour.

"My nephew is a quiet man for the most part," Olnar's sister said, a matronly woman who had taken on the mantle of leadership. "At least until Olnar passed. After that he became prone to rages, finding fault where there was none and such. A few times, I caught him ranting when there was no one else around. I put it down to grief for his father."

"The Uhlwald's illness was sudden?" Thera asked.

"That it was, Vellihr. Terrible painful too. A malady of the stomach that none of the healers could remedy, and they tried their best. To his credit, Lohdur stayed by his father's side till the end, and him screaming the place down half the time."

I'm sure he did, Thera thought before proceeding to instruct the woman to see to the mustering of the port's warriors. "Fill your largest boats with all who can fight and sail for Danith's Bay. Be sure they arrive within four days."

Later, as they rode away from a port now filled with frantic activity, Aldeyn spoke a word that had been at the forefront of Thera's mind, "Volkrath."

"It seems so," she said. "You know this Lohdur by sight, I hope?"

"I do. Though I'll not claim knowledge of his nature. As his aunt said, he was always taciturn."

"A useful trait for a spy."

"As is finding a place to hide. This is a big island with much unsettled land. He could be anywhere."

"I'll find him. And when I do, I feel sure he'll be persuaded to a more talkative mood."

Her confidence was borne out a day later, although any intelligence Thera might have forced from the Uhlwald's son was now beyond her reach. Lohdur hung from the leafless branch of a willow tree atop a cliff where the coastal track curved away from the Wolf's Tongue. From the grey desiccation of his skin, Thera judged he had been there for days. Her practised eye roved his corpse for signs that his current state had been achieved by hands other than his own, finding none.

"I didn't know they were capable of guilt," she mused, looking up at the bunched, bloodless features above the noose.

"Poisoning your own father is not an easy thing to bear," Aldeyn replied. "And I speak as one who often contemplated just such an act. Still, his guilt redeems him not. As a traitor, he deserved a worse fate. We should leave him to rot." His hands tightened on his reins as he prepared to ride on.

"Wait." Thera unhooked the dreadaxe from her saddle and stood tall in the stirrups. Sweeping the engraved blades, she severed the rope suspending Lohdur from the willow branch. "Even the dead can tell us something."

Rifling through the traitor's damp, foul-smelling garb revealed a strip of hack silver and a few coins. "No cyphers, no parchment at all," Thera muttered, her disappointment fading when she noticed a chain about Lohdur's neck. Drawing it forth, she found it to hold an inexpertly crafted silver knot. *Just like the one Annuk wore*, she realised. Thinking back over the Volkrath she had encountered, she felt a conclusion form, like the meeting of a perfect seam. *You found the trinket on that fool in Buhl Hardta*, Eshilde had said just before she died. *Did you think your great-grandfather was the only one to walk in dreams?*

The realisation summoned a measure of shame, for it was something that should have occurred earlier. Thera pushed aside the excuse of her wounding and the distracting pains that lingered in her chest. *Great-grandfather commands his spies with trinkets like this*, she thought, fist closing on the silver knot. *Why would the Volkrath not do the same? And, if they do, what would I see if I were to dream wearing this?*

"Vellihr?"

Thera blinked at Aldeyn's puzzled frown, then rose from Lohdur's body, pocketing the silver knot. "You're right," she said. "We leave him here to rot. How many miles to the next village? I find myself in want of a comfortable bed."

CHAPTER SIX

Elvine

E lvine was no stranger to penning words that would bear the signature of others, overseeing Hemund's correspondence in the Olversahl Dockmaster's house having been one of her principal duties. Yet, never before had she written something to be spoken by another, especially not a queen. When setting about the task, she worried that the language of Sister Lore's first address to the people of Skar Magnol had been too florid. The text was rich in allusions to the Altvar and the great heroes of Ascarlian history. But what troubled Elvine most of all was the fact that it was all such a blatant pack of lies.

"Weep for my sisters, as I weep!" Lore implored the gathered folk of the port. Elvine reckoned their number at five thousand or more, crowding the main market square and the streets beyond. "Weep for their precious blood spilled upon the sacred stones of Nerlfeya's Chamber. Both slain by the worst treachery."

Lore faltered then, wavering a little as she stood atop the platform Ilvar's *menda* had constructed that morning. Putting a hand to her forehead, Lore closed her eyes tight against welling tears and took a moment to banish the catch from her voice.

"I must tell you, good people of this port," she went on, having apparently mastered her grief, "that, unbeknownst to myself and my sisters, the Verungyr has for years been infested with traitors intent on overthrowing the sacred compact between Altvar, queens and Ascarls. It was these wretches who did strike down my sisters as we met in sacred council. These vile dogs who would have claimed my life but for the swift courage of Vellihr Ilvar and his *menda*."

As Lore paused to cast a grateful smile in Ilvar's direction, Elvine studied the reaction of the crowd. She saw mostly bafflement mixed with shock.

Many were too dumbfounded to speak, but she heard a murmur of disbelief begin to break through the hush.

"Who were these creatures of deceit, I hear you ask?" Lore continued, Elvine finding herself grudgingly impressed by the power and command of the queen's speaking voice as it echoed across the packed square. "Who could have secreted themselves in the heart of this realm and spent years awaiting the moment to strike? It shames me now to present you so obvious an answer, so stark a truth, one that I have failed you in not realising sooner. Who else, friends, but our eternal enemy? Ever has the pestilent, envious kingdom to the south sought our defeat. Ever have they sought our destruction. But do they confront us in honest battle, as we would? No. Theirs is always the path of the weakling and the coward. Instead of a fleet, they send emissaries of their vile, heretic covenant into our lands to corrupt our youth with carnal rites and empty promises of eternal life. Instead of warriors, they send spies and assassins. Never have they forgiven our just rescue of the Fjord Geld from their oppressive dominion. Now, in the murder of your queens, they have had their revenge."

Elvine's hands bunched within the folds of her cloak, her face as passive as she could make it. However, she couldn't prevent tears beading her eyes. *I wrote that*, she thought, finding guilt a curiously potent pain. It didn't cut like grief, but instead birthed a deep, sickening ache in the core of her being. *I wrote those lies.* Her pain was worsened by the crowd's reaction. A good deal of confusion remained, but the burgeoning growl and increasing number of angry faces made it clear many, if not most, believed the words she had written. She was, it transpired, a very good liar. *Perhaps I get it from my father.*

The thought provoked a shrill laugh to her lips, one she caged by clamping her jaw tight and lowering her head, but not before Ilvar caught the gesture. Darting a glance at his hard, frowning face, she saw the same suspicion she always did. Lowering her gaze, she hoped the tears now streaming down her cheeks would convince him she was putting on a show of grief. When she risked another look, Ilvar had resumed his careful scrutiny of the crowd, but she knew the doubts he harboured would continue to fester. *How long?* she wondered. *How long until he decides to act?* Sister Lore's protection was vital, but could end at any moment. Thus Elvine's willingness to concoct the lies the queen now spoke. *Guilt is a hard pain to bear*, Elvine decided, *but pain is at least the province of the living. And mine is not the only life in the balance.*

"And the villainy of our enemy ends not with assassination," Lore was saying now, her fine features set in a mask of noble resolution. "You will have heard many a rumour in recent days of discord in the Outer Isles, and elsewhere. Sadly, these tales are not the folly of idle tongues. Albermaine-ish spies have been busy spreading discord among the subjects of this realm, kindling feuds and setting kin against kin. Thus do they seek to sap our strength and distract us as they prepare to once again seize the Fjord Geld. Nor should you imagine they will stop there. With Ascarlia so weakened, they will sweep north, spreading fire, pillage and slaughter until the Ascarls are no more."

The growl had become a discordant, angry chorus now, shouts of defiance punctuated by raised fists and brandished swords. *Are they really so foolish?* Elvine asked herself. *Can it be so easy to bend others to your will with just a few lies?*

"I hear your anger," Lore said, raising her hands to placate the growing tumult. "And will not rebuke you for it. Yet, in anger there resides the treachery of fear. This I will not allow. Nor is it justified. For be it known to all present that we are not without allies in this struggle. Soon they will come to our aid. A people of fierce courage and stout hearts have appeared from the west in this our hour of greatest need. Who can they be, I hear you ask? Know that I, as custodian of the lore of our people, have discovered them to be the descendants of the Uhltvar themselves, scions of that most blessed race first set upon the earth by the Worldsmith. Far across the sea, beyond the Fire Isles have they lived for centuries, awaiting the moment when they were needed. For they are the swords of the Altvar, warriors born for but one purpose: our salvation!"

This climax to Lore's dishonest screed had troubled Elvine the most during those fraught hours of authorship. It seemed outlandish, even absurd, to suppose that mention of allies of such curious origin would win the hearts of an already shocked audience. Yet, as Lore raised her arms high and her voice pealed out, Elvine saw a fervent ardour sweep across the crowd. It was by no means universal, for she picked out many sceptical faces in the throng. But there were more than enough believers to fill the air with wild acclaim. Those closest to the platform were the most enthused, straining against the cordon of Ilvar's warriors to reach out to the queen, faces lit with near desperate adulation.

No questions, Elvine realised, watching Lore lower her arms to clasp hands, her expression now one of serene surety. *None have asked when the new queens will be appointed.* It was set in law that, when a Sister Queen died, her replacement must be chosen within two months. Yet none thought to ask why Lore had made no mention of this long-cherished rule. Nor had she explained precisely how she had identified the assassins and their

Albermaine-ish masters. These people had been served a cup of falsity and drank it down without hesitation. From here on, Elvine harboured no doubt that Ascarlia would have but one queen.

"Sounds like she has a portion of my mother's gift," Colvyn said. "Father always said she could tilt the world entire with just a few words."

"Did he write them for her?" Elvine asked, dabbing a cloth dampened with liniment to the bruise on Colvyn's forehead. One of the warriors conveying him to this cell had been overly keen in applying his sword pommel to his prisoner's back, and suffered a broken jaw for his efforts. It had cost Colvyn a beating, although he exhibited scant rancour over his injuries, commenting, "I learned something: your queen wants me alive."

"Actually, as far as I know, her speeches were never composed in advance," he said now after a moment's reflection. "Father penned a large body of her correspondence, but the oratory was all hers. He said it flowed out of her in the moment, and he never saw her fail to capture an audience."

"A perhaps important difference, then." Elvine shifted the cloth to the purple patch on Colvyn's cheek. "Sister Lore likes to plan for everything. The world doesn't need another Blackheart." She sighed, moving back from him, feeling the guilty ache once more. "Or those who would serve her."

"Stop that." Colvyn put a hand to her chin, lifting her face. His gaze was warm with sympathy, but voice hard with purpose. "We do what we must. *You* do what you must, or it's likely we'll never get out of here."

They conversed in softly spoken Ishtan, but his words still provoked a careful glance at the cell door. It was thick and the slat closed, but the lingering image of Ilvar's suspicious glance compelled her to excessive caution.

"Not just us," she said. "I will not leave without my mother. She's been busy ingratiating herself with the other servants. Those that are left, that is, seeking allies. Most are fervent, even fanatical in their loyalty to Sister Lore. She chose them carefully, it seems. But there are a few, mostly the elders, or those who served the other queens and were somehow spared."

"Tell her to be careful of those who appear most keen," Colvyn said. "Or others who say very little beyond an encouraging word or two. I suspect your queen will have been smart enough to seed spies among her servants. It's the ones who seem the most scared you want. Remember." He leaned closer, eyes hard now. "Spying is often called a game. It is not. It's business, and it's deadly. If you identify one you are sure is in Lore's employ, they have to be silenced. A nasty fall down the stairs, or some such. Stamp on their neck to make sure."

She shot him a hard glare. "I'm not a killer."

Colvyn let out a faint snort. "I saw you stick a spear in a man's guts on the *Sea Hawk*. It was a mortal wound, Elvine. You're already a killer."

Truth, it transpired, could hurt even more than guilt, though it was a sharper pain.

"Sorry," Colvyn said as she drew back from him. She said nothing, head lowered as she fought tears until he took her hands in his. "I'm sorry."

Her brother was plainly a practised liar, but she fancied she heard some genuine contrition in his tone. Drawing a breath, she swallowed hard and opened her eyes. "You spoke of getting out of here. Do you have any notion how we might do that? I'd hazard this isn't the first time you've been compelled to escape a prison."

He gave a small grin, features softening in relief. "And you would be right, honoured sister. Twice, in fact. Although, the last time I had a good deal of help. The time before that, I was obliged to rely on my own resources but—" he looked around the windowless stone box "—that was a far easier cage to slip than this. The only way I leave this cell is when someone unlocks that door and lets me out. Father once told me that prisons aren't governed by rules, but by keys. Pay close attention to who your queen allows to hold them, and what doors they unlock."

He fell silent as a heavy fist thumped the door, signalling Elvine's time was over.

"And remember what I said in regard to spies," he whispered as the lock rattled and the door swung open.

"If you please, Scholar Elvine," the gaoler said with gruff respect. He was a large man with an expansive gut and a briskly efficient manner she assumed came from many years overseeing this darkest corner of the Verungyr. Gathering her various ointments into her satchel, she briefly clasped Colvyn's hand before exiting the cell. As she edged past the gaoler, she let her gaze linger on the plentiful keys dangling from the ring on his belt, counting twenty-three in all. *Prisons are governed by keys.*

As she stepped into the gloomy stone corridor, she started at a sudden commotion from the neighbouring cell. The door was open and from within she heard a harsh grunt followed by the thwack of something hard meeting flesh. "Get your treacherous arse from my sight!" roared an unseen but familiar voice, quickly smothered by a chorus of shouts and a flurry of additional blows. The door slammed shut as something heavy impacted it, muting the ongoing struggle within.

"Best if you don't linger, Scholar," the gaoler said. Elvine saw a deep frown of distaste on his brow before, noticing her scrutiny, he moulded his features into its prior state of wrinkled neutrality. She replied with a strained smile and followed him along the corridor as he led her to the exit. The sounds emanating from the cell faded, although she heard another shout, the words too vague to discern. Once again, she had little difficulty in identifying its owner. Here, at last, she had discovered the whereabouts of Margnus Gruinskard.

"So, he's still alive." Berrine ran a hand through her hair, brow creased in calculation. "As ever, when it comes to him, I'm unsure if that's a good thing."

"At least we know he's not allied with Lore," Elvine pointed out. "Nor, from the sound of things, is he willing to be persuaded."

"That won't last." Berrine sat on her narrow bed, still scowling in thought. "Something he told me once: 'When it comes to torture, everyone breaks. It just takes time.' And, when he does break, that old swine has a great many secrets to share, not least about your honoured mother. The kind of secrets I'm sure our queen would be keen to exploit."

"Then there really is no choice." Elvine lowered her voice even further, despite the fact that this time she had made her way to Berrine's room without an escort. Either Sister Lore felt secure in her scholar's loyalty, or didn't see her as sufficient threat to warrant a guard. "We have to get away from here."

"I had hoped it could be different." Berrine's frown shifted into something more reflective, and regretful. "That we could garner enough allies from the servants of the Verungyr to . . ." She gave a helpless shrug. "Do something. But those who share our sentiments are few."

"If even they can be trusted. My brother had some insights on the subject."

Berrine's eyes narrowed. Elvine had noted before how her mother disliked hearing her daughter speak of Colvyn in such a way.

"Allow me to guess, honoured daughter," she said. "Trust no one."

"More that we should be wary of those who seem too keen, or too reserved. And . . ." Elvine swallowed. "Take measures should we find any to be a traitor."

"Measures?" Berrine snorted a laugh. "Are we to become assassins now? I had my fill of killing many years ago. And I'll not have your hands stained with blood."

They already are, Mother. Elvine smothered the words. She hadn't told Berrine all the details of her sojourn aboard the *Sea Hawk*, and hoped she never would. "You spoke of a kitchen maid who seemed enthusiastic," she ventured. "Are you sure of her heart?"

"Fildra?" Berrine seemed about to voice more disparagement, but paused, her thoughtful frown returning. "It appears you've rekindled some habits I'd long thought lost," she murmured after a moment. "Obsessive suspicion being the one I liked least."

"What have you told her?"

"Nothing that would see us slung into the bowels of the Verungyr alongside the Tielwald. Just vague allusions to a certain discontent, and sorrow for the murdered queens."

"Even that might have been too much."

"I'll watch her."

"That may not be enough . . ."

"I said I'd watch her!" The words were loud enough to echo through the halls beyond the door. Even spoken in Ishtan, Elvine worried that they would draw unwelcome notice. They both sat in silence, matching stares until it became apparent no one was coming to investigate.

"What of Lore?" Berrine said, evidently keen to change the subject. "Does she have you penning more speeches?"

"Not as yet, thankfully. I am to report to her early on the morrow. Apparently, she has another task to set me."

"Whatever it is, however distasteful or disgusting, do it well. Keeping her trust means keeping our heads, at least until we can reckon a way out of this cage."

Elvine met her mother's gaze, ensuring she wouldn't mistake the sincerity in what she said next. "When we do, I will not leave without Colvyn."

To her surprise, Berrine didn't argue the point. Instead, her brow now drawn in an expression of weary resignation, she asked, "Are you entirely sure he would do the same for you?"

"How would you define history, Elvine?" Sister Lore asked from atop one of the ladders ascending to the upper reaches of her library's shelves. She spoke with a distracted air, preoccupied by the book she held. Elvine could make out a portion of the spine, recognising it as an Alberic text: Trumaine's *Chronicle of the Algathinet Dynasty*.

"The study of past events—" Elvine began, only to be interrupted by the echoing thump of Lore closing the book.

"No, no, no," she said, slotting the volume back into its place. "History, dear heart, is not a matter of study. Not when one gains an insight into its true nature." Lore descended the ladder, the severity of her tone belied by the warmth of her smile as she took Elvine's hand. "History, you see, is a weapon. But one that must be used with expert care if it is to be effective. Come."

She tugged Elvine to another towering stack. "This," she said, waving a hand at the volumes crowding the shelves, "is all the scholarship regarding Ascarlian history that is in any way worthy of the name. Collected under my authority over the course of a decade. And even though I have been a careful curator, much of it remains a collection of myth and legend rather than a properly attested and credible account of our people. Did you know there is no complete chronicle of Ascarlia? Some Alberic scholars have attempted the task, but their efforts remain far from complete. In any case, the great work I require of you must be written in Ascarlian, if it's to be of any use, that is."

"Great work, my queen?"

"Why yes. A work I would trust to no other. For you, Elvine Jurest, will write the first complete history of the Ascarls."

Elvine looked again at the book-laden shelves looming above. Her scholar's mind knew that, copious as it was, even such an archive as this was inadequate to the task. "That would require the labour of years, my queen," she said.

"Of that I have no doubt." Lore laughed and put an arm around Elvine's shoulders. "Fortunate then that you are so young, is it not? Besides, the immediate task is not so daunting. Before compiling what I'm sure will be a voluminous work, I should like you to pen a more abbreviated version. I require a book of no more than a few hundred pages, written in modern Ascarlian so that it can be as widely understood as possible. It must also leave no doubt as to the greatness of our people, especially in comparison to the weaklings to the south. In such vein, I should like you to be unambiguous in depicting the villainy of our enemy and their many crimes against us. The most recent visitation of the Blackheart upon the folk of the Fjord Geld being a particularly important example. Above all, any Ascarlian who reads it must know that we are a people favoured by the Altvar. Their blessing raises us above the lesser races of the world."

More lies, Elvine realised as the guilty ache lurched again. Perhaps, if she had not already proven so adept in falsehood, she might have been spared this. Yet, looking into Lore's earnest, fond gaze, she could see no alternative. *Whatever it is, do it well.*

"I shall endeavour to work quickly, my queen," she said, lowering her head in formal obeisance. "And I thank you for this honour."

The following days saw her labouring in Lore's library, hard at work on a task she had swiftly come to despise. Although the other servants had been instructed to leave her be, she was rarely completely alone. Functionaries and messengers came and went while Lore herself was a frequent presence. She would drift in at various times throughout the day to peruse the pages Elvine filled with her scholarly lies. Sometimes Lore suggested changes, usually to include a reference to the Altvar, especially in relation to Ascarlian victories. The defeats, of course, were to be glossed over or completely ignored, except when they provided fuel for revenge. In truth, Elvine had been surprised to discover that, when tallying the confrontations between the Ascarls and their southern neighbours, the balance of victory to defeat was roughly even. Many of the battles had, in fact, been inconclusive. Such nuance was not for Sister Lore, however, and Elvine anticipated her approval in transforming these pointless slaughters into Ascarlian triumphs, and always thanks to the Altvar's blessing.

There did come a day towards the end of the first week when she found herself properly alone. Ilvar, more grim faced than usual, had arrived that morning with tidings for the queen. Elvine hadn't been privy to his news, but the swiftness with which Lore departed the tower indicated some form of emergency. Risking a foray to the library's largest window, Elvine spied a column of smoke rising above the dockside quarter of Skar Magnol. Fires were not uncommon in the close-packed houses that tended to proliferate near the seafront of many a harbour, but she doubted a mere accident would have commanded Lore's immediate attention.

Riot? Elvine wondered, resuming her seat. *Revolt, even?* Perhaps there had been more unbelievers in the crowd that day than she imagined. Whatever the reason, for the next two hours she found herself in solitude. Although, of course, there was another presence in this library. Lore had propped the Spear of the Altvar on an iron frame in the centre of the table. While the queen continued to regard the object with only vague interest, Ilvar and the servants exhibited a cowed awe at the sight of the weapon. No one save Lore and her favoured scholar dared to lay a hand upon it.

Finishing a passage in which the self-imposed exile of King Velgard resulted not from his own fratricidal guilt but the perfidy of an Albermaine-ish seductress, Elvine set her quill aside and rose from her chair. Once again, the cold iron of the spear warmed at her touch, and the voice within spoke to her without pause.

Your heart is burdened, child, it said, Elvine shuddering at the compassion she sensed in this trapped soul. *What has sickened you so?*

"Lies," Elvine said. "She makes me tell lies."

Lies, the voice echoed, musing. *Strange to think that once I had no conception of that word's meaning. Your kind are very complex creatures. You profess to despise falsehood, yet without it, your world would fall apart.*

The comment led Elvine to wonder at the age of the spear's inhabitant. It wasn't just the insight evident in its words. She could feel its vast experience, a sensation that resembled peering into a well so deep the water was beyond the reach of the sun. "What are you?" she asked it. "Are you . . . a god?"

A god? Elvine felt a pulse of amusement from the spear before the voice spoke on. *One day, I hope you come to understand the absurdity of that question. Until then, suffice to say that I am, like you, a prisoner.*

"And how did you come to be imprisoned?"

As with any soul that finds itself in a snare, I was lured by irresistible bait. He that lured me wanted much in return for my freedom, more than I was willing to give. I punished him for his arrogance and his cruelty, driving him far away so that I might linger here. I do not regret it, for he was unworthy of any gift that I might bestow, as, I suspect, are most of your kind. But you, child, are a notable exception.

It happened without warning, the warmth beneath Elvine's palm surging into a searing fire before she could draw her hand back. The fiery heat tore through her in a brief but jarring pulse. It wasn't exactly pain, more like a deep-seated sense of having touched something dangerous, something forbidden. As she staggered back from the spear, the library spun in a blur. She thought she would fall, but the burning sensation faded as quickly as it had arrived. Staring at her hand and flexing the fingers, she saw no injury, though it possessed a tremble she ascribed more to fear than any unseen wounding.

"What did you do?" she demanded of the spear, but, since she no longer grasped it, no answer was forthcoming.

Hearing the echo of footfalls from the direction of the tower stairwell, Elvine hurried to resume her seat. She picked up her quill and set down a few meaningless words before Lore strode into the library. Her features were hard now, beauty rendered austere by anger. Ilvar trailed behind the queen, for once failing to afford Elvine the customary distrustful glare. His face was downcast, even cowed.

"At a time like this, merciful impulse is, in fact, cruelty," Lore told Ilvar in a clipped tone that bespoke a self-control maintained with an effort. "For it will only force us to more severe measures later. Be so good as to remember that."

"I shall, my queen," Ilvar said, bowing with grave assurance.

"And don't grovel so," Lore snapped. "I'll have no weakling customs in this court."

"My apologies, my queen."

Lore let out a sigh, composing her features into something more akin to the typical mask of warm consideration. "Your efforts of late are commendable and greatly appreciated, Ilvar. But bear in mind that we stand not at the pinnacle of success, but merely at its threshold. Much still needs to be done. Soon our allies will be here and I am intent that they shall be greeted by not even the smallest sign of discord."

Elvine saw Ilvar resist the urge to bow again. "I shall see it done, my queen. Yet, to achieve your aim . . ." His gaze slid briefly to Elvine. "Additional measures must be taken, measures that have been avoided until now."

"The lists, you mean?" the queen enquired, letting out an annoyed huff when Ilvar directed another hesitant glance at Elvine. "My scholar has my trust," Lore said. "Speak freely."

"Yes, the lists, my queen. Compiled over many months with diligent care by our . . . loyal agents."

"How many names?"

"Near three hundred. At least those on the primary list. The secondary lists are longer."

"Very well. Start with the three hundred. We'll decide on the others if that fails to have the desired effect." Lore gestured to the door, forcing a smile. "Leave me now, if you would."

She waited until Ilvar had gone before sinking down into the chair next to Elvine. She was surprised to see a genuine sorrow marring the queen's brow, and the tightness with which she clasped her hands together on the table. Elvine was pondering the wisdom of asking if she was all right when Lore spoke.

"This is all very regrettable," she said, turning to regard Elvine with a sad smile. "Your speech went so well. But some hearts will always be shielded against the truth."

Of the many questions threatening to spill from Elvine's lips, she felt safe in voicing only one. "Has something happened, my queen?"

Lore's smile was joined by an arched eyebrow. "Don't pretend you didn't see the smoke from the window, dear heart." She laughed and reached to clasp Elvine's hand when she lowered her head. "Yes, something has happened. A few townsfolk still cleaving to the old ways and inflamed by vile rumour saw fit to cause trouble. There was fighting, some fires lit, but nothing Vellihr Ilvar couldn't deal with. Worry not. It was all settled with a minimum of bloodshed. You know, I would suspect Gruinskard's hand in this if the old goat wasn't so securely chained downstairs. Worry not, however." She squeezed Elvine's hand and stood. "It won't happen again. Of that, I'm certain. I believe some tea is in order."

As the queen turned away to pull the cord that would sound a bell in the servants' quarters, Elvine was shaken by a sudden, unexpected shudder. The same fiery sensation that had pulsed from the spear flared anew, but this time in her chest. The feeling of being shifted descended once more and the sight of Lore shimmered as the library whirled into formless mist. Lore, however, remained, the surrounding fog settling into a different form Elvine recognised as the main wharf of the Skar Magnol docks. Lore stood alongside Ilvar regarding a line of kneeling men and women. There were a dozen in all, their arms bound and each stripped to the waist. A stiff, chilly breeze swept in off Linsker Fjord, but Elvine could tell their shudders were born more of fear than cold.

"Insufficient," Lore told Ilvar, flicking a hand to the whip he held. Her tone was unlike any Elvine had heard from her before. Even in the aftermath of the massacre in Nerlfeya's Hall, Lore's voice had retained that curious note of warmth. Now, it was stripped of all emotion save for a brisk impatience. "Behead them all. Stake the heads in the market square, each to be branded as a traitor."

The shifting sensation came again, and the wharf swirled, re-forming itself into the library once more. Lore stood perusing a book she had plucked from the shelves, apparently ignorant of the vision Elvine had just experienced. *It was all settled with a minimum of bloodshed.* Lore's words revealed as a lie in the starkest clarity. Elvine's gaze fixed upon the spear, unmoving and unremarkable in its iron cradle. *What did you do?*

CHAPTER SEVEN

Ruhlin

Before entering Speltsaer, they donned the armour they had acquired during the escape from Turihmvek. "All ports have a nightly curfew six days a week," Sygurn explained. "The Vortigurn likes an orderly kingdom. Once we're through the gate, we head straight for the docks, then make out we're a patrol from the town garrison."

"What happens on the seventh day?" Julette enquired.

"What d'you think? Everyone gets drunk. If it's a special occasion, you can count on them rioting and wrecking the place." He tightened the strap on his greaves and cast a caustic eye over Aleida. Her lithe form was not especially suited to armour and she would seem an odd figure to any inquisitive soul. "Try to stand a bit taller and keep to the middle of the line. All right," he went on, addressing them all while Iyaka translated for the Morvek. "There's bound to be a guard on the ship's gangway. I'll take care of it, then the rest of you get aboard and do what's necessary." He turned to Julette. "The tide changes in about an hour, so we need to be quick sailing clear of here."

"I can do quick," Julette said. "Just get me to the tiller and haul the oars when I say."

Before climbing into the carriage, Ruhlin spared a glance at the bear. It sat on the side of the road regarding their preparations with what he felt to be a doleful cast to its eye. He wondered if it knew it was about to be left behind and felt an absurd urge to offer some manner of apology. But, given the beast's aggressive rejection of all prior attempts at communication, he just raised a hand in a tentative wave. In response, the bear blinked, rose from its haunches and shambled into the undergrowth.

Sygurn, still clad in the garb of a wealthy merchant, sat alongside Tuhlan on the duckboard as he steered the carriage towards the largest gate in the town walls. The busier an entry point, the less likely they were to attract the notice of any overworked guards. Concealed within the carriage, Ruhlin listened to Sygurn provide a series of impatient answers to the watchman. "One carriage, two wagons, no goods," he said. "Here to collect slaves for the market in Turihmvek."

The watchman asked more questions, Ruhlin gaining the impression of a man deliberately prolonging a task. "Where are you lodging?"

"The Black Pot inn on the wharf," Sygurn said. Additional questions followed until Sygurn, huffing out a convincing display of parsimonious annoyance, handed over a bribe. "Best not be any more pissing about or searching my wagons," he grumbled. The sum he provided must have won the watchman's favour because the caravan trundled through the gate without further delay. There followed a tense interval as they made their way through winding cobbled streets to the docks. The night air was punctuated by the shouts of neighbours calling to each other and the clatter of many shutters and doors closing in quick succession.

When they came to a halt, Sygurn rapped a hand on the carriage roof and they decamped. Looking around, Ruhlin saw they were in a yard at the rear of a large two-storey building. He assumed it to be the inn Sygurn spoke of due to the appetising aroma and cheerful voices issuing from its windows. As their party assembled into some semblance of martial order, a door opened, revealing a matronly woman with features set in professional welcome.

"Back inside!" Sygurn barked. Having hastily clad himself in breastplate and helm he now appeared every inch the Nihlvarian warrior. "Best be moving," he muttered to Ruhlin as the door slammed closed. "The town watch doesn't patrol in carriages and she'll soon be telling her customers of the curious sight she just saw."

They duly trooped past the inn and into the broad and thankfully empty expanse of the wharf. The larger ships occupied most of the quay, each one lit with lanterns and emitting the sound of song or conversation from their unseen crews. Their quarry was anchored at the furthest reach of the docks, a sleek and silent contrast to its bulky neighbours. As Sygurn predicted, two armoured men stood at the base of the vessel's gangplank. Their hardened, brutal faces stirred more unwelcome memories in Ruhlin, the heat sparking to life at the sight of the coiled whip on the belt of the tallest one.

"Quiet night?" Sygurn asked by way of greeting as their party drew near.

"Quiet enough," the tall guard replied. "Makes a welcome change, in truth."

"Troubled voyage?" Sygurn came closer still, resting a hand on the pommel of the dagger at his belt.

"One of the bastards we've got chained up below has a habit of causing a ruckus," the guard said. "It's like the fecker wants to die. We'd have happily obliged him, but the Aerling said he's too valuable. Reckons he'll get three strips of gold for him at the *wuhltra*. Not that we'll see a share of it."

Sygurn gave a sympathetic grunt and, moving without hesitation, smoothly drew his dagger and slashed the taller guard's throat open. His companion reacted with impressive swiftness, sidestepping Sygurn's next thrust and whirling clear, sword scraping from his sheath as he raised his head to shout a warning to the ship. His cry died in a guttural choke when Tuhlan darted forward to lance his sword through the guard's neck.

"Come on!" Sygurn hissed, already climbing the gangplank. Ruhlin drew his sword and followed, Aleida and the others close behind. He saw the flash of Sygurn's blade before he crested the rail and jumped onto the deck, finding the Nihlvarian standing over the twitching body of a youth in seafarer's garb. Ruhlin's face tightened upon seeing that the lad hadn't been armed. *Can't be helped*, he decided, clamping down on the welling pity with a stern reminder: *This is a slave ship.*

Julette hurried to take charge of the tiller while the rest of them scoured the upper deck for more sailors, finding none. "Go aft," Sygurn told Ruhlin. "I'll take the rest forward. We'll meet in the middle."

Ruhlin nodded and gestured for Aleida to follow as he headed for the hatch at the rear of the ship. Finding it unlatched, he levered it open, pausing to survey the steps leading into the flickering lamplight below. "Close that, you little shit!" an aggrieved voice called from below. "The breeze'll put my fires out."

Descending the steps, Ruhlin found himself matching stares with a stocky man standing amid a circle of steaming pots. He paused in the act of stirring the contents of a large urn, his broad, sweaty face registering both surprise and mystification. *Kill him*, Ruhlin commanded himself, yet didn't move. Nor did the monster consent to stir. In this moment, this man presented no threat. It occurred to Ruhlin that the only man he had actively tried to kill in his untransformed state had been Radylf, an act that had been driven as much by necessity as hatred. Now, confronted by a stranger exhibiting only bafflement instead of aggression, lethality had deserted him.

The frozen instant evaporated when Aleida leaped down the steps to Ruhlin's side. Instantly spying the cook, she rushed for him with her dagger in hand. He reached for a cleaver as she closed on him, but couldn't match the feline speed of her attack. Her dagger lashed across his eyes then his wrist, causing him to drop the cleaver into his soup before she finished him with two blurringly fast thrusts, one to the neck and the other the chest.

"Come on!" she snapped, beckoning urgently with her bloodied dagger and plunging into the gloom beyond the cook's alcove. Jostled into motion by the harshness of her command, Ruhlin stumbled forward. He covered only a few feet before he found Aleida locked in a vicious embrace with a large, bare-chested man. His thick muscled arms bore the scars of her dagger as they pressed her against a beam, his face a rictus of deadly rage. This time, there was no hesitation. Ruhlin's hours of training in the circle showed themselves in the fast and accurate sword stroke he delivered to the leg of Aleida's assailant. He followed it up as the man reared back in shock, Ruhlin putting all his weight behind the blade to drive it deep into the sailor's unprotected chest. Ruhlin shuddered in revulsion as his victim convulsed and vomited up a thick wad of blood, the spatter warm against Ruhlin's skin. Momentarily captured by the light fading from the sailor's eyes, he blinked at the sudden upsurge of alarm throughout the ship. Shouts of fear and anger were soon accompanied by the thuds and screams of combat. Sygurn and the others had evidently been discovered.

"Keep going," he told Aleida, now busy venting her anger by driving a series of kicks into the fallen sailor's head. Taking a shuddering breath, she resumed her rush through the ship's shadowed innards. Another crewman came at them a few yards on, looming from a stack of barrels to swing a hatchet at Ruhlin's back. He parried the blow, deflecting it and leaving an opening for him to deliver a thrust to the sailor's belly. Hearing a rattle ahead, he left the man to his death throes and moved on, finding Aleida working the lock of a sturdy iron-braced door.

A new sound joined the burgeoning cacophony raging through the ship then, a low, ominous whoosh accompanied by a shudder to the vessel's timbers. Soon, they heard more screams echoing from the lower deck. These were different to the yells of combat, riven with panic as well as pain.

"That sounds . . . bad," Aleida whispered.

Ruhlin couldn't argue that point, but the urgency of their mission remained. "Not time to look for keys," he said, casting a meaningful look at the lock. Nodding, she pressed her hand to it, blood-smeared face tensing in concentration. It took only seconds for her effort to be rewarded by a dull snapping sound, whereupon the door swung open to reveal the pale, empty-eyed features of another dead man.

His head was cocked at a curious angle and his brows drawn in a near comical expression of surprise. His back was pressed to the bars of a cage and the cause of his demise obvious in the well-muscled arm encircling his neck. The arm flexed and the man's neck emitted a grinding crack before it was released, slumping lifeless to the deck.

"Are you pirates?" the arm's owner asked in unaccented Ascarlian, blue eyes glittering in the dim lantern light. He was a good deal taller than Ruhlin, with an unruly mane of matted blond hair and an impressive frame that bore several scars, a few old but most recent. Ruhlin's experienced eye picked out the marks of a whip on his shoulders and chest, making him recall the tall guard's talk of a troublesome slave.

"No," Ruhlin said, stepping over the corpse to check the other cages. "We're the new owners of this ship and you are now part of her crew, if you're willing."

"That's a voice from the Outer Isles, if I'm not mistaken," the tall captive said. "You're a long way from home, lad."

"As are you, I'd guess." There were two more cages in this hold. One contained a tall woman with the colouring of the southern seas who glared at Ruhlin with a mix of suppressed hope and suspicion. The other held a youth a few years Ruhlin's junior. He looked up at Ruhlin with his teeth bared in a grimace of pain and desperation. Like the blond man, he had been whipped, recently judging by the raw gleam of his scars.

"Just you three?" Ruhlin asked the blond man.

"Just us," he confirmed, pursing his lips at Ruhlin's evident disappointment. "Sorry."

"Keys," Aleida said, straightening from the broken-necked corpse to toss Ruhlin a jangling bundle. As he caught it, another whoosh sounded from below, louder than before. A thick stream of smoke began to issue from between the deck boards, accompanied by a rising heat.

"Someone's put a torch to a great deal of lamp oil," the blond man observed, offering Ruhlin a regretful grin. "Looks like you won't be stealing anything tonight, my friend."

Looking down at the thickening smoke, Ruhlin swallowed a curse. Stealing the ship was one thing. Doing so while battling a fire at the same time was an impossibility. This plan had come to nothing.

"We need to go," Aleida said, echoing his thoughts.

"Don't wait." He jerked his head at the upper deck. "I'll follow."

She grimaced in reluctance but thankfully chose not to argue, turning and disappearing into the hazy gloom.

"I trust you're willing to fight," Ruhlin said, opening the youth's cage first, then the woman's.

"If it gets me clear of this shite-bucket, I'll fight whoever you want," she said.

"Dead men back there," he said, nodding to the empty door. "Take their weapons and get ashore."

As he moved to the blond man's cage, the growl of flames from below blossomed into a roar. Deck boards splintered and blackened as flames erupted all around, forcing Ruhlin towards the door.

"Looks like you're out of time, my islander friend," the blond man said. Through the smoke, Ruhlin could see a faint grin on his face, a man accepting his fate, perhaps even welcoming it. "Take care of those two, will you?" he added. "They're the only ones left."

Another gout of flame from below compelled Ruhlin to back further away, but not before a tongue of fire lapped at his arm. The pain birthed an instant surge of anger, lighting the torch to an already simmering ball of frustration. They had been so close. All those miles travelled, just so he could leave this man to the death he seemed to want. The leather breastplate covering Ruhlin's chest swelled, then split at the seams as a familiar red hue filled his vision. The flames rose yet higher, licking at his flesh, but he barely felt their fiery caress. Tearing the scraps of the breastplate away, he leaped through the fire to the blond man's cage, mangling the lock with a single squeeze of his massive fist. Shoving the barred door aside, he reached for the man inside, glimpsing his startled features before turning and casting him through the open portal as if he weighed no more than a child.

Fire and smoke flooded the cabin, the heat now so intense he finally felt a jolt of pain. As ever, the monster fed on his agony, claiming him entirely. For a time, all was confusion, a chaotic whirl of colour and shadow. He was aware of timbers shattering as he barrelled his way through bulkheads, smashing a course through the ship's hull until greeted by the sudden coolness of night air and the hardness of the wharf's cobbles beneath his feet. Then shouts of challenge turning to terror as wet spatter covered his arm and chest.

He returned to himself with his hand buried in the red grey mush that had been a Nihlvarian warrior's skull. Behind him, the still burning slave ship prickled his mostly unclad flesh. The bodies of several more warriors sprawled across the wharf, perhaps a dozen. It was difficult to tell the full number since they had been torn into so many pieces. As in Turihmvek, the aftermath of a rampage summoned a great weariness, although not as burdensome and he found he was able to stand when he felt a familiar soft hand on his shoulder.

"It was just for an instant," she said, eyes full of sorrow as she touched the *stagna*. "I hoped it wouldn't be so bad this time."

"It wasn't," Ruhlin assured her, then staggered as his legs threatened to give way. Strong arms kept him from falling. Raising his head, Ruhlin found the blond man regarding him with a narrow appraisal that lacked the usual wide-eyed cast of fearful awe.

"Might I know your name, my friend?" he asked.

"Ruhlin ehs Kestryg of Ayl-Ah-Swahl." Ruhlin sagged as a fresh wave of fatigue swept through him, the blond man keeping him upright so that their eyes met.

"A quiet man, eh?" He laughed, casting a glance at the disordered bodies littering the wharf. "I'd guess whoever named you didn't know you very well. Come, Ruhlin ehs Kestryg." He draped Ruhlin's arm over his shoulders and began to drag him towards the town. "I think it's time we got clear of these docks, don't you?"

Ruhlin's head lolled as he was borne away. He felt a pulse of relief at the sight of his companions following close behind. At least this abortive foray didn't appear to have cost them any lives. The woman and the youth he had freed were also there, both casting wary glances around them. People were emerging from the buildings alongside the wharf to watch the fire rage on the slave ship while sailors on the neighbouring vessel were busily raising anchor to draw away.

"What's going on?" someone called to Sygurn, marked as a person of authority thanks to his armour and tattoos.

"Slaves got loose and fired their ship," he replied. "We rescued the crew. Fetch buckets and form a chain. Hurry!" he added in a bark when the onlookers hesitated, sending them into startled activity and clearing the way into the town. Ruhlin felt his awareness begin to ebb as the dark maze of alley and street closed in.

"Your name," he groaned, head swivelling back to the blond man. His stature and bearing made Ruhlin suspect he may have heard of him, one of the celebrated warriors or seafarers remembered in song at the Uhlwald's hall when the mead was flowing. But when the blond man grunted his answer, the name he spoke was unfamiliar.

"Guthnyr of Skar Magnol," he said, carrying Ruhlin onwards as his mind finally slipped into the dark. "And it appears I'm in your debt."

CHAPTER EIGHT

Felnir

After two more days of sailing through a choppy swell and frequent rain, the sea calmed and became noticeably richer in life. Falk caught an increasing number of fish and dolphins appeared below the prow, diving and spinning in the wash. This was much to Sygna's delight, as she had a fondness for playful beasts. Leaning over the figurehead, she tossed some of Falk's catch to their visitors, laughing as they leaped even higher in gratitude. The first sight of land hove into view a day later, a thin green line above the western horizon. Felnir wanted to head directly for shore but Wohtin advised against it, insisting they steer south-east for another two days and keep well clear of the coast. Finally, on the morning of the third day, he pointed to a dip in the distant landscape.

"There," he said, Felnir noting the evident trepidation on the old man's weathered brow.

"What awaits us ashore?" Felnir demanded, voice laced with warning that he would tolerate no more riddles.

"A port," Wohtin replied. "At least there was when I left."

"And are the people of this port likely to be more welcoming than the *Ahrkun Krayl*?"

The faint shrug of Wohtin's shoulders was less encouraging than his words. "As long as Arnhilt Volksora still holds sway in the Greencrest, we should find a welcome."

Volksora, Felnir repeated inwardly, parsing the archaic phrasing of old Ascarlian. *Wavestrider*. A worthy name, but he had learned long ago that titles didn't always reflect a man's character. "Another ancient, like you?" he asked. "A friend?"

"Ancient yes. A friend, no. Arnhilt is . . . was my brother-in-law. Still, he always liked me more than my wife ever did."

"If I'm to put into harbour, I must be sure it's a safe berth."

"A man as well travelled as you should know. There's no such thing. I have not lied to you, my king. You knew this was a risky enterprise when we set forth. I believe the Greencrest will offer the least risk when you first set foot upon Vorunvahl. But my absence has been long, although—" Wohtin's cheek twitched a little "—hopefully longer than Arnhilt's memory, should he still draw breath."

Eyeing the anonymous strip of land ahead, Felnir felt the strongest urge yet to turn back. *We sailed across these Red Waves once and survived. We can do so again.* Yet, he was sharply aware there was no guarantee of that, nor of successfully navigating the Fire Isles. To come so far and turn away from a prize so rich was cowardice, more shaming than any defeat he could suffer.

"Sygna!" he called out, pointing to the dip in the landscape. She nodded and angled the tiller accordingly while he and Falk set about altering the pitch of the sail.

The port came into view as the sky began to dim. Felnir trimmed the sail to allow the evening tide to carry the *Dehlgra* into a natural harbour formed of steep bluffs enclosing a deep-water bay. The port extended in a sprawl of buildings up the shallowest slope to the ridge beyond. Walls protected its flanks to either side and he could make out a procession of watch towers on the ridge. The absence of all but a few houses outside the walls made it plain they were not for show.

As Sygna steered towards one of the jetties extending from the dockside, Felnir noticed an increasing commotion among the many boats and ships at anchor in the bay. The shouts and gesticulations of the sailors soon spread to the shore where a large crowd began to gather.

"This lot seems awful excited about just one small ship, my lord," Falk commented in puzzlement.

"Not the ship," Felnir said, jabbing his thumb upwards, "the sail."

The colourful silk forming King Velgard's crest hadn't faded during the *Dehlgra's* incarceration in his unused tomb, standing out bright despite the fading sun. As they drew nearer to the jetty, Felnir saw crewmen pointing and assumed it had been a long time since any had seen this sigil emblazoned upon a sail. The sight appeared to arouse as much fear as fascination. Many sailors on the ships moored at the long jetty backed away, while others began to arm themselves. Fortunately, none saw fit to launch an arrow or voice an outright challenge before they moored up. Felnir and Falk lowered the sail while Sygna's expert piloting brought the *Dehlgra* close to the jetty.

Seeing no one waiting to receive a rope, Felnir leaped over the side and onto the boards to set about securing the lines.

"Not the warmest welcome," Sygna observed as she and Felnir manoeuvred the gangplank into place. A dense knot of people had formed at the far end of the jetty, mostly milling about in agitation, though Felnir's experienced eye picked out the more orderly lines of armed warriors forming among the confusion. Their concerned babble transformed into hushed surprise when Wohtin descended the gangplank. The crowd was too distant to make out speech, but Felnir felt certain the word "Diretongue" featured prominently.

Five centuries and some still remember him, he thought, watching Wohtin assume a placid, inexpressive stance.

"What now?" Felnir asked.

"We wait," Wohtin replied. "For Arnhilt or his heirs, whereupon I shall introduce them to their new king." He afforded Felnir a brief, appraising glance. "Until then, perhaps try to appear more . . . regal."

Felnir grunted a laugh and patted the pommel of the sword at his belt. "This should be all the finery I need."

The wait was long, the people on the docks continuing to throng as ever more warriors appeared among them. The sky was fully dark and a line of torches flickered to life along the wharf by the time the crowd parted and a man of impressive size strode onto the jetty. His bulk was enhanced by the bearskin about his shoulders, Felnir reckoning him at least equal in stature to his great-grandfather, which was no mean boast. He also noted the man's purposeful stride and the sword at his belt, also the fact that he felt no need for an armed escort. Only two figures accompanied him, a man and a woman. They were both tall, the woman of handsome bearing and about Felnir's age. The man was several years his junior and near as tall as the man he followed, though not so broad.

The man in the bearskin came to a halt a dozen paces off, standing in silent regard of Wohtin after casting a cursory glance over the *Dehlgra* and her crew. His beard was mostly grey but laced in black about his chin, face lined with age but not so degraded by experience as Wohtin's. It was in his gaze, however, that Felnir saw the true span of his years. Its shrewd appraisal bespoke considerable experience and displayed obvious recognition when regarding the old man before him.

"Angmund," he said finally in a voice like gravel. The name held a faint note of greeting, but not much else.

"Arnhilt," Wohtin replied, inclining his head. "It's good to see you."

Any suggestion that the sentiment might be shared was quickly dispelled by the hardening of the large man's features. Turning to Felnir, his shrewd eyes scanned him from head to toe, briefly settling on the Sword of the Altvar before shifting to the ship at his back.

"Still a thief, I see," Arnhilt observed. "Too much to hope you might leave his tomb un-desecrated, I suppose."

"No one was using it," Wohtin replied.

Felnir saw a faint twitch to Arnhilt's lips, though his gaze remained hard as it flicked back to Felnir, once again focusing on the sword at his belt. "Finally found someone fool enough to claim it, then?" Arnhilt asked Wohtin, though he continued to study Felnir, as if searching for something.

"He remains whole in mind and body," Wohtin said. "A worthy claimant, and now your king." Stepping forward, Wohtin raised his arms and called out to the people thronging the docks. "Behold, for I have brought unto thee the king that was promised." Sweeping an arm towards Felnir, he went on, "Show honour to Velgard's heir!"

The declaration heralded a buzz of conversation among the crowd, but no expressions of obeisance.

"Does he have a name, this king of yours?" Arnhilt enquired.

"I do," Felnir said before Wohtin could answer. "Felnir Skyrnrak of Skar Magnol." He had briefly considered either failing to mention his given name or adopting another, but spoke it now with unhesitant habit. Apparently, he had borne the name for so long it had become part of him, despised though it was.

"Redtooth, eh?" Arnhilt stroked his beard. "A noteworthy name for a man who hails from a clutch of hovels beneath the great mountain." He arched an eyebrow at Felnir. "Although, I imagine it's changed since my day."

"It has," Felnir said. "Now it sits at the heart of Ascarlia as the capital of the Sister Queens."

Arnhilt's brow furrowed in both amusement and surprise. "Sister Queens, is it? Ulthnir alone knows what calamity brought you to that." He paused to offer Felnir a formal nod as he introduced himself. "Arnhilt Volksora, Gyrwald of the Greencrest. This—" he nodded to the woman on his right "—is my great-great-granddaughter Freyna Kreemehr, who sits highest at my table. This one—" he flicked a hand at the young man "—is her grandson Tulvik, who does not. But since he's likely to be the last bearer of my blood for a while, I'm obliged to drag him along whenever something happens."

Felnir watched the youngster strive to keep his features neutral, but caught the glimmer of resentment before he lowered his face. His grandmother was much more practised in concealing emotion and Felnir could see why she had earned the name Owlsight. Her gaze was near as shrewd as Arnhilt's, and no less interested in the Sword of the Altvar.

"Sygna," Felnir said, gesturing to the figurehead of the *Dehlgra* where Sygna had perched herself, bow in hand. "My queen," Felnir added before inclining his head at Falk. "This man is Falk of the Southlands, leader of my *menda.*"

"*Menda?*" Arnhilt cast a pointed glance at the *Dehlgra's* empty deck before speaking on without waiting for an answer. "It's getting colder by the minute. As ever, Angmund has given me a lot to think about. My hall stands open to receive you." He stood aside, extending a hand towards the port. "I Arnhilt Volksora do swear, witnessed here in the sight of my closest kin, that no hand will be raised against you nor insult offered while you remain my guest."

Felnir exchanged a glance with Wohtin and, receiving a faint nod, told Falk and Sygna to disembark.

"You'll have to excuse my people their gawping," Arnhilt said as he led them along the jetty. "Not often a figure of legend returns from the dead, with a king in tow, no less."

Like near every building in the port, the hall of Arnhilt Volksora had been constructed from wood, although Felnir couldn't reckon the manner of tree from which such mighty beams might have been hewn. The dark timbers had a hint of red and few joins that he could see. The hall appeared to consist of great slabs of the stuff, creating a tall structure where Arnhilt's voice echoed as he led them inside.

"Hewn from the trunk of a single tree, if you can believe it," he explained, noting Felnir's interest in the building's construction. "There's a whole forest of them ten miles inland. The scarlet giants, we call them. Monsters standing two hundred feet high and twenty feet thick. I remember my brother-in-law guessing the tallest to be over two thousand years old. He was ever full of shit, of course, but I reckon he might actually have been right about that."

Wohtin exhibited no rancour at the unsubtle barb, merely commenting in a dry tone, "Indeed I was. There was a strange comfort to knowing that there was something in this land even older than you and I."

Arnhilt let out a grudging laugh as they entered the broad, high-beamed chamber at the heart of his hall. Torches blazed alongside thick timbers ascending towards a ceiling the light couldn't reach. "Bring benches, tables, food and drink!" Arnhilt called out to the dozen or so servants standing in the shadowed recesses of the chamber. "We have guests to honour."

Shrugging off his bearskin, he placed it on the high back of a raised chair, the only one in the hall. As he sat, he let out a grateful groan that made Felnir wonder if he appeared more hale than he was. However, Felnir saw no sign of decrepitude in the gaze he levelled at his guests, so naked in its mix of appraisal and calculation that it stirred a knot of worry. *He gave an oath in front of kin to do us no harm*, Felnir reminded himself, looking around the chamber to note the armed warriors taking up station in the gloom beyond the beams. *But do oaths hold true here as they do at home?*

"Tulvik usually sits to my left at a feast," Arnhilt said. "But tonight, Felnir of the Redtooth, that honour shall fall to you. I am keen to hear your tale. And—" his eyes slid towards Wohtin "—would prefer to do so without any interruption from my brother-in-law."

The Gyrwald of the Greencrest sat in silence as his servants brought tables and benches for his guests, nor did he speak while they waited for the food to arrive. No other kin or friends were invited to this welcoming feast, which Felnir felt said much for Arnhilt's summation of his guest's claim to kingship. It was only with the arrival of a roasted bird of some kind, unusually large to Felnir's eyes but possessed of a highly appetising aroma, that their host consented to stand and utter a few words. He spoke with solemn, if pointed formality, Felnir catching a squint in Wohtin's direction.

"I bid Felnir Skyrnrak and his companions welcome to this hall, where meat and drink shall serve as evidence of my good will. Let no hand be raised against them within the domain of the Greencrest. Any who break the given word of their Gyrwald shall suffer his fury unto death." Lifting a goblet into which a servant had poured some form of red-hued liquor, he drank and said, "Thus speak I, Arnhilt Volksora."

Seeing Tulvik and Freyna mimic the gesture, Felnir followed suit. The liquor in his goblet turned out to be a thick and potent type of wine. It grated on the palate compared to the more subtle vintages he preferred, but after so long at sea with only water, it was still welcome. The roasted bird was even more so, the meat rich and possessed of a sweet taste.

"We call it a gobble bird," Arnhilt said, "on account of the sound it makes. They're easy prey since they can't fly more than a few feet off the ground. The forests were full of them when we first set foot on this land. You have to travel a good way inland to find one these days." The Wald paused to sip some wine, Felnir seeing a shadow in his eyes as he added in a softer tone, "Much was different then, and not all the prey so easily hunted."

He brightened quickly, turning to Felnir to ask, "So, how did you come by your name? If you're to be king of Vorunvahl, the story should be told, should it not?"

"I bit a man's throat out in a duel," Felnir said, seeing little point in lies or obfuscation. He sensed this insightful and ancient soul would have little patience for either.

"Nasty way to go," Arnhilt grunted. "I trust he deserved it."

"No, he didn't. But I was younger then, and not yet in full mastery of my anger."

"Such is the way with age. Although I find it's not so much a matter of wisdom, but rather fatigue. Anger requires energy, and I've little enough of that these days." Arnhilt cast a sour glance at Tulvik eating his meal in stoic silence at the far end of the table. "Although some of my kin do occasionally manage to relight the fire from time to time. Do you have children?"

"Not as yet."

"Good. Do yourself a considerable service and keep it that way. Over five hundred winters upon this earth and Freyna's the only product of my blood worth a turd, and even she irks me more than I'd like."

Freyna, unlike her carefully inexpressive grandson, responded to this with a weary sigh that bespoke the forbearance of a trying and elderly relative.

"Are there many like you and Angmund in this land?" Felnir asked. "Ageless souls, I mean."

"Ageless? Hah!" Arnhilt thumped the table in amusement. "Nay, age harries me as it does all others, just more slowly. There are fewer of us these days, the *Ehilkun* they call us, the ancients. Our people are long-lived thanks to the Altvar's flame unleashed the day Velgard disappeared from Skar Altvar. Although, with every new branch to the tree of kin, their span of years grows shorter. My grandson saw nigh two hundred winters, but my great-grandson barely half that. Tulvik there will be lucky to make a century, that's if his doltish ways don't see him fall prey to a stumble down the stairs or a trip into the harbour."

Felnir saw the tendons of the young kinsman's jaw stand out in stark relief as he continued to eat, refusing to rise to the old man's jibes.

"In truth, there aren't so many *Ehilkun* left these days," Arnhilt went on, the lines of his face softening in sombre reflection. "So many years weighs upon the soul. People are not made to live to so long, and many eventually succumbed to what we call the *senflah*, the great weariness. Sickness and war took the rest, principally war. I imagine my brother-in-law has educated you in the many conflicts of this realm."

"In truth, he has not," Felnir said, glancing at Wohtin, who appeared mostly interested in his meal. Unlike Tulvik, his indifference gave every indication of being genuine. "However, our voyage to your shores was not without incident. We were met upon the seas by a ship bearing a raven upon its sail. Her crew were far from friendly."

At this Arnhilt stiffened, Felnir seeing him exchange looks with Freyna. "You fought them?" he asked.

"Yes. They rest now in Ulfmaer's embrace. Had to burn their ship too, which was a shame. She was a fine vessel."

A faint, bitter smile curled Arnhilt's lips as his eyes shifted to Wohtin. "So that's why you chose him," he grunted. "Makes sense, I suppose. If you're to unite this land, you'll need a killer, and that—" he looked to the Sword of the Altvar "—will surely make a great talisman. I think it's time, Redtooth, you told me the tale of how you came by it. I assume it was found in the Vaults of the Altvar?"

"It was. I was sent to find them by Queen Lore, and, with the aid of a scholar of great learning and insight, I did." As memories of the Vaults crowded his head, Felnir fought down the sudden welling of grief, although he couldn't keep the grating note from his voice as he spoke on, "Sadly, I regret to inform you that the Vaults are no more. The entire chamber fell to ruin when . . ." *Guthnyr hefting the spear, his face lit with satisfaction and triumph, utterly ignorant of his imminent fate.* Felnir gritted his teeth and continued, "When the treasures of the Altvar were claimed."

"You lost someone, didn't you?" Arnhilt asked, shrewd eyes intent upon Felnir's face. "Who was it?"

"My brother. And good friends. A man named Kodryn I had sailed with for years. And the scholar I spoke of."

"A hard loss, to be sure. But, when you've lived as long as I, you know that anything of great value will always extract an equal price from those who would claim it. How much did Angmund tell you, I wonder? I recall how he always liked to lacerate himself for his role in it, how he brought that vile foreign wretch Moyirn into our midst and led our blessed king into the worst folly."

Felnir noted how Wohtin's brows began to tighten, Arnhilt's words seemingly penetrating his reserve now he had fixed upon this particular subject.

"But, although he was there for the moment of calamity," the Gyrwald went on, "he wasn't there for the worst of it. In those days, to my great honour, King Velgard had made me warden of Ostan Hardta, the city on the shore. Those of us who dwelt there felt it too, but it was a passing thing, a fogging of the mind joined by a pain deep inside. We didn't know then what that pain meant, the great change that had been wrought upon us. So, while our minds cleared quickly, it was a different story for those in the mountain. Angmund came to us a gibbering madman, frothing at the mouth, barely able to speak a single word we could make sense of. But it was clear something terrible had happened. And so I gathered my *menda* and set out to investigate." Arnhilt paused to reach for his goblet, taking a hefty swig and swallowing it down, eyes distant as he continued his tale. "And there in the flame-lashed halls of Skar Altvar did I find my sister, laughing as she regarded the mess of guts she had cut from her own stomach."

Wohtin had become very still now, though he refused to turn and regard his brother-in-law, who wasn't yet done. "I it was who faced the horror that Skar Altvar had become," Arnhilt went on. "The city of the gods fallen into savage madness. It's a hard thing for a man to cut down his comrades, his own kin even, all of them crafted into ravenous, crazed beasts by forces that should never have been unleashed."

"My king commanded," Wohtin said, voice soft. "I obeyed."

"You were his most trusted counsel!" Arnhilt cut in, wine spilling from his upended goblet as his hand slammed the table. "The one voice that could have turned him from his folly. But no, the great and sagacious Angmund couldn't forgo his ambition. Couldn't cage the creature he had nurtured and raised up to orchestrate our destruction."

Arnhilt turned to Felnir, the anger on his face joined by a certain, urgent entreaty. "We searched, and we searched. Every corner of the Vaults and Skar Altvar scoured for any sign of our king, but we found nothing. It was as if he had been plucked from the world. And so, even now, all these many years later, there are those in Vorunvahl who believe he abides amid the Altvar themselves, awaiting the day he will return to us. You met a few such believers on the sea, Redtooth. Given that they regard any claim to kingship of this land as blasphemy, expect to meet many more. But you will do so alone."

Getting to his feet, the Gyrwald of the Greencrest stared hard at Wohtin, speaking in formal but emphatic tones. "Your words only ever bring destruction, Angmund. Diretongue they called you, and it was fitting. I'll raise no hand against you, Felnir Skyrnrak, but I will not send the folk of the Greencrest to war for the glory of a man I do not know. I thank you for your company this night, and will bid you fair sailing on the morrow."

"At least he didn't want us to starve," Sygna grunted as she and Felnir hefted casks of pickled fish onto the *Dehlgra*'s deck. The supplies, which included wine and oatmeal as well as fish, were waiting on the jetty when they returned to the ship the night before. Felnir reckoned there was enough to sustain them as far as the Fire Isles should he choose to forsake this enterprise. Last night he had enquired of Wohtin where they might head next, but the old man had sunk into one of his prolonged silences. He sat in his nook, eyes distant and expressionless, his position unchanged come the morning. *Did he sleep?* Felnir wondered. *Or just sit there all night wallowing in the misery provoked by his brother-in-law's words?*

"Visitors, my lord," Falk said, stepping up to the port rail with his axe in hand. Joining him, Felnir saw a large group approaching along the jetty. There were about thirty, all armed, led by Tulvik.

"Doesn't look like they're here to see us on our way with a hearty cheer or two," Sygna observed, reaching for her bow and quiver.

"Hold a moment," Felnir said. "Arnhilt Volksora didn't strike me as an oath breaker."

"Perhaps his kin are less honourable," Sygna replied, but kept her bow lowered as they watched the party approach.

They came to a halt just short of the *Dehlgra's* prow, whereupon they spent a moment in uncertain dithering. Watching Tulvik share glances with his companions, Felnir saw that they were all much the same age, men and women in their early twenties or younger. After some whispered urgings from the youths clustered at his back, Tulvik stepped forward and sank to one knee with his head lowered. The entire group followed suit as their apparent leader began to speak: "Mighty King Felnir Skyrnrak," he began, voice strained and faltering so much he was obliged to cough before continuing, "we come in search of your blessing . . ."

His voice died as Felnir's boots thumped onto the jetty. "Stand up!" Felnir snapped. "All of you," he added to the kneeling group. "Are you not Ascarls? You do not kneel to a man you don't know. A man who has done nothing to earn your obeisance. Stand up!"

Hesitantly, they complied, rising to the feet with uncertainty on many faces but also a hard determination on others. The decision to come here was evidently one they hadn't taken lightly.

"State your business," Felnir told Tulvik, who promptly responded with more downcast dithering.

"Ah, my king. We, ah, we come . . ."

"Oh, Ulthnir's arse, Tul," a beefy young man said in exasperation, stepping forward to afford Felnir a respectful nod. He was almost Tulvik's height but broader and, judging by the unabashed stare he directed at Felnir, also possessed a good deal more confidence.

"Beyorn of the Greencrest, my king," he introduced himself. "Come to pledge my sword in service to your cause." That said, he drew the blade at his belt and held it out to Felnir, lowering his head once more. Studying the proffered weapon, Felnir made out some nicks and scratches to the steel.

"This has seen battle," he said. "Who have you fought, Beyorn of the Greencrest?"

"The *Ahrkun Krayl*, my king," the youth replied promptly. "And more than once. I've killed three and consider it far too few. Our Gyrwald is a good man, but . . ." Beyorn's jaw tightened and he shot a look at Tulvik before speaking on. "Age gives him wisdom but makes him cautious, too cautious. The vile cult of the Raven Hearts ravages our outlying villages, slays our kin and steals our children, my cousin Huhlda amongst them. And my tale is but one of dozens. Too long has this been suffered. You have fought the *Ahrkun* once. To claim this land, you will have to fight them again, and I will stand with you when you do."

Felnir gave a soft grunt and stepped around Beyorn to survey his companions. A decent sized *menda*, if younger than he would like. But the *Dehlgra*, though small by the standards of an Ascarlian warship, would require a crew if she were to face battle again. He doubted they would enjoy so much fortune in their next encounter with these Raven Heart cultists.

"Sheath that," he told Beyorn, gesturing to his sword, then fixing his gaze on Tulvik. "I assume you are here without your Gyrwald's knowledge?"

Tulvik swallowed and nodded.

"And have you, like this man, tasted battle with the Raven Hearts?"

The narrowed eyes and twitch of resentment to Tulvik's lips made his answer plain before he voiced it. "No. The Gyrwald would not allow it. My blood is too precious, he tells me. Besides—" a bitter smile twisted Tulvik's lips "—it's his opinion that my oafish clumsiness would see me cut my own foot off before I got a chance to swing at the enemy."

"If you join with me," Felnir told him, "you'll have ample chance to prove him wrong. Just be sure of your choice before you make it."

"Surety I can give you, my king," Tulvik said, straightening, his voice taking on a new steadiness. *Disapproval,* Felnir decided, *that's what he fears most.* A sentiment he had felt often growing up in his great-grandfather's house.

"Don't call me that," Felnir told him. "When my business in this land is complete, any who wish to call me their king may do so. Until then, my name is Felnir, and all I have to offer is blood and hardship. For, despite what the sagas tell you, that is the true lot of a warrior. Nor will I promise you victory, for only a fool claims to know the outcome of war. But I will promise you this: join my *menda* and your enemies will be made to pay for their crimes. And, perhaps, if the Altvar bless us," he added, clapping a hand to Beyorn's shoulder, "we might even find your cousin."

Receiving a relieved smile in response, Felnir stepped back. "Now then, where do I find the closest nest of these pestilent birds?"

CHAPTER NINE

Thera

I t surprised her to discover that trying to dream was far more difficult than she expected. Every night since finding Lohdur's body, she had bedded down as comfortably as circumstance allowed. Having replaced her great-grandfather's gift about her neck with the traitor's trinket, Thera sought to compose her thoughts before succumbing to sleep. She hoped to conjure memories that would craft a coherent stage for whatever insights the silver knot had to offer.

Yet, the first night she dreamed nothing, at least as far as she could recall, despite having slept in an abandoned crofter's cottage featuring both bed and straw-filled mattress. The second night was much less pleasant, endured amid a copse of trees, and her dreams were a vague, ugly swirl of recent horrors. She caught her first glimmer of potential success on the third night in a small fishing port where the Uhlwald had provided a comfortable room in his hall.

She would have preferred a different dream, for this one brought a pang to her heart. She was a girl again, practising swordplay with her brothers and Sygna in the grounds of her great-grandfather's house. This was several months after the taking of Olversahl, and the mood was sour between the siblings. Felnir was a bundle of bitter, glowering resentment and Guthnyr, although recovering much of his habitual cheer, was given to sudden bouts of rage or tears. Sygna was different. Spared the horrors of battle, she was an untarnished soul, and a welcome one since Thera's brothers spoke to her so little now.

She recalled this particular day because she and Felnir, not for the first time, had inflicted some telling bruises on each other with their wooden swords. In Thera's mind, this was the moment her affection for Sygna had first been kindled. Admonishing Felnir for being a brute, she had tended to the welt on Thera's shin with a damp cloth. Sygna's smile had been a wondrous thing, a bright spot of genuine warmth and beauty after all the ugly memories of Olversahl and the loss of Thera's parents. Yet this dream was treacherous, for it changed Sygna's smile. The sympathetic wince and soft curving lips became the twist of a malicious, duplicitous heart. Instead of casting a reproachful glare at Felnir, Sygna's gaze was now filled with dark, lustful admiration.

It wasn't like this, Thera protested, watching her brother return Sygna's interest in full measure. *She hated him then.* But was that true? They had quarrelled a good deal, but had those recurrent exchanges of insults been a mask? Had they always been in league? Driven by jealousy and dark hearts to plot against Felnir's more celebrated sister . . .

Stop that! Thera barked, causing the dream version of Sygna to retreat in fright. Around them, the sunlight bathing the grounds of her great-grandfather's house became a matrix of twisting shadows as the sky above roiled with clouds. *Not real*, Thera reminded herself, recalling the trinket she wore. *Nothing here can be trusted. Not even my own thoughts.*

A stiff gale swept across the grassy field then, the lacerating chill of it jolting Thera into a gasp. Blinking, she realised she was alone now, her brothers and Sygna vanished. Yet, the sense of another presence was strong. Rising, she looked around, eyes probing the swirl of shadow and grass until they fixed upon a confluence of darkness at the edge of the nearby forest. She saw no true shape in it, beset by a strong intuition that something looked back at her from the formless gloom. So too was a mounting certainty that it would be folly to venture closer.

I came here to learn of my enemy, she reminded herself, resisting the urge to seek a way back to the waking world. Forcing herself forward, she traced a series of faltering steps towards the conjoined shadows. It had grown in the space of a few seconds, as had her fear. Wrongness seemed to flow from it, a disorientating sense of looking upon a thing that simply shouldn't be. Steeling her heart against a terror threatening to spill tears from her child's eyes, she stepped closer still and peered into the shadow.

"What are you?" she demanded, straining to discern shape or substance in the blackness. "Tell me the names of your spies!"

The response was immediate, and violent. Emitting a savage growl, the darkness lashed at her, an inky tendril uncoiling to whip at her face. As it touched her, Thera felt a chill more deep and painful than she had ever known. It went far beyond the icy gales of the frozen north, cutting so deep she wondered if her skull would crack. Reeling back from the blow, the dreamscape shattering around her, Thera saw something in the depths of the shadow. A face, the features mostly lost to the blackness, but catching a sliver of light so that she could make out the eyes and the mouth. It was laughing.

She came awake to the sound of pounding on her door, Aldeyn's voice loud with alarm. "Vellihr! Are you well?" More pounding until, groaning, Thera rose from her bed to open the door.

"I heard screaming," Aldeyn said, eyes darting about the room. He held his sword and had evidently come fearing assassins.

"It's all right," she told him, finding some both amusement and gratification in his panic. "Merely a dream." She took hold of the chain about her neck and held up the silver knot. "It worked."

"So you learned nothing of use?" he asked the next morning. Their business concluded, they were once again on the coastal track heading for Danith's Bay. By Thera's reckoning, they had mustered perhaps eight hundred warriors from a dozen villages, plus two score of boats. Not a great number, but every sword would be needed when they sailed south.

"I learned that whatever commands the Volkrath is truly vile," Thera replied. Touching a hand to her face, she added, "And powerful. I can still feel its touch." She didn't elaborate, thinking it best not to relate how the face in the shadow had laughed at her. The sound of its mirth lingered in her mind, not just for its evident cruelty, but also its note of surprise. *It hadn't expected me*, she realised. *It came in search of Lohdur and instead found me.* She knew distance meant nothing to those who could walk in dreams. Her great-grandfather had reached into hers all the way from Skar Magnol. Therefore, the Volkrath's spymaster could reside anywhere, most probably in the heart of the Nihlvarian realm since nothing about his face had been familiar. She also recalled the pain he had inflicted on her, resolving to repay it in full should she ever get the chance, but also recognising the import of it. Although her face showed no sign of injury, the chilly ache persisted. *If he could hurt me in a dream*, she pondered, *could I not do the same to him?*

Arriving at Danith's Bay, she was heartened to find it filled with vessels, counting nigh three hundred craft of all sizes. Most were fishing boats, but there were several dozen ships among them, though none as large as the *Great Wolf.*

"Fifteen hundred swords gathered to our cause," Ossgrym said, greeting her at the gate to the stockade. "And we can count on more when Kahlvik returns. Seems we'll have us a decent-sized *menda* after all."

"Too many small boats," Thera said, casting a critical eye over their fleet.

"We need to do some organising. Each fishing craft will be given a ship to follow into battle."

"Like a wolf leading cubs, eh?" Ossgrym teased a thoughtful hand through his beard. "Not a bad notion, Vellihr." His gaze darkened as it alighted on his nephew. Neither offered the other a greeting. "No trouble during your travels, I trust?"

"Found another Volkrath spy," Thera told him, going on to describe Lohdur's treachery and suicide.

"Olnar's boy?" Ossgrym sighed, shaking his head. "Gifted one of my best horses to that little shit when he came of age. Suppose I'll have to name a successor soon."

"Then I would suggest your nephew. He was of great assistance in spreading your summons. He also commands a good deal of respect among your people."

"I have no nephew," Ossgrym muttered before stalking off towards the makeshift wharf. "Kahlvik's due back tomorrow," he called over his shoulder. "We need to make all preparations to sail south without delay."

The following day, Kahlvik Vahrimdorr sailed into the bay with the evening tide, standing at the prow of perhaps the finest vessel Thera had ever seen. More narrow of beam than the *Great Wolf*, she was almost her equal in length, but had none of the brutish aspect that marked a warship. This was a sleek-hulled craft built to catch the wind on the open ocean, featuring two masts instead of one. The figurehead was also unusual in being of non-Ascarlian origin, the carving a brightly painted depiction of a beauteous woman in serene regard of the sea. This, Thera knew, must be the *Ohlira*, the ship that had carried Kahlvik of the Grey Eyes across countless miles to make him the most celebrated Ascarlian explorer of the modern age. Her name equated to the Ishtan word for princess and, according to rumour, had been chosen in honour of Kahlvik's lost love, a daughter to the Saluhtan himself. This tale of doomed romance had always seemed fanciful to Thera, and Kahlvik himself famously never spoke of it.

Trailing behind the *Ohlira* was a pair of bulky, wide-beamed craft Thera recognised as merchantmen of Albermaine-ish manufacture. Each sat low in the water due to the men and women crowding their decks. Behind them came a disparate gaggle of smaller ships and fishing boats, all laden with warriors. Even a cursory glance told Thera that the size of their *menda* had just doubled.

Perhaps we have a chance after all.

Turning, Thera found Lynnea standing nearby with Mohlnir perched on her shoulders. The apprentice had forsaken her makeshift crutch but still walked with a limp, often in defiance of Thera's instructions to keep to the *Great Wolf* and not exert herself.

"Do you doubt our success?" Thera enquired, surprised at what she sensed in Lynnea's thoughts. Uncertainty and fear were rare for her, or had they just been well hidden until now?

My experience of battle convinces me that nothing in war is certain, Lynnea responded. *But I have never doubted that what lies ahead must be done, whatever the outcome.*

Thera looked back at the *Ohlira* as she shipped oars and dropped anchor in the bay, hearing the many shouted greetings from the surrounding vessels as kinfolk and old friends hailed each other. She concealed a grimace as the dark calculation of how many would be alive in a few days began to churn in her brain. Thera forced the bothersome numbers away, knowing no good would come of it. Lynnea was right: their course was set now and battle inevitable. But then, Lynnea was right about most things and Thera had come to value her counsel, even when it came to matters best kept secret.

"You told me your mother knew much about those who bear the Altvar's blessing," she said. "Did she ever make mention of a dream walker?"

Frowning, Lynnea shook her head.

"You recall the trinket we took from that Volkrath spy?" Thera reached into her pocket and extracted the silver knot she had taken from Lohdur's body. "I found another. I believe this is how they communicate, how they receive their instructions." She paused, surprised by how difficult it was to speak a simple name. "Eshilde had one, too. It wasn't on her corpse, so perhaps Snaryk ate it."

Lynnea regarded the bauble with a furrowed brow. *How is it done?*

"In dreams. Somehow, the wearer of this thing allows a dream walker to share their mind." Thera went on to disclose her great-grandfather's ability, and his visitation that had set them on course to union with Ossgrym. She also related her own attempt to discover the puppeteer behind the Volkrath's treachery.

I have never heard tell of such a thing. Lynnea shook her head, fascination creeping into her gaze as she reached for the silver knot. Her thoughts exuded a pulse of reluctant criticism as she went on. *Although, Vellihr, I am bound to tell you that I believe your actions to have been very foolish.*

"We needed to know," Thera returned, annoyed both by her chiding tone and the knowledge that she was probably right.

The one who can walk dreams possesses the Altvar's blessing, Lynnea continued, still squinting at the trinket. *But the wearer of this does not. The dream walker would therefore possess all the power in such a meeting.* She paused, her face taking on a thoughtful cast. *Unless they were to share a dream with another blessed soul.*

Detecting the suggestion in her thoughts, Thera shook her head. "No. The risks are too great."

You want to know our enemy's mind, here lies the answer. I do not fear it.

"But I do." Thera plucked the trinket from her apprentice's grasp. "Let me ponder this further."

Lynnea's brow creased in consternation, but she confined her response to a short nod before turning and limping towards the gangplank. *As my Vellihr wishes. Veilwald Ossgrym has sent word summoning us to a feast. I think it would be rude not to attend.*

The feast proved to be a surprisingly raucous affair, largely free of the tension and morose fatalism Thera had expected. The assembled warriors of the Kast Geld drank and revelled with thirsty abandon. Clustering around the many fires blazing upon the shore of Danith's Bay, they gorged on roasted meat, bawled out various songs with varying degrees of tuneless enthusiasm, betwixt engaging in mostly good-natured brawling.

Thera made a point of visiting as many groupings as possible with Aldeyn in tow. She exchanged greetings with dozens of folk, striving to cement their names in her memory despite the guilty knowledge that most wouldn't stick. Once again, grim calculations crowded in with every meeting and forced word of encouragement she offered. She had seen enough of battle by now to guess which of these Kast Gelders would fall in the coming storm. A grey-bearded man with clouded eyes who had insisted on accompanying his granddaughter to the *menda*, brandishing his old, ragged-edged sword and loudly refusing all entreaties to leave. A youthful braggart who twirled and tossed his axe with a skill and boisterousness that couldn't mask the fear Thera saw every time he paused to gulp fulsome horns of liquor. Cowards were found in all battles, but rarely noticed in a confrontation at sea. After all, aboard a ship, there was nowhere to run. Even so, amid such fury, fear could be more fatal than courage.

She paid particular attention to the fisher folk who had been instructed to follow the *Great Wolf.* They all hailed from the same port on the northern coast of Ayl-Ah-Vahrim, hardy people of mixed ages and, if she was any judge, little experience of war. There were a half-dozen exceptions, older folk who had followed the Tielwald to Olversahl, but the rest were novices. Even so, she saw the firmness of their resolve, and could discern no obvious cravens in their ranks. In any case, the test of combat would quickly sort fearful braggart from steadfast warrior. Although she tried not to, she couldn't help but count them. Of the two hundred and twenty-three souls set to follow her ship to war, she would consider the Altvar kind if half were left when it was done.

Although never one for excessive indulgence in drink, she found herself taking ever more gulps from the wineskin Ragnalt handed her early in the evening. She knew little of wine, but could tell this was an expensive vintage from across the southern seas, potent too. Her worries dimmed as the wineskin grew thinner, although it also birthed a desire to separate herself from the throng. When a fist fight erupted at a nearby fire, she used the distraction to drift away from Aldeyn's side and wandered along the shore, enjoying the sight of the bay in moonlight. The weather was calm, and the ships bobbed on a gentle swell beneath a sky mostly bare of clouds. However, her pleasant contemplation of the stars glimmering above the forest of masts was soon interrupted by the sound of discordant voices. This was not the drunken shouts of brawlers but the hard-edged and sober declarations of those broaching a grievance. Also, they spoke in Alberic.

". . . not our war, Kahlvik," she heard one say as she moved closer, seeing three men on the beach. Kahlvik stood tallest among them. The other two were easily marked as foreign seafarers by their garb. The speaker was a stocky man with a bald pate and extensive beard, his teeth showing white in the gloom as he stabbed a finger at Kahlvik's chest. "You promised reward, not battle, remember? I've seen nothing of one and much promise of the other."

"And my crew grows anxious," the other seafarer said. He was taller than the bald man, his Alberic lightly accented and the hue of his skin told of far southern origin. "It takes a lot to ask a sailor to risk his neck for a cause not his own."

The captains of those merchantmen, Thera concluded, recalling the two bulky freighters that followed the *Ohlira* into the bay. *Kahlvik has enlisted reluctant allies, it seems.*

"I told no lies when we joined hands in this," Kahlvik replied. "Truth was spoken and a fair bargain struck for your services."

Thera was impressed with his command of Alberic. It flowed smoothly from his lips with little trace of an accent, unlike hers, which she knew possessed a stilted, grating quality. It was harsh enough to cause both captains to start in fright when she spoke, stepping from the shadows to regard them with an uncompromising glare.

"What did he promise you?" she asked, taking another gulp from her wineskin. "Silver, was it?"

"Vellihr Thera Speldrenda," Kahlvik said, greeting her with a nod before introducing his companions. "I present Captain Obryn D'Shaine of the *Northern Star*." The stocky man responded with a cautious nod. "And Captain Nahim Din Rabahs of the *Saffihr*." The taller man favoured her with a low bow and a smile of practised solicitation. "I am pleased to call them old friends and allies in our cause," Kahlvik added.

"Didn't sound much like allies," Thera observed, not bothering to smother a burp. "Sounded like hired hands grumbling over an already agreed price. Out with it, then." She fixed the two captains with a demanding glare. "What did he offer you?"

The two captains exchanged uncertain glances before Nahim coughed and provided an answer. "Our initial agreement was for a hundred silver pieces each," he said. "And surety that any goods we landed in Ascarlian ports would be free of all duties for a period of ten years."

"Really?" Thera turned her glare upon Kahlvik, who, to his credit, bore it with a steady-eyed resolve. "You have been generous, Grey Eye," Thera observed. "Making promises that reside within the province of the queens alone."

"In a time of extremity," Kahlvik replied, his tone lacking any contrition, "extreme measures are warranted, are they not?"

Thera grunted and turned back to the two captains. "As Vellihr of Justice, I judge the terms of your bargain to be more than fair. Therefore, they stand unchanged and you will be subject to just punishment should you attempt to break them. I bid you return to your ships and be ready to sail with the morning tide."

Captain Obryn was quick to lower his head and retreat a step, but Nahim did not. "Might I enquire," he said, "as to the nature of such just punishment."

"Certainly." Thera swigged more wine, then grimaced when she found the skin mostly empty. Tossing it aside, she went on, "I'll make you kneel on the deck of your own ship and cut your head off with my axe. It's very old, but also very sharp."

Nahim bridled, but his response faded when Obryn, presumably more accustomed to Ascarlian ways, silenced him with a firm grip to the shoulder. "The word of a Vellihr is always fair," he said, bobbing his head and tugging Nahim away. They exchanged clipped farewells with Kahlvik before hurrying across the beach towards a pair of waiting boats.

"You left a good-sized guard on both their ships, I trust?" Thera asked Kahlvik.

"I did. Not that I'd expect them to flee, in any case. For all their greed, they remain trustworthy friends at heart. They didn't forsake me when we faced pirates together upon the Green Tides. I doubt they'll do so now." He paused, shoulders stiffening in discomfort. "As regards the bargain I struck with them, if there is judgement to be made . . ."

Thera waved him to silence and sat down heavily on the beach. "Extreme measures, as you said." She reclined, resting her elbows on the sand and casting her eye over the ships once more, her gaze settling on the unique figurehead of the *Ohlira*.

"I confess myself envious of your ship," she told Kahlvik. "Built to your own design, was she not?"

"The man who crafted her hull would disagree, but he did have to suffer my constant hectoring. I told him I wanted the fastest ship ever to be birthed by an Ascarlian yard, and he didn't fail me."

"But she did not always bear the same name, I believe. Her birth name was the *Eastern Star*, so the tale is told. Yet you changed it. Tell me," she prompted, kicking a spray of sand at him when she saw his reluctance, "is she truly named for your lost love, a princess of Ishtakar, no less?"

Kahlvik's lips formed a rueful grin as he sat down beside her, though the humour faded quickly, replaced by the distance of sorrowful recollection. "She called herself a princess," he said. "As she called herself many things. But, for all her fine speech and bejewelled adornments, I doubt she shared a drop of blood with the Saluhtan, or even the most distant branch of his family. She told me many tales of her origin, each more fanciful than the last. There were only two truths I ever learned of her. First, she was the greatest love of my life. Second, she was perhaps the most dangerous being I have ever encountered, man, woman, or beast."

"And where did you find her, this singular and dangerous woman?"

"In different places, for she never tired of travelling. We first met in Assyrna, that teeming pit on the Sylmarian coast. She was posing as a merchant then, trading silks and spices. We engaged in a . . . lively round of bargaining that began with bared blades and ended in her bedchamber." Kahlvik paused to let out a brief laugh. "In days to come, it would be the reverse and I have the scar to show for it. There was a darkness in her, Vellihr. The gifts that made her great, also made her terrible."

He fell silent, but Thera, curiosity piqued and circumspection eroded by wine, prompted him for more. "You said she posed as a merchant. What was she really?"

"In her own way, she was like me, I suppose. A soul in search of all the spectacle the world had to offer. But, whereas I have always been succoured by the sheer joy of discovery, she lusted for the power inherent in fresh knowledge. Or—" a shadow passed over his face then, the sorrow in his gaze deepening "—ancient lore best left buried."

Abruptly, he got to his feet, forestalling any further enquiry with a formal nod. "I'd best shepherd my *menda* into the boats. I bid you good night, Vellihr, and fair sailing on the morrow."

"Does it look like her?" Thera asked before he could walk away. She pointed to the *Ohlira's* figurehead, the beauteous curves silhouetted against the stars.

"It should," Kahlvik said. "For she carved it. The morning after the last night we spent together, I returned to the *Eastern Star* to find the orca that had been her figurehead reshaped into the image of the woman who called herself a princess. How she did it, I never knew, nor could any of my crew explain it. The carving never weathers, nor does the paint fade or crack, and my ship has been favoured by the greatest luck ever since. Changing her name was the least I could do."

"Luck, eh?" Feeling suddenly sober, Thera rose, her gaze still captured by the gentle bob of the wooden woman. "We'll surely need plenty of that in days to come."

"The Altvar will bless us, Vellihr." Kahlvik extended his hand, and she took it, finding his grip fierce and his tone hard with certainty. "Trust the word of one who has sailed beyond the reach of any map. I can smell fortune on the wind, be it good or ill. And tonight, I smell victory."

By prior agreement with Ossgrym, the *Great Wolf* was the first ship to weigh anchor. Thera instructed Althsten to steer for the middle of the bay, then ordered the oars raised high so that all eyes would be drawn to the ship. Standing tall on the prow, she lifted the bronze striker above her head to catch the rising sun. Although most of those watching from the dense assemblage of boats and ships wouldn't be able to make out the crossed spears motif that formed the implement, she knew they would still divine the meaning of this ritual. Other captains were also taking up position on the prows of the vessels with strikers in hand, waiting to repeat her action.

"To Silfaer Rendwohlar, daughter to Ulthnir and Nerlfeya!" Thera called out. "The Battle Maiden, arbiter of victory to those who honour the Altvar and call themselves Ascarls! May she bestow her favour so that our swords cut deep, our arrows fly true, and our foes fall into the embrace of her brother, Ulfmaer!"

A cheer went up as she scraped the iron rod to the striker, casting a flurry of sparks into the sea as every captain in the fleet followed suit. She was gratified by the volume of the response, and the way the warriors crowding the decks waved their weapons as they cheered. She seized on it, used it to smother any further dark introspection, for with battle ahead, she could afford no more doubts. *Certainty trumps all when leading a* menda, Sister Iron had told her once. *Strategy and courage have their place, but if a warrior is to risk their life at your command, they must trust your word above all else. And so must you.*

"Steer south!" she called to Althsten as she stepped down from the prow. "Raise high the sail and set the oars to steady stroke. Our foes await, and I've no wish to disappoint them."

CHAPTER TEN

Elvine

The first Nihlvarian vessel to appear on Linsker Fjord was the largest ship Elvine had ever seen, and she had seen many. The warship dwarfed even the most hulking Alberic freighters in both breadth and length. Three tall masts rose from her deck, a feature usually unique to the southern seas barques that came to trade in iron and copper. However, her hull was an enlarged version of the arched, overlapped planking that distinguished vessels of Ascarlian design. The many oars that propelled her through the placid waters of the fjord sprouted from her hull, all sweeping with a precision that would have put veteran crews to shame. Behind her, many more red sails resolved out of the morning mist. These ships were not so large, but still possessed of impressive bulk. Elvine made a careful count of every ship, striving to estimate the number of warriors carried by this fleet. The figure she arrived at made it plain Skar Magnol was about to play host to a sizeable army.

As the huge ship drew up to the dock, Elvine was surprised to find she could read the gold-painted characters carved into her stern planking. *Ancient Ascarlian*, she realised. *Northern dialect.* Despite its familiarity, her practised eye picked out a few flourishes and additional punctuation that marked it as a form of writing that had evolved over time. The letters read: *The Vortigurn's Blade.* Although she had no trouble reading it, her memory supplied no immediate translation for the word "Vortigurn" though it chimed a distant echo in her mind. *Something from the sagas*, she decided, but not the Altvar Rendi, otherwise she would know it. She resolved to speak to Berrine about it later. Not even Lore possessed a greater knowledge of Ascarlian myth than her mother.

There was a considerable palaver in mooring the huge ship to the dock, with many lines thrown and much confusion between the stevedores and the Nihlvarian crew. It was only after some careful listening that Elvine realised they were speaking a heavily accented version of Ascarlian rather than a completely different language. It jarred on the ear, sounding coarse, not least due to the Nihlvarian sailors' liberal use of profanity.

"Catch the fecking thing, y'fecking shite brain!" one man called to a stevedore on the docks as he tried for the second time to toss him a rope. It wasn't just their ugly words and manners that made them disconcerting. The red-inked tattoos on many a face summoned raw memories of the attack on the *Sea Hawk*. *The warrior whimpering as the spear pierced his side while folk she had come to regard as friends died around her . . .*

The thud of the great ship's gangplank meeting the wharf dispelled the unwanted reverie, Elvine blinking to see a tall man in a bearskin cloak and black leather armour descend to the quay. His face captured her attention instantly, not least due to its undeniable, if gaunt, handsomeness, but also the sense of recognition it engendered. It blossomed with nagging elusiveness as he strode across the cobbled dockside, hands extended in greeting to Sister Lore. She raised her face to regard this apparent stranger with evident warmth, perhaps even a measure of concealed joy. But, although the Nihlvarian's hair was an inky black contrast to Lore's flaxen tresses, the similarity in the curve of nose and chin was unmistakable. *These two share blood*, Elvine realised as all she could recall about Lore's origins began to churn in her mind. *An orphan found alone on a ship drifting in northern waters. The only survivor of an attack by white whales, her memory destroyed by the horror of the ordeal . . .*

"Do I have the honour," the tall man began, cutting through Elvine's thoughts, "of addressing Sister Lore, Queen of the Ascarls?"

His tone was measured, the words spoken carefully to ensure they were comprehensible despite his accent. Even so, Elvine detected a knowing edge to it, conveying a sense of a man sharing a joke. The suspicion was confirmed when she saw a brief tension in Lore's face that told of a smothered laugh.

"You do," she said, affording him a gracious nod. "And who, may I enquire, might you be?"

A small shift to the head and thinning of the lips heightened the impression of performance as the tall man returned her nod. "Vahlak Tahrimsturm," he said, pressing a leather gauntlet to his breastplate. *Golden blade*, Elvine thought, her eyes slipping to the sword at the Nihlvarian's belt. The blade was hidden by the scabbard, but the hilt and handle gleamed with the untarnished shine of true gold.

"I come as both ambassador to and defender of the Ascarls and their most excellent queen," Vahlak continued, raising his voice so that Lore's assembled entourage of servants and warriors could hear. "As Tuhlvyr of the Buhl Aylis, I bid you greetings on behalf of the Vortigurn, King of Nihlvar, Emperor of the Volkrath Dominion, and Servant of the Altvar."

Although still preoccupied by her recognition of kinship between Lore and this Nihlvarian luminary, Elvine caught the additional weight he put on the word "Emperor." She also saw how Lore's expression faltered slightly upon hearing it, and this time there was no suggestion of humour in the grind of her jaw. *This Vortigurn is an emperor,* Elvine surmised. *Yet she remains but a queen.*

"Behold these gifts bestowed by my great lord," Vahlak continued, extending a hand to the gangplank where warriors were porting a procession of locked chests to the wharf. "Gold and jewels hewn from our mountains. Adornments fit for a queen."

"Adornments," Lore repeated, casting an eye over the stacked chests. Her voice held a clear note of annoyance, the smile she afforded the Nihlvarian forced. "Received with thanks, Tuhlvyr. The gold will be added to our treasury, and will be much needed in this time of strife and peril. The jewels will be sold to succour the families of those slain in the attack that claimed the lives of our sisters." She spread her hands, displaying fingers free of rings and wrists bare of bracelets. "For I have no need of finery, save this." Lore touched a hand to the moon and stars medallion hanging about her neck, sigil of Trieya, goddess of learning and wisdom.

A frown creased Vahlak's brow at this, Elvine reading the expression as surprised puzzlement rather than anger. He appeared to be about to voice a response when Lore spoke on with smooth assurance: "Now, you must allow me one introduction before we repair to the Verungyr, where a feast of welcome awaits you." Elvine's heart lurched when the queen beckoned her forth, offering a smile of encouragement. "This is Scholar Elvine Jurest," Lore told Vahlak. "Who, despite her youth, is quite the brightest and most accomplished mind in my realm. She is, I assure you, very clever."

Stepping from the line of assembled servants, Elvine caught the emphasis Lore placed on this last word. She could only wonder at its meaning as she afforded the Nihlvarian a respectful nod. "It is my honour to meet you . . . Tuhlvyr," she said, halting at the unfamiliar term, but thankfully free of the stammer she feared.

"I assure you, Scholar," Vahlak replied, eyes tracking her from toe to head, "the honour is truly mine."

Elvine had been the recipient of male attention since girlhood, most of it unwelcome and, in a few cases, annoyingly persistent until firmly rejected. So she knew lust when she saw it, yet the evident interest in the Nihlvarian's gaze failed to stir the usual welling of repugnance. There was an honesty to it that negated any impression of lasciviousness. There was also much the same warmth in his smile as in Lore's, although in his case it actually appeared to be genuine. Unlike many of his countrymen, Vahlak's face was mostly bare of red ink, save for an intricate motif curving around the brow of his right eye. Elvine felt the design tended to enhance rather than negate the pleasing angles of his features. Incredibly, she felt a warm flush to her skin as she lowered her gaze, smothering the sensation by summoning more ugliness from the attack on the *Sea Hawk*. *Druba bleeding his life onto the deck boards. Guthnyr fighting like a hero from the sagas, his sword sending crimson arcs into the air as he hacked and hacked, all to no avail . . .*

"Should you have an interest in perusing my library," Lore was saying, "I am sure Scholar Elvine would make the most excellent guide."

"I've little doubt of it," Vahlak said, Elvine reading a certain reluctance in his gaze as he returned it to the queen. "I am very pleased, my queen, to find your welcome so warm. I trust sufficient accommodation and supplies have been allotted for my warriors."

"All in hand. They shall be garrisoned close to the docks. My Vellihr of Lore," she gestured to Ilvar, "has overseen the preparations personally."

"Excellent." Without turning, Vahlak raised a gauntleted hand, whereupon a stocky man descended the gangplank followed by a dozen warriors. Unlike the Tuhlvyr, their faces were all liberally decorated in red ink, the stocky man in particular being so extensively tattooed it was difficult to make out the pale skin beneath the interwoven mass of designs. "This is Gonvyr," Vahlak said as the stocky man came to his side. "My bondsman and leader of my personal *menda*. He shall oversee the disembarkation of our forces. I have also requested that he survey the defences of this port. This is, of course, no reflection on your own preparations, my queen, but you must understand that I am charged by the Vortigurn with the success of this enterprise and therefore cannot leave anything to chance."

Once again, Elvine gained the impression of hidden communication, especially in Vahlak's emphasis when he spoke the word "anything". Lore's eyes narrowed a little in response, but her smile was its old radiant self when she nodded and stepped aside, extending a hand towards the misted holdfast rising above the town. "Of course. Assuming you are content to leave matters in the hands of your bondsman, please accompany us to the Verungyr." As she started off and Vahlak fell in alongside, Elvine saw their hands touch, just for a second, as the queen added in a soft, affectionate tone, "I'm afraid it's a bit of a climb, but I suspect you've scaled many a peak in your time."

* * *

The feast was a trying affair, overlong and filled with a strained atmosphere made worse by the fact that neither the queen nor her honoured guest seemed to notice. *Or*, Elvine thought, watching them laugh together, *they just don't care.*

She had worried that the Tuhlvyr might prove a pest this evening, but, though courteous, he afforded almost all his attention to Lore. Seated to the queen's left, Elvine was privy to the entirety of their conversation. Lore spoke at length of her ascension to the role of Sister Queen, Elvine noting that she made only a brief mention of her status as an orphan foundling.

"I had the good fortune to be placed with a childless merchant and his wife in Skar Magnol," she said. "They were as kind and loving as I could have wished for. Also, my new father's principal trade was in books. He insisted I learn to read, although I sometimes wonder if he regretted his choice for, once the flame of knowledge had been lit, I proved near impossible to separate from his stock. Every day my mother would have to drag me from the stacks in the storeroom. After a while, she gave up and would bring my meals to me, fearing I might starve." Lore paused to smile in fond remembrance before her features grew sombre. "I do miss them, terribly."

"They are no longer with us?" Vahlak enquired.

"They were old when they took me in. Father went first, a malady of the lungs. Mother not long after, a broken heart, I believe."

"I've little doubt your achievements gained them high honour in the Halls of Aevnir." Elvine wondered if the Tuhlvyr's reassurance might be more mummery, but she saw genuine concern in the way he clasped Lore's hand. The gesture dispelled any marginal doubt Elvine harboured about their relationship. *They grew up together*, she concluded. *Lore was not a seaborne gift from the Altvar. She was sent here. How long has this all been planned?*

Apart from the queen and Vahlak, conversation in the feasting hall was muted. Ilvar sat at one of the lower tables amid the more senior members of his *menda*, none of them exhibiting the raucous manners expected from warriors at feast. The other tables were filled with servants and various functionaries. Elvine calculated that there was considerable space for more seating, heralding the grim realisation that there were far fewer living bodies to fill them these days. A sickening mix of anger and hatred rose within her then, causing her to almost choke on the slice of boar she had been chewing. Though she tried not to, her eyes inevitably slipped towards Lore, the nauseous rage welling at the sight of her laughing at some witticism of Vahlak's.

You murdered dozens before my eyes, Elvine thought. *You slaughtered the queens with your own hands. You who are naught but a foreign intriguer, the grandest and worst of liars. And here I sit in this hall of cowards and traitors eating your meat and drinking your wine.* The fork in her hand began to shake as her gaze lingered on the elegant, pale curve of Lore's neck. She could see the faint line of a vein beneath the skin. *So close.* Her fist began to ache as it clutched the fork tighter. *How easy it would be. And have I not killed before . . .*

"Are you well, Scholar Elvine?"

Her gaze snapped to Vahlak, his conversation stalled as he regarded her with a frown of concern. Setting down her fork as gently as she could, Elvine swallowed with difficulty before grating out a reply. "I find myself embarrassed by so rich a feast, Tuhlvyr." Reaching for a goblet, she swallowed down a mouthful to banish the dregs of boar from her throat. "Too much of this, I think," she added with a laugh, raising the goblet.

"Don't be fooled by her pretence of delicacy," Lore said, arching an eyebrow at Elvine, though her smile was all indulgent fondness. "This one sailed all the way to the Fire Islands and returned with the greatest treasure, risking life and limb in the process."

"Treasure, eh?" Vahlak pursed his lips in mock judgement. "And I thought my queen had no need of finery?"

"Not that kind of treasure," she chided, lightly tapping his hand. "Something far more valuable than any bauble. In fact—" she frowned and rose "—it occurs to me I have been remiss in not showing it to you sooner. Please," she added, raising a hand as the assembled feasters also began to get to their feet, "stay and enjoy, good people of the Verungyr. I shall return shortly." She inclined her head at Elvine. "Come, dear heart, I would have the Tuhlvyr hear the story from your own lips as we ascend the tower."

"It's . . ." Vahlak paused, regarding the Spear of the Altvar with a quizzical frown, arms crossed and one hand tapping his chin ". . . just a spear."

"Indeed," Lore agreed. "Plain as an old stick. Yet I've no doubt of its provenance."

The Tuhlvyr extended a hand to the spear's haft, then hesitated. "I assume it's safe to touch?"

"I find it so. So does Elvine. No others in the Verungyr dare venture near it, however. But I sense you are fashioned from more courageous stuff, Tuhlvyr."

He grimaced a little at the taunt in her voice, then plucked the spear from its cradle. Holding it aloft for a second, he let out a soft grunt. "Mere wood and iron," he said, smoothing his hands over the haft and the blade.

It was as his fingers touched the metal that he betrayed a small, nearly imperceptible shudder.

He hears it! Elvine thought, fighting panic.

However, the moment passed quickly and Vahlak merely grunted again before setting the spear down. Turning to Lore, he said something in a language Elvine was surprised to find, not without some chafed pride, she had never heard before. Yet, it was obvious that Lore understood every word. Also, from the way her gaze briefly settled on Elvine, it was equally clear that the queen's scholar had been the subject of his question.

"You can speak freely," she told Vahlak in Ascarlian. "I expect my dear scholar has divined far more than either of us could suspect already. Have you not, dearest one?"

Unable to summon a response, Elvine could only lower her head.

"Don't be tedious, Elvine." Lore's instruction was inflected with a rare curtness. "Tell me and don't obfuscate. What have you deduced about Tuhlvyr Vahlak?" Her voice softened as she added, "And know that you have nothing to fear from me."

Another lie, Elvine decided. Yet, as the resentful fear set her heart thumping, she experienced the same sense of dislocation she had felt before receiving the vision of Lore ordering the execution of the rioters. However, this time, there was no vision. Instead, she saw a glow surround the queen, accompanied by a wave of reassurance. The meaning was unexpected, also unmistakable. *No lie.* Elvine blinked, eyes snapping from Lore to the spear and back again. *This woman truly loves me.*

"I . . . believe," Elvine began, grimacing as she fought to strip the stammer from her words, "Tuhlvyr Vahlak to be your brother, or close kin of some kind."

Lore's smile took on a smug curve as she turned to Vahlak. "Told you she was clever."

"That she most certainly is." The Nihlvarian's gaze tracked over Elvine's face with even more intensity than he had shown at the docks. This time, however, she was sure she saw as much lust as curiosity. Meeting her eyes, he smiled and said, "You are right, of course." He extended a hand to Lore, and she took it, coming closer to press herself to his side. "For many years, I longed to see my sister again." Vahlak cupped Lore's cheek. "Now, thanks to the Altvar, it has finally come to pass. Along with much else."

Elvine knew she should cage the words she spoke next, but they tumbled from her mouth before wiser instinct could take hold. "You are Nihlvarian," she said to Lore. "Sent here to bring down the Sister Queens."

"Yes," Lore replied, her tone one of simple honesty. "And a long and difficult business it has been."

Murderer! Assassin! Spy! This time, Elvine managed to swallow the words, face reddening with the effort.

"It had to be, Elvine," Lore said, seeing her distress. Unclasping her brother's hand, she moved to take hold of Elvine's shoulders. "You know this better than anyone. Were you not persecuted by the queens' laws? If not for my intercession, they would surely have tortured and killed you. Don't waste your grief on them. Their time was over many years ago, but still they clung to power, unable and unwilling to grasp the greatness that is the destiny of this realm. A destiny ordained by the Altvar at the founding of the world, and now once more set in motion." She enfolded Elvine in her arms, drawing her into a tight embrace. "With you at my side, I can make it happen," she whispered in Alberic, too soft for her brother to hear. "But you must trust me above all others."

She squeezed Elvine tighter then stepped back, briskly clasping her hands together. "Now then. While I did want my brother to hear the fascinating tale of your recent adventures, I had another reason for calling you here. I should like you to tell Tuhlvyr Vahlak all you can about the port of Olversahl."

"Olversahl, my queen?" Elvine asked, her voice made small by sudden, icy foreboding.

"A pertinent question," Vahlak said. "While this war has gone reasonably well, I still have unfinished business in the Outer Islands. The locals are proving irksomely hard to subdue. I hear tell they destroyed one of my stockades not long ago. It is not wise to leave our line of supply to Nihlvar threatened so, yet you talk of a port I believe lies far to the south."

"Not so far as to be out of reach," Lore replied. "And supply lines are also my concern. Olversahl is the principal port of call for southern trade with Ascarlia. At least three times the number of foreign vessels arrive there every year than arrive in Skar Magnol. Perhaps the one thing my sisters did right was agree to seize Olversahl back from the Algathinets. The Dowager Princess of Albermaine has undoubtedly been informed by her spies of recent events here. She knows well that opportunity often arises from chaos. And I've little doubt there are many in Olversahl who would welcome the return of Albermaine-ish rule. Would they not, Elvine?"

Unable to think of any reply other than the simple truth, Elvine responded with a flat, "Some, my queen. But far from all."

"A confused picture then, which makes it a city ripe for sowing of discord in advance of seizure, at least in the ever cunning eyes of the Dowager Princess. Besides, we'll need to secure it for later. Skar Magnol, as you've seen, lacks the harbour to properly provision a full-sized invasion force."

Vahlak let out a small chuckle. "It seems my sister has learned to think like a warrior."

"Hardly." Lore afforded her brother a thin smile. "You remember what he told us that day before I was sent away?"

Vahlak's face clouded, brows growing heavy. "He said many things that day."

"He did. But one has always stayed at the forefront of my mind. 'Warriors,' he said, 'Don't win wars. They merely fight them.' And you, my cherished brother, are here to fight for me." She turned to Elvine, the smile shifting into a businesslike frown. "While my scholar will provide you with all the intelligence required to secure victory. For a start, we need lists. I'd guess there are few better acquainted with the workings of governance in Olversahl. Elvine, you will list those most likely to support our cause, and those most likely to oppose it. If the task is burdensome, I'm sure your mother can assist."

She loves me, Elvine thought. *Yet never balks at threats, however carefully phrased.* The notion stoked her fear, for it meant that Lore's love was genuine, born of knowledge rather than delusion. *She knows me. Knows I want no part of this. What else does she know?*

Lowering her head, Elvine replied in a soft tone of grave assurance, "As you wish, my queen."

"Olversahl." Berrine's voice echoed softly in the stairwell, but still too loud for Elvine's liking. Glancing at the steep, arcing curve of steps to their rear, she tugged her mother into an alcove and didn't speak until she was sure no curious ears lurked above or below. Unwilling to risk another whispered conversation in Berrine's chamber, she had visited that morning with a loudly spoken request to view the ancient documents stored in the Verungyr's vaults. As far as either of them could tell, they hadn't been followed, but Elvine made sure to descend to a suitably remote depth before relating what she had learned in Lore's tower.

"She's too clever to forgo securing it," Elvine murmured. "Skar Magnol is a prize, but Olversahl is the true jewel of Ascarlian trade. And, unless I'm mistaken, she and her brother have plans that extend far beyond this realm."

Berrine pursed her lips, brows drawn in calculation. "I saw the way he looked at you during the feast. He's as smitten as . . ." She paused and Elvine knew she had just stopped herself speaking Uhttar's name. The fate of the unfortunate apprentice shipwright, and would-be suitor, remained a raw subject between them, not least for the guilt that surged whenever Elvine's thoughts turned to him.

"Such interest may prove useful," Berrine added, drawing a glare from her daughter.

"What exactly are you suggesting, Mother?"

Berrine rolled her eyes. "Don't look at me like that. You don't have to lie with a man to win his heart or secure his assistance. Sometimes, merely the possibility alone will suffice. Just be nice to him, is all. We can't afford the luxury of not playing all the cards in our deck, given that we have so few."

Elvine folded her arms, muttering, "I'll consider it."

"Do that. While you do, also consider that our need for escape is now more urgent than ever. We have to bring warning to Olversahl."

"Lore has no intention of letting me go. And Ilvar's *menda* are ever vigilant. Not to mention the thousands of Nihlvarians now crowding the docks and their fleet at anchor in the fjord." Elvine shook her head. "This cage is too well made, Mother."

"There never was a snare that couldn't be slipped," Berrine replied, a thoughtful distance in her eyes. "Something someone told me once. Perhaps the only soul who could reckon a way out of here." She blinked, fixing Elvine with a purposeful stare, albeit tinged with reluctance. "You need to prevail upon the queen to grant you access to the Tielwald, assuming he hasn't already been tortured to death."

CHAPTER ELEVEN

Ruhlin

He awoke to the sound of a blade biting wood. Groaning, Ruhlin raised his head from a bed of leaves, blinking the fog from his eyes to behold the sight of Guthnyr hacking away at a tree branch with a sword. The morning air was chilly and Ruhlin saw steam rising from the blond man's bare, muscular frame as he worked, making him wonder how long he had been at it.

"He took the sword from a guard in Speltsaer." Ruhlin turned to find Aleida crouched at his side, a concerned frown creasing her brow as she scanned him for sign of injury. "The only one we encountered on the way out, unlucky for him." Grunting in satisfaction at Ruhlin's absence of wounds, she glanced over her shoulder at the Ascarlian, still busily swinging the sword. "That one snapped his neck before he knew what was happening. And he seems very keen to find more to snap."

"Did we lose anyone?" Ruhlin asked, looking around the camp. They were in a small clearing amid a dense patch of woodland. Through the frosted overlap of branches he made out the others clustered around a fire leaking grey smoke into the air.

"They're all still here," Aleida confirmed. "Apart from Tuhlan, who went off to hunt."

Nodding, Ruhlin got to his feet, smiling in gratitude when Aleida handed him a jerkin and fox fur cape. "What few treasures we have left," she explained. "We had to leave the carriages behind in Speltsaer." The worry on her face mirrored his own. Having failed to seize a ship, they were now just a group of beggared people hiding in a forest. He forced the encroaching self-pity away with an annoyed grunt. *Beggared or not, I'd rather starve free than eat chained under another's whip.*

"So, you're awake!" Guthnyr greeted him with hearty good cheer, breath billowing as he paused his exertions. "Feels good to hold a blade after so long."

"I owe you thanks," Ruhlin said. "For carrying me clear of that place . . ."

"You owe me nothing, Ruhlin ehs Kestryg," Guthnyr cut in. "The debt between us is so great I doubt I'll ever balance it."

Catching a small movement to Guthnyr's rear, Ruhlin saw the youth and the woman they had rescued from the slave ship huddled in the lee of a wide oak. Their eyes shone bright with the wariness of folk confronting unfamiliar and potentially dangerous circumstances.

"Forgive my crewmates," Guthnyr said. "Their time aboard that fucking ship did them scant favours. Come here, you two!" he instructed, raising his voice. "Time to properly greet our benefactor."

Hesitantly, the pair rose and moved to Guthnyr's side, eyes constantly darting between Ruhlin and the others clustered around the fire. "He's Jolnyr, and she's Behsla," Guthnyr said. "Late of the *Sea Hawk*."

"Welcome," Ruhlin said, offering them both a nod and putting a hand to his chest. "Ruhlin ehs Kestryg of Ayl-Ah-Swahl." He hoped his accent and mention of an Ascarlian island would allay their fears, but both continued to exhibit only fearful anticipation. "We'll eat soon," Ruhlin assured them. "One of our party is out hunting, and he never fails to return with meat. Please—" he gestured to the fire "—go and warm yourselves. You'll find only welcome in our party, for all here have suffered the chain and the whip."

At an encouraging nod from Guthnyr, the two of them moved towards the fire, Ruhlin gratified to see the others make room for them. "Jolnyr's just a lad," Guthnyr sighed. "But Behsla was one of the fiercest souls I ever met, quick with a laugh but quicker with a knife. The whip-man liked to torment her more than us, said breaking her will was a matter of professional pride. Wish I'd taken longer over choking the bastard." He flicked his wrist, the sword sending splinters flying from the nearest branch.

"You were their captain?" Ruhlin asked.

"Aye." A shadow passed over the seafarer's face. "For a short time. The *Sea Hawk* was my brother's ship . . ." He trailed off, shoulders hunching and expression darkening yet further.

"The Nihlvarians killed him?" Ruhlin prompted, which earned no answer save a shake of the head before Guthnyr sniffed and straightened.

"It would please me to know where exactly we are," he said. "And if you have any notion of how we might get home."

"We are some miles north of the port of Speltsaer in the realm of Nihlvar, which sits far west of the Fire Isles. As for getting home." Ruhlin pulled his cloak about his shoulders and turned to the fire. At first he couldn't see Sygurn, then picked out his hunched, unspeaking form sitting apart from the others. "We have another plan to make, it seems."

"We can forget about trying for another ship." Sygurn's voice was quieter than usual but still emphatic. Tuhlan had returned bearing a small deer across his shoulders. Swiftly butchered, it now hung on a spit over an expanded fire, the aroma doing much to revive the spirits of this disparate and recently disappointed company. Ruhlin had worried the smoke and the smell would attract unwanted notice, but Sygurn assured him they were too deep in the forest for it to matter.

"Word of that mess in Speltsaer will have spread to every town and village within reach," the Nihlvarian said. "Soon, it'll reach the local Tuhlvyr's ears and he'll have every warrior under his command scouring the country for a band of murderous escaped slaves. Getting anywhere near another port will be impossible." His hard, weathered features held a note of apology as he met Ruhlin's eye before casting a reluctant glance at Iyaka. "We have to run. And I can think of but one direction."

"As I wanted to from the beginning," the Morvek pointed out. "When the distance to our lands was shorter."

"We gambled and lost," Ruhlin cut in as Sygurn began to bridle. "And it was my choice. So cast the blame at me, if you must."

Upon waking he had half-expected to find the Morvek gone, but Iyaka and the others remained. Nor did he sense any urge to separate from the group now as they exchanged glances. He had no argument to offer should they decide to leave, or at least insist on different leadership. Yet, when Iyaka spoke again, her voice and bearing lacked any recrimination or defiance.

"It will be a hard trail," she said. "And long. We'll have to avoid all roads and settlements." Iyaka paused, features bunching in thought. Ruhlin saw her lips curve in an unexpected smile, but it faded quickly. "Save for when we need to steal supplies," she continued. "Which we surely will with the change of seasons upon us."

"But you can guide us?" Ruhlin asked. Receiving a nod, he went on, "And will your people accept us?"

This heralded a longer pause and more unspoken communication between the Morvek. "My words hold weight among certain clans," Iyaka said. "With luck, we'll find them."

"And what if we happen upon a clan who don't give a shit for your word?" Sygurn enquired.

Iyaka shrugged. "Then they're just as likely to kill me as they are you."

Until now, Ruhlin had thought of the Morvek as a single people, all sharing the same language and customs. Now it seemed they could be as disunited as folk everywhere. Still, they were severely lacking in options. "It's settled then," he said, looking around the group. The way they hung on his word disturbed him, all eager to lend him their trust. *Is it the monster?* he wondered. *Instead of an affliction, they see a mark of greatness.*

"Iyaka will guide us into Morvek lands," Ruhlin went on. "Any who disagree are welcome to follow your own path. For now." He forced a smile, gesturing to the spitted deer carcass. "We eat."

For four days, they followed Iyaka as she set a punishing pace through the forest. By Ruhlin's reckoning, they headed due west rather than the northward course he expected. Although reluctant to question her judgement so soon, on the third day he took advantage of a brief rest stop to venture a soft-spoken observation. "I thought Morvek lands lay to the north-west."

"They do," she said. "But, as agreed, we need supplies. There is a place I know not far from here where we will find all we need."

"Is it defended?"

Iyaka let out a grunt, Ruhlin hearing an anticipatory growl when she added, "Not as well as it should be."

Another day and half of marching, during which the air seemed to grow colder by the hour, the trees thinned and gave way to pasture. Herds of shaggy-haired, long-horned cattle grazed on grass stunted by the onset of winter, given to mooing loudly at two-legged intruders.

"Plenty of meat to be had, at least," Sygurn commented as Iyaka led them to the crest of a hill.

"More than that," she muttered back. Nearing the crest, she dropped to her hands and knees, gesturing for them to do the same. Crawling to her side, Ruhlin looked down upon a sprawl of buildings. There were about a score of varying sizes, linked by tall fences that resembled more the walls of a stockade than the pens of a farm. People laboured in the surrounding fields and among the buildings, working in groups of half a dozen, each overseen by a figure in armour.

"Slaves," Ruhlin said. Turning to Iyaka, he saw her features now set with predatory hardness, eyes flicking from one overseer to the other, as if searching for someone she knew. "You were enslaved here," he realised, recalling her smile back at the clearing.

"I said there would be supplies," she said. "And there are, in plenty. But one purpose can fulfil another. Would you begrudge me some revenge,

Telchak?" She still used the name she had afforded him when they wore chains. When first spoken, he had taken it for an insult. Now he heard something new in the phrasing, the sound less harsh and more elongated, almost reverential.

"Our numbers are few," he reminded her. "We cannot afford a battle."

"I can." The words came from Guthnyr, spoken in a low growl. Like Iyaka, his gaze was focused on the whip-men below, fingers twitching on the handle of his sword. "How many guards?" he asked the Morvek.

"Twenty, when last I was chained here. But many more slaves."

"Twenty is a lot for us," Sygurn said, shuffling to Ruhlin's side. "Unless . . ." He gave a meaningful arch of his brow, the hopeful suggestion obvious.

Ruhlin ignored the Nihlvarian and turned back to Iyaka. "I assume you know a way in?"

"The west-facing fence borders a stream. There's a small gate for when they toss out the worst of the filth from the pig pens." She cast an eye at the sky. "We'll wait for darkness."

The stream flowed fast, emitting a loud and welcome gurgle that masked the sound of their approach. The banks were also thick with tall grass, the ground being too broken and strewn with rocks for grazing. They lay under cover for hours as gloom crept across the sky. Above the stream's busy churn, Ruhlin heard the raised voices and occasional whip cracks of the field slaves being harried back to the farm buildings. When the noise faded, he caught the flicker of Iyaka unsheathing a dagger.

"There's a man here," she said. "He has a scar down this side of his face." She traced a thumb over her right cheek, then cast a hard glare around them all, lingering most on Guthnyr. "You can have all the others, but no blade touches him but mine."

"Sounds fair," Guthnyr said with an amicable shrug. Drawing his sword, he set it flat on the grass, leaning forward to cover the blade's gleam with his bulk. "Can we get in?"

"There's a chain on the gate," Iyaka said, shifting her gaze to Aleida. "Just two of us," the Morvek added when Ruhlin began to rise alongside Aleida. "More risks attracting notice. And you're not the stealthiest among us, *Telchak*."

The two women approached in a crouch, slipping into the rapid flow of the stream and keeping low as they made their way to the far bank. Once there, they became vague shapes against the backdrop of the fence. Aleida reappeared after a short delay, beckoning them across. Entering the water, Ruhlin bit down hard to cage an exclamation at the chill. Sygurn was unable to match the feat. "Fecking ball shriveller!" Fortunately, his profane hiss was swallowed by the stream and no alarm came from the buildings ahead.

"Once past the pig pens, the slave hut is to the left," Iyaka said when Ruhlin came to her side. She crouched at the opened gate, dagger in one hand and sword in the other. Although she spoke in a whisper, he could hear the hunger in her voice. "The guard house is to the right."

"Take the pens," Ruhlin told Aleida. "Free any willing to fight. Sygurn, Julette, go with her." He drew his own sword and began to follow as Iyaka started through the gate, then paused at the weight of Guthnyr's hand on his shoulder. "Crave your pardon," he said, affording Ruhlin a wink as he slipped ahead of him. "Wouldn't want to let your friend out too soon, would we?"

He and Iyaka moved on before Ruhlin could voice a response. Sighing, he followed with Tuhlan and the other Morvek close behind. Traversing a narrow channel with stone walls to either side, Ruhlin's nostrils were briefly assailed by the stink of pig muck before he emerged into the inner precinct of the farm. Iyaka and Guthnyr had already drawn blood. The Morvek crouched over the body of a guard, wiping her dagger on his trews, while Guthnyr had another pinned to the pig pen wall. The man grunted wetly as Guthnyr pressed his sword blade into his neck, not stopping until steel met spine.

The pair moved on swiftly, heading for a large thatch-roofed building to the right. Glancing over his shoulder, Ruhlin saw Aleida leading her party towards a longer but more squat structure. As he turned away he heard a stifled cry of pain followed by the thud of a falling body.

Nearing the thatched building, he was puzzled to find no guards posted outside. The windows were lit by the glow of hearths within and he could hear the murmur of voices engaged in tired conversation. He found Guthnyr and Iyaka standing in contemplation of a large door.

"Twenty, eh?" the Ascarlian asked, drawing a small laugh in response. "Two less now."

"Wait," Ruhlin warned as Guthnyr raised a boot to kick the door open. Nodding to the thatching above, Ruhlin remembered a favourite phrase of his grandmother's: "It's easier to smoke out a rat than go looking for it."

Fortunately, the farm precincts featured several stanchions supporting blazing torches. They hacked planking from the fences to make more. Before they were lit, Iyaka sent the other Morvek to seal the entrance at the rear of the building. Guthnyr threw the torches, casting them in a high arc to land at the apex of the thatched roof. It took longer than Ruhlin expected for the fire to take hold, and when it did, it proved disappointing, birthing more smoke than flame. The inhabitants of the guard house, however, found it sufficiently alarming to raise a chorus of shouts and commence a stampede into the open.

Guthnyr killed the first to appear, a large man who had neglected to don armour or carry a weapon in his haste towards safety. The wide-eyed glare of surprise lingered on his face even after Guthnyr's sword stroke cleaved his back open, sending him sprawling onto the muddy ground. A woman followed, her hacking coughs cut short when Iyaka's dagger lanced into her throat. For the next few moments, the two of them killed with vicious efficiency, maimed and slain bodies piling up at the door. Inevitably, the remaining guards realised the danger and began to fight back, driven to desperate courage by the flames licking at their rear.

One man managed to make it past Guthnyr when the warrior was distracted by disembowelling another. Clothes smoking and axe flailing, the guard let out a shrill scream of triumph and terror as he stumbled into Ruhlin's path. This time there was no repeat of the frozen moment aboard the slave ship, Ruhlin cutting the man down with an overhead swing of his sword. The blade bit deep into the guard's unprotected shoulder, sending him to his knees. For an instant, he stared up at Ruhlin, recrimination vying with a desire for mercy in his eyes. Ruhlin kicked him free of the blade and left him twitching on the ground.

Nearby, Behsla and Jolnyr set about finishing the wounded guards, moving from one stricken form to another and stabbing with murderous fury. Of the two, the south seas woman appeared the more controlled, although clearly relishing the task. The youth, however, went about his business with an expression of such manic joy that Ruhlin concluded his trials aboard the slave ship had driven him beyond the reach of reason.

A scream drew his gaze back to the door in time to witness Guthnyr lift a bloody-faced guard and cast him back into the flaming interior of the building. No more came forth after that. "Didn't see your scar-faced friend," Guthnyr observed to Iyaka, wiping the mingled sweat and soot from his brow.

"No, he wouldn't be here," she said. She started towards the northern end of the farm, where a large house rose above the drifting smoke. "I can do this alone," the Morvek added, slipping into the hazy gloom. Ruhlin began to debate the wisdom of following her when an upsurge of shouting drew his attention to the slave hut.

"Still work to do," Guthnyr observed, charging off with a cheerful twirl of his sword. Ruhlin began to follow, then paused at the sight of Jolnyr using the tip of a dagger to pluck out the eye of a still living guard.

"Stop that!" Ruhlin snapped, the youth responding with an empty-eyed glance of confusion, the wet, glistening orb slipping from the tip of his blade while the guard guttered out his last few breaths. Sighing, Ruhlin turned and hurried in Guthnyr's wake.

"I told you I'd come back." Although Iyaka's words were spoken to a severed head impaled upon a fence post, she seemed annoyed by the absence of a reply. Upon finding her contemplating this grisly trophy outside the burned-out husk of the house, Ruhlin was unsurprised to note the scar marring the right cheek of the impaled head. From what he had been able to gather from the freed slaves, this man had been the Aerling of this farmstead, feared and hated in equal measure for his many cruelties. There were over forty slaves in all, and not one free of scarring from whip or brand. Ruhlin thought about asking Iyaka for the Aerling's name, but decided not to. Like Eldryk, this man deserved death, but not remembrance.

"There are several Morvek among the slaves," he said. "It would help if you could talk to them. Perhaps persuade them to come with us."

Iyaka didn't appear to hear him, continuing to regard the Aerling's slack, death-bloated features with the same irked cast to her brow. "You didn't beg," she muttered. "I wanted you to beg. For your family, if not yourself."

Ruhlin's gaze shifted to the smoking ruin of the house, blackened bricks piled amid charred beams with no sign of life. According to the Nihlvarians among the freed slaves, the Aerling had a wife and three sons, two full grown and one still a lad, all claimed by the blaze. *If she didn't get to them first,* he added inwardly, returning his focus to Iyaka and wondering if she wasn't just as insane as Jolnyr. *Can a madwoman be trusted to guide us to safety?*

"Iyaka!" he said, loud enough to capture her attention. "The Morvek slaves."

A brief spasm of irritation passed across her soot-smeared features before she got to her feet. "From what I recall, most will be too cowed to join us," she grunted. "Some will want to stay and will surely betray our path to any *Rulchakin* warriors who come looking."

Ruhlin ignored the obvious suggestion in her words. "Then tell them we're heading back to the coast to try to seize another ship. A false trail may serve us well."

Pursing her lips, Iyaka shrugged before slouching off towards the slave hut. "*Telchak* is wise."

Making his way through the farmstead, he heard a rhythmic ring of metal upon metal from one of the sheds. Venturing closer, he blinked at the heat gushing from the open door. Inside he found Sygurn pounding a hammer into a length of glowing steel, a coal-stoked forge glowing bright at his back.

"Found a sword left unfinished," he said, pausing in his work. "Couldn't stand the thought. Won't take long." Raising the red-hot bar from the anvil, he sniffed in appreciation. "Fine work. Shame we killed the smith last night."

"We need to be gone by midday," Ruhlin reminded him, receiving a vague nod in response as the Nihlvarian returned to his labour. Ruhlin recalled how Sygurn had made mention of being raised to the forge and had the burn marks to prove it. Seeing the half-grin on his face as sparks fountained with each blow of his hammer, this was the first time Ruhlin could remember the Nihlvarian exhibiting anything close to true happiness.

Iyaka's judgement of the slaves' demeanour proved accurate. Only four, three Morvek and a Nihlvarian, agreed to join their band. The others either fled into the fields at the first opportunity or sat in the miserable hovel of the slave pen, trembling in mortal fear, as if their refusal to be liberated meant death.

"That's the thing about the whip," Sygurn opined when he finally emerged from the smithy. "Cuts its way into the soul as well as the body."

Rigorous looting yielded copious supplies from the storehouses, while the stables provided a quartet of pack horses to carry it all. Before leaving, Ruhlin made a point of engaging in a loud discussion about their route within earshot of the cowed slaves. He had Sygurn mention the names of several ports to confuse any pursuers. When they set off, they followed a southward route until the farm was out of sight before turning north. They were obliged to navigate near ten miles of bare fields before a welcome sprawl of woodland came into view just as the sun began to dim.

At Iyaka's insistence, no fires were lit when they camped beneath the trees. They were still too close to cultivated lands to risk the betraying glimmer of flame. Settling down amid the roots of a yew, Ruhlin scanned the intricate shadows for any sign of the bear. The creature hadn't reappeared since that day outside Speltsaer and he found its absence curiously discomfiting.

"She's gone," Aleida said, appearing out of the gloom. Lying down, she pressed herself against him, the embrace fierce in its need for comfort. "I don't think she's coming back."

Ruhlin smiled with joy at their unhesitant intimacy. As his arms enfolded her, she rested her head against his chest, trembling a little. He thought it due to the chill but her whisper revealed another reason: "I didn't like doing that."

The distress he heard in her voice reminded him that, while never formally a slave, Aleida had also been a captive subject to the cruel whims of a harsh master. Yet, unlike Iyaka, she felt no desire to match cruelty with cruelty.

"No," he said, pulling her closer. "Neither did I."

"I don't want to do that again."

Ruhlin hesitated, stroking a hand through the silken tresses of her hair. "Let's hope we won't have to."

CHAPTER TWELVE

Felnir

Beyorn called the settlement Kahl Hardta, the Silver Port, which Felnir considered a jarringly inapt name for a place of such grim and mean appearance. It consisted of several dozen houses straggling along a rocky shore broken by a narrow inlet where a clutch of fishing craft bobbed on the morning tide. To Felnir's eye it appeared almost deserted, the boats un-crewed and the walled pens around the houses bare of all save a few sheep and goats.

"Scurrying inside at the first sight of strangers has become habit here," Beyorn explained. "They expect a raid by the *Ahrkun Krayl* every year, but sometimes they come more often."

"You're familiar with this shit-hole?" Sygna asked him.

Beyorn's reply was coloured by a wry grin that lacked any sign of offence. "I should, my queen. I was born here."

Felnir swallowed his chastising snap at the honorific. Getting his newly acquired *menda* to observe his injunction against kingly titles had required some harsh reminders over the last few days. However, they continued to address Sygna as a queen, a habit she did nothing to discourage.

"And this is the closest port to the *Ahrkun* stronghold?" he asked Beyorn, receiving a nod in response.

"Aye, the biggest one they have in the Greencrest. There are larger nests further east and north. The Hahl-Trova, the nest where the *Sindra* himself resides, is said to be the largest fortification in all Vorunvahl, though I've never seen it."

"Nor have few outside their cult," Tulvik added. As usual, when the heir to the Greencrest spoke, Felnir gained the impression of a youth quelling nervous uncertainty. It was as if he expected every utterance to result in ridicule or a punishing cuff. Felnir hoped Tulvik's fear of voicing an opinion wasn't matched by any apprehension over combat. If only a fraction of what was said of the *Ahrkun Krayl* turned out to be true, defeating them would be a bloody business.

"How many folk live here?" he asked Beyorn.

"Perhaps four hundred. As a lad, I remember there being more, but many fled to the Gyrwald's protection when the raids started."

"And they come to steal children?" Sygna said.

"That they do, my queen," Beyorn confirmed. "And much else besides. The *Ahrkun* neither fish nor farm and live entirely on stolen supplies and forced tribute, replenishing their numbers with the children they kidnap and raise in the cult's mad beliefs." From the anguish he tried unsuccessfully to quell, Felnir knew he was thinking of his cousin, stolen away in a raid months back.

"For that alone," Sygna said, casting a dark, purposeful look at Felnir, "they deserve eradication. Do they not, my king?"

Felnir kept the rueful grimace from his features. Of them all, only she could address him with such honours. Falk too, but he still insisted on calling Felnir a lord.

"Will these people fight?" he persisted, turning back to Beyorn.

"I would have said no." The young warrior's broad face broke into a smile. "But that was before Felnir Skyrnrak sailed into the Greencrest bearing the Sword of the Altvar. They won't fight for Arnhilt Volksora. But they will fight for you."

"Come out, you craven dogs!"

Beyorn's features turned a deeper shade of crimson with every shout he cast at the closed doors and shuttered windows that greeted their landing. "Come forth and greet one who has come to save us! He will return our children and defeat our hated foe!"

So far his exhortations had yielded no reaction, the only sound Felnir could detect being a faint whimpering from an outhouse. Fixing a baleful gaze on one particular door, Beyorn stomped towards it to assail the sturdy oak barrier with a hefty kick.

"Farryk! It is I, Beyorn! Your kin. Will you not face me, Uncle?"

With no answer immediately forthcoming, Beyorn assailed the door with successive kicks until he was rewarded with the sound of a bolt being drawn. The door opened to reveal a man of ragged appearance, much the same height as Beyorn, but far less well fed.

"Nephew," he said, voice fatigued rather than shamed. His heavy-lidded eyes widened at the sight of Felnir before narrowing in suspicion. "Have you brought more trouble to your uncle's door?"

"I have never done so! All I have ever done is try to defend my kin—"

"Enough," Felnir cut off the youth's burgeoning diatribe with a raised hand before affording his uncle a respectful nod. "My name is Felnir Skyrnrak," he said. "Know that I come with no hostile intent. Merely, I seek guidance to the place where I might find my enemy, there to slay them for their many crimes."

"You are not of Vorunvahl," Farryk said after subjecting Felnir to a prolonged stare of appraisal.

"No, I am not. I hail from the land of your forebears, guided here by the blessings of the Altvar to vanquish any who would transgress their laws."

"The *Ahrkun Krayl* say the same thing," Farryk muttered back, though his expression softened. "But they're rarely so polite about it." He shifted, casting his eye over the *menda* arrayed at Felnir's back, no doubt recognising many, but fixing upon one in particular.

"Are you here with the Gyrwald's blessing?" he asked Tulvik.

The youth turned an uncertain glance towards Felnir. Curious to see if Tulvik would pass this test, Felnir responded only with a raised eyebrow. Letting out a small cough, Tulvik straightened and addressed Farryk in clipped and formal terms. "I am not. I have joined the *menda* of Felnir Skyrnrak, bearer of the Sword of the Altvar. I have given my service freely, for I believe only he can rid this land of the scourge of the *Ahrkun Krayl*. Come with us, Farryk of Kahl Hardta, reclaim your daughter and your honour. If there is a vestige of a father's duty still left in your heart."

Well said, Felnir mused. *If a touch harsh*. Nevertheless, the words had a definite effect on Farryk. Face darkening, he stepped clear of the door. "Talk not to me of duty," he growled. "For years we have suffered while you sit pampered and safe in the Gyrwald's hall."

"I am here now," Tulvik cut in. "Ready to fight and die to see this village safe and your children recovered. Can you say the same?"

Felnir saw the words strike home, a glimmer of shame shining amid the anger on Farryk's face as he took another forward step. "We do not come to sow discord," Felnir said, placing himself between the two. "Merely for guidance, as I said." He moved closer to Farryk, offering a smile of grim reassurance and grasping his shoulder. "I see in you a good man," Felnir told him, voice pitched to a low, solicitous tone. "But pushed too far, I think. Tell me where to find the *Ahrkun* and I offer solemn promise you will be pushed no more."

Farryk shuddered in his grasp, the shame shining brighter as he fought down welling emotion. "They took our arms in the first raid," he said. "The sword my great-great-grandmother bore to this land from Ostan Hardta. We had nothing to fight them with when they came again."

"I will give you weapons," Felnir said, tightening his grip on Farryk's shoulder. "The weapons of a king, no less. Then you will come with me and reclaim your heirloom." He raised his free hand, palm open in invitation. The lean muscles of Farryk's face bunched as he blinked tears and grasped Felnir's hand, the grip trembling but fierce.

"You will swear this before the entire village?" he asked in a rasp. "With Ulthnir as your witness?"

"I'll swear it in the name of all the Altvar," Felnir replied. Releasing Farryk's hand, he drew the sword, stepping back to raise the flawless blade high. "For I bear the sword they forged for Velgard himself. And now I see its sacred purpose in the destruction of the Raven Hearts and their pestilent creed."

"Bit dramatic, don't you think?" Sygna squinted at him in the dim glow cast by the blazing bonfire the people of Kahl Hardta had raised on the shore. After addressing a crowd assembled through Farryk's hectoring and occasionally ungentle persuasion, Felnir ordered half the supplies from the *Dehlgra* distributed to the villagers. This sudden glut of food and liquor, coupled with Felnir's speech, kindled a feast. Songs were sung amid increasingly voluminous revelry, fuelled as much by relief as wine and mead. Felnir had witnessed similarly paradoxical scenes in the Ishtan borderlands. The unlucky denizens of towns and cities laid waste by the Fulminar's Rebellion would emerge from the ruins to lose themselves in joyous abandon at the sight of the Saluhtan's army. It had always struck him as odd that people who had lost all they possessed retained a capacity for celebration.

"Kingship requires drama," he said. They sat together atop a rocky outcrop overlooking the inlet. Sygna, although never one to shun a gathering, had slipped away come nightfall. Sensing a desire to talk, Felnir followed. She sat with her legs folded beneath her, the Bow of the Altvar resting on her shoulder as she played a finger along the string.

"Not so long ago," she said, "we found ourselves upon the empty shore of the Fire Isles with nothing, save our stolen treasures." The bowstring hummed as she plucked it, the note unnaturally loud and long to Felnir's ears. "Now we have a fine ship and the beginnings of an army. As ever, your resourcefulness impresses me, my love."

Felnir detected a genuine warmth to her words, but also an undertone of worry. "And yet?" he prompted when she lapsed into silence.

"It strikes me we have come a very long way only to find another war, is all." She plucked the string again, the thrum louder still. The way she stared at it stirred a question in Felnir's mind.

"Is it still just a bow?" he ventured. "You still sense nothing else in it?"

"Mostly." She frowned, running a hand over the stave. "And yet, some-times, usually at night, I feel . . . something. It's faint. So faint at first I thought it merely my imaginings. Yet I know it's there, like a snake moving under a blanket you can never quite catch." Her gaze narrowed as she turned it upon the sword at his belt. "One question deserves another, my love. Has that thing gifted you another vision?"

"No." Felnir shifted, surprised by how discomfiting it was to think back on the only blessing the Altvar had seen fit to grant him.

"Yet that one glimpse of the past still suffices to keep us to that old man's course." Sygna's eyes drifted to the *Dehlgra*, where a single lantern glimmered upon her deck. Wohtin hadn't deigned to come ashore, nor had he spoken little beyond a grunt since they departed the Greencrest. Advised by Beyorn that the presence of the Diretongue might be more a hindrance than an aid to their cause, Felnir had been content to leave the old man to his misery. Yet he felt a growing certainty Wohtin's part in all this was far from done. Grudgingly, he also suspected it could be crucial.

"He hasn't lied to us yet," Felnir pointed out. "He promised there would be a kingdom for the claiming, and here it is."

"A soul so old will know a thousand tricks," Sygna said. "If Thera was here, she could parse the truth from him quick enough."

Felnir frowned in surprise, for Sygna rarely made mention of his sister. "Aided by a variety of sharp instruments," he pointed out. "The ways of a Vellihr of Justice are not subtle."

"No. But they are effective when dealing with the untrustworthy, and I can't shake the notion that's what he is. If all we've heard of him is true, he helped raise up a king only to bring him down. Who's to say he won't do it again? And why is he so keen for you to claim this land?"

Pertinent questions to which Felnir had no answer. "He's useful. That you can't deny."

"That spy we plucked from the Albermaine shore would have had his uses too, yet you pitched him into the sea quickly enough."

"And I shouldn't have. Anger is my worst weakness, as you know."

He saw a good deal of resignation in Sygna's face as she turned, but also a hard resolve to her gaze. "Even in my most fanciful childhood whims, I never once dreamed of being a queen, but I'll wear the mantle for you." She ran her hand over the bow stave. "And I'll wield this as best I can in the wars to come. But when it's done, I want the only thing you have so far denied me, Felnir. I want a child. If we are to rule this land, we need an heir."

He knew there was more to her need than a desire to secure a legacy. It was not the first time she had raised this subject, but always he had resisted. Ever respectful of his wishes, Sygna had continued to drink the protective herbal brew she bought from an old woman in Skar Magnol, and cleanse herself after they made love. For him, it was simple expedience. He remained a disgraced former exile, living a life of continual danger at his great-grandfather's behest. It was no life for a child. At least that's what he told her, and himself. But, faced by her stark demand, he was forced to confront the true reason: he was afraid of fatherhood. The sheer responsibility of it had always scared him. He recalled his parents fondly, but still they had perished and left him, Guthnyr and Thera, to the clutches of Margnus Gruinskard. Who was to say what dark inheritance the Redtooth would leave a son or daughter? But he couldn't deny Sygna's reasoning. If he was to truly reign here in the manner of a king from legend, shorn of the customs of the Sister Queens, then his bloodline must be established and all cowardice set aside.

Shifting closer, he drew her to him and kissed her softly. "As my queen commands," he whispered, feeling her lips curve against his.

Kahl Hardta yielded only twenty fighters to Felnir's *menda*, fifteen men and five women. All had children to reclaim or scores to avenge and were older than he would have liked. Most of the young folk had either fled to Greencrest or died vainly contesting the *Ahrkun's* raids. A few possessed arms they had successfully hidden from the cultists, but Felnir was obliged to equip the rest with the weapons they had found aboard the *Dehlgra*.

"A sword once wielded by the hand of the Exiled King himself," Farryk breathed as he drew a blade from its sheath. It had an ornately decorated hilt and pommel of silver and ebony. Centuries in the sealed tomb had also spared the steel corrosion. However, the steel bore some dark patches resulting from weeks of exposure to sea air. Farryk didn't seem to mind, nor did his kin exhibit anything other than awe and gratitude as they examined the swords, spears and axes Falk handed out. While they had sufficient bladed weapons for all, they possessed only one shield, an intricately worked silver inlaid treasure that Felnir wouldn't entertain subjecting to the depredations of combat. So, before setting off inland, he insisted on fashioning enough shields for the entire *menda*. Setting them to the task, he was appalled to discover that few had any understanding of the craft.

"What manner of Ascarls are you?" he demanded in exasperation upon witnessing their fumbling attempts to properly cut the hardwood panels that formed the heart of a shield. It was the simplest task in the process, yet hardly any of them had done it before.

"Such things are usually left to artisans," Beyorn said. "Shields are expensive in Vorunvahl, as is all weaponry."

Felnir bit down on an angry reminder of the first injunction set down in the Altvar Rendi: *Let every hand know the sword, for the Ascarls shall be warriors all.* After five hundred years of isolation, it was clear to him that, while these people might still cleave to the Ascarlian gods, they had drifted far from their wisdom.

Sighing, he ordered the *menda* to leave off their toil and gather round. "Witness this and learn the lesson well," he said, laying down the boards on the *Dehlgra's* deck before setting out the glue and nails he would use to bind them together. "Next to your sword, spear, or axe, your shield is your most precious possession upon a battlefield. For, without it, your life shall be forfeit before you can slay a single foe."

He refused to begin the march until every warrior had fashioned their own shield, or at least assisted in its making. Their ineptitude was irksome, and made for a trying few days, but he saw that the shared toil also bound them to each other. Despite his disdain at their loss of tradition, Felnir felt a burgeoning respect for these people. None complained at the tedium or the delay, and when it finally came time to depart the village, all mustered without hesitation, backs straight and faces set with purpose.

Not the crew of the Sea Hawk, he mused, looking them over. *But they'll do.* "Farryk," Felnir said, inclining his head at the forested hills to the north. "Lead the way and let's get this done."

"Not so much a stronghold as an eyrie," Sygna said, face bunching in dismay as she eyed the *Ahrkun* stronghold. After a five-day march, Farryk had led them to a steep hill which had taken another day to climb. Once atop the crest, they beheld the sight of the *Ahrkun* stronghold, or Raven's Nest, as the villagers insisted on calling it. The fortification had been constructed upon the tiered heights of a sandstone promontory rising from the forested valley below. It appeared an intricate matrix of walls and towers, ancient judging by the dark weathered stone. A banner bearing the same crest as the ship they had burned on the Red Waves fluttered from the tallest tower, making its ownership unmistakable.

"One narrow track leading to the gate," Sygna added. "Overlooked by high walls all the way." Turning to Felnir, she shook her head and spoke a word also at the forefront of his mind, "Impregnable."

"We thought the same of Castle Granoire," he pointed out. "Yet found a way in."

"And barely made it out again, and what a prize you brought back."

Her voice hardened as she glanced in Wohtin's direction. He stood apart from the group, silent and apparently lost in thought. "No sage insight to offer, old man?" Sygna enquired. "Some clever stratagem born from centuries of experience?" Her tone indicated she expected little by way of response and Wohtin didn't disappoint her.

"I have never been here before," he muttered, sparing her a brief, irritated glare. "And war is not my province."

Shaking her head in disdain, Sygna turned back to Felnir. "The only way this place will fall is if we ring it with an army and starve them out. And you may have noticed, my love, that we currently lack an army."

Turning to Falk, Felnir could tell the outlaw had formed much the same conclusion. "Best to wait a while, my lord," he said. "Watch the comings and goings. That gate has to open some time, else how would they do their raiding?"

"Ambush," Sygna said, pursing her lips in approval. "Disguise ourselves in their garb, then seize the gate once we're inside."

"Won't work." Felnir pointed to the upper tiers of the stronghold. "Once through the lower gate, there's half a dozen more before you reach the main tower, and you can bet we'll be assailed by arrows from the walls at every step."

Lapsing into silent contemplation of the Nest, he saw how the buildings were clustered on the south-facing side of the promontory, and that the tower was partially overlooked by a narrow peak to its rear. It was difficult to judge the distance between rock and tower, but from here they appeared to be almost touching. Beckoning Farryk to his side, he asked, "What lies on the northern side?"

"Just a cliff," the villager replied. "Sheer from bottom to top. Not even the most sure-footed goat could scale it."

Felnir shared a grin with Falk. "Now that sounds like a challenge."

"Should be me, my lord." Falk gazed up at the cliff, that old shrewdness shining in his eyes as they tracked from one handhold to another. "No offence and such, but I am the better climber."

"No offence suffered." Felnir tightened the sword belt across his chest and clapped Falk on the arm. "For it's surely true." He leaned closer, lowering his voice. "But some deeds must be reserved for kings."

Seeing the confused frown on the outlaw's brow, Felnir wondered just how much he understood about their current endeavour. Felnir had thought the outlaw changed by their recent trials, the ordeal perhaps reordering his mind into something sharper. Yet, while he exhibited a greater level of comprehension, there were still moments when bafflement clouded his gaze, as if he couldn't recall why or how he found himself in such an unfamiliar place. Also, the memories of his days prior to joining Felnir's crew remained as dim as ever.

Taking the grappling rope from the outlaw, Felnir settled it over his shoulder so it criss-crossed with his sword belt over his chest and back. He had stripped down to a thin leather jerkin, darkening his skin with soot. It was not quite evening yet, since attempting such a climb in the dark would be suicide. With luck, by the time he reached the summit, the encroaching gloom would conceal him.

"The risk in this is great," Sygna said as he stepped towards the cliff. "We could range the woods, kill any raiding parties they send out. Wear them down until their numbers are too reduced to contest an attack on the gate."

"That would take weeks," Felnir said. Reaching for the first handhold, he hauled himself up. "And legends must be born somewhere."

"Don't fall," she instructed with a sigh as he continued to climb.

"I won't," he grunted back. "Make for the base of the path and be ready."

A dozen feet off the ground, he paused to watch the pair of them slip back into the forest before resuming his toil. Climbing was something he had taken to at an early age, despite being advised by his father that he would grow too big for it one day. The prediction had proved partially correct as Felnir found it increasingly hard to haul his expanding frame up the mountains ringing Skar Magnol. Yet he kept at it, not least because it was one of the few skills his sister failed to match. Shifting from one notch or crack in the red stone edifice, he discovered it contrasted with the hard granite of home, more powdery and rounded at the edges than he was used to. It made for a difficult climb and, as the distance to the ground increased, hazardous.

This is nothing, Felnir told himself, muscles straining as he ascended to a ledge barely wide enough to fix a toe upon. *After Skar Magnol, no peak can defeat me.* Although he tried to imbue his resolve with firm conviction, it was tinged with the inescapable knowledge that surviving his most famous climb owed more to luck than skill, but also something he preferred not to dwell upon. Now, with the wind stiffening the higher he climbed, memories of that day began to assail him with distracting persistence.

You weren't really alone up there, were you? His great-grandfather's question, never given an answer because the old bastard surely knew it already.

"No," Felnir sighed, pausing to press his forehead against the sandstone in a vain effort to stem the unwanted remembrance. "No, I wasn't."

The upper reaches of the great sacred peak of Skar Magnol, it transpired, were not bare of life. Goats proliferated on the rocky slopes above the treeline, and if you were lucky, you might catch sight of a snow cat. Felnir had seen one that day: a fleeting glimpse of mottled silver-grey fur and a snarling, sharp-toothed maw. For all its feral aggression, it remained one of the most beautiful creatures he had ever beheld. It was as he watched the cat bound from view that the first flurry of snow assailed him. It was late summer, and the weather had been kind for most of the climb, but the higher slopes of the mountain were notoriously treacherous. As Felnir forced himself on, he was continually beset by thick cloud and intermittent blizzards feeding the ever-deepening snow banks. He knew he should turn back, but didn't. This was only a few weeks since his fateful duel with Volund Strongback. It had been a time of suffering the fearful, disparaging glares of others while he awaited the Sister Queens' word on his fate. Climbing Skar Magnol was to be his deliverance, a feat sure to win enough renown to spare him the disgrace of exile.

You're a fool to think so, boy, his great-grandfather had advised in a growl. The old man's fury at Felnir's misdeed was a towering thing then, his gaze perpetually filled with dire disappointment. Of course, he had been proven right. Felnir's triumph was noted by many, but not the queens, nor did he seek to make mention of it when he stood before them, ready to receive their judgement. His spirit had been laid low by Skar Magnol, for it was upon her mighty flanks that Felnir Redtooth came closest to death in a life rich in dangers.

The climb that almost killed him was not particularly steep, a craggy slab of frosted rock he could have scaled in a trice if not for the weather. He wore gloves of thin leather, better to allow his fingers to find a hold, but at this height they proved too flimsy against the cut of the wind. Clamping a hand to the edge of the slab's crest, he found a patch of ice and lost purchase trying to haul himself the final yard. He recalled the moment of weightless dread before the jolting pain of his back connecting with an outcrop, forcing all the air from his lungs and robbing his body of strength. The cold attacked like some formless, ravening beast, invading his flesh all the way down to bone and organs. Unable to catch more than a small gasp of air with each agonised spasm of his chest, he lay staring into the swirling pale cloud, feeling his life ebb away as the chill ate ever deeper into his being.

He never knew how long he lay there, for pain soon gave way to delirium. The drifting mist formed itself into a parade of faces, Volund being the most prominent. His gaunt features, bleached of colour save for the spatter of blood on his chin, regarded Felnir without the accusation or hate he expected. Instead, the Strongback's lip curled in a grimace of utter contempt. *Coward*, he sneered. *Fearing mere shame more than battle.*

You shouldn't have laughed, Felnir had tried to groan in response, but the all-consuming chill stole his voice.

I was going to clasp your hand, Volund continued. *For you had fought well enough to win my regard. I would have given those who taunted your brother a sound thrashing and we would have shared meat and drink in my father's hall that night.*

"You shouldn't have laughed!" The defiant snarl emerged as little more than a whimper, bringing yet more pain as he drew breath that felt like a thousand needles in his throat and lungs. He shuddered on the outcrop, his spasms coming close to tipping him over the edge. That would have surely brought an end to the tale of Felnir Skyrnrak, had not Volund's wraith transformed into a different face.

Oh Felnir, it said, soft with exasperation. *What are you doing?*

If his eyes were capable of shedding tears, he would have done so at the sight of his mother's weary, if fond, smile. "I am disgraced," he whispered back. "This . . . will wash it . . . clean."

No, it won't, she stated. *Some stains are just too deep, my foolish son. Cleansing yourself of this one will be the work of years. A lifetime, in truth. Would that I could spare you all the many trials that lie ahead, but I cannot. Now.* The face loomed closer, taking on a familiar parental sternness that birthed an ache in Felnir's heart. *Stop lolling about and get up. Climb this mountain if it pleases you. Or don't. It doesn't matter. All that matters is that you live. Your brother and your sister need you.*

"They don't . . . Thera hates me . . . Guthnyr will be . . . better off without me . . ."

Cease your whining and get up this instant!

Ingrained obedience, and shame at the recrimination he heard in her voice, sufficed to shake him from his frozen torpor. Groaning, he had forced himself to crawl to the cliff face, pressing himself to the unyielding rock, pounding his hands against it until feeling returned. The invading cold retreated before his resolve, allowing him to reach for the handholds once more.

"Mother?" He looked for her, squinting into the clouds, but she was gone. "Mother . . ."

Felnir jerked as the memory faded, his vision now filled with the varied crimson hues of the sandstone cliff. Looking down, then up, he realised he was almost at the top. The knowledge that he had completed such a climb while subsumed in an unwanted memory made him sag. Muscles burning from the effort, he let out an angry grunt and reached for the inch-wide ledge a few feet above his head.

The sky had taken on the shades of sunset by the time he reached the top of the cliff. It ended in a shelf below the conical summit of this miniature mountain. Felnir crouched in deepening shadow, allowing his strained body to recover as he viewed the *Ahrkun* stronghold below. He found the distance between the summit and the tower greater than he thought, but still within reach of a thrown grappling hook. He saw no guards atop the tower and only dim light glimmering in the narrow slits in its walls. The air was laced with woodsmoke undercut by the sharper taint of human effluent. Looking over the structures spread out beneath the tower, he saw unwashed walls and scattered detritus. These cultists were plainly a slovenly bunch.

Too idle to even post a sentry, Felnir mused in satisfaction as he unlimbered the rope. He waited for the sun to dip fully below the horizon before casting the iron grapple across the divide. It caught at the first throw, the iron hook latching onto the tower's edge and refusing to yield despite a hefty tug. Gathering in the slack, Felnir tightened his grip and prepared to leap.

All that matters is that you live, his mother had said. Although he cherished every word she had ever imparted to him, in life and in death, he was forced to disagree.

No, Mother. All that matters is that I win.

It was time for the King of Vorunvahl to begin writing his legend.

CHAPTER THIRTEEN

Thera

By good fortune, the wind was at their backs that morning, so Thera saw the smoke before she smelled it. It rose in a tall grey column above the southern headland of Ayl-Ah-Elkor. It was the largest of the four islands that ringed the stretch of placid waters, those of the Aiken Geld called the Lyx Helv, the Mirror Sea. On a calm night, it was said the surface of the Lyx became a mirror to the heavens, allowing communion with the Altvar. For Ascarls of devout leanings, it was a place of pilgrimage, a site where souls beset by a malady of the heart or mind would come for guidance and succour from the gods. As the *Great Wolf* followed the *Silver Hawk* into the channel separating Ayl-Ah-Elkor from its southern neighbour, Thera doubted there would be much succour to be found here today.

She had ceded the leading place in the fleet to the *Silver Hawk*, trusting to Skahlvyr Estrynlud's familiarity with these waters to plot a speedy and safe course. Next came the gaggle of skiffs and fishing boats laden with warriors. To his credit, Aldeyn had chosen to place himself among them, hoping the presence of the Veilwald's kin would buttress their courage. To starboard, Kahlvik Vahrimdorr managed to keep the swifter *Ohlira* in check so as not to outpace the *Great Wolf*. Instead of a cluster of fishing craft, the Grey Eye sailed in company with the two Albermaine-ish merchantmen, their decks heaving with warriors. To port, Veilwald Ossgrym led another flotilla aboard his warship, the *Storm Fist*. Behind this vanguard came the entire fleet assembled in the north.

Although Thera's tactic of clustering boats around ships had imposed a certain sense of order upon the mass of disparate craft, the need to draw closer as they neared the constricted mouth of the channel conveyed the impression of a near chaotic seaborne horde. She could only hope they would regain some cohesion once they were through the strait. However, as the *Great Wolf* rounded the southern shore of Ayl-Ah-Elkor, she knew there would be no time to tidy this fleet, for battle was fully joined.

The source of the smoke became dreadfully obvious in the dozen or more burning ships drifting towards the long, pale beach to the north, victims of the furious struggle raging in the centre of the Lyx Helv. Despite the lingering banks of smoke, Thera found she could distinguish between the two contesting fleets, indicating this battle was still in its early stages. The Nihlvarians, marked by their red sails and the more impressive size of their vessels, were mostly clustered to the north. With the wind partially against them, they were relying on their oars to provide forward momentum as they pushed against the mass of Aiken Geld ships. As with Thera's fleet, it was a mix of large and small craft. If Veilwald Hakkyn had adopted any kind of formation at the dawn of battle, it had been lost now. The Aiken Gelders were spread out in a broad crescent, their centre bowed in by the oncoming mass of Nihlvarians. Salvos of fire arrows arced between the swaying forest of masts. Intense fighting raged on several decks, the shouts and screams of combat mingling with the increasing roar of flames and the thud and crack of splintered hulls. It was a fierce struggle, but Thera had no doubt of the outcome should the Nihlvarian assault continue. They simply had too many ships and too many warriors.

"There!" she called to Althsten, pointing to the centre of the mass of red sails before adding an order to her *menda* labouring at the oars. "Fast stroke!"

Shifting her gaze to the *Storm Fist*, she took satisfaction in seeing that Ossgrym had needed no instruction to follow suit. The Veilwald led his flotilla towards the point where the Aiken Geld fleet met the Nihlvarians. Off to starboard, Kahlvik kept the *Ohlira* to steady stroke so as not to leave behind her two escorting merchantmen as she led them to the rear flank of the enemy formation. This had all been preordained by Thera at their last council before departing Danith's Bay and represented the most influence she could have over the initial stage of this struggle. Once her fleet was committed, such tactical niceties would swiftly become irrelevant.

Checking the disposition of their contingent of smaller craft, she was gratified to see most were keeping pace with the *Great Wolf*, the toil of their oarsmen aided by the wind filling their sails. Soon, however, they were mostly obscured by a descending pall of smoke when another burning ship, fully alight from prow to stern, drifted across their path. Thera couldn't tell if it had been crewed by friend or foe.

"Steady!" she warned Althsten. "Keep the course!"

The thickness of the smoke meant that she was almost too late in calling the order to ship oars, the dense wall of entangled hulls looming out of the haze barely forty yards beyond the prow. "To arms!" she cried out, raising the dreadaxe high as her *menda* dragged in their oars and scrambled to gather weapons and shields. One fortunate effect of the smoke was that it spared them the attention of the Nihlvarian archers until the *Great Wolf* bore down upon the smaller vessel directly ahead. A few shafts thudded into the deck but failed to find a victim before the prow crunched against the enemy's timbers.

Preparing to leap onto the opposing deck, Thera spared a glance for Lynnea. As instructed, the apprentice stood close to Althsten at the tiller, Snaryk at her side. Her ostensible task was to protect the helmsman during the battle, but the resigned taint of resentment and shame Thera sensed when their thoughts touched made it apparent that Lynnea knew she was being spared combat. Still, as Thera turned and hurled herself over the rail, she felt more concern and warm regard than anger.

Thera landed on a deck tilted by the impact of the *Great Wolf*'s prow. It spared her the attentions of any nearby archers, but also made it hard to kill the first Nihlvarian she saw. A lithe fellow in sparse leather armour, he regarded her with a glare of consternation, clinging on to a rope with one hand, a long dagger in the other. He nimbly avoided the first blow of the dreadaxe, dodging aside as the double blade raised a cloud of splinters. Grunting in annoyance, Thera aimed her second blow not at him, but at the rope he held. He attempted to dodge again but this time with less luck, the deck shifting to place his arm directly under the axe as it fell. Screaming in shock at the sight of blood spouting from a shortened limb, he still managed to slash wildly at Thera with his dagger before she finished him with an efficient chop to the head.

She turned in time to parry the spear thrust of a charging Nihlvarian, the counter sweep of the dreadaxe forcing him to sway back, whereupon he was borne down by the descending figure of Ragnalt. The warrior's boots pinned the spearman to the deck before Ragnalt's sword stabbed into his forehead.

"Form up!" Thera shouted to the warriors now leaping to her side from the *Great Wolf*. A cluster of enemies was gathering at the stern, commanded by a large, brawny man with a bushy black beard Thera assumed to be the captain of this stricken vessel. Wielding a nail-studded club, the black-beard cried out exhortations to his sailors, his accent too thick for Thera to catch the words beyond an impression of snarled and profane defiance. Despite his efforts, the Nihlvarians' subsequent charge was a feeble thing. She saw several sailors linger in the rear as their crew mates rushed forward, one craven even choosing to leap over the side and take his chances in the sea rather than face combat. Only a dozen threw themselves at Thera's hastily assembled shield wall, failing to break through and most being swiftly cut down when they were shoved back. The captain lasted longest. Thumping his club into the surrounding shields, he kept them at bay for a few seconds until Achier darted forward. Ducking low with a hatchet in both hands, the Morvek delivered two precise blows to the Nihlvarian's legs, sending him to his knees, whereupon he was skewered through the chest by a trio of swords.

"Clear this deck," Thera instructed her *menda*. As they completed the business of dispatching the remaining Nihlvarian sailors, she moved to the ship's rail, finding that the impact with the *Great Wolf* had created a gap between this vessel and the neighbouring ship. Thera ducked at the thrum of multiple bowstrings, arrows thunking into the timber around her as the archers on the opposing ship sought retribution for fallen countrymen. The barrage was short-lived, Thera risking a glance over the rail to see the first of the fishing boats draw up to the Nihlvarian ship's prow, grappling ropes flying. Three more followed quickly, the occupants swarming up the vessel's hull to overwhelm the crew vainly attempting to hold them back. Thera quelled the lurch in her heart at the sight of several Ascarlians tumbling into the sea, hacked by blades or pierced by arrows. She searched for Aldeyn among the frenzied chaos of the struggle that followed, but couldn't find him.

"Thera!" Ragnalt's shout drew her to the prow of the seized ship, finding him and the rest of her *menda* crouched as a flurry of fire arrows arced across the divide separating them from the dense mass of the Nihlvarian fleet. It appeared the captains of the closest vessels had angled their tillers to draw away, creating a stretch of open sea. Luckily, the fire arrows were ineffective, most falling into the sea and the few to land on the deck quickly extinguished with water buckets. Thera knew such fortune wouldn't hold unless they could close the distance to their foes. Looking around, she spotted an open hatch and peered at the lower deck. She was confronted by the thick, fetid stink of unwashed bodies and two rows of upturned faces, eyes bright in the gloom. The slaves were all grimy with dirt and sweat, some staring at her in stark desperation, others with the hollow-eyed resignation of hopeless souls.

"Achier!" She pointed into the hatch as the Morvek rushed to her side. "Talk to them. Tell them if they want freedom, they have to row. Promise that we'll break their chains as we broke yours. But get this ship moving."

She commanded Ragnalt to take over the tiller and busied herself with dousing more fire arrows, while Achier's voice echoed below. He was plainly a man of persuasive talents, for the ship quickly lurched into motion, the oars sweeping urgently to close the gap to the Nihlvarian ships. Glancing to her either side, Thera experienced a pang of joyful pride at the sight of more fishing boats keeping pace with the *Great Wolf*. Looking forward, she found the smoke too thick to gauge the course of the battle. However, the increasing din of combat and the flares of newly kindled fires indicated a fierce struggle now raged all along the eastern flank of the Nihlvarian fleet.

"Brace!" Ragnalt called out an instant before the prow of this seized vessel slammed into the hull of an enemy warship. Moving to the slain body of the black-bearded captain, Thera unhooked the keys from his belt. "Free them," she said, returning to the hatch and tossing the ring to Achier. "Gather what arms you can and join the fight. Tell them if we don't win, they'll either be dead or back in chains by nightfall."

Returning to the prow, she found Ragnalt and the rest of the *menda* throwing grappling ropes to prevent the ship they had rammed from pulling away. A brief scan of her deck revealed a crew of at least two dozen, resolved to fight judging by the way they brandished their weapons and hurled abuse at the oncoming fishing boats.

"It seems," Thera said, turning to Ragnalt, "this is going to be a very long day."

He replied with a grin, newly acquired scars wrinkling as he hefted his shield before slamming the pommel of his sword into it. The *menda* quickly followed his example, pounding their shields to create an irregular but constant drumbeat as they formed up on the prow. "Vengeance!" Ragnalt shouted, raising his blade. "For the slain of Ayl-Ah-Veyn!"

"For the slain!" his fellow warriors roared back, then, as one, leaped onto the opposing deck, hurling themselves at the Nihlvarians. Before following, Thera paused to glance back at the *Great Wolf*, seeing a slender figure standing at the prow. Thera could feel her thoughts even at this distance, consisting of the same mix of worry and shame: *Don't die.*

"I won't," Thera muttered. Gripping the dreadaxe in both hands, she turned and leaped, bringing it down to crunch through armour and flesh the instant her boots met the deck.

In Thera's experience, land battles were shorter than those at sea. Fighting from deck to deck amid a chaos of heaving ships, many of them alight, was characterised by intense bouts of frenzied combat interspersed with prolonged pauses. She wasn't entirely sure how long it took for her combined force of warriors and freed slaves to fight its way to what she guessed to be the heart of the Nihlvarian fleet, but the sun was beginning to wane by the time the dreadaxe claimed its final victim of the day.

The warrior she slew had been a man of impressive stature, standing an inch taller than her in dark armour etched with some form of script. His square-jawed features were tattooed in red from brow to neck, which failed to obscure their undeniable handsomeness. Wielding an axe even larger than her own, he might have proven a more formidable opponent but for the two arrows jutting from his back. Revealing bloodstained teeth in a snarl, he had managed only a few decent swings at Thera before the dreadaxe crunched into his side, cleaving the leather breastplate to bite deep into his ribs. As he collapsed to his knees, the surrounding Nihlvarians lost heart. Some let out despairing cries that told of great devotion to this fallen captain, attempting to rush to his side even as Thera's *menda* cut them down.

Head sagging, the stricken captain tried to say something. Whether his words were worthy of note, Thera would never know, for they emerged as an incomprehensible red sputter. Kicking him off the dreadaxe's blade, she ordered two of her warriors to throw him overboard.

"But keep that," she added, pointing to his axe. "We can't afford to waste decent arms."

The onset of evening heralded a shift in the tide and a stiffening of the wind. The smoke wreathing the Lyx Helv thinned while the changing current created a chaotic spiral of battling or ruined ships. The revealed scene was so confused Thera couldn't make sense of it at first. Burning hulks drifted among vessels making headway with oars sweeping. Here and there, masts jutted above the water, bobbing as they slowly sank from view. Patches of wreckage twisted on the swell, clung to by survivors, both friend and foe. Incredibly, some were still trying to fight amid the flotsam. Thera saw a trio of slaves, marked as such by their manacles, churning the water white as they attempted to drown a flailing Nihlvarian.

It was as the sky darkened further, the flames reflecting with unwelcome clarity on this well-named sea, that she spotted the line of red-sailed ships making for the strait to the west. There were perhaps two dozen in all, many trailing smoke, their sails ragged and oars worked with poor rhythm. These, Thera knew, were the fleeing vestige of a routed fleet. The cheers built gradually, faint and tremulous at first but mounting in volume as the last skirmishing faded and the realisation of victory dawned.

"What a day!" Ragnalt laughed. "To think I should have lived to see such glory."

As he removed his helm, Thera was gratified to find no fresh scars upon his smiling, soot-stained features. Turning to survey her *menda*, she counted more than she expected. Three of her veterans were nowhere in sight. Of the rest, only two bore wounds that appeared serious. Achier was also still with her, slumped in exhaustion alongside the slaves they had freed in the struggle. The sight of the Morvek's weariness brought awareness of her own fatigue. The sealed wounds marring her flesh burned like cinders, sending fiery pulses through her torso. The pain was fierce enough to double her over if she hadn't stiffened her back, teeth gritted with the effort.

More bothersome than physical discomfort was the horror of the past hours. Although much of it was rendered vague by the heat and rush of battle, some instances shone with dire clarity. A Nihlvarian archer trying to draw her bow even as a thin stream of blood jetted from the cut in her neck. One of the Morvek they had freed at Danith's Bay, lying dead with his brains leaking from a sundered skull. The screams of slaves trapped aboard a burning ship she had been forced to abandon.

"Vellihr!" Looking up, Thera made out the figurehead of a ship looming out of the haze. It was a carving of Fearnyl, the scythe-bearing god from the Lower Hall of the Altvar with dominion over the change of seasons and cultivation of land. Standing to the right of the wooden god was a tall, broad-shouldered figure in armour that bore the marks and rents of recent combat. His heavily bearded face was blackened, but still recognisable.

"Veilwald Hakkyn!" Thera attempted to call back, the words emerging as a croak from a throat made dry by exertion and smoke. Accepting a flask of water from Ragnalt, she drank deep and raised a hand to the Veilwald of the Aiken Geld. Beneath a covering of sweat and grime, Hakkyn Rohnlank's features were flushed with the joy of an unexpected victory. Behind him, she could see the jabbing blades of his jubilant *menda*.

"I knew the queens would never forsake us!" the Greenhand shouted across the divide. The depth of relief she heard in his voice made her wonder if his faith in the queens had been as firm as he claimed. Deciding it wasn't the best time to enlighten him to the fact that she was not here on their agency but her own, she pointed to the north.

"We have many ships to take charge of!" she told him. "And wounded to tend. Best anchor off Ayl-Ah-Elkor while there's still some of light left in the day."

"Aye, that we will!" Hakkyn laughed and waved, turning a little so his crew could hear his next words. "Tonight we feast in victory, where I'll raise my drinking horn in honour of the Blackspear and the Sister Queens!"

Thera could summon only a smile of thanks as the Veilwald's *menda* roared in acclaim. Loud as it was, it couldn't drown the echoing screams of those burning slaves.

"So, the queens sent no aid." Veilwald Hakkyn's face was now a stark contrast to his prior jubilation. He stared into the glowing coals of a brazier set upon the *Great Wolf*'s foredeck. The hour was well past the apex of night and the victory feast still raged on the shore. Campfires dotted the white sands of the long beach, flickering as those around them danced and revelled. In addition to slaves, weapons, and sundry goods looted from the Outer Isles, the Nihlvarian ships had also yielded a copious store of liquor. The combined *menda* of the Kast and Aiken Gelds had wasted no time in tapping the casks and roasting whatever meat they could find. It was often the way in the aftermath of battle, warriors keen to lose themselves in drunken celebration. Thera supposed it was preferable to sober reflection on recent experience and felt a pang of envy that she couldn't afford the luxury of such abandon. Calling her captains to the *Great Wolf* for council, she had told Hakkyn the unvarnished truth regarding the mustering of the Kast Geld.

"Not a single sword, nor even a messenger," Ossgrym confirmed. "The Outer Isles have been abandoned to their fate, old friend."

"I do not believe the queens would do so willingly," Thera said. "With the Isles beset by foes, it stands to reason the same has happened at Skar Magnol."

"Beset or not," Ossgrym said, eyes steady upon hers. "They were not here, and this victory is not won in the queens' name."

"Careful, Veilwald," Thera told him, voice soft but intent. Wisely, he confined his response to an un-cowed stare, allowing her to continue without further warning of potential treason. "It is my intention," she said, "to sail to Skar Magnol forthwith and discover their plight."

"One victory does not mean a war won," Kahlvik pointed out. "A good many *Skyrnlohk* escaped and we have no way of knowing how many more prowl these waters. Or how many will be coming across the Styrnspeld to reinforce them." Straightening, he addressed Thera in formal tones. "I should sail for Skar Magnol in your place, Vellihr. I believe the warriors in this great *menda* take too much heart from your presence for it to be cast away." He inclined his head at the beach. "Hear how many call your name. Even the slaves we freed speak of a fearless warrior queen who came to break their chains."

"Then they should be told clearly that I am not a queen," Thera replied.

"Queen or not," Ossgrym said, "my cousin is right. This victory was yours and every warrior who fought here knows it. Removing yourself from this fleet bodes ill, while the war remains unwon."

"And you know well the *Ohlira*'s swiftness," Kahlvik added. "I could be back with word on the queens' fate within twenty days, if Ulfmaer is kind with wind and weather."

Thera resisted the urge to rub a hand to her wounds. The burn had lessened since the battle but continued to linger, making her wonder if it was a burden she would bear for the rest of her life. *Not a burden*, she chided herself, recalling Eshilde's gleeful betrayal. *A gift that warns against incautious trust.* Turning an appraising gaze upon Kahlvik, she saw no artifice in his gaze, just the honest surety of a steadfast warrior. Still, she couldn't prevent her eyes tracking over his neck, seeking a cord or chain that might indicate a hidden silver trinket.

He's no liar.

Thera saw Lynnea leaning against the port rail, face pale and tired in the brazier's glow. Thera had made her way back to the *Great Wolf* to discover that she hadn't remained unmolested during the battle. Spying her mostly bare deck, a swift Nihlvarian warship had separated from the main struggle and attempted to board. Thera hadn't yet obtained fulsome details of what happened next, but when she returned to the ship, she found Althsten casting bodies over the side. Nearby, Snaryk licked reddened chops and barked a greeting while Lynnea sat huddled at the stern. Thera's query as to her wellbeing earned only the faintest smile, her apprentice's thoughts closed against contact.

Nor is he Volkrath, Lynnea added, gathering her shawl more tightly about her shoulders. *And you should trust his judgement. These people need you more than the queens do.*

"I shall think on this," Thera told her captains. "For now, let us give thanks to the Altvar for their favour. On the morrow, I shall seek from you a full accounting of our gains, and our losses."

After they had boarded the boats to take them ashore, Thera went to Lynnea's side, noting her preoccupation with a dark stain on the starboard rail. Thera recognised the signature hue of timber discoloured by recently spilled blood. It was but one of several blemishes to the *Great Wolf*'s deck, most scrubbed clean, but not this one. She didn't ask any questions, instead waiting for Lynnea to allow access to her thoughts. When she did, Thera winced at the pain she sensed, a raw mix of grief and confusion.

Strange it is, Lynnea commented, looking up from the bloodstain, *to feel sorrow for someone you killed. A soul you didn't know in life, and now never will.*

"Who?" Thera asked, nodding to the stain.

Just a man. Lynnea pursed her lips as she regarded the mark once more. *Angry and desirous of my death, or so it seemed. Rage, I have learned, is a mask for fear in battle.*

"True enough. Did Snaryk do it?"

Lynnea shook her head. *He was otherwise engaged with the bunch who climbed up the port side. This one was more cunning. I spotted him, but Mohlnir got to him first.* As if hearing his name, the cat came bounding across the deck, leaping up onto the rail to rub his head against Lynnea's arm until she consented to pet him. *Tore one of his eyes out. But that didn't stop him.* She spared a glance at her staff propped nearby, whereupon Thera's mind became filled with the sight of the weapon in Lynnea's hands. It blurred as she brought it down on the head of a snarling Nihlvarian with a bloody, gaping eye socket. The blow was strong enough to send his face into collision with the rail before he tumbled into the sea, flailed briefly, then sank from view. Lynnea continued to peer at the crimson water sloshing against the hull, but the Nihlvarian failed to reappear.

"Your form has improved," Thera commented. "Though you still need to lean forward more when you strike."

Lynnea's thoughts receded, her brow furrowing into a disapproving scowl.

"You wanted to taste battle," Thera pointed out. "Now you have. Bitter, isn't it?"

Lynnea turned away from her, Mohlnir jumping into her arms as she made for her shelter. *Yes,* her thoughts said simply, though Thera could feel the tinge of disappointed anger. *She wanted comfort,* she realised, quelling the urge to go after Lynnea, pull her close. As she had once done for Eshilde after her first battle. She remembered how full of bravado Eshilde had been that day. They had cornered a southern seas pirate ship in a cove on the shore of the Skor Geld, the fight that followed short but fierce. Eshilde seemed to exult in the victory feast that followed, brandishing a scimitar taken from the body of the pirate she killed. Later, Thera found her shivering in her shelter, tears streaming from her eyes, and drew her into a tight embrace. Eshilde's lips had found hers and comfort became something more, something that now caused Thera greater hurt than the ache of her sealed wounds. *Had it all been an act?* she wondered. *Even then?*

She turned away from Lynnea's retreating form and went to her own shelter, sighing in annoyance at the persistence of irksome memories. Casting off her armour, she lay back on her furs, contemplating the trinkets sitting in each palm. *Which one?* she pondered. *Perhaps neither.* Tonight of all nights, she doubted she could face another trial by nightmare, especially since her great-grandfather remained stubbornly absent from any dreams she conjured when holding his gift. Yet, she had a decision to make come the morning, and scant information upon which to base it.

Setting aside Lohdur's more crudely fashioned silver knot, she kept hold of the other and settled onto her back. Sleeping on her side made her wounds hurt too much. For a time, memories of the battle swirled, the cries of slaves trapped in burning hulls, the mighty, arrow-pierced man she had slain. *He must have had a name of great renown*, she mused, remembering his vain attempt to speak some final words. The notion stirred neither empathy nor regret. She knew her enemy now, and they were worthy only of extermination. Curiously, her grim resolve served to calm her mind, and she drifted into sleep moments later. The dream followed swiftly, whereupon she found herself staring into the bloodied, scarred face of Margnus Gruinskard, screaming in pain.

PART II

"Beware the skilled liar, for they will conceal their deceit within a garnish of truth, as with a worthless bead that gleams bright among pearls."

Ulthnir Horuhnklehr – the Worldsmith – from the Altvar Rendi

CHAPTER FOURTEEN

Elvine

The stink that greeted Elvine as the gaoler opened the door to the Tielwald's cell was an acrid melange of piss, unwashed flesh, and damp. As such, it contrasted with Colvyn's cell, which was at least dry. "Had stopped using this one years ago," the gaoler explained, Elvine noting again the poorly concealed shame in his downcast gaze. "Water leaks in from a crack in the ceiling, makes for bad air. Vellihr Ilvar insisted on it, though. Won't let me wash it out, either." He lowered his voice, stepping closer after a careful glance in the direction of the warrior standing at the far end of the passage. "Don't know why they don't just kill him, to be truthful."

Then his secrets would die with him, Elvine thought, forcing a reassuring smile. "The queen has her reasons, I'm sure." Entering the fetid space, she paused to blink until her eyes adjusted to the gloom. The large form of Margnus Gruinskard slumped in a corner, barefoot and clad in besmirched rags. His face was lost to shadow and the concealing mass of his uncon-strained hair. He was so still that Elvine considered he might be dead, but then she noted the slight shift of his head.

"Has . . ." he began in a grating croak that resembled old twine scraped by a copper knife. His words faltered into a cough before he tried again, his voice betraying a painful effort but lacking a stutter. "Has she sent you to torment with Covenant scripture now?" The matted spikes of his beard twitched as he emitted a grunt that might have been an attempt to laugh. "I think I'd prefer another round with the knuckle clamps."

Elvine's gaze went to the hand resting in his lap, seeing the swollen joints and bruise-darkened flesh. She had thought herself hardened to ugliness now, but the cruelty on display summoned a shudder of revulsion.

"I bring no torment," she said, moving to crouch at his side and unfasten her satchel. She extracted a flask of clean water and a muslin-wrapped bundle of bread and cheese. In addition to persuading Lore of the need to extract from this man all he knew of Ascarlian history, she had also convinced her that attempting to torture it out of him would be counterproductive. Ilvar had objected, of course. His naked suspicion shone bright in the glare he directed at Elvine while addressing his argument to the queen.

"The old fool won't talk, my queen," he said. "Not for us. And not for her."

"I believe he will," Elvine insisted, striving to maintain a tone of polite insistence. "If I am allowed to speak to him alone, and offer a few comforts. Since I seek only his knowledge of history, it's possible such consideration could loosen his tongue. It's worth trying, at least."

Lore was often inscrutable, her inner calculation hidden behind that perfect and composed mask. Yet, since receiving the mysterious blessing of the spear, Elvine found she could sense the train of her thoughts in the shifting hues of the aura it conjured. The colour remained the same warm, golden glow as before, indicating Lore's abiding love for her scholar. But it was also tinged with a pink hue Elvine interpreted as amusement at Ilvar's anger. As the queen turned to address her Vellihr, the colour darkened into crimson, providing Elvine with a new and surprising insight: *She detests him. He would cast his life away in a heartbeat for her. Yet, for him, she harbours only revulsion and contempt.*

"A fresh approach is not to be dismissed so easily, Ilvar," she said, voice measured as usual but with a hint of reproach. "Especially since your own efforts have yielded us nothing. The former Tielwald has a mind filled with at least a century's worth of secrets, and I mean to have them."

"In which case, a more . . . robust approach might be in order," Ilvar said. Elvine could tell it took considerable effort for him to strip the burgeoning rage from his voice. "As you know, there are members of my *menda* with the skills to keep a man breathing despite grievous injury—"

"He's too valuable to risk in such hazardous business," Lore cut in. "And, I suspect, would be all too willing to let us bleed him lifeless rather than succumb to any manner of torment. No." Flicking a dismissive hand at the Vellihr, Lore turned back to Elvine, her aura once again shimmering with affection. "I believe my scholar has, as usual, arrived at a more elegant solution. Of course." She came closer to Elvine, cupping her cheek. "Once you've won his confidence satisfying your historical curiosity, I shall expect further information to be of a more contemporary nature. I'm especially keen to learn what he knows regarding the likely movements of his great-granddaughter. And, more importantly, the names of his as yet undiscovered agents, for I am sure there are many."

Now, as she looked into Gruinskard's one good eye, glaring with baleful suspicion amid a mass of bruised and swollen flesh, Elvine understood the folly of the queen's ambition. This man would never divulge a single secret in his head, not unless it served his purpose.

"Please," she said, removing the stopper from the flask and holding it to his lips. "It's untainted. I promise."

"They already tried drugs, anyway," the Tielwald grunted. "I recited the tale of Ihryka the Deceiver over and over again until they lost patience and beat me unconscious." He huffed another laugh before gulping down a good portion of the contents. "I assume," he went on when finished, "that treacherous bitch has decided to try the gentle approach."

"I am not here as an interrogator. But as a scholar. The queen has afforded me the honour of writing the first complete history of the Ascarls. I find my sources lacking in many respects." Elvine touched her fingers to the back of his mangled hand. Meeting his eyes, she spoke on as her fingertip traced the symbol Berrine had taught her the night before: a circle with a line through it. "Please, Tielwald. For the sake of scholarship, if nothing else, allow me to partake of your wisdom."

Gruinskard's eye narrowed, flicking towards the half-open door. "Who's outside?" he asked in a whisper.

"One of Ilvar's warriors is posted here," she replied, voice equally soft. "And the gaoler lingers close by."

"Hulnath's a good man. It's thanks to me he got this job. Took a slash to the back years ago and couldn't row any more." His cracked lips formed a small grimace. "Kindness doesn't always breed trust, however."

"Trust may have to be risked, for time grows short. A foreign fleet sits in Linsker Fjord and a foreign army garrisons Skar Magnol while our queen looks south, to Olversahl."

"Then, whatever she might be, she's not stupid." A long bitter sigh escaped Gruinskard's lips as he reclined, closing his eye as he pressed his head into the stone wall behind. "I always knew something wasn't right about her. That whole orphan story struck me as strange. Yet, every enquiry I made turned up nothing. I had so many opportunities, girl, so many chances to have her quietly poisoned. But she kept being so damnably useful. That alone should have warned me."

Elvine was about to enlighten him as to Lore's true origins when she heard a scuff of boot leather on stone from beyond the door. "Your willingness to help pleases me greatly," she said, raising her voice as she reached into her satchel to extract a quill, ink bottle and parchment. "As I'm sure it will please the queen. She might even see fit to providing some additional comforts. Now." Smoothing out the pages on her lap, she dipped the quill in preparation. "What can you tell me regarding the later Broken Age, particularly the years leading up to the ascendency of King Aeric? The sources for the period are particularly sparse."

Over the course of the next hour, it transpired that Margnus Gruinskard did indeed possess a remarkable repository of knowledge regarding Ascarlian history. While painfully chewing his way through the bread and cheese, he related portions of sagas Elvine had never heard before, and others that differed from those set down in Lore's books. She found herself wishing her true mission hadn't been so pressing, and her notes less hastily scribbled, for this old man was surely a treasure trove for any scholar. Even so, some of his tales inevitably piqued her historian's curiosity, not to say scepticism.

"Aeric was illiterate?" She squinted at the Tielwald, unsure whether he might be subjecting her to some form of jest. "The founder of the great library in Olversahl, famed for paying vast fortunes for the rarest volumes, you claim that this man was unable to read?"

"Not a single word his entire life." Gruinskard winced as a broken tooth found a seed in the mouthful of bread he chewed. Spitting it out, he added, "But I'm sure he liked looking at the pictures. It's one of the quirks of history that Aeric, a monumental dolt, has been remembered as the most sage and learned of monarchs. In truth, it was his wife, Sehlda, who did most of the thinking while he did the fighting. The library was her idea."

"How could you possibly know this?"

The Tielwald's eyepatch had been taken, meaning Elvine was now subjected to the sight of both eye and empty socket narrowing in annoyance. "The same way I know most things, girl. Human memory is a curious thing. Has a life of its own, a way of persisting beyond death that has nothing to do with words scribbled in books." His expression softened into sorrow, head slumping as he muttered, "Though, in times of trial such as this, reaching for it becomes . . . difficult."

A creak of hinges drew Elvine's gaze to the door. "That's an hour, Scholar," the gaoler, Hulnath, said with a tight smile of apology.

"Just one moment longer, please," she said, waiting until he nodded and stepped from view before turning back to Gruinskard. She leaned closer to him as she went about gathering her things, the Tielwald speaking in a low, rapid murmur.

"There's a servant of mine named Coelnyr."

"I should seek him out?"

The Tielwald gave a fractional shake of his head. "Tell Lore you need to visit my house. There's a bundle of hidden papers in the attic I'd guess Ilvar's scum missed. Look for the plastered section of wall under the window. It'll come loose with a little work. It's not much, old cyphers and a list of contacts in far-away places. But it should help win her approval for continuing these visits."

"And this Coelnyr?"

"Once you've been to the house, he'll find you."

"Would not Ilvar have hunted down any servants of yours by now?"

"Not this one. There are rats less gifted in survival. When he turns up, be careful of him. His appetites can sometimes get the better of his loyalty. Best if you keep a knife close to hand at all times."

"And what am I to ask of him?"

"To arrange passage out of this port, of course. But, before all else, go to the kitchens."

"The kitchens?"

"There's a woman there, Aldunna the pie cook. Make the same sign for her you did for me." Grunting in pain, he traced a stubby finger over the back of his hand, describing the circle and the line. "Tell her it's time she awoke from her long slumber."

"And then?"

Gruinskard's answer was forestalled by another squeal of door hinges and a pointed cough from Hulnath. Closing her satchel, Elvine offered the old man a polite nod. "My thanks, Tielwald. I hope to visit again shortly."

Sneering, Gruinskard flicked his maimed hand at her. "I tolerated your presence only to fill my belly." Elvine assumed this was mummery for Hulnath's benefit, but as the old man spoke on, the spear's gift revealed his aura. The colour was a complex, shifting shroud covering his aged form, but she had learned to parse its meaning by now and saw a flicker of genuine contempt in its darker hues. "You really are more like your father than your mother," he said. "He was a traitor too, so I'm told." Turning away, he huddled into the corner. "Off with you and leave me in peace."

The pretty kitchen maid was a spy. Of that Elvine had not the slightest doubt. The young woman's aura was a strange mix of cheerful pale blue, frequently supplanted by a darker red as her gaze tracked over Berrine and Elvine. These, she knew instinctively, were the colours of a deceitful soul who delighted in subterfuge. Watching the maid smile as she greeted Berrine, clasping both hands in ready, even eager welcome, Elvine couldn't help but marvel at her facility for deception.

"Fildra," Berrine said. "This is my daughter, Elvine."

"The famous scholar who brought back the Spear of the Altvar?" Fildra's eyes widened in apparent awe even as Elvine saw her aura take on a grey pall of suspicion. The colour was shot through with sickly yellow flecks Elvine interpreted as a combination of resentment and envy. Still, that smile, so open and true. *A nasty fall down the stairs.* Colvyn's advice rang loud as Elvine suppressed a flinch at the feel of the maid's hands on hers, momentarily distracted by the blue ink tattoo of a dragonfly betwixt the maid's thumb and wrist. *Does it mean something?* she wondered. *A signal to other agents in Ilvar's service?* Swallowing a sigh, Elvine admonished herself for her endless suspicions. The tattoo was a common design seen on many a youth's arm. The game of secrets she had been forced to play within the walls of this stronghold was making her see signs and portents where there were none.

"You are well?" Berrine asked Fildra. Elvine concealed a grimace of dismay at the genuine concern in her mother's voice. For one who had spied in the Tielwald's service, it was odd that she should have missed this treacherous scullion's deceit.

"I am well enough." Fildra's expression was a perfect simulacrum of muted worry as she afforded a cautious glance around the kitchens. Cooks and maids were hard at work preparing meals for the populace of the Verungyr, recently increased substantially by Tuhlvyr Vahlak and the warriors of his personal *menda*. Meeting Berrine's gaze, Fildra added in a softer tone, "Especially since I took your advice as regards too much chatter to heart."

"I'm glad to hear it."

Fildra lowered her voice further, hefting the basket of crockery she held and stepping closer. "Have you come with more news?"

"Sadly no. We—"

"We're looking for a pie cook," Elvine cut in before Berrine could speak the name. "In a week it will be ten years since Sister Lore ascended to queenhood. We would like to honour the occasion with a treat or two. She's especially fond of fruit tarts."

"Ah." Fildra's aura flickered, the sickly yellow becoming more prominent as she hid her frustration with another smile. Elvine knew they had already revealed too much just by coming here. Also, the aura confirmed the need to follow her brother's advice, and quickly, before this one could convey what she knew to Ilvar. *Stairs. Neck.* The thought of it stirred an uncomfortable roil in Elvine's belly. *I have killed before,* she reminded herself, attempting unsuccessfully to quell the rising nausea.

"Best if you talk to Aldunna, then," Fildra said, nodding to the far recesses of the kitchens. "Don't expect too warm a welcome. She hates to be interrupted. And—" she arched an eyebrow at Berrine "—she'll want paying for extra work. Just so you know."

"Our thanks." Berrine touched Fildra's arm, murmuring, "We'll talk again soon. I promise."

Aldunna, the pie cook, gave no response to their greeting. The only sign that she had heard Berrine's words came in the form of a very brief squint before she slammed a fist-sized lump of dough onto her countertop. Sprinkling some flour, she set about kneading it with the strong but deft hand of an expert.

"We require tarts," Berrine ploughed on with cheerful resolve. "A gift for the queen from her most grateful servants." When this failed to produce a response, she added, "Of course, we'll pay you for your time."

"Time I don't have can't be paid for," the cook responded in a distracted mutter, though this time her hands paused in their work as she noticed the depth of Elvine's scrutiny. Unlike Fildra, this woman either possessed no aura at all, or the spear's gift had chosen not to reveal it. Elvine had noticed its capricious nature before. Sometimes the auras were clear, sometimes dull and vague or, as in the case of this taciturn cook, completely absent. *Is it the fickleness of a god?* Elvine wondered. *Or does it only show me what I need to see?*

"Got no time for gawping girls neither," Aldunna said, her voice hardened and her squint transformed into a glower. For all her apparent fierceness, Elvine felt no fear as she returned the cook's stare. Instead of true anger, she saw well-controlled fear in the steadiness of the woman's gaze.

"Oh, I'm sure we can persuade you to make a little time for us," Elvine said. Moving closer, she put a finger to the thin covering of flour on the counter and drew a circle bisected by a line. "It's time for you to wake up," Elvine added quietly before wiping the symbol away. She had asked Berrine its meaning only to learn that it had none. It was just a means by which agents of the Tielwald made themselves known to one another.

Aldunna's expression didn't change, but Elvine saw how the knuckles of her capable hands whitened, squeezing the dough until it bulged between her fingers. "Tarts I can make," she said, voice clipped. "Cherry and apple. I'm told they're a particular favourite of the queen." She resumed kneading, her tone gaining surety as she continued. "It'll cost a silver. A coin. No hacked strips, and no haggling."

"Perfectly acceptable," Berrine said.

Aldunna spared a short glance at the other servants toiling in the kitchens. "I'll have to work extra to make them, so come back two evenings from now, after the eighth bell."

"Is Fildra likely to work late also?" Elvine asked. Her words once again brought the cook's hands to a halt, looking up at Elvine with a question in her eyes.

"It would be best if she weren't," Elvine said, voice barely above a whisper.

She saw a small shift in Aldunna's expression, a tightening of the mouth that bespoke understanding. "She's always so nice," she sighed with a faint note of regret. Giving a brisk sniff, she gathered up the dough and slammed it down again. "No. She won't be here. Two days. Eighth bell. Don't be late."

CHAPTER FIFTEEN

Ruhlin

The blood of the slain had frozen by the time they came upon the camp, creating crimson rivulets that glittered in the meagre sunlight slipping through the trees. Ruhlin reckoned about thirty people had resided here, making a home of deer-hide shelters nestled into the broken ground of the forest. Everything had been ransacked, tools and shattered cookware scattered among the fallen. At first, Ruhlin assumed them to be Morvek, as Iyaka said a few isolated bands of her folk still ranged these woods. Yet, looking closer at the first corpse he encountered, he made out the red designs inked into the man's forehead.

"Savaged by a dog, this one," Sygurn grunted, crouching next to another body, a woman sprawled face down on the frosted earth. "Hunters. My guess is they came looking for us, found this lot instead."

"Why slaughter their own people like this?" Ruhlin asked.

"These are *Travka*, dispossessed and landless, usually because of debt owed to an Aerling. With no other means of making a living, they take to the woods, living like the Morvek. Having abandoned their Aerling's land, they're considered outlaws."

"Doesn't explain the slaughter," Guthnyr said, face grim as he gazed at the body of a child lying amid the ashes of a campfire. The blaze had burned through clothing down to the flesh, exposing blackened ribs. "Why go to the trouble?"

"Insult offered to whoever had charge of the hunting party, maybe. Or just venting their anger. We've led them quite a dance these past weeks." Shrugging, Sygurn rose, casting a wary eye at the surrounding trees. "I'd guess this happened yesterday. The feckers who did it won't be far off. It's fair odds their hounds will have our scent before long. We can't linger."

"Why not?" Guthnyr's expression lacked any concern as he scanned the forest. "They come back this way, they'll be expecting just a camp of corpses. I'd very much like to prove them wrong."

"We've no notion of their numbers," Ruhlin pointed out. "To wreak this much havoc, they must outnumber us."

"Given how quickly they've dogged our trail, I'm not so sure," Guthnyr returned. "Takes a small party to move so fast."

Ruhlin was forced to concede the warrior had a point. Their first week of tracking through the increasingly dense northern forest had been blessedly free of pursuit, allowing for steady progress under Iyaka's guidance. Then came the morning when Tuhlan shook him awake, whispering of dog scent on the wind. Since then, each day had been a trial, a joyless game of attempting to cover as many miles as possible before nightfall. This wasn't the first time Guthnyr had suggested laying an ambush for their pursuers. Running from an enemy was not in his nature. Yet, only now did Ruhlin seriously consider it. Ridding themselves of the hunters would make the daily slog easier. Also, as he cast another glance around this place of massacre, it occurred to him that these people deserved a reckoning.

Hoping for a more sober perspective, he looked for Aleida, finding her crouched and peering into the disordered remnants of a shelter. Before he could seek her advice, Tuhlan's arrival forestalled further discussion. Bursting from the trees at a run, the Caerith came to a halt, chest heaving as he pointed a finger south.

"They draw near?" Ruhlin asked.

Tuhlan shook his head and dragged in a gulp of air. "Another group," he gasped. "Moving fast."

"How many?"

Tuhlan displayed his typical disregard for numbers with an exasperated shake of his head. "Many times more than us. Many dogs also. They are close. We have to run."

Calling out to the others, Ruhlin got them moving. After checking to ensure the pack horses had set off at a fast walk, he paused in annoyance when he noticed both Aleida and Guthnyr had failed to move. She was still crouched at the shelter, her hand extended as if trying to coax something forth.

"What is it?" Ruhlin said, moving to her side. Aleida didn't answer him, instead inching forward, beckoning as she spoke in a gentle tone.

"It's all right," she said, smiling in reassurance. "You're safe now."

Squinting into the shadowed gloom of the shelter, Ruhlin saw two bright blue eyes staring back. They blinked, then dimmed as their owner retreated at the sight of him.

"Don't be frightened," Aleida said. "He's a friend. So am I." She reached deeper into the shadow, but the eyes faded from view completely.

"We don't have the time," Ruhlin grunted. Dragging aside blood-matted hides, he looked down on a small oval face staring up at him with blank incomprehension. The girl was at most four years old, her skin pale as ice and her hair the shade of burnished copper, the same as the murdered woman lying only feet away. Lifting the girl from the shelter's remnants, he pushed her into Aleida's arms. "Go!"

As she hurried off, he shifted his attention to Guthnyr, sighing in dismay at the sight of the warrior drawing his sword. He steadied his feet, twirling the blade, eyes lit by an anticipatory glower. The first faint yapping of hunting dogs echoed through the forest, Ruhlin judging the distance at less than a mile. Deciding the time for reasoned debate was over, he spoke in harsh, unvarnished terms.

"Stay here and you die. And your death earns us nothing."

Guthnyr's shoulders tensed at the words, but he didn't move.

Gritting his teeth, Ruhlin tried again. "You are needed, and this is utter folly."

Guthnyr cast a baleful glance at him, Ruhlin seeing the tears that brimmed in his eyes. "I lost all," he grated. "My brother. My ship. My crew. All of it. I was captain for a day and I lost it all. Would you take a good death from me too, Ruhlin ehs Kestryg?"

"I take nothing. I offer the chance of life. The chance to win a true victory. If you want vengeance rather than just a release from the torment of guilt, then come with me." Watching Guthnyr grit his teeth against a sob, Ruhlin gentled his tone, adding, "Besides. You still owe me a debt, remember? By any honest reckoning, your life belongs to me. And I forbid you from spending it so cheaply. Now, let's be on our way."

He turned and set off at a steady run, forcing himself not to look back. For the first few strides he thought he had miscalculated, then huffed in relief at the sound of Guthnyr's boots crunching on the frosted ground.

They pressed on past nightfall, Ruhlin allowing no rest while the baying of hounds echoed to their rear. Labouring at his side, Tuhlan slowed, eyes narrowed as he cocked his ear to the south. "There are more," he said. "More hounds. More hunters."

"Two groups coming together," Ruhlin concluded. The knowledge stirred the familiar heat in his core for the first time in many days. It had faded so completely he had begun to wonder if the monster might have chosen to leave him be for good. A forlorn hope, he knew as he felt the muscles of his legs ripple. *It smells them too. And wants to come out.* He was tempted to allow it. Stop, tell the others to keep going, then wait for the monster to unleash itself on their pursuers. But it was clear they were hunted by many and there were some odds even his transformed self couldn't overcome. Also, if he did stop, he knew most, if not all, of this company would refuse to abandon him. Guthnyr would get the death he longed for, but how many of the others would join him? Indulging such a chance-ridden whim felt like a betrayal, so Ruhlin kept running.

They finally stopped when Iyaka came to a halt, Ruhlin almost stumbling into her in the deepening gloom. Seeing her moving from tree to tree, hands exploring each trunk, Ruhlin whispered, "What are you looking for?"

"The path we seek is hidden," she said, clicking her tongue in frustration as she shifted her touch from one trunk to another. "But there are signs. Marks left by my people pointing the way."

It took a moment for the meaning behind her words to dawn, the realisation putting an edge to his next question. "You mean to tell me you haven't walked this path before?"

"Only in my mind," she muttered back, distracted by her search.

Ruhlin bit down on further words, the effort of containing his anger adding fuel to the simmering heat. If he spoke now, he knew his tongue would be twisted by the monster's growl. Feeling the veins of his wrists and forearms swell, he forced himself to rigid immobility while the inner fire mounted. His garb began to tighten on expanded muscles when he saw Iyaka straighten in relief. Her hand rested on what appeared to be just a stunted branch jutting from the gnarled trunk of an aged birch. Stepping closer, Ruhlin made out a collection of marks carved into the weathered stump. To Ruhlin they seemed just a meaningless cluster of intersecting lines, but not to Iyaka.

"This way," she said, moving off and waving for the rest of them to follow.

"How far?" Ruhlin asked, hearing another echo of yapping hounds, still distant but closer than before. As they didn't rest at sunset, neither did the hunters.

"It's close," Iyaka said, scrambling up a slope, one of several they had navigated in the past hour. The higher they climbed, the steeper the ground, now also peppered by patches of snow. It wasn't the fulsome drifts of winter but still enough to make for occasionally hazardous going, especially for the pack horses. The beasts had been pushed to near exhaustion and now, faced with another obstacle, they came to a stubborn halt.

"Move, you fecking nag!" Sygurn raged, tugging on the reins of the larger horse. The animal neighed in protest, head bobbing as it threatened to tear free.

"Leave off," Ruhlin said. Moving to the horse, he calmed it with a few strokes to the neck before setting about undoing the ties to its pack. "Grab what supplies you can, then loose them. With luck, the dogs will follow their trail instead of ours."

With the horses unburdened and sent trotting off on a separate track, they gathered up what they could carry and followed in Iyaka's wake. Ruhlin hefted a pair of grain sacks on each shoulder and ported them up the slope with relative ease thanks to his swollen frame. The rest of the party could manage no more than a sack between them, save for Guthnyr, who carried a bag of turnips on one shoulder and their remaining cask of apple brandy on the other.

"Keeps the chill off," he said upon cresting the slope. His grin faded when the sound of pursuing dogs grew abruptly louder, this time accompanied by a chorus of human shouts. Looking back, Ruhlin could see dark shapes loping through the trees. None appeared to have been distracted by the fleeing horses.

"Drop it all!" he called out, dumping the sacks and moving along the line. "Run!"

Sprinting on, he caught sight of Iyaka silhouetted against a tall, snow-speckled cliff face. At first he thought she had led them to a dead end, but then saw the narrow crack running through the cliff from summit to base. Reaching her side, he peered into a channel wide enough to permit the passage of two people at a time. The shadows were too thick for him to see the end. "How long is it?" he asked Iyaka

"It leads to Morvek lands," she said, shrugging. "That is all I know."

"Then don't tarry." Ruhlin jerked his head at the channel. Iyaka shook her head, unsheathing her sword and dagger.

"The *Rulchakin* are too close. If any are to escape, we have to hold them off."

With the baying hounds so loud, he couldn't argue the point. Beckoning the others on, he pushed them into the gloomy passage two at a time. Aleida, carrying the girl from the *Travka* camp, paused before entering, clasping his hand, eyes glistening. For her part, the child seemed unperturbed, reaching out to prod curious fingers at Ruhlin's partially distorted features.

"I'll be along soon," he told Aleida.

"You better be," she said. "Else I'll have to come looking."

Predictably, Guthnyr refused to go, along with Tuhlan and, to Ruhlin's surprise, Sygurn. Julette had also dithered at the portal until Ruhlin told her to get on. "Watch over Aleida for me," he said, by way of permission. A mingling of shame and relief played over the pirate woman's face before she disappeared into the shadow. Jolnyr and Behsla were more reluctant to leave Guthnyr's side, but he pushed them both into the passage with forceful good humour.

"You seem to think I won't be victorious this night," he admonished with a laugh. "Why must you insult me so? Now, piss off the pair of you. I've work to do."

Facing the wall of trees barely fifty yards off, Ruhlin realised the tumult of hounds had diminished to a muted yapping. He could see faint movement, but, for the moment, the hunters appeared to be content to wait.

"Gathering the dogs together for a final rush," Sygurn surmised, crouching low behind the shield he had purloined in Speltsaer. "Gives them less fighting to do."

"They're wrong about that," Guthnyr growled, his face a grim but eager mask. Having kept hold of the brandy cask, he set it down on the frosted ground and unsheathed his sword. The blade flickered in the dimming light as he limbered his arm in readiness.

Feeling the heat build to an uncomfortable pitch, Ruhlin shrugged off his cloak and jerkin. He could smell both the dogs and their masters now, an acrid mingling of beast and human sweat adding hunger to the fire spreading through his body. He grunted at the feel of his hands swelling, accompanied by the grind of his spine stretching and muscle thickening across his back. Instinctively, the others edged away from him, all save Tuhlan, who once again stared at him with undisguised awe, whispering something in the Caerith tongue.

The dogs burst from the trees without warning, more than twenty pelting up the slope, yapping hungrily as they ran. The sight of them, all impressive beasts bred to kill as well as track, sent a pulse of eager heat through Ruhlin's body, his form swelling even more. To his right, Tuhlan loosed an arrow and the leading hound tumbled. The Caerith killed another two hounds before they had covered half the distance to their prey, then cast his bow aside and drew his long-hafted hatchet from his belt.

Time slowed as Ruhlin watched the hounds draw near, the red tinge of the monster's rage crowding the edges of his vision. Yet, he remained aware. The all-consuming fury that stole his mind failed to blossom this time, even though his body continued to assume bestial form. So, when he heard a familiar huffing growl from above, his reaction was one of surprise rather than aggression.

The bear peered down at him from a ledge a dozen feet above, gaze filled with a knowing, part judgemental light. Grunting, either in greeting or disapproval, the beast leaped from the cliff face and sped towards the oncoming dogs. Confronted with an unexpected opponent of such size, they came to an immediate halt, milling about and yapping in confusion until a second surprise arrived.

The arrows descended from the clifftop in a dark blizzard, felling the hounds in an instant, each one skewered by at least four shafts. The arrow storm shifted then, arcing into the forest, birthing an uproar of surprise and pain from the unseen hunters. The chorus of screams increased when the bear charged into the trees a heartbeat later.

Stalled by bafflement, Ruhlin grunted when a man appeared to his left, nimbly descending the cliff via a rope. He was tall, near equal in stature to Guthnyr, pale of face with long black hair bound into tight braids. His garb was a mix of buckskin and sparse steel armour. Unslinging the iron-headed spear strapped across his back, he spared Ruhlin a short, curious glance before sprinting off towards the forest. More followed, men and women all similarly clad, bearing a variety of weapons, roping down from the clifftop before charging into the trees.

"Hold!" Iyaka shouted when a wary Guthnyr raised his sword to one of the newcomers. "These are friends."

Morvek, Ruhlin concluded, watching them disappear into the forest as more descended the cliff. He reckoned their number at well over a hundred. The tumult bespoke a fierce struggle, one Guthnyr was keen not to miss. Watching him pelt down the slope with sword raised, Ruhlin felt obliged to follow, even though the fury was fading fast. It seemed the monster had a well-tuned sense for when danger had passed. By the time he reached the trees, he had mostly returned to his usual size, and begun to feel the fierce chill of a high place on the cusp of winter.

"Shite on it," Guthnyr grumbled, stomping into view with his sword untarnished. "They might have left some for us."

Squinting into the surrounding shadows, Ruhlin made out the bodies of Nihlvarian hunters and warriors. Some were pierced by arrows, but most appeared to have fallen to blade, spear, or the more gruesome effect of a slashing bear claw. Judging by the number lying face down, he concluded many had died attempting to flee. A few distant screams sounded, indicating their Morvek saviours were disinclined to offer mercy to cowards.

The tall man with the long braids approached to within a few feet from Ruhlin, his face and spear dark with blood, a group of Morvek gathering at his back. His expression was stern but also coloured by much the same bafflement as when he had first looked upon Ruhlin.

"My . . . thanks," Ruhlin said, unsure of what else to say.

The man's expression remained unchanged until his eyes alighted on

Iyaka. A smile played over his lips, though Ruhlin sensed a certain guardedness when he spoke a few short words in the Morvek tongue. Iyaka's demeanour was one of resignation rather than welcome, as she responded with what sounded like a question. In response, the tall man pointed to the shaggy mass of the bear ambling towards them, tongue lapping over a gore-darkened maw.

"So," Ruhlin said. "That's where she went."

The bear surprised him by coming close enough to sniff him, letting out a series of grunts Ruhlin felt held a note of approval. Although, for all he knew, they could equally mean the opposite.

"Tirohk says she guided his war band here a week ago," Iyaka said. "They've been growing impatient for our arrival."

"Tirohk?" Ruhlin asked.

"I am Tirohk," the tall man said in clear Nihlvarian. "War chief of the *Vehlkasa*. And you are the *Telchak*, the one we were promised."

"Promised?" Ruhlin asked only for Iyaka to interrupt in rapidly spoken Morvek. Tirohk nodded and called out to the surrounding warriors, busily divesting the Nihlvarians of weapons and valuables. The war band quickly gathered up their loot and began to ascend the slope.

"I told him there are likely more on our trail," Iyaka said. "We shouldn't loiter here."

Labouring up the slope, Ruhlin paused to don his discarded garb, noting how Iyaka's eyes tracked Tirohk as he led his warriors into the channel in the cliff. "You know this man?" he asked.

Iyaka's lips formed a sour, rueful grin as she said, "I do. He's my husband." Letting out a heavy sigh, she entered the passage, her next words echoing loud. "I hoped he'd be dead by now."

"Well, that looks like a fecking shite-hole." Sygurn turned from the sight of the dilapidated settlement, asking Iyaka, "Can't they find somewhere better for us?"

"*Rulchakin* belong in shelters of their own fashioning," she replied with a shrug. "My people consider this place cursed and home to many ghosts, so it remains untouched. Count yourself lucky they offer any refuge at all."

Once through the channel in the cliff, Ruhlin had enjoyed a brief reunion with Aleida and the others before Tirohk harried them into a rapid march through the steep mountain country beyond. The weather worsened as they made their way along a series of narrow tracks, the air taking on a frigid edge as flurries of snow became every more frequent. Three days on, they came to a ridge overlooking a canyon, the far slope marked by a cluster of buildings.

The settlement was clearly long abandoned, the surviving structures in varying states of disrepair. However, Ruhlin was able to discern signs of Nihlvarian manufacture in the *kehlgruin* walls still standing in defiance of the elements.

"The *Rulchakin* came years ago to dig metal from the mountain," Iyaka explained. "But lasted only one winter."

"Your people killed them?" he asked.

She shook her head. "They didn't have to. The mountain spirit here is jealous of her privacy. She killed them with cold, hunger, and the madness that comes with both. But she'll probably tolerate you as long as I'm here." Her face bunched in reluctance as she began to descend the ridge. "But first, we'll have to clear out the bones."

Upon closer inspection, Ruhlin found the settlement less ruined than he expected. The stone walls had fallen in places, as had many of the roofs, but those buildings constructed mostly from *kehlgruin* remained largely intact. Most of the houses lay close to a mineshaft. The sturdy beams forming the entrance were undamaged, as was the tunnel beyond, at least as far as the reach of Ruhlin's torch. Hearing a loud huff to his rear, he stood aside as the bear lumbered into the mine. The shaggy bulk slipped quickly into shadow and soon Ruhlin heard the regular grating wheeze of its snores. One of them, at least, would have a roof this night.

Only Tirohk and a handful of Morvek accompanied them to the settlement. The rest of the war band had gradually taken their leave during the march, along with several Morvek from Ruhlin's band. Those that remained exhibited a potent wariness towards Tirohk and his warriors, an attitude reflected in full measure. *They are not* Vehlkasa, Ruhlin concluded. According to Iyaka, the word translated as 'Grey Mountains', the clan with dominance over this northern high country. Although no violence occurred between the *Vehlkasa* and the other Morvek, the pitch of their mutual hostility made him wonder how often these people warred with each other.

The *Vehlkasa* provided deer and goat hides for use as makeshift roofs, along with a stock of firewood and provisions for several days. "You'll find the hunting fair nearby," Tirohk said. "The goats come down from the high slopes in winter. But so do the leopards, so be wary. We'll bring more before the snows come."

"You're just leaving us here?" Aleida asked as Tirohk turned to walk away. As he paused to regard her, the expression on the war chief's face stirred a flicker of heat in Ruhlin's core. He had noticed it during the trek here: dislike, bordering on outright repugnance. While Tirohk and his fellow warriors exhibited a measure of contempt for the Nihlvarians in this company, it was scant in comparison to their disdain for Aleida. *Her blood is mixed,* Iyaka had explained. *Many among my people see those of mixed blood as both tainted and dangerous. And she is the daughter of an Aerling.*

"A fair question," Ruhlin said, the heat putting an edge to his voice. "Why save us just to abandon us?"

"You will be safe here," Tirohk replied. "And fed. We saved you because of her." He jerked his head at the mineshaft where the bear continued to snore. "But we cannot have you live among us."

Clearly ill disposed to answer further questions, he turned and addressed his next words to Iyaka, speaking in Morvek. Her response was short, delivered with a stone-faced expression that invited no argument. Muttering something, Tirohk hefted his spear and began to descend the slope to the canyon floor, his warriors following.

For a short while they stood surveying their new home, eyes tracking over roofless houses. Iyaka had been right. Each structure was home to at least one aged corpse, stripped of flesh down to bare bones.

"Do your people have burial rites?" Guthnyr asked Sygurn.

"Just pile them up over there and cover them with rocks," the Nihlvarian said, gesturing to a nearby gully. "The ground's too hard for digging." Stroking his chin, he cast a critical eye over the largest structure, a broad, one-storey building that Ruhlin assumed had served as the village hall. "Before I was sold to the Aerling, I slaved for a builder's whip-man," Sygurn went on. "If we can gather enough slate, I reckon I might be able to put a roof on that."

"A task for tomorrow," Ruhlin said. "Guthnyr, Tuhlan, scout the upper slope before nightfall. We need to know if our new friends left sentries to watch over us. Or if we're likely to have other visitors."

"And if we find anyone?" Guthnyr asked.

"Leave them be unless they offer violence. Also, see if you can bring down one of the goats he spoke of. It would be good to bless this place with a feast. As for the rest of us." He offered them all an apologetic smile. "We have bones to gather. And if you catch sight of a ghost, please say nothing."

"This is a bad place." Aleida managed to maintain a cheerful expression as she fussed over the *Travka* girl. She sat in Aleida's lap, letting out occasional giggles as her hair was combed and braided. Attempts to elicit a name from her had produced nothing and when she did speak, it was only in an incomprehensible babble lacking true words. Ruhlin worried that the sights she had witnessed might have disordered her mind, perhaps robbed her tongue of speech. But she remained a mostly happy child, only resorting to tears when separated from Aleida for more than a few moments. For want of another, she had named the girl Ryma, her grandmother's name.

They had taken over a *kehlgruin* walled hut about half the size of his grandmother's cottage, one of the few dwellings with a partially intact roof. Although, judging by how many stars Ruhlin could see through the sparse tiles and beams, he doubted it would serve when the snows came. Loud voices rose from the large building where they had convened the feast. Tuhlan, as usual, had not disappointed, returning with a goat carcass across his shoulders, swiftly skinned and butchered for the spit. He and Guthnyr reported no sightings of any watchers, but both felt sure they had been observed.

"Got that itch between the shoulder blades that tells of hidden eyes," Guthnyr said. "Be easier to spot once we learn the lie of the country. Reckon I'll do some more scouting on the morrow, if you can spare me from the toil."

"Go with Tuhlan when you do," Ruhlin had told him. "See if you can find other settlements nearby. Miners don't typically sink just one shaft into a mountain. We'll need to scavenge materials for building."

Thanks to Guthnyr's brandy cask, the remainder of the night was spent in reasonable good cheer, even the occasional song. Ruhlin and Aleida had departed the feast early when Ryma began to tire.

"We have been in worse places," he told Aleida. "And we've yet to see a ghost."

"They're here. She knows." Aleida nodded to the un-shuttered window where the glow of a small fire could be seen. Iyaka had built it at sunset, remaining in the same spot for hours, eyes closed and head bowed as she canted something in her own tongue.

"She asks the spirit of the mountain to keep them at bay," Aleida explained. "And not to kill us as she killed those who came before."

"This mountain spirit is a god?" Ruhlin ventured, earning a disparaging roll of her eyes.

"Always gods with your kind," she said, keeping her voice soft and gently setting Ryma down on a bed of furs. The child's head lolled, and she let out only a small groan of protest as Aleida covered her. "My father spoke of the Altvar endlessly. When I was young, he would force me to learn their many names and stories, but they never had purchase on my heart. My mother had seen to that. 'Why look to unseen halls and mighty beings who only make themselves known through ancient tales and random chance?' she asked me. The spirits that reside in rock, earth, wind and water are so easily touched. They speak to us every day, if only we allow ourselves to hear them."

"Can you hear it now?" he asked. "The spirit of this mountain?"

She smiled and moved to his side, covering herself with his cloak as she settled against him. "The wind cuts, but not so sharp as it could. The snow is kept at bay. The rocks do not tremble or tumble into our midst. I think she's content to let us stay, for now."

She pressed a kiss to his neck, her lips lingering as her hand reached into his jerkin, exploring with obvious intent.

"What about . . . ?" Ruhlin glanced at Ryma's small, slumbering form.

"She sleeps like a stone," she murmured, nuzzling at his ear. "And I feel we have waited long enough, Ruhlin ehs Kestryg."

He pulled her closer, feeling heat of a different kind building within. But this time, he was happy to surrender to it.

CHAPTER SIXTEEN

Felnir

Felnir's first victim was a large man with a copious belly slouching his way up the winding stairwell of the stronghold's tower. He plodded with head downcast and a low, expletive-filled mutter issuing from his lips.

"My fucking turn," he slurred, Felnir catching the taint of liquor on his breath while noting the irregularity of this gait. "Always my fucking turn—"

His words came to an abrupt halt at the sight of Felnir's bare feet upon the steps. As he raised a baffled, gape-mouthed face, Felnir was struck by the density of black ink tattooed into the cultist's skin. He saw little artistry in it, small pictograms and what may have been ancient Ascarlian text stretched across the man's flabby jowls in ugly discordance. They wobbled as his drink-addled mind belatedly decided that, having discovered an intruder, he should raise the alarm. He died before the shout escaped his throat, Felnir stabbing the Sword of the Altvar into his open mouth, aimed perfectly to sever the spine on the way through.

He caught the body about the waist before it fell, grunting with the effort of preventing the bulky encumbrance tumbling down the stairwell. The cultist gurgled out his last few breaths as Felnir laid him on his side. A brief inspection of the corpse revealed only a dagger not worth taking and a leather flask filled with a more acrid-smelling version of the wine that seemed so prevalent in this land.

Moving on, he enjoyed an uninterrupted journey to the base of the tower. An empty walkway linked the structure to the lower tier of fortifications, Felnir crossing it in a crouched run. More steps led him through a series of bastions. The first was vacant, but he found another cultist slumbering in the second. He was less broad of girth than the man Felnir had killed in the high tower, but more drunk. Perched precariously on a stool, he swayed back and forth, heavy eyelids fluttering in a vain attempt to reacquaint a pickled mind with his surroundings. Felnir quickly slit his throat, dragged the body into shadow, and descended the next stairwell.

Here, the stronghold became more substantial. A narrow passage gave way to a broad chamber where more cultists slumbered. They lay on bedrolls amid a chaotic mess of discarded clothes and uncleared rubbish. Weapons were stacked in haphazard order, none of them within easy reach of their sleeping owners. The atmosphere mingled liquor with the sharp sting of bodies unwashed for days. Felnir was as disgusted by the smell as he was by their slovenliness. If any of his *menda* had neglected themselves and their arms to this degree, he would have beaten them bloody. Moving carefully through the untidy space, he began to wonder if the *Ahrkun Krayl's* fierce reputation might be undeserved. If so, he would find out in short order.

Once through the chamber, he descended another series of stairwells. Again, he encountered no sentries and detected little sound beyond the snores emanating from various closed doors. That changed when he passed one outlined in firelight and heard a very distinct scream from within. A child's scream. It was cut short by the shouts of an enraged adult male, punctuated by the hard slap of something striking flesh. Coming to a halt, Felnir discerned an overlap of whimpering and sobs, indicating that more than one child faced torment on the other side of this door. The voice became clearer then, taking on an instructive note.

"Again! The names of the gods of the Lower Hall! All of them! And don't mumble!"

A distraction, Felnir told himself. *Deal with the gate and come back.*

Another slap of punished flesh accompanied by a shrill cry, this one yet more riven with pain and despair than the first, banished any further calculation. Reaching for the door's iron handle, he found it unlocked. Upon hauling it open Felnir beheld a bald-headed man of cadaverous aspect stalled in the act of raising a long leather strap. The intended target of his anger huddled on the floor. A boy of perhaps ten, naked but for a threadbare set of trews, his back striped with red welts from recent blows. Looking closer, Felnir saw that the lad wasn't alone. Peeking out from beneath his skinny form was the face of a girl several years younger. Plainly, the boy had been trying to shield her.

Anger is my worst weakness. An inarguably true statement that, had it risen to mind in that instant, might have compelled Felnir to a more stealthy mode of attack. But it didn't. Hissing in rage, he stepped into the room and lopped off the bald man's hand at the wrist. As both appendage and the leather strap it held fell to the floor, the maimed man let out a scream that was even more high-pitched and piercing than that of his victim. It continued as he collapsed to his knees, manic eyes fixed upon the jetting stump of his wrist, his animalistic distress echoing long and loud through the halls at Felnir's back.

He curtailed the bothersome tumult by slashing open the bald man's neck, kicking his twitching body aside as he moved to the children on the floor. "Can you walk?" he asked the boy. The lad regarded him with blank astonishment until a nudge from the little girl brought focus to his gaze.

"Yes," he said, raising a hand to point beyond Felnir's shoulder. "But, them . . ."

Turning, Felnir saw a line of small bodies along the wall. Each was secured by a strap about the waist fixed to the stone. He counted eight, all slumped and unmoving. At least one was dead, his head lolling at an angle that only a body devoid of life could adopt. Felnir saw no signs of animation in the others.

"We'll come back for them," he said, hauling the boy upright. The girl he had been shielding hopped to her feet quickly, her small face showing markedly less confusion than her protector's.

"Are you Turmvek?" she asked, referring to the god of the Lower Hall with dominion over blades and those who wield them.

"Of course he's not," the boy said. Felnir could tell he was struggling to control his trembles and the sob that threatened to escape his throat.

"But he looks so much like that picture they showed us," the girl responded with a pout, then frowned as she noticed Felnir's feet. "But Turmvek was wearing shoes."

"He's right," Felnir told the girl, casting a glance at the door as alarmed voices began to echo. "I'm no god. And we have to go."

The girl seemed about to ask another question when the boy took firm hold of her hand, dragging her along as Felnir ushered them from the room. Once outside, he led them down the next series of stairwells until they came to a tower where the walkways forked.

"Which one leads to the gate?" Felnir asked the boy.

"I don't know." The lad shook his head in confusion. "They put sacks on our heads when they brought us here."

"It's that one." The girl pointed to the walkway on the left. "I could see through mine a little."

Unsure as to the wisdom of trusting an infant's judgement but lacking any other clues, Felnir moved left, gesturing for them to keep up. They were halfway across the walkway when a trio of armed cultists emerged from the base of the squat tower ahead.

"Wait here," Felnir told the children before accelerating into a fast run. The oncoming cultists reacted with all the confusion he hoped from amateur warriors faced with a quarry that attacked instead of fleeing. Coming to an untidy halt, they stumbled into each other, the one in the lead barely managing to raise her sword before Felnir closed to sweep it aside and deliver a blinding lateral stroke to her eyes. He sidestepped the thrust of the man to her left, then kicked the screaming woman, sending her into collision with the one behind. It required a swiftly delivered series of blows aimed at the head of the man on his right to drive him to the walkway's balustrade, and another kick to send him over it. His yell was brief and terminated by a satisfying thud from below.

Turning to confront the unwounded member of the trio, Felnir glimpsed a bleached, terrified face before the cultist turned and ran back the way he had come, crying out a garbled warning as he disappeared into the next tower. The woman Felnir had blinded shuddered on her knees, sobbing out some form of ritualised words as she clutched at her ruined eyes.

"In the Altvar's light I serve . . . For their glory do I toil . . . In the Altvar's light I—"

Her devotions ended in a wet choke when the boy, having retrieved her fallen sword, jabbed its point into her throat. "She would help the teacher sometimes," he told Felnir, watching the cultist gasp and shudder into stillness. "She was worse than him." His features bunched at the onset of tears. By contrast, the girl appeared more angry than distressed, stepping forward to deliver a sharp kick to the slain woman's head.

"Keep hold of that," Felnir said, seeing the sword begin to slip from the boy's grip. "And stay close to me."

Rushing into the tower at the end of the walkway, he saw that it formed a bastion at the far end of the wall where the stronghold's gate was located. The craven who had run was aloft somewhere, his pleas for support echoing down the stairwell. For the moment, no one nearby seemed inclined to respond. Stepping out onto the battlement, Felnir could see only a portion of the track below, the slope and the forest beyond, lost to the darkness. He headed for the gate with the coward still calling out from atop the tower behind. Felnir considered going back to silence him, but, as he turned, his eye caught the flicker of an arrow arcing out of the darkness beyond the wall. Looking up, he saw a flap of clothing and flailing arm, whereupon the cultist's cries were silenced.

Bow of the Altvar, Felnir thought, squinting at the shadowed landscape.

Such a shot would have been extremely difficult in daylight. In the darkness it seemed impossible, yet Sygna had done it.

"Turmvek!"

Feeling the tug of the girl's small hand to his sleeve, Felnir turned to see a number of cultists scaling a ladder propped against the wall ahead. Sprinting forward, he reached the first climber just as he set his foot upon the battlement, the Sword of the Altvar cleaving his unarmoured skull before he could raise the hatchet he held. Felnir grabbed hold of the slain man, positioning him so that his tumbling form would clear the ladder of climbers, then letting go. Looking down, he saw a dozen or so cultists milling about, one raising a bow. The arrow thrummed the air as Felnir crouched, beckoning the boy closer.

"What's your name, lad?"

"Ehdlur," the boy said, then nodded to the girl. "My sister, Yuhlla."

"It's my honour to meet you both. I am Felnir Skyrnrak, and I must ask you to lend me your blade." He gestured to the sword in the boy's hand. "I promise I'll return it shortly."

"What are you going to do?" he asked, handing over the sword without hesitation.

"Open the gate. My friends are waiting, you see. Both of you stay here." He fixed them with a stern glare. "No wandering off until I come back, all right?"

Ehdlur replied with a grave nod, clasping his sister's hand tight. For her part, the girl seemed more curious than scared. "Are you going to kill them all, Turmvek?" she asked, staring up at him with bright, eager eyes.

"Felnir," he corrected. "And yes, I am. Remember what I said." Then, with a sword in each hand, he turned and leaped from the battlement.

Life as a mercenary had imparted many a hard lesson, one of which was the value of the unexpected attack, especially when visited upon a weak enemy. Had he faced more expert opponents, they would have reacted with either instant aggression or drawn back to form a solid defence. The *Ahrkun* warriors did neither. Instead, they mostly stood and gaped in astonishment as he landed in their midst, the sole exception being the bowman, who was quick to set another arrow to his stave. Felnir killed him first, an overhead swing of Ehdlur's sword biting deep into his shoulder. Dragging the blade free, Felnir whirled, letting out a feral war cry as his two blades hacked at legs, arms and faces. In response, those cultists who had survived the onslaught scattered. A couple fled into the stronghold while the others retreated several paces, all exchanging uncertain glances verging on panic. Luckily, their cowardice gave Felnir a clear run to the gate. Warding off jabbing spears with his swords, he hurled himself against the timbers, stooping to put his shoulder under the hefty crossbeam, then straightening to lift it.

"Stop him!" one of the *Ahrkun* yelled, charging forward with a battle axe raised. Felnir crouched lower as the poorly aimed blow fell, the axe blade sinking into the crossbeam an inch from his head. He replied with an upward slash at the cultist's groin as he vainly tried to tug his weapon free. The shrillness of his scream, and subsequent writhing upon the ground as he clutched at the bloody ruin between his legs, sufficed to dissuade his comrades from following his example.

Yelling with the effort, Felnir gave a final heave, successfully dislodging the crossbeam from the gate. It swung open instantly, the two large doors forced apart by the pressure of bodies from outside. Sygna was the first to charge into the gap, swiftly followed by Falk and Beyorn. Tulvik, Farryk and the warriors from Kahl Hardta came next, streaming through in a dense mass, every face snarling with a hunger for retribution. Of the cultists who had gathered to defend the gate, only two stayed to contend the onslaught, both quickly cut down while their comrades ran.

"To the walls!" Felnir called out, pointing one of his blades at the ladder. "We must move quickly. Tulvik, take half and go left. The rest of you follow me."

Once back atop the battlement, he paused to return his borrowed blade to Ehdlur. "Wait here a while longer," Felnir told the pair, both staring wide-eyed at the warriors crowding the wall. "I'll be back before morning. Then we'll have us a feast, eh?"

Turning, he started along the wall at a run, Sygna falling in alongside with bow in hand. "New friends?" she asked.

"You wanted a child. I found you two."

It required less than an hour of fighting for the stronghold to fall. Felnir's estimation of the *Ahrkun*'s martial abilities was borne out by their failure to organise any form of meaningful defence as his vengeful *menda* rampaged through the stronghold. Most of the cultists appeared to have been roused from inebriated slumber, many dying as they struggled free of their beds, still unaware of the danger they faced. Those in the upper levels were more alert and likely to offer resistance, but most exhibited only a desperate desire to flee. Felnir saw a few begging, crouched in corners with hands raised to ward off the blades of folk disinclined to mercy.

The only fight worthy of the name occurred in the large sleeping chamber near the main tower. Here, two dozen *Ahrkun* contrived to organise a shield wall that successfully repelled the first rush. However, a few well-placed arrows from Sygna, and the arrival of Tulvik's contingent via a door the cultists had neglected to seal, ensured the subsequent melee was both brief and one-sided. Felnir found himself impressed by both Tulvik and Beyorn. The latter showed a natural gift for leadership in the way he marshalled his warriors, nor was he lacking in skill and courage at arms. Tulvik, by contrast, presented an example of unreasoned ferocity. Hurling himself into the midst of the few remaining *Ahrkun*, he hacked away with tireless energy, seemingly unaware of the fresh cuts to his face and hands.

With their meagre defence broken, what remained of their foes were swiftly dispatched. In accordance with Felnir's prior experience of battles between folk bearing genuine hatred for each other, the aftermath to this one was ugly. The men and women from Kahl Hardta began to inflict a frenzy of mutilation upon the dead before scouring the other bodies for signs of life. The torment they inflicted inflamed their hunger for more and soon the victors were searching every room for survivors, the screams of those they found growing harder to bear as their tormentors explored ways to prolong their suffering.

Drawing Falk aside, Felnir imparted some soft-spoken instructions. "There's bound to be a few hiding they'll miss. Find one and keep them hidden until this calms down, then bring them to me. I would know more of this cult."

Any impulse towards clemency he might have felt was quelled when he returned to the room where he had discovered Ehdlur and Yuhlla. He and Sygna undid the bonds of the children secured to the wall, finding all but one dead. "Should've kept that one breathing a little longer," Felnir grunted, glancing at the one-handed corpse near the door.

"Yes," Sygna said, smoothing the blood-matted hair of the only survivor, a girl no more than eight years old. "You should."

They took the girl to the lower tiers of the stronghold, finding a room with a bed in one of the towers. Felnir fetched Ehdlur and Yuhlla, both obediently waiting where he had left them, and set about lighting a fire in the tower room's hearth.

"Her name's Huhlda," Ehdlur said as Sygna, having found a bucket of clean water, setting about tending to the girl.

"Farryk's daughter," Felnir said, recognising the name. It occurred to him that he hadn't seen the man during the battle, and a sombre glance from Sygna confirmed his suspicions.

"He went with Tulvik," she said, pressing a damp cloth to the unconscious child's forehead. "Caught an arrow at the second wall."

"Will Huhlda be all right?" Ehdlur asked. "She would always talk back to the teacher, so he hurt her more."

"She just needs to sleep for a good while," Sygna told him. "There's a pot over there. Why don't you boil some water for us? I'll need it to clean her cuts."

"If he's Turmvek, you must be Denhild," Yuhlla said, coming closer to peer at Sygna. Denhild was the goddess of healing. Clearly the child was clinging to the notion that her saviours were scions of the Altvar's Lower Hall.

"Hardly," Sygna muttered, touching a finger to the pulse in Huhlda's neck. "Strong," she murmured, pursing her lips in satisfaction. "Good."

Hearing a distant but piercing upsurge of screams from outside, Felnir closed the door. "Come," he told the two children, beckoning them to the hearth. "Let's fix a meal, and you can tell me all about where you're from and how you came to be here."

The man Falk brought him was perhaps the most wretched, pathetic and patently devious soul Felnir had encountered in a career rich in less-than-admirable characters. The captive grovelled at first, falling to all fours and pressing his head to the flagstones in abject subjugation. However, the calculation Felnir saw when the fellow darted glances at his captors made it clear his fear hadn't driven him beyond reason.

"Such mercy you show me, great captain," he said in a humble whisper. He was sallow of face with a spindly bearing that bordered on emaciation. Felnir saw the bones in his neck shift in stark clarity as he bobbed his head with every word. "Long have I prayed to the Altvar for deliverance from this vile place. Such torments I suffered here . . ."

"Quiet!" Felnir snapped. Having ordered all the bodies in the sleeping chamber cleared, and the floors scrubbed clean of a great many stains, he had adopted it as a temporary throne room. Beyorn found a suitably grand chair to serve as the royal perch, though it was unevenly balanced with a tendency to put an ache in Felnir's back. Rising, he moved to the narrow window, looking down at the descending tiers of walls and walkways. His *menda* were at work dragging the remaining bodies away to be dumped in the forest with no rites spoken. The slaughter had gone on for hours until no more victims could be found, whereupon the victors turned their attentions to the plentiful wine and brandy stored in the lower rooms. Felnir allowed their drunken revels for a night, knowing it would serve to extinguish their residual rage. Come the morning, he made a point to berate them all for their excesses and had Beyorn smash the remaining liquor casks.

"Where did you find him?" he asked Falk, not turning from the window.

"Behind a false wall in one of the cellars, my lord. Well crafted. Most eyes would miss it."

"But not yours, eh, old friend?"

"Fresh scraped dust on the floor gave it away. I suspect this one hid in haste."

"As well he might." Felnir turned, finding the captive squinting up at him again with his calculating eyes. It was plain he wanted to say a great many things, but wisely kept his tongue in check. *This one's not to be underestimated*, Felnir decided. "You have a name?" he asked.

The prisoner bobbed his head again. "Olvynd, my lord."

"Only Falk gets to call me that. You don't get to call me anything at all." Felnir angled his head, studying Olvynd's face as he continued, "This place was home to a deluded perversion of Ascarlian beliefs. The *Ahrkun Krayl* are a cowardly scum. The very existence of their vile cult is an insult to the Altvar."

No glimmer of offence or outrage, Felnir judged, seeing only tense expectation and the faint flicker to the eyes that told of a very busy mind. Grunting in satisfaction, Felnir moved to crouch in front of Olvynd, speaking with soft intent. "You do not strike me as a man of firm conviction. Which makes me wonder how you came to be here. And—" he held up a finger in warning when the captive opened his mouth "—I caution you to speak only the truth, for I have a very keen ear for lies. If I hear the slightest note of falsehood, I'll allow my *menda* to choose the manner of your execution, and you've seen how inventive they can be."

Felnir returned to his uncomfortable throne, gesturing for Olvynd to rise and speak on, which he did after a brief pause to swallow. "I was recently obliged to leave my home of many years," he began. "The port of Speldhelven to the north. Perhaps you are familiar with it?" He halted his tale long enough to register that his question would remain unanswered before ploughing on. "In any case, the manner of my departure was both rapid and unfortunate, for I was compelled to leave behind my purse. Such privation I suffered on the road, for this land is not kind to the destitute."

"So," Felnir interrupted, "you got caught thieving in this Speldhelven. Forced to flee, you threw your lot in with the *Ahrkun* despite the fact that you couldn't give two shits for their beliefs. Do I misconstrue?"

"Forgive me, but yes." A smile played over Olvynd's lips, ingratiating and repellent in equal measure. "I was never a thief. Merely a broker of information. Can I be blamed if certain parties take exception to the truths they are told? As for the *Ahrkun*, I had the ill luck to make my way to a village barely an hour before they arrived to raid it. I knew enough of their peculiar dogma to convince them that I was of like mind. Sadly, this obliged me to accompany them to this hideous rat hole. Living among them has not been easy." Felnir saw a small spasm to Olvynd's features then, a genuine flicker of disgust and, he was surprised to see, guilt.

"Did you have any part in what happened to the children they stole?" Felnir asked, leaning forward to maintain his stare.

"I did not. Though I'll confess to the crime of failing to speak or act against it. If that earns me the noose or the knife, I'll not argue the point."

A *gamble*, Felnir concluded, watching the careful composure of Olvynd's lean, elongated features. Whether his noble contrition would survive an encounter with imminent death was a moot point. Like the late Sir Aurent Vellinde, this one had uses. Unlike Vellinde, he failed to stir Felnir's anger to a murderous pitch. He wasn't wholly convinced by Olvynd's story, but remained certain he hadn't been a genuine recruit to this cult.

"I would guess," Felnir said, "that a man so well versed in the value of information would have kept his ears and eyes very much open in a place like this."

"I'm very happy to say I did." Olvynd stood a little straighter. "I learned the names of the villages they raided, and those they intended to raid. Of little consequence now, I suppose. But," he went on quickly in response to Felnir's frown, "I also learned that this stronghold is due a visitor in the very near future."

"A visitor?"

"A very important visitor, in fact. The *Ahrkun* here were tasked with collecting children and spoils, as you know. They also stored a good deal of silver, gold and various other loot, all of which is regularly turned over to the *Sindra*, or rather the agent of the *Sindra*. He's expected in a few days. And when he arrives—" Olvynd's small tongue emerged to lick at his lips, Felnir thinking it the ugliest thing he had done yet "—his retinue will be carrying all the riches collected during his travels. Also, possibly some more children in need of rescue, since I suspect that to be your principal object."

"My object is to make myself king of this land," Felnir told him. "The first step towards that goal being the destruction of the *Ahrkun Krayl*. To do that, I require an army, one that will need to be paid in more than just vengeance. Falk, bring another chair and some refreshment for us. My newly appointed Scribe of Records and I have much to discuss. You can read and write, I assume?"

Olvynd nodded, Felnir's estimation of his intelligence increased by the fact that he had enough wit not to bow. "I do, my king."

Felnir didn't correct him as he would the others. Instinct born of experience warned him that this man would need a constant reminder as to their respective status. "Excellent. Now, sit with me and tell me all you know of the *Sindra*, and our soon-to-arrive guest."

CHAPTER SEVENTEEN

Thera

Reeling away from the screaming face of her great-grandfather, Thera's back connected painfully with something hard. The impact and, as she discovered in trying to keep herself upright, hard frozen ground succeeded in tipping her onto her rump. Air billowed from her lips in a cloud, the icy caress of winter playing over her skin. Looking around, she found herself in a snowbound forest, dark trunks sprouting from tall drifts, their whiteness marred by crimson streaks. Bodies littered the snow all about. Some bore the armour of warriors, others were clad in the garb of townsfolk or fishermen. Some were young, some were old. Most showed only marginal signs of injury, but a few lay amid dismembered limbs, and a smaller number had been subjected to spectacular mutilation. Thera grimaced at the sight of a man suspended between two saplings, his back cut open and ribs broken so that the organs within could be drawn out and laid upon his shoulders. *The Crimson Hawk*, she recalled. A rare punishment reserved for the worst traitors to the Sister Queens, one she counted herself fortunate never to have inflicted.

"He broke the queens' law," the words came from her great-grandfather. Phrased in a tone of such raw, piteous defensiveness, she found it hard to credit they had emerged from his lips. "The Fjord Gelders had been told," he went on, Thera shocked to discover that, in this dream, he still possessed both his eyes. They blazed at her in a desperate desire for understanding. Gruinskard began to crawl towards her, reaching out with trembling hands. "They had all been told. No trade with Olversahl. An example had to be set . . ."

Beset both by repulsion and a conviction she was subject to some form of arcane deceit, Thera scrambled away from him. Bracing herself against the tree she had collided with, she levered herself upright, demanding, "Who are you? Where is the Tielwald?"

The sound of her voice brought an abrupt halt to Gruinskard's movements. Recognition flickered in his eyes, which abruptly became one, the surrounding flesh wrinkling with age until she looked upon the true face of her great-grandfather. "You're here," he said, relief and annoyance colouring his tone. "You're finally here."

"I've been searching my dreams," Thera replied. "I couldn't find you before."

Gruinskard grunted and climbed to his feet, casting a dour glance at their surroundings. "Back to this again," he murmured. "Always when pain assails the body, the mind flees to the worst place."

"Where are we?" Thera asked. "I don't recognise this forest."

"You wouldn't. It exists only here. The receptacle of my crimes. My form of the Altvar's blessing is often more of a curse."

His crimes, Thera thought, looking again at the corpses. They stretched away into the gloomy recesses of the forest in an ugly sprawl. *So many.* "You killed them all?"

"Or had them killed. It's the same thing in the end." Gruinskard's eye lingered on the man who had received the Crimson Hawk before he turned away. "All an unneeded distraction now you have deigned to appear, great-granddaughter of mine."

The forest disappeared in an instant, Thera blinking in disorientation as her surroundings shifted into a place she recognised. They stood upon a shingle beach lapped by the shifting tide of Linsker Fjord. Through the mist drifting across the water, she could see the ascending sprawl of Skar Magnol. The Verungyr rose above the town in all its grim majesty, itself outshone by the yet more impressive sight of the great mountain beyond. As children, she and her brothers had come here to skim stones, one of the few games in which Guthnyr regularly triumphed over both his elder siblings. She had once seen him earn twelve splashes from a throw while she never managed more than ten. Felnir, much to his poorly concealed annoyance, couldn't do more than eight. This morning there were no children on the shore and the sluggish swell of the fjord remained undisturbed. *Drawn from the old man's memory*, she realised. *Not mine.*

"This was where I came to think sometimes," Gruinskard said. "When you and your brothers were being more irksome than usual."

Turning, Thera was struck by how much older he looked. Always ancient to her eyes, he had at least conveyed a sense of vitality, a figure that even age could not diminish. Now, he leaned upon his great stone axe more heavily than before, his beard and hair almost entirely grey. Furthermore, she saw a terrible weariness in his face, the single eye gazing upon Skar

Magnol with only a dull gleam. If this was how he appeared in his own mind, she wondered what his actual body must look like.

"They killed Myhsta," he said. "One of Ilvar's scum smashed her skull with an axe. She had bitten his arm down to the bone, so I supposed he felt justified. I managed to strangle him before they hauled me off." His beard twitched in muted satisfaction. "That's something, at least."

"One of Ilvar's?" Thera said, mystified as to why or how the Vellihr of Lore should set his *menda* against the Tielwald. "What has happened here?"

"A great many things, first and foremost among them being the fact that Sister Lore has revealed herself an agent of the Volkrath." He turned to regard Thera's stunned visage with a rueful grimace. "Yes, it was a surprise to me, too. All those years and I never thought her a traitor. An accomplished liar, certainly. Careful of concealing her ambition, too. But that's hardly rare among those who seek power. But this . . ." He shook his head. "An orphan found at sea appears an obviously contrived tale now."

"Sister Lore is an agent of the Volkrath," Thera repeated. The words felt so absurd in her mouth as to be near blasphemous. "Do Silver and Iron know of this?"

For all his insights, her great-grandfather had never been gifted in gauging the emotions of others, especially when it came to imparting bad news. In the aftermath of Olversahl's fall, she and her siblings had learned of their parents' demise via a gruff, short statement that, henceforth, they would be living under his roof and had best mind their manners. Guthnyr had cried a good deal. Thera and Felnir hadn't. Now, for the first time, she saw Gruinskard struggle with the dilemma of how to voice something yet more terrible. Watching him clutch his axe and fumble for the words left her the leisure to form the inevitable conclusion.

"They're dead," she said. "She killed them."

"With her own hands, so the tale is told. She used a supposedly Altvarblessed spear her scholar brought back from Felnir's mad jaunt to the Fire Isles. He's probably dead too, by the way. Caught a few glimpses of you when I had chance to dream, but none of him."

The shingle shifted under Thera's backside, damp and uncomfortable. She couldn't remember sitting, nor could she manage to conjure a single coherent thought beyond a curiously firm conviction. "Felnir lives," she said. "I'd know it if he died."

Gruinskard flicked his beard with a non-committal huff before slowly easing his aged bulk down beside her. "I'll take your word for it. But it helps us naught. Skar Magnol is under Lore's control and she now has a Nihlvarian fleet and great *menda* on hand to enforce her will."

"And you? Are you in hiding?"

"If I was, you would have heard from me sooner. No. Due to indifference, I shunned Lore's invitation to the gathering where she wrought her massacre, so was waiting at home when Ilvar came for me. He's spent a good amount of effort since trying to persuade me to spill all my secrets. The distraction of pain makes it so hard to dream, and when I do, I find myself back in that fucking forest surrounded by bodies."

"I have a fleet of my own now. I'll come for you . . ."

"No!" His old self shone bright in the fierceness of the command. "The enemy's strength is too great here. I assume you gathered this force in the Outer Isles?"

"I did. We just vanquished a Nihlvarian fleet. The Outer Isles stand liberated in the queens' name."

"There are no queens now, Thera. Regardless of what transpires from here on, that dynasty is gone for good. It was a brilliant move, I must admit. Shattering the centre of Ascarlian power with one stroke. Whatever Ascarlia becomes, it will be something new." His gaze settled into a commanding glare. "Do not come here. The Fjord Lands are closed to you. Look elsewhere for reinforcement."

"Where? Skar Magnol seized. Lore a traitor. Where can we turn?"

"There are places in this realm where our enemy's hand has not yet reached. Start in the Inner Isles, then the northern gelds. Gather all the allies you can. Tell them you have the Tielwald's authority. Tell them the truth if it helps. Lie if it doesn't. These Nihlvarians are much more numerous than I could have imagined. Defeating them may require more strength than we can muster, but we're not done yet. Besides, we have a momentary advantage. I'm reliably informed that Lore's gaze is fixed upon Olversahl. While I've little doubt her Nihlvarian war leader will send some of his strength after you, the bulk of it will soon be sailing south. In war, all opportunities must be seized, however slender."

He shuddered then, a hiss of discomfort escaped his lips. "I have visitors," he said, Thera feeling a nauseous sense of dislocation as the dream began to fragment, dark cracks snaking through the fjord and the mountain. "Dream again when you can," Gruinskard grunted, the many lines on his face deepening into scars with the strain of maintaining this shared illusion. "You may not find me, but keep trying. And remember, above all else, gather strength . . ."

Thera jerked into wakefulness with the feel of a hand on her brow, the chill air of Linsker Fjord replaced by the musty warmth of her shelter aboard the *Great Wolf*. Blinking sweat from her eyes, she looked up at Lynnea, her pale oval face set in a frown of concern. *I heard you shouting*, her thoughts said, gaze narrowing in understanding as it slipped to the trinket on Thera's chest. *What did you find?*

Thera tried to speak, but no words came. The full measure of grief that had eluded her in the dream descended like an axe blow, allowing only sobs to escape her throat. Lynnea's arms embraced her, holding tight as Thera Speldrenda, for the first time in many years, wept until she had no more tears to shed.

In the morning, she convened a council of captains on the shore to impart what she had learned. She spoke in clear and unambiguous terms, detailing not only the dire news but also precisely how she had received it. Thera reasoned that the import of her intelligence outweighed any need for secrecy regarding the Tielwald's arcane abilities. She found it odd that none of them questioned the veracity of her tidings. She suspected that Aldeyn had already enlightened Ossgrym as to Gruinskard's means of communicating with his agents. As for the rest, all appeared to feel that doubting her word was simply out of the question. *The main spoils of victory lie not in loot or glory*, Sister Iron had told her once. *But in the loyalty it breeds.*

Thoughts of the murdered queen sent a pang through Thera's chest. That blunt-mannered woman had been hard to like, but Thera had found reason to do so anyway. Also, since stepping from her great-grandfather's shadow, Iron had been her principal source of sage council. Now, faced with a dozen or so stunned and bewildered faces, Thera would have dearly liked the veteran queen's advice on how to proceed. But Iron was dead, struck down by the most accomplished liar Thera had ever encountered. She clung to this fact, grateful for the anger it stoked. Regardless of what Gruinskard had said regarding the demise of the Sister Queens, Thera Speldrenda remained Vellihr of Justice.

"My duty is clear," she said, recapturing the attention of all present. She spoke on in as strident and purposeful a tone as she could manage, the need to shout above the stiff wind blowing off the Lyx Helv, adding to the impression of forceful certainty. "Sister Lore must be judged for her crimes. Henceforth, this will be my sole object. To achieve it, we will defeat those who have transgressed our lands and visited countless outrages on our people. The Sister Queens have fallen, but this realm has not. You will return to your ships and tell them all I told you. Omit nothing and speak no lies. All who follow me from this day on must know the scale of the task we face and the depravity of our enemy."

She paused, making a point to meet the eye of every captain present. She saw no flicker of doubt or cowardice, save for D'Shaine and Din Rabahs, the two foreign merchant captains wisely keeping to the rear of the gathering. Even they appeared more calculating than afraid. *No doubt hoping to negotiate a steeper price for their services,* Thera surmised. She could just seize their ships and have done with it, but they were tricky vessels to sail, requiring expert handling. Also, thanks to her victory, the fleet now boasted a good many ships of near equal size.

"That said, I can no longer claim to speak on the queens' behalf," Thera went on. "Now my only authority lies in the law. Therefore, any who wish to depart from my command may do so without fear of punishment. As for those who stay, make sure they know that the many hardships of war shall be their lot in the days ahead. Possibly for many months. We won a great triumph upon the Lyx Helv yesterday, but it came at a cost. None should doubt the price of victory will grow ever steeper."

"And I'd pay it a thousand times!" Ossgrym growled, heralding a chorus of fierce agreement from the other captains. "To avenge the fallen of my geld, and the kin I have lost, I'll bathe in a sea of blood!" The Veilwald drew his sword, raising it above his head, he turned to the assembly. "Are there any cravens here who would do otherwise?"

The scrape of many blades was instantly followed by a loud, emphatic "NO!" as they all pointed their swords and axes to the heavens.

"You commanded us to victory, Vellihr," Ossgrym said, turning back to her. He then did something that surprised her, more so when the others followed his example: he knelt. *Ascarls do not kneel to any save the queens,* she wanted to say, but didn't. *Now there are no queens.*

"I, Ossgrym Styrntorc," Ossgrym began, holding his sword out to her, "Veilwald of the Kast Geld, do hereby give oath in the sight of the Altvar to follow the commands of Vellihr Thera Speldrenda unto death if need be."

Veilwald Hakkyn spoke next, proffering his sword while repeating the oath, the words swiftly echoed by the rest of the assembly. D'Shaine and Din Rabahs were notable exceptions, although they did consent to kneel as the oaths were spoken.

The unexpectedness of their obeisance gave Thera pause. She had foreseen a good deal of alarm and discord at this meeting. Instead, faced with such unswerving and unhesitant devotion, she found her throat constricted by a fresh welling of grief and the discomfiting certainty of her own unworthiness.

They hunger for leadership. Lynnea's thoughts intruded, coloured by hard insistence. She knelt alongside Ragnalt at the fringes of the gathering, her blue eyes intent and unblinking. *Direction dispels fear. Give it to them.*

188 · ANTHONY RYAN

"Rise!" Thera snapped. "We'll have no more kneeling in this *menda*, to friend or foe." Once they had resumed standing, she spoke on, tone clipped of all doubt. "Blind hope will not avail us. Winning a war requires the acceptance of hard truth. While we have garnered strength here, we are still too few to fully contend with our enemy. They are certain to send more ships into these islands to recover what they have lost. Veilwald Hakkyn, though it pains me to say it, the Aiken Geld cannot be held. You will send Skahlvyr Estrynlud, and the three fastest ships in your charge to spread word to all the folk of this geld to board every craft that floats and flee north to Ayl-Ah-Vahrim. Any goods that cannot be carried that might give aid to our enemy must be destroyed, including livestock."

She paused, turning to Kahlvik standing at Ossgrym's side. She was perturbed to find the famed seafarer's expression just as grimly earnest as his kinsman. *Even he can't tell how undeserving I am*, she thought, pushing the notion away and speaking with all the authority she could muster. "Kahlvik Vahrimdorr. You will carry news of the Sister Queens' fate to the upper gelds. Tell the Veilwalds there that the Vellihr of Justice will come to treat with them soon and expects their *menda* to be mustered and war fleets gathered in full. Find me at Ayl-Ah-Skorna in thirty days."

"I sail with the evening tide, Vellihr," Kahlvik responded with a lowering of the head that wasn't quite a bow.

"This fleet will sail immediately for Ayl-Ah-Vahrim," Thera went on, addressing them as a whole. "Where a great redoubt will be constructed on shore to ensure sound defence and supplies stockpiled to feed our Aiken brethren. The petty concerns of trade and taxes must be put aside for now. So must all prior feuds and grievances. Only in holding to our shared blood as Ascarls can we triumph."

Unhooking the striker from her belt, a bronze effigy of Ulthnir's crossed hammer and sword, she held it up. "Let the Worldsmith, first among the Altvar and father of all who call themselves Ascarls, show his favour and lend his strength to our cause."

Before scraping the steel rod to the striker, she waited for every Ascarlian captain present to raise their own. The varying sigils on display indicated that all the gods of both the upper and lower halls would hear their call. "Ulthnir!" Thera cried out, sending a flurry of sparks into the wind, the gesture immediately copied by her captains, each of them calling out the name of the god whose sigil they held. The sparks flared only briefly in the harsh seaborne wind, dwindling to nothing in the blink of an eye. She hoped it wasn't an omen.

Chapter Eighteen

Elvine

The hiding place was precisely where Gruinskard said it would be. Prising open the plaster-covered board beneath the attic window, expertly rendered to appear as just a rough patch of wall, she uncovered a gap in the stonework filled with scrolled parchment. Before she could reach into it, she was unceremoniously shouldered aside by Ilvar. Upon reporting the results of her interview with the Tielwald to Lore, the Vellihr had insisted on escorting her to his house, accompanied by two nervous-looking warriors. They were both younger than most in his *menda* and shuddered in patent alarm when he turned from the hiding place, snarling: "You pair of useless fucks!"

This time, the spear's gift chose to reveal both their auras. The one on the right, a stocky man with a sparse beard that told of ambitions towards manly hirsuteness he didn't yet possess, exhibited a black cloud of basic fear. The one on the left, tall with more fulsome facial hair, was different. Of fear, he had plenty, but it was laced with equal parts resentment and, even more surprising, shame. *Doesn't like Ilvar, nor what he's been set to do,* Elvine concluded.

"Get downstairs and tear this place apart," Ilvar instructed. "There's bound to be at least one more hidden nook. The old fucker wouldn't be content with just one."

As the unfortunate duo descended the creaking staircase, Ilvar plucked one of the scrolls from the nook. Unfurling it, he frowned in irked confusion. "What does this say?" he demanded, handing the scroll to Elvine with evident reluctance.

Briefly scanning the symbols neatly inscribed on the parchment, Elvine shrugged. "I have no idea. It's cyphered. Codes and such lie outside my field of study."

His baleful glare made it plain he didn't believe her. "Don't think I don't see you," he grated, looming closer. "The queen may have blinded herself to the treason in your heretic's heart, but you haven't fooled me, girl."

"Scholar Elvine," she reminded him, taking no small delight in seeing how her mild tone stoked his anger. "My title. As ordained by the queen, who you consider to be *foolish*. Unless I mistake your words, Vellihr."

Like Aldunna, the spear's gift failed to reveal Ilvar's aura. But it didn't need to. She watched him swallow his rage and return his focus to the scrolls, gathering them all into a sack. "Return to the Verungyr," he told her. "You are no longer needed here."

"Without escort?" Elvine asked in surprise.

"Why would you need one?" He fixed her with a glare. "Are you so disloyal that you require a constant guard?"

"Of course not." She attempted a dignified air as she rose and departed the attic, feeling the heat of Ilvar's gaze upon her. Making her way past the two warriors busily wrecking the already disordered rooms of the Tielwald's abode, she stepped out into the chill, smoke-tinged air of Skar Magnol. Ilvar hadn't lied; a few townsfolk made their way along the cobbled street, eyes scrupulously averted from Gruinskard's house, but there were no warriors waiting to escort her.

A trap, she concluded, eyes flicking across alley and doorway. She had no doubt she was being observed and her steps would be dogged by hidden eyes all the way back to the Verungyr. *Wants to see who I talk to.*

Making her way through the maze of narrow streets, she recalled Gruinskard's warning that his servant would find her after she visited the house. She could only hope this Coelnyr would have the skills to spot the fact that she was being followed and the good sense to steer clear. As her journey continued, she caught the scents of the market square. The aroma of cooked meat and spices proved a potent lure. Also, she suspected forcing Ilvar's unseen spies to trail her through such a busy throng would provide some measure of amusement.

Entering the busy square, she experienced a paradoxical sense of liber-ation. Despite the jostling and the press of bodies, the anonymity of moving through a large group of people felt like a welcome release from constant suspicion. Her lightened mood was dimmed a little by the tension evident in the townsfolk. From the guarded glances of some, and avoidance of eye contact of most, it was clear to Elvine that she was now a recognised as a trusted servant of the queen. Conversation hushed at her approach, the speakers quickly disappearing into the throng. Here and there she glimpsed brief scowls of resentment she did her best to ignore. As time wore on, however, the atmosphere of distrust began to weigh upon her and she quickened her step, keen to be gone. That is until she spied the bookseller. The stall owner stood shorter than Elvine by a good two inches, narrow of feature with the complexion of the southern seas. His face was all wrinkled good humour, albeit with a glimmer of mercantile shrewdness as he noted her immediate interest in his wares.

"Now that's a discerning eye," he said when she opened the cover on a small volume of Alberic poetry, only to close it again upon recognising the author's name. "Liselle is dreadfully clichéd, don't you find?"

His Ascarlian was good, if heavily accented. "A pretentious noble reaching for artistry beyond his talents," she replied in Ishtan, the words creasing the bookseller's face yet more, this time with delight.

"Too long has it been since my ears were graced by such fine speech, most honoured lady," he said, also in Ishtan, bowing low. His phrasing was excellent, but also tinged with a lilt that told her this was not his native tongue.

"You flatter me, esteemed sir," she said, returning the bow. "For I am not honoured in this land. Merely a servant, albeit one whose duties include the administration of a library."

Looking over his wares, she was saddened to find that she wouldn't be adding to his purse, for there was little of interest. Mostly, his stock consisted of a mix of mundane Alberic texts and equally uninteresting Ascarlian translations. There were a few volumes in Ishtan, but nothing she hadn't already read.

"What you see are not my best wares," the bookseller said, apparently skilled in reading the expression of a disinterested customer. "I can see that you possess a far more discerning eye. If there is a particular field of study you require, I shall be happy to scour my stock for a suitable tome."

"My studies at present have a very narrow focus." She shook her head in apology. "Unless you can offer a book on the more obscure reaches of Ascarlian history, I will not occupy more of your time."

"Wait," he said, tentatively touching a hand to her sleeve as she began to move on. "Esteemed lady, if you would indulge me. I believe I may have something."

Holding up a hand, he moved to the chests stacked behind his stall. As he rummaged, Elvine allowed her gaze to track over the crowd. Surveying the wary townsfolk revealed no obvious spies, but, she reasoned, they would be severely lacking in skill if even her inexpert eye could find them.

"Here we are." The bookseller's voice held a note of triumph as he returned with a tome in hand. Taking it from him, she found it another Alberic text, albeit one she had heard of but never read. "*The Collected Plays of Jeanivere*

D'Ambrille," Elvine murmured, tracing fingers over the faded letters embossed onto the frayed leather of the binding. She began to enquire why the farces of an oft-derided actor turned playwright would enhance her studies when she recalled Berrine had made mention of her during the voyage from Olversahl. Opening the book to the contents page, she found 'The Ice Bound Treachery' included in a long list of plays with unfamiliar titles, many of them featuring references to Ascarlian history.

"The sagas of this land provided her with much inspiration," the book-seller said.

"It appears so," Elvine agreed. "However, if I recall correctly, her work is not highly regarded."

"Some of her plays are overly sentimental in places and garishly violent in others. Clearly, they pander to the tastes of an unsophisticated audience. However, those tend to be the works written in collaboration with her husband. I think you'll find that the fruit of her own pen is far more inter-esting. She certainly had an ear for elegant verse." He paused, watching Elvine leaf through more pages, before adding, "The scholar who compiled this collection saw fit to include an afterword speculating on her sources, which may aid your endeavour."

Elvine resisted the urge to flip to the back of the book. It would have been rude. "How much?" she asked, slipping back into Ascarlian. Although her native tongue was far from the most elegant, when it came to haggling, there was none better.

"For the uneducated, I would seek a higher price," the bookseller said. "But for one clearly so learned, I will ask merely for four silver strips, or two coins if you prefer."

"Merely?" Elvine laughed before regretfully handing the book back. No amount of bargaining could inflate her purse so much. "I have not such riches at present. But keep it for me and I shall return . . ."

"Here," a voice said, Elvine catching the flicker of a tossed coin, nimbly caught by the bookseller. Turning, she found Tuhlvyr Vahlak regarding the small man with a quizzical look. She was surprised to see that the Nihlvarian chose to walk a crowded marketplace without an escort. He also wore no armour today, clad in mostly simple garb with his dark sable-trimmed cloak and gold-hilted sword the only concessions to finery.

"One silver seems fair to me," Vahlak said, speaking with careful delib-eration, so the words were not mangled by his accent. "Unless your intent is to cheat the queen's scholar."

Elvine felt a pang of regret at the stark alarm on the small man's features. Unlike most market-goers, it was plain he had no notion of her status.

"Certainly not, your honour," he said, accent growing both coarser and more pronounced as he bowed again. "In fact, the book is a gift." He proffered the coin, but Elvine stepped between them before Vahlak could take it back.

"My thanks," she said, taking the book from his hand, dismayed at how much it trembled. Lowering her voice, she added in Ishtan, "I'll return with the second coin when I can, esteemed sir. My thanks for your consideration this day."

He bowed lower and backed away as Vahlak came to her side, frowning at the books on display. "These are valuable here, then?"

"Your people do not value books, Tuhlvyr?" she asked. Her tone was imprudently sharp, but the bookseller's fearful reaction had soured her mood.

"Not so," Vahlak replied, his tone lacking any sign of offence. If anything, his muted grin bespoke amusement. "In the Vortigurn's citadel there are great vaults filled with books, though only those who carry his special favour can read them." He stepped aside, gesturing at the looming bulk of the Verungyr. "I should very much like to accompany you back to my sister's tower. Only if you wish it, of course."

Given that he had just purchased her an expensive gift, and the fact that he was inarguably the second most important personage in this port, she could hardly refuse. "It would be my honour," she said, silently berating herself for failing to strip the sardonic edge from her voice. *Just be nice to him*, Berrine had said. It was proving harder than Elvine expected.

"May I see?" he asked, nodding to the book as they made their way clear of the marketplace.

"If you like."

Taking the book, he pursed his lips as he perused the first few pages. "This is not the script I learned before sailing here," he said.

"No," she said. "It's Alberic. The language of the kingdom to the south."

"Ah." He handed the volume back to her. "Another one I'll need to learn before long, it seems. It pays to know well the ways of your enemy. Perhaps you can teach me."

"Of course." She was proud of her neutral inflection this time, although the prospect of spending hours per day instructing this man in Alberic was hardly appealing. "If the queen allows me the leisure."

His marginal grin broadened. "I've little doubt that she will. She has always loved learning new things, especially languages. It was a task we shared as children, although, of course, she was always more accomplished in such things than I."

His openness surprised her, while also stirring a question she had wanted to ask Lore but so far hadn't found the opportunity. "At our first meeting, you both spoke in a tongue I had never heard before. Might I know what it is?"

"Certainly. It was Morvek. In particular, the dialect spoken by the clans of the southern hill country."

"Morvek?"

"The people who once flourished in the land we now call Nihlvar. Many of my countrymen insist on naming them bestial savages who wrought massacre and all manner of vileness upon our people when we first came to their shores. But such tales are nonsense concocted to justify enslaving a conquered people."

Slaves? She caged the word before it could escape her mouth, it being phrased with so much shocked disgust. However, he read her expression well, his gaunt, handsome face growing sombre. "A regrettable necessity, you might call it," he said. "Or, as most of my people believe, merely the rightful order of things as ordained by the Altvar."

"There is nothing in the Altvar Rendi that justifies slavery," Elvine said, striving for a moderate tone and failing.

"True," Vahlak admitted with a shrug. "But also nothing that forbids it. And it must be said that the great realm of Nihlvar, and the Volkrath Empire we are in the process of building, would not exist without slaves to work our oars and till our fields. Greatness can arise from cruelty. Though I wish it were not so. I myself own no slaves, nor do I have them aboard my ship. It is a condition of joining my *menda* that every warrior takes an oar. Those who consider it beneath them are dismissed."

He paused, apparently expecting some expression of admiration for his principled stance. When Elvine continued to regard him with evident disapproval, he gave a rueful grimace. "Our ways are different, I know. In time, I hope they will change. But the task that lies before us is vast, and cannot be achieved without sacrifice, be it of the body or the spirit."

There was a stilted inflection to his words that told her they were not truly his, merely a quotation. "Did your king tell you that? The Vortigurn?"

His grin returned, brows arched in pleased surprise. "Why, yes, as a matter of fact, he did, during the one audience I had with him." Vahlak's expression took on a distant cast, Elvine finding herself perturbed by the reverence she saw in it. "It's hard to describe what it is to be in his presence. To see him with your own eyes, hear his voice . . ." He shook his head, wincing in faint embarrassment. "I hope, one day, to have the pleasure of introducing you to him. Then you will understand how it feels to converse with one who has stood in the presence of the gods themselves . . ."

He trailed off and came to a halt, features hardening. They were upon the lower steps of the long, winding track leading to the Verungyr's gate. The Tuhlvyr's attention was focused on a copse of trees further down the slope. Elvine saw a faint twitch to the bushes, something she would have ascribed to the wind, but Vahlak had keener eyes. "Best wait here a moment, Scholar Elvine," he said, hand going to his sword as he started back down the steps. "It appears I have attracted unwanted company."

"It's all right," she said, halting him with a touch to the arm. "Vellihr Ilvar likes to keep a close watch on the queen's servants."

"He spies on you?" Vahlak's face darkened, Elvine wondering if his apparent anger on her behalf might actually be genuine. The absence of an aura indicated it was.

"He is . . . scrupulous in ensuring the queen's safety," she said. Enlightening this man to the true source of Ilvar's suspicion struck her as unwise, especially in light of Lore's cautionary words regarding espousal of Covenant beliefs. "It's of no matter. Come." She resumed climbing the steps. "I am curious to learn more of your people's origins. You said they came to the land once occupied by the Morvek. How long ago was that?"

Vahlak spent a moment longer in hard-eyed contemplation of the trees before falling in alongside. From the persistence of his glower, she felt sure this was a matter he would raise with his sister. It was therefore possible that her footsteps might not be dogged by Ilvar's spies in future. *Mother was right*, Elvine thought. *As usual.*

"More than five centuries ago," he said, features softening as his ire faded. "Or so the tale is told. My sister has a far better grasp of history than I."

"Five centuries," Elvine repeated in a murmur, sorting through the mental repository of her recent studies until a singular realisation struck. She laughed at the obviousness of it, drawing a curious glance from Vahlak.

"Scholar?"

"The Age of Discord," she said, laughing again. "Its end is marked by the defeat of the Volkrath. They fled into the Fire Isles and were assumed destroyed. Your people are the descendants of the Volkrath Cu—" She stopped herself finishing the word "cult", fearing his reaction. However, Vahlak appeared unperturbed.

"Why yes, I suppose we are. Some tales of those early days upon the wild shores of a new land persist, but they are few, and scarcely believable. What is clear is that it was a time of great trial and we would surely have perished but for the rise of the Vortigurn. He brought order to chaos. Ending all feuds, he united us, led the *menda* that won victory over the Morvek, made us truly Nihlvarians."

"And his dynasty has ruled ever since?"

Vahlak's brow took on a puzzled crease. "Dynasty?"

Elvine's reply was forestalled by the sound of bells. Looking towards the entrance to the Verungyr, she saw a small group making their way through the gate. The leading figure, a tall woman in a sombre grey robe, bore a tree branch which she shook with every other step, causing the eight bells dangling from it to chime. The presence of the branch bearer confirmed the reason for this procession before Elvine saw the body. It was borne upon a litter by four women, also clad in grey, matching the hue of the shroud covering the corpse.

"Funeral rite?" Vahlak asked, as Elvine stepped from the path, motioning for him to do the same.

"Yes," she said, lowering her eyes and pitching her voice to a murmur. "Your rites are different?"

"Less elaborate, and we ring no bells." Moving to her side, he mimicked her downcast pose, whispering, "What are they for?"

"There are eight, as you see. One for each of the Altvar of the Upper Hall. They are rung to gain their notice so that the deceased's spirit will suffer no delay in entering the Halls of Aevnir."

"Very considerate of them. In Nihlvar, we leave it to the dead to find their own way into the halls. As you forge your own path in life, so should you in death."

He fell silent at her insistent glare. As the procession passed by, Elvine saw that the shroud failed to cover the body completely. As was custom in some places, the hands were bare so that they could be clasped together, clutching a medallion bearing the eye of Aerldun. Like the bells, this appeal to the goddess with dominion over the darkest paths was intended to ease the passage of the departed soul in their journey to the Halls. As her gaze lingered on those pale, limp hands, Elvine shuddered in shock. Inked onto the skin between the thumb and wrist of the left hand was a dragonfly, one Elvine had seen only the day before.

The nausea that had lingered in her gut since meeting Fildra in the kitchens blossomed into a sickening shudder, one she was unable to conceal from Vahlak.

"What's wrong?" he asked, turning to her in concern.

"I . . ." She swallowed. "I knew this woman," she managed in a hoarse rasp. She knew her distress was perverse, absurd even. Had she not plotted Fildra's demise? Yet, when confronted by her corpse, she realised any notion that her tribulations had hardened her heart was revealed as optimistic fantasy. She remembered Aldunna's hands pausing in their work when she spoke Fildra's name. The tightening of her mouth Elvine had taken for understanding. Now she felt sure it had signified decision.

"A moment, please," Vahlak said, holding up a hand to halt the procession in place. Normally such an interruption would have earned a severe rebuke from the branch bearer, but she was too cowed by the Nihlvarian to offer more than a disapproving scowl.

"My companion wishes to pay her respects," Vahlak said, motioning for the litter bearers to lower their burden. Standing aside, he gestured for Elvine to come forward. Moving on numbed legs, Elvine stooped to gently pull aside the shroud covering the corpse's face. Although slackened in death, Fildra's pretty, youthful features were still recognisable. She saw no sign of injury, neither on the face nor the neck. She wanted to ask the cause of death, but feared she had already associated herself with this dead spy too much. Fortunately, Vahlak saw no reason for such circumspection.

"She's so young," he said. "How did it happen?"

"A vessel burst in her gut," the branch bearer said. "So the healers say. She awoke this morning spewing blood, in terrible pain, too. Nothing could be done."

Terrible pain. The words repeated in Elvine's mind with insistent cruelty, along with three more: *I did this.*

"Did you know her well?" Vahlak asked gently as Elvine continued to stare at Fildra's empty face.

"Not . . . especially," Elvine replied, feeling a numbness creep over her. Showing excessive emotion now would be a mistake. "She was a bright soul," she added. Covering Fildra's face, she stepped back, allowing the procession to continue. "I shall miss her smile."

She stood and watched the party carry their burden down the path to the port. There, according to her family's custom, she would either be cremated upon a pyre on the shore or placed in a barrow with her most treasured objects. In addition to the guilt churning in Elvine's heart, there rose an additional flare of worry. *What will Ilvar do when he learns of his agent's death?*

Chapter Nineteen

Ruhlin

After only a few paces into the shaft, Ruhlin concluded that he would never make a miner. The musty air felt heavy in his lungs and the rough-hewn walls of the passage narrowed the deeper he went. Raised to the vastness of the sea and grassy hills of Ayl-Ah-Swahl, he was acutely conscious of the massive weight of rock above his head. To Ruhlin's eye, this shaft lacked the solid appearance of the one near the village. His gaze constantly flicked from one wooden beam to another, searching for wear and damage. The fact that they had held for decades failed to assuage his fears, since how long could such aged timber be expected to last?

Finally, Tuhlan led him into a larger chamber where Sygurn was busy piling rocks into a bucket. A half-dozen others were stacked nearby, each one brimming with loose stone. Looking closer, Ruhlin made out its dark hue and shiny texture.

"Coal?" he asked the Nihlvarian, receiving a cheerful nod in response.

"Tons of the stuff," he said, nodding to the absolute gloom of a downward sloping passage. "A thick vein of riches runs through the heart of this mountain. And it's not just coal."

Guthnyr and Tuhlan had found this second shaft during one of their scouting trips. Upon investigation, Sygurn had quickly dispatched the Caerith to fetch Ruhlin with news of an important discovery. Rising, he beckoned Ruhlin to one of the buckets. The stones piled into it differed markedly from coal, possessing a reddish-brown hue and a gnarled surface. "What is it?" he asked, baffled by Sygurn's evident excitement.

"Ore." Taking a stone from the bucket, the Nihlvarian rapped it against a nail in one of the beams. It gave off a faint, metallic ting. "Iron ore, to be precise. And copper too, if you can credit it. Curious thing, it's clear the folk who dug it out stopped after a few days so they could dig a deeper shaft away from the main seams."

"They came for gold," Ruhlin said, recalling Iyaka's words the day they arrived here. "The storytellers say it has a way of blinding a soul to other rewards."

"Silly feckers. I haven't seen even a glimmer of the yellow stuff anywhere down here. But this—" Sygurn plucked a chunk of coal from another bucket, tapping it and the ore together "—is true wealth. Coal and iron. Use one to heat the other and you have steel. And is there not a forge in the village?"

"Keen to get back to smithing?"

"It'll be something to do, at least. Now we've got the village into a half-decent state. Besides, with winter coming on, the coal will be welcome."

Ruhlin cast his gaze over the assembled buckets. Although hardly expert in such matters, he knew this was but a small portion of what could be extracted from this mine. "Leave it here for now," he said. "I must speak to Iyaka first."

Sygurn let out a caustic laugh. "Worried the mountain spirit will punish us for stealing her riches?"

"Yes," Ruhlin replied honestly. "But I'm more worried about how the Morvek will react to us plundering their land."

To his surprise, Iyaka responded with only partial interest when he imparted news of the discovery. She and the other Morvek had spent the weeks since their arrival establishing their own encampment at a short remove from the village. Despite the slate roofs that now covered most of the surviving Nihlvarian buildings, the Morvek exhibited a marked dislike for the dwellings. The deer and goat hide shelters they constructed appeared flimsy at first glance, but withstood the increasingly fierce weather with impressive fortitude. In addition to the shelters, they had recently begun journeying to the foot of the mountain to harvest timber for a larger, round structure. It was only partially complete and Ruhlin remained unsure of its purpose.

"Of stone, the mountain has plenty," Iyaka said, continuing to interweave the many thin branches that formed the roof of the round house, as he and the other non-Morvek had taken to calling it. "I doubt she will punish you for taking it. Still, if it will ease your mind, I will sing to her tonight and seek her leave."

"How will we know if she gives it?" Ruhlin asked.

"If the shaft is still there in the morning, then you can be sure she is content for you to keep digging."

Ryma's happy laugh drew Ruhlin's gaze to the upper tier of the village. The girl was perched atop the bear's back, giggling and clapping her small hands in excitement as the beast slowly ambled back and forth. Much to Ruhlin and Aleida's alarm, they had awoken to find the girl missing one morning, a frantic search revealing her at play with her new friend. Ruhlin's instinct had been to pull her away, but Aleida persuaded him otherwise. "She'll do no harm to her," she said, Ruhlin noting a flicker of annoyance as she watched the girl bounce on her shaggy perch. "My aunt has her favourites, it seems."

"I have puzzled over something for a while now," Ruhlin said, turning back to Iyaka. "How did the *Vehlkasa* know to follow the bear? Would they not have seen her as just another beast of the forest?"

The Morvek woman paused in her work for a moment, a guardedness showing in the tightening of her features. "Among all clans, there are those who can see beyond mere appearance," she said. "Those who can tell when a bear is not merely a bear, but host to something more." Ruhlin saw her hesitate, then fall silent. *Something she doesn't want to say*, he concluded. *Why?*

"Tirohk used your name for me," he persisted. "*Telchak*. But he spoke it as you do sometimes. As if the word holds more meaning than just the bearer of a curse." When this failed to elicit an answer, he went on. "He also spoke of me as one who was promised. What did he mean?"

Sighing, Iyaka straightened to face him, her frown bespeaking both reluctance and resignation. "It means you should be grateful for your curse, for it earned us this refuge. But that doesn't mean there won't be a price to pay when Tirohk returns."

"What price?"

She gave a mirthless laugh. "The same one you have been paying since you came to this land, Ruhlin *Telchak*: blood."

That night he heard Iyaka sing her song to the mountain and in the morning, the second shaft remained intact. With no pack horses to carry the stone to the village, he organised a party to haul it down the winding, half-mile long track. It was an arduous business requiring a full day's labour, but when done, Sygurn pronounced they had sufficient coal to fire the forge.

"Smelting steel from ore will be harder," he advised. "While the folk who built this place were good enough to leave us a smithy, it looks like they had neither the foresight nor the skills to build a smelter."

"Do you?" Ruhlin asked him, finding the Nihlvarian's shrug less than encouraging.

"Seen one being used, so at least I know what it looks like."

"I can build it," Guthnyr said, frowning at their surprised glances. "As a lad, I was fond of loitering in smithies. The smelters would need to be rebuilt every year come summer. They'd let me help out." He pursed his lips in sombre reflection. "Until my great-grandfather put a stop to it. He said my hands were made for the sword, not the hammer. I suppose it was for the best."

"What do we need to do?" Ruhlin asked him.

"Well, first of all—" Guthnyr cast a doubtful eye around the village and the snow-covered ground beyond "—we need some clay. Though I've no notion where we'd find any here."

"We won't." Ruhlin's gaze drifted back to Iyaka. "But there are those who might."

She led them down the mountain the next day. They followed the busy stream tracing along the narrow valley below for about a mile to where it cascaded over the edge of a low cliff to merge with the fast-flowing river below. "There," Iyaka said, once they had descended the short drop to the riverbank. She pointed to the bare earth behind the curtain of falling water, Ruhlin making out a familiar pale brown hue among the roots and rocks.

They had found a number of dusty but intact pots in the village, and filled them with the soft, loamy clay before porting them back up the mountain. There, Guthnyr set about fashioning what appeared to be a large conical basket from gathered twigs. Once complete, it resembled a giant bottle, Guthnyr positioning it over a bowl-sized pit he had scraped in the ground. Taking the clay, he covered his creation in a thick layer of the stuff, leaving an opening at the top and another smaller one level with the ground.

"We need to let it dry overnight," he said, sniffing in satisfaction as he plucked brown matter from his beard and eyebrows. "Cover it in furs to keep the snow off."

The following morning, Guthnyr smeared a second layer of clay over the hardened shell to which he added a covering of loose rocks. Thus complete, the smelter resembled a chimney sprouting from the frosted earth. Before pronouncing it ready, Guthnyr pushed kindling into the opening at the base and lit a fire. Building it with additional timber, he tended the blaze throughout the rest of the day, the smelter belching a thick stream of ember-laced smoke as it burned away the wooden framework within. The next day, they spent several hours using the hammers from the village forge to pound the ore into smaller fragments. Before tipping them into the opening at the top the smelter, Guthnyr lit another fire in the base, this time using coal to craft a far more intense blaze.

"Equal parts coal and ore," he insisted when it came time to attempt their first smelting.

"What happens next?" Ruhlin asked as they upended the last of three buckets of mingled ore and coal into the smelter.

"The coal will burn away the slag and the steel will melt together in one big lump." Guthnyr took a seat on his near empty brandy barrel and leaned down to hold a drinking horn to the tap, draining the dregs. "Just have to wait for it to burn down, if you'd care to join me."

It required two days for the smelter's blaze to fully extinguish itself, then several more hours before Guthnyr pronounced it cool enough to extract the promised steel ingot, or "bloom" as he called it. The soot-blackened object he dragged from the ashes with a pair of tongs was about twelve inches long and four wide. It also didn't resemble any workable metal Ruhlin could remember. However, after a few wipes of Guthnyr's cloak, he made out a silvery gleam among the grime.

"So," Guthnyr said, holding the object out to Sygurn, "what do you want to make first?"

The heat of the forge and the unfolding craft within soon drew a small crowd of spectators to the door. However, the novel sight of Sygurn pounding away at a glowing length of steel wore thin after a while and most drifted away. Despite the thickness of the heat and the recurrent wafts of smoke, Ruhlin stayed, fascinated by the gradual emergence of a recognisable object from the misshapen ingot. Although he had witnessed the forging of various tools in Buhl Hardta, he had never seen a sword fashioned. He was surprised to find that the blade was formed of separate steel rods rather than a single length of metal. Having flattened the ingot, Sygurn then used a hammer and chisel to segment it into three, two short, one long. Leaving the longer section flat, he and Guthnyr twisted the other two into tight spirals. That done, he reheated the twisted rods and hammered them into union. The longer section he fashioned into an edge, dividing it in two, then using thin strips of iron to bind it to the two central rods before plunging it into the blazing coal of the forge. Several more hours at the anvil produced a recognisable sword blade a yard long.

Despite Ruhlin's satisfaction with their achievement, both Guthnyr and Sygurn exhibited only frowning disappointment as they inspected the blade. "Worth quenching?" Guthnyr asked.

"Better off trying again," Sygurn grunted, tossing the fruit of their labour onto a bench. "Might have better luck with the next bloom."

"What's wrong with it?" Ruhlin asked.

"The steel is poor," Guthnyr replied. "'A tarnished soul lies within', as the old smith back home used to say. Means the metal's been weakened by too much dirt from the smelting. We quench it, it'll crack. Even if it doesn't, it'll shatter the instant it meets another blade."

"Could try pounding for longer next time," Sygurn mused. "Or melt it until it's liquid, then forge it when it's cooled. Might at least give us something usable, if not exactly pretty."

"Like this?"

Turning, Ruhlin found Aleida had taken up the blade from the bench. However, in place of the blackened object Sygurn had discarded, it now gleamed bright in the glow from the forge.

"How . . . ?" Guthnyr breathed, extending a tentative hand to the blade.

"A way with metal," Ruhlin said, sharing a smile with Aleida as she placed the shining sword in his hands. It was cool to the touch and possessed a mirror-like sheen. A thin line of yellow light played over the edge, which appeared keen as a razor. When Ruhlin softly pressed a fingertip to the edge, it drew forth a small bead of blood.

"I know warriors who would sell their mother for a blade like that," Guthnyr said, gaze fixed upon the sword.

"Whereas you get it for nothing," Ruhlin said, holding the weapon out to him. "Take it," he prompted when Guthnyr hesitated. "I can't think of a more fitting hand. Besides—" he turned back to Aleida, smile broadening "—I've a sense it's but the first of many."

Winter tightened its grip over the next few weeks, draping ever deeper snowdrifts over the mountainside. It also made any venture beyond the walls of house or shelter a trial of suffering. Fortunately, before the freeze closed in, Ruhlin had organised a working party to shift the remaining ore and coal from the second mineshaft to the village. A dozen more steel ingots had been smelted by the time the chill and the snow forced a retreat indoors, and all the while Sygurn and Guthnyr kept the forge working. Upon visiting the forge after a tedious day's labour in the mine, Ruhlin discovered their long hours of labour produced a further surprise.

"Found it this morning," Sygurn said, wiping soot from a wooden roof beam. The revealed carving was formed of several characters in an unfamiliar script. "'Tahrim Kyrn'," the Nihlvarian translated. "Looks like the poor feckers who came before us named the place. Not sure I like it." Sygurn squinted at the carving, shaking his head. "An ill-fated name for an ill-fated settlement."

"'Village of Gold'," Ruhlin said, reflecting on the optimism of doomed souls. "As good a name as any, I suppose. We have to call this place something."

"As you wish." Sygurn shrugged, hefting a hammer and returning to his anvil. "But I'd've thought 'Village of Ghosts' more fitting."

Their next weapon to emerge from the forge was of unfamiliar design. A twin-headed hammer affixed atop a spiralled iron haft. Guthnyr named it a "maul", a weapon often employed by armoured Albermaine-ish warriors. It was just as besmirched and unusable as the sword until Aleida set her hands upon it. Ruhlin found the change she conjured both disturbing and fascinating. Under her touch the colours in the metal shifted and swirled, transforming into an untarnished sheen in the space of seconds. The sight forced a realisation that, in her own way, Aleida possessed as much power as he did. Nor was it limited to simply banishing the impurities from poor steel. As he watched her remake the maul, he saw lettering appear at the join between the twin hammerheads, forming an ancient Ascarlian script he couldn't read.

"It says '*Telchak*'," Aleida said, raising her hands from the weapon. "A union of Morvek and Nihlvarian. Seems fitting."

"It's yours," Sygurn elaborated when she placed the weapon in Ruhlin's hands. "We thought it best given what a fecking terrible swordsman you are."

During a break between blizzards, Ruhlin made an experimental swing with the maul and succeeded in shattering a block of granite twice the size of his head. *What might you do with a weapon such as this?* he asked the monster, but as had become typical, it failed to stir.

By the time the snows finally began to abate, Sygurn and Guthnyr had produced weapons enough for the entire village. The Nihlvarians all received swords or axes, while the Morvek preferred spears and knives. Julette was gifted a curve-bladed sabre, remarkable in both its lightness and the sharpness of its edge. The weapon they made for Tuhlan was the most unusual. Produced under the Caerith's direction and fashioned entirely from steel, its haft was curved like an elongated snake, with a long, sickle-shaped blade protruding from one end.

"*Tahlik*," Tuhlan called it, a rare grin playing over his lips as he whirled the weapon around with blinding speed. "Long has it been since I held one. Now I have the finest ever made."

With everyone armed, the remaining steel was used up in fashioning arrowheads, broad headed for hunting and narrow and barbed for war. "Expecting a fight, then?" Sygurn asked as they watched Aleida play her hands over a cluster of arrowheads, soot-stained metal instantly altered into shining steel. The Nihlvarian kept his voice low as he went on, "If you're thinking our hosts might not be too friendly after all, I can't say I disagree."

"If they wanted us dead, it would have been easily done," Ruhlin pointed out. "These—" he touched a hand to his maul then gestured at the arrowheads "—are for when we leave here. It stands to reason we'll have to fight again when we venture back into Nihlvar."

"You intend to go back?"

"I promised a return home to those who want it. Which means we still require a ship and I doubt one will be forthcoming from the Morvek."

"You think they'll just let us go?" Sygurn grimaced, shaking his head. "Couldn't say what their reasons are for taking us in, but I know they have some. Something my mean old shit of a pa used to say comes to mind: 'When a man opens his door to you, beware of two things: a knife in the back when you're sleeping, or the price he demands come morning.'"

"Oh, I'm sure the Morvek will demand a price. Luckily—" Ruhlin nodded at the forge "—thanks to you, we have a means of paying it. Tomorrow, we return to the mine for more ore and coal. I'm afraid your labours are not yet done, my friend."

Tirohk arrived alone and unheralded while they were celebrating Ryma's birthday, his tall form appearing on the lower slopes at midday. The child had begun to speak recently, albeit mostly by repeatedly shouting "No" leavened with the occasional giggling "Yes". Attempts to elicit any information about her parents or childhood, including the date of her birth, proved unsuccessful. Reasoning every child needed a birthday, Aleida had chosen an arbitrary date and convened a feast. Thanks to Tuhlan, they had a goat to roast, and the weather proved kind, enabling the gathering to linger and make a fuss of Ryma. Although initially delighted with the attention, she quickly grew both bored and tired, subsiding into sleep in Aleida's arms.

Guthnyr, aggrieved by the absence of liquor, was loudly proclaiming his intention to start brewing ale come the spring, when Tirohk's appearance abruptly ended his good humour. The Morvek strode into the village with his gaze fixed upon Ruhlin, although he did spare a glance in Iyaka's direction.

"You must come, *Telchak*," he said without offering a greeting.

"Come where?" Ruhlin asked.

"A council awaits you." Tirohk spoke with a guarded impatience, frowning in annoyance when Iyaka asked a question in Morvek. He snapped his response, provoking her to an angry injunction.

"Speak plain and in their tongue!" she stated. "Have the elders of the northern clans gathered already? And in winter?"

"Not just the northern clans," Tirohk replied. "Word of his coming spread fast and far. Even the people of the plains have sent their wisest. The journey was hard and long, but still they came."

"What do they want of me?" Ruhlin asked.

Watching Tirohk's expression soften, Ruhlin gained the impression of a man acting against his own best judgement. "Many things," he said. "But mostly, they either want to be proven right, or very much proven wrong."

CHAPTER TWENTY

Felnir

One glance at the two dozen mounted cultists making their way through the forest convinced Felnir that these were warriors of a very different kind to those slaughtered at the stronghold. They rode with an alertness and ease in the saddle that bespoke extensive experience, as did their well-maintained armour. They also differed from that unfortunate gang of drunkards and cowards in the uniformity of their facial tattoos. Instead of a mishmash of gibberish and barely legible ancient script, each bore the silhouette of a spread-winged raven on their foreheads. Their scalps were shaved down to stubble in a fashion that would have been considered laughable in Ascarlia. However, their lean, unsmiling faces, most marked by more than one scar, told of men and women hardened by violence.

"The wretch didn't lie, my lord," Falk murmured at his side. The two of them had ridden out before dawn. The stronghold's stables had yielded a number of horses. Most were draught animals unsuitable for riding, save for a mare and a stallion with the length of leg and leanness of muscle that marked them as bred for the hunt. Olvynd had told Felnir of a trail that intersected with the more commonly used track through the forest. Such intimate knowledge of the surrounding country indicated the newly appointed Royal Scribe's tenure amid the *Ahrkun* had been more prolonged than he claimed. Felnir was disinclined to punish him for his dishonesty, reasoning it would be akin to whipping the rain for being wet.

Upon reaching the track, Falk's keen eye for hidden vantage points led them to the hollowed trunk of a long dead oak where they waited for the *Ahrkun* to appear. Upon hearing Olvynd's tale, Felnir's instinct had been to gather his *menda* and set an ambush. But, if there was one lesson his days as a hired blade had taught him, it was the value of taking full measure of an enemy before launching an attack. This company's keen awareness of their surroundings, and habit of ranging out in pairs to scout the trail ahead, meant they would most likely spot any decent-sized force lying in wait. Although Felnir didn't doubt the courage and vengefulness of his *menda*, they were far from being a disciplined and trained fighting force. Matching them against these warriors in a melee would result in a great many dead and wounded at best, and defeat at worst.

He kept watching as the full company rode by, counting each cultist until he spotted the figure he assumed to be the leader. Olvynd said the man's formal title was the *Sindra's* Factor, a tall man of baleful appearance. While his warriors peered into every shadow with careful discernment, the Factor glared at his surroundings with a mix of disdain and resentment. *Does he hate his task?* Felnir wondered. *Or just harbour an aversion to trees?*

Following the Factor came another cultist, a stocky, lank-haired woman leading a train of four pack horses. Unlike the escorts, she wore no armour and, while they were alert, she rode with her head lowered, dark, unwashed tresses veiling her face. The heavy chests swaying atop the beasts she led made it plain several tributes to the *Ahrkun Krayl* had already been collected. Even so, Felnir judged it insufficient. To win kingship of this land, he would need a true army, and he knew well how expensive a business war could be. Every chest so far acquired by the *Sindra's* Factor wouldn't have paid the wages of the Saluhtan's host for a month.

"Noticed a spot at a river crossing a few miles on, my lord," Falk said once the cultists were out of earshot. "Catch 'em midstream with a volley of arrows, then finish the rest at the water's edge."

It was a decent plan, worthy of Falk's outlaw expertise, but Felnir still judged the risk too high. Besides, he had begun to hatch another scheme. "I think it best to wait a while," he said. "Let this fruit ripen before we pluck it. Come on." He began to lever himself free of the oak. "We need to be back before midday."

While Beyorn and a few others exhibited a measure of bafflement at being ordered to abandon a place they had spilled blood to seize, no voices were raised to question it. Felnir had all the *Ahrkun's* loot and weapons packed onto the draught horses, instructing his *menda* to carry all the supplies they could. He considered setting light to the stronghold, but since it was mostly stone, it seemed a futile and time-consuming gesture. He also reckoned the mystery of empty halls would both unnerve and enrage the Factor, more so when his party discovered the hacked and mutilated remains of their fellow cultists dumped in the forest.

Olvynd guided them to a glade some miles west of the stronghold, and well away from the forest track, where they made camp. Come nightfall, Felnir quizzed the former captive on where the Factor, having made his grim discovery, would go next.

"The River Belt, my king," Olvynd said. "It's a string of villages spread along the bank of the Hol Ledda. They've been under the *Ahrkun's* boot heel for a few seasons now. It's a fair bet the Factor will be seeking answers to what happened at the Nest, and he won't ask gently."

"Will he resort to killing?" Sygna asked. She sat beside Felnir at the fire, Yuhlla's small head resting in her lap. So as not to wake the girl, Sygna spoke softly, but Felnir heard the edge in her voice. He had known she wouldn't like his plan. For that matter, neither did he. But he had seen far more of war than she had. It was always a series of hard choices, and he had made one.

"Perhaps, my queen," Olvynd replied. "Though he's more likely to hand out a few floggings. Mayhap take an ear or two. Dead folk don't fish the river or grow crops, and the *Ahrkun* are always keen to keep the tributes flowing."

"An earless man can still fight," Beyorn said, chewing a morsel of the salted pork they had liberated from the Nest. "And perhaps be keen to do so."

At his side, Tulvik frowned but remained silent. The youth couldn't be accused of possessing a complex mind, but Felnir still found him difficult to read sometimes. It was hard to tell if his expression indicated disapproval or confusion. Either way, Felnir knew it would be best to allay any concerns now rather than wait for the ugliness to come.

"You may think this harsh," he said, eyes shifting between the faces arrayed around the fire. "Cold, perhaps. Even cowardly. If so, you are right on the first two counts, but not the third. War compels us to dreadful acts. This is the simple truth. The worthiness of our cause lies in the fact that we endure one outrage to prevent others, not to prolong them. The *Ahrkun's* cruelty is their weakness, and an enemy's flaws should always be accepted as the most precious of gifts. If any would gainsay my judgement, speak and be heard without fear of recrimination. I have ever welcomed the counsel of all who sit at my fire."

"For my part," Beyorn said, "I believe the folk of my homeland have too long dishonoured themselves with their shameful acceptance of the *Ahrkun's* dominion. If briefly tolerating their crimes will shake these people from their cowed torpor, then I'm all for it."

"Tulvik?" Felnir prompted when the youth didn't speak. Leaving him to stew in silence might have been wiser, but as kin to the Gyrwald of the Greencrest, his agreement would carry weight with any waverers in this *menda*.

"It . . . lies heavy on my heart," Tulvik said, fingers playing over the scar on the back of his hand he had earned at the Nest. "And may sit ill with others. But, our cause being just, and the blessings of the Altvar upon our actions so evident, I believe the burden may be borne. Providing," he added, forestalling Felnir's next words. He was surprised by the sudden steadiness of the youth's gaze as he regarded him across the fire. "The *Ahrkun* must receive all due punishment for their cruelties." He cast a short, disgusted glance at Olvynd. "Unwarranted mercy is also a heavy weight upon the soul."

Since revealing his new scribe, Felnir had been acutely aware of the detestation he engendered. So far, the protection afforded by the would-be king of Vorunvahl had served to preserve Olvynd's life. But Felnir had little doubt that, should he fall in this war, the scribe's demise would follow swiftly after.

"You would have me kill them all?" Felnir asked Tulvik.

The young warrior's gaze didn't waver. "I would. For that is their due. And can any doubt that is what they would offer us? The bearer of the Sword of the Altvar should not hesitate to wield it in the cause of justice."

Felnir made a show of stroking his beard, furrowing his brow in sombre reflection. He watched the others around the fire nod in agreement, many casting glares in Olvynd's direction. *I carry a sword forged by the gods themselves,* Felnir thought. *And yet must still strive to win their loyalty. If Velgard sat before them with this sword at his belt, would they even dare meet his eye, let alone seek to bargain the terms of their service?*

His gaze slid towards the hunched figure silhouetted against the glow of a nearby fire. The *menda* knew who he was and, while some regarded the fabled Angmund with awe, all avoided his company. For his part, Wohtin seemed content in his isolation, features perpetually set in a frown of deep, troubled contemplation.

"Have no fear," Felnir said, turning back to Tulvik. "All *Ahrkun* will receive justice in full measure. Go now and rest." He got to his feet, smiling in tactful dismissal. "For I've no doubt tomorrow will be a day of hardship."

When they had gone and Sygna retired to their shelter with the children, Felnir made his way to Wohtin's fire. For a time, he watched the old man stare into the flames without troubling himself to acknowledge his king's presence. Not for the first time, a singular question rose to the forefront of Felnir's mind: *Do I still need you?*

As if hearing his thoughts, Wohtin spoke, his voice a tired drawl. "You want to know if Velgard would do the same thing?"

Actually, I was pondering the wisdom of cutting your head off and throwing it into the fire. "Would he?" Felnir asked, scraping the frost from a fallen yew branch before sitting down.

"No. When it came to war, he was ever straightforward: find the enemy and attack them with all his strength as swiftly as possible. Yet, when it came to politics, he was far more subtle and calculating. He was fond of saying that the endless weave and weft of alliance and diplomacy was a far more dangerous game than war."

Felnir plucked a twig from the branch and tossed it into the fire. "Perhaps not if he had ever carried the Sword of the Altvar."

"Do you find it so, Felnir Skyrnrak?" For the first time in many days, a measure of humour showed in the faint curve of Wohtin's lips. "I think not. Did you imagine it would be easier to twist these people to your will with a blade at your side that shimmered with the Altvar's blessing?"

"I do not twist them. I offer what they have been too craven to claim before now."

"All due to your heroic and unselfish heart, no doubt." Wohtin's amusement shifted into open contempt. "Do not seek to measure yourself against Velgard's example, Redtooth. It will always be utter folly."

Just one stroke. Felnir's gaze lingered on the old man's neck. *Who would even care?* "This thing is not what you promised," he said, drawing the sword and angling the blade to catch the firelight. "It's sharp enough, I'll grant. Doesn't tarnish, nor does the edge chip in battle. But it remains just a sword. But for one cryptic vision, it has given me nothing."

"It gave you them." Wohtin jerked his head over his shoulder at the camp. "A totem worth following. A symbol around which you can weave your legend."

"I'll need more. Today I saw true warriors, not the fools we slew at the Nest. The *Ahrkun* will not fall easily. And even should I defeat them, this land is far from united. Forging it into a true kingdom will be the work of years."

"Are you so impatient?"

Felnir watched the flames dance in the steel, a clear reflection lacking the blurring or distortion of even the finest mirrors. "Yes," he said. "You promised me a kingdom, old man. Not a lifetime of war and toil that might never end. To do that, I must be able to call upon the power of this thing."

Wohtin grunted, his mirth returning. "Another marked difference between you and Velgard. Even he never dared dream of commanding the gods."

"Don't seek to distract me with insults. I don't like it." Felnir spoke in a low growl possessing enough threat to capture Wohtin's gaze. His eyes narrowed as they flicked between Felnir and the sword.

"It has truly shown nothing since that first vision?" he asked, grunting again when Felnir shook his head. "There may be a way. But it can't be done until the *Ahrkun Krayl* are vanquished."

"Why?"

"Because it demands greatness, my king. Not mere ambition."

"I recall telling you once, quite clearly, that I would tolerate no more riddles."

"Not a riddle. Just truth. If the power that resides in that blade can be unlocked, it must recognise the wielder as one worthy of its blessing. Even then . . ." Wohtin trailed off, doubt creasing his brow. "It won't be easy." He forestalled further questions by getting to his feet and stalking off towards his shelter. "Ask me again when the *Sindra* lies dead. Until then, you must trust to your own skills, Felnir Skyrnrak."

Felnir assumed the man hanging by his wrists from a post in the village marketplace had been chosen for his impressive stature. Visiting punishment on a weakling only emphasised the weakness of the punisher. Instead, the Factor had wisely opted to flog a tall, well-muscled fellow. Felnir recognised the many ragged wounds on his back as the work of a studded whip and calculated only a few more strokes would have seen this unfortunate to the Halls of Aevnir.

"What are you doing?" a shrill old woman called out as Felnir strode towards the post. "They said to leave him. They'll come back if we don't."

Felnir ignored her, cutting the flayed man's bonds with his dagger and gently guiding him to the ground while Sygna came forth to inspect his wounds. "Bad," she murmured, a trace of bitterness to her voice. Felnir could tell she was striving to keep the accusing glare from her gaze. "He needs salve and water. Poor bastard's near dead from thirst."

"Tend him as best you can," Felnir said before rising to cast a hard glare at the surrounding villagers. Most had hidden at their approach. The rest slowly emerged from their homes when it became apparent this new group of armed strangers would visit no further violence upon them. Apart from the old woman, now clutching at her apron in teary-eyed terror, none of the villagers dared to speak.

"It was you!" she sobbed, stabbing an accusing finger at Felnir. "You're the ones they were looking for. They punished us for your crime."

"No," Felnir replied, pointing to the flayed man. "They punished him, while you all looked on and did nothing."

His words carried enough truth to shame the woman into silence, Felnir casting a baleful eye over her fellow villagers as he spoke on. "My name is Felnir Skyrnrak. I have sailed countless miles through storm and hunger to bring justice and freedom to this land. I came here to return to you what has been stolen, having visited just execution on the thieves that took it from you. Now, I wonder if this nest of cravens is worthy of such reward."

"They were many," a man called out from the burgeoning crowd. "They had arms. We have none—"

"The folk of Kahl Hardta had none either," Felnir interrupted, pointing to the coast-landers in his *menda*. "Yet they chose to stand, not to cower and snivel as one of their own is tormented to the point of death. The blood of the Ascarls flows in your veins, but you dishonour it."

"And who are you to judge us?" the old woman demanded, rediscovering her voice, though it now held a plaintive note. "We know you not, outlander. Nor do we owe you fealty . . ."

"You owe him more than that!" Beyorn cut in, striding forth to cast out a declaration that impressed Felnir with its booming volume. "Know that you behold this day the Altvar's chosen, the bearer of their very sword." Turning to Felnir, he gave a formal nod. "Show them, my king. I beg you."

Drawing the Sword of the Altvar, Felnir held it aloft. The untarnished gleam of the blade succeeded in capturing the crowd's attention, but he saw as much doubt on their faces as awe. *Still just a length of shiny metal*, Felnir sighed inwardly, noting how the mere sight of the fabled weapon failed to capture their hearts. Fortunately, it transpired that Beyorn's rhetoric could craft its own form of magic.

"Know that this blade has been recognised by Arnhilt Volksora, the Gyrwald of the Greencrest himself, as the Sword of the Altvar," the warrior boomed on. "He who stood at Velgard's side the day he was gathered unto the Altvar. He saw this blade with his *own* eyes. His blood kin, Tulvik, stands here, proud to serve in the *menda* of Felnir, future king of Vorunvahl. I have followed this man in battle. I have seen his undaunted courage and his great skill in combat and have no doubt that he was sent here at the Altvar's behest to deliver us from the *Ahrkun's* yoke."

Felnir swallowed a grunt of satisfaction at the effect of Beyorn's words. The villagers' mingled shame and confusion was slowly being replaced by hope, even resolve. *Best leave the speeches to him in future*, Felnir mused.

Beyorn then further demonstrated his gift for oratory by falling silent, head bowed and jaw grinding as he sought to control a raging well of emotion. "Has not our suffering been long enough?" he asked, raising his face to regard the villagers with moist eyes, a choked rasp now colouring his tone. "Have you endured enough? Have you not watched enough of your children carried away? Here!" He began to boom again as he cast a hand at Felnir. "Here, in this man, stands the hammer that will shatter your chains. All he asks is that you stand with him. Who here can still feel the blood of our forebears in their veins? Who here will stand with the Altvar's Blade?"

"I will!" The girl who rushed from the crowd was perhaps sixteen summers old and of slender build. She stumbled to the side of the flayed man and collapsed to her knees, clasping his hand before looking up at Felnir in stark appeal. At first Felnir thought her subject to some form of disfigurement, but then realised her nose had been broken, recently judging by the blood spattering her face and garb.

"He is your father?" Felnir asked, seeing the fierceness with which she clutched at the flayed man's limp hand.

"My brother," she said, stifling a sob as she looked at the ruined flesh of the man's back. "For years he hid me from the *Ahrkun*, lest they steal me away. Whenever they came, only he had the courage to speak to them. When the Factor demanded to know what had happened at the Nest, he had no answers. I tried to stop them . . ." She touched her misaligned nose, wincing in pain. "It did no good. All the times he saved me, yet I couldn't save him."

"But you can avenge him," Felnir told her. Stooping, he offered her his hand. "What is your name?"

She sniffed, wiping blood-flecked snot from her nose before taking his hand. "Tyrheld . . . my king."

"Stand, Tyrheld," he said, guiding her to her feet before addressing the crowd once more. "In this fierce maiden, I feel this village has given all it can to our cause. So I'll waste no more words appealing to fearful hearts. We will leave you supplies to make good what has been taken by the *Ahrkun*. This maiden's brother will be taken into our care. If he possesses one-tenth of his sister's courage, then I'll consider him a fine addition to my *menda*. Beyorn, hand out the supplies and let's be on our way."

"Wait!" The man who had spoken of being outnumbered stepped forward. A figure of brawny stature, his heavy jaw was set in a grimace of hope and wariness. "You give us food, but ask for nothing in return?"

"If you will not fight, what more can you give?" Felnir beckoned Tulvik forward and the two of them draped the flayed man's arms across their shoulders to raise him up. From the chill feel of his skin, Felnir doubted he would last much longer.

"I will fight," the brawny man said. "If you promise enough food for the winter and vengeance upon the *Ahrkun*, I will fight."

Still, I am forced to bargain, Felnir mused, although the sight of a dozen more villagers moving to the brawny man's side brought some measure of satisfaction. "No subject of my kingdom will ever go hungry," Felnir said. "As for vengeance. Of that, you'll have so much you may be sickened by it."

Despite Sygna's best efforts, the flayed man, named as Ulgriff by his sister, died before morning. Tyrheld's grief was raw and echoed loud through the village but Felnir made no effort to quiet her. Such piercing cries would be a clarion call for any waverers and, come the dawn, he had another ten grim-faced recruits to his *menda*.

It was local custom for the dead to be set adrift on the river in a boat stocked with firewood and set ablaze. Although impatient to get on, Felnir made time for the ritual. This moment of shared grief and shame would further cement the resolve of his newly acquired warriors.

He armed them with the weapons captured at the Nest, swords and axes of undistinguished but serviceable manufacture. He was also pleased to see most sporting their own hunting bows, long-staved and fashioned from ash and yew. Vehldur, the brawny man, organised a brief demonstration of archery. Although a wheelwright by trade, he succeeded in sinking a shaft into a tree trunk from sixty paces, a feat matched by his comrades. Felnir placed them under Sygna's command, knowing well the value a cohort of skilled archers brought to any war band.

They departed the village before midday, Felnir keen not to allow his recruits time to reconsider their choice in the face of families distressed by the prospect they might never return. The *menda* kept close to the riverbank for the next two days, maintaining a steady pace and scouting the forested country on their right flank to ward against ambush. Felnir was glad to find that, while the Factor's escort were vigilant, they were also overconfident. A wise commander would pay close attention to his rear when on the march.

They're accustomed to intimidation, not war, Felnir concluded. The notion boded well for the outcome of this foray. With the strength he expected to add at the next village, the advantage in numbers would put the eventual confrontation beyond question. Unfortunately, upon viewing the cottages sprawled along the riverbank ahead, it became clear that his plans would have to be adjusted. Each dwelling was a blackened ruin, the thinness of the smoke indicating this had been done the previous day. Not content with arson, the *Ahrkun* had also chosen to mark their work.

The heads were impaled on wooden stakes in the centre of the village. A dozen in all, their age difficult to judge thanks to the effects of violent death, but some were plainly children. Each one had been branded on the cheek, the sigil burned into the flesh identical to the raven that adorned the foreheads of the Factor's warriors. An inspection of the ruins yielded no survivors, Felnir peering through windows at blackened bones and seared skulls lying amid the ash.

"The dead don't fish or grow crops," he muttered to Olvynd, the scribe squirming under the weight of his stare.

"Must've gotten angrier," Olvynd muttered. "Or perhaps they had no tribute to offer."

"More likely one of them said the wrong thing," Vehldur said, his attention fixed on one of the heads. Felnir guessed it to be a young woman from the long hair partially veiling her mutilated features. "Ehdsa," the wright murmured, Felnir hearing the pain in his voice. "My niece. Married a man here last year. Her mother said no good would come of it."

"Cowardly wretches," Tulvik spat, turning to Felnir. "Such outrages cannot be permitted to continue."

The angry growl from the rest of the *menda* made it plain to Felnir that he had stretched this stratagem as far as it would go. "No, they cannot," he said, straightening in the saddle. "Falk. Beyorn. Ride ahead and find the trail of the Factor's party. Return when they've camped for the night. Do not be seen."

Once the pair had ridden off, he dismounted from the hunter's back. "Come. Let us see to the fallen."

The *Ahrkun* had seen fit to sink every boat in the village but, rather than forgo the ritual, Vehldur and the other river folk insisted on lashing salvaged timber together to make a raft. The heads and bones were piled onto the makeshift craft, whereupon they pushed it into the river to be set ablaze by a fire arrow. The current carried it into the reeds covering the far bank, where it continued to burn until nightfall.

"They've about a five-mile lead on us, my lord," Falk reported when he and Beyorn returned. Felnir nodded, his gaze captured by the raft still blazing in the darkness. He found himself resenting its stubborn refusal to burn itself out, and the unpleasant taint to the smoke drifting over the water. It was almost as if he could smell accusation in the acrid, meat-laced stench.

"Moved away from the bank a few miles too," Falk went on. "Nested themselves in the forest amid a clutch of tall stones." He paused, adding when Felnir didn't speak, "Won't be an easy place to storm."

"Yet storm it we must," Beyorn said, voice hushed but fierce with insistence. "These folk were promised vengeance, my king. After this, they'll demand their due. That's if you want to keep them following your banner."

"I don't have a banner," Felnir replied, pursing his lips in consideration. "Something I should see to, I suppose."

He lingered a moment longer, drawing the Sword of the Altvar as the raft continued to burn. Once again, he watched flames dance in the steel, failing to impart any meaning. *It must recognise the wielder as one worthy of its blessing,* Wohtin had said. *You think me unworthy?* Felnir asked the sword silently. *Witness this.*

"Nested amid a clutch of tall stones, you say?" he asked Falk, striding towards his horse.

"You're going now, my king?" Beyorn asked, watching Felnir mount up.

"I think it best," he replied, settling himself into the saddle. "There are a good many *Ahrkun* in need of killing and the hour grows late. Feel at liberty to join me if you're so minded."

Raising high the Sword of the Altvar, he kicked his heels, sending the hunter into a fast gallop towards the trees.

CHAPTER TWENTY-ONE

Thera

Watching the many folk toiling upon the shore of Danith's Bay, it occurred to Thera that she had inadvertently founded a new port. The partly destroyed stockade established by the Nihlvarians had been repaired and greatly expanded. The defensive wall now extended a quarter-mile inland while the number of buildings within tripled. Thera had also ordered watchtowers constructed atop the headlands flanking the bay. Already, those who laboured to build this nascent settlement had taken to calling it Vellihr Hardta: the Vellihr's Port. *All done without Sister Silver's permission, too,* she mused, imagining the old woman's profane anger at such unsanctioned intrusion into her responsibilities. Her humour evaporated as the thought summoned images of the queens' murder. Even though she hadn't seen it, Thera's mind conjured all manner of ugly sights. Chief among them the beauteous face of Sister Lore twisted into murderous glee.

She must have known I would come for her, Thera thought. *Her scheme was so well planned, yet she chose to leave me alive.* Or had she? Thera recalled the assassin in Skyrn-Hardta. At the time she assumed his arrow had been intended for Lynnea, now Thera wasn't so sure. *Perhaps his orders were to kill us both. In which case, why send only one assassin?*

Thera sighed, shaking her head to dispel the swarm of questions that had beset her since the shared dream with her great-grandfather. *I'll have answers when she's under my knife,* she decided, finding she greatly relished the prospect of putting Lore to the question. On that day, she felt certain her usual detestation for the ugliest part of a Vellihr's role would fade very quickly.

Her thoughts were interrupted by raised voices further along the jetty. Leaning over the *Great Wolf*'s rail, she saw Ossgrym remonstrating with the occupants of a captured Nihlvarian warship. "Get off or I'll flay the lot of you!" the Veilwald shouted, the crimson hue of his features making it plain this was no idle threat.

"Make us, y'fecking pig's arse!" a voice called back from the ship. "This one's ours. We earned it."

Leaning out further, Thera recognised Veltta, the one-eared Nihlvarian slave freed when the stockade fell. Since their last meeting, her garb had been replaced by a motley collection of armour. She punctuated her words by brandishing a spear in Ossgrym's direction, the gesture mimicked by the dozen other former slaves at her back.

"Why?" the Veilwald returned. "So you can steal it and piss off to who-knows-where? I think not."

"We aren't beholden to you!" Veltta yelled back. "And no one's taking what's ours. Not any more."

The argument continued to escalate as Thera made her way down the gangplank and along the jetty. Ossgrym's face had taken on a purple-ish shade and his hand gone to his sword by the time Thera reached his side. "Allies should not fight, Veilwald," she told him quietly. There was a time when even such a gentle interjection from her would have stoked the Ironbones' ire to a higher pitch. Now it brought calm, albeit tinged with a sullen scowl.

"These *Skyrnlohk* scum are set on thievery," he growled, voice low, but it transpired that Veltta had very keen hearing.

"We won this ship at the Lyx Helv," she declared amid a chorus of approval from her fellow Nihlvarians. "Lost three of ours doing it, too. It's their blood on these timbers, not this old fool's."

Thera raised an eyebrow at Ossgrym, receiving a grudging shrug in return. "Might have. Doesn't change the fact that it's not theirs to take."

"We freed a good many other slaves after the battle," Thera pointed out. "They need to know they'll receive fair treatment and just reward if they join us. Besides, do we not currently have more ships than hands to sail them?"

Ossgrym's creased brow twitched in reluctant acknowledgement, though his scowl lingered. "And what's to stop them just sailing off?"

Thera glanced up at the array of red-tattooed faces above, all uniformly defiant and, more importantly, lacking any vestige of fear. "I would ask that you leave that in my hands, Veilwald," she said, smiling but with a note of dismissal.

Once again, instead of anger, Ossgrym showed only deference as he offered a respectful nod. "Spoken like a queen," he murmured before stomping off along the jetty, gesturing for his pair of escorting warriors to follow.

Thera took a moment to survey the Nihlvarian vessel, concluding that the freed folk had chosen well. She was small for a warship, but possessed of sleek lines. The lack of weathering and barnacles to her hull also bespoke a craft fresh from the yard. "Very fine," Thera said, shifting her gaze back to Veltta. "But she'll take some handling. Are you up to it?"

"Three years chained to an oar was a fine teacher in sea craft," Veltta replied. "We know which ropes to tighten and which to slacken, if that's your meaning. And you won't find any who can haul an oar faster than us."

"I don't doubt it." Thera gestured to the gangplank. "May I come aboard, Captain?"

A dim flicker of emotion altered Veltta's frown for an instant. Whether it was amusement, or perhaps pride, Thera couldn't tell. "You may," she said.

Thera counted close to two score Nihlvarians as she stepped onto the deck. Not all were those freed from the stockade. A handful were evidently survivors of the Lyx Helv. Lacking the more fulsome if mismatched armour of their comrades, they reacted to her presence with markedly more suspicion, edging away with hands twitching on their weapons. *Worried they've exchanged one set of masters for another*, Thera concluded. She also took note of the barrels stacked below the deck planking, reckoning the ship had been provisioned for a lengthy voyage.

"Planning on leaving us?" she asked Veltta.

"Are we not free?" A measure of accusation coloured the freed woman's question. "And did we not repay you? With our own blood, no less?"

"That you did. Take the ship and sail where you will. I'll raise no hand to stop you. But I am curious as to your destination. You can hardly sail for home, after all."

"When last we met, you said there was nowhere for us to go. Now there is. I hear much talk of the southern seas where a great many ships carry riches from port to port."

"Piracy is your object, then?"

A grin played over Veltta's lips. "I thought we'd try the merchant trade first. Captain Din Rabahs says a fast ship like this can earn a great deal in the tea trade."

"That it can. But what if I said you could earn more in my service?"

Veltta paused to exchange glances with her comrades. Some replied with shrugs, but most appeared at least amenable to hearing Thera's offer. "How much more?" Veltta asked.

"You will have title to any Nihlvarian ship you seize, to be sold or kept as you see fit." Thera paused, watching the calculation play out on Veltta's face. Shorn of grime, with her hair grown an inch or two, the prettiness

Thera had noticed before had become undeniable feline beauty. Although she possessed none of the inscrutability unique to cats. Thera saw greed in those fine features, but also reluctance. *Does she find the taste of war too bitter?* she wondered. Perhaps this deal needed sweetening.

"Can any of you claim to have had full measure of justice?" Thera said, addressing the question to the crew rather than just their captain. "Or do you not still feel the lash upon your backs? There are many others now suffering aboard Nihlvarian ships who can only dream of freedom. Will you not offer them what you have received?"

This heralded another round of shared looks until one of the crew broke the silence. A man of brutish aspect and at least forty summers, he spoke to Veltta in a tone of surprising gentleness. "My son, Vel," he said, grimacing in apology. "You know they took him to punish me. He's still chained to an oar in one of the Tuhlvyr's ships. If there's even the smallest chance of freeing him . . ."

"I know the fecking story, Alryhk," Veltta cut in. "You've told it enough times." Sighing, she settled a narrow, demanding squint on Thera. "Not just the ships. We want all the cargos, too."

"Done." Thera held out her hand. Once they had shaken, she moved to the gangplank. "In six days, I sail for Ayl-Ah-Skorna. You will be my escort." She paused before descending to the jetty. "By the way, what do you intend naming her?"

Veltta's grin returned. "The *Chainbreaker,*" she said. "What else could she be?"

"You're sure of the count?"

Skahlvyr's face was grim as he replied, "Trust me, Vellihr, it's my fervent wish I had miscounted."

"More than three hundred warships," Hakkyn said, shaking his head. "How could they gather that many so soon after such a crushing defeat?"

"I believe I witnessed a union of two fleets, Veilwald," Skahlvyr said. "One sailing east, the other west."

"Fresh reinforcements from their homeland joining with ships drawn from the fleet at Skar Magnol," Thera concluded. "It appears Lore, or whoever commands her, is very keen to see our end."

They had gathered in a newly built structure dubbed, without her blessing, the Vellihr's Hall. The high ceiling and imposing scale said much for the industry and skill of their workforce. However, Thera felt the toil and timber could have been spent on more housing for the Aiken Gelders arriving in ever larger numbers. Yet, she gave no order halting construction, recalling Lynnea's words: *They hunger for leadership.* Any Ascarlian holding rank of note always had their own hall.

"Not yet one-tenth of my people have made the journey north," Hakkyn said. "With our strength concentrated here, a fleet this size could enslave all who remain and lay waste to the geld entire."

"Then we sail out and meet them," Ossgrym stated. "We beat them once. I've little doubt we can do so again."

"We have many ships, it is true, but scant hands to sail them well. A battle upon the open sea will not favour us. Even should we triumph, our losses would be terrible. And who's to say our foes will not simply conjure another fleet to plague us?"

Thera focused on her map of the Outer Isles spread out on the table before them. Her eyes lingered on the point where Skahlvyr had spotted the two Nihlvarian cohorts coming together. *A good thirty miles from the lower Aiken Geld,* she mused before shifting her gaze north-east to the Inner Isles. They were depicted only in part on this map, but enough of the coast had been detailed to stir the beginnings of a fresh stratagem. *Gelmyr always hated the approach to Vorun Hardta. The Crusher's Strait, they call it . . .*

"I think I should sail for the Inner Isles sooner than planned," she said.

"Now, Vellihr?" Hakkyn stared at her. "Surely you are needed here to rally our strength—"

"I am needed where victory will be won, Veilwald," she interrupted, not looking up from the map. "Having suffered a defeat, I believe our enemy's object will be to eliminate the most present threat."

"They come for you," Ossgrym said, nodding in agreement. "It's good odds one of their many spies will have told them all about the Vellihr who won victory at the Lyx Helv and now rules the Outer Isles."

Thera quelled the urge to correct him. There were more pressing issues at hand than arguing the niceties of her status. Besides, he had a point. In any way that mattered, she now ruled these islands, which made the necessity of abandoning them harder to bear. But she saw no other course.

"Veilwald Hakkyn," she said, meeting his gaze. "You will remain here with a third of our strength to guard against an assault on Danith's Bay and continue to provide succour to those fleeing the Aiken Geld. Veilwald Ossgrym, you will take command of the remainder and sail south."

"You wish to meet them in battle, then?" the Ironbones asked.

"I do," she confirmed. "But not quite yet. You will head south until you sight their vanguard. Tarry long enough to ensure they've seen the fleet entire, then sail with all speed for Ayl-Ah-Skorna." She went on to describe the dispositions he was to adopt upon reaching the Inner Isles. Ossgrym didn't argue his orders, but she saw the doubt he struggled to conceal.

"There's a lot of steps to this dance, Vellihr," he said, stroking his beard and contemplating the map. "Just one stumble and we're done."

"War is often decided by who stumbles last," Thera told him. "And I don't intend it to be me."

The south-easterly approach to Vorun Hardta, the principal port on the southern coast of Ayl-Ah-Skorna, inevitably called forth memories of those times she had watched Gelmyr steer the *Great Wolf* through the channel. This comparatively short and seemingly unremarkable stretch of water troubled him more than any in Ascarlia. It was named the Crushers' Strait for good reason. Despite appearing both broad and deep, in fact it was only navigable at high tide and even then passing vessels needed to keep to a narrow avenue between the hull shredding rocks below. It required a skilled hand on the tiller and intimate knowledge of the local currents. While Althsten was a deft helmsman, his knowledge of these waters was but a pale shadow of her former *Johten Apt*. Consequently, the *Great Wolf* was obliged to follow the *Northern Star* through the strait. Captain Obryn D'Shaine was well acquainted with the port and the valuable cargo to be found there. The merchantman's copious hold would also prove useful for what lay ahead. Behind the *Great Wolf*, the *Chainbreaker* followed closely, Veltta having been sternly warned of the danger of straying off course.

As expected, Thera found the *Ohlira* waiting in the waters beyond the strait, but was surprised to see Kahlvik had anchored her offshore rather than in harbour. More concerning was the sight of a tall fire burning on the fringes of Vorun Hardta. At first she worried that the Nihlvarians had arrived in advance of her coming, but a shouted exchange with Kahlvik allayed her fears. "Veilwald Synghild uncovered a clutch of traitors in her household!" the seafarer called out as the *Great Wolf* drew alongside the *Ohlira*. "She asked for privacy in settling the matter, as it pertained to family."

"Family?" Thera called back in puzzlement.

"Her daughter and two of her sons were unmasked as Volkrath agents. A grim business, Vellihr. She spared them the Crimson Hawk, but not the fire. I advised her of your arrival. She will receive us come the morn."

The fire continued to burn throughout the night, only dwindling past midnight. Lynnea came to Thera's side as she watched the blaze fade into a flicker. *She burned her own children alive.* Lynnea's thoughts were laced with both mystification and repugnance. *What manner of woman could do that?*

"One fierce in her attachment to law and custom," Thera replied. "And Veilwald Synghild is no stranger to spilling her own blood. She had a difficult passage to the Veilwald's chair. Chosen by the queens upon her father's death in favour of her two elder brothers, she faced much discord, then outright rebellion. In those days, I was apprenticed to the Vellihr of Justice, who would later become Sister Iron. We sailed on the queens' orders to lend our swords to Synghild's cause, but the struggle was over by the time we landed. Both her brothers awaited us at the harbour, splayed on scaffolds, having suffered the Crimson Hawk. Burning alive is considered the more merciful punishment for treason."

Yet you did neither to my father.

This was a mostly unspoken topic between them. Despite witnessing Thera put a spear through her sire, Lynnea had never exhibited a morsel of resentment over the act and Thera sensed only curiosity in this question.

"He was mad," she said. "And his crime could be termed thievery rather than treason, though some would argue the point. While I couldn't spare him, it felt wrong to torment one already driven beyond reason."

The soft patter of Mohlnir's paws drew Thera's gaze to the sight of him trotting across the deck, a freshly killed mouse dangling from his mouth. Depositing the trophy at Thera's feet, he let out a soft meow before leaping into Lynnea's arms.

"I'll need you at my side on the morrow," Thera said, stooping to take hold of the mouse's tail and toss the tiny corpse over the side. "I find it hard to credit Veilwald Synghild would lie. I'm not even sure she knows how. But if three of her own children were Volkrath, there must be more. Find them for me, but make sure they don't know they've been found."

A faint grin played over Lynnea's lips as she ran a hand through Mohlnir's fur. *I am your spy hunter now?*

"Why not? Given that you're so very good at it."

Thera had always found Vorun Hardta a place of grim aspect. Although the island it sat upon had been named for its thickly forested shore, its principal source of wealth lay not in timber but stone, hence the name of Veilwald Synghild's dominion: the Speldmeara Geld, the Land of Black Marble. Only here, in all the lands ruled by the Sister Queens, was marble found, and it was unique. Black as shadow in hue and veined in white crystal, it was highly prized in even far-flung places where it adorned the most opulent palaces and temples. Consequently, Vorun Hardta had long been sought out by many a foreign merchantman. While the stone's rare beauty did much to enhance the coffers of both the Veilwald and Sister

Silver's treasury, the business of quarrying it had, over the course of many years, done much to spoil a once beauteous coastline. The surrounding hills had been largely denuded of trees and the soil beneath scraped away to reveal the stone. Successive decades saw Vorun Hardta ringed by quarries, dark bites into the landscape conveying an impression of a place increasingly removed from nature.

As the boat carried them towards the wharf, Lynnea's thoughts revealed an even more potent dislike of this ugly, human-crafted spectacle. *One day they'll surely run out of stone,* she surmised with a grimace. *But by then there'll be no more island left to plunder.*

"A day too distant for most minds to contemplate," Thera said. "It looks marginally better when the sun shines. Makes the marble glitter."

They were greeted on the wharf by a dozen warriors from Veilwald Synghild's *menda*, hard-faced men and women begrimed in soot from the previous night's work. The veteran in charge offered Thera all due courtesy before leading her along the quay. They halted a good distance short of where a woman of slight build and steel grey hair stood in contemplation of the ashen remnants of the fire. Three blackened posts jutted from the smoking detritus, steel manacles dangling empty, but Thera picked out the stick-like bundles clustered around the base of each. She also saw that the woman was not alone. A naked man knelt close by, his hands bound behind his back and signs of recent torment showing on the impressive muscles of his bare body. He shuddered continually, either in pain or fear. *More of the latter,* Thera concluded, noting how the captive strove to keep his head lowered, long, dark hair covering his face.

A questioning glance at Lynnea confirmed her suspicions. *One less spy I won't have to find,* she thought with a nod. *He reeks of desperation and deceit in equal measure.*

"Vellihr," the veteran prompted, gesturing towards the grey-haired woman. "The Veilwald wishes to speak to you alone."

"Wait here," Thera told Lynnea before striding towards the woman. She didn't turn from the ashes at the sound of Thera's approach, merely raising her head.

"Vellihr Thera Speldrenda," she said in a voice that Thera found unnerving in its unhesitant calmness. "What tidings from the queens?"

"Then you have not heard news from Skar Magnol, Veilwald?"

"A veritable plague of rumours has assailed me these past weeks. But I have learned recently that truth is now a rare thing in this realm." She paused, turning to regard Thera with a pair of steady green eyes. "It's true, then? The queens are slain?"

"It is, Veilwald. But, though our queens have fallen, Ascarlia has not. I stand against our foes and call upon all true Ascarls to do the same."

"Our foes," Synghild echoed, turning back to the fire. "Another source of pestilent rumour. Are they truly ten feet tall with faces inked in arcane substances that burn when the battle rage is upon them?"

"No. They are merely men and women who bleed and die like any other."

"Well, that's something, I suppose. Certainly, if this one has anything other than blood in him, I've yet to see it." She made no move against the bound man, but he cowered yet lower. Thera could see a portion of his face now, discerning an undeniable handsomeness despite some livid bruises.

"But he is merely their creature," Synghild went on. "I thought his masters would be more impressive."

"They can be fierce," Thera conceded. "But their strength lies in their numbers, and their capacity for deceit. I am sorry your family fell victim to it."

This earned another glance from those green eyes. When Thera had first encountered this woman, she had been handsome, her hair a shade that earned her the name Vyrnvest, the Flamehair. Time had marked her face with creases and turned red to grey, but her eyes remained bright as ever, even when beset by grief. Beneath the sorrow, Thera saw something more, a mingling of emotion she had seen from many assailed by the worst of circumstances: guilt and shame.

"She didn't beg," Synghild said, her brow furrowed in puzzlement as her gaze slipped back to the ashes, focusing on the post in the centre. "Her brothers did. Screamed their promises of contrition and future loyalty until the smoke choked them to silence. But not Syred. She was always the strongest. 'Unto the Altvar I consign my soul,' she said. 'In the name of the Volkrath do I die. When next we meet, Mother, I shall deny you entry to the Halls.' I was going to spare her the worst of it. Put an arrow in her chest before the flames reached her. But after those words, I couldn't."

Slowly, she lowered her gaze to the bound man. When she spoke on, her previously placid tones were coloured by hungry anticipation. "I had allowed myself the delusion that it was all for him, this mad design she and her brothers had concocted. Apparently, they had gone to the trouble and expense of purchasing a swift-acting but painless poison from some far distant apothecary. Foolishly, they opted to await its arrival before dribbling it into my nightly tankard of mead."

As she spoke, the bound man shrank ever lower. His athletic frame shuddered rhythmically as he let out a series of piteous sobs, a pool of piss discolouring the ash covered cobbles around him. Disgusted, Thera looked away.

"Might I ask, Veilwald," she said, "how you came to know of their treachery?"

"Thanks to this one, of course. The problem with those skilled in seduction is that they're never satisfied with but one conquest. To win Syred's heart he had to spurn another, a maiden of sweet aspect but, it transpired, viciously jealous temperament. She came to me and confessed all, suitably tearful and abject too. It was all an act, of course, but I appreciated her efforts, so took but one of her ears before sending her off into exile. I regret that now. I would have much preferred she stay and watch what I'm going to do to her lover."

She stepped closer to the shuddering wretch, head angled as she surveyed his bruised form. "This creature would sit in my hall and sing songs. Such a fine voice he had. Such a winning smile. You will not be surprised to hear, Vellihr, that my hall was often described as austere, my company cold, a thing to be endured. But when this one turned up at my door with mandolin in hand, and that smile at the ready, I welcomed him, and those who had once made excuses when I invited them to table, no longer did so. Warmth and joy became the norm. Dancing and revels, much to my children's delight." She stopped, letting out a thin, bitter sigh. "It's a hard thing to know yourself a fool. To look into the glass and see a gullible old woman. I have punished those who deserved it, but the true blame here lies with me. I should have known better."

"The Volkrath are skilled in deception and treachery, Veilwald." Thera coughed, finding she had to summon the fortitude to speak her next words. *A hard thing to know yourself a fool.* "I myself was almost slain by one of their agents. An apprentice who had been at my side for years. Do not reproach yourself too harshly. And I would ask that you give thanks to the Altvar, for they have seen fit to bring vengeance within your grasp. A vengeance more potent than the death of one spy."

A faint smile played over Synghild's lips. "You come with promise of battle, then?"

"I do, Veilwald. An enemy fleet will arrive here within weeks, whereupon, with your help, I will orchestrate their destruction."

"Good. Then my geld is at your disposal. You should know that when our foes arrive, it is my intention to die in battle as swiftly as possible. Since I have no remaining children, I leave the choice of my successor to you. Now, if you will excuse me." She drew the dagger from her belt, beckoning two of her warriors forward to raise up the captive. "I have to make the

Crimson Hawk fly. It's been many a year since I conjured it, so it might take a good long while. Don't feel obliged to stand witness."

Watching the warriors drag the spy to the waiting scaffold, Thera resisted the impulse to request a pause in his execution. Although he no doubt possessed a great deal of useful information, extracting it would take more time than she had, and there was much to do in this port. Turning, she strode back to Lynnea as the first screams began to echo across the dockside.

"Find out where that one made his home," she said, voice low enough not to be heard by the nearby guards. "He was masquerading as a travelling balladeer, so check the taverns first." Noting how her apprentice strove not to flinch with every fresh scream, she added, "Can you deal with this alone, or do you need help?"

Lynnea's answer consisted of a pulse of indignation atop a welter of suppressed revulsion. *I can cope.*

Thera jerked her chin in dismissal. "Then get about it. Find me at the Veilwald's hall when you have something."

"Although I won't be here to see it," Synghild said, flicking her hands to banish the bloody droplets from her freshly washed hands, "it strikes me that your plan may have a debilitating effect on the future prospects of my geld, Vellihr."

Thera found the matter-of-fact manner with which the Veilwald referred to the imminence of her own demise jarring, but not so much as her mostly unchanged demeanour since inflicting the Crimson Hawk on the spy. When the grisly task was done and the balladeer's cries finally silenced, a gore-spattered Synghild had cordially invited the Vellihr of Justice to her hall. Alone together in her private chambers, the Veilwald had stripped off her besmirched garb to wash herself clean in a basin of water. Her nakedness seemed to trouble her no more than her recent actions, and Thera was impressed by the litheness of her form. But for her grey mane and creased face, it appeared she had aged little since their first meeting.

"The stone found in this geld will retain its value regardless," Thera replied. "It might even increase, given the added difficulty of acquiring it."

Synghild gave a faint grunt and began to dry herself with a flannel. "A great deal of labour will be required too. My lot have grown used to being well paid for their toil, and my coffers have become ever more empty of late. With Sister Silver gone, and a treasonous bitch playing queen in Skar Magnol, persuading them to work the quarries at the required pitch may prove difficult."

"I'll speak to them, explain the direness of our plight. If necessary, I can also promise a share of all loot captured when we are victorious."

"That might well suffice." The Veilwald worked the flannel under her armpits before casting it aside. "Assuming we are actually victorious."

"Of that, I've no doubt."

One corner of Synghild's mouth twitched before she reached for a plain woollen shift, pulling it over her head. "Such confidence, Vellihr. Two queens may have fallen, but it strikes me another one rises in the Isles."

"I have no wish for power. Only victory."

The Veilwald let out a short bark of mirth. "You talk like you have a choice. In times like these, choice is a luxury. Take me, for instance. Some might say I had a choice whether to kill all my children, but you and I know that I did not."

Her words brought a puzzled frown to Thera's brow as she remembered something. "Forgive me, Veilwald, but I was under the impression the Altvar had blessed you with four children. Or has some calamity befallen your third son? Teylhar, was it not?"

She saw the tendons in Synghild's neck stand out as she tightened a belt about her waist, the first true expression of anger Thera had seen from her. "Vellihr," she said, tone clipped, "while I am happy to lend all aid to our cause, if relations betwixt us are to remain cordial, please never speak that name to me again. I cast that wastrel from my hall two winters back, and have no cause to regret it."

Moving to a table, she poured a generous measure of mead into a tankard and raised it to her lips. "A word of advice, my friend," she said. "Never fuck drunk." Draining the tankard in a few gulps, she set it aside and reached for a pair of boots. "Now then, let's set about girding my mob of lazy bastards for war, shall we?"

CHAPTER TWENTY-TWO

Elvine

Intent on keeping her promise, the day after Fildra's funeral procession, Elvine returned to the market to give the bookseller the second coin. Once again she walked the streets of Skar Magnol unescorted. Rising that morning, she had descended Lore's Tower and taken a chance on simply striding through the Verungyr's main gate. The quartet of warriors offered only respectful nods as she passed by, untroubled by the sense of being observed. She knew that didn't necessarily mean anything; whoever Ilvar had set to watch her this day was probably just more skilled than those who had drawn Vahlak's notice. Although, recalling the Tuhlvyr's ire at discovering her observed status, she wondered if he might have interceded on her behalf.

Reaching the market, she found the diminutive bookseller absent. His stall had been taken by a woman selling inexpertly crafted trinkets who avowed no knowledge of the previous occupant. Elvine's questioning of the neighbouring stallholders elicited only nervous denials.

"Didn't know him," a nearby shoe peddler muttered when she pressed him for information as to where the bookseller made his home. "I'm not given to conversing with foreigners."

Seeing how the man avoided her gaze, she thought it best to leave him be and wandered the market for a time. While her ostensible reason for coming had been to settle a debt, she hoped Gruinskard's elusive servant might make an appearance. Yet, after an hour of fruitless and uninterrupted browsing, it became clear that this would be a doubly fruitless trip.

Before commencing the weary trudge back to the Verungyr, she had to quell the mischievous impulse to test her potentially unobserved status with an impromptu return to the Tielwald's house. While she might not be followed today, she was sure Ilvar had set a watch on Gruinskard's home.

Any further rummaging she would do there would surely attract the notice of Ilvar's agents. Elvine found she relished the possibility of offering an innocent face to his angry questions. *I merely recalled your words regarding another hidden store of documents, Vellihr Ilvar. Or is it your desire to prevent me properly serving our queen?* Although tempting, such a confrontation was also reckless, especially at a time when one of the Vellihr's spies had suffered a mysteriously sudden and fatal illness. She remembered what Colvyn had said about spying not being a game. *It's business, and it's deadly.*

The image of Fildra's bloodless, empty face returned as she made her way through the crowd. She and Berrine would meet with Aldunna today and Elvine didn't relish the confrontation, resolving to guard her words carefully lest the cook find further reason for murder. *A murder I ordered,* Elvine reminded herself.

Distracted by such dark pondering, she failed to note the angry shout of a stallholder or notice the small boy hurtling through the throng clutching a turnip. Their collision was painful, the lad's speed sending both he and Elvine into an untidy tumble.

"Grab that little fucker!" A red-faced man pushed through the crowd, lunging for the boy, but he proved too nimble. Scrambling free of Elvine's tangling legs, he spared her a quick, impish grin before sprinting away with his prize. The aggrieved turnip seller continued to shout as he lumbered in pursuit, but, given the thief's speed, Elvine didn't think much of his chances. None of the onlookers nearby appeared inclined to help her to her feet. Most averted their gazes for fear of arousing the ire of a queen's servant. Although, as she stood, she caught a few poorly concealed grins.

The tedium of the subsequent climb back to the Verungyr's gate was made worse by the bruise she had suffered to her hip. As she paused to rub at it, her gaze wandered to Linsker Fjord, whereupon she forgot her pains. When she departed the Verungyr that morning the fog had concealed much of Vahlak's fleet, but now she saw that the number of ships had thinned. Shifting her view to the eastern end of the fjord, she could see sails fading into the haze. They were too distant to count, but, after a swift survey of the remaining vessels, she estimated that about a third of the Nihlvarian ships previously at anchor off Skar Magnol had departed with the morning tide. The question as to where they were going summoned a shudder of panicked concern that Lore had finally launched her campaign against Olversahl. Yet, pondering further, she felt that unlikely. Although hardly expert in matters of war, Elvine knew taking a port of such size required a stronger force. The threat of intervention from Albermaine meant Vahlak would need as much strength as he could muster. *Then why send away so many now?*

Resuming her climb, she winced at a fresh ache in her hip and, as she reached lower to massage her protesting thigh muscle, she felt something small and hard beneath the fabric of her skirt. Exploring it, she identified a cylindrical shape a few inches long. The fact that it barely budged as she probed it made her realise it had been stuck to her skin with some kind of glue, pressed hard enough into her flesh to bruise, hence her ache. *The boy with the turnip*, she thought, recalling his fleeting grin.

Elvine resisted the urge to pluck the thing clear of her skirts for proper examination, wary of drawing the notice of the guards on the gate. Although, as she re-entered the stronghold, she found she had to conceal a grin of her own. As promised, Gruinskard's agent had found a way.

Opening the door to the tower, she drew up short at the sight of Lore and her brother engaged in a full-throated argument.

"Never leave an enemy at your back!" Vahlak shouted while his sister regarded him with an expression that came closest to outright rage that Elvine had seen upon her face. Anger, it transpired, could actually make the queen appear ugly. She faced Vahlak across the table, eyes blazing and features drawn in a veritable snarl. Although Elvine required no assistance in reading her mood, the spear's gift still deigned to display her aura as a roiling cloud of dark grey shot through with flashes of crimson lightning.

"Thera Speldrenda is not worthy of being called my enemy!" Lore shouted back. "She is barely even a distraction at this point. You piss our strength away while Olversahl lies ripe for the taking."

"And take it we will. Our intelligence is sound and the ships on hand are more than sufficient. Our respective roles were made clear to us years ago, Aylsa. Concern yourself with politics and leave war to me."

"They're the same fucking thing!"

The grey hue of Lore's aura darkened to near black, the luminescence coursing through it pulsing like veins swollen with blood. *Is that her mind?* Elvine wondered, unable to prevent herself staring in appalled fascination. *This is what she keeps hidden behind that perfect face.* Instinctively, she retreated from the sight, hoping to back out of the room without being noticed. However, the scrape of her foot on the floor tiles betrayed her.

As Lore turned to her, her aura changed with a jarring swiftness. The black storm became a confusion of colours while the crimson veins dissipated into a vague, pinkish web Elvine thought might signal annoyance, or at least the concern of one who had finally let slip her mask. Taking a deep breath, Lore straightened, resuming her regal bearing with practised alacrity. Casting a faintly rueful smile at Vahlak, she said, "We appear to have inadvertently provided my scholar with a demonstration of how we were as children, brother."

"A ghastly sight indeed." As usual, Vahlak lacked an aura, but Elvine could read the pitch of his embarrassment in his lowered gaze and tightened jaw. "One I would not visit upon anyone, but especially her." He inclined his head at Elvine. "My apologies, Scholar."

"Altogether unnecessary, Tuhlvyr," she replied, forcing a smile.

"In fact, I'm glad you're here, Elvine," Lore said. Her aura had diminished into a dark shimmer. Elvine couldn't tell if it indicated a reduction in her rage or simply greater self-control. "I believe," the queen continued, "Tuhlvyr Vahlak has waited long enough for the fruit of your researches into Olversahl."

"Time is not so pressing," Vahlak said. "The flotilla I sent east required most of our stores. I'll need another ten days for additional provisioning—"

"Excessive caution will not aid us now," Lore cut in. "Your fleet can resupply itself from the stores captured at Olversahl, with the aid of my scholar's detailed intelligence, of course." Although just as practised as usual, the slight increase in Lore's aura indicated her smile required some effort. "Assuming it's ready."

Meeting her expectant stare, Elvine abruptly became aware of two things. The first was the as yet unexamined object glued to her thigh. The second was the Spear of the Altvar residing in its iron cradle upon the table no more than three steps away. *Kill her.* At first, she thought the instruction came from the spear. But, given that she wasn't touching it, she quickly recognised it as her own. *Kill her and save Olversahl.* One quick lunge to grab the weapon, another to thrust it through Lore's slender throat. Vahlak would be near certain to cut Elvine down a heartbeat later, but what was one life weighed against so many?

"Elvine?" Lore prompted as Elvine's gaze lingered on the spear. "Are you well?"

"Apologies, my queen." Elvine swallowed a cough. "The document is prepared. I intended to show it you before providing the finished version to Tuhlvyr Vahlak."

"No need. I have the fullest confidence in your abilities, you know that. Fetch it and we shall allow my brother to be about his most urgent business."

Nodding, Elvine hurried to her chamber. Behind her, a more quietly voiced argument commenced between the siblings.

"This is foolish," Vahlak said. "Stretching our forces so thin while so much remains unconquered."

"It is more vital than ever to seize Olversahl now before the winter storms come. Remember, I know this realm and you do not."

Closing the door to her chamber, Elvine slumped against the wall, weakened by relief and self-reproach. *Why couldn't I kill her?* The question raged in her head, loud enough to make her choke down a sob, for she knew well the answer. *Because I still want to live.*

Moving to gather the papers containing her detailed and unedited report on Olversahl, she found a crumb of solace in a singular realisation: she had learned Lore's true name. *Aylsa.* It was not a name she had heard before, but there was one who might.

"It's a fragmentary tale," Berrine said. After Elvine had told her the name, her mother's brow creased in the manner that indicated a deep delve into the well of her archivist's memory. "Not included in the Altvar Rendi, I imagine due to it being incomplete."

"But it's connected to the Altvar?" Elvine asked. "Could Aylsa be some forgotten god of the Lower Hall?"

"No, but the story goes that she was born of one, if born is the right word. Ihryka, the divine trickster, found herself shunned for her endless deceit by the Uhltvar warrior Holsvein, one of many mortal lovers, but the only one to truly win her heart. Intent on reclaiming his love, she concocted a plan to present him with a daughter as the fruit of their union. But Ihryka's womb was barren, a punishment for her villainy inflicted by the Worldsmith himself. And so she took clay from the earth, and mixing it with her moon blood, did form it into a living babe she named Aylsa. For a time, her plan worked, for Holsvein was of noble heart and would not shun his own issue. Succoured by the warmth of his hall, the child grew into a maiden of great beauty, with her father's strength but her mother's passion for dark design. Jealous of her brothers, she poisoned Holsvein's mind against them, so much so that they were all exiled from his lands. Thereafter, Holsvein sickened as Aylsa dripped a nightly dose of poison into his meals. The story ends with Holsvein's three sons returning from exile to save their father and reclaim their birthright, but the outcome is not recorded." Berrine sighed a humourless laugh. "Whatever Lore might be, it seems she is at least well named."

"One mystery solved," Elvine said, her mother frowning as she gathered up her skirts to reveal the object glued to her thigh. "Now, you must help me solve another."

The cylinder was fashioned from wood and its presence had grown ever more uncomfortable over the course of several hours. The flesh surrounding the thing had taken on a maddening itch, irritated by the glue that held it in place. Fortunately, the mingling of oil and sweat on her skin had combined to weaken the substance. Removing it still stung, however, but at least she suffered no injury in the process. The wooden cylinder appeared completely solid until Elvine noticed a seam halfway along its length. She had to scrape away more glue to pull it apart, revealing a scrolled scrap of parchment.

"What is that?" Berrine said, mystified by the scroll's seemingly abstract contents.

"I've no idea." Elvine could find nothing in her memory to correspond to the symbol on the parchment; seven intersecting lines, some shorter than others. From Berrine's baffled shake of the head, it had plainly defeated her too. The only other mark of interest was a small line of script in a language or cypher beyond Elvine's knowledge.

"Looks vaguely like Ishtan," she said, squinting at the characters. "A dialect from the eastern reaches of the empire, perhaps?"

"No, it's courtly script." Berrine went to a small chest in the corner of the chamber, opening it to rummage briefly before returning with a small steel mirror. "Reversed writing," she said, settling the reflective metal alongside the scribbled words. "One of Gruinskard's favourite tricks."

Although still riven by nerves after her meeting with Lore and Vahlak, Elvine managed to conjure a delighted smile at the sight of the reflected script, now completely legible. "'When Gahil Din Fahrik walked the shadowed path,'" she murmured.

"You know it?" Berrine asked.

"You should expand your studies beyond Ascarlian lore, Mother. The 'Trials of Gahil Din Fahrik' stand tall in Ishtan legend. He was a fabled explorer and adventurer, collector of rare treasures, and frequent rescuer of imperilled maidens. The tale of the Shadowed Path sees him venture into the catacombs beneath an evil sorcerer's castle in order to save a kidnapped princess."

"And how does that help us?"

"Because the entrance to the catacombs was made via a secret passage he discovered in the sorcerer's wine cellar." She picked up the parchment, displaying the symbol. "This, I believe, is the key to finding another."

The Verungyr possessed several vaults filled with casks of mead, ale and brandy, but only one given over to wine. Berrine had wanted to accompany her, but Elvine insisted on going alone. "Gruinskard's agent will expect me, but not you. From what I gather, he's the type who won't react well to the unexpected."

Although tempted to return to the tower and await nightfall, she opted to go immediately. Coming and going at odd hours was bound to attract notice and making the trip while some daylight remained would arouse less suspicion. Should she be challenged, Elvine would claim she had come to choose a bottle of wine as a gift for Vahlak. Such a display of apparent affection would be bound to please the queen.

Berrine insisted she take a knife, strapping it about her calf and making her practise drawing it free several times over. "If you have to use it, go for the neck," she said. "Strike swiftly and don't stop until he's down."

"You suspect a trap?"

"In this nest of traitors, we have little choice but to suspect everyone and everything."

Descending the narrow spiral stairwell to the vaults with lantern in hand, Elvine peered into several arched chambers until she found the wine store. First, she sought out a bottle of suitably impressive vintage in case an inquisitive guard appeared. The chosen wine hailed from Alundia, the most southern of Albermaine's duchies. Thanks to her tenure at Olversahl's docks, Elvine recognised the wax seal on the cork, which marked the wine as the product of the duke's own vineyards.

Consigning the bottle to her satchel, she began to scour the store for the symbol from the parchment. Close to an hour of profitless searching later, she started to wonder if her satisfaction at deciphering the riddle had been misplaced. She cast the light into every corner of the chamber, cleared cobwebs from racks and shelves, and swept dust from ancient glass, all to no avail.

"How did Din Fahrik find it?" Elvine muttered. She had read various versions of the tale but recalled one that described how the intrepid adventurer had found the entrance behind the lid of a huge wine cask. To open it, he had to turn the tap four times in a counterclockwise direction, one turn for each of the cornerstones of wisdom beloved by Ishtan philosophers. This wine store didn't feature a huge cask. Instead, it had a row of barrels lined up against a wall. From the depth of the cobwebs and dust covering them, their contents had either been exhausted or long ignored. She had already inspected the barrels, finding nothing of interest, but the tale of Din Fahrik caused her to look again. Yet the lantern revealed only old, scarred wood and no sign of the seven intersecting lines. *Fahrik had four cornerstones. I have seven scratches.* She paused as the notion stirred a fresh conclusion.

Seven, she thought, counting the barrels. *Seven lines. Seven barrels.*

She began another, more thorough examination, performed with the aid of clearing away the cobwebs and dust, much to her begrimed and choking annoyance. Once cleaned, she found that the lids of each barrel bore a scratch that was deeper than the others. Surveying them all, she noted that each scratch was in roughly the same place but had been carved in differing directions. Unfurling the scroll, her excited eyes saw that, were each scratch on the barrel lids to be combined into one mark, they would be identical to the symbol.

Smothering a delighted laugh at her discovery, Elvine pressed a hand to the closest lid, feeling it give. It was a small movement, but not one any reputable cooper would have allowed in a barrel. Removing her hand, she waited, but nothing happened. She tried again with the other. The same slight movement, but no result when she removed the pressure.

A sequence? she wondered, looking again at the parchment and noting the mismatched length of each line. *Shortest to longest or the other way around?* Shrugging, she opted to try pressing the lid with the shortest scratch first, then the second shortest, and so on. With all seven lids pressed, she stood back and waited, breath stilled in anticipation. After several more laboured heartbeats, her optimism faded, and she resolved to try again.

The muted rumble of shifting stone came as she reached for the barrel with the longest scratch, the unexpectedness of it causing Elvine to almost drop her lantern. The casks vibrated as the sound continued, now joined by the grind of some hidden mechanism. An echoing boom heralded a sudden halt to the barrels' shudders, whereupon the one in the centre receded into the wall behind. All sound ceased as Elvine stooped to gaze into a dark portal about three feet high and the same wide. Glancing over her shoulder, she detected no sign of another presence. Still, while her pulse had calmed, she retained a strong sense of transgression. She felt sure this revealed passage was unknown to Lore, and probably had been equally unknown to the fallen queens. This thing was of the Tielwald's making, a secret way into and out of the Verungyr.

Slipping to her knees, she held the lantern out before her, the glow illuminating only the curve of the receded barrel and a small portion of the passage's interior. Crawling forward, she wrinkled her nose at the musty redolence of a place undisturbed for years. She had to squeeze past the barrel to enter the passage proper, the lantern illuminating a long straight tunnel with rough-hewn walls streaked in damp. Even for one of such slight dimensions as herself, making her way along it proved an uncomfortably constricted task. Elvine made a point to count her steps, reckoning she had covered fifty paces by the time the tunnel broadened into a junction where two other tunnels branched off. Unsure which one to take, she halted and cast lantern light into the passage on the left when a softly spoken voice brought her to an abrupt halt.

"Didn't take you as long to reckon it out as I thought. He said you were a clever one."

The voice was male and came from the tunnel to the right. It mostly lacked inflection, however Elvine detected a faint note of strain to it, as if its flatness was the result of some effort on the part of the speaker. "The . . ." she began, faltering thanks to the combination of the tainted air and trepidation. Swallowing, she forced the words out. "The Tielwald sent me . . ."

"I know." A face appeared from the shadow of the tunnel mouth. It was narrow and beardless, bordering on handsome if it hadn't been so sharp of nose and chin. His hair was paler than his skin, cropped short in the Albermaine-ish manner, though his accent was pure Ascarlian. Like his voice, his expression was stripped of emotion, but his gaze held a piercing quality as it tracked Elvine from head to toe. "You are the queen's scholar," he said. "As I am the Tielwald's servant in all things."

"He said your name was Hahlfur," Elvine said.

The sharp-faced man straightened as he emerged from the tunnel, Elvine finding herself distracted by the fineness of his clothing. Clad in an expertly tailored jerkin and trews, hemmed with silver thread, and a sable-trimmed cloak, he resembled more an Albermaine-ish noble than a native Ascarlian. "No," he said, voice as flat as before. "He didn't. But he did tell you my true name. What is it?"

As he spoke, his aura flared into life around him, Elvine smothering a gasp at the sight. It was the ugliest she had seen so far, a coiling mess of colour surrounding his form, black tendrils shifting like snakes, each one tipped in red. While his bearing betrayed no threat, his aura left her in no doubt of the danger this man posed. More than the colours was the sensation it birthed in her, as if she could sense the inner chaos of emotions that produced it. Lust, anger and a need to hurt all swirled together, kept in check by a sickening wall of hate. While his other emotions were all projected outwards, the hatred was the opposite. *He detests himself above all*, Elvine realised, taking an involuntary step back even though he made no move to approach her.

"My name," the man insisted, the faint but potent edge now colouring his voice reminded Elvine of the knife strapped to her calf. "What is it?"

"No," she said, annoyed by the tremble accompanying the refusal. Showing fear in front of one such as this was a very poor idea. "You tell me your name, since you evidently know mine."

His aura flared, the coiling dark snakes spasming, although his features showed no change at all. Elvine concealed a shudder as she felt the accompanying emotion: outrage mixed with a contrasting delight. *He wants to hurt me very much*, she concluded, recalling Gruinskard's warning about his servant. *His appetites can sometimes get the better of his loyalty.* Suddenly, her hidden knife felt worryingly out of reach.

"Coelnyr." He spoke the name with the same absence of inflection, the animation of his aura calming.

"I bring a message from the Tielwald—" she began, but Coelnyr cut her off.

"I am to arrange passage from this port. I know. The arrangements are in motion." He inclined his head at the tunnel to his back. "This leads through the mountain to a bay on the northern shore. In three days' time a boat will be waiting there. It will linger from midnight for one hour only."

"Three days," Elvine repeated. "I understand."

"I hope you do. For if the Tielwald is not with you, the boat leaves empty."

This wasn't unexpected. Gruinskard would hardly have troubled himself if not to facilitate his own escape. "Very well," Elvine said. "I shall also be bringing my mother and an Albermaine-ish prisoner. And Aldunna, if she wishes it. I suppose you know her name, too."

"I do. Three days, Scholar. This will be your last opportunity. I urge you not to waste it."

Then he was gone, slipping into the shadow of the tunnel without a sound. As she turned to go, Elvine realised she couldn't hear the echo of his footfalls. Drawing her knife, she kept her eyes on the junction as she retreated back towards the wine store. She didn't turn around until she was forced to crawl through the passage entrance. Closing it required pressing a hand to the barrel lids in reverse sequence. With the tunnel sealed, she let out a long sigh, beset by an urgent need to bathe. Climbing the stairs to the upper halls of the Verungyr, she resolved that, should Gruinskard's servant present the slightest threat during their escape, she would have Colvyn kill him, regardless of how much use the old man saw in so wretched and perverted a soul.

CHAPTER TWENTY-THREE

Ruhlin

A leida and Guthnyr had both wanted to accompany him, but Tirohk
forbade it, stating that only Ruhlin *Telchak* would be welcome at
the impending gathering of elders.

"And what if I don't give a shit for your elders?" Guthnyr growled, resting
a hand on the hilt of his new sword.

"Then you'll die less than a mile from this mountain." Turning to Ruhlin,
the Morvek inclined his head at the valley below. "We must go."

Ruhlin had hoped to show Tirohk the fruits of the forge, the opening
gambit in what might be a mutually beneficial negotiation. But the man's
evident urgency and tension made it clear there was no time for such niceties. Whatever awaited Ruhlin at the gathering of elders was clearly of grave
import. So, he tarried long enough only to collect his maul, some provisions
for the journey, and a cloth-wrapped bundle he hoped would prove useful
in what lay ahead.

"If I don't return . . ." he told Aleida, falling silent when she held a finger
to his lips.

"You will," she said. "She won't allow any harm to you." She nodded to
the bear, now shambling free of the mineshaft. As the beast paused to yawn,
scratching a claw to its neck, Ryma tottered up to it. Laughing, she raised
her arms, expectant of another ride upon its back. Her laughter turned to
a pout when the beast licked its long tongue over her face but failed to
lower itself and allow her to climb aboard. Ryma's stern disappointment
transformed into tears when the bear started down the slope to the valley
floor. Aleida gave Ruhlin a swift fierce embrace, then hurried to gather up
the weeping child.

"I'm not happy about this," Guthnyr said when Ruhlin clasped hands with
him. There was a calculating glint in the warrior's eye that made Ruhlin pause.

"Don't try to follow," he said. "These lands are not ours, remember? Besides, I would ask that you stay and watch over my family and our friends. With me gone, they will look to you."

Guthnyr's beard shifted in a reluctant grimace. "Then you'd best hurry back. My last attempt at leadership did not end well."

Ruhlin expected Tirohk to prove a taciturn companion but, once through the valley and into the rolling hills beyond, the Morvek became a persistent source of questions.

"You were a warrior in your land?" he asked as they crested a rise. Up ahead, the bear's dark bulk stood out against the snow-covered slope. It had led throughout the day and Ruhlin wondered how it knew the route to follow. *Aleida's aunt must have walked these lands in life,* he realised. *And perhaps attended an elders' gathering.*

"A fisherman," he replied. "Like my father before me. Though he had been a warrior in his youth and fought battles in distant lands."

"Then he taught you to fight?"

"No. Learned that myself, with some help from an Aerling's whip-man. My father never let me touch a hand to a weapon. For many years, I thought it due to his dislike of war, for I could tell his taste of battle had been bitter. Now I know he worried training me in combat would rouse the monster."

Tirohk frowned. "Monster? What is this word?"

"It's what I call the thing inside me. A great and terrible creature conjured into being by my worst instincts."

"I thought your kind saw you as blessed by your gods."

"Some do. I don't. *Telchak* you call me; cursed one. It feels more fitting."

The Morvek's questions continued throughout the day. Where had Ruhlin been born? What manner of place was Ayl-Ah-Swahl? He seemed particularly interested in Ascarlian customs, reacting with both bafflement and curiosity to their form of governance.

"You are ruled by three women? And they are all sisters?"

"Not blood sisters. It's a title. The queens are not born to their role, but chosen after many years' service. It ensures wise rule untroubled by prior allegiance to family or forebear. Such things have often been the downfall of many a realm." Seeing the puzzlement lingering on Tirohk's brow, he asked, "Do the Morvek not have rulers? Are you not a chieftain of the *Vehlkasa*?"

"War chief only," Tirohk grunted. "When there's no one to fight, they stop listening to me."

"So, there are other kinds of chiefs?"

"Of course. There is the chief of healing, the chief of hunting, the chief of reading the stars, another who reads the wind and the moods of the earth. We had a chief of wisdom, but she died last winter and another is yet to prove themselves fit."

"But there is no chief set above the others?"

"One cannot be set above another, for all hearts are worthy in different ways." Tirohk paused to survey the landscape ahead, pointing his spear at a tree-filled gulley. "We'll camp there tonight and you can tell me more about these white-skinned great fish that eat people."

"They're whales," Ruhlin corrected. "And, so far as I know, they only kill people. They don't eat them."

"Why?"

"No one is entirely sure, except that they dislike us a great deal."

As daylight ebbed, they encamped beneath the trees and crafted a fire, the bear settling down nearby to fill the chill night air with a steady grate of snoring. Tirohk had finally lapsed into silence. However, from the tension in his jaw, Ruhlin could tell he still had more to ask. "Iyaka," the Morvek said finally. "You were slaves together."

"We were. Bought by the Aerling Eldryk to fight in the Meidvang, so that he might win the approval of the Tuhlvyrs." Ruhlin sighed as he contemplated Eldryk's fate, wondering why it failed to summon more than vague satisfaction tinged with a regret he didn't fully understand. The man had been terrible, to his daughter as well as his captives. Yet his desperate desire for the favour of those set above him had been pathetic, even tragic. Ruhlin also knew that taking her father's life had hurt Aleida more than she would ever admit.

"So, Iyaka suffered the whip?" Tirohk went on. He sat with his back hunched, staring into the fire, hands enfolded in a tight double fist. "And was tormented into fighting?"

"We all were," Ruhlin said. Concerned that Iyaka's captivity might have dishonoured her in the eyes of other Morvek, he added, "She was also among the first to agree to join me in trying to escape. Without her, we would most likely all be dead."

Tirohk let out a soft grunt, but said no more, continuing to gaze into the fire with a troubled frown upon his brow. For a time, Ruhlin debated the wisdom of voicing the question poised on his lips, but decided the answer might prove useful.

"She said you were married," he ventured.

Tirohk's eyes flicked to meet his. "For a time," he said. "Morvek are not like the *Rulchakin*. We do not marry for life, though some unions last longer than others." He surprised Ruhlin by grunting a laugh. "Iyaka was my sixth wife, and our marriage was by far the shortest. The old chief of wisdom to the *Vehlkasa* had a saying: 'Even when fashioned from the same branch and shot from the same bow, no two arrows will ever fly the same course.' So it was with us. Iyaka was ever restless, driven by the old ones' tales to venture over the mountains and see our enemy with her own eyes. I felt no such urge, having witnessed my fill of them when I joined a war party in my youth. We killed some and captured a few. It's how I learned your tongue. It dismayed me to find that the *Rulchakin* were neither ravening beasts nor cunning wielders of strange powers. They were stupider than us, it's true. Greedier too, and prone to such a depth of hatred, it was as if their pestilent gods had engraved it upon their bones. But, at heart, they were not so different. I soon came to understand that they had stolen so much from us simply because there were more of them, and they had weapons of steel.

"I told all this to Iyaka, but she didn't listen. So intent was she on her mission to walk the lands stolen by the *Rulchakin* and learn their weaknesses. 'One day we will sweep them back into the sea that birthed them,' she told me. I told her to forget her mad scheme and be content." He laughed again. "She did not react well. Her leaving was a great loss to the *Vehlkasa*, more so than we realised at the time. One day she might have become the chief of wisdom, but now she is too sullied by *Rulchakin* ways. I see it, their hatred, burning in her veins like a sickness."

"She has much to avenge. As do all Morvek, judging by what I have seen."

"Do not make the mistake of thinking us all of one mind. As you'll find when we stand before the elders, it's a rare thing for Morvek to agree on anything. Despite what some claim, this was not a peaceful land before the *Rulchakin* came. The clans have always warred with each other, and were not merciful in victory. On the third moon of every year, the *Vehlkasa* feast and sing songs to celebrate the day they wiped out the people who once made their homes in these very hills. A wise man would have thought that the coming of the *Rulchakin* would have united us. It did not. We war less these days only because there are less of us to fight. Discord has ever been our way." His gaze grew sharper as he turned it upon Ruhlin. "Except when it comes to you. The *Telchak*, as all elders know, is the herald of change. Iyaka knows it too. Why else would she try so hard to bring you to us?"

"She didn't. She led us into Morvek lands because we had no choice. We tried to steal a ship, but it burned."

"And how did it come to burn?"

Ruhlin thought back to their attempt to seize the slave ship in Speltsaer.

Iyaka and the other Morvek had followed Sygurn to the bow while he and Aleida made for the stern. Until now, he had assumed the fire broke out due to a lantern shattered in the chaos of combat, or a Nihlvarian sailor unwilling to lose his vessel to a mob of escaped slaves. *She couldn't persuade us to follow her,* Ruhlin concluded. *So left us no choice.*

"Don't be too angry with her," Tirohk said, lying down and resting his head on a rolled deer hide. "She believes you will be our revenge. The long-promised gift who will return to us all the *Rulchakin* stole."

"And what do you believe?"

Tirohk didn't reply at first, Ruhlin watching the firelight dance in his eyes until he closed them and turned onto his side. "I believe you don't yet know what you are," he said. "So how can you truly be the *Telchak?*"

They travelled for four more days, making their way through the snow-covered hill country and across a plain where Ruhlin saw a great herd of shaggy, wild cattle. They covered at least half a mile square and were too numerous to be easily counted. Their size was beyond any similar beast Ruhlin had seen before, standing over six feet at the shoulder, each bearing a pair of long, curved horns they used to tease grass from the snow in order to graze. "*Altahnk*", Tirohk called them, insisting on keeping a distance from the herd. However, when the wind shifted, the mingled scent of human and bear caused a disturbance in their ranks, raising a lowing chorus as several trotted towards the intruders. Fortunately, they soon abandoned their pursuit when Tirohk ordered Ruhlin to run, although the Morvek insisted they maintain the pace until the herd was a long way to their rear. For its part, the bear had ignored the *altahnk*, continuing to plod along without deigning to increase its speed.

After another day's journey, a broken green line appeared on the horizon, thickening into a forest as they drew closer. The white dappled trees stretched away to either side as far as Ruhlin could see, causing him to stop and stare in unabashed wonder.

"The *Teyracha,*" Tirohk said. "The Green Heart, in your tongue. The greatest forest in all Morvek lands, perhaps in all lands everywhere." Although he spoke with a note of pride, Ruhlin saw the caution in his gaze as the wall of trees loomed closer.

"You've been here before?" he asked.

"Once. It is home to the *Teyrak*. They do not welcome the *Vehlkasa*. 'Mountain dogs' they call us." He grinned. "We call them 'tree fuckers.'"

Despite evident trepidation, Tirohk's steps didn't falter as they ventured into the shade beneath the trees. The bear, curiously, was more circumspect.

Halting at the forest's edge, it sniffed the air, huffing and swinging its great head up and down.

"What is it doing?" Ruhlin asked Tirohk, receiving a shrug in response. "Why do you think I know?"

Ruhlin's mystification deepened when the bear lowered itself to its belly, paws extended and head laid upon the ground. It remained in the same position for some time until a gentle gust of wind rippled the bushes and drew a creak from the branches above. He heard a clear note of satisfaction in the bear's grunt as it raised itself up and plodded past its human companions, the shaggy brown bulk soon swallowed by the trees.

"We should keep up," Tirohk said. "I think she knows the path we should follow."

"Meaning you don't?"

Before spurring to a run, Tirohk glanced back at him with an amused cast to his brow. "Of course I don't. I've been following her since we left the mountain."

Running through a forest, it transpired, was a tricky business, especially in winter. Drifts often concealed deep ruts or treacherous roots. Their pursuit was also frustrated by the bear's speed. The animal made no concession for their two-legged slowness, and it wasn't long before they lost sight of its loping bulk.

"What now?" Ruhlin asked as he and Tirohk came to a halt, breath steaming. The Morvek gave no answer and Ruhlin saw that his companion's composure had been supplanted by a deep, busy-eyed wariness. Sweat beaded Tirohk's skin as he gripped his spear tighter, gaze darting from one shadow to another. Ruhlin was about to suggest they wait for the bear to return when he heard a soft crunch of snow to his rear. He whirled towards the sound, but Tirohk was faster, dropping into a crouch with his spear levelled at the shape emerging from the frosted undergrowth. Ruhlin's attention was instantly snared by the creature's teeth, long and white in a maw quivered by an ominous growl. A pair of yellow eyes blazed above a wrinkled nose, framed by silver-grey fur. The sight summoned the memory of the dog that had once menaced him on the shore of Ayl-Ah-Swahl, inevitably rousing the monster from its slumber.

The heat building in his core flared brighter as more snarling faces loomed out of the trees, Ruhlin turning to find they were encircled. He had heard stories of wolves all his life, but never seen one with his own eyes. They were larger than he expected, making him wonder if these were a breed distinct from those in Ascarlia. The monster, however, had no interest in such conjecture. As ever, when faced with a threat, it responded in kind.

Ruhlin felt the bones of his spine begin to strain as muscle swelled across his back, the tendons of his neck thickening into rope-like cords. A familiar crimson mist began to cloud the edges of his vision as the monster answered the wolves with a growl of its own. He felt a pulse of amusement at Tirohk's startled face. The Morvek retreated, uncaring of showing his back to the wolves as he found himself in proximity to something far more dangerous. The wolves were also alarmed by the monster's burgeoning appearance, but not cowed. Withdrawing a few paces, they continued to snarl until a sharp female voice cut through the bestial chorus.

"*Tek, tahw aktcha!*"

The pack's silence was jarring in its suddenness, each wolf retreating further with ears flat and brows creased as they stared at the woman striding through the snow. She was tall and clad in buckskin garb like Tirohk, a cloak of rabbit pelts about her shoulders, her long hair an inky cloud in the breeze. Ruhlin felt the monster calm as she drew nearer, caused either by the removal of a threat or the fascination he saw in the woman's face. Her features were paler than other Morvek, and seemingly youthful. Her eyes, however, were not those of a young woman. Despite the absence of creases, he saw a depth of insight that spoke of much hard-won experience. She continued to stare in unabashed examination as Ruhlin recovered his prior form, her eyes narrowing at the sight of shrinking vein and muscle. When she spoke, it was in the Nihlvarian dialect, but far more accented than Tirohk's more practised tones.

"Does it hurt?" she asked.

"More so at first," Ruhlin said, seeing no reason for dishonesty. "Not as much now."

She shook her head, something he read as an expression of consternation rather than disagreement. "A curse should hurt," she murmured, then frowned in irritation when Tirohk addressed her.

"We come for the gathering . . ."

"I know why you've come, *ka-tchen!*" she snapped. "Even though you are not needed." She nodded at Ruhlin. "Only him."

"The *Vehlkasa* must have a voice here. Our *Krisch-tuhk* has not yet been chosen. So I, Tirohk, will speak as war chief."

"Then I hope you speak better than you fight."

Tirohk bridled at this, glowering and raising his spear while the woman glared back and her wolves resumed their growling. The patent antipathy Ruhlin saw between these two might well have escalated if the bear had not reappeared. While the wolves had been wary of the monster, they were instantly afraid of the bear. Whining, they clustered around the woman, somewhat to her annoyance. Castigating them in what sounded like an insult in the Morvek tongue, she spared the bear a grimace of annoyance before turning back to Ruhlin.

"I see you brought an elder, after all."

"She has been our guide," he said. Curious as to how the woman might react, he added, "Her name was once Achela. Though, I know not her clan—"

"She never had one," the woman cut in. Sighing, she beckoned to them to follow as she began to walk away. "I am Velkar, *Krisch-tuhk* to the *Teyrak*. I will guide you to the *Vikra-sah*."

Ruhlin assumed this word meant "gathering", but from the way Tirohk hesitated at the sound of it, he wasn't so sure. "What does it mean?" Ruhlin asked him, but the Morvek was already hurrying to catch up with the woman. Ruhlin felt certain he was trying to avoid his gaze.

The wolves fanned out to either side as they made their way through the forest. Velkar walked in silence, casting occasional glances at Ruhlin that worried him more than her bestial coterie. If he truly was the *Telchak* of Morvek legend, supposedly some kind of promised saviour, then would not his arrival be an occasion for joyous celebration? But he saw no joy in the furrow of this woman's brow. She, he was sure, looked upon him as a mystifying and unwelcome complication, if not an outright threat.

A trek of about a mile brought a thinning of the trees and a scent of woodsmoke. Soon people began to appear, all clad in similar garb to Velkar and Tirohk, but with subtle variations to clothing and adornment that marked them as hailing from different clans. Some wore white beads braided into their hair, others amber. Many had faces daubed in various hues of red and blue, but most were undecorated. However, they were unified in the unrestrained fascination with which they regarded Ruhlin. He counted a few dozen at first, then several more. By the time he reached a hundred, he stopped trying to gauge the size of this gathering. The clans of the Morvek, it was plain, had a great many elders. More curious was the fact that, for the most part, they weren't particularly old. He caught sight of a few aged faces among the throng, but the majority, while certainly possessing more years than he did, would not be termed old in his homeland. "Elder", he realised, was merely a poor translation of a Morvek word carrying a different meaning.

They stood among shelters similar to those Iyaka and the other freed Morvek had fashioned at the village. However, these had a less permanent appearance, and the campfires leaking smoke into the air were small and recently crafted. This was a temporary encampment established by people who had arrived not long before he had. As with Velkar, Ruhlin saw no jubilation here, only stern and wary inspection. As they made their way through the loose ranks of elders, he began to resent the weight of their collective examination, a small kernel of heat stirring the monster to a soft but potent inner growl.

The crowd thinned as they came to the edge of a slope. The forest had fallen away completely here, leaving a wide clearing around a bowl-shaped depression in the ground. It made for a curious sight. The bare earth that formed its sides was darker than seemed natural, also lacking even the smallest speck of snow. Its base was a mass of overlapping tree roots and fallen trunks, all long rotted into near abstraction. This tangle of dead vegetation stretched away for at least a mile, the ugly scar upon the forest forming a long, shallow vale.

"The *Vikra-sah*," Velkar said, and Ruhlin understood the meaning of the word: *the Hollow.*

He noticed that her perennial frown now held an expectant cast. He saw it also in the silent, watchful faces of the other Morvek lining the edge of this curious feature.

"What is this place?" he asked.

"The *Telchak* would know." A tall man pushed his way through the throng. He marginally exceeded Tirohk in stature, his broad chest clad in a bearskin vest that left his thickly muscled arms bare. His hair was shaved down to the scalp and his face painted with a black stripe across his nose and upper cheeks. His Nihlvarian dialect was coarser than either Velkar or Tirohk, its harshness matched by the hostile demand writ large in his expression. Turning, he addressed the gathering, this time in Morvek. From the brevity of the statement, Ruhlin concluded he was repeating his words for the benefit of those not familiar with the *Rulchakin* tongue.

"This one knows nothing," the stripe-faced man went on, turning to gesture at Ruhlin with one of the long-hafted, narrow-bladed hatchets favoured by the Morvek. "He speaks not our words." He stepped closer, Ruhlin clenching his jaw as the monster growled again, sensing an increasing threat. "And—" he poked at Ruhlin's chest with his hatchet "—he is weak."

"He is not," Tirohk stated. "I have seen his strength. So has she." He jerked his head at Velkar. "He is the *Telchak*." Stepping forward, he raised his voice to cast a long statement in Morvek to the elders. Judging by the murmured voices and exchanged glances, all lacking any indication of agreement, Ruhlin felt a dispiriting certainty that Tirohk's words had fallen on mostly deaf ears.

"You speak as an elder," the man with the hatchet said. "But are not. You claim wisdom, but have none."

"I speak as *Vakil-tuhk* of the *Vehlkasa*," Tirohk returned with a dangerous glower. "We, who for seasons uncounted, have stood against the *Rulchakin* while you, *Sohlcha* dog, cower on the other side of your lakes."

The hatchet wielder snarled at this, shoulders hunching into a fighting stance. One Tirohk was quick to match. The confrontation ignited a wave of discord throughout the throng. Murmured voices grew into shouts as men and women jostled each other in a stark demonstration of Tirohk's words: *It's a rare thing for Morvek to agree on anything.*

The chorus of raised and increasingly angry voices grew louder as Tirohk and the *Sohlcha* elder began to circle each other, weapons poised. Ruhlin looked to Velkar, hoping she might have enough authority to calm the rising storm. But her face showed only weary disgust as her wolves drew close around her. He considered calling out to the gathering, but what could he say? Most of those present surely couldn't understand his words, and he had no inkling of what might be expected of him in this place. Seeing Tirohk poised to deliver the first blow, Ruhlin resolved to call out regardless, but a new, rhythmic sound forestalled him. It wasn't particularly loud, a repeated crack of wood upon wood, but it swiftly captured the notice of the gathering. Voices stilled, and the jostling ended. Tirohk and the *Sohlcha* elder straightened and stepped away from each other, all eyes turning to regard a small figure making its way through the parting throng, clacking two sticks together.

With silence restored, the figure came to a halt, planting both sticks upon the ground to rest its weight upon them while peering at Ruhlin with a narrow squint. Returning the scrutiny, Ruhlin beheld what must surely be the oldest of these elders. The bunched features were creased and weathered like old wood, the figure's back bent, a human being so old that Ruhlin found it difficult to discern their gender until they spoke.

"I apologise," the voice began, the cracked, rasping tones that of a man. "For my people." He began to hobble closer, planting each of his sticks with careful deliberation. "We are unpractised in greeting visitors." His wizened lips formed a smile as he came to a halt, a measure of humour showing in his narrowed gaze. Unlike any Morvek Ruhlin had encountered so far, his Ascarlian lacked an accent. But for the aged tones, it would have resembled the cultured delivery of an Aerling or Tuhlvyr.

Pausing, the old man cast a baleful eye at his fellow Morvek, none of whom were willing to meet his gaze. Ruhlin caught a flash of sullen resentment on the face of Tirohk's would-be opponent, but it was plain he didn't dare raise his voice. *Cowed by a small old man*, Ruhlin thought, looking closer at the figure before him.

"I am Olchar," the old man said, inclining his head in greeting. "*Krisch-tuhk* to the *Vulksa*, the people of the western plains. I bid you welcome to our lands."

Ruhlin returned the gesture, patting his chest. "Ruhlin ehs Kestryg, of Ayl-Ah-Swahl in the realm of Ascarlia."

A soft grunt escaped Olchar's lips. "A place I have heard of, but often wondered if it might be no more than *Rulchakin* legend." He came closer still, the many wrinkles of his ancient brow deepening as his scrutiny increased. Despite his age, there was no cloudiness to his eyes, their gleaming insight putting Ruhlin in mind of a kestrel eyeing prey. The thought stirred another growl from the monster, one that didn't reach his lips. Nevertheless, the fractional widening of Olchar's gaze convinced Ruhlin the old man had heard it.

"So, here you are at last," Olchar murmured, lowering his head with a sorrowful shake. The collective hush of the gathering continued as the bent-backed ancient remained still, broken only by the faint, grating breaths of his labouring chest. Finally, the old man looked up. Straightening as much as his crooked spine would allow, he turned and called out to the other elders in a surprisingly strong voice: "*Telchak ver chtaw ka!*"

While the meaning was lost to Ruhlin, the words had an immediate effect. The murmuring resumed, but the fractiousness from moments before had vanished. All eyes now regarded Ruhlin with a mix of awe, fear and wary anticipation.

"*Krisch vora resk sahkra Vikra-sah lohs chtaw!*" Olchar proclaimed, raising his sticks for emphasis, although he was only able to hold them aloft for a short, trembling instant. As the gathering engaged in voluble and excited discussion, the elder turned to Ruhlin with his face set in an apologetic cast.

"I told them the truth I see, Ruhlin ehs Kestryg," he said. "You may be the *Telchak*, but for us to know with no shred of doubt . . ." he paused to point a wavering stick at the hollow ". . . first you must walk the *Vikra-sah*, a path so riven with the darkness of the world that no Morvek who walked it has ever returned."

CHAPTER TWENTY-FOUR

Felnir

During his days in Ishtakar, Felnir had once been invited to eat with the High Velzir of the Saluhtan's armies. Such an honour was rarely extended to mercenaries, but the exploits of the man Ishtan soldiery referred to as "the Desert Plague", had aroused the interest of the emperor's general of generals. Felnir found him a slim man of undistinguished appearance but a paragon of the peerless manners to which Ishtan nobility aspired though often failed to achieve. His every word was considered and phrased in tones designed to avoid any suggestion of offence and he exhibited none of the condescension, or outright contempt, Felnir had come to expect of other commanders in this army. Felnir's Ishtan had improved enough to be serviceable by then but, having been learned from soldiers, lacked the formalities and gentility expected in such company. The Velzir, however, was too polite to match the wincing or smirks of his fellow nobles provoked by Felnir's lack of etiquette in responding to the general's questions. He asked about Felnir's origins, displaying honest curiosity at what must have seemed to him a bizarre array of customs. He also enquired as to how Felnir had earned his singular name.

"It began as a joke, my Velzir," Felnir replied. "After a skirmish, an Ishtan cavalry captain remarked that I had killed more rebels than the plague. Sadly, it stuck."

The Velzir's neatly trimmed moustache twitched with amusement before he asked his next question: "Tell me, for it is a question I ask of all who rise high in my command, what would you say is the most potent weapon in war?"

Various replies flitted through Felnir's head, from the value of a well-handled horse to all manner of cunning battlefield ploys. However, a glance at the noble's shrewd, expectant features told him that the man expected something that delved beneath the obvious. "Hunger, Velzir," Felnir said. "Deprive an enemy of sustenance and he'll perish before you even need to cross swords."

The Velzir pursed his lips in consideration. "A good answer, esteemed sir. But, you will, I hope, forgive me if I disagree. For I have found that the most potent weapon in war is surprise. To win absolute victory, and crush your enemy to the point where they would not dare to dream of further resistance, your army must strike as swiftly as a thunderbolt, with no warning, and often at the least expected time. Soon, my friend from distant lands—" he raised his wine cup to Felnir, another rarely bestowed honour that scandalised the other Ishtan nobles present "—you will be my thunderbolt, the lightning strike that ends this pestilent revolt for good. Then, I'm sure, all will know you by a different name."

A week later, the last vestige of the rebel army that had ravaged the borderlands for nigh a decade was discovered on the slopes of a place the local tribes called the Iron Ridge. There did Felnir Skyrnrak lead a charge of two thousand mounted mercenaries in the dead of night that succeeded in breaking the rebel defences. The great mass of the Saluhtan's army had been quick to exploit the breach and, by morning, the entire rebel horde lay dead upon the sands. After that, the "Desert Plague" became the "Velzir's Thunderbolt" and, as Felnir rode through the darkened forest towards the *Ahrkun* encampment, he summoned all the trust he could in the great general's words regarding the value of surprise.

Upon spying the cluster of tall stones ahead, he thumped his heels into the hunter's flanks to spur the beast to a full gallop. Falk had been right about the soundness of the cultists' choice of campsite. The stones formed a tight circle, each one close to twenty feet high and separated from the other by a gap of only a few yards. As he hurtled towards it, Felnir wondered if this place might be a ruined fortification, even though it sat upon level ground. He heard a flurry of shouts as he closed, aiming the hunter at the widest gap between the stones. Normally he would have considered charging through a forest in darkness a mad gamble. The ground was rich in leg-snapping ruts and roots, but, as that fine Ishtan noble had said before commanding the nighttime charge to the Iron Ridge, "To be effective, surprise also requires the abandonment of all caution."

His charge was so swift, and unexpected, that only a single arrow was launched before he closed on the gap between the stones. The shaft was hastily loosed but well aimed, scoring a cut on Felnir's cheek as he swayed to avoid it. The sting birthed a flare of rage in his breast, much to his relief. He always killed more when properly angry. The archer was the first to fall, trampled by the hunter's hooves as he drew his bow for a second try. The two cultists to either side died next, skulls cleaved open by a left and right slash of the Altvar's sword. A trio of warriors hurried to bar his path, but he spurred the hunter into a leap, its hooves crushing another skull as it carried Felnir into the heart of the camp.

Tugging the reins hard, he guided his mount in a tight circle, slashing the sword at any cultist within reach. Sparks erupted and burning logs flew as the hunter sped through a succession of campfires. Felnir was impressed by the beast's aggression. Despite not being bred for battle, this fleet stallion clearly possessed a warhorse's heart, lashing out with his fore hooves at any *Ahrkun* foolish enough to linger in their path.

For a time, Felnir wreaked havoc amid a welter of confusion. The embers from the scattered fires caught canvas and soon several tents were ablaze, the shouts of the cultists joined by the panicked screams of their horses. The burgeoning pall of smoke and the chaotic shadows playing over the towering stones aided Felnir as he rode through the camp once more. It may have been due to the exhilaration of combat, but the sword felt lighter in his hand now, describing a series of flashing, blood-laced arcs as he cut down one *Ahrkun* after another. Not all wore armour, the unnaturally sharp blade slicing through flesh and bone as easily as a baker's knife parted dough.

His earlier estimation of his foes' abilities was soon borne out by the speed with which they reacted to his incursion. He ducked repeated salvos of thrown knives and axes, thankful for the concealing smoke that spoiled their aim. Felnir completed one more charge, hacking down a warrior who attempted to unseat him with a jabbing spear, until, inevitably, the cultists recovered enough discipline to form a circle, hemming him in. Others tossed water buckets over the blazing tents, thinning the haze enough to fully reveal their target. He halted the hunter, turning in the saddle to regard the surrounding warriors, every face set in determined hate. But they were all looking inwards, when at least one should have been looking out.

Tulvik was the first to charge through one of the gaps between the stones. Perched unsteadily atop one of the lumbering draught horses, he yelled a war cry filled with vengeful, if shrill, fury, an axe whirling in his hand. His bulky mount crashed through the *Ahrkun* line and promptly fell to its knees, unseating its rider. Tulvik hacked at the surrounding legs as he regained his feet, uncaring of the fresh scars the cultists scored into his face and arms. Despite his unreasoning ferocity, it was clear to Felnir the youth had but seconds to live. He began to spur the hunter forward when Beyorn arrived with three more riders at his back. Plunging into the untidy melee, they succeeded in completely disordering the *Ahrkun* defence. Knowing the time for any further tactical nuance had passed, Felnir kicked his heels and sent the hunter charging into the heart of the fray.

There were a few occasions in his career when it could be said he had lost himself in the frenzy of battle. His duel with the unfortunate Volund Stolntalv was one. The night he fought his way free of the rebel's desert encampment was another, as was the climax of his charge at the Iron Ridge. But it was a rare thing. Throughout his childhood, his great-grandfather had drummed into him the need to maintain control in combat. *Rage has its place, boy, but it also blinds, and a blind man will not live long on a battlefield.* But this night, Felnir knew, was a time for unfettered rage.

He recalled only brief instants later, the wonderfully weightless sword opening throats and parting limbs from bodies. A cultist screaming her defiance at him even as he skewered her through the belly. Another fumbling on the ground for the hand he had lost, a frown of childlike peevishness on his face, as if he reached for a broken toy. Felnir lopped off the crown of his skull and kicked him aside before bringing the sword around in a two-handed blow that cleaved another *Ahrkun*'s waist down to the spine.

Calm descended with a bracing suddenness, Felnir snarling as he whirled to confront more foes only for his blade to meet empty air. Blinking, he realised two things: he now fought on foot and the *Ahrkun* had drawn back. Their circle was smaller but ranks tighter. Bodies twitched or lay still on the ground between them. Nearby, Tulvik attempted to stand, blood leaking from a wound in his thigh as he issued a wordless, crimson-flecked growl of un-sated bloodlust. Behind him, Beyorn, Falk, and the wheelwright, Vehldur, stood with swords held ready, all bloodied but unbowed. The sight of them brought a grin to Felnir's lips, one of satisfaction rather than pride, although they surely read it as the latter.

"Command us, my king!" Beyorn said, his voice booming once again. "We'll slay all these dogs this night!"

"Aye!" Vehldur agreed, chest heaving from exertion but eyes blazing. "Vengeance!"

Instead of cowing their opponents, their defiance served to fire their resolve, the surrounding warriors tensing for another rush, then pausing as a voice rang out, sharp with command. "Hold!" A tall figure shouldered his way through the *Ahrkun* line. The Factor's narrow features were riven with a mix of anger and indignation as he snapped further instruction to his escort. "Bowmen forward! We've lost enough for one night."

As he waited for the archers to fetch their bows, he settled a steady, demanding glare on Felnir. "Before you die for your heresy, wretch, tell me who you are? Tell me who set you to this?" When Felnir merely laughed, the Factor's face took on a feral, manic aspect. "Tell me! Was it that old bitch Jorhyld?"

His rage deepened as Felnir's laugh grew louder and longer. His mirth faded when a trio of *Ahrkun* archers stepped forward to level their shafts at his chest. Meeting the Factor's eye, he said, "I am Felnir Skyrnrak, as of tonight, the King of Vorunvahl. And you just wasted your last chance to kill me."

The arrow described a shallow arc, flicking Felnir's hair before striking the Factor in the centre of the raven tattoo on his forehead. As he tottered, lips squirming and brow creased in a comical frown of annoyed confusion, three more arrows flashed over Felnir's head, felling the archers. A savage roar heralded the arrival of his *menda*, villagers and warriors hurling themselves through the gaps in the stones to assail the cultists. The *Ahrkun* fought back with impressive fortitude, but disarrayed by the shock of their leader's sudden demise and the unheralded arrival of a more numerous enemy, they were overwhelmed in mere minutes.

Inevitably, none were spared in the ensuing slaughter. The lucky died quickly, and the unlucky did not. After what he had seen on the riverbank, Felnir was not inclined to intervene, not that there would have been any chance of assuaging the villagers' wrath. Once again, the *Ahrkun* impressed him even as they died a variety of gruesome deaths. *Not one has begged*, he mused, watching a cluster of villagers hold a cultist over a fire. They had doused him in lamp oil and his writhing body burned bright. Though he screamed, Felnir heard only exhortations to the Altvar among the shrieking agony.

"There's going to be an awful mess to clean up tomorrow," Sygna said, coming to his side with the Bow of the Altvar slung across her shoulders.

"My thanks for the arrows, my love," Felnir said as she pressed herself to him. "Timely as ever."

Sygna drew back, frowning at the troubled cast to his brow. "What is it?"

"This," he sighed, glancing at the burning corpse the villagers had abandoned to the fire, "is going to be harder than I thought."

"I think I'll call you Bolt." The hunter's flank twitched as Felnir smoothed a hand over it. Come the morning, he had found the horse beyond the circle of stones, sheltering in the lee of one of the taller monoliths. His hide was marked with several cuts, but none so deep as to require a merciful slash to the neck. "We'll get you some salve for these," he murmured, peering closer at the beast's wounds before holding a carrot to his muzzle. As well as a fat purse of gold, the Factor's caravan had yielded an impressive stock of victuals. "And more of these."

He chuckled, watching the beast chomp the carrot into oblivion until his eye alighted on a curious mark in the stone beyond. Moving closer, he saw it was a carving of some kind, a spiral design etched into the rock. Further examination revealed that the symbol lay at the centre of a circle of smaller carvings. They were weathered, but not so much as to be truly ancient in manufacture. They were also completely unfamiliar, bearing no resemblance to any written language he knew. Had the Ascarlians who settled here and raised these stones developed their own script? The notion summoned a pang of sorrow for Elvine. *The brightest mind I ever knew,* he mused, fingers exploring the spiral. *If anyone could have reckoned some sense from this, it was her.*

Felnir stepped back, eyes roving the stone's surface for more carvings. There were others around the base, but a sudden chorus of shouting to his rear drew his notice before he could stoop to investigate. It had snowed overnight, blanketing the forest in white. Vehldur and a number of his fellow villagers had surrounded a cluster of bushes, blades jabbing at a stocky figure struggling free of a deep drift. From their excited exclamations, Felnir judged they had found another cultist to torment. As he approached, he recognised the target of their ire as the lank-haired woman he had seen attending to the Factor's wagons on the road to the Nest.

"I told you fuckers!" she yelled, brandishing a rock at the encircling villagers. "I am not *Ahrkun*! I'm a fucking captive, for Ulthnir's sake!"

"Then where's your chains, you lying bitch!" Vehldur demanded, edging closer, his sword poised to slash. "I saw you. Standing and watching when they flogged her brother." The wright jerked his head at Tyrheld, barely recognisable now as the slight, grieving girl Felnir had met only days before. With her torn clothes, blood-matted hair, and broken-nosed features besmirched by soot and gore, she resembled a feral creature drawn from the forest to scavenge this place of death. The impression was enhanced by the twin daggers she clutched in both hands, dark with dried blood up to the elbows. She lurched towards the stocky woman, a garbled, hissing insult issuing from her lips.

"Stop that!" Felnir barked, placing himself between the villagers and the woman. His appearance sufficed to cow all of them save Tyrheld. Sinking lower, she tried to edge around him, a manic grin on her face and eyes locked on her prey.

"I said enough," Felnir growled, barring her path. "This woman is under my protection. All of you, get back to the camp."

Tyrheld glared at him, mouth twitching as she grated a reply. "You promised vengeance . . ."

"And you've had it, with more to come. Now heed your king's word or suffer for your disloyalty."

The girl's glare became a snarl and she would surely have had more to say if Vehldur hadn't dragged her away. "Apologies, my king," he said, bobbing his head while pushing Tyrheld towards the stones. "No holding her when her blood's up. Her brother was the same."

Felnir made sure they had retreated into the shade of the stones before turning to the stocky woman, still holding her rock. Although she could have fled into the forest, she stayed, eyeing Felnir with wary suspicion but saying nothing. *Smart, but too proud to beg,* he concluded, his interest piquing.

"It was a fair question," he said. "Where are your chains?"

"They have my son at Hahl-Trova," the woman replied. "Hostage to my good behaviour. He is my chain."

Hahl-Trova. Felnir had heard the coast-landers talk of this; the Great Nest where the *Sindra* himself held court. "You have been there?" he asked.

"I live there." The woman sagged, shoulders slumping as she let the rock slip from her grasp. "Since they took us four years ago. Killed my man and all my kin save my boy. Kept me alive because I have a way with horses and wagons. Kept Taynvar to turn him into one of them."

"And have they?"

She met Felnir's gaze, expression growing fierce. "Never. He's too strong. He says the words but their nonsense creed has no purchase on his heart. This I know as his mother."

"You must have travelled far with the Factor. Perhaps more than once."

"Three times I made this trip with him, each journey worse than the last. Folk always have less to give. This one was the worst of all, though. I'm guessing thanks to you."

"You guess right . . . ?" Felnir paused, raising an eyebrow in expectation until she consented to give her name.

"Dyssha." She squinted at him, eyes flicking over his garb until they settled on the sword. "Are you truly a king?"

"I am now, but you can just call me Felnir if it pleases you." He stepped aside, extending an arm to the stones. "Come, Dyssha, and warm yourself at my fire. Hiding under snow all night must have put a chill in your bones."

"Froze more in Hahl-Trova last winter," she grunted, shaking flakes from her hair. "S'pose you'll be wanting me to tell you all I know about the *Ahrkun,* then?"

Felnir grinned as he led her towards the stones. *Smart indeed.* "In time. But let's get some warm food inside you first, eh?"

They remained at the stones for another two days, Felnir prolonging the stay to allow any shirkers to depart quietly. A dozen left the first night, their thirst for vengeance slaked and bellies full of war. Although Beyorn raged at their cowardice and begged leave to hunt them down, Felnir forbade it. Any army worth its salt needed to be formed of committed souls and he knew well the folly of trying to compel waverers to unwilling service. Only a handful disappeared the following night, leaving him with a *menda* of some two hundred and forty souls. Hardly the Velzir's host, but a decent start to what he knew, thanks to Dyssha, would be a protracted campaign.

"There's about three thousand warriors at Hahl-Trova," she advised around a mouthful of Falk's stew. "And the same number who do little but abase themselves to the *Sindra* all day. You can be sure they'll all fight if need be."

"Too many for a direct assault," Sygna concluded. "At least until we gather more forces."

"They won't let you." Dyssha accompanied her words with a shrug. "When what you did here becomes known throughout middle-Vorunvahl, the *Sindra* will send all the strength he can muster to crush you."

"What can you tell us of him?" Felnir asked.

"He's *Ehilkun*, like him." Dyssha nodded at Wohtin, seated at Felnir's left. "But doesn't look so old. The *Ahrkun* claim he's been preserved by a blessing of the Altvar, but there's another story that he was only a child when Velgard was gathered to their breast. Could all be horse shit, though."

"Is he a warrior?" Felnir persisted. "Has he commanded armies in war?"

"Fucked if I know." Dyssha rose, going to the stewpot to help herself to more. "Barely caught sight of the bugger. He's big." She sat, continuing to speak as she spooned more food into her mouth. "Bit bigger than you, come to think of it. His grovellers are full of stories about all the battles he's fought, but I doubt he's left the Hahl-Trova for years. But don't make the mistake of thinking him weak or stupid. He'd have to have something about him to command that bunch of mad bastards for so long."

"An ancient," Felnir mused, turning to Wohtin. "Someone you know, perhaps?"

"There were thousands caught in the wave unleashed that day," the old man said. "Old and young." He grunted. "Now we're all old." The flatness of his tone and avoidance of Felnir's eye were clear signals of dishonesty. Once again, he found himself eyeing Wohtin's wrinkled neck. *The sword,* he reminded himself. *I still need him to awaken it, unless that was another lie.*

"Where was the Factor headed next?" Felnir asked, turning back to Dyssha.

"Vorl Arna, the Moon Lake." Her mouth quirked in amusement as she chewed. "Usually the most dangerous part of the trip. The eastern bank pays tribute to the *Ahrkun*, but the western bank doesn't. They're a wild lot, those lake-siders, always prone to living apart. Got a funny accent and strange customs, so they say. Wouldn't know, m'self. Never met one. But I know the *Sindra's* been trying to conquer them for years. Any *Ahrkun* that strays too close to their lands . . ." She paused, drawing a thumb across her throat.

Felnir exchanged a glance with Sygna, finding her brow creased with an obvious question: *Allies?* "Anyone else know anything of these lake-siders?" he asked, casting his gaze across the other faces at the fire. At first, none spoke, but then he saw Vehldur deliver a nudge to Tyrheld. Still smarting from Felnir's frustration of her vengeance, the girl spoke with a sullen frown.

"I do . . . my king. My father came from the eastern banks of Vorl Arna. They traded with the Vorl Tuhrk back then. It's what they call them."

Vorl Tuhrk, Felnir considered. *Moon touched.* A phrase often ascribed to the mad in Ascarlia. But, in war, he had often found the mad just as useful as the sane. Sometimes more so.

"Tomorrow we break camp," he said. "Beyorn, you will take two-thirds of our strength and bring word of my coming to the eastern lake-siders. Tell them of our victory here and call all who are willing to fight."

"They would be more willing if you were at our side, my king," Beyorn said.

"I know," Felnir replied. "And I'll join you shortly. But first—" he favoured Tyrheld with a smile which failed to alleviate her frown "—with the aid of my guide, I shall head east and treat with the Vorl Tuhrk."

CHAPTER TWENTY-FIVE

Thera

The youthful barmaid's smile was perfect, Thera failing to catch even a glimmer of falsity in her eyes. Yet Lynnea's judgement was firm in its conviction. *She and the traitor lived in the same inn*, the apprentice explained as she led Thera into the establishment, marked as "The Golden Cask" by the sign hanging above the door. The title matched neither the unwashed exterior nor unadorned interior. *Yet spoke hardly at all*, Lynnea added. *Of all the women in this place, she was the only one he never tried to bed. Plus, behind that pretty smile, she stinks of lies and hatred.*

As she conversed with the innkeeper, Thera kept her gaze from lingering on the barmaid mopping the floor nearby, humming a soft, cheerful ditty to herself. "The traitor executed by the Veilwald two days ago lived here, I believe," Thera told the flush-faced proprietor, a far more nervous soul than his employee. "I need to see his room."

The man's gaze flicked between Thera and Lynnea, who he had undoubtedly spotted among his customers the previous night. Licking his lips and forcing a smile, he said, "The Veilwald's *menda* already searched it, Vellihr. Took all his stuff. So I'm afraid there's not much to see."

"Even so." Thera extended a hand. "The key, if you please."

She had been wary of tipping her hand in coming here, but reasoned that the Vellihr of Justice inspecting the home of an executed traitor would not arouse suspicion. If anything, it would be thought strange if she failed to turn up at some point.

"I take it you found no silver knot?" she asked her apprentice after a cursory inspection of the room. As the innkeeper said, the place was bare. The bed had been turned over and the straw mattress shredded. An empty chest lay partially smashed in the corner.

Mohlnir was able to get in via a hole in the roof. I had him check every board in the floor and scoured the walls for hiding places, Lynnea confirmed. *If the balladeer had one, it's not here. Though the maid has a chain about her neck she conceals beneath a silk scarf.*

Thera noted that the balladeer had been something of a vandal, scrawling song lyrics upon the wall plaster, she assumed for want of paper. Peering closely at the ill-formed script, she made out a series of clumsy rhymes. *He wasn't much of a poet,* she reflected, concluding that the author's charm must have compensated for a lack of true talent.

"Copy these down, just in case," she told Lynnea, gesturing to the scrawled lyrics. "It's possible there's a code hidden in there somewhere."

Lynnea nodded, then put a finger to her lips before pointing at the floor. *There's a linen cupboard below. She's listening.*

Thera went to the window, looking towards the docks, where a forest of masts rose above the rooftops. In accordance with her request, Veilwald Synghild had taken charge of the ships on hand and sent word to all the ports under her dominion to send more. Every spare pair of hands in Vorun Hardta had been marshalled for labour in the quarries, a necessary expedient that couldn't be concealed. However, at Thera's instruction, its true purpose hadn't yet been disclosed. She had instructed Veltta's crew to spend the previous two nights touring the town's taverns spreading a variety of rumours. They ranged from fortifying the harbour with a wall of quarried stone to building a redoubt further inland. This seeding of misleading gossip served two purposes. First, to conceal the true reason for the work. Second, the presence of these strangely accented, red-faced strangers would ensure the folk of this port entertained no doubts as to the peril they faced.

"Have you detected any sign the townsfolk know what we're about?" she asked, turning to Lynnea. She waited for a moment before speaking on, Lynnea regarding her with patent bafflement. "Good. If word got out that we are intent on carrying away as much of this Kast's wealth as we can carry, the locals may react poorly." She paused again, as if listening to a response. "I know, but it can't be helped. War is an expensive business. While the marble isn't quite worth its weight in silver, it's still going to bring a fat purse when D'Shaine carries it off to foreign ports."

Understanding dawned on Lynnea then, her brow smoothing and a smile curving her lips. *Clever.*

Thera shrugged in acknowledgement. She was about to gild her deception with some false allusions to sending her battle fleet into the northern Fjord Lands, when the muffled, annoyed tones of the innkeeper sounded from below. "Velka! Stop dawdling in there and haul up another cask from the cellar!"

How long until she tells her masters? Lynnea asked once they had departed the inn.

"Most likely tonight," Thera replied. "She won't want to wait. And neither can we." She came to a halt, turning to fix her apprentice with a steady, intent gaze. "In three days, it will become obvious to anyone with a shred of intelligence what we're truly planning here. The maid, and any other Volkrath you can find, need to be silenced before then."

Lynnea's face tightened, Thera sensing the reluctance in her thoughts. *Seized then? More Crimson Hawks to line the harbour?*

"No. The people here, and their Veilwald, have been unnerved enough by the unmasked Volkrath in their midst. This needs to be done quietly. I'll give you Ragnalt to help. He's well skilled in wielding a knife in the dark."

Lynnea shook her head. *Unnecessary. I'll take care of it myself.*

"You're sure?"

Lynnea's response was shot through with a vein of resentment, but also firm resolve. *If I am to wear your brooch one day, some things cannot be shirked.*

Thera's hand went to the adornment on her jerkin. It hadn't occurred to her before, but it was possible she remained the only living Vellihr in Ascarlia. *Apart from Ilvar,* she remembered. *And he cannot honestly claim the title any longer.* "True," she told her apprentice with a tight smile. "Though I've no notion of who might pin it on you."

Lynnea's reply was faint and accompanied by a small grin, as if trying to conceal its meaning, but not very well. *I think I do.*

"You're certain you can build this?"

The sailor performed one of the deep bows with which Albermaine-ish commoners greeted their supposed betters. The woman was somewhere north of her fortieth year with an impressively muscled build and the weathered features of one who had spent much of her adult life at sea. Yet she seemed girlishly shy in Thera's presence, hands clutching the woollen hat she had swiftly torn from her head when D'Shaine called her forward. The hour being late, Thera was forced to squint to make out the details on the parchment in the light from the *Northern Star*'s deck lanterns. The sailor had handed it over with trembling hands before quickly retreating a step. Thera had heard of the contraption it depicted, but to her eyes it appeared merely a triangle topped by a long, narrow rectangle.

"Given enough timber and hands to work it, y'highness," the woman said, a wavering smile playing over her lips. "They're designed to be put together quick, y'see. Give me ten days and I'll make two, if you like."

"I'm not a highness," Thera told her, turning a quizzical eye on D'Shaine.

"Luissa is the finest sail rigger I've ever sailed with," the captain said. "And, as a girl, was apprenticed to none other than Aurent Vassier." In response to Thera's baffled frown, he elaborated, "Vassier was perhaps the greatest artisan of engines who ever lived, Vellihr. Although he built many a bridge in his time, it was his battle engines that brought him most renown. They called him the 'Siege Master', and many are the wars that fattened his purse. Regardless of all the nonsense spoken about the Scribe these days, it was Vassier's engines that broke the walls of Highsahl. And Luissa here helped him build them."

Looking again at the diagram, Thera asked, "How far can it throw a stone?"

"Depends on the weight of the stone, y'high—m'lady," Luissa said, clearly having difficulty in slotting Thera into Albermaine-ish noble hierarchy. Still, Thera's interest had bolstered her confidence. She spoke on with clear enthusiasm while darting cautious glances to gauge Thera's expression. "This one will be the same size as those that carved the breaches at Highsahl, and they could sling a half-ton stone over two hundred paces."

Looking up from the diagram, Thera strode to the *Northern Star*'s starboard rail, gauging the distance to the shore. She had boarded the ship at sunset with the intention of overseeing the first shipment of freshly quarried marble. With Volkrath spies possibly still at large, she reasoned, it would be best to obscure the nature of the transport for as long as possible. As the hulking merchantman made her way to the strait, D'Shaine had surprised her with this intriguing addition to her plans.

"It's one hundred and eighty paces to the eastern shore," he said as Thera turned her gaze from starboard to port. "To the west, less than one hundred and twenty."

Thera's frown deepened as she pondered the possibilities. Even should her initial stratagem work perfectly, she still expected a fierce battle to unfold in the aftermath. Victory would be assured, but, like the Lyx Helv, it would also be costly. "Ten days to build two, you say?" she asked Luissa.

"Mayhap eight if I have enough skilled hands," the sailor said. The way her salt-kissed features flushed in pleasure rendered her into an apple-cheeked child, eager to please.

"I'll get you the hands, and the timber," Thera assured her. "For now, the night's work awaits." She gestured to the quarried marble piled onto the deck, each chunk chiselled down to dimensions that enabled them to be ported by one strong-backed labourer. "Let's get this lot dumped over the side."

* * *

The silver knot felt heavier in Thera's hand than the others she had held, making her wonder if it had become burdened by Lynnea's guilt. Four days after the *Northern Star*'s first trip to the centre of the Crusher's Strait, she had placed it wordlessly in her Vellihr's palm. Her thoughts formed no words, but Thera could feel the rawness of her apprentice's feelings. *She's killed before, but that had been battle,* Thera recalled. *Plain murder is always harder to bear.* As far as the townsfolk of Vorun Hardta knew, Velka, the pretty barmaid from the Golden Cask, had taken an unfortunate tumble into the river when doing laundry. Her body had been found that morning, pressed into the iron grate where a drain channelled the fast-flowing current into the harbour.

"Did you get anything else out of her?" Thera asked. "The names of other Volkrath?"

Lynnea shook her head. *I watched her carefully. Read her moods. If there are other agents here, she didn't meet with them.*

"Keep looking. If I were to seed spies in so busy a port, I would make sure at least some were unknown to each other." She rubbed the trinket between her thumb and forefinger as she spoke. *Why is it always knots?* she wondered, resolving to ask her great-grandfather about it when next he deigned to appear in her dreams. Night after night she had tried to summon him again, without success, though the nightmares remained as vivid as ever. It made for groggy awakenings and a frequently soured mood. Seeing the troubled cast to Lynnea's brow, she realised her tone had been overly curt.

"I ask nothing of you that is not absolutely necessary," she said. It wasn't much by the way of comfort and did little to assuage the maiden's angst. *Does she begin to hate me?* Thera wondered. *For what I make her do.*

However, she detected no bitterness when Lynnea tightened her lips and nodded. *There's a few taverns in the quarrymen's quarter I've yet to visit. I hear rumours of discontent despite their recent increase in pay.*

Inclining her head at Thera, she made for the *Great Wolf*'s gangplank. "Leave it for now," Thera told her. When Lynnea turned back to her in surprise, she nodded to the huge dog and his far smaller feline companion lying at the base of the mast. "These two become a pair of miserable lumps when you're not here. Snaryk's been growling of late. It makes the crew nervous. Stay the night and resume your mission in the morning."

In response to an unspoken summons, Snaryk and Mohlnir both immediately rose and rushed to Lynnea. The cat swiftly climbed upon her shoulders while the great dog gambolled about her legs in puppyish excitement. Lynnea laughed, but her thoughts remained troubled. *Your plan becomes more obvious by the day. If there are still spies to be found—*

"We can't conceal the work forever," Thera interrupted. "War has a tendency to force unwanted wagers on its participants. With the trap baited, we must gamble that the enemy will oblige us by walking blithely into it."

And if they don't?

Thera went to the brazier in the centre of the mid-deck, holding her hands out to the warmth. The night breezes were taking on a sharper edge as winter's chill deepened. "Then battle will still unfold here," she said. "And a far bloodier business it will be."

She caught a flash of the Lyx Helv as Lynnea joined her, a brief spasm of ugly memory in which a flailing hand grasped at nothing before disappearing beneath the crimson churn. It was swiftly supplanted by the sight of Velka tumbling into the river. Before the frothing river bore her away, she gazed up at her killer, previously cheery features now set in a mask of furious hatred. Her ire turned to desperation as the river carried her off, a plaintive cry smothered when the current dragged her under. Thera let out a gasp at the swirl of guilt and revulsion accompanying the images. Lynnea had shared sensations with her before, but this was far more potent, and unwelcome.

Sorry. Lynnea blinked at her, the memory instantly fading. *I didn't mean to.*

Thera rubbed at her temples, head aching and a ball of nausea forming in her gut. "Don't do that again."

I won't. I promise. I didn't even know I could. Lynnea's thoughts tumbled rapidly, shot through with a rising panic. Her alarmed, guilt-riven features reminded Thera just how young her apprentice was. *I've never . . . Well, apart from Mother . . .*

"It's all right," Thera said.

I tried with Father. When the madness started to take him. I tried to calm his mind, but it never worked . . .

"Lynnea!"

The babbling stream of thought stalled when Thera took hold of Lynnea's shoulders. Breathing hard, she stared into Thera's eyes, her next thought so riven with self-recrimination it was hard to bear. *It shouldn't be so easy. Taking a life should hurt more.*

Thera opened her arms, drawing Lynnea into an embrace. "I think it hurts you enough," she said. The tears came shortly after, the maiden's slender form shuddering while Thera smoothed a hand through her hair until she felt the mental torrent fade into a semblance of calm.

"You've never told me," Thera asked her, still holding her close. "Why do you want the Vellihr's brooch so badly?"

Lynnea shifted, looking up at Thera with a faint smile. *I don't suppose you would believe me if I said I wanted to be like you?*

"You'd be right."

Settling her head against Thera's chest, Lynnea's thoughts settled further, albeit now coloured by sorrowful remembrance. *My mother should have been a Vellihr. You know she was often called to Sister Iron's service to provide healing. What Iron didn't tell you was that, when she first became queen, she offered to make my mother the first ever Vellihr of Healing. It wasn't possible by then, of course. She had me to take care of, and my father's changeable moods to manage. Even though I was small when she passed into the Halls, I can still recall the bitter sting of regret that she didn't accept the honour when it was offered.*

"So that's it? A desire to honour your mother?"

Lynnea's slender form moved in a shrug as she pressed herself closer, raising her lips to Thera's until they almost touched. *Partly. But mostly because I knew she saw in me the chance to do good, perhaps great things. While I don't have her healing touch, you know I have other talents . . .* Their lips brushed, Thera's mind filling with a new sensation that sent a warm flush through her body.

She moved back, releasing Lynnea from her embrace. "I can't . . ."

I'm not her. Lynnea's expression lacked the hurt of rejection, but her thoughts held a small note of reproach. *I will never betray you.*

Thera needed no accompanying image to know who she meant. Although she didn't doubt the loyalty of this apprentice, ever since she had been hauled bleeding and near death from the waters of Danith's Bay, Thera had known her dalliance with Eshilde to be a mistake. It wasn't only that it had left her open to treachery, it had blinded her to things she should have seen. Lynnea would never betray her, that was true. But that didn't mean Thera could afford the luxury of this curious connection between them to grow into something more. *One day, I may have to order you to your death.* She didn't speak the words, but the sudden hardening of Lynnea's features made it plain she had heard them, nonetheless.

She forced a strained smile before turning away, her parting thought riven with suppressed pain. *Once again, spoken like a queen.*

The first test of what Veilwald Synghild insisted on calling "that foreign contrivance" came precisely eight days after Thera had viewed the diagram aboard the *Northern Star*. Upon receiving Thera's request for skilled labour to build the thing, the Veilwald had expressed a marked scepticism, revealing a prejudiced attitude to outland novelties, especially those of Albermaine-ish origin. "We haven't fought those swine for generations to take on their ways now." Thera's counter argument that the task before them required the adoption of every advantage, regardless of origin, only partially served to mollify the Veilwald's misgivings. "You can have fifty pairs of hands from the shipyard," she said by way of grudging accedence. "They're the most skilled woodworkers to hand. The fucking thing better work, mark you."

Thera had hoped that seeing the fully constructed engine in all its impressive glory would erode any lingering doubts Synghild might harbour. Yet, as they stood together on the eastern shore of the Crusher Strait and watched the tall throwing arm of the engine raised into union with the crossbeam, Thera saw a darkening of the Veilwald's mood. As the device came together under Luissa's occasionally shrill direction, Thera discerned that Synghild's glower was focused not on the device itself, but one of the shipwrights. A tall, well-muscled man with skin several shades darker than his comrades, but what drew Thera's eye most was the reddish hue of his hair. He appeared to enjoy a good deal of regard among his fellows, even a modicum of authority, as she saw several defer to him as they set about organising the many ropes required for this complex task. When one of them called upon him for guidance, Thera was unsurprised to hear his name. "Teylhar. Where d'you want this block?"

This then was the famously detested and disowned third son to Veilwald Synghild Vyrnvest. Judging by the man's evident skill and capability, Thera saw little to mark him as the wastrel described by his mother. Her unabated glower, however, indicated an undiminished pitch of disapproval.

"We'll be ready soon, Vellihr!" Luissa called amid a tumult of pounding mallets and overlapping voices. Her face was even more flushed than before, and she constantly clenched her gloved hands together. *At least she's learned my proper title*, Thera thought, confining her reply to a nod as she surveyed the nearly completed engine. The great arm was narrow at one end where an iron hook had been fixed. At the other, it was considerably broader and connected by an axle to a sturdy basket-like construction.

"The counterweight, Vellihr," D'Shaine explained, noting her interest. "It's what powers the throw. The engine of the engine, you might say." He chuckled at his own wit, something Thera noticed he did quite a lot.

After another round of hammering and rope fixing, the builders piled the counterweight high with loose stone, while others enclosed a far larger slab of marble in a large canvas sling attached to the throwing arm. Drawing the great oaken pole back for the throw took longer than Thera expected, Luissa's commands growing ever more strained as she marshalled the wrights into hauling the rope. The huge engine creaked and groaned with each heave, iron fittings squealing until at last the counterweight was raised and a lever thrown to lock into place.

"That took a good long while," Synghild observed. "Battle does not often afford such leisure."

"Practice will surely improve matters," D'Shaine said. "In the east, I've seen well-drilled crews launch three stones in as many minutes."

The Veilwald appeared unconvinced, squinting at Luissa as the engineer returned, bowing once again. "I thought perhaps the Vellihr would like to launch the first stone," she said.

"My thanks," Thera replied. "But that honour must go to Veilwald Synghild. She is paying for all of this, after all."

"And I'll expect my successor to receive full reimbursement in due course," Synghild muttered before gesturing impatiently at Luissa. "All right. What do I do?"

The engineer continued to bob her head as she led the Veilwald to the machine, handing her a rope attached to a locking lever. The shipwrights all stood at a respectful remove and Thera noted how Synghild avoided looking in their direction. Teylhar had seen fit to place himself at the rear of the gathering, standing with his head lowered.

"Just one firm tug will do, my lady," Luissa told Synghild before backing away in a crouch. The Veilwald spared her a faintly disgusted glance before yanking the rope. Thera had hoped for an impressive demonstration this morning, while also nurturing a grim suspicion that the engine would tear itself to pieces. All her expectations were immediately exceeded when the great arm swung upwards, hauling the marble slab to its full height, whereupon the sling slipped its hook and the huge stone sailed free. It tumbled slowly as it described a lazy, almost graceful arc through the air before plummeting down, birthing a water spout twice as tall as a ship's mast dead in the centre of the Crusher Strait.

"Fuck me!" Synghild laughed, a less harsh sound than her usual caustic bark. "It actually works. Let's do it again." Turning, she quieted the jubilant shipwrights with a snapped command. "Hurry up! You buggers will have to be quicker when the *Skyrnlohk* get here."

While they set about manoeuvring a fresh stone into place, Thera drew Luissa aside. "You say you can make another?"

"Certainly, Vellihr."

"How long?"

"Now that these fine folk know what to do, mayhap four days. Three if we work in shifts."

Three days. Thera looked to the waters beyond the strait, knowing that somewhere to the south, two fleets were now racing to reach this island. Her plan had always involved more risk than she liked, but with engines like these, the odds could well be tipped in her favour.

"Then get to it and waste no more time talking to me," she told Luissa.

The *Ohlira* sailed with the evening tide, Thera breathing a relieved sigh at the sight of her successfully navigating the strait into open water. Kahlvik's instructions were simple: find the Nihlvarian fleet and be seen doing it. If Ossgrym had followed instructions, the enemy force would have followed his ships north, only to lose them when they tacked east upon drawing close to the Inner Isles. With luck, upon catching sight of the *Ohlira*, the Nihlvarian commander would be eager to chase fresh prey. Thera hoped any caution they might harbour would be overcome upon realising they were heading for a port where the Vellihr of Justice could be killed or captured. Once Kahlvik was safely on his way, the heavily laden *Northern Star* once again lumbered from her anchorage to complete her task, the waters of the strait churning white as ever more stone was dumped over her sides.

Thera spent the next three days agreeing to the final deployments with Synghild. With all the necessary stone quarried from the surrounding hills, the Veilwald began to muster her *menda* for war. All the townsfolk of fighting age were instructed to present themselves with arms at the docks each morning. There they were drilled in speedy embarkation upon the many boats and ships moored along the wharf. Thera was disappointed to find relatively few with bows among them, but the number of archers steadily increased as hunters from the surrounding villages answered the Veilwald's call.

Each day, Lynnea would come to advise on progress in her mission. While she could find no more Volkrath agents, her reports were useful in gauging the mood of the people. *They're scared, as well they might be.* Lynnea's thoughts were mostly stripped of emotion now, although Thera could still sense the undercurrent of hurt. *But determined too. The engines have done much to bolster their resolve.*

"So they'll fight?" Thera asked.

Of course. Let every hand know the sword, after all. A sardonic smile ghosted across Lynnea's lips. She was not often given to allusions to the Altvar. *They'll fight because they have no choice,* she added. *And they'll fight for you. They harbour loyalty to Synghild, but most think her driven mad by what she did to her children. It's in you that they place their trust.*

Luissa's crew completed the second engine in less than two days, a remarkable feat of industry that left them all exhausted. Even so, when Thera asked for a third, no complaints were voiced. She began to spend more time at their worksite, helping with the less skilled tasks. She hoped that Lynnea's judgement was true and that her mere presence would inspire them to yet greater efforts. All the while, her gaze strayed repeatedly to the waters south of the strait. Not so long ago, several ships a day would sail to and from Vorun Hardta, but now the channel was empty. *Nothing empties a purse so fast as war*, Sister Silver had said once, although Thera couldn't recall precisely when or why, which saddened her. That miserly old woman's wisdom had often been harshly spoken, but could rarely be gainsaid.

It was another two days before she spotted the *Ohlira*'s sail resolving out of the morning mist. Thera saw a single fire arrow sail free of her deck, arcing high before splashing into the channel as Kahlvik veered away, making for the fjord to the west. The signal was prearranged, so Thera knew its meaning clearly: the Nihlvarian fleet was here.

Chapter Twenty-Six

Elvine

"There are three doors barring the dungeons from the rest of the Verungyr," Aldunna said. "Each have but one guard. Their meals are all delivered twice a day. The cook who prepares them fell sick yesterday, so I have been allotted the task. The next delivery is in one hour's time." She cast a glance at the pot of porridge bubbling on the stove nearby. "I also prepared the cakes you requested." Aldunna gestured to a tray of freshly baked cherry and apple tarts on the bench before her, her lips curved in a barely noticeable smile. "For the queen. I hope she likes them. Fildra certainly did."

As before, the spear's gift revealed nothing of Aldunna's aura, but, if it had, Elvine thought it might resemble Coelnyr's mass of writhing snakes. Evidently, the Tielwald was fond of choosing servants with unpleasant proclivities.

"Very thorough," Berrine said, voice low as she cast a careful glance around the kitchens. "We'll be ready to follow you when you deliver the food."

"No," Elvine said. "I'll go in first. The gaoler is a good man. He deserves a chance to join us." Seeing a disapproving frown on Aldunna's brow, she added, "I'm a regular visitor, so they won't suspect me. Besides, it'll work to our advantage to have someone on the other side of the third door in case of . . . complications."

"As you wish. But if the gaoler proves loyal to the queen, you know what must be done."

Elvine's calf muscle gave an involuntary twitch, reminding her of the knife strapped there. "I do."

The doubtful line in Aldunna's forehead eased a little, but not fully. "The Tielwald trusts you, so I am obliged to do the same. But know this well,

Scholar, failure to act when needed means death for us all." She looked again at the tarts. "I'll arrange these on a suitably dainty plate for presentation to the queen. Tell her they go especially well with black leaf tea. Should it be necessary for you to share them, choose this one." She pointed to a tart with a little extra icing on the crust.

"How long will it take?" Elvine asked, surprised by the thickness of her voice. She also found she had to clench her fists to keep her hands from trembling.

"A few hours. The most immediate effect is drowsiness. It should give you an excuse to leave her alone."

After arranging the cakes and covering them with a glass bowl, she afforded mother and daughter a hard-eyed stare of unmistakable intent. "One hour," she said, voice curt. "Do not be late."

The climb to the top of Lore's tower felt longer than any Elvine could remember, even though she made every effort to hurry while encumbered by the plate of tarts. She continually rehearsed what she would say upon greeting Lore, reminding herself not to offer the treats immediately. *My mother is friendly with one of the cooks. She had some spare.* She would then set them down and start to her rooms, fully expecting Lore to draw her into another lengthy conversation. She would surely send for tea and they would enjoy the tarts together while discussing the finer points of Alberic poetry, which had become one of the queen's principal distractions of late. *Then wait for her to get sleepy and retire to her chambers for a nap.*

Elvine came to a halt at the top of the stairwell, stomach roiling. For no reason she could fathom the word "sleepy" kept repeating in her head. *Sleepy. But she won't be sleeping, will she? She'll be dead. Just like Fildra, and that man you killed on the* Sea Hawk.

"One hour," Elvine murmured to herself, pushing the door open. It was with both relief and alarm that she found the tower rooms empty. A quick check of Lore's chambers confirmed her absence, leaving Elvine with a particular quandary. *Wait for her, or go now?* She winced as another thought chimed with cruel honesty. *Wait to kill her, or leave, you mean.*

It was rare for Lore to be gone this late, but not unheard of, especially recently as all manner of other business demanded her attention. Concluding that it might be hours before she returned, Elvine set the tarts down upon the library table and hurried to her own rooms. She took little, only her quills, ink and a few more cherished notes, the fruits of her interrogation of Lore's archive. The name "Alwyn Scribe" featured most prominently among the text.

As she made her way back through the library, she was presented with another dilemma. The Spear of the Altvar sat upon its iron frame, as outwardly unremarkable as always. Elvine's hand hovered over the haft, frozen by indecision. *If I touch it, what will it tell me?* A memory rose as she continued to dither. That terrible day in Nerlfeya's Hall when the spirit in the spear had hissed in alarm at the prospect of Lore's touch, and the accusation it spoke later. *"You gave me unto dark hands."*

Letting out a grunt of annoyance, Elvine returned to her room. Stripping the blanket from her bed, she went back to the library and threw it over the spear before lifting the weapon free of its frame.

"What are you doing with that?"

Elvine froze, heart hammering. Taking a breath, she forced herself to turn. Vahlak stood in the doorway, regarding her with amused puzzlement. "She hasn't set you to polishing it, has she?" he enquired, coming closer. "Hardly work fit for a scholar."

"She . . ." Elvine swallowed. "The queen requested further research regarding its . . . construction. I'm to show it to the master of the smithy. She thinks he may have some insight as to when and how it was forged."

"If it's truly a gift from the Altvar themselves, wouldn't it have been conjured into existence?" Vahlak's voice held a lightly taunting note, also pleasure at finding himself alone in her company. "Shall I escort you? A visit to the smithy intrigues me. The forging arts are endlessly fascinating, don't you find? Or are you so completely lost to the written word?"

"I'm sure it will be interesting." Elvine continued to wrap the blanket around the spear, finding it strange that, while her heart continued to pound, her hands were now free of any tremble. "But first," she said after swallowing again to banish the rasp from her voice, "I brought some cakes. Would you like one?"

Vahlak's gaze shifted to the plate, pursing his lips. "A present for my sister, I assume?"

"Yes. I don't think she would mind if we enjoyed a few in her absence."

"I'm not so sure about that." Vahlak gave a small chuckle as he removed the glass cover from the plate. "I can still feel the bruise from when she punched me for hiding one of her dolls." He peered closer at the cakes. "Still, she won't miss a couple, I'm sure . . ."

Elvine never knew why she did what she did next. Allowing him to eat one of the cakes would surely serve their cause well. The commander of the Nihlvarian great *menda* slain by poison in the midst of war was inarguably a good thing. But instead of standing and watching as he took the first bite, she swung the butt of the spear as hard as she could into the back of his head. Given his size and strength, she expected another blow would be needed, but the Tuhlvyr surprised her by collapsing instantly, his temple suffering a second collision with the table edge before he slumped to the floor.

Standing over him, with the blanket fallen away to reveal the iron head of the spear, she knew driving it into his neck was undoubtedly the smart thing to do. Quicker than poison. An act sure to send Lore into maddened grief.

Are we embarking upon a journey, child?

Elvine jerked at the sudden intrusion of the spear's voice, realising that she had inadvertently grasped the metal above the haft. "Yes," she said.

This is pleasing to me. I find this place increasingly tedious. Despite all the intriguing your queen and her brother engage in. Did you know she was planning to kill your mother and blame it on assassins loyal to the fallen queens? A means of binding you closer to her.

"No." Elvine's gaze returned to Vahlak. Blood trickled from his temple where it had connected with the table, his unprotected neck now seeming even more vulnerable. "No, I did not know that."

Better if you don't, the spear cautioned. *He persuaded her it was a poor idea. So I suppose you owe him a debt. Killing without need weighs heavy on the heart. The choice is yours, of course.*

Despite her anger, Elvine felt no urge to kill as she continued to regard Vahlak's unmoving form. Debt or no, as Lore's brother and the Nihlvarians' general, he deserved death. But, unlike the man on the *Sea Hawk*, this one presented no threat. This kind of killing was simply beyond her.

Wrapping the blanket around the spear, she shouldered her satchel and hurried to the stairwell, descending as fast as she dared.

"I shall see the foreigner first today," she told Hulnath a short while later, hoping he didn't notice her flushed features and strained tone. She had presented herself to the gaoler as she usually did, having left the blanketed spear in her mother's care. It required some effort to stop her eyes straying to the main door to the dungeons, expecting Aldunna to arrive any second with the evening porridge delivery. One of Ilvar's *menda* stood guard and, as she entered, had afforded her a glare that was both intense and worryingly alert. With luck, his hostility wouldn't spoil his appetite.

"As you wish, Scholar." Hulnath levered himself free of his chair and lumbered towards Colvyn's cell, keys jangling. "He's been teaching me Alberic these past few days. Did you know they have about sixteen different ways of telling someone to fuck off?"

"I did not," Elvine confessed honestly.

"Should get him to teach you too." Hulnath laughed as he hauled the cell door open. "Mayhap you'll write a book about it."

Elvine forced an appropriately bashful grin before slipping into the cell. As had become his habit, Hulnath failed to lock it behind her, leaving only a small gap as a concession to privacy.

"I trust you've brought me more entertaining fare," Colvyn remarked, setting aside the book he had been reading. "I'm finding Lucuria a somewhat dry read."

"She's an excellent historian," Elvine said, crouching beside him. Instead of opening her satchel as usual, she began to hitch up her skirts, gesturing at Colvyn to continue talking.

"Also one of the dullest prose writers ever to inflict herself on the Ishtan language," he said, his bemused frown shifting into serious understanding as she revealed the knives strapped to each of her calves. She had added another before coming here, knowing the guard would check her satchel, but not, in deference to the queen's regard for her scholar, her person.

"When?" Colvyn whispered as he leaned close, fingers working loose the strap on her left calf.

Elvine tensed, hearing the distant echo of one of the outer doors opening. "Any moment now. Be ready."

"Pity." Colvyn drew the knife from its sheath, affording the blade a quick, expert examination. "I'd grown fond of the gaoler."

"He's to be spared, if we can. Keep talking nonsense about Lucuria."

Smiling, he got to his feet, working his arms and legs to loosen muscle as he continued in a louder tone. "I find it odd that her prose should be so lifeless when she was so famously interesting. Is it true she had a hundred lovers?"

"Some accounts say two hundred." Elvine drew her own knife and stood facing the door. "Though much written about her after her death can be dismissed as the calumny of lesser scholars intent on degrading her reputation."

"It certainly doesn't count against her in my book. Two hundred lovers should be celebrated as quite the achievement, especially for one so apparently charmless."

As in the instant before she struck down Vahlak, Elvine's nerves steadied upon hearing the dungeon door grind open. She heard the guard greet Aldunna before asking after the cook, who usually performed this chore. "A malady of the guts," he was told. "Poor cow can barely leave the privy. Eat up lest it gets cold." Elvine heard the slop of porridge being ladled into a bowl, then a brief pause before Aldunna exchanged more cheery greetings with Hulnath.

"Dengryd said you preferred a bigger bowl," she said. "And a spot of honey."

"May the Altvar bless you all your days," the gaoler responded with anticipatory relish, his voice accompanied by the scrape of a chair as he took position at his small table.

"Wait here," Elvine whispered to Colvyn. Concealing her knife behind her satchel, she pushed the door open, seeing Hulnath already dipping his spoon into the steaming bowl of porridge. "I'm done!" she said, voice a notch louder than it should be, but it succeeded in interrupting the passage of the spoon to his lips. "I'll see the Tielwald now."

Huffing in restrained annoyance, Hulnath set down his spoon and got to his feet. Moving to Colvyn's cell, he jangled his keys again as he prepared to lock it, then stopped as the guard at the main door let out a loud, agonised retch. The warrior's bowl clattered to the floor, the stool he had been perched on kicked away in his sudden convulsion. A grey froth covered his lips, his eyes bulging wide as he collapsed against the wall before doubling over. Slipping to his knees, he retched again, sending a dark red spatter onto the flagstones.

"Please give me the keys," Elvine said, stepping into the gaoler's path as he started towards the guard. She revealed her knife, holding out her free hand. "There's no need for there to be any more trouble."

Halting, he gaped at her, broad, fleshy features paling. Understanding brought a frown to his brow and an instinctive reach for the cudgel dangling from his belt. His movements came to an abrupt halt when Aldunna's knife pressed into the flesh beneath his chin. "The fucking keys," she said with soft, intent precision.

Hulnath winced when the guard let out an agonised whimper. He lay on his side, hands clutched to his belly and a crimson pool expanding from his mouth. "Is . . ." the gaoler began, chins wobbling as he swallowed hard before speaking on. "Is this wise, Scholar?"

"I think we all left wisdom behind some time ago," she replied, stepping forward to pluck the keys from his belt. "Free the Tielwald," she told Aldunna, tossing her ring. Hulnath remained still as the key rattled in the lock, fresh sweat beading his brow when Colvyn emerged from his cell.

"My thanks for being such a diverting host," he told the gaoler, blinking in the comparatively brighter confines of the dungeon. "So glad we didn't have to kill you."

"Put his garb on," Elvine said, keeping her knife pointed at Hulnath as she nodded to the fallen guard.

"How do you intend to get clear of the Verungyr?" the gaoler asked, eyes flicking to the sight of Aldunna helping Gruinskard from his cell.

"Don't concern yourself," Elvine told Hulnath. "Unless you'd like to come with us. I know you have no liking for this task."

"Tempting." He licked his moistened lips. "But I'm too old to be running about. You'll have to tie me up. A few punches wouldn't go amiss either. Lest the queen think I had a hand in this . . ."

His words ended in a wet choke when Gruinskard, having relieved Aldunna of her knife, plunged it into the base of Hulnath's skull. Grunting with the effort, the Tielwald worked the blade back and forth several times before drawing it clear, letting the body fall.

"His ears were always too keen for my liking," Gruinskard said, handing the knife back to Aldunna. Meeting Elvine's furious gaze with weary impatience, he said, "Too much dawdling, Scholar. Let's be gone from here. I trust Coelnyr has a boat waiting."

As they made their way past the other guards, all slumped and twitching in pools of their own blood, a mounting clamour began to echo from above. It grew into loud constancy by the time they reached the alcove where Berrine waited with the spear. The words were indistinct, but Elvine could discern a sense of urgent alarm among it all.

"Must've found the others," Aldunna commented.

"Others?" Berrine demanded.

"This holdfast is filled with traitors," the cook returned. "You didn't think this lot would be the only ones to enjoy my supper tonight, did you?"

"You stupid, vicious bitch!" Berrine hissed at her. "You've roused the entire Verungyr against us."

"Bicker another time," Gruinskard stated. Although he walked unaided, he was obliged to support himself by reaching out to the passing wall.

"He's right, Mother," Elvine said, relieving Berrine of the spear. "We must hurry."

She and Colvyn led the way as they descended successive stairwells and passageways, navigating a complicated course towards the wine cellar. "I hope that old bastard's worth the trouble," Colvyn muttered, casting a dark glance over his shoulder at Gruinskard's lumbering form.

"Without him, the boat doesn't sail," Elvine replied. "And, though it pains me to say it, he'll have other uses too . . ."

She trailed off as they rounded a corner into the vaults, halting at the sight of three of Ilvar's *menda*. Elvine recognised them all. The two youngest had been the pair of unfortunates roundly castigated for failing to find the hiding place in Gruinskard's house. The third was older by several years and had been aboard the ship that carried her and Berrine from Olversahl to Skar Magnol. As expected, upon sighting her, his heavy, bearded face took on an instant grimace of suspicion, though it turned to mystified surprise when Colvyn let out a relieved laugh.

"Thank the Worldsmith himself!" he exclaimed in his near flawless Ascarlian, striding forward with hands raised. "I was starting to think we were all alone down here."

The older warrior was not easily gulled, however. Sinking into a crouch, his hand going to his sword, he growled, "Stop there! Who the fuck are you?"

"He's with me," Elvine said, hurrying to Colvyn's side. "We're here on the queen's business. Stand aside."

The warrior's suspicion only deepened at her approach. "What would a scholar be doing down here?" The sight of the iron head of the spear poking from her blanket transformed suspicion into alarm. "To arms!" he shouted to his two companions, his sword scraping from its sheath. Colvyn was faster, lunging forward to lance the point of his dagger through the warrior's right eye. Pressing his weight against the now screaming man, Colvyn forced him against the wall, pushing the blade in up to the hilt. The warrior's two youthful companions reacted differently. The tall one stood back, failing to draw his weapon while the stocky one with the sparse beard rushed at Colvyn with his sword raised high. Darting forward, Elvine jabbed at him with the spear, an inexpert thrust that succeeded only in forcing him to abandon his attack and turn on her.

Ducking a swipe of his sword, she scrambled back. A bruising collision with the wall sent her sprawling, the spear clattering to the floor, while the stocky warrior loomed closer. A challenging shout from Colvyn forced him to turn once again. Blades clashed as the two engaged in a frenzied fight.

"Halkyr!" the stocky youth called to his comrade as he desperately tried to fend off Colvyn's blurring steel. "Kill him, you bastard!" For his part, Halkyr appeared disinclined towards involving himself in this fracas, retreating further into the shadows, his sword undrawn.

Wincing from what she was sure would be a spectacular bruise to her back, Elvine gathered up the spear and began to rise. Her progress halted when a large, gnarled hand closed upon the haft. "Give me that," Gruinskard grunted. As he pulled it from her grasp, he attempted to secure his grip with the bruised misshapen digits of his other hand, the twitching fingers alighting on the iron head below the point, whereupon he stiffened in sudden pain. Staggering back, the Tielwald gaped at her, eyes wide with shock, the spear clattering the stone floor.

"What is that?" Gruinskard demanded, clutching his wounded hand as if it had suffered even worse torment than Ilvar's torture.

"The Spear of the Altvar," Elvine said, quickly gathering up the weapon. "Best approached with care." She heard the voice within let out a disgruntled huff as her hand brushed the metal. *You do seem to have a gift for placing me in the most unpleasant hands, child.*

Turning her back on Gruinskard, Elvine prepared for another lunge at Colvyn's opponent but found her intervention unnecessary. The stocky youth lay on his side, features bunched in pain as he clutched at a seeping wound in his thigh. Halkyr had now retreated to the far wall, both hands raised in a signal of either surrender or neutrality.

"Finish them both!" the Tielwald commanded. Having recovered from whatever pain the spear inflicted, he stomped forward to recover the wounded man's sword. When Colvyn responded with a disgusted glance, Gruinskard snarled in annoyance and stepped towards the stocky warrior.

"Don't!" Elvine hurried to bar his path, keeping the spear between them. Although she didn't point it at him, it was clear from Gruinskard's backward step that the mere proximity of the thing was a sufficient deterrent.

"This isn't a game, girl . . ." he began.

"I know it's not a game!" she snapped. "And I've seen enough wanton murder from you."

"Leave them alive and they'll signal our passing." The scarred granite of the old man's face betrayed the thinning patience of a wise soul forced to argue with idiots.

"Not necessarily," Colvyn said. Stooping, he slammed the pommel of his sword into the side of the wounded warrior's head. As the fellow slumped into unconsciousness, Colvyn straightened and started towards his comrade. "Just a little bump on the noggin, my craven friend. Tell them you were taken unawares."

"Wait!" Halkyr raised his hands higher, staring at Elvine in stark appeal. "Take me with you, Scholar. Please. I want no further part in the queen's evil."

"He's one of Ilvar's scum," Gruinskard said. "Fanatics all. Trust him and you're a fool."

Elvine could see Halkyr's aura clearly, finding it flickering with flashes of fear, but no indication of deceit. Also, she could still discern the hue of shame she had noticed back at the Tielwald's house. Her impression was confirmed by an arch observation from the spear: *Offer a guilty soul a chance at redemption, and you'll win their loyalty forever.*

"Then I'm a fool," Elvine said. "And we're wasting time here." She jerked her head at Halkyr. "Move ahead of us. Make for the wine store."

The babble of pursuing voices was still a distant echo by the time she pushed the barrel lids to unlock the passage. However, it wouldn't be long before they discovered this place, and they had no means of sealing the tunnel behind them.

"Leave it to me," Gruinskard said, gesturing impatiently for them to proceed. Elvine took the lead, lantern in hand as they crawled inside and hurried along the passage to the junction. Seconds after reaching it, a long, grinding tumult of displaced stone echoed through the tunnel, followed by a blinding cloud of grit and dust. When it settled, the Tielwald's bulky form appeared. "Lynchpin in the roof," he explained, tossing aside a piece of rusted iron. "Installed at my insistence sixty years ago. Take weeks to dig through all that." He shot Elvine an urgent glare. "But we still shouldn't linger."

Entering the right-hand tunnel, she soon understood it to be a far longer passage than she expected. It was also possessed of an incline, gentle at first, but grew steeper the further they went. Her legs had taken on a deep, growing ache by the time she caught a faint lessening in the gloom ahead. The tunnel ended at a broad ledge overlooking the lower reaches of Skar Magnol's northern flank. The moon was bright, illuminating the narrow cove below where a boat waited. As they descended the slope, her view of the craft became clearer; a single-sailed fishing craft with three pairs of oars and a crew of four. She marked Coelnyr's silhouette easily thanks to the silver trim of his cloak, then blinked in surprise at recognising the three others.

"Ahlgrun!" she exclaimed when they reached the shore. A torch flared into life aboard the boat, illuminating the three siblings who had plucked her and Colvyn from the Styrnspeld Sea.

"Scholar," the fisherman replied before casting a look of grudging appreciation at Coelnyr. "Seems this one wasn't lying after all. Here." Ahlgrun began tossing ropes over the side. "Best get aboard before the tide changes."

To do so, they had to wade into the chill waters of the cove and suffer the buffeting waves of a changing tide. Getting Gruinskard's bulky, ancient form over the rail required a good deal of hauling. By the time it was done, Elvine was soaked and shivering.

"H-how come you to be here?" she asked Ahlgrun through chattering teeth.

"Got stuck in Skar Magnol after all the trouble in the Verungyr, didn't we?" The fisherman handed her a blanket, jerking his head at Coelnyr. "This one found us a few days back. Last few weeks we'd only been allowed to fish the fjord under watch of those red-faced filth. He said he had a pass to allow us to fish further afield, and our catch would be very valuable." A grin showed on Ahlgrun's weathered features. "Veilwald Hakkyn said to take good care of you, and so we have."

Elvine returned his smile, wrapping the blanket tight about her shoulders. "And appreciated it is."

"Are you well, Tielwald?" Coelnyr enquired as he helped Gruinskard to his feet. Elvine was struck by the shift in hue of Coelnyr's aura, seeing pulses of warm yellow she interpreted as genuine concern. *A man who sees the world as populated by potential victims*, she thought, *yet finds compassion in his heart for this aged spymaster.*

"Oh yes," Gruinskard groaned, "weeks of lying in a damp cell while being tortured every few days has left me in the best of health." He glanced around the boat, squinting in disapproval. "Not much, is it?"

"Anything larger would have attracted undue attention," Coelnyr responded. "She's fit for the open sea. We require only a destination. While war continues to rage in the Isles, I'm reliably informed the northern gelds remain free of invaders."

"No. We go south, to Olversahl."

Coelnyr nodded and shot a commanding glare at Ahlgrun. "You heard the Tielwald. Set your course."

"Not a good notion to sail south just now," the fisherman replied. "Better to head for the inlets to the west and await the morning fog."

"The Tielwald has given his order . . ." Coelnyr began, but fell silent at an ungentle nudge from Gruinskard.

"He's right. We raised quite a clamour in the Verungyr. Lore will soon have her fleet scouring Linsker Fjord and beyond for us, and the moon shines bright. With luck, the fog will let us slip by." He favoured Ahlgrun with a respectful nod. "It's your boat. Plot whatever course you think best. Just get us to Olversahl as swiftly as you can." His eyes slipped to Elvine before shifting to Berrine. "Where it seems I will soon be destined to fight another battle. But this time, I'll wager more than just the library will burn."

CHAPTER TWENTY-SEVEN

Ruhlin

"Any notion of what's waiting for me in there?"

Ruhlin's question provoked an apologetic wince from Tirohk. "No one has ventured inside for a very long time," he said. "And when they did, they didn't come out again. Old tales speak of a place where the earth has been sullied, corrupted like a festered wound. Quite how or why is not known, though there are stories aplenty. Some say the spirits of the forest came to war with each other, and their discord created the *Vikra-sah*. Others claim that a *kess-tuhk* of the *Teyrak* reached too far beyond her knowledge and awoke something best left to slumber. But all stories agree that it's a place so terrible only the *Telchak* could hope to survive it."

Since Olchar's announcement, the gathering of elders had become an expectant audience. In some ways, they reminded Ruhlin of those who had crowded the *wuhltra* to watch the monster wreak havoc, but lacking the same frenzied bloodlust. While he saw anticipation on many faces, he continued to discern an equal pitch of wariness. "Would I be wrong," he commented quietly as he shrugged off his pack, "in thinking not all here are keen for the *Telchak* to become real?"

He had addressed the question to Tirohk, but Velkar answered. "Not every obligation is welcome." While he saw the same carefully controlled trepidation on her face, he also perceived a glimmer of contempt as she surveyed her fellow elders. "If the *Telchak* is proven real, then the Morvek have no choice but to follow him to war with the *Rulchakin*."

"Even if war is not his object?"

Velkar's expression made him wonder if her grasp of Ascarlian had failed her, it being so rich in mystification. "There is no other path for the *Telchak*," she stated, voice soft and brow furrowed by doubt.

It seems, Ruhlin mused inwardly, hefting his maul, *whatever transpires here, I am destined to be a disappointment.*

"Why would the *Telchak* require a weapon?" the *Sohlcha* elder demanded, pointing to the maul in Ruhlin's grasp. His voice held a shrill edge that spoke of increasing desperation. Ruhlin concluded that the *Sohlcha* were a clan who greatly desired peace, which at least made this man worthy of his title as Chief of Wisdom.

Instead of the prior murmur of agreement or discord, the elders reacted to this question with utter silence. Olchar regarded the Sohlcha with a steady, inexpressive glare until the man once again lowered his head and retreated into the crowd.

"You do not have to do this, Ruhlin ehs Kestryg," the old man said as Ruhlin approached the edge of the slope. "You may leave. No hand will be raised to stop you."

"And my people's place within these lands?" Ruhlin asked.

"I cannot speak for the *Vehlkasa*," Olchar replied. "But my clan will welcome you if they do not." He stepped closer, reaching out with a trembling, liver-spotted hand to grasp Ruhlin's arm. "You do not have to do this," he repeated with slow emphasis, his unnervingly clear eyes far more steady than his grip.

Looking away, Ruhlin peered into the dark depths of the hollow. Gnarled roots rose from dark earth like snakes frozen in the act of coiling for a strike beneath a roof of entangled branches, all twisted like diseased limbs. *What do I lose by turning from this?* he asked himself. Even if they were forced to give up their place in the mountains, his people could still settle here. But then, there would be no return home, not for him, nor Guthnyr, or any of the others to whom he had made a solemn promise. Furthermore, the Nihlvarians and their endless greed would not simply vanish. Nor would the war he was sure now raged far away, laying waste to how many more villages? Claiming how many more slaves? Vengeance did not burn in his breast as it did in Guthnyr's, but he had seen enough of the Vortigurn's realm to know it needed to fall. Its people had been forged into something unnatural, something fundamentally wrong. If the monster that lived within him had a purpose, this was surely it.

"Yes," he told Olchar with a smile of apology, "I do."

A quick spasm of disappointment flickered over the old man's face before he withdrew his hand. Leaning heavily on his twin walking sticks, he retreated, saying softly, "Then walk your path, my young friend. I wish I had guidance to offer, except to say: tread carefully."

As Ruhlin began to descend the slope, the bear let out a long, keening groan. The animal hovered at the edge of the *Vikra-sah*, claws scraping at the earth, a snarl rising and falling from its quivering lips. Ruhlin couldn't recall seeing it so fearful before, nor had he been able to read the meaning in its gaze so clearly: *Don't do this.* He felt a chilling certainty that whatever awaited him in the shadowed depths of this hollow, the spirit inhabiting the bear's mind had a far clearer notion of what it was than any other soul present.

"I have to," he told the bear before resuming his descent.

The weight of the elders' collective stares was so oppressive that he actually found the shadows of the hollow a welcome respite. Beneath the canopy of entangled branches, the air was cool but scented with damp rot, although the ground felt firm enough beneath his boots. He walked with slow deliberation, peering into every shadow, the maul held tight in his hands. Curiously, despite the increased thud of his heart, the monster failed to stir. If there was danger here, it couldn't sense it. *Or perhaps*, he reflected, *it fears it.*

A few minutes of traversing the hollow found him walking in deeper shadows as the roof thickened. He could feel himself descending a gentle slope, his eyes straining to discern detail and making him regret his lack of foresight in not bringing a torch. Shafts of light still penetrated the canopy, catching motes of drifting dust but failing to reveal much of his surroundings. Save for his footsteps, all remained silent, until something crunched beneath his boot.

Stepping back, he squinted, making out pale fragments upon the earth. Stooping, he found them to be pieces of bone dislodged from a spine. It snaked across the ground to a skull that caught a gleam from one of the shafts. Its undamaged state puzzled him. The spine, and smaller pieces he took to be remnants of a ribcage, appeared to have been crushed, but the skull remained intact. *One of those who tried to walk the* Vikra-sah *in ages past*, Ruhlin decided, working the relic loose from the soil. Turning it in the light, he saw no cracking or scars that would indicate an injury.

"What did you find down here?" Ruhlin asked it, huffing a rueful sigh when no response was forthcoming. He began to set it down, then stopped as he heard something, a wordless sound that startled the skull from his grasp. Rising, he whirled, maul held ready. Nothing. Only shadows lanced by thin beams of light. Still, he was sure he had heard it. Had it been a voice? Or earth scraped by movement?

When no further sound came, he lowered the maul and resumed his trek. The sense of descending ever deeper into this gloomy recess became more acute. The light streaming through the weave of branches thinned, becoming less frequent. He found it difficult to gauge distance, unsure if he had yet walked a mile. He tried counting his steps, but stopped at two hundred when his surroundings failed to show any appreciable change. Occasionally, he heard another crunch of fragmented bone underfoot but, beset by a mounting desire to get this task over with, didn't stop to inspect the remains.

Finally, a break in the pervading gloom arrived in the form of a flickering swirl of luminescence in the dark. Drawing closer, Ruhlin made out the wavering glimmer of light on water. The reflection cast a dim glow over the scene, revealing a pool. The path he walked ended at the water's edge, its other sides enclosed within thick banks of tangled roots. He saw specks of white among the overlapping mesh of coils; more skulls of those who had once dared to traverse this hollow.

Approaching the pool's edge, he crouched, peering into water so dark he could see nothing of what lay beneath. He began to dip a hand to the surface, then stopped, his gaze caught by the gap-toothed grin of a skull staring out from the roots nearby. Something had killed all these people. Could it be as mundane a thing as tainted water? As if in answer, the sound came again, louder this time. It was more a creak than a voice, but the sense that it had been produced by a living thing was strong. Also, he was sure he had heard a note of mirth in it. Something here was laughing at him.

As he rose, hefting the maul once more, he caught a flicker of movement in the corner of his eye, a raised gout of displaced soil. It was gone in an instant, leaving silence in its wake broken only by Ruhlin's labouring breath. Despite the chill, sweat trickled between his shoulder blades, his eyes darting from one tangle of roots to another. Yet, the monster still failed to stir.

Once again, he wondered if the monster might fear this place. The notion seemed absurd, but so did the failure of his inner beast to emerge now, when before it had done so at the slightest provocation. *What keeps you at bay?* he asked it, anger rising along with his fear. *Now when I need you most?*

He was warned by the drip of water to his rear, the small noise accompanied by the same creak from moments before. Spinning, Ruhlin lashed out with the maul. He had time to perceive a long, gnarled length of root stabbing towards him before the hammerhead impacted it. The root's point shattered, the rest of it recoiling as if stung while a new sound filled the air. It was loud enough to pain his ears, a screech that could never have come from a human throat. Yet, he still detected a similarity to the laugh he had heard when approaching the pool.

A splash drew his gaze to the water as a dark shape retreated. The gloom was such that he couldn't make out details, but he saw enough to know that this thing, though unquestionably alive, was neither human nor animal. Roots sprouted from a central mass like limbs, coiling and slapping at the water while it continued to back away from him. Upon reaching the rearmost edge of the pool, it seemed to expand, its flailing tendrils calming. Ruhlin heard the creak again, this time joined by an overlapping chorus of straining and twisting wood. He realised the creature had merged itself with its surroundings, though not completely. As he stood, staring in both disgust and fear, he saw a protrusion emerge from the densest portion of the thing. It was thicker than the limbs, extending several feet. Ruhlin discerned smaller growths appearing at the protrusion's blunt end, entwining and merging until he beheld something that should have sent him fleeing. Either through the immobility of terror, or repulsed fascination, he continued to stand in place, returning the regard of a face formed from tree roots.

It had placed itself within one of the shafts of light, so he could see the features clearly. The eyes and mouth were three black holes in the snaking mass. When the mouth opened to issue a sound, Ruhlin gave an involuntary shudder. It was similar to the laugh and the scream, but more controlled, a gust of air forced through this thing's innards to produce an approximation of speech. Ruhlin couldn't understand any of it, although, as the thing continued to assail him with its mangled vocals, he realised it was speaking in Morvek.

"I know not this tongue," he told it.

In response, the thing fell abruptly silent, the suspended head angling to and fro as it bobbed over the water. He fancied he saw the writhing features form into a frown of sorts before it spoke again, this time in words he understood. The creature's speech was both dry and sibilant, continually underscored by that same creak. "One of those from far away," it said, slowly swaying from side to side, the black recesses of its eyes fixed upon Ruhlin. "Long has it been since one such as you came . . ."

Without warning, it darted closer, Ruhlin jerking back and raising the maul to strike. However, the creature stopped a yard short. Ruhlin felt a breeze on his skin as it drew in the surrounding air. For a moment it seemed to savour the scents it had gathered, then gave a sudden, convulsive spasm, letting out a wordless gasp of disgust.

"I smell you. Hide not from me . . ."

"I'm not hiding . . ." he began, then trailed off when, at last, he felt the familiar heat build in his core. *It wasn't talking to me*, he realised. It burned hot this time but, unlike every other instance when it had stirred before, it failed to signal a transformation. He stood unchanged and vulnerable before this impossible beast.

The thing's mouth opened again to voice a clack, a sharp exclamation Ruhlin took as either frustration or understanding. "Not whole . . ." it gusted in its broken voice. "Just a remnant . . ." The eye holes narrowed. "Rent and torn you were when they lured you here. Or were you one of those who sacrificed themselves?" The notion seemed to amuse the creature, the mouth gaping to issue a far more voluminous and ugly laugh than its previous faint titter.

In response, the heat within Ruhlin flared hotter, causing him to stagger. Yet still no stretching muscles nor grind of lengthening bone. He did, however, detect an emotion among the inner storm, one he had often felt himself during this long and difficult sojourn: the enraged hatred for a justly detested enemy.

"What are you?" he asked the creature. "How come you to be here?"

"So the puppet speaks, but not . . ." the dark maw of its mouth formed a taunting curve ". . . the master."

It's not my master. Ruhlin kept the words caged. Instinct warned him that it would be foolish indeed to impart any information to this thing. Besides, was such a denial entirely true? He would not be here if not for the monster. But then, he wouldn't be alive either.

The creature seemed not to care if he answered. Swaying back a little, it raised one of its root limbs from the water. The tendril coiled around a skull, clean and unstained like the others. "This one found this place in ages past. A place where the veil is thin. From it she drew power and, like all her kind, thirsted for more. She baited the trap with herself. Imagining she possessed the knowledge to bend one of us to her will. Long did I make her pay for her ignorant conceit."

"You were . . . summoned here?" Ruhlin frowned, fumbling for the right words. "From somewhere else? Somewhere beyond this world?" The thought that this being could be one of the Altvar seemed absurd. Yet what other worlds were there?

"Another ignorant wretch." Water splashed as the creature's limb loosened, letting the skull fall. "Of scant value, save for the remnant woven into your soul. A mere spark, true. But a spark can kindle a flame." It appeared as if the surrounding water began to boil, churning white as a thicket of limbs rose to thrash the surface. "A flame that will burn this prison to ash . . ."

Its voice became ever more garbled as it rose from the pool, revealing a body of writhing roots that resembled the broken corpses of ten men forced into ugly union. More skulls lay within the mesh of its being, grinning out at Ruhlin as he began to back away. A limb lashed at his legs, swiftly blocked and shattered by the maul. Once again, the thin point of the tendril exploded at the mere touch of the weapon, the limb recoiling as if burned. *Something in the metal,* Ruhlin concluded, recalling Aleida reshaping it with her gift. *This is more than mere steel.* Other limbs swung at him, all fended off with rapid swings of the maul while he continued to retreat.

"You should thank me . . ." the creature sputtered amid a mass of writhing roots, dragging its bulk from the water. "How long have you endured your cages of flesh? How long have you suffered the stench of this realm? These wretches are filth! Their mere existence pollutes us . . ."

A blunt, gnarled root resembling a mace thrust at Ruhlin's head, too fast to block, and barely ducked. The movement distracted him long enough for another limb to whip around his legs, bearing him down. Falling, he swung the maul, shattering more roots, but not enough. He shouted in frustration as his arms were snared, dragged apart and squeezed until the maul fell from his grasp. His cries ended when more encircled his chest, forcing the air from his lungs. Still, he writhed in the creature's grip, silently imploring the monster to come to his aid. Yet, while the fire of hatred continued to burn, it refused to fully wake.

"So frail . . ." The creature's head loomed above him, the coiling features moulded into something that resembled genuine puzzlement. "So pitifully weak . . ." A root protruded from its forehead to play over Ruhlin's face, exploring his eyes before moving on to his mouth. "So unworthy of your largesse. Why did you and your kind sacrifice so much for them, I wonder? All for nothing. For soon it all ends. I can feel them, my brethren, drawn by the endless conflicts of this realm. The ruler of this land works dark wonders to entice us. It feeds our hunger for more. A hunger that will break the veil in a thousand places . . ."

The root probing Ruhlin's mouth thickened and went deeper. The rotten, earthy taste of it made him gag, his vision dimming as it pushed towards his throat.

"And then, my little flame . . ." The creature's face was bare inches away now, the holes of its eyes remained blank, but within them Ruhlin saw a depthless well of malice. "Then you know what we will feed on next . . ."

A new sound echoed through the hollow, muted at first by the pounding pulse in Ruhlin's ears. The tendril invading his mouth paused, the sound growing in volume until he recognised it: the enraged roar of a charging bear. He caught the blur of a dark, fast-moving shape before the root pushing into his throat withdrew with painful swiftness. The coils snaring his limbs remained in place, jerking him from side to side with jarring violence as the creature they sprouted from did ugly battle with a furious foe.

The bear continued to roar as it tore into the flailing mass of root and bone, tearing shreds from its central mass with repeated swipes of its claws. Screeching its inhuman cry, the creature was forced back into its pool, the contest soon obscured by a welter of raised water as they continued to thrash at each other. Then a flash of red amid the grey white spray of tainted liquid, accompanied by a whimpering groan that told of a beast suffering mortal injury. As the water calmed, Ruhlin beheld the bear speared through the chest by one of the creature's tendrils. Blood gushed from its mouth as it tried to continue the fight, the slashing of its claws brought to an abrupt end when another tendril slammed into its abdomen, piercing the hide with ease and erupting from the bear's back in a cloud of gore and bone.

As he watched the bear's death throes, the stricken beast held aloft by the creature which seemed intent on prolonging its agonies, the raging fire deep inside Ruhlin stilled, just for an instant, and then blossomed into an inferno. Never before had the transformation been so rapid. In the space of a heartbeat Ruhlin's body pulsed and swelled to its largest and most bestial form yet. He spat the foul-tasting dregs of the invading root from his mouth and tore his arms and legs free of the coiled snares, shredding roots as thick as tree trunks as if they were formed of wet paper.

The monster roared as it came free, leaping high to launch itself at the creature, clamping huge hands on its head and mashing it to pulp with one mighty squeeze. The thing failed to die. Multiple screeches of alarm issued from the many fissures of its body as it fought back, myriad limbs whipping in a frenzy. Cast away by the sheer violence of the response, the monster landed hard on the fringes of the pool. There it lay for a second, staring into the empty eyes of the bear lying close by. They were black, devoid of all life. The mystery of just how much of Aleida's aunt had remained in the beast would now never be answered. The thought seemed to inflame the monster's passions yet more. Grunting, it righted itself and, as it did so, felt the cold metal of the maul's haft upon its palm.

Roaring anew, it leaped again, the maul raised high. Clearing the whipping limbs, it landed atop the bulkiest portion of the creature's body and brought the weapon down, tearing a deep hole in its wooden flesh. Ruhlin felt his grip on consciousness begin to ebb as the monster raised the maul for another strike, bringing it down again and again with blurring speed and force. He perceived the shredded and powdered debris raised by the monster's efforts, but the familiar red fog robbed him of detail and sensation, save a growing heat in his palms. It was different from the fire that signalled his transformation, more intense and born of an external source. Even as the crimson mist closed in, he saw that it came from the maul. A bright silver glow shone from its edges as it wrought ever more havoc on the creature. The monster had pounded through so much of its mass that the pool lapped around its enlarged feet. Steam billowed where the blazing weapon met the water, the monster altering the angle of its blows to destroy ever more of its enemy.

The pulverised remnant of the creature flailed its way across the pool and began to merge with the bank. Its movements were spasmodic, rich in frantic desperation as it began to weave itself into the wall of roots. Roaring, the monster pursued it, the maul shining ever brighter in its grasp. Before the thickening mist claimed him entirely, Ruhlin watched the monster plunge the blazing weapon deep into the mass of writhing tendrils. A shout of savage triumph escaped its throat as flames erupted and all turned to fiery oblivion.

He awoke to the feel of cinders upon his skin. Blinking, he beheld his hands, still monstrous but slowly reducing in size. He walked through a swirl of embers, the feel of them against his flesh muted by the lingering grasp of the monster upon his body. He was naked, what remained of his clothes now burned rags, though he saw no scars or blisters upon his skin. Around him lay the charred remains of the *Vikra-sah*, the tangled roots rendered into a scorched mass, the earth covered with a blanket of ash. A few feet away, the bear's corpse was a vague grey hump. Glancing back, he found the pool at the heart of the hollow vanished, steamed into nothingness by the inferno that had destroyed this place.

He carried the maul in his right hand, its glow vanished. He struggled to drag forth any vestige of what had just happened from his memory, but found only a swirling miasma of confusion. *What did you do?* he asked the monster. There was no reply, the heat in his core diminishing in concert with his thinning muscle and shortening bone.

After a dozen paces, the smoke and slow blizzard of embers fell away, revealing the gathered Morvek elders lining the edges of the hollow. All stared down at him in either horror or wonder. When he paused at the foot of the slope, he heard the same word uttered over and over again, first in a whisper, then in firm acclamation. "*Telchak* . . . *Telchak. Telchak!* TELCHAK!"

They were all chanting it, arms raised and faces lit with a manic light. Even the *Sohlcha* elder, who had been so vociferous in his doubts, joined the chorus, as did Tirohk. The only exceptions were Velkar and Olchar. The forest woman regarded him with her features tightened in an unconcealed mix of doubt and dismay. The frail old man with the bright eyes, however, favoured him with a smile of placid acceptance. For his part, Ruhlin felt a deep desire for them all to shut up.

Now fully returned to his human state, his body had quickly begun to assail him with a plethora of aches. He wanted to get away from this place. Find some soft patch of ground to lie upon and slip into the refuge of sleep. Furthermore, the absurdity of their sudden adulation irked him. Despite all the centuries they had spent regarding this place with mythic dread, they had no more understanding of what had lurked here than he did. Nor did they know the nature of the monster they saw as a saviour. Yet, both rest and contempt were luxuries, indulgences he couldn't afford. His confrontation with the creature had left him with a new, not altogether welcome, certainty. *The ruler of this land works dark wonders to entice us.* He couldn't pretend to know the full meaning of its words, but one thing was clear: the Vortigurn and his schemes had to be defeated.

"Enough," he croaked, finding he had to swallow before raising his voice to a shout, lifting the maul above his head for emphasis. "Enough!" Their silence was jarring in its sudden obedience, the subsequent hush thick with expectation. "Tirohk," Ruhlin said. "Please bring me my pack."

The *Vehlkasa* was quick to oblige, gathering up Ruhlin's pack and scrambling down the slope to place it at his feet. He found the reverence on the war chief's face dispiriting. Their shared journey from the mountains had nurtured a friendship of sorts, but that was gone now. A figure worthy of worship could not befriend a mere man.

Opening the pack, Ruhlin extracted the cloth-wrapped bundle he had carried from the mountain. Casting away the covering, he revealed a curve-bladed dagger. Next to his maul and Guthnyr's sword, this was the finest weapon so far produced by the mountain forge. "Relate my words in full," he told Tirohk, raising the dagger and the maul.

"These are my gifts to the Morvek," he called out, turning so that all present could behold the weapons while Tirohk provided a translation. "Forged from iron gifted to me by the spirit of the mountain upon which my people dwell. Know that these are no ordinary weapons. This—" he raised the dagger higher "—can cut through any armour worn by the *Rulchakin*. This—" he brandished the maul "—can shatter their weapons, and you have witnessed its power in vanquishing the evil that dwelt in this place. We will forge more, enough for every warrior from every clan that pledges itself to the destruction of our enemies. All that was stolen will be regained. All blood spilled will be avenged. This I swear to you as *Telchak*. Will you, the true inheritors of this land, swear to me?"

Their answer came in a deluge of sound, flooding the hollow with the name *"Telchak!"*, chanted with fervent cadence. Ruhlin forced himself to maintain a pose of noble acceptance while his gaze drifted to the bear's corpse and shame replaced his contempt. Whatever he might be, he felt an absolute certainty that he was not these people's saviour.

CHAPTER TWENTY-EIGHT

Felnir

"So, yer a king, are yer?"

Baldyr Klarresk, the Foe's Bane, Gyrwald of the Vorl Tuhrk, resembled a crow inspecting freshly slain carrion as he leaned forward to peer at Felnir. A thin man, the Gyrwald's face and head were shaven to reveal in full his raddled, blotched skin. Felnir might have ascribed his appearance to overindulgence in liquor or drugs if his gaze hadn't been so clear. It tracked over Felnir in careful examination that surely missed nothing of import. Baldyr's hall stood upon a hillock enclosed within a stockade of tall, spike-topped timbers rising from the forested bank of the Vorl Arna. It was an impressive contrivance of timber and stone, artfully melded into a high-ceilinged structure. As his party had been led through the gate, Felnir's practised eye noted the recent application of daub and fresh, unworn rope binding the stockade. This was a necessary wall overseen by a leader who knew well the value of regular repairs.

"I am," Felnir replied. "King Felnir of Vorunvahl, come with offer of alliance and mutual benefit."

Baldyr reclined a little, the squint of his gaze taking on a thoughtful glint. He sat upon his chair, flanked by neither kin nor counsel. Nearby, a dozen warriors occupied some tables, watching the meeting in inexpressive silence. They were tough-looking men and women clad in garb that differed from the other Vorunvahl folk Felnir had encountered. Before coming here, the people he met could have easily been mistaken for Ascarlians, their attire being so similar. This lot were more colourful, though not garishly so. Their cloaks and trews were fashioned from a patterned, densely woven wool, dyed muted shades of crimson or gold, and fastened with brooches of silver. Their appearance bespoke a level of wealth and craft beyond most in this land, making Felnir wonder if that was why the *Ahrkun* were so keen on conquest.

"And who made yer a king, might I ask?" Baldyr said, arching a hairless eyebrow.

"I did." Felnir patted the sword at his belt. "With this, the Sword of the Altvar."

"Very nice," the Gyrwald commented, although his tone was far from impressed. "Give it yer themselves, did they?"

"No. I found it at the foot of a statue to the Worldsmith in the Vaults of the Altvar. The place your ancestors called home."

"Really?" Baldyr pursed his lips before turning to address his watching *menda*. "Just like those useless old fuckers to leave the important stuff behind."

This drew forth a muted chuckle, although Felnir caught them sharing a few intrigued glances before their leader recaptured his attention. "Gods blessed sword or not," he said. "I don't know yer. Know her though." Baldyr shifted his scrutiny to Tyrheld, who stood with Tulvik, Falk and Sygna at Felnir's back. He had also included Dyssha and Olvynd in the party, but thought it best to leave them with the horses before entering the hall.

"Come forth, girl." The Gyrwald flicked his hand in summons at Tyrheld. Separated from her kin, she had assumed a far more taciturn and timid demeanour than the vicious creature that Felnir recalled from the standing stones. Casting a nervous glance at him, she shuffled forward to afford Baldyr a respectful nod. "Gyrwald. I thank you for the warmth of your hall."

"As well yer might." Baldyr's gaze flicked from her to Felnir's companions and back again. "Where's yer brother? There was a man whose word could always be trusted."

"Slain, Gyrwald," Tyrheld replied. She hesitated to take a breath before speaking on, her tone growing more forceful with each word. "Tortured and killed by the *Ahrkun Krayl* not ten days since."

Baldyr's discoloured brow took on a sombre crease. "Sorrowful tidings. He was a good man. Though, if he'd accepted the offer to join my *menda* years back, he'd still be breathing. I told him the *Ahrkun* couldn't be bargained with any more than yer can bargain with a starved wolf. So, come to me for vengeance, have yer?"

"Vengeance has already been taken, Gyrwald. By my hand, and by the hands of my kin." Tyrheld paused and nodded to Felnir. "And by this man's blade. More than a hundred have we slain under his kingship, and he has made solemn oath before the Altvar to rid this land of the *Ahrkun* for once and all. On this promise have my kin and I pledged ourselves to him. In my brother's name, I beseech you to join us."

The line creasing Baldyr's forehead shifted into one of contemplation, although Felnir found little upon his face to track his thoughts. *Got some wit about him*, Felnir decided. *A useful ally, but also a dangerous enemy.*

"You lot." The Gyrwald broke his silent reverie with a harsh bark at his *menda*. "Go and hunt me a boar or two." As the warriors trooped from the hall, Baldyr offered Felnir a bland smile. "If I'm to host a king beneath my roof, a decent meal seems the least I can offer."

The feast that night contrasted greatly with that provided by Arnhilt Volksora in the Greencrest, for Baldyr filled his hall with several dozen kinfolk and favoured friends. Felnir's initial estimation of the Vorl Tuhrk as a grim people was disproven once the liquor began to flow, and the air sweetened with the aroma of roasted boar. They sang, danced and laughed in rowdy good humour while a trio of musicians conjured many a jaunty tune from instruments of unfamiliar design. One blew into a double-piped flute while another scraped a bow along the strings of something that resembled a concoction of harp and mandolin. The loudest, however, was a fabric-covered bag from which several pipes protruded. Upon hearing its first few notes, Felnir had entertained the notion that these people had nurtured a very peculiar taste in music. Yet, as the piper played on, the sound became more tuneful and possessed of a low, compelling tone sure to capture the ear.

While Felnir and his fellow outlanders were regarded with wary respect, Tyrheld was made far more welcome. Swept into the swirl of dance and song, many soon clustered around her to hear the tale of King Felnir's triumph at the standing stones. Many of the listeners were plainly sceptical as to its truth, but he noted how they seemed to relish the details of the *Ahrkun's* slaughter.

The sole exception to the revelry was the Gyrwald himself, slumping in his chair with goblet in hand, his features cast in an expression of morose calculation. Felnir made a few attempts at conversation, only to be rebuffed with wordless grunts. He contented himself with wolfing down the well-cooked boar meat placed before him and trying to gauge the mood of the Vorl Tuhrk. Their response to Tyrheld's tale was encouraging, but the suspicion he saw whenever they glanced in his direction bespoke a people not easily persuaded to anything.

"Did yer really find that in the vaults?"

Blinking in surprise, Felnir turned to find Baldyr directing his shrewd gaze towards the Sword of the Altvar. Felnir had unbuckled the blade on taking his seat, propping it against his chair. "I did," he replied. "Would you like to hold it?"

"No," the Gyrwald mused after a brief pause. "Don't think I would. Come on." He got to his feet, gesturing for Felnir to follow. "Time we had a proper chat."

The music and revels dimmed when Baldyr rose, resuming again at his growling command as he led Felnir from the hall. The night air was bracing, a stiff wind sweeping from the north to sway the trees and ripple the surface of the lake beyond.

"I heard Tyrheld speak of an *Ehilkun* among yer company," Baldyr said, striding towards a tall watchtower. "One of the more famous ones, unless my ears played me wrong."

"Angmund," Felnir confirmed. "The very same Angmund who stood at Velgard's side throughout his reign."

"Thought it sounded familiar. Yet yer chose not to bring him."

"Tyrheld suggested it might be a poor idea. The old ones are not so welcome here, she said."

"And she wasn't wrong." Halting at the base of the watchtower, Baldyr called to the two warriors stationed atop it. "You pair. Get down from there and piss off to the feast."

Once the sentries had descended and hurried off towards the hall, Baldyr inclined his head at the ladder. "Thought yer might care to see my domain, yer kingship."

"Just Felnir will suffice," he said, reaching for the first rung.

Once atop the tower and buffeted by the yet fiercer breeze, he beheld the entire length of the Vorl Arna. The clouds were sparse and the half-moon bright, casting a shimmer on the ruffled water. To the east lay the hills and forests he had traversed to get here. This western bank of the long lake was characterised by cultivated fields and grazing land for the herds of cattle he could see clustering together for warmth. A range of hills rose on the western horizon, beyond which lay a flat plain.

"The Swathe, we call it," Baldyr said. "Goes on fer mile after mile, so flat and featureless it's said to have driven men mad through sheer boredom."

"What lies on the other side?" Felnir asked.

"Not a bugger among us knows. Every soul who ever ventured to cross it either failed to return or came back with their brains addled by hunger and solitude. It might go on forever fer all we know. This, y'see, is the very edge of Vorunvahl, where my kin were driven many years ago." He paused, turning to regard the far richer lands to the east. Felnir resisted the urge to prompt him. It was plain the Gyrwald had a good deal more to say but would do so only in his own time.

When he spoke again, it was with a sombre, reflective air lacking his previous undercurrent of scorn. "We have always been different, y'see. Set apart from those who first came to these lands. For while they enjoyed an unnatural span of years, thanks to the Altvar's blessing, our forebears did not. They lived as long as men and women are s'posed to. Not more, not less. No one truly knows why, but my grandfather told an old tale about how those of our bloodline had been at sea when the great calamity befell the city beneath the mountain and the Altvar's blessing swept over the shore.

"So their descendants had been denied the favour of the gods, though I like to think we had been spared it. The *Ehilkun* came to despise our ancestors, watching them wither with age while they stayed young. They were considered cursed and cast out. Banding together, they came here, hounded to the very edge of the earth. They would have been driven into the Swathe if they hadn't stood and fought, and bloody was the day they defeated their persecutors. Henceforth, the Vorl Tuhrk have ever stood apart from Vorunvahl. We trade with them as needed, but we take no part in their affairs, nor they in ours. Their hatred dimmed as the centuries passed and the ranks of the *Ehilkun* began to thin. Their children and grandchildren slowly became as we are. But still, we remember if they do not. Their wars are not our wars, and any king they might choose to grovel to is not our king."

"I didn't come here in search of grovellers," Felnir told him. "But fighters. For we share a common enemy, do we not?" Baldyr replied with a short nod, but said nothing. Clearly it was Felnir's turn to set out his stall for this bargain. "As for kingship," he went on, "I'll make no claim upon you or your folk. Pay no tribute and offer no obeisance, I don't care. Even name yourself king of the Vorl Tuhrk, if it pleases you. We will be brother kings. Our people bound together in victory over a vile foe. That's a tale worth telling, don't you think?"

Baldyr retained a neutral expression, turning to regard the snow-dappled hills and forests stretching away from the eastern bank of the Vorl Arna. "The *Ahrkun* were not always as they are now. This feud began in my father's time and he spoke of them as friends once. The *Sindra* was not cruel then, whatever madness claimed him not yet blossomed. It's said he was once a Gyrwald himself, ruling his stretch of coastline with both strength and wisdom. But something changed. A crack in his mind, some say, while his followers claim the Altvar blessed him with a vision. And so he abandoned his people and wandered alone for many years, speaking to any who would listen of the great secret revealed unto him by the gods. In time, he gained a following. They were a peaceable lot at first, keeping to themselves and not seeming to mind so much when folk laughed at their prattle. But, slowly, they grew tired of being laughed at. Where before they would trade for food, they simply began to take it. Once they only accepted those into their ranks who came to them willingly, then came the tales of them stealing children. It was this that set us to war with them.

"Late in my father's time upon the Gyrwald's chair, the *Ahrkun* crossed the lake and laid waste to a village on the shore, killing many and carrying off the young folk. My father was a man of gentle manners, but like most such men, his anger was a terrible thing when roused. I was barely more than a lad when we set out to hunt the bastards down. We cornered them in a gulley some miles from the lake. They killed the children they'd stolen, then threw themselves at us, screaming cants to their beloved *Sindra*. My father had their heads set on spikes along the eastern bank, a warning he hoped. It didn't stop them. Not then. Not now. The feud waxes and wanes, but never ends. Long have I dreamed of leading my *menda* to the Hahl-Trova and wiping it from the earth. But we have always been too few. My question for you now, King Felnir of Vorunvahl, is how few are those that follow you?"

"My *menda* is small," Felnir admitted. "But it will grow. I have my trusted bondsman spreading word of the victory we won at the standing stones. I know war, brother. I've fought battles from here to the most distant borders of the world's greatest empire. I know how to build a host, and how to wield it. Those who have suffered the *Ahrkun*'s yoke will seize the chance to throw it off, especially when they see the strength of my ally."

"And is this yer plan, or the scheme of that *Ehilkun* who walks at yer side?"

"Angmund does not command me." Felnir paused to quell the heat in his tone. "But only a fool would blind himself to useful insight. The old man knows much, but do not imagine that I trust him in all things. I owe him a meal each day and the protection of my *menda*. Nothing more."

"Best keep him away from my lot on the march then," Baldyr said, offering his hand. "And be sure they'll expect their fair share of the loot . . . brother." His features betrayed resignation rather than zeal as they shook hands, though his grip was fierce. "Just one other thing," he added. "The *Sindra*'s head. When this is done, I want it. You can kill the fucker if yer like. But the head is mine. I intend to make a cairn of *Ahrkun* skulls, and his will sit at the very top."

"Take it," Felnir said, grinning. "A gift from one king to another."

It required close to two weeks for Baldyr to muster his full *menda*. Messengers were sent to every village in the Gyrwald's domain and the response had been swift, the first warriors arriving only two days later. Once the full host had gathered at the stockade, Baldyr convened another feast, a great celebration too large for the confines of his hall. As he walked with Sygna and Falk among the many fires where the Vorl Tuhrk played their strange music amid a welter of dance and drink, Felnir made a rough count of their numbers.

"Near a thousand, wouldn't you say?" he asked Sygna.

"I make it closer to nine hundred," she said. "Less those left behind to guard his lands when we march. Plenty of archers, though. That's something to be thankful for."

"Good steel and sound shields, too," Falk put in. "But not a scrap of armour among them."

"Hatred can make up for a lack of armour," Felnir said. "And I've a sense these folk have plenty of that, too."

Once again, Tyrheld proved a popular figure, regaling repeated audiences with the tale of the standing stones. Felnir noticed that the scale of his victory had grown with the telling, as had the number of *Ahrkun* slain and the manner of the Factor's demise.

"Filthy coward that he was, he begged our king for his life," Tyrheld proclaimed to a rapt group of warriors from one of the lakeside villages. "Upon his knees he wept in contrition for the lives he had taken and torments inflicted on the poor folk of the River Belt. But Felnir is a man of justice above all and took his head with but one stroke of the Altvar's blessed blade."

"You have to admit," Felnir murmured to a peeved Sygna, "it's more dramatic than an arrow through the forehead."

There were other story-spinners at neighbouring fires retelling the sagas of old. Yet, as Felnir listened, he found the tales differed from those he knew. Some changes were subtle, such as the colour of Ihryka's hair being golden yellow rather than jet black. Others were more pronounced, so much so that they altered the meaning of the original. Turmvek the Blademaster's justified slaying of his treacherous son in battle was presented as the act of a prideful warrior jealous of his son's prowess. Thus, a polemic of disappointed parentage and the inescapable chains of duty became a cautionary tale of the perils of envy.

"They've forgotten," Sygna said as the story-spinner completed her recitation to appreciative applause. "Forgotten who they are. Too many years removed from the truth of our history."

"Were the sagas ever truly history?" Felnir wondered, once again feeling a pang at Elvine's absence. She would surely have found this fascinating. "These people are the descendants of those shunned and despised for no fault of their own. I'll not begrudge them the freedom to write their own stories."

A blaring of pipes drew their gaze to the largest fire where all the musicians were now gathered. They played no tune but pealed out the same low, ominous note. In response, the Vorl Tuhrk all abandoned their revels and began to gather about the great stack of burning timber. All attention was fixed upon their Gyrwald, silhouetted against the flames with his arm raised.

"King Felnir Skyrnrak!" he called. "Come forth! We have oaths to make in sight of my people!"

A hush settled over the crowd as Felnir made his way to Baldyr's side. He expected to find the Gyrwald holding a striker, yet as he drew closer, he recognised the object in his hand as a wooden effigy carved into the shape of a man. The motif of a spread-winged raven had been scorched into the thing's forehead.

"Here is our enemy!" Baldyr proclaimed, raising the effigy higher. "The *Sindra* himself. In the name of Silfaer, do I vow my vengeance for his many crimes. In the name of Karnic, do I call upon his blessing in our hunt so that our blades may darken with the blood of our prey. In the name of Ulthnir, do I state my words are true and fear not his justice, for I am no oath breaker. So have I spoken, so shall our enemy perish." With that, he cast the effigy into the flames, the act greeted by a great shout from the onlooking warriors.

"Now you, Felnir Skyrnrak," Baldyr went on as the raised voices faded. "Make your oath in the sight of the gods, to be witnessed by my *menda* so that they will hold you to your word unto your dying breath."

Stepping closer to the fire, Felnir unhooked the striker from his belt. He had chosen to bring the bronze sigil of Ulthnir, knowing that tonight he would make the most sacred of oaths. "In the land of your forebears," he said, holding up the striker, "an oath is made by the conjuring of fire from a sigil of the gods. This is Ulthnir's sigil, the sign of the Worldsmith. No secret can be kept from his eye. No lie unheard by his ear. Know then that in Ulthnir's sight do I name myself a friend and ally of the Vorl Tuhrk, for now and always. Your struggles will be my struggles. Your battles, my battles. No denizen of this land who finds themselves in need shall ever be turned from my fire. A great mission lies before us, for it is glorious to strike down an enemy so vile as the *Ahrkun*. Ulthnir knows this, and will bless our blades when I seal this compact in fire."

Taking the steel rod attached to the striker, he scraped it across the metal, scattering sparks into the air. The crowd's reaction was less voluble than that afforded their Gyrwald, more a loud murmuring of grim approval.

Felnir took heart from the absence of any discord, turning to offer Baldyr his hand. As they gripped, forearm to forearm, the Vorl Tuhrk's murmur became a hungry chorus of shouts, many brandishing swords or beating their shields with axes. Their evident keenness for the fight to come caused Felnir to recall another jewel of wisdom from the High Velzir: "Be not deceived by numbers in war, my thunderbolt. A thousand swords wielded by those willing to die in their cause can win against the tallest odds."

"I hope yer fight as well yer talk, my kingly brother," Baldyr said, leaning close to be heard above the cries of his *menda*. "The *Ahrkun* won't fall easy."

Chapter Twenty-Nine

Thera

Come the dawn, Thera positioned herself at the prow of the *Great Wolf*, dreadaxe in hand. Before her, the strait was thick with a morning mist so far undisturbed by red sails. To port, the *Chainbreaker* rested at anchor, Veltta and her crew arrayed on deck in their mismatched armour. To starboard, Veilwald Synghild waited aboard her personal warship, *Ulfmaer's Gale*, with as many warriors as could be carried. While only two-thirds the *Great Wolf*'s size, she was still a substantial craft, and Thera didn't doubt the value of her service in the struggle to come. Still, she couldn't help but harbour a kernel of worry over Synghild's avowed goal: *It is my intention to die in battle as swiftly as possible.* No aspect of the Veilwald's actions since had given Thera any reason to think her insincere.

A far larger number of warriors had been crammed aboard the *Northern Star*. The merchantman lay to the rear of the three warships, trailed by a flotilla of smaller craft that stretched all the way back to the Vorun Hardta docks. In normal times, Thera would have thought it an impressive force. Now, facing the might of the Nihlvarian battle fleet, she knew it to be paltry. With luck, so would their enemies.

As she waited, her gaze strayed continually towards the banks of the strait, even though they were rendered into vague grey slopes by the fog. She told herself this worked to their advantage: if she couldn't see the engines, then neither could the Nihlvarians. But she was nagged by the knowledge that Lynnea had been far from certain she had found every spy in this port, and who could say what her opposing commander might know? This inevitably summoned thoughts of her apprentice and the lingering hurt Thera sensed in her presence. It had been worsened by Thera's order that she remain ashore during the battle.

"If the day goes against us, you will secrete yourself in this port and report the enemy's actions to the Tielwald." She handed Lynnea the silver knot her great-grandfather had gifted her. "I know not if this will work, but you must try. If you can reach him, you will follow his orders in all things." The prospect of placing Lynnea under Gruinskard's direction stirred a welter of guilt in Thera's breast, but, should she fail today, she saw no other option. Lynnea's abilities, and her newly acquired skills in spy-hunting, made her too valuable an asset to risk in the chaos of battle.

For her part, the maiden had taken the trinket and accepted her orders with a stiff, wordless nod. Thera could feel her restraining the many thoughts behind her eyes, catching a faint impression of anger mixed with resignation. No words accompanied the sensation, for which Thera was grateful. She was sure they would haunt her final moments if they were to come this morn.

"There . . ." Ragnalt murmured, shifting at Thera's side. Ever the hunter, he had his ear cocked to the waters beyond the prow, brows drawn as he strained for the slightest sound. "Oars," he added, a relieved grin joining the grim anticipation in his gaze. "Coming on at fast stroke. They took the bait."

"Stand ready," Thera snapped, keeping her voice low. Ragnalt swiftly relayed the command to her *menda*, warriors setting their shields and drawing weapons while archers climbed ropes to the platform they had constructed atop the mast. Thera kept her gaze on the swirling mist. Her ears were not so keen as Ragnalt's, so it was a few moments before she heard the overlapping creak and splash of many oars cutting the water. The first sail resolved into view soon after, a scarlet square emblazoned with the invaders' perversion of Ulthnir's sigil. The hull below was narrow, built for speed, her oars churning the water white as she hurtled through the strait. Her course was unerring, bespeaking a knowledge of the famously treach-erous channel leading to Vorun Hardta. *Fruit of the Volkrath's labour*, Thera concluded, watching the ship draw ever nearer. Three more sails appeared to her rear, sailing in line, most likely with the intention of assuming battle formation once through the narrows.

When the leading ship had closed to within three hundred yards of the *Great Wolf*, her crew let forth a collective cry of challenge as they spied the awaiting flotilla. Their voices were rich in confidence, the bombast of warriors prematurely drunk on victory. The manner in which it faltered into surprised dismay would have been comical to Thera, had she not been keenly aware of all the slaughter to follow. The war cry died amid the splintering crash of their ship's hull colliding with the newly created marble reef below. Thera had worried that even the huge amount of stone they had tumbled into the strait over the past weeks might prove ineffective against shallow draught ships. But even with the channel swollen by the morning tide, the submerged mountain sufficed to bring the swift Nihlvarian vessel to an abrupt halt.

Mast tilting, she slewed to port, her oars flailing like the legs of a bug caught in honey. From the way her prow dipped, Thera concluded her hull must have been holed. The suspicion was confirmed by the sight of frothing water and Nihlvarian sailors hastily trying to launch a boat as their ship began to sink. The current covered only half her deck, however, prevented from sinking lower by the mass of stone beneath. It was a short reprieve, for the next warship in line smashed into her stern a heartbeat later. Timbers shattered and sailors tumbled as the two ships met in an ugly embrace of mutual destruction. The captain of the third ship evidently saw the danger and tried to veer away, only to steer their vessel into the ragged submerged flanks of the strait. Through the fog, Thera made out a forest of wavering masts and lowering sails as the bulk of the Nihlvarian fleet attempted to halt its charge. The leading ships, however, were moving too fast to avoid the inexorable collision with the pair of conjoined and ruined vessels aground on the marble barrier.

"Now!" Thera hissed in hungry expectation, eyes flicking from one bank of the channel to the other. The crews serving the engines had been instructed that the moment to launch would be obvious from the cacophony of colliding hulls and panicked screaming. As the tumult of catastrophe filled the fjord, Thera worried that these instructions had been too vague, then huffed a deep sigh of relief at the sight of the first stone arcing above the fog shrouding the western bank. The engines had been sighted carefully the preceding day to ensure their projectiles would assail the enemy fleet from end to end. The first stone plummeted down not far from the mass of stricken vessels forming the vanguard. The haze obscured the sight of its impact, but the explosive crunch of smashed timbers told the tale clearly enough.

Two more stones descended in quick succession, launched from the eastern bank, birthing similar unseen destruction. Luissa had hoped to have a fourth engine ready in time for the battle, but it remained only partially completed when the *Ohlira*'s warning arrived. As another salvo came crashing down and Thera heard the signature screams of many people struggling in troubled waters, she concluded that three was more than enough.

"Might not have to stain our steel at all today," Ragnalt commented as the din continued, growing louder by the second. For a time, Thera allowed herself the hope that he was right. Stone after stone fell, wreaking ever more havoc upon their enemies. The manic sway of masts visible through the mist, and the ongoing chorus of fearful cries, bespoke a fleet beset by chaos. Yet, as the destruction wore on, the burgeoning sun began to dispel the fog, whereupon it became clear their foe was far from spent.

While the bulk of the Nihlvarian vanguard had been sunk or run aground, the larger ships forming the heart of their fleet were busily drawing back. Thera winced at the sight of their dense banks of oars sweeping with desperate energy to reverse the course of the huge vessels. A great many slaves would surely be suffering under the whip to produce such a feat. The engines continued their barrage as the enemy dispersed. She saw one large warship smashed from deck to hull by a stone, the wreck sinking within mere moments as her crew tumbled from her rails like ants. Once again, Thera's thoughts went to the slaves chained below. For them, there would be no escape. More stones fell, but with the gaps between the Nihlvarian ships widening, most failed to find a target.

"They'll run if they're smart," Ragnalt grunted, eyes dark with battle lust below the rim of his helm. "Let's hope they're not, eh?"

His words roused a growl of agreement from the nearest warriors, Thera noting how they fidgeted with impatience or the inner turmoil of suppressed fear. Once again, she was struck by the irksome nature of sea battles. Long intervals of waiting interspersed with furious combat and deadly peril. So she and her *menda* were obliged to stand and watch for a full hour as their enemy decided their next course of action. Ragnalt was right: the Nihlvarian commander would be wise to turn back rather than make another attempt to run the gauntlet of engines and a hull-shredding reef. While their force had been badly mauled, most of it remained intact and there were other approaches to Vorun Hardta. Yet that would entail a delay of at least a week, and who knew what surprises Thera could orchestrate in the interim?

You came for me, she thought, eyes flicking from one great warship to another, wondering upon which deck her adversary stood in worried calculation. *And for the riches of this port. Why leave with such a prize within your grasp?* She nurtured a fervent hope that, however much the unseen commander feared her, he feared Sister Lore, or his far-away king more. If so, this trap would be fully sprung. So it was with considerable relief that she saw the enemy ships once again drawing together. They had retreated beyond the reach of the engines now, smaller vessels clustering around their larger sisters. It was too distant to make out much detail, but after another hour the purpose became clear.

"They're launching boats!" came the cry from the platform atop the mast. A pause, then another call: "A lot of fucking boats!"

By the time the last dregs of the mist had dissipated, the water surrounding the Nihlvarian fleet was so thick with boats it resembled a huge lily pad. Ever more warriors descended the hulls of the great ships to fill the smaller craft. Thera surmised that their commander had, rightly, concluded that carrying an additional quota of boats would be a useful asset when assaulting a port.

It was near noon by the time the mass of bobbing craft began to separate from their ships, at first with a great clatter of oars before they struggled into a semblance of order and set off towards Vorun Hardta. Untroubled by the jagged flanks of the strait or the marble reef, they came on in a dark tide, oars moving at a slow pace to ensure they retained some measure of cohesion. As they neared the wrecks still perched atop the barrier, the engines resumed their barrage. The two on the eastern bank cast forth the same huge boulders as before, producing impressively tall splashes as they impacted the oncoming horde, but sinking only one or two craft at a time. Whoever had charge of the engine on the western bank was more astute, filling the sling with smaller chunks of marble that wreaked a great deal more damage. Still, it wasn't enough, the Nihlvarians sweeping on despite the ragged holes torn in their ranks.

"Archers!" Thera barked, the warriors aloft responding with a well-aimed volley. The range was still long, but she needed to kill or wound as many foes as possible before the two sides joined battle. To either side, the archers aboard the *Chainbreaker* and the *Ulfmaer's Gale* added their bows to the effort, and the air separating the ships from the fleet became a dark blizzard of arcing shafts. Thera once again found much to regret in the dearth of skilled bowmen under her command. The continual volleys inflicted a good amount of damage on the leading boats, the crew of the foremost so liberally feathered that they slumped at their oars, all lifeless or injured, to drift away on the current. But there were too many boats and too few archers, and soon the Nihlvarians were barely a dozen yards off.

"Signal the rest to fan out!" Thera called to the stern, where Althsten began waving a blazing torch back and forth. In response, the long trail of boats and merchant ships began to separate into two wings, spreading to either side of the warships in the centre. Hefting the dreadaxe, Thera turned to face her *menda*. "Stand ready to repel boarders and hold fast to your oaths!"

Replying with a hearty shout, they immediately arranged themselves into two ranks, lining the *Great Wolf*'s port and starboard rails. In accordance with their agreed plan, Veilwald Synghild ordered her ship's anchor raised and her port oars to fast stroke, causing the warship to turn and create a barricade against the oncoming onslaught. To port, the *Chainbreaker* mirrored the manoeuvre just as the first Nihlvarian craft butted up against her hull. Grapples flew, the barbed hooks sinking into the *Great Wolf's* timbers around her bows. Thera and Ragnalt drew daggers to cut away as many ropes as they could before a volley of arrows and thrown axes forced them back. Taking a firm grip on the dreadaxe's haft, Thera waited for the first Nihlvarian warrior to appear above the rail.

She saw his hands first, clawing at the rope to haul his considerable bulk into view. He was impressive, broad and tall, with a shaven head and thick beard, scalp and face tattooed in a dense maze of red. His expression was one of angry determination rather than unreasoning battle lust. She considered allowing him time to reach for the sword strapped to his back. Better a brave soul died with a sword in hand, after all. But in the midst of war, sentiment had no place. As she stabbed the tips of the dreadaxe's blades into his chest, the ancient metal piercing his leather armour with ease, he let out a sound that was as rich in annoyance as it was pain. Before he tumbled from view, Thera caught his final expression, reading in it the aggrieved despondency of a man suffering a terrible theft. Casting her gaze to the warrior's comrades now climbing the ropes to either side, she saw the same resolve on their faces, men and women intent on securing their moment of glory. *These are different to those we faced at the Lyx Helv,* she decided. *Lore sent her best.*

"Thera!" Ragnalt shouted in warning, hauling her back as a thrown knife whistled close to her head. Its owner followed swiftly, a lithe, unarmoured woman who hopped onto the rail with a hatchet in hand and a small dagger clenched between her teeth. Nimbly dodging the swing of Ragnalt's sword, she threw herself at Thera, hatchet whirling as she snatched the dagger from her mouth. She moved with a quickness that seemed inhuman, ducking the sweep of the dreadaxe to hack Thera's legs. The move was revealed as a feint when, taking advantage of Thera's imbalance, she leaped, dagger extended. The blade might well have pierced Thera's eye if a fast, blurring shape hadn't hurtled past her shoulder to latch itself to the quick woman's face. Mohlnir yowled and hissed as she tore at the Nihlvarian, claws and teeth rending skin into ribbons. Cat and human engaged in a brief, chaotic dance, the woman vainly attempting to prise the thrashing beast away until she collided with the rail and tumbled over, taking Mohlnir with her.

The prospect of having to explain the cat's demise to Lynnea birthed a new sensation in Thera's breast. Up until this point, she had been too fixated on her unfolding plan to allow for the luxury of anger, but now it blossomed into a fiery battle rage. Spying a trio of Nihlvarians clambering over the prow, she charged, the dreadaxe felling two with the first stroke, and the third with the second. The thunk of more grappling hooks biting timber drew her gaze to the starboard rail where a half-dozen strong group of red faces were in process of securing a foothold upon the deck with more following behind. Thera's grasp on the world fractured into the disjointed haze of combat as she threw herself into their midst, the twin blades of the dreadaxe lacing the air with crimson arcs. Severed hands and limbs littered the deck as she continued her rampage, catching glimpses of shattered faces and crushed helms.

"Why did you come here?" The strident, enraged demand echoed through the red mist, Thera only vaguely recognising the voice as her own. "Why? WHY?"

She came back to herself shouting the question into the slack, tattooed features of a stocky man with the dreadaxe's blade buried in his shoulder. Beyond a few shudders and a dribble of blood from his squirming lips, he had no answer for her. Straightening, she drew in a deep draught of air and surveyed her ship, finding both rails free of attackers. She saw a red-muzzled Snaryk roving about, whining in distress as he peered into every shadowed corner, searching for his feline friend. A dozen bodies lay upon the deck, most red-faced, some not. The ship remained hers.

Returning to the prow, she clapped a hand to Ragnalt's shoulder, relieved to find him among the living, before climbing up on the prow, seeking to gauge the course of the battle. To port, the *Chainbreaker* had drifted a dozen yards from her prior position, her deck roiling with combat. The frenzy with which the freed slaves assailed their former masters ensured the scene was too chaotic to discern who might be winning, but the trail of wrecked boats in her wake gave Thera heart that the contest was going Veltta's way. Beyond the *Chainbreaker*, the waters were filled with dozens of boats locked in deadly combat as Synghild's folk strove to contest the Nihlvarian assault on the port. The smaller merchant ships crashed into the Nihlvarian boats, capsizing some, while the fishing craft became embroiled in duels, which often saw the destruction of both combatants. Still, for all the evident cost-liness of the struggle, the line appeared to be holding.

Looking to starboard, Thera found a less encouraging sight. The *Ulfmaer's Gale* had drifted much further away than the *Chainbreaker*, and her deck two-thirds covered in Nihlvarians, with more clambering up the many ropes fixed to her rails. She couldn't see the Veilwald, but it was starkly clear that her ship would soon become a prize of the enemy.

"Althsten, steer to starboard!" Thera called to the helmsman before addressing her next command to her *menda*. "To oars! Port side, reverse stroke! Starboard, fast stroke! Be quick about it!"

The *Great Wolf* had ever been sluggish to manoeuvre at slow speed and it required several aggravating moments of wallowing before she began to close the distance to the *Ulfmaer's Gale*. From below, Thera heard the screams and shattered timber that told of Nihlvarian boats being crushed between the two hulls. Calling her *menda* to her side, she leaped across the gap and began to hack her way through the red-faced throng. Once again, the crimson veil of battle descended, the nightmarish confusion punctuated by a few stark horrors. She saw Snaryk bite a Nihlvarian's leg nearly in two as the hound bore him to the deck before crushing his head, helm and all, between its massive jaws. At one point she realised she had fallen, her boot scrabbling on boards made slippy with spilled guts. A red-faced warrior loomed above her, sword raised for a killing stroke. His triumphant yell ended when the boss of Ragnalt's shield smashed into his face. Ragnalt finished the foeman with a thrust to the belly, then turned to help Thera regain her feet.

Looking around at the ongoing struggle, Thera saw with satisfaction that her *menda* had succeeded in forging a path across the mid-deck of the *Ulfmaer's Gale*. Half the surviving Nihlvarians had drawn back to the prow while the rest were still battling Synghild's warriors at the stern. The Veilwald stood tall atop a stack of barrels near the helm, sword lashing tirelessly at the surrounding enemy. Thera took some heart from the absence of more boarders scaling the rails, but then grunted in frustration at the sight of a half-dozen grappling ropes sailing over the stern.

"Push this lot off the deck," she instructed Ragnalt, nodding towards the enemy contingent clustered at the prow. "Then find me at the Veilwald's side."

With her battle rage faded, the process of hacking her way towards the stern swiftly became a dire, methodical chore. Now there was no red mist to obscure the detail of every injury or death she inflicted, nor block their screams from her ears. She was aided by their weariness. Rowing through the engines' barrage, scaling a ship's hull, then fighting a ferocious enemy had left many too fatigued to contest Thera's charge. Snaryk's presence greatly assisted her progress. The hound's bulk repeatedly barrelled Nihlvarians aside while his snapping jaws dissuaded already tired warriors from attempting to bar their path.

Hacking down a pair of enemies close to the helm, Thera faltered to a halt in surprise. She had expected to find the Veilwald dead, or borne down and surrounded by foes. Instead, she was propped against a barrel, face drawn in both pain and anger as Teylhar applied a wad of cloth to a bleeding wound in her side.

"You . . ." Synghild grated at her son ". . . were supposed to stay with the fucking engine!"

"There was nothing to aim at, Mother," Teylhar replied amiably. "We thought we'd be more use here."

A tight cordon of his fellow shipwrights surrounded them, all bloodied from recent combat. Thera recalled the grapples she had seen arcing over the stern and sighed in relief. There were no more Nihlvarians to fight, at least for now.

"Couldn't even—" Synghild choked off into a shout of pain, features taking on a dark hue as she railed at Teylhar. "Couldn't even let me die!" she managed through her shudders. "Can't you do one thing right, boy?"

"I'll happily accept any punishment you deem fit, Veilwald." Teylhar smiled and tightened his grip on the bloody dressing. "Now hold still." Noticing Thera's presence, he looked up, face stark with worry. "She needs a healer, Vellihr. This wound must be closed."

Thera went in search of Achier, finding the former slave near the stern slitting the throat of a wounded Nihlvarian. "Whip-man's mark," Achier explained, pointing to a cluster of tattoos on the slain man's cheek. Nearby, her *menda* were busy tossing bodies over the side, some dead, some not. A quick count of her warriors sent a shudder through Thera. The fighting most likely wasn't over and she had already lost at least half.

"The Veilwald is wounded," she told Achier. "See to her." Nodding, he got to his feet, then paused when Thera caught his arm. "Stitch it if you can," she said, voice low. "If not, do what you must."

"It doesn't work on all wounds," he replied softly. "You were . . . an unusual case, Vellihr."

"Even so. She has to live."

Releasing him, she joined Ragnalt at the rail. She had to fight the desire to slump against the timbers, her body beset by such a wave of weariness it was almost an ache. A similar pitch of tiredness showed in Ragnalt's eyes, but his face was lit by a growing smile.

"By Ulthnir's mighty balls, that's a welcome sight," he breathed, gaze fixed on the distant reaches of the fjord. Turning, Thera quickly beheld the source of his joy. The Nihlvarian fleet was moving again. Having turned about, they were now heading for open water, yet beyond them, she saw the many sails of another fast-approaching host of vessels. *Ossgrym's fleet*, she realised, *come to close the trap*. She found she couldn't contend with the needs of her body and collapsed against the rail. Only Ragnalt's embrace kept her from slumping to the deck.

For a time, she lost track of events. She learned later of how the Nihlvarian ships, shorn of their warriors, were unable to fend off Ossgrym's attack. A few of their ships were burned and sunk, but most were captured in the brief but bloody fighting. The lingering clusters of boat-borne warriors assaulting Vorun Hardta were systematically destroyed. A few even managed to reach the docks, only to be slaughtered upon the quayside by the townsfolk.

Eventually, a hefty gulp of mead and the burgeoning cries of the survivors as they greeted Ossgrym's leading ships brought Thera back to full awareness. The noise lacked cohesion at first, just a great wordless expression of victory mixed with the exultation of survival. As it wore on, however, words began to form, and it took on a definite meaning.

Thera found herself jostled and raised up, gazing around through bleary eyes at the surrounding mass of ships and boats. Everywhere people were cheering, and each throat cast forth the same cry. The clamour grew so loud it filled the fjord, echoing from the flanks of the mountains and casting its proclamation to the sky so that even the gods could not mistake it: "HAIL THERA! QUEEN OF THE ISLES!"

PART III

"If war must be fought, let it be fought unto the most bitter end, lest the Ascarls grow too fond of its taste."
Ulthnir Horuhnklehr – the Worldsmith – from the Altvar Rendi

CHAPTER THIRTY

Elvine

As Ahlgrun predicted, the fog descended in a thick pall a good hour before dawn, whereupon he and his brothers set about steering a south-westerly course. They had spent the previous night sheltered in a narrow inlet. Ahlgrun had allowed a small, coal-fired brazier to be lit, enabling Elvine and the others to banish their chill. Now, it had to be doused and she once again found herself shivering despite the blanket wrapped tight about her. The boat moved by benefit of wind only, Ahlgrun shunning the use of oars.

"Too loud," he explained. "An experienced ear can hear an oar in a rowlock from miles off. And fog has an uncanny way of carrying sounds further than you'd like."

He had charge of the helm while Kelvyrn, the middle brother, worked the sail and the youngest, Teryk, perched himself at the prow. The least talkative of an already reticent trio, he maintained a silent vigil. Every now and then he would flick a hand to port or starboard, sometimes raising a fist above his head in a signal for Kelvyrn to trim the sail.

"Does he know these waters?" an intrigued Colvyn enquired of Ahlgrun.

"Teryk knows all waters," the fisherman grunted back, clearly disinclined to elaboration.

The morning wore on in mostly tense silence, broken occasionally by Gruinskard's snores. In accordance with the Tielwald's instructions, Coelnyr was obliged to nudge him awake whenever he made a sound, suffering the old man's caustic tongue for his pains.

"Get off me, you filthy reprobate," he groaned, pushing the spy's hand away at his third such rousing. Getting to his feet, Gruinskard cast a baleful eye at the thick haze surrounding the boat. "Aren't we clear of this stuff yet?"

"Be thankful for a cold and cloudy morn," Ahlgrun said. "Means it'll linger long, which is no bad thing for us. Now, all of you hold your tongues. One of those red ships could be no more than fifty paces off and we'd still not see it."

The flanks of the fjord they sailed through were lost to the haze, preventing Elvine from gauging their progress. She watched Teryk constantly, hoping to read some meaning into the frequency of his signals to his brothers. After a time, his movements slowed, giving her hope they had reached open water. However, a sudden raised fist had her heart lurching. Turning, the younger brother shot an ominous scowl at Ahlgrun while Kelvyrn hurried to trim the sail and slow the boat. The reason for Teryk's alarm became clear when Elvine spied a small smudge of yellow light a few points to the left of the prow. More glimmered into view as Ahlgrun angled the tiller to steer them away, a row of flickering torches describing the sweep of a ship's rail. Despite the change in direction, the fjord's current conspired to force the two vessels closer, the boat passing in front the larger craft's bow.

Elvine stilled her breath as she watched the slow passage of the torchlit stern. She could see only vague outlines of rigging and crew, but no agitation that would indicate they had been spotted. Several long moments later, the torches had faded into the fog. Elvine's explosive sigh of relief stalled in her breast at the sight of more ahead. This time the flickering specks of flame were more numerous and positioned higher above the water. This was one of Vahlak's great warships. Fortunately, the current drew them clear of the huge vessel by well over a hundred paces, rendering them invisible to those on board.

"Elvine!"

She shuddered as the call echoed across the misted waters, shocked both by hearing her own name, and her immediate recognition of the voice that called it.

"Elvine!" it came again, clear and strong, though lacking the anger she expected. "I know you're there. Will you not speak to me, dear heart?"

Involuntarily, Elvine moved to the port side of the boat, staring at the indistinct flare of torchlight as Lore spoke on: "Come back to me. It's not too late. I can forgive. But you must come back and return what you stole."

The queen's voice held an unexpectedly plaintive note, Elvine hearing in it a genuine, even raw need. *She actually believed us friends*, she reminded herself, wondering at the sorrowful ache rising in her chest.

"There is much blood on your hands, Elvine!" Lore's voice took on a chiding tone. "Many faithful servants now lie dead in the Verungyr thanks to your treachery. And yet, still, I offer forgiveness. As does Tuhlvyr Vahlak, though he does complain of a headache." She paused, as if in expectation of an answering laugh. When none came and she spoke again, her voice had hardened further. "Look to Gruinskard and ask yourself if he would ever be so merciful."

Elvine didn't need to spare the Tielwald a glance to know the answer. Should she prove false, the old man would orchestrate her death without hesitation. She was also certain of Lore's sincerity. In this moment, should Elvine call out and reveal herself, the queen would take her back. For the first time, Elvine realised the source of Lore's affection for her. "How terribly lonely you are, my queen," Elvine whispered, the sound barely passing her lips. "And have been all your life."

The subsequent silence stretched and the row of torches dimmed to mere pinpricks in the fog by the time Lore's voice came again. All solicitation had been stripped away now, replaced with implacable purpose.

"Do you remember your bookseller?" Lore demanded. "He insists he is just a simple peddler and not a spy. Ilvar isn't so sure. Shall we see if we can get the truth from him now?"

The scream that followed lacked any words, its sole meaning one of deep, excruciating pain. Elvine couldn't know if it truly came from the throat of the bookseller, but didn't doubt it, nonetheless.

"He knows nothing . . ." The words emerged in a breathless rush, choked off when Colvyn placed his hand over her mouth. Berrine came to her side, gripping her hand tight while the screams continued. Eventually, they died into piteous sobs and the queen's voice came again.

"A one-eyed bookseller can still make a living. Would you beggar this poor man, Elvine? Speak! Tell me of his innocence!"

Elvine clenched her teeth against a sob, falling to her knees while Colvyn and Berrine held her. A short pause, then the screams came again, louder and longer. The sound lashed at her, sinking deep enough to birth a nauseous chill in her gut. Her stomach lurched, and she cast a spatter of vomit onto the deck.

"Only your word will save him, Elvine! Blind though he is! Will you force me to take his tongue, too?"

Elvine clamped her hands to her ears, hugging herself tight as tears swam in her eyes. The urge to voice a scream raged, so much so that she reached for Colvyn's hands and pressed them to her mouth again.

"I will chase you wherever you go!" Lore's fury cut through the book-seller's agonies. "I will burn every city that harbours you. I will kill everyone you have ever called friend . . ."

Berrine cupped Elvine's face, blinking her own tears while Lore ranted on and the cries of a blameless man echoed through the fog. Elvine still heard them even after the torches had faded completely. Later, as the last vestiges of mist were burned away by a late blooming sun to reveal the open sea, she knew she would be hearing them for the rest of her life.

Incredibly, borne down by sheer fatigue, she managed to sleep that night, despite fearing the dreams that would greet her. For reasons she couldn't fathom, her slumber was undisturbed by nightmares, though her rest proved briefer than she would have liked. Upon awakening some time before sunrise, she was sure she heard the bookseller again, but it was only the groan of the sea breeze through the sail. Yet, as she lay nestled between the deck boards, she heard other voices. Blinking, she saw Berrine and Colvyn seated nearby, facing each other as they conversed in low, whispered Ishtan. Understandably, neither wished for Gruinskard to hear what they had to say.

"So, how is your father these days?" Berrine asked. Her Ishtan had never been as accomplished as Elvine's, being harshly accented and lacking the expected formalities and honorifics.

"Rendered quite furious by my absence, I imagine," Colvyn replied in his far more refined tones. "Making him angry has been one of my principal amusements since childhood."

Berrine gave a small laugh, muttering, "If I had any doubt as to your parentage, it's gone now." After a short pause, she went on. "So that's why you embarked upon this mad journey? To annoy him?"

"No. I came to find my sister."

"And now you have? What are your intentions?"

"Presently, to keep her alive, for it appears she is in dire need of my protection."

"And when she isn't?"

"Are you, perhaps, afraid I'm going to steal her away? Carry her off to foreign lands never to be seen again?"

"I'm afraid of what happens should she be drawn into your father's orbit. Rarely has a man attracted more trouble."

"From what I have seen, she seems perfectly capable of attracting it herself. I'm beset by the suspicion it might be a trait of our bloodline. Rest assured, esteemed lady, her choices regarding her future will be hers to make. But, whatever she chooses, she will forever remain my sister. That, I assure you, will not change."

Berrine's response was swift and hard with warning. "Nor will she ever stop being my daughter. When this nightmare ends, it is my intention she live as safe and quiet a life as possible, even if I have to drag her to the other side of the world to find it."

"Then I wish you good fortune in your search. Although, I must advise you, speaking as a well-travelled man, there are few truly safe places in this world."

They lapsed into silence, leaving Elvine to reflect on how, not so long ago, she would have made an angry interjection, expressing her indignation that anyone but her should determine her fate. Yet, with the bookseller's screams still echoing in her ears, such things felt small, the petulant tantrum of an ungrateful child. She had a mother and a brother willing to die for her. Not all souls were so fortunate. But, as she tried vainly to slip back into sleep, Colvyn's words and Lore's dire promise lingered. While Lore still lived, where could she go that could ever be considered safe?

The boat entered Aeric's Fjord on the morning of their fifth day at sea. The rising sun was bright, dispelling the fog well before noon to reveal the port of Olversahl in full. Elvine had expected the sight of home to bring comfort. Instead, she found the city below the cracked mountain a grey, unwelcoming sprawl. Her mood was not leavened by the grim calculation she saw on Gruinskard's brow as Ahlgrun steered the boat towards the harbour. The inhabitants of this port had held the Tielwald in dark esteem ever since he sundered the mountain to drive out the foreign occupiers. Even those loyal to the Sister Queens tended to speak of him only in mutters. The terrible cost of their liberation from Albermaine-ish tyranny remained an ugly memory.

Elvine's sense of foreboding deepened at the sight of the docks. Save for a few merchantmen and fishing craft, the wharf was mostly bare of ships. Her gaze lingered most on a lone warship, its furled sail concealing the sigil of its allegiance. The absence of sailors upon her deck provided some reassurance, although even that was short-lived when the boat passed by a row of tall poles jutting from the harbour waters. Elvine knew she should be immune to grisly sights by now, but the two dozen partly rotted, impaled heads still birthed an icy clutch at her belly.

"Helvryn," Halkyr said, squinting at one of the passing heads. The youthful warrior had said little during the voyage, maintaining what distance he could from Coelnyr and the Tielwald. Judging by Gruinskard's frequent, baleful glares in his direction, Elvine felt his caution well justified.

Forcing herself to behold the head in full, Elvine saw nothing recognisable in the greyed mask of desiccated flesh. The slack jaw and empty eye sockets, the orbs presumably torn out by gulls, conveyed the impression of being gaped at by a diseased stranger. "You knew him?" she asked Halkyr.

"A little. He was one of Ilvar's more trusted lieutenants, not seen in the Verungyr for some time. I did wonder where he'd gone."

Gruinskard let out a soft laugh, turning to the fast-approaching dockside where a dozen or so people had begun to gather. "Then, I'd wager we may well receive a friendly reception after all," he said.

Upon drawing up to the quay, Elvine's initial impression of the party's mood made her doubt Gruinskard's judgement. Their ranks had swollen to nigh three dozen by the time Teryk and Kelvyrn leaped onto the wharf to tie the lines. She saw much glowering suspicion among the throng, also many weapons.

"State your business!" demanded a large, broad-shouldered man positioned at the forefront of the group. He bore an axe in his meaty hands and spoke in a grating snarl. Despite his aggression, Elvine could see the twitch of his fingers upon the haft of his weapon and the animated darting of his hollowed eyes.

"Hemund," Elvine said, stepping forward and drawing back the hood of her cloak. "It's me . . ."

"Elvine Jurest!" The harbour master stared at her, his aggression shifting into joyful surprise. "Ulthnir's eyes, girl, I thought you dead these past months. Your mother too!" His countenance brightened further as his gaze lit upon Berrine.

"Hello, Hemund," she said, offering a warm smile. "How goes it in Olversahl?"

At this, the big man's demeanour recovered much of its prior grimness. "We've had some trouble," he said, pointing his axe at the poles in the harbour. "As you've seen. Turned up weeks back and told us there was but one queen now. Also kicked the eldermen out of their hall and got too free with their swords when folk objected. You know how we can be once blood gets spilled. Wasn't no saving them when the riot got going, not that any were inclined to. Kept their ship, though." He inclined his head at the warship moored nearby. "Though I'm buggered if I know what we'll do with it. As you can imagine, commerce has been slow lately . . ."

Hemund's voice trailed off as Gruinskard stepped forward, a disconcerted murmur rippling through the crowd at the sight of the Tielwald. He allowed a short pause before speaking, voice pitched to a low gruffness, but Elvine was sure all present heard every word. "Who has charge of this city?"

Hemund exchanged glances with his fellow townsfolk before offering a response. "Not sure anyone can make that claim, Tielwald. The Veilwald was cut down by the queen's *menda*, along with some of the eldermen. Others took ship as soon as they could. The one or two that's left seem keen to keep to their houses."

Gruinskard fixed him with a hard stare before repeating his question. "Who has charge of this city?"

Some among the crowd resumed their discontented muttering, and Elvine saw no sign upon any face that told of a warm welcome for this most infamous old man. Yet, nor was any voice raised in objection when Hemund replied, "Well, since there's no one else, I s'pose that would be you, Tielwald. As long as you haven't come to claim the port in the false queen's name, that is."

"Indeed, I have not," Gruinskard grunted before jerking his head at Elvine. "Show it to them."

Fetching her blanketed bundle, she unfurled the wooden covering to reveal the Spear of the Altvar, holding it above her head for all to see. *A new place,* the spirit inside commented as Elvine gripped the iron shaft. *I sense a great welling of fear, child. I trust you haven't brought me here to witness another massacre.*

"Behold a spear forged by the gods themselves," Gruinskard said, all gruffness gone now as he held forth in commanding tones. "Recovered from the very Vaults of the Altvar by this maiden of Olversahl. With this blessing shall we stand against the forces of the false queen and her foreign allies." Turning, he reached out to press his uninjured hand to the spear, Elvine noting how he avoided the metal. Even so, she caught the spasm of fear on his face before he turned back to address the crowd. "Upon this most sacred relic do I, Margnus Gruinskard, swear that here shall I make my stand, though it cost me my life. No further will I run. All true Ascarls of stout heart are commanded to stand with me or know themselves cravens in the sight of the gods."

No affirming clamour followed his words, the crowd's reaction varying between exchanges of uncertain glances and grimacing concern. The spear's gift revealed contrasting auras, some flickering in pale uncertainty, but others emitting a more constant crimson glow she read as firm resolve. However, she noted that the gazes of these stalwart souls were more rapt by the sight of the mythic weapon she held than the Tielwald's defiance.

"Is it true, Elvine?" Hemund asked, stepping closer, his eyes fixed upon the spear. Noting the intensity of his gaze, and the questioning crease of his brow, she understood that her word would carry far more weight here than Gruinskard's.

"It is," she stated. A sudden catch in her throat forced her to cough before speaking on, voice raised to what she hoped would be a strident certainty. *Like Lore when she read the speech I wrote*, she recalled with a pang of guilt. *The lies I wrote for her*. Yet, what else could she do? If the people of this port were to fight, their courage had to be buttressed by something.

"This is the very Spear of the Altvar," she said, raising the weapon higher. "Once set at the feet of a great statue of Ulthnir himself, which resides at the heart of sacred vaults once thought lost. Know that I have walked there, and know that this spear is the gods' blessing made flesh." She faltered, just for an instant, jarred by the inevitable, unavoidable necessity of her next words. "Know that the heresy of Covenant belief that once soiled my soul has been burned away by the truth of the Altvar's light. I stand before you a true servant of the gods, washed clean of the foreign faith. Know also that, as we speak, our enemy marshals a great fleet to come and seize this port for the false queen, and they will deal bloody murder to any they think disloyal. To save this city, my home that I love, I will wield this spear. And if I must wield it alone, I shall."

"You will not be alone!" Gruinskard proclaimed. Casting an accusing glare at the crowd, he demanded, "Who will stand with Elvine, Spear Maiden of Olversahl, Blessed of the Gods?"

Those with the crimson auras were quick to call out their allegiance. Elvine took heart from seeing Hemund among them, although she caught the cautious glint in his eyes as he cheered. Some who had wavered before also cheered, but most stood in silence. She took small comfort from the fact that at least they hadn't raised their voices against her.

"Fewer than I'd like," Gruinskard muttered, surveying the less-than-enthusiastic throng. "But it's a start."

The Tielwald was quick to establish himself in the Elderman's House. Once home to the infamous traitor Maritz Fohlvast, the red brick, Albermaine-ish-styled manor house had become the seat of town governance following the city's seizure by the Sister Queens. Keeping much of Olversahl's traditions in place was another measure of the late Sister Silver's wisdom. Although a Veilwald had been appointed to oversee the port in the queens' name, they were selected from the ranks of the local eldermen. Thus was the port allowed to function much as it always had, albeit with new strictures against Covenant worship and a marginal increase in crown taxes.

Gruinskard's first act was to summon all the port's luminaries to an audience in which Elvine was required to recite an embellished version of her speech at the dockside. This audience of merchants, town guards and various civic functionaries responded with more enthusiasm than those on the quay. But, thanks to the spear, Elvine saw plenty of concealed doubt among the outward display of zeal. She also saw how the Tielwald took the measure of those present, his shrewd gaze presumably engaged in sorting the capable from the incompetent, and the brave from the craven. She realised that she hadn't seen Aldunna since they stepped ashore. Coelnyr remained in attendance, but had an uncanny facility for finding the least-glanced-at corner of any room. The roiling snakes of his aura had taken on a darker hue now, Elvine identifying it as the colour of unbridled predation. Like his master, he was passing very astute judgement on the great and good of Olversahl.

"I won't be party to murder," she told the old man once the audience was over.

Engaged in sorting through a collection of city maps, he barely glanced at her. "I don't recall requesting such a service of you, Scholar," he said. They were alone in the large meeting hall, save for Coelnyr and Colvyn. Berrine had gone to check on their house, avowing a faint hope it had remained unoccupied in their absence. Halkyr had been allotted the role of additional protector to the Spear Maiden and stood guard outside the door.

"Really?" Elvine replied. "So I can assume Aldunna is not currently scouring the apothecaries of this city for fresh ingredients?"

A brief, amused bunching of Gruinskard's beard confirmed her suspicions.

"Have you made a list already?" she asked. "Lore was also fond of making lists."

Sighing, the Tielwald raised his gaze to meet hers, all amusement gone now. "I had thought us of shared mind in this. Olversahl must be held against the Nihlvarians. Do you doubt it now?"

"I do not. What I doubt is the need for unwarranted murder of those you judge as disloyal. Understand this: if I suspect this has been done, I will speak against it." She watched the webbed creases of the old man's forehead draw into tighter arrangement, seeing his beard twitch in patent annoyance. *Doesn't like being dictated to by a mere girl*, Elvine decided. She knew she should fear this ancient schemer, and his deadly servants, but found it out of reach. After all, she could do something he couldn't.

"You named me Spear Maiden," she went on, hefting the spear. Once again, she had wrapped it in a blanket to ward against the voice of the spirit within. No doubt it had much to say about this change in circumstance, but she would need privacy for that. "You did that because you know these people won't follow you blindly. Too much blood spilled on your account for that.

If you want me at your side for what's coming, you will heed my words. No murder without my sanction."

Gruinskard stared at her for a moment before straightening, groaning as he rubbed at his back. "Inherited your mother's attachment to tedious ideals, didn't you? Though, I'd guess your insight comes from your father. Tell me, Spear Maiden, do you think the folk of Olversahl will be so heedful of your words if they knew you a bastard sired by the Blackheart's scribe?" His narrowed eye slipped to Colvyn. "With another of his bastards at your side, no less. I imagine many here would take it ill."

Colvyn stirred, unfolding his arms, features hardening until Elvine put a restraining hand to his chest.

"I've known about your parentage since your birth," the old man went on. "And his wasn't hard to reckon. Alwyn Scribe made more of an impression on me than most. But then, you never forget a rat that bites you."

"He remembers you too," Colvyn said. Summoning a grin, he added, "Not fondly."

"Perhaps you're right," Elvine said, forestalling Gruinskard's next words. "Some in this city would hesitate to follow the scribe's daughter, as I'm sure many will hesitate to follow you, the man who once nearly rendered all of Olversahl into ash. Please enlighten me, for I've always been curious, did you deliberately burn down King Aeric's Library, as my mother believes?"

"My actions are not for you to judge, girl," he growled, the ancient stone of his face reshaping itself into a furious grimace. "Without me, this realm would have fallen to ruin long ago—"

"Well, now it has," she cut in. "So your efforts appear to have been wasted." She moved closer, facing him across the table. Gruinskard's fists quivered on the maps, his glaring eye rich in warning. She should fear him more than she did, but took confidence from the fact that the old man had no aura, at least not one the spear felt compelled to show her.

Unfurling the spear from its covering, she set it down on the table. She saw how Gruinskard failed to conceal a flinch at the weapon's proximity. "Pick it up," Elvine told him. "If you can. Then you will be the bearer of the Altvar's blessing and will have no need of me."

Nostrils flaring, the old man continued to glare, but made no move to touch the spear. *What did it show you?* Elvine wondered. *When you touched it, what scared you so?*

"I am not one of your creatures," she informed him, casting a pointed glance at Coelnyr. "And you will do no murder in this city without my leave. You will also let it be known that my authority is not to be questioned by any guard or official." She stared into his eye, wondering if she didn't find a glimmer of respect in its unblinking stare. If so, it was gone quickly.

"You think yourself fit to lead these people in war?" Gruinskard asked.

"No. That I'll leave to you. But I also know you are not fit to lead them in anything else. That you will leave to me."

Finally, the eye blinked, and he lowered his head. When he spoke again, it was in a reluctant grunt. "There are certain to be agents of the enemy here. The Volkrath, they call themselves. I'm sure you've heard the name. They cannot be suffered to live if we are to hold this port."

"Then find them, by all means. But none shall die without my consent, and your evidence had better be compelling."

Gruinskard's shaggy head moved in a fractional nod and he drew in a deep breath before continuing. "You'll need to speak again. Proclaim the Altvar's blessing and show the spear to as many as we can gather. All who are able will be required to prepare the city against attack, and fight when it comes. I smell both uncertainty and fear among this lot. Banish one and you banish the other."

"Very well." Elvine gestured to the maps spread out on the table. "I trust you have some notion of how to defend this port, having taken it once."

The Tielwald let out a grudging huff, fingers splaying over the various charts. "When the Blackheart held the place, my plan was simple. Draw her gaze to the fjord, then attack through the rent in the mountain. But the mountain could only be cracked once, so at least they won't be coming that way. In truth, they have but two options." He leafed through the charts, placing the largest on top. Elvine remembered a copy adorning the walls of Hemund's office, a rendering of the entire city.

"They either come at us in a mass ship-borne assault," Gruinskard said, his overlarge finger tracing over the docks. "Or—" the finger moved to the Gate Wall guarding the eastern land approaches "—they land their forces and attempt to storm the wall."

"Why not both?" Colvyn enquired.

"A possibility," the old man conceded. "Depends on how numerous they are. We know they sent some of their ships to the Inner Isles, but that still leaves a sizeable fleet and many warriors to contend with."

"The Gate Wall has never been breached," Elvine said. "Vahlak is no fool. He'll know that." She didn't add that this particular fact had been one of many truths contained in the report she compiled for the Tuhlvyr at Lore's request. "He also knows full well the story of how you took the city, so the path through the mountain should still be guarded."

"It will be. But here is where he'll attack." His finger tapped the docks again. "With numbers on his side, it's by far the best option."

"Then what's to be done?"

"The same thing city folk have always done when facing an attack. We build a wall. And a back-breaking task it will be." Gruinskard's beard bunched in a bland smile. "Fortunately, I'm not the one who has to persuade this bunch of near-foreigners to do it."

CHAPTER THIRTY-ONE

Ruhlin

He stayed in the forest for another day, an honoured guest of the *Teyrak*. The great gathering of elders had dispersed swiftly, keen to carry word of the *Telchak's* coming to their clans. Olchar was a notable exception. Professing himself too old for such things, he entrusted the task of mustering the *Vulksa* clan for war to a younger companion.

"Best if I wait here," the old man said. He had settled himself at Ruhlin's side at the feast the *Teyrak* organised the night Ruhlin returned from the scorched hollow. Many Morvek had emerged from the forest as word spread that the *Telchak's* arrival had been sanctioned by the elders. Freshly hunted deer were roasted and gourds filled with a sweet, honey-tasting liquor distributed. The *Teyrak* were clearly a musical people, gathering together to cast a variety of lilting choral melodies through the trees. While the atmosphere was rich in celebration, Ruhlin detected an undertone of tension in the songs and occasional speeches, even though he understood no more than a fraction of the words.

"It's a song of mourning," Olchar explained, noting Ruhlin's interest in one particular singer. A tall man with a beardless face of statuesque handsomeness, he sang alone. Despite his lack of understanding, the elegant sorrow of the song still managed to twinge Ruhlin's heart. "Not for those lost," the elder went on as the handsome singer's voice faded, "but those yet to be lost. It's often sung in advance of battle. Your people have similar customs, do they not?"

"The Ascarls are rich in battle odes and such," Ruhlin agreed. "Though I rarely found them so pleasing to the ear."

Olchar laughed, but beneath his avuncular kindliness, Ruhlin detected a keen desire for knowledge, especially regarding what had transpired that day. While the events churned continually in Ruhlin's mind, he found he didn't want to talk about it.

"I don't know what lurked in the *Vikra-sah*," he said, deciding to forestall Olchar's questions. "I doubt I ever will."

"But there was something," the old man said. If he was irked by Ruhlin's reticence, he hid it well, bright eyes and perennial smile undimmed.

"There was." Ruhlin swallowed a sigh. It was clear Olchar was not about to let the matter drop. *Telchak* or no, Ruhlin couldn't afford to offend these people, especially not their most respected elder. "It was old," he said. "I suspect far older than either of us can imagine. A prisoner, it called itself."

The old man's eyes widened, gleaming brighter. "You spoke to it?"

"Yes." Ruhlin paused, unsure of how much he should reveal. Olchar was a compassionate and trustworthy soul, that much was clear. Yet, the way the creature had talked of the monster left Ruhlin with much to ponder. With no answers, he thought circumspection the best course. "It was nonsense, mostly. Gibbering about things beyond my understanding."

"But what form did it take?" Olchar leaned closer. "What manner of thing was it?"

"The hollow was its form. Roots and branches twisted to its will. I don't believe it had a true body."

"And yet you still succeeded in destroying it. How?"

"I had help." Ruhlin's gaze drifted back to the hollow. It was a good distance from the scene of celebration, but its position was marked by the thin stream of smoke it continued to leak into the forest air. Incredibly, the many embers birthed by its destruction had failed to kindle blazes among the enclosing trees. It was now an ashen furrow, a grave to the unknowable thing that had lurked there, and the bear that had died trying to vanquish it. Ruhlin had pondered creating some better resting place for the creature. Given its sacrifice and all it had done to ensure his safe passage into these lands, it seemed the least he could do. But he couldn't do it alone and the Morvek continued to shun the *Vikra-sah*. As he stood at the hollow's edge regarding the bear's ash-covered corpse, Ruhlin found he had not the heart to venture into it again either. He assuaged his guilt by reasoning that whatever spirit had inhabited the bear was now vanished, like the vileness it had fought. But still, he felt himself a coward for leaving her to rot.

"Some things are unknown, even to me," he told Olchar. "But I suspect its being was bound up in the *Vikra-sah*." *A place where the veil is thin*, he recalled, but left unsaid. "Without the hollow, it couldn't persist. Or, at least, I hope so." Ruhlin reached for a wooden cup, downing the sweet liquor to ward off a shudder. For all he knew, some vestige of the creature still lingered in this forest, perhaps sunken into the earth awaiting the day it could emerge renewed.

"I'll pester you no longer," Olchar said, jostling Ruhlin's arm. "But I would ask about these marvellous steel weapons of yours. How long do you think it will take to make all we need for the war?"

War. The word hung in Ruhlin's mind like a stain. This was his path now, one he couldn't turn from. The Morvek were intent on following the *Telchak* to war, with all that entailed. "Some time," he said. "We have but one forge at the mountain. More will have to be built, and the skills of our smiths shared. It will be the work of months, at least."

"Be careful it does not become the work of years, my young friend. The Morvek's passions run high thanks to your . . . demonstration. But no passion ever persists forever. Take it from an ancient who's seen more war than he ever wanted to. To have any chance against the *Rulchakin*, we must strike quickly, while their great Vortigurn's gaze is fixed upon his newest conquest. Yes," he added with a small grin at Ruhlin's surprised frown. "We know about that. He has sent his great ships and warriors to reclaim the land that spawned his kind. Your land." For the first time, all vestige of humour slipped from Olchar's wrinkled features, his eyes dimming a little in sombre reflection. "Strange that the source of all our troubles should also be the wellspring of our salvation," he murmured, peering closer at Ruhlin's face. "No *Kess-tuhk* ever foresaw the true nature of the *Telchak*. Although many foresaw the war to come, and terrible it will be."

His gaze lingered and Ruhlin saw it flicker for an instant, as if the old man had come to a decision. If so, it remained unspoken, and soon he smiled again. "I am very keen to hear how you came to these lands," he said, reaching for his own cup. "Even at my age, my head still harbours room for another interesting tale."

Ruhlin and Tirohk set out the next morning, accompanied by Velkar, who avowed a desire to witness the forging of what had been dubbed "the *Telchak*'s blades" with her own eyes. She proved an even more persistent interrogator than Olchar, making little effort to conceal her abiding distrust while quizzing Ruhlin on his past and what had occurred in the hollow. Her questions were phrased with far less solicitation, causing Ruhlin to be increasingly terse in his answers.

"I told you, I don't know where it comes from," he said when they halted for the night, Velkar's wolves forming a loose cordon around the camp. This time Velkar had asked about the nature of his transformation, especially the means by which he summoned the monster.

"But you must have some notion of what caused it," she persisted. "Were you cursed by some spirit? Did you transgress in some way?"

"It first happened when I was a child. I assume it's always been part of me."

"Can you stop it?"

Ruhlin paused. This was a question that hadn't occurred to him before. Could he keep the monster at bay? Every time it had emerged so far had been in response to dire peril, leaving no time for thought or any desire to prevent its much needed intervention. "No . . ." he began, then trailed off as he remembered the time Aerling Eldryk had matched him against a seemingly bestial opponent in the circle. It had been an attempt to rouse the monster, one that almost succeeded. Yet, ultimately, it hadn't worked. *Because that poor wretch was no threat*, Ruhlin reminded himself. Even so, the beast had begun to emerge, and, despite suffering for it, Ruhlin had remained himself. But, of course, there were other means of quelling the monster. The icy agony of the *stagna* had muzzled it. So had Angomar's dart that terrible day in Buhl Hardta. If one Nihlvarian noble had possessed the elixir that coated the dart, it stood to reason so would others.

"Why would he want to stop it?" Tirohk asked. "It is thanks to his might that we will triumph in the war to come. He will lead us in every battle and the *Rulchakin* will tremble at the sight of his fury. Ignore her, *Telchak*," he told Ruhlin. "The *Teyrak* were ever a miserable, pessimistic lot. Gift them a brace of rabbits and they'll moan about having to skin them."

"As if we ever received a single gift from the *Vehlkasa*," Velkar shot back, which led to a round of bickering in the Morvek tongue. Although it went on for some time, Ruhlin was grateful, as it distracted Velkar from her endless questions. However, once the two Morvek had lapsed into resentful silence, she allowed only a brief interval before recommencing her litany, only for him to cut her off with a curt injunction.

"You came to witness the forging of weapons," Ruhlin snapped. "Attend to that and assail me no more. I have said all I will say."

The sharpness of his tone roused her wolves. Rising, the pack all turned to face him, lips quivered by the same ominous growl until calmed by a quiet word from Velkar. She said nothing for a time, regarding him with a steady glare of appraisal, her brow riven by doubt. Finally, she said, "Much have you promised, Ruhlin ehs Kestryg. I know not what you are, not truly. But, I also know that neither do you. And that troubles me."

Ruhlin considered ignoring her. She was a lone dissenting voice among the Morvek, after all. Olchar's word carried by far the most authority and had he not proclaimed the *Telchak*'s coming? Still, Ruhlin couldn't begrudge Velkar her doubts. She was right: he had no more notion of what he was than she did.

"I know that we share a common foe," he told her. "I know that I possess the means of defeating them. For now, that must be enough, for both of us." He turned away, slumping onto his side. "Now, in the name of the gods and your forest spirits, let me sleep."

He sensed as much relief as joy in the greeting he received upon arriving at the mine. Aleida came running to crush herself against him while Ryma wrapped her small arms around his leg. "Beh-behr?" she enquired, frowning at the absence of her favourite playmate.

"Beh-behr had to go away," Ruhlin told her, sinking down to meet her saddened gaze. "She found a wonderful forest where there was much to eat and I couldn't persuade her to leave." Looking up at Aleida, he could only offer a grimace at the grim understanding he saw on her face. "She died saving me," he murmured, rising to draw her close again.

"She died before," she whispered back. "Could it be that she will . . ." She trailed off when he shook his head.

"Not this time. I'm sorry."

"By Trieya's tits, you're a welcome sight!" Ruhlin was abruptly drawn away by Guthnyr's fierce embrace, the warrior lifting him off his feet while muttering in his ear, "It's easier teaching a cat to swim than getting this lot to do a day's work."

"Ill tidings, my friend," Ruhlin told him as the larger man set him down. "For we have much to do."

Despite Guthnyr's complaints, Ruhlin took heart from the sight of the shed next to the smithy. Swords, axes and spearheads were arrayed along the walls, all gleaming in the sunlight shafting through the patched roof. "We tried to keep the damp out at first," Sygurn said. "Then we realised they don't rust. Nor do the edges seem to dull." The combined soot and grime covering the Nihlvarian's face told of many hours in the forge, as did his hollowed eyes and hunched back.

"Quite the feat you've achieved here," Ruhlin said, gesturing to the stacked weapons.

"Would've been more," Sygurn said with a tired shrug. "Now we've used up all the loose ore, we're having to carve more out of the mountain."

"A problem for tomorrow," Ruhlin said. "Go and rest."

Sygurn shook his head. "I've three blades near ready—"

"Rest, Sygurn," Ruhlin cut in. "You're no good to us if you're too weary to lift a hammer. When you've slept for two days, I have something new for you to make. Until then, we'll find a way to ease the passage of ore from the mountain."

He expected some measure of resistance from Tirohk, but the war chief reacted with only firm assurance when Ruhlin told him they would require his clan to help hew rock from the mountain. "As the *Telchak* wills it," he said.

"We also need folk who know how to work metal," Ruhlin added. "Those who can shape it with tools and—" he gave a short glance at Aleida "—those who can do so by other means."

This summoned a cautious crease to Tirohk's brow. "There is . . . one, perhaps, among the *Vehlkasa* who can do this. He is old, and stubborn. I cannot promise he will come if asked."

"There are others among the *Teyrak* with the same skill," Velkar put in. Having inspected their growing armoury, she appeared to have acquired a good deal more enthusiasm for this enterprise. Arching a pointed eyebrow at Tirohk, she went on, "*They* will not shirk in providing needed labour. I'll send for them now."

Ruhlin's question as to how she might accomplish this task faded when Velkar turned to one of her wolves. The beast stiffened as she met its gaze, the two sharing an unbroken stare for several seconds. Finally, the wolf blinked and immediately bounded away, scattering frost in its wake.

"They shall arrive within ten days," Velkar assured him. She didn't elaborate on how a wolf would convey such instructions to a person, but Ruhlin felt it best not to ask.

"*My* warriors will arrive in five days to work the mine," Tirohk said, a peeved edge to his voice. Hefting his spear, he set off down the mountain at a steady run.

"They seem awful eager to please all of a sudden," Guthnyr observed. "Something important happen on your travels, did it?"

"A tale for another time," Ruhlin said, pushing away the memory of the thing in the hollow. Turning, he tracked his gaze over the trail leading to the second shaft. Steep in places and strewn with boulders, it described a wayward course up the mountain's flanks that made for slow and sometimes hazardous passage. "It strikes me that our task would be made easier with a better road to follow, and more carts to carry the ore."

The next week was taken up with clearing the track and doing what they could to level its steeper sections. Iyaka and the other Morvek harvested timber from the lower slopes, which was reworked into carts and employed in buttressing the fringes of their new road. Guthnyr once again revealed hidden skills in carpentry, as did the still mostly silent Jolnyr who took charge of fashioning the wheels.

"Always plenty of woodworking to be done aboard ship," Guthnyr explained. "And Jolnyr here practically grew up at sea, didn't you, lad?"

The youth responded with a faint smile before returning to his task of chiselling a sapling trunk into an axle.

"Be best if he's left to this kind of toil from now on," Guthnyr added to Ruhlin in a quieter tone. "Battle doesn't suit all souls. He's brave enough, but thinks far too much."

"As you wish." Ruhlin's eye strayed to Iyaka, dumping a stack of freshly hewn branches nearby. Nodding to Guthnyr, he moved to the Morvek woman's side. She greeted him with a smile that faded when she saw the hardness of his gaze. "I know what you did," he told her without preamble. "On the slave ship."

He saw a measure of regret in her subsequent frown, but no real contrition. "Your plan wouldn't have worked, *Telchak*," she said. "Without a wayfinder, you would all have perished in the Fire Isles."

"It wasn't your decision to make."

Her features tightened into defiance. "No. It was mine, and I would do it again. Finally, the *Telchak* is here and my people rise to take back what is theirs. I seek no pardon for my actions, whatever punishment you inflict."

He hadn't noticed it before, but saw now how deeply this woman feared him. He remembered she had seen the monster wreaking bloody slaughter in the *wuhltra*. It would be a strange soul indeed that failed to find terror in such a sight, although it hadn't dissuaded her from burning the ship that could have taken him home. Yet, he found he couldn't summon more than a vague resentment for her actions. They had shared so many dangers, and so much had changed since. Harbouring a grudge felt petty, the indulgence of an aggrieved youth, not a leader.

"Truth," he said. "That is your punishment. From this moment, you will speak only truth to me. Swear it or take yourself from my sight."

Iyaka spent a silent interval grinding her jaw. Fear him though she did, he had also come to know her as prideful to a fault. "I so swear," she muttered through gritted teeth, avoiding his eye.

"Well and good." Ruhlin lowered his voice, sparing a short glance at Guthnyr. "Best if you say nothing of this to the others. I doubt they would be so forgiving."

Work on the road required a full week's toil, by the end of which Tirohk's promised warriors failed to appear. "Most likely they fight among themselves,"

Velkar concluded, Ruhlin detecting a certain smugness in her judgement. "The *Vehlkasa* were ever a pack of squabbling mountain cats."

With no additional hands to work the mine, they were forced to do the labour themselves. Ruhlin and the Nihlvarians took on the task of hewing the ore from the seams while the Morvek transported it to the forge. The arrangement worked reasonably well, although he knew the amount of ore they produced was but a trickle of what would be needed to produce arms for every Morvek warrior who answered the *Telchak's* call.

Fortunately, in Ruhlin's absence, Sygurn had possessed the foresight to forge a number of pickaxes and chisels. Thanks to Aleida's touch, these tools had the same unnatural hardness as the weapons. During his second day in the mine, Ruhlin marvelled at how his pickaxe could transform hard granite into powder with only a few swings. The monster's strength would have greatly aided their endeavour, but it failed to stir, making Ruhlin wonder if it felt such drudgery to be beneath it.

Crouching to toss the recently hewn ore into a bucket, he paused at the sound of Julette calling his name. He found her at the shaft entrance, panting in exertion while standing well back from the mine. Her aversion to being underground was palpable. Consequently, he had set her and Tuhlan the task of patrolling the lower slopes for signs of trouble.

"We have a visitor," she panted.

"Tirohk?"

She shook her head. "One of his warriors, Iyaka says. She's talking to him now. Whatever he's saying, it doesn't sound like good news, dear boy."

The *Vehlkasa* warrior wore only thin buckskin, despite the cold, and carried no weapon. He was a lean man of medium height and, from the flushed state of his features and evident fatigue, Ruhlin could tell he had been running for several hours. He was engaged in an animated discussion with Iyaka, but, upon seeing Ruhlin approach with Guthnyr in tow, the man lowered his head. "*Telchak,*" he said, voice soft with reverence. He spoke on in a rapid stream of Morvek Ruhlin couldn't follow, although he did hear one word clearly. "*Rulchakin.*"

"*Vehlkasa* scouts spotted their approach three days ago," Iyaka said. "A far larger number than we faced last time. Many on horses."

Ruhlin didn't bother asking for a more accurate count, recalling the Morvek's disdain for numbers. "Where?" he asked instead.

"They make for the *Sahlrak,*" Iyaka said. "The word means 'scar' in our tongue. It's the only passage through the mountains that isn't fully closed by snow until the height of winter." She paused as the warrior spoke again.

"He says the *Telchak* must come. There are too many for the *Vehlkasa* to face alone, but they will die defending the *Sahlrak* if you wish it."

"How long until they reach the pass?" Guthnyr asked.

"Six days, perhaps sooner," Iyaka related. "They are pushing hard. The scouts talk of *Rulchakin* warriors left to perish if they can't keep up."

"Making war in the midst of winter is a fool's game," Guthnyr said. "They'll lose more to cold and hunger than they will battle."

"I doubt the Vortigurn cares much for the lives of his people," Ruhlin said. Looking to the messenger, he asked, "Tirohk takes his warriors to the *Sahlrak*?"

Upon hearing Iyaka's translation, the man nodded. "All who can carry a weapon have been gathered by the *Vakil-tuhk*."

Seeing Velkar nearby, Ruhlin beckoned her closer. "The *Rulchakin* have not allowed us time to prepare. Can you send another wolf to your people? Tell them the *Telchak* summons all the warriors they can send. And warning must be given to the other clans."

She replied with a grave nod, one of her wolves instantly trotting to her side.

"Once he's rested, I need him to take a message back to Tirohk," Ruhlin told Iyaka, gesturing to the warrior. "Can he do that?"

The messenger's face darkened in offence when she related the question, responding with a few clipped words. "He needs no rest," Iyaka said.

"Good. He's to tell Tirohk that the *Telchak* is coming with all his strength, and his steel."

With no pack horses, they had to carry the weapons on their backs, along with provisions for the four-day trek to the *Sahlrak*. Before they set off, Iyaka canted a request to the spirits of the air for clement weather. For the first two days, her efforts appeared to have borne fruit, for they marched beneath a clear sky and, though the wind was cutting, suffered neither gale nor blizzard. The morning of the third day was different, with dark clouds obscuring the mountain tops and sending repeated flurries of snow into the valleys. Once again, Ruhlin found himself wishing the monster would emerge to spare him the pain of carrying a pack laden with swords and axes. Fortunately, despite the worsening weather and poor visibility, Iyaka was able to guide them to the *Sahlrak* before nightfall on the fourth day.

Ruhlin could see why the feature had earned its name. A great jagged rent through the join between two tall peaks. He could only wonder at what ancient calamity of nature had created it. Drawing closer, he reckoned its width at between fifty and a hundred paces, more than enough to allow the passage of an entire *menda*. It was also too broad to be easily blocked with tumbled stone or some kind of barricade. The shadowy confines of the pass were liberally covered in snow, but not so much as to impede the Nihlvarian advance.

They were met at the mouth of the pass by a party of *Vehlkasa* who led them through the mountains to where Tirohk had encamped his warriors. The war chief had established his band in a semicircular stockade covering the *Sahlrak's* southern end. Ruhlin estimated the Morvek's strength at close to six hundred, wishing Aleida was with him to provide a more accurate count. However, he had insisted she stay behind, ostensibly to oversee continued work in the mine and the forge, but they had both known the truth. Despite obvious reluctance, she surprised him by not arguing, handing him a cloth-wrapped item. "Sygurn said to give you this," she said. "I've reshaped it a little." She forced a smile. "Since I know your face so well."

"*Telchak!*" Tirohk greeted him with a hearty smile, dimmed when he caught sight of Velkar among Ruhlin's party. The *Teyrak* elder returned his glare with one of her own but, to Ruhlin's relief, for once their enmity failed to blossom into words.

"We are prepared," Tirohk went on, gesturing to the rough stockade his people had crafted. It was about four feet high and fashioned from a mix of recently felled trees and piled stone. A glance at Guthnyr's judgemental frown confirmed Ruhlin's estimation that such a barrier wouldn't last long against a determined enemy attacking in large numbers.

"The *Rulchakin*," Ruhlin said. "I need to see them."

Taking only Guthnyr with him, Ruhlin followed Tirohk through patchy forest and low hills until they came to a ledge overlooking a shallow vale. Snow continued to fall but not so thick as to obscure the sight of a dense column following the stream tracing through the valley floor.

"They keep together," Tirohk said. "Send no warriors ahead to scout their route. At night, they cluster in a great mass and mark their camp with many torches."

Letting out a disgusted laugh, Guthnyr asked, "How fast do they march?"

"By your reckoning, no more than six miles a day. Their fear, and the mountain spirits' hatred, prevent them moving faster. Whenever the *Rulchakin* venture into our lands, the weather worsens."

Ruhlin concentrated on the approaching column, watching the warriors in the vanguard come fully into view. Most of them were mounted, horses plodding through the snow with heads lowered and breath steaming. The figures on their backs rode hunched against the chill. The sole exception was the rider at the forefront of the column, Ruhlin starting in recognition as she drew close enough to make out her features.

"Deyna," he breathed, his mind returning to that day in Eldryk's mountain lair. Then the Tuhlvyr had appeared the image of confident assurance. Now, even though she was still too distant to discern her expression, her straight-backed posture and constantly shifting head told of a far more pensive soul.

"You know her?" Guthnyr asked.

"I met her but once," Ruhlin said, striving to recall all words this woman had spoken to him. She had been the one to name him Amundyr, a figure of legend to garner the crowd's interest in the *wuhltra*. Sometimes, when lying next to Aleida at night, the tattoos bearing that name she had inked into his skin still burned. Deyna had also been insightful enough to spot his hatred of Eldryk, and the escape plot Ruhlin failed to conceal behind his eyes.

"She shouldn't be underestimated," he said. "She sees much and knows much."

"Whatever she knows," Guthnyr replied, "it doesn't include how to command a *menda* in war. Look at those poor bastards." He nodded to the column of plodding infantry. While their ranks were close-packed, the pace of their march was slow. The mass of warriors swayed and twisted as it wormed its way along the valley, bespeaking discordance and ragged discipline. Ruhlin saw one man stumble free of the ranks and collapse, failing to stand when a pair of more sturdy figures came to kick his prostrate form. After a sound beating, they gave up and crouched, stripping him of armour and weapons before stomping back to the column. Watching the weak flailing of the man's limbs, Ruhlin knew he would never rise again.

"I'd wager he's not the first," Guthnyr said. "Nor will he be the last. No scouts or outriders and they're forcing already exhausted warriors to march in foul weather."

"I reckon their numbers at about two thousand," Ruhlin said, watching the larger man's brow constrict in shrewd calculation as he surveyed the Nihlvarian force.

"Closer to fifteen hundred," he said, fingers tracing thoughtfully through his beard before he turned to Tirohk. "At this rate, they won't make the pass before nightfall. Where's the most likely place for them to camp?"

"The valley ends two miles north. If they are wise, they will camp atop the higher slope and wait for morning before attacking the *Sahlrak*."

"If I'm any judge, their leader is both impatient and far from wise."

Guthnyr shuffled back from the ledge and got to his feet. "Let's go and see, shall we?"

His prediction was borne out a few hours later. Concealed in a dense copse not far from where the valley flattened out into a snow-covered plain, they watched the Nihlvarian *menda* continue its painfully slow course for another few miles before coming to a halt. Viewed from a distance, their camp resembled a dark stain upon a great white sheet dappled in torchlight when the sky began to darken.

"This is our chance, my friend," Guthnyr told Ruhlin, voice fierce with conviction. "They're already beaten. They just don't know it yet. Let's teach them."

"You mean attack now?" Ruhlin squinted at him. "Wouldn't it make more sense to wait for them to assault the pass? If they're as weak as you claim, they'll break themselves on the stockade."

"Perhaps," Guthnyr acceded. "Perhaps not. A foe prepared for battle is always harder to kill than one taken unawares, and weary after a long day's march. And, even if we beat them back at the pass, many are likely to escape. For all we know, there's a larger force following this one. Why allow them reinforcements?"

"I see wisdom in this, *Telchak*," Tirohk said, previously unseen respect showing in his eye as he regarded Guthnyr. "If your enemy offers a gift, take it. And my people have never liked the notion of fighting from behind a wall."

Ruhlin was about to argue that, bedraggled as the Nihlvarian *menda* was, they still outnumbered his force by a considerable margin. The words died when a small but potent pulse of heat flared in his core. While he might have misgivings over Guthnyr's plan, the monster did not.

"Then we attack," he said, rising. "But first, I have gifts for the *Vehlkasa*. I promised you steel, Tirohk. Now it's time to see how well it cuts."

CHAPTER THIRTY-TWO

Felnir

He found Beyorn in the market square of the largest settlement so far encountered on the eastern bank of the Vorl Arna. Felnir had taken his companions and ridden ahead of Baldyr's *menda*, telling the folk they met along the road not to fear the approach of the Vorl Tuhrk, for they came as allies. It was clear that Beyorn had done his work well, for the locals knew of Felnir's coming. Many were vocal in hailing him as king, though an equal number displayed a cautious reserve. This land and its people contrasted greatly with their neighbours on the other side of the lake. He saw many a face hollowed by hunger, underfed livestock, and houses either abandoned or in need of repair.

"The *Ahrkun* have been ravaging these lands for far longer than ours, my king," Tyrheld explained. "My folk called them the Dragyr, the defeated." She gave a bitter laugh. "As if we would not have become just as wretched in time."

"See him now and know me no liar!" Beyorn proclaimed upon spying Felnir's approach. Beneath the usual bombast, he detected a certain relief in the young warrior's tone. "King Felnir himself is come! Hear his words and know yourselves blessed by his courage and wisdom!"

The assembled villagers parted ranks in silence as Felnir guided Bolt towards the centre of the square. Beyorn stepped down from the cart where he had perched himself, taking the reins. "How goes it?" Felnir asked quietly as he dismounted.

"Well in some places, worse in others, my king," Beyorn murmured back. "Many of the smaller villages were happy to swear fealty, even without seeing you with their own eyes. But, the larger the village, the more deaf they are to your tidings. This lot are the most deaf of all."

"Hunger saps courage. It's the way of things." Felnir clapped him on the shoulder and stepped up onto the cart. He stood regarding the throng in silence for a time, seeing many a haggard face. Most were drawn in a mix of curiosity and fear, while a smaller number scowled in suspicion. Some fidgeted at the edges of the crowd, no doubt worried the *Ahrkun* would punish their mere attendance at such a gathering. Such cowardice should have disgusted him. Yet, to his surprise, he found it merely pitiable. *They did not ask for a king*, he thought. *Nor to be saved from their misery. But I cannot allow them the choice.*

"You," he said, pointing to a man at the forefront of the crowd. Felnir chose him for his gaunt appearance and bedraggled clothes, consisting of a matted sheepskin and threadbare trews. His feet were clad in stitched together patches of leather that wouldn't last the winter. "What did the *Ahrkun* take from you?" Felnir demanded.

The gaunt man squirmed under this stranger's fierce glare, casting nervous glances at those nearby before answering in a thin grating voice. "I was a shepherd. They took my flock in the autumn. Took half the year before."

"A shepherd without a flock," Felnir said. "How to live now, friend?"

The shepherd's bearing stiffened, pale cheeks flushing as he spoke without meeting Felnir's eye. "I hunt, when I can. Not much game in the winter. Cut wood for those that can offer a meal in return, not that there's many who can."

"And when there is nothing to hunt and no wood to cut?" Felnir pressed.

The shepherd's jaw clenched, his head dropping further. Felnir thought he might say nothing or walk away. But, drawing a breath, the gaunt fellow forced himself to meet Felnir's eye. "I beg," he stated, voice raw and lips twitching. "From my kin at first. Then anyone who might have a kindly heart."

"And yet, do you have a full belly on this day?"

Clenching his teeth, the shepherd shook his head.

"No, you do not. Because those you would beg from are hungry, too." Felnir shifted his gaze to the crowd, finding them now rapt with attention. At the edges, the fearful waverers had stopped dithering to move closer, merging with the throng.

"All Beyorn has told you is true," Felnir went on. "I am king of Vorunvahl, named as such by Angmund himself, who once stood at Velgard's side. But I'll not claim kingship merely on the word of an ancient soul. I have won it, in battle. At the *Ahrkun* nest south of here and at the standing stones. With my sword and the faithful courage of my *menda*, I struck down two hundred *Ahrkun* and considered it too few. As I speak, the Gyrwald of the Vorl Tuhrk has gathered his *menda* and marches in alliance with my cause, not only to settle a righteous grudge but also because he heard my words and knew them as truth."

He paused, moulding his features into a frown of sorrowful reflection, the pitch of his voice lighter when he spoke on. "Are you not tired of beggary?" he asked them. "Are you not shamed by your servile obeisance to the *Ahrkun*? How long since you felt pride in your labour, knowing all you have worked for will soon be stolen?" Hardening his tone, Felnir put a hand to the Sword of the Altvar. "No doubt you wonder what it is I promise, and I shall tell you. But first I shall tell you what I do not promise. Do not look to me for ease or comfort, for I have neither. Do not look to me for peace, for war will be my province until this land is free of oppression and thievery. As for what I promise, know this: I promise blood. I promise toil and battle until the *Ahrkun* are wiped from the earth like the filth they are. I promise the chance to live as true inheritors of Velgard's legacy. As Ascarls in both blood and spirit."

Drawing the sword, he held it high. A bank of grey cloud concealed the sun, but the blade's edge still caught a gleam, the sight of such perfect steel engendering a satisfying fascination among his audience. "By this gods blessed sword I so swear," Felnir told them with grave conviction. "In sight of Ulthnir the Worldsmith and all his mighty kin. And may they visit eternal torment upon me if I speak false. Now—" he lowered the blade and cast a baleful glower over the crowd "—gather what weapons you have and march with me, or stay here and be a beggar."

They didn't cheer, but they did growl, an ugly sound rich in hunger and hatred, which was good. Felnir knew that few wars were won by noble hearts. The shepherd was the first to step forward and recite the oath at Beyorn's instruction, a short but unambiguous pledge in the Altvar's name to fight in King Felnir's *menda*. A dozen more quickly followed his example, mostly younger men and women. With the spark lit, more followed and soon it seemed the entire population of this village clamoured for the chance to fight in the king's cause.

"Nicely done, my king," Beyorn said when Felnir stepped down from the cart.

Nodding, Felnir cast around for a decent place to stay the night, finding little appeal in the grey-walled and sparsely roofed hovels. Looking beyond the confines of the village, he spied a stunted structure atop a nearby hill. Too large to be a house, but too small for a holdfast. "What's that?" he asked, pointing it out to Beyorn.

"The old Gyrwald's stronghold, my king. The *Ahrkun* tore it down when they cut his head off some years ago."

A ruin was little more appealing than a hovel, but a king needed some semblance of grandeur in his dwelling place. Also, the hill offered commanding views of the surrounding country. "Gyrwald Baldyr will arrive before nightfall," he told Beyorn. "Ask him to find me there."

"A little over four thousand, as of this morning," Sygna said. "Including Baldyr's lot. Feeding so many will soon present a problem, my love."

Responding with a non-committal grunt, Felnir continued to play the light of his torch over the foundation stones of the partly tumbled stronghold. The slain Gyrwald of this land had fashioned his home entirely from stone, but the surviving sections displayed a curious mismatch between upper and lower levels. Small, irregular boulders had been piled atop a far more substantial and finely crafted base.

"Also, there's the prospect of marching in winter," Sygna went on. "Getting a half-trained mob to traipse across open country when beset by snow and ice will not be easy." She paused when Felnir crouched lower, letting out a pleased huff at what his torch revealed.

"Also, I've decided to take a lover," Sygna went on, voice edged in annoyance. "Several, in fact. I suspect they'll pay more heed to your queen than you do."

"Choose wisely," Felnir advised, his fingers exploring the foundation stone. "Come, look at this."

"Supplies," Sygna stated, crossing her arms. "And marching in the snow."

Sighing, Felnir said, "I spoke to Baldyr. He's agreed to supply our *menda* from his lands, they being so much richer than these plundered fields. As for marching in winter, I doubt it'll be necessary. Dyssha assures me the *Sindra* will come to us. All we need do is remain here and prepare to meet him. Now—" he beckoned to her, pointing at the stone "—what do you make of this?"

Stepping closer, she peered at the faint spiral etched into the rock. "Mason's mark?" she suggested. "It's custom in many places for those that built something to mark their work."

"True, but I've never seen a mason's mark quite like this. I saw something similar back at the standing stones. And look." He stood, raising his torch to illuminate the wall above. "The stones set into the earth are far larger and more expertly worked than these."

Sygna crossed her arms again, shrugging. "And what does that tell you, my love?"

"It tells me this holdfast was built upon something far older."

"Velgard's people came here centuries ago. Stands to reason they'd have buildings dating back that far. Ask the old man if it troubles you. Although," she added with a peeved note, "I've no notion why it should, given our many distractions. You'll be hearing petitions tomorrow, remember? Beyorn's got a list of requests. We should at least pay some heed to it."

"Petitions I leave in the hands of my very capable queen." Reaching out, he drew her closer, planting a kiss on her forehead. "She being the recipient of my fullest confidence hereby empowered to pass judgement in my name."

"They swore themselves to you, not me," she pointed out, only partially mollified. "How should I explain your absence?"

"Tell them their king is doing what he swore he would do. To wit: orchestrating the defeat of our enemies."

Training these people, Felnir quickly discovered, offered a marked contrast to his prior experience. In Ishtakar, young men were raised in the knowledge they would one day be conscripted into the Saluhtan's armies. Accordingly, they responded to discipline and instruction mostly with dutiful resignation. Ascarlians, of course, considered themselves warriors from birth. As a result, they tended to compensate for a lack of battlefield cohesion with enthusiasm and the ingrained fear arising from even the slightest suggestion of cowardice. The folk of Vorunvahl, however, seemed to harbour little more than a vague attachment to such sentiment. Only a small number maintained the ancient custom of keeping weapons in their household. Consequently, those who answered the mustering call of their new king carried either a wood axe or some form of farming implement. At least half bore no arms at all, and very few displayed much in the way of fighting skill. For all their adherence to Ascarlian lore, it was clear to Felnir that, at heart, these were farmers, not warriors.

His first order of business, therefore, was to set them to work rather than drill. The weapons captured at the Nest and the standing stones sufficed to equip only a fraction of his new host. The local smithies were tasked with forging spearheads and parties were sent into the forests to cut wood for shafts and shields. As with the coast-landers, the toil served as a useful exercise in bonding the recruits both to each other and their leaders. Felnir put Beyorn in charge of the newer recruits while those who had already sworn to his cause came under Tulvik's authority. Felnir toured both encampments constantly, helping to fashion shields and fix newly forged spearpoints to four-foot-long shafts. He had ordered the spears kept short, making them easier to wield in conjunction with a shield. Moving among this nascent host, he could sense an undercurrent of fear, but also a grim determination. They all knew this to be an all-or-nothing enterprise. Defeat at the hands of the *Ahrkun* meant only one thing.

He gave Falk the task of scouting the southern and eastern approaches, placing the few decent riders they possessed at his disposal. In addition to warning of the *Ahrkun's* inevitable approach, they were also charged with spreading word of the new king's cause to any settlement within reach. He would have preferred allotting this task to Beyorn, but the young warrior's facility for leadership was too valuable to be spared. Of the scouts, Tyrheld proved to be the most successful recruiter. Over the course of a few weeks she persuaded dozens in the outlying villages to pledge themselves to a man many were now calling the King from Beyond the Sea, a title swiftly abbreviated to the Sea King. Felnir found he quite liked it. Certainly it was an improvement on the name that had burdened him for so long.

"They move like a pack of drunkards at a wedding," Baldyr observed, casting a caustic eye over the several hundred lake-landers attempting to form a shield wall. He stood at Felnir's side atop a hill overlooking the flattest expanse of grazing land in the region. It was hard to argue with the Gyrwald's judgement. Below, a line that had taken far too long to form resembled a thin, wavering snake upon the frosted grass.

"It's their first proper day of drill," Felnir pointed out. "Given a few weeks, they'll be solid enough."

"A few weeks of eating my food and supping my ale. Our stocks won't last forever, brother."

"When the *Sindra* gets here, we'll have plunder aplenty. And that head I promised you."

"The bugger still hasn't turned up, though, has he?" Baldyr turned his squint upon the eastern horizon. Away from the fertile terrain fringing the Vorl Arna, the country became flatter and more barren, in places resembling the great emptiness of the Swathe to the west of Baldyr's domain. Felnir didn't relish the prospect of marching across such ground, but, if Dyssha was to be believed, their enemy wouldn't shirk it. *The* Sindra *can abide no threats*, she had said. *He once skinned one of his more trusted grovellers because he suggested a small change to the nightly invocation to Ulthnir.*

"He'll come," Felnir assured the Gyrwald. "And when he does, know that we'll have a shield wall worthy of the name to greet him."

In addition to arming his host, Felnir oversaw the rebuilding of the tumbled stronghold atop the hill. He enlisted the older folk for this task, those keen to offer their service but lacking the fortitude for battle. Even so, their progress was impressive, raising two-thirds of the outer wall and constructing a temporary timber-roofed hall for the Sea King. Here, every five days, Sygna would receive petitioners, a chore she professed to detest but performed with considerable skill. Land disputes between neighbours, or kin squabbling over inheritances, were heard in full and decided upon without bias. Thanks to her years under the Tielwald's roof, Sygna possessed a sound grasp of Ascarlian law and how to apply it. Not all her decisions were popular, but such was the way when diligence and fairness were applied to petty feuds. As yet, none had dared to openly defy the queen's judgements.

It required a full month of training before Felnir was satisfied with the speed and soundness of Beyorn's shield wall. Tulvik's more seasoned company was also required to perform the manoeuvre, but not so often. When the time came, Felnir would have another role for them. With winter's chill beginning to bite, Sygna advised that their stocks were now less than half that needed to see them through to spring. Baldyr, with grudging ill grace, sent for more supplies from his lands. He also organised sustained fishing of the Vorl Arna while griping that the lake would soon sit empty if they kept on at this rate. All the while, the treeless, increasingly snow-covered land to the east remained unblemished by an advancing host.

Two weeks into the second month, lookouts spotted Falk and Tyrheld riding hard towards the stronghold. Going to greet them, Felnir noted their sagging fatigue and the sweat bathing the flanks of their mounts.

"The *Sindra* has finally consented to join us, I take it?" Felnir asked as Falk slipped from the saddle.

"He's moved, all right, my lord," the outlaw said. His legs buckled and he might have collapsed if Felnir hadn't caught him. "But not towards us."

"Then where?"

"The Craggens, my king," Tyrheld said, groaning with the effort of dismounting.

"Where?" Felnir asked, bemused by the unfamiliar name.

"The rocky land twenty miles north-east of here. Long have the folk of the Craggens suffered the *Ahrkun* yoke. It seems that when word reached them of the Sea King's coming, they rose in rebellion. Sadly, they didn't realise the *Sindra* had already marched his host from the Hahl-Trova, and was well placed to visit swift vengeance upon them."

"It's an ugly scene, my lord," Falk said, his face grave. "Whole villages put to flame and sword. None are spared, not even children."

"And they're far from done," Tyrheld put in. "The Craggens is a region of scattered settlements, and the *Sindra* intends to lay waste to it all."

Felnir felt the weight of her stare, seeing both accusation and expectation. In strict military terms, his choice was clear. The *Sindra* might spend weeks indulging his cruelty in these Craggens, no doubt losing warriors and expending supplies in the process. Meanwhile, the Sea King's *menda* would only grow stronger, and more capable. Yet, there was truth in Tyrheld's gaze. He had made a mistake in allowing the *Ahrkun* to run amok in the river belt, useful though it had been. He could obfuscate, of course, pretend to suffer an agonised dilemma while he continued to delay. Beyorn would surely be persuaded, but not Tulvik or Baldyr. Above all, Felnir feared the judgement of his queen should he fail to act.

"Get what rest you can," he told them both. "For tomorrow, the Sea King's *menda* marches for the Craggens where, so the tale will be told in years to come, the *Ahrkun* met their doom."

CHAPTER THIRTY-THREE

Thera

Years at sea had provided Thera with plentiful experience of gulls. Consequently, she shared many a sailor's antipathy towards the thieving, often aggressive creatures that thronged the skies of every port and filled the morning air with their aggravating keening. The bird perched on the chimney stack jutting from the roof of the merchant's house was larger than most of its kind, with a wingspan that could match an eagle and a vicious gleam to its beady eyes.

"You're sure that thing's tame?" Thera asked Lynnea, the question provoking a small laugh from her apprentice.

They're never tame, she replied. *But he is willing to help.*

"Because you command it."

Not . . . command, precisely. Lynnea's brow furrowed, as if this was something she hadn't considered before. *They become attached to me, you could say. And it doesn't always work. There was a seal in the harbour at home that refused to come near me, despite the many times I called to him.*

Thera looked to the gull again, disturbed by a nagging suspicion that this creature understood far more than she wanted it to. "You'll see what it sees? No matter how far away it is?"

Provided he's not too distracted by food or some other amusement, yes. Lynnea raised her eyebrows expectantly. *Where do you want him to go?*

Ideally, Thera would have liked to send one of these avian spies to every corner of Ascarlia, but Lynnea had been clear that she could perform this feat with but one bird at a time. "Skar Magnol," she said. "I need to know how many ships Lore has left."

Nodding, Lynnea reached out to trace her fingers through the gull's plumage. Its eyes blinked white before, with a piercing cry, it launched itself from the chimney stack, broad wings beating to gain the sky. Thera watched it wheel across grey cloud before it glided away on the southerly winds.

So, Skar Magnol is our destination? Lynnea prompted, her thoughts coloured by amusement as she added, *My queen?*

Thera bit down on the admonishment before it escaped her lips. *Best if I get used to it.* What had begun as a victory chant in the aftermath of battle had quickly solidified into a snare she couldn't escape. Synghild, still suffering the effects of her wound but refusing to take to her bed, had been the first to formally address Thera as queen, but far from the last.

"I'll tell you our destination when I know it," she told Lynnea, trying to keep the snap from her voice but not quite succeeding. Lynnea displayed no hurt this time, however, merely flattening her lips to conceal a smile. It appeared any bitterness engendered by Thera's rejection had been dispelled by their triumph in the Crusher Strait. Thera also suspected the maiden's lightened mood partially arose from Mohlnir's reappearance. Thera had begun the difficult chore of informing Lynnea of the cat's demise only for him to hop up onto the *Great Wolf*'s rail. Yawning, he shook water from his fur before leaping into Lynnea's arms. Snaryk soon came bounding over, barking loudly in welcome. It had been good to see Lynnea smile again, although Thera worried her improved mood might not survive the day's business.

"Come on," she said, making her way to the skylight. "Best get it over with."

Synghild's gift felt heavy in Thera's hand as she stood in the large dining hall of the merchant's house. The building had belonged to the richest trader in Vorun Hardta. A prescient fellow, he had taken ship when rumours of trouble in the Outer Isles began to harden into dire reality. Despite his avowed intention of conducting an extensive survey of his foreign holdings, Synghild had promptly pronounced the merchant both a coward and a traitor and seized all his property, including this fine house. It was only marginally less grand than her own and therefore made for a fitting, if temporary, residence for the newly proclaimed Queen of the Isles. As befit the audience chamber of an Ascarlian queen, table and chairs had been removed, requiring all to stand.

"It's bronze, my queen," Synghild said as Thera continued to regard her gift. "Gold is in short supply and silver seemed . . . inappropriate." The Veilwald spoke with a pronounced croak to her voice, her eyes and cheeks hollowed and skin several shades paler than before. However, she insisted on standing in the queen's presence. "I do wonder," Synghild added after a pained cough, "how it would look upon your head."

"As do we all, my queen," Ossgrym put in with soft but insistent emphasis.

Thera's gaze tracked across all present. She had kept this gathering small, inviting only the two Veilwalds and the principal captains of her fleet. Besides Synghild, the only denizen of the Speldmeara Geld in attendance was her son. Teylhar, much to his mother's patent annoyance, hovered at her back with the only chair remaining in the room, holding it ready in case her legs failed.

"Then you are all intent upon this?" Thera asked them. She entertained a faint hope for at least one dissenting voice. Perhaps Skahlvyr, as the sole representative of the Aiken Geld, would voice his discomfort of hailing a new queen without his Veilwald's approval. But the seafarer's response only mirrored the unambiguous affirmation of his comrades.

"The *Skyrnlohk* murdered our queens," he stated. "The lessons of our history are clear. The Isles do not prosper without a queen to lead them. And we will accept none other than you, Thera Speldrenda, Victor of the Lyx Helv. Victor of Vorun Hardta. There can be no clearer sign of the Altvar's favour."

Thera managed to resist the impulse to lower her head, although she couldn't stop herself closing her eyes, nor stem the sigh that hissed from her mouth. *Whatever Ascarlia becomes, it will be something new,* her great-grandfather had told her. As ever, events had conspired to prove the old man infuriatingly correct.

"Once this rests upon my head," she said, opening her eyes and raising the bronze crown, "it can only be removed but one way. You all know this. I will be a lone monarch in a land where law dictates rule must reside in our three wisest souls. You know this too, I assume."

"We do, my queen," Ossgrym said. "But the Sister Queens allowed themselves to be infiltrated and corrupted, and so they fell. Their time is over. Long did I serve them, as did Veilwald Synghild. It grieves us to set a cherished custom aside, but in the face of such dire circumstance we are left no other course."

Noticing that the hand holding the crown had begun to tremble, Thera stilled it. "Then the two Veilwalds of the Isles present should be the ones to place this upon my brow," she said, wondering why her voice held no vestige of a quaver.

"And gladly we shall," Synghild rasped. Coming forward, she stumbled, grimacing in annoyance at the need to take Ossgrym's arm in order to reach Thera's side.

"Let all present witness this act and know it as the will of the Isles," Ossgrym said. He and his fellow Veilwald took hold of the crown and lowered it onto Thera's head. It felt lighter than she expected, but that, she knew, was a terrible illusion.

"My first command as queen," she said, clasping Synghild's hand as she began to retreat, "is to tell you, in Ulthnir's name, to sit down, Veilwald."

Synghild grimaced but consented to sink onto the chair Teylhar hurriedly placed at her back.

"A queen must have servants to ensure her will," Thera said, trying to inject a brisk tone into her voice. "Accordingly, Ragnalt, my loyal apprentice of many years, will be my Vellihr of Justice. Henceforth, he will be named Ragnalt Mihrlyndir, Truth Hunter." She paused, finding her next words harder to say than expected. "My ship, the *Great Wolf*, I place in his care. May she serve him as well as she served me."

At first, Ragnalt could only stare at her, eyes moist. When the silence began to stretch, he blinked and stuttered out a reply. "My . . . my queen honours me more than I deserve."

Thera considered responding with some witticism, an allusion to the fact that he would be unlikely to thank her after his first year as Vellihr. But she didn't. A salient feature of her audiences with the Sister Queens had been their general absence of humour.

"Skahlvyr Estrynlud and Kahlvik Vahrimdorr," Thera went on, "I name you both as Vellihrs of the Sword, charged with protecting this realm and its people for all your days." She offered them both an apologetic smile. "If you accept, then your far-flung voyages will be done, my friends. I hope you can forgive me."

Skahlvyr was the first to speak, voice and bearing lacking equivocation. "My queen commands and I obey. And it is my honour to do so."

By contrast, Kahlvik's response was accompanied by both a shrug and a rueful smile. "I've seen enough of the world for one lifetime, my queen. My sword and ship are yours, for now and always."

"Veilwald Ossgrym Styrntorc will continue as commander of the Queen's Fleet," Thera said, inclining her head in acknowledgement of the Ironbones' satisfied nod before turning to Synghild. "Veilwald Synghild Vyrnvest, if she is willing, I appoint as Guardian of the Queen's Treasury, for I feel there is no soul better suited to the role."

"Trying to keep me clear of any more battles, eh?" Synghild asked, unsuccessfully smothering a cough.

"A task surely beyond any mortal, Veilwald. But wars, as I need not tell you, are expensive and your geld is the richest in the Isles. Your queen requests your service. Will you give it?"

"Could hardly fucking refuse, since it's me who just helped put that crown on your head." Synghild winced, forcing herself to half rise. "As my queen commands."

Thera waved her back into her seat, then raised her gaze to the young man holding the Veilwald's' chair. "Teylhar," she said, causing him to blink in surprise. Until now, he had no doubt assumed his presence here had been only to aid his ailing mother. "I name you the Queen's Master of Engines," Thera said. "With authority to requisition all goods and labour required to build more. I also require you to fashion a new device suitable for carriage aboard a longship."

Teylhar gaped at her until a sharp nudge of his mother's elbow compelled him to speak. "A great honour, my queen," he said. "But, as you know, the engines' design came from Luissa—"

"Yes, and I am grateful for her service," Thera interrupted. "But, as a foreigner, she can hardly be appointed servant of the queen. You are, however, at leave to employ her at crown expense. I shall expect reports on your progress with the new engines within one week."

Thera paused, girding herself for what came next. Her final appointment would certainly be the most controversial, and unexpected, not least to its recipient. "Lynnea Trahleyl."

Standing to Thera's right, the maiden's blue eyes widened as Thera turned to her. Her thoughts were a wordless jumble of surprise and warning, but Thera was not to be dissuaded. "I name you Tielwald to the Queen of the Isles," Thera said. "You will be my eyes in dark places, charged with the identification of all threats to this realm, be they from within or without. You will answer only to me and all here present are commanded to render unto you all assistance without question." Thera shifted her gaze to the other attendees, speaking on with harsh certainty. "Also, no word of the Tielwald's appointment or actions is to be spoken of outside this room. Nor is she to be impeded in any way. This I command on pain of death."

She didn't demand confirmation of their understanding, trusting that they knew her well enough to recognise her sincerity. She saw frowns of surprise on some faces, particularly Ossgrym and Skahlvyr. Of the rest, Synghild appeared the least perturbed. Thera assumed the Veilwald had her own agents in the port who had advised her on the silent maiden's activities.

"Very well," Thera said, clasping her hands together. "To more detailed business. Let's have the table and chairs back in and some food brought. Ossgrym, be so good as to advise on the current state of the fleet and our newly acquired ships . . ."

She had expected being a queen to be tiresome, but not truly tiring. Yet her first full day of monarchical duties had left her yearning for the comparative ease of the *Great Wolf*'s deck. Even clinging to ropes in the midst of a storm was preferable to such tedium. It wasn't simply the minutiae of administration, although that was burdensome enough; Synghild had been swift in transporting a veritable library of ledger books to the merchant's house for the queen's inspection and approval. Moreover, it was the interminable need of every soul who appeared before her. A queen's role, she quickly understood, was not simply a matter of issuing edicts and expecting compliance. Everyone wanted something, and she had to decide whether they should have it.

Despite enjoying licence to take whatever he needed for his work, Teylhar still faced objections from various quarters, especially the local timber merchants. Having supplied the material for the engines gratis, with the danger of defeat and enslavement passed, they now began to demand payment for their lumber. Initially, Thera wanted to have the most vocal complainants beaten, but Synghild advised a more conciliatory course. Roundly admonishing the merchants for their opportunistic avarice, she made a begrudged offer of silver equivalent to one-tenth the value of goods already supplied, with the balance to be paid with interest at the close of the war.

"Merchants are like whore chasers," the Veilwald explained. "Except, instead of tickling their balls, you have to tickle their purse."

Curiously, the business of orchestrating a war proved to be by far the least taxing of her duties. Thanks to their recent victory, Ossgrym reported no less than thirty new additions to the royal fleet, including eight of the hulking Nihlvarian warships. A good number of slaves had been freed from their fetid hulls, more than enough to make up the losses aboard the *Chainbreaker* and crew three more ships of similar size. Of the Nihlvarian warriors who had come against them at Vorun Hardta, not a single one had been captured. Those found clinging to wreckage in the strait had either been picked off for sport by Ascarlian archers or, when it became apparent they were about to be made prisoner, surrendered themselves to the water.

"Seems we've got two new reefs now," Synghild had commented. "One of marble and one of bones." She went on to petition the queen to have the channel cleared for commerce at the close of hostilities. "Teylhar has reckoned out a way to do it. Lots of pulleys and ropes involved, as you'd imagine."

"A worthy project, and happily approved," Thera assured her. She considered adding an observation regarding the Veilwald's transformed attitude towards her previously shunned son, but decided against it. At the very least, a woman who had sacrificed so much deserved her privacy.

Three days after the meeting at the merchant's house, Thera's newly appointed Tielwald reported on what the gull had witnessed in the waters off Skar Magnol. *Ships lined up at the docks, taking on a great many warriors,* Lynnea related, sharing the image with Thera. It was jarringly clear, but coloured in strange hues that, while muted, still birthed an ache in her head. *Birds see the world through different eyes,* Lynnea explained. *Best if you don't look too long.*

She withdrew the image, but Thera had seen enough to confirm her judgement: the Nihlvarian fleet was preparing to set sail with a great *menda.* But to where?

The main bedroom of the merchant's house was both too large and too comfortable, a feature shared by the four-poster bed that dominated the space. Thera had intended to replace the eiderdown-stuffed mattress with something her body might recognise as a typical resting place, but it had slipped a mind beset by competing distractions. The outcome was a solid hour of restless shifting as she strove for elusive slumber. The silver knot hung on its chain about her neck, the metal cool against her skin, which she felt to be a poor omen. This night would be like all the others recently, dreamless or populated by whatever meagre and vague conjurations her brain consented to provide.

So, when sleep finally arrived, the looming, grizzled visage of Margnus Gruinskard came as a shock. "Where have you been?" he demanded, eyes flicking from Thera's startled expression to her head. "And what, in the name of the Ulthnir's gizzard, is that?"

Thera reached up, her fingers playing over the cool bronze of the crown. The fact that it existed in this world of dreams made her ponder the notion that her reluctance to accept it hadn't been as deep as she believed.

"A crown," she said, recovering her wits enough to find a morsel of enjoyment in the effect her next words would have. "They made me Queen of the Isles."

To her acute disappointment, Gruinskard reacted with neither outrage nor baffled disbelief. Instead, his brow crinkled as calculation took hold. She should have known he would instantly latch upon her changed status as a prospect for advantage.

"I suppose that might prove useful," he grunted finally. "I trust you made a decent show of reluctance."

"It wasn't show," Thera replied, knowing the crown's presence undermined her heated tone. "I find it not much to my liking."

Her great-grandfather's eye flicked to the bronze band on her head but, for once, he chose to guard his caustic tongue. "Where are you now?" he asked instead.

"Vorun Hardta, where a good portion of the Nihlvarian fleet was recently sunk or captured. I have reliable intelligence that the remainder is preparing to depart Skar Magnol. Might you know where they're heading?"

The old man didn't answer. Huffing another grunt, he resumed his silent pondering. Quelling her annoyance, Thera surveyed their surroundings. They were back on the shingle beach at Linsker Fjord. It was even gloomier than before, the waters so shrouded in fog she couldn't see the city rising from the far bank. Looking deeper, she discerned an ugly roil to the mist, tendrils clumping together in sickly yellow coils. She didn't know how, but she felt sure this indicated a deep resentment in her great-grandfather's thoughts.

"Are you still imprisoned?" she asked him, wondering if his distress arose from yet more torment at Ilvar's hands. The question earned her an irritable flick of his hand before he returned to his musing. As time wore on, Thera saw the sickly swirls in the fog grow ever thicker.

"To answer your questions," Gruinskard said, recapturing her attention with the sharp growl, "no, I am no longer a prisoner. And the Nihlvarian fleet is coming for me, at Olversahl, where you will soon lead your loyal forces, oh great Queen of the Isles."

"Olversahl," Thera repeated, her seafarer's mind immediately sorting through distances, courses and tides. "You're sure?" she asked, provoking another flare of irritation.

"Of course I am." He paused, glowering as he spoke on in a softer tone, "There's something here Lore wants. Something besides me."

"Which is?"

"Does it matter? Your enemy sails to seize an Ascarlian city, and will surely do great slaughter when they take it. A noble warrior queen has no option but to sail to the rescue."

"I'm Queen of the Isles, not the Fjord Geld." Thera crossed her arms, brow arched to an expectant angle. Once again, her great-grandfather's lack of anger surprised her.

"Maybe you have enough arrogance to wear that crown, after all," he said. "Always thought it would be your brother who got one first. But then, he'd have had to steal his, while yours was doubtless a gift."

It occurred to Thera that he could actually be attempting to impart a compliment. And might that be a glimmer of pride in his eye? If so, it was gone quickly, her great-grandfather continuing in a gruff tone, indicating the divulgence of a secret he would rather have kept to himself.

"You recall the mad expedition that got your brother killed," he said. "Well, it transpires that the scholar who led him on his chase not only survived but returned from the very Vaults of the Altvar with a spear, one forged by the gods themselves. When we escaped the Verungyr, she brought it with her. I've little doubt Lore will be desperate to get it back."

"You've doubts over the origin of this spear?" Thera asked. The old man appeared to be putting an uncharacteristic amount of faith in the word of a lone scholar.

"I would have," he admitted, "if I hadn't touched the fucking thing. I regret to say it's all too real." His lips twisted in a sneer of annoyance. "Far better to leave the artefacts of the gods where you find them. Placing them in mortal hands always has unpredictable consequences. In any case, it's done now and Lore will be coming with all her might to claim it."

"I'll sail to you with all the ships I can muster. As swiftly as I can."

"No." Gruinskard gave a firm shake of his head. "Strike too soon and the blow will be wasted. Gather allies from the upper gelds first. While you do, I will forge this city into a shield, one Lore will waste the blood of her warriors trying to break."

"How can you be so sure she will oblige you in this? Olversahl is a port, more likely to fall to blockade than outright assault."

His eye narrowed and beard bunched in a grin. "Something I learned during my escape. Lore is in love with the scholar. And there is no rage more certain to unreason a mind than that of love betrayed. Gather your forces and come to me when they're ready, my queen. Do this right, and we have a chance to end this war at one stroke."

CHAPTER THIRTY-FOUR

Elvine

Only one cell in the Rent still held a prisoner in these fraught times. Despite the fact she had come to free him, Elvine found its occupant wasn't pleased to see her.

"When the gaoler told me the name of the Altvar's Spear Maiden, I laughed," Bahn said. "Now I see he wasn't lying."

When the door to his cell swung open, his expression had been one of rigid expectation. Upon seeing Elvine's face, it softened at first, a measure of the respect and affection she recalled showing in the upturned brows and widened eye. But, after a few seconds of wordless mutual regard, his face hardened into a mask of mingled resentment and accusation.

Elvine didn't reply, instead turning to the gaoler and asking him to leave them alone. The stern-faced fellow afforded Bahn a glare before stomping away into the shadowed recesses of his domain. Turning back to Bahn, she saw how his once husky frame had been denuded by months of captivity. His skin had a sallow tint and his eye was sunken. Like Gruinskard, he had lost the other the night Olversahl fell to the Sister Queens. His patch had been taken, and he had tied a rag over the empty socket. Looking into his remaining orb, she couldn't be sure if the glimmer it held was one of defiance or condemnation.

"I will not recant," he stated. An answer to a question she hadn't asked, spoken with the grating harshness of oft-repeated refusal. She knew that, alone among the congregation seized that terrible night by Ilvar's *menda*, Bahn had held true to the Covenant.

"I know," Elvine said. Standing back, she gestured to the open doorway. "Come. You're free."

Bahn continued to sit upon the thin mattress covering his bunk. Blinking, he turned away from her. "Do you know why I'm still alive, Elvine?" he asked, voice softer now. He didn't wait for her answer, not that she had one to offer. "I am alive because they forgot about me. Slung into this cell to await death while all manner of chaos raged outside. When first they caged me here, they would bring our fellow congregants to plead with me, beseech me to cast aside the heresy of Covenant faith and accept the Altvar. Your friend Dehny was the most persistent. I marvelled at how quickly she had acquired so deep a knowledge of the sagas, reciting them at length for many an hour. In the end, I told her if she didn't leave me alone, I'd drown her in my shit bucket. Do I have to threaten you so, Elvine?"

She resisted the urge to evade his gaze. Dehny had been there that morning when she spoke to the assembled masses of Olversahl. Elvine stood atop a platform raised at Gruinskard's instruction on the site of the ruins of Aeric's Library, since it offered the most expansive stretch of open space in the city. Word had already spread of Elvine's return, and her apparent acceptance of the Altvar. Consequently, the foremost ranks of her audience were filled with fervent local adherents of the gods. One youthful figure cried out louder than the others, beseeching the Spear Maiden with arms raised and face set in manic adoration. It had been a stranger's face until Elvine realised she looked upon a woman she had known since childhood. Once the Spear Maiden's words roused the crowd to a suitably voluminous roar and she stepped down from the platform, she told Halkyr not to let them get close. As Colvyn hustled her away, she could hear Dehny's voice cutting through the others, as much a stranger as her face: "Bless me, Spear Maiden! Command me and my blood is yours!"

"I am not here for your conversion," Elvine told Bahn now. "If you have any inkling of what has befallen this realm, you'll know that everything has changed. Olversahl stands threatened with destruction, and all strong hands are needed in her defence."

"Even those of an unrepentant heretic?"

"I find I prefer those at my side with unclouded minds. Those I trust to provide honest advice when asked."

A faint, hissing laugh escaped Bahn's lips. "My mind is unclouded, eh? What about yours, Elvine? Have you truly given your heart to the Altvar?"

"I've given my heart to the cause of saving this city and defeating our enemies." Hearing the harshness of her tone, she paused, drawing in a breath before entering the cell and sitting at his side. "I have journeyed far, Bahn. I have seen wonders and terrors. I have seen battle, and I have taken lives. I have learned many, many things. But most of all, I have come to understand the vastness of my own ignorance. I cannot tell you that the Covenant has the same hold on my soul as it once did. Nor will I lie. I know not whether the Altvar are real. But I do know with no shred of doubt that the spear that bears their name was not born of this world. Most of all, I know I've lost too many friends to lose another."

Bahn's shoulders slumped, and he said nothing for a time. When he spoke, it was to ask a question, one she had dreaded but thought might well be spoken here: "Did you ever truly love my nephew?"

She could lie. Tell this man of her unbridled devotion to poor, slain Uhttar and how her heart still yearned for him. But Bahn deserved the truth. "I loved him," she said. "Not as he wanted me to, but that was all I could offer him. In time, it may have become something more. I don't know."

Bahn's head dipped lower. "He never believed," he muttered. "Not even as a boy when I would take him to secret supplications. I could tell it meant nothing to him. It was only when you joined us that he seemed to develop a passion for the Covenant. It was never his faith. You were."

Drawing in a breath, he got to his feet. "Would I be wrong in assuming the Spear Maiden might be able to provide a meal or two?"

Pausing to blink a tear from her eye, Elvine rose, smiling and taking his hand. "You would not. Come, as you eat, I'll tell you of the Tielwald's battle plan. I'm keen to hear any opinion you might offer."

While Elvine doubted she would ever feel any semblance of affection towards Margnus Gruinskard, his preparations for the impending Nihlvarian assault did at least engender a modicum of reluctant admiration. Placing the warship of Lore's unfortunate *menda* in the hands of Ahlgrun and his brothers, he recruited additional crew from the experienced sailors stuck in port since the foreign merchant vessels fled. Most were glad of the chance to tread a deck once again. With the ship fully crewed, Gruinskard instructed Ahlgrun to sail to the mouth of Aeric's Fjord and watch for the arrival of the enemy fleet.

A workforce several thousand strong was assembled, all set to one task that had swiftly become the overriding purpose of the port's denizens: the building of the harbour wall. Elvine had expected it to be a straightforward if arduous proposition. However, it soon transpired that constructing a sufficiently tall and robust barrier atop a sea-facing structure was a complex enterprise requiring all the skill of every mason and builder in Olversahl. Stone was quarried from the base of the mountain, hacked from the granite fringing the huge, cracked carvings of the Altvar. More building materials were sourced via the simple expedient of tearing down a number of warehouses close to the wharf and gathering up the tumbled bricks. The larger stones were placed along the edge of the quay to form a foundation. The massive blocks were manoeuvred into place with a small forest of timber cranes and pulleys, some of them perched on the decks of merchant ships pressed into service as work platforms.

Watching the labour progress over the course of the first week, Elvine wondered if the Tielwald's grand design would ever be complete. Some foundation stones had been laid, but they covered only a few feet of the dockside. It appeared a meagre result given the scale of labour employed.

"It'll grow," Bahn assured her. Although he had spent much of his adult life as a wool merchant, he had overseen many a construction in the course of his business. "It always seems slow at first. Give it another week, and it'll start to look like something."

Elvine didn't voice her doubts that Lore might well not grant them the grace of further delay. As Spear Maiden, it had quickly become clear to her that outward displays of anything other than zealous belief in victory, as ordained by the Altvar, was not her role.

"Like it or not, you're a character in a play now," Berrine told her one night as they collaborated on the Spear Maiden's next public address. Her mother had been pleased to discover their house both empty and unmolested, expressing a suspicion that most folk were too scared to venture near it. Despite her desire to settle back into a long-cherished home, it soon became impossible thanks to the persistent crowd of adoring believers who dogged Elvine's every step. Halkyr had shown creditable initiative in quickly recruiting a dozen unemployed sailors, all Ascarlians with battle experience, to serve as her personal guard. Their principal role so far had been keeping Elvine's worshippers, for she couldn't think of a better name, at bay. To her considerable dismay, Dehny had emerged as the group's leader. Elvine suspected this to be the result of their prior friendship. Of them all, only Dehny addressed her by name when the mob was baying its delusional cries for her attention.

Consequently, she, Berrine and Colvyn had been forced to take up residence in the city archive. Built in the aftermath of the old library's destruction, it was a substantial building of many large rooms, although still but a lesser shadow of a greatness it couldn't hope to match. Gruinskard had made a surprisingly cordial invitation to join him at the Elderman's House, but Elvine refused. She still met with him every other day, but felt it best for the Spear Maiden not to be too closely associated with the Tielwald.

"Speaking of which," Berrine said, reaching for a freshly inscribed piece of parchment. "I found a speech in that volume of D'Ambrille you gave me. A battle exhortation from her 'Triumph of King Mathis'. It's a tad flowery in places. Woefully inaccurate historically, too, since Mathis the First famously couldn't speak above a whisper thanks to an arrow he took in the throat as a youth. But, with a few alterations, it'll serve well enough."

"How well you've taken to this, Mother," Elvine observed dryly. "Perhaps it's not just my father I have to thank for my facility with lies."

Her mood was sour this night. While she continued to shun Dehny, earlier that day she had sought out her other sole remaining childhood friend. Senhild's home was a substantial building located in the city's most affluent quarter, close to the Elderman's House. Its three-storey grandeur reflected her father's status as one of Olversahl's more successful lawyers. Senhild's mother had been reluctant to admit Elvine, but the presence of Halkyr and several armed escorts forestalled any outright objections to welcoming the Spear Maiden into her home. The thin girl Elvine found alone in the upstairs bedroom shrank from her the moment she entered. Lank, unwashed hair veiled Senhild's face as she huddled into a corner, whimpering. Elvine's attempts to allay her fears had produced only sobs, then a spittle fleck diatribe. It was mostly gibberish but Elvine heard the words "They made me!" among the babble before it trailed off into piteous weeping.

"I'm not here to punish you," Elvine had told her, grasping one of her trembling hands. "I know you had no choice."

She glimpsed Senhild's eyes through the matted curtain of hair, bright and unblinking. "You should be," she whispered. "For my betrayal of our congregation damns me in the Martyr's eyes for all time. The gates are ever closed to me, Elvine. Please." She gripped Elvine's hand. "Please, when you kill me, call upon the Martyrs to beseech the Seraphile to have mercy. They will listen to you. Please . . ."

All the comfort and reassurance Elvine offered yielded only more sorrow, growing in despair and volume to the point that she fled the house. Since then, the shame of her cowardice had stirred a bitterness she couldn't explain.

"This city must stand," Berrine said. A measure of hurt showed in her eyes, though Elvine could tell she was striving to keep any anger from her voice. "If the words we weave can buttress the courage of our people, even by the smallest amount, then that is our role. We are not fighters, Elvine. At least, not with weapons. And a well-chosen word can cut as deep as any sword, or spear." Her gaze narrowed in clear dislike as it slipped to the Spear of the Altvar. Elvine had set it close to the fireplace because the spirit inside professed a liking for warmth. Like Gruinskard, Berrine avoided proximity to the weapon, never once touching it. Although her mother voiced no reason for this aversion, Elvine knew it didn't arise from the spear's arcane, possibly divine, nature. No, Berrine's resentment stemmed from the fact it had claimed her daughter, made her a figure of adulation to the deluded, but also a target for Lore's hatred.

"A Spear Maiden who can't even wield it properly," Elvine sighed. Frowning, she rose from the table to take up the spear. "Write the speech, Mother," she told Berrine, moving to the door. "I'll look it over in the morning."

"This is not a good idea." The reluctance in Colvyn's voice echoed loud in the archive's central hall. Elvine had ordered the tables stacked against the far wall, leaving a bare space suitable for her purposes. "Learning the proper handling of any weapon requires months," he went on. "True proficiency only comes after years of practice."

"Then teach me what you can in the time we have," Elvine said, hefting the spear. When he continued to regard her with a doubtful squint, she added, "At least enough so that it appears the Spear Maiden of Olversahl actually knows how to wield the Altvar's divine instrument."

"Or knows enough to get herself killed when the red-faces assault the wall. I've stayed at your side all this time to keep you safe. I won't be party to your death."

Seeing the stern resolve on his face, she bit back a retort. Colvyn could not be commanded to the Spear Maiden's will, but there was one who could. "Very well." She turned, footsteps echoing as she strode for the door. "If you won't teach me, I've no doubt Halkyr will . . ."

"Wait." Grimacing in resignation, he beckoned her closer and nodded to the spear. "For a start, your hands are too close together on the haft . . ."

He spent the next hour teaching her what he called the basic forms of spear-based combat. In practice, this required much standing in various poses and learning the fundamentals of the thrust and the parry. It was all much more tedious than she expected, and Colvyn proved to be a harsh tutor.

"Balance," he snapped, nudging a toe to her feet as she adopted a fighting stance. "Always in line with your shoulders, otherwise this happens." He delivered a gentle shove to her hip, sending her sprawling onto her side. "And then—" his sword came free of its scabbard in a flash, the cool metal chilling the underside of Elvine's chin "—you're dead, dear sister."

"You think if you bruise me enough I'll give up?" she asked, scrambling to her feet.

"Bruise you?" Colvyn shook his head, letting out a small laugh. "The man our father hired to teach me to fight considered it a dishonour if he didn't make me bleed at least once a week. I'm fairly certain he genuinely tried to kill me on more than one occasion. Battle is not forgiving, so don't expect your lessons to be."

Although she was sure he hoped she would abandon this notion after the first lesson, she insisted he spend an hour teaching her every night. At the start of the next session, he told her to put the spear aside and handed her a wooden stave roughly the same length. "Let's see how much you remember," he said, before promptly thumping his own stave into her upper thigh. Hissing in pain, Elvine jabbed at his face only for him to duck the thrust and sweep her legs out from under her.

"Dead again," he said, tapping the tip of his weapon to the top of her head. "Get up. And this time bear in mind the folly of succumbing to anger."

For the next week, her routine became one of touring the dockside works during the day, collaborating with Berrine on inspiring doggerel in the evening, after which she would spend an hour training with Colvyn. Of it all, she found her visits to the docks the most trying. Her repeated presence, insisted upon by the Tielwald, was supposed to inspire the labouring towns-folk to greater efforts, but the collective weight of their hopeful regard was oppressive. Her speeches were semi-regular affairs but always well attended, even by folk wearied after long hours of toil, and she couldn't deny their effect. At first it had been her gaggle of worshippers who shouted loudest in acclaim. Now they all did. She appeared before them in warrior garb now, a collection of resized leather armour and a cape of white satin. A gift from Gruinskard, the fact that the ensemble fitted perfectly irked her. Clearly, the old man, or more likely Coelnyr, had paid uncomfortably close attention to her person.

"Unless I'm very much mistaken, dear sister," Colvyn observed during their nightly practice, "your fine oratory today was not entirely original." He punctuated the last word with a swipe at her head, their staves clattering together as she blocked it and dodged clear of the thrust he aimed at her chest. "'When a ravening bear is at your throat, know that only stout heart and keen steel shall be your saviour,'" he quoted, circling her in a low crouch. "Remarkably similar to Velzir Din-Matun's proclamation during the siege of the Emerald Citadel. Except he spoke of a lion instead of a bear."

"Inspiration arises from many sources," Elvine said, fending off a thrust at her belly and then replying with a quick swipe at his forearm. It failed to land as he twisted away, angling his stave to deliver a downward poke, too fast for her parry. She grunted as the ash point pressed hard into her flesh, stepping back and smothering her annoyance with a rueful laugh. "I keep falling for that."

"Yes." Colvyn's expression lacked any amusement. "You do." Lowering his stave, his features took on a far more serious and worrying cast than usual. "I haven't been teaching you properly," he said. "As I was taught. Time we rectified that."

Moving to the wall where the Spear of the Altvar rested, he picked it up, displaying none of the hesitancy she saw in Berrine or Gruinskard. "Here," he said, taking her stave and replacing it with the spear before stepping back. The stave clattered on the floorboards as he tossed it aside and drew his sword, saying, "Now, Spear Maiden, defend yourself."

He struck without warning, a lightning fast thrust at her midriff she barely managed to parry, his plain Ascarlian sword of good steel ringing loud as it rebounded from the coarse iron of the spearpoint. He attacked again without pause, feinting to the left then slashing at her right, this time evading the flailing spear. She wore a blouse and trews today, easier to move in than her armour. Colvyn's blade slashed the blouse open, coming within a whisker of scoring the flesh beneath.

"I said!" he growled, teeth clenched. "Defend yourself!"

His blade described a silver arc as he brought it down in an overhead slash at her shoulder. Elvine back-pedalled, the sword point missing by inches. Colvyn came on undaunted, hacking left and right while she tried vainly to retreat faster than he could advance. She parried as best she could but panic made her clumsy, more cuts appearing her blouse, her brother's rage increasing every time he evaded her inexpert attempts to block his attacks.

"Are you going to make me cut you?" he demanded, voice rising to a shout as he brought the sword round, handle gripped with both hands. She could tell the blow was aimed at the spear, not her, designed to jar it from her grasp and leave her defenceless. As she adjusted her hands on the weapon, her skin touched the base of the iron point, whereupon time instantly slowed. Colvyn's blurringly fast strike became a languid whirl, his shirt and hair rippling as if submerged in water.

You know he's not truly trying to hurt you, I assume? the spear's inhabitant enquired as Colvyn's sword continued its incremental approach. For the first time, Elvine perceived an aura around him. It was more complex than most, shot through with anger, but mostly roiling in a mix of fear and frustration.

You asked him for something he can't give, the spear said. *To impart skills that are simply beyond you.*

"I need them," Elvine replied, experiencing a jolt of disorientation when she realised her lips hadn't moved. She and the spear were communicating via unknown means, and far faster than she thought possible.

You're sure? The spear's tone held a cautionary note. *Your kind is terribly prone to misusing our gifts. And I have already given you so much.*

"I need them!" Elvine repeated, shouting now even though no sound escaped her throat.

As you wish. The words held a note of disappointment, but also weary inevitability. *Remember, this was your choice.*

The spear pulsed in Elvine's grip and Colvyn's aura changed. Instead of a formless cloud, it swirled into a shadowy echo of his form, but moving at normal speed. It described his oncoming blow, revealing how he intended to alter the trajectory of the blade at the last instant to slap the flat of it to her thigh. A stinging rebuke he hoped would dissuade her from further practice.

Time resumed its normal course as Elvine moved, taking a forward step and lowering the spear to parry Colvyn's blade. Pausing in surprise, he blinked at her and tried again, flicking his sword point at her face then delivering a downward slash at her forearm. Once again, time slowed and his shadow form revealed it all, Elvine sidestepping the attack to deliver a thrust of her own. The spearpoint jabbed within a hand's width of his face before he batted it aside.

Retreating a few paces, Colvyn's gaze narrowed, focusing on the spear. His aura darkened with both realisation and foreboding. "I knew that thing had power," he said, shaking his head. "But this is beyond any strangeness I've seen before. And I've seen quite a lot."

A little annoyed that he hadn't ascribed her new-found skill to her quick learning, Elvine shrugged. "If it's any comfort, before today I didn't know it could do that."

His furrowed brow deepened as he continued to regard the spear. "When we were adrift on the Styrnspeld, I considered taking it when you were sleeping and casting it into the sea. Now I wish I had. It would have spared you all this."

"I don't think it would've let you," she told him, forcing a smile and coughing to banish the catch in her throat. "But your concern . . . pleases me, brother."

After another baleful glance at the spear, he summoned a smile of his own and raised his sword with a flourish. "Let's see what else it can do."

CHAPTER THIRTY-FIVE

Ruhlin

The mask was icy in his grip, chilled by the stiff mountain breeze that grew colder as night fell. Ruhlin's instructions to Sygurn had been simple: make a steel covering for the monster's face. Yet the smith had seen fit to embellish his work with iron, adding deep brows above the slits of the eyes and a gaping, many-toothed maw around the narrow grate over the mouth. The result was a snarling visage that, Ruhlin suspected, bore more than a passing resemblance to his transformed features when the monster had been roused.

He paused when the many torches of the Nihlvarian camp flickered into view through the gusting snow. The weather had worsened with the onset of night, no doubt increasing the misery of the unfortunate warriors clustered in their tents. Ruhlin felt a curious jab of sympathy as he donned the mask. Unpleasant as their night was, it would soon get much worse. Sygurn had fashioned an ingenious strap for the mask, fixing coiled springs to a thick piece of leather designed to stretch as its wearer's form expanded. Ruhlin had to trust the monster would understand its purpose and not cast it off in irritated fury. With the mask in place, he sloughed off his cloak and removed his jerkin and shirt. The lacerating caress of snow and wind upon his unprotected flesh set him shuddering, but the heat flaring in his gut confirmed that his suffering would be short-lived. The monster smelled battle.

The change began as he started towards the Nihlvarian camp; the maul growing light in his grip, his boots and trews ripping as his form swelled with every step. His vision was limited by the mask, but the monster's wrath was fed as much by scent and sound as by sight. Ruhlin hadn't noticed before, but the transformation heralded a sharpening of his senses. The campfire smoke staining the mountain air blossomed from a faint, ashen taint to an acrid stench laced with the sweat of huddled warriors. He could hear their muttered conversation, a low murmur of complaint and shared discomfort, soon overridden by alarmed shouting when the pickets noticed Ruhlin's approach.

The monster fully emerged when the first arrows flew, most going wide thanks to the wind, but one rebounding from his chest as if it had struck a castle wall. The monster let out a sound that mingled laughter with deep, dire hunger and spurred to a run. The red fog that typically accompanied these moments closed in when it reaped its first victims, a pair of archers smashed and torn without breaking stride. However, the obscuring mist was not so thick this time, making Ruhlin a witness to all the havoc that followed.

The monster shredded ox-hide tents like rice paper then did the same to the occupants, the maul hammering bones into shards before the monster tore limbs from sockets. Men and women ran screaming or, foolishly, tried to stand against a rampaging nightmare made real. Blades failed to even scar his skin, and their owners never had a chance for a second blow. It punched through armour to drag forth spines from the chests of its victims. Slab-like feet pulped the ribs and heads of the maimed. For a time, all was slaughter, and the monster's hungry laugh rang loud enough to smother the screams of the dying or the terrorised.

The sharp ping of something small impacting the mask brought a sudden halt to its onslaught. Standing in the midst of a scattered fire, a dying warrior dangling from its massive fist, the monster paused. A slender figure stood twenty paces off with a thin metal tube raised to her lips. Her cheeks swelled and a second dart flew. This one was poorly aimed, perhaps because Deyna's hands shook so badly. The barbed missile impacted just below the monster's collarbone, spinning away without managing to penetrate its hide. It watched Deyna fumble for another dart, fishing in a leather pouch at her belt, only to scatter the contents as her hands failed her. Dropping to her knees, she scrabbled in the snow, succeeding in finding a lone projectile. The monster reached her as she vainly attempted to slot it into her blowpipe.

To Ruhlin's surprise, it didn't kill her. Instead, it clamped one massive hand around her neck and lifted her off her feet. As it pulled her close, Ruhlin caught the stink of her fear. The Tuhlvyr's nostrils flared and bulging eyes leaked tears as she beheld her imminent demise, yet still, he saw a small glint of prideful resolve in those quivering features. *She won't beg*, Ruhlin realised, recalling how the unfortunate Tuhlvyr Feydrik had displayed much the same defiance in his last moments.

Her courage dwindled when the monster drew her closer still and, for the first time, Ruhlin heard it speak. The sound was part snarl and part sigh, the words ill formed but still comprehensible through the mask. "My name is not Amundyr," the monster informed the Tuhlvyr, whereupon she tried to scream. It emerged as only a piteous squeal, the abject knowledge of impending death shining bright in her bloodshot gaze.

Something fast and hard impacted the monster's back then, failing to inflict injury, but causing it to turn. Through the red haze, Ruhlin saw a cordon of Nihlvarian warriors forming a circle around the monster. They closed ranks with practised efficiency, overlapping shields locked together. These, Ruhlin knew, must be the elite of Deyna's force. Hardened veterans capable of braving both the harsh mountain climes and the inhuman beast that had put their less resolute comrades to flight. Levelling their spears and swords atop their shields, they began to inch closer.

Grunting in anticipation, the monster opened his hand and let Deyna fall. She collapsed onto the snow, retching. Ruhlin expected the monster to crush her beneath his foot at any second, but it didn't. Instead, it hunched low in readiness, hefting the maul and casting a throaty roar of challenge at the closing circle of enemies. Surveying their number, Ruhlin guessed at least a hundred. The monster had never faced so many at once before, but its bloodlust only grew as they drew nearer. He wondered if it was even capable of fear. Or perhaps, some corner of its mind contrived to remember the plan he had hatched with Guthnyr and Tirohk.

The first volley of Morvek arrows, all launched at close range to negate the effect of the wind, felled at least a score of the veterans. The second was not so successful, most of the shafts deflected by their shields as they turned to face the new threat, but by then, the *Vehlkasa* were already among them. These were Tirohk's hand-picked best, all armed with the fruits of Sygurn's forge. Their blades shone bright in the chaotic light of scattered torches and blazing tents, swords and axes wielded with skill and speed. Ruhlin saw several Nihlvarian swords shattered in the unfolding melee, also shields splintered and cracked by axe blows.

A fierce cry drew the monster's notice to a frenzied knot of battling figures, Nihlvarians clustering around a tall warrior who had hurled himself into their midst. Guthnyr's sword sliced through iron helms and leather greaves with ease, his ferocity wedded to a wicked artistry. Ruhlin had been impressed when seeing him fight before, but this was Guthnyr unbridled, his vengeance unleashed at last. Watching the Nihlvarians wither around him, Ruhlin found the sight of his friend's bloody, exultant features more forbidding than inspiring. What could such skilful fury achieve were it to be matched by ambition?

It was a human thought, summoning the realisation that his form was returning to normal. The chill lashed at his bare flesh once again as he watched his hands diminish in size, a downward glance revealing the sight of Deyna trying to crawl away. "Forgive me," Ruhlin said, planting a foot on her back and forcing her into the snow. "But I must insist you favour us with your company a while longer, Tuhlvyr. For I believe you have much to tell me."

The complete destruction of the Nihlvarian force wore on through the night. With Deyna's best warriors slain, the already disrupted and terror-stricken rump of her command mostly fled or, pathetically, attempted to surrender to a foe disinclined to mercy. Besides the warriors chosen for the main assault, Tirohk had arranged the rest of his war party in a wide circle around the camp, ensuring there would be no survivors. When dawn broke, the burgeoning sun revealed a white field streaked in crimson for near a half-mile all around. Despite their bloody exertions, the Morvek were in a celebratory mood, capering about in captured armour as they brandished looted swords, or more grisly trophies. Faced with such ugliness, Ruhlin had to remind himself that these people, like Guthnyr, had many a score to settle.

"Do you intend to play with me a while before giving me to these savages?" Deyna enquired. She sat close by, wrists and ankles bound, while Ruhlin warmed himself at a bonfire of piled tent hides. He had acquired clothing from the plentiful dead, but the chill lingered.

"Your people force the enslaved to fight like animals for public amusement," he reminded her, grinding his jaw to banish the chatter of his teeth. "I would say you have no right to call anyone a savage."

"Still clinging to your weakling ways, I see." She sighed, shaking her head. "To think of the glory that could have been yours." Beneath the poised disdain, Ruhlin could see the fear that made her eyes dart between him and the corpse-strewn ruin of her camp. Still, her refusal to cower stirred a grudging and annoying admiration. The sentiment, however, was not shared by his companions.

"My wolves are still hungry," Velkar said, fixing an unblinking stare on the captive. Her pack were arrayed alongside her, reddened snouts quivering and yellow eyes as steady as their mistress. "So rare to capture one of her rank," the elder went on, coming closer, her wolves hunching in preparation.

"Enough," Ruhlin said, stepping into Velkar's path. "She has knowledge we need and remains under the *Telchak's* protection."

He hadn't thought Velkar a particularly bloodthirsty soul, but the snarl that twisted her lips as she retreated made him ponder just how much she shared with her wolves. "Please try to run," she told Deyna before stalking away with her pack in tow.

"*Telchak*?" Deyna asked, managing to infuse her tone with a measure of taunting amusement. "That's what they think you are? Their mythical saviour made flesh?"

Ruhlin ignored her, turning to greet Guthnyr as he approached carrying a stack of Nihlvarian helms. "These were the captains, as far as I can tell," he said, dumping the burden at Ruhlin's feet. "One of them lived long enough to share his opinion of their commander." He cast a disgusted glance at Deyna. "It wasn't favourable."

"He was honoured to die in the Vortigurn's service," she replied, attempting a defiant pose despite her bonds. "As am I."

"And I'll be more than happy to oblige when the leader of my *menda* gives the order," Guthnyr said, jerking his head at Ruhlin. "Y'see, he knows how to command." Turning to Ruhlin, he added, "I'm not gifted with torture, but I gather Sygurn knows a thing or two about it. We should take her back to the mountain. Since she's such a courageous soul, it'll most likely require hot irons to get anything out of her."

Ruhlin watched Deyna struggle to maintain her composure as the words sank home. Fear, he knew, could be as potent as any device of torment when it came to extracting information. "For now, I have but one question, Tuhlvyr," he said, sinking to his haunches before her. "Is yours the only *menda* to venture into these mountains? I caution you, speak true, for our scouts will soon reveal the truth."

Deyna grunted in frustration, tipping over as she strained against her bindings. Her struggles came to an abrupt end when Guthnyr dragged her to her feet. "A question requires an answer," he growled. "How many more of your filth will come against us?"

The swirling scarlet tattoos about her eyes stood out in stark contrast to her skin, pale with fury and fear. Lowering her head, she spoke in a soft mutter. "The Vortigurn granted me the honour of recovering this one." She shot a glare at Ruhlin. "A task I was to perform alone, since it was by my agency that he had first been brought to the king's attention."

"You mean this was your punishment for my escape," Ruhlin said. "Sent into Morvek lands to either bring me back or die in the attempt. Your great king appears to place scant value on your life, Tuhlvyr."

Deyna's features twitched, her voice dwindling yet further when she replied, "My life is his to spend as he sees fit."

"Then you're just as much a slave as I once was." Ruhlin nodded at

Guthnyr, the warrior dumping Deyna to the snow before they moved away, voices lowered. "Ask Velkar to send her wolves to scout the southern approaches," Ruhlin told him. "You, Julette and Tuhlan stay with her. Meet me at the pass when it's done." He met Guthnyr's gaze. "If you find any Nihlvarians, leave them be. Even a small number. Best if they don't know we're here." Seeing a wry smile play over Guthnyr's lips, he asked, "What is it?"

"It's just, sometimes you sound like . . ." Guthnyr trailed off, shaking his head. "No matter. Trust me." He patted the hilt of his sword as he strode away. "This beauty's tasted enough blood, for now."

They remained at the *Sahlrak* for five days, during which time more *Vehlkasa* arrived to buttress their numbers. The wolf Velkar had dispatched to her people also returned, after which the elder confirmed that a strong *Teyrak* war band was already making its way to the pass. The rest of her pack, and Guthnyr's scouting party, brought confirmation that Deyna had spoken true; hers was the only Nihlvarian force to venture into the mountains.

"Doesn't mean there aren't more of the bastards," Guthnyr said. "Could be camped further south, awaiting a break in the weather."

"How far can your wolves range?" Ruhlin asked Velkar, the question summoning a crease to her brow, as if it hadn't been asked before.

"To the other side of the world if need be," she said. "But if the *Rulchakin* were anywhere close, their scent would taint the wind. And it does not."

"Meaning we have another opportunity," Guthnyr said. "The north of the red-faces' realm appears undefended, while we will soon have an army here."

"An army still lacking the weapons needed for victory," Ruhlin pointed out. "Besides, I thought only a fool campaigns in winter."

"Not if he has sufficient supplies." Guthnyr's gaze slid towards Deyna. The Tuhlvyr's ankles were now unbound, though her movements were constrained by the chain fixed about her neck, the other end hammered into a nearby rock. "And," Guthnyr added, "there's one among us who would know where to find them."

"The risk is too great," Ruhlin said. "The *Vehlkasa* and the *Teyrak* will hold the pass while we produce more arms and await the spring thaw. By then, all the clans will have mustered their war bands. These people put great trust in me, my friend. I'll not squander it on a gamble."

He could sense Guthnyr's frustration at such caution, but the larger man voiced no further argument. "What about her?" he said, jerking his chin at Deyna. "If we don't need her to tell us where to find supplies, what use is she?"

"That I've yet to discover," Ruhlin admitted. "But it's not her knowledge of our enemy's dispositions that interests me. It's the man she serves."

To Ruhlin's surprise, Deyna proved far more forthcoming regarding the Vortigurn than expected. He began questioning her during the trek back to the Tahrim Kyrn, anticipating a terse refusal to speak. Instead, her initial response had been a clipped enquiry as to what might befall her if she failed to talk.

"The hot irons that Teilvik brute spoke of, I assume?"

"We can't spare the metal," Ruhlin said. "I could hand you over to the Morvek, but I doubt you'd be capable of saying much when they're done." He watched her features as he spoke, reading a spasm of fear, but also a narrowing of the eyes that told of insightful judgement.

"You won't," she said. "I've suffered enough cruel hearts to know when I meet one, and I haven't now. The beast within you is not cruel either, just ferocious. He's the same." She nodded at Guthnyr, striding at the head of their party. "For all his talk of torment."

"I wouldn't test him," Ruhlin warned. "All he's suffered at the hands of your kind has made him vengeful. And I find vengeance is a form of cruelty in itself. Still—" he sniffed "—you're right. I've no stomach for torture. Nor do those that follow me. So, perhaps I should just let you go. You can make your way back to the court of your king and tell him of your defeat and capture at my hands. I wonder how he would respond."

Coming to a halt, he drew his dagger. The rest of the party stopped, turning to witness what came next. Deyna's features showed a rigid lack of expression as he took hold of her wrists and began to cut away her bonds. "Go," he said, gesturing towards the dark notch of the pass. "I'll tell the Morvek to leave you be, and even give you enough food and water to last you a week or more. Go and tell your king that the *Telchak* sends greetings, and looks forward to the day we face each other in his hall."

"You are an ignorant, low-born fool," Deyna stated, gaze dark with anger. "A child at play in a cage of hungry beasts."

"If that's your judgement, feel free to share it with the Vortigurn."

Deyna massaged her wrists, eyes narrowed in calculation as they flicked from him to the pass and back again. After a full ten seconds, she had still failed to move.

"He'll kill you, won't he?" Ruhlin asked. "And I suspect he will have no qualms when it comes to torture. He already sent you here to die. Your survival would therefore be a severe disappointment, would it not, Tuhlvyr?" He resumed walking, gesturing for the others to do the same. "You should come with us," he told Deyna over his shoulder. "Since I can't think of anywhere else in this world you could go at this juncture. But if you do, I would very much like to hear more of the Vortigurn's court."

"He has no court, as such." Deyna spoke in a flat tone, occasionally coloured by a reflective note, the firelight painting her near-white hair a soft shade of gold. They had camped for the night atop a low rise a day's march from the *Sahlrak*. "He has slaves to see to his needs and service his hall, but no actual courtiers, save one." Her lips curled in an unconscious spasm of disgust. "The vilest, most grasping soul you could ever meet. He guards the Vortigurn. Not against attack, but unwanted visitors. Only those who win his favour are allowed to petition for an audience with the king, and the price is extortionate. Even then, the few who ever find themselves in his presence rarely speak of the experience. Myself included."

"But you have met him?" Ruhlin pressed. "You were granted an audience?"

"Yes, I met him. Once Feydrik and I had handed over a mountain of gold to his creature, we were granted the ultimate honour of a personal audience. He wanted to hear what we had to say about the very special slaves we had been gathering for the Meidvang, and our plans for the grandest and most spectacular event the great *wuhltra* in the capital had ever seen."

"By this you meant to win his favour? Enhance your status yet further?"

Deyna shrugged. "Of course. That is the endless game of the Tuhlvyr caste, one that often turns deadly."

"But your caste sits at the top of Nihlvarian society. How much higher could you climb?"

"While there are other Tuhlvyr to contend with, the game never ends. It's my belief the Vortigurn prefers it this way. While we plot against each other, we do not plot against him." She spoke with an off-handedness that belied the guarded tension of her face. She tried to hide it, but Ruhlin saw a measure of the same calculation he had noticed at their first meeting. There was more here than just the power-hungry squabbling of the privileged.

"When we met before, you spoke of presenting me to the Vortigurn," he recalled. "Something that seemed to appeal to you greatly. Why?"

"He has a famed fascination with those blessed by the Altvar, especially those said to possess the fire blood. It's one of the few things certain to gain his notice. Nihlvarian law holds that any such person found within or without the realm are to be tested in the Meidvang and brought to him should they survive. It has been many years since this happened. Feydrik and I would have won great honour and reward by presenting you for the Vortigurn's inspection."

The sense that she concealed something lingered, but Ruhlin decided not to press her. The Tuhlvyr's candour undoubtedly had an unspoken purpose. Perhaps she intended to win his trust and, in time, twist him to her will. He found the prospect of witnessing her eventual disappointment highly appealing.

"You say the Tuhlvyr vie with each other constantly," he said. "But speak of Feydrik as an ally. Were you lovers?"

Her laugh, rich in disparagement, surprised him. Until now, she hadn't displayed the smallest shred of humour. "Were our circumstances different," she said, once sobered, "I would have you whipped to death for even whispering such a suggestion. Feydrik was a very limited man, but useful. I heard about his death at your hands, of course. They say he was brave, but I wonder if that is merely a story spun by his relatives to garnish an otherwise dishonourable end."

"Brave he was," Ruhlin said, offering her a smile. "And dead a heartbeat later."

"You slew him, but spared me. Why?"

"I didn't do either. The monster inside me did. I suspect it saw use in you, but none in Feydrik."

"So when the fire blood burns, it is not you that rages." She angled her head, and he almost heard her keen mind at work. "How interesting."

"I'll have more interesting things to show when we reach the mountain. Of course, I'll have to persuade the Morvek among us not to kill you on sight. I'm afraid I can't offer any promises in that regard." He rose and went to his bedroll. "Sleep well, Tuhlvyr."

The following day saw an end to the recurrent snowfall, but also the descent of a thick, freezing mist that made each breath a painful gasp and obscured their course. Fortunately, Velkar's wolves proved expert navigators even in the fog, enabling the party to make steady progress until they came to an abrupt halt. A long, plaintive howl echoed towards them, stirring Velkar to instant alertness.

"Someone comes," she said, eyes taking on a distant cast. After a brief interval of silence, she relaxed. "They are friends. My people's war band has found us, but they bring an unusual visitor to the mountains."

Peering into the drifting swirl, Ruhlin made out a large shape drawing closer. At first he assumed it to be a horse, which was certainly out of the ordinary, for he hadn't yet seen a Morvek ride. But, as the form approached, his alarm returned as he discerned the long horns and shaggy hide of an *altahnk*. However, the beast appeared placid enough, picking its way carefully over the winding trail with no indication it might be about to charge. Once it had slipped fully from the fog's embrace, Ruhlin saw the small figure perched atop its broad back.

"How good it is to find you well, *Telchak!*" Olchar said, raising a hand in greeting. To his rear, the vague forms of *Teyrak* warriors emerged from the mist. Ruhlin could count only a dozen, but the combined murmurs of many more echoed loud.

"Don't worry," the *Vulksa* elder said, running a hand through the thick mop of hair covering the *altahnk's* head. "He's a sweet-natured soul at heart."

Despite the old man's reassurance, Ruhlin still kept well clear of the beast's horns. "I wasn't expecting you to lead the *Teyrak* to war," he said.

"And I haven't," Olchar laughed. "Merely attached myself to their war band, since they were kind enough to let me." His countenance took on a far more serious aspect when he noticed Deyna among Ruhlin's company. "I take it you have won a victory, then?"

"We have. Though the *Teyrak* will still be needed at the *Sahlrak* to guard against further assaults. I intend to return to the mountain, where there is much work to be done."

"Then it pains me to interrupt your homecoming." The elder offered an apologetic smile. "But I must ask that you accompany me on yet another journey. You see, it's time the *Telchak* sought the favour not only of the people of this land but also the spirits that rule it."

Chapter Thirty-Six

Felnir

In Felnir's experience, a twenty-mile forced march was an arduous but achievable task for most armies, one that could be completed in a single day. A few hours into the advance of the Sea King's host proved that, despite their weeks of training and recent improvement in diet, they simply couldn't manage it. When Felnir judged they had covered ten miles, leaving a trail of stragglers in their wake, he called a halt. There was little point marching an army to battle if they would be in no state to fight when they arrived. At camp that night, he heard reports from his scouts of riders glimpsed on distant hilltops.

"So, he'll know we're coming," Baldyr reasoned. "Gives the bastard the advantage of choosing his ground."

"And also the chore of gathering his *menda* to meet us," Felnir pointed out. "He'll have split his force into smaller parties, the better to wreak havoc upon the Craggens. Pulling them together will take time. And, if he's wise, he'll draw back a distance to do it."

"I've heard the *Sindra* described as cunning many times." Baldyr gave a mirthless laugh and swigged a gulp of mead. "But never wise. I'll wager he scrapes up as many warriors as he can and comes at us on the morrow, trusting the gods to grant him victory."

"I hope you're right, brother. Then this war will be over before the next dawn."

Baldyr afforded Felnir an appraising squint, mouth crooked in a grin. "Such surety from the Sea King. I wish I shared it."

Despite the Gyrwald's prediction, the next day's march passed without encountering the *Sindra's menda*. By late afternoon, the king's host had reached the outer fringes of the Craggens. Although far more verdant, the country put him in mind of the eastern reaches of Ishtakar, where a series of ridges rose to mark the boundary between the Saluhtan's domain and the endless dune sea. Here, the ridges were more like miniature plateaus, the granite flanks varying in height from a dozen feet to nigh fifty in places. The folk of the Craggens mostly made their homes along the banks of the narrow rivers running between these promontories, although Felnir glimpsed one settlement carved into the top of a tall cliff. It appeared unoccupied but undamaged. He found it curious that many in his *menda* paid the sight scant notice, some even appearing to shun it. Was it an ill-omened place? Perhaps the scene of some plague or calamity? Wohtin proved to be a notable exception. The old man stared up at the silent structures with nervous animation, as if he feared what he might see but couldn't look away.

"An impressive piece of engineering," Felnir observed, guiding Bolt along-side Wohtin's pony. "The *Ahrkun* must have driven the inhabitants away."

"No," Wohtin replied. Blinking hard, he tore his gaze from the carved settlement. "No one has lived there for a long time."

"Why? Are the buildings unsafe?"

He could tell the old man didn't want to answer, but feared the conse-quences if he didn't offer at least some response. "Time, my king," he said. "The only thing certain to claim us all in the end." Before Felnir could ask more, Wohtin kicked his heels to send his pony into a canter. Felnir consid-ered seeking answers from one of the river-landers, but with battle in the offing, decided to let the matter drop for now. Although, something told him that, should he take a closer look at the clifftop settlement, he would find another carved spiral adorning its stones.

Further into the Craggens, the wind carried the signature taint of ash and death shortly before the remnants of wasted villages came into view. Each one had been burned and littered with corpses, many mangled by terrible tortures. As Tyrheld and Falk had said, the *Ahrkun* showed no discrimination in their slaughter, young and old lying hacked or scorched among the fallen.

"Tracks leading in all directions, my lord," Falk reported when the host halted at the end of the second day's march. Felnir had placed his army atop a hillock, forming a saddle between two plateaus. It made for a constricted encampment, but Felnir was unwilling to surrender the advan-tage of high ground. "The freshest are heading north, however," the outlaw added.

"Found some Craggen folk making their way here too, my king," Tyrheld put in. "Only a few dozen, and in a ragged state, as you'd imagine. They'll be looking for succour from the Sea King."

"And they'll have it," Felnir assured her. "Tomorrow, you'll both ride north and find me the *Ahrkun menda*. It's time we ended this."

He toured the camp at dusk, ordering a double watch set and ensuring all warriors had their weapons to hand rather than allowing them to be stacked. Moving from fire to fire, he exchanged words with as many clustered groups as he could. Long experience of war had ingrained an instinct for looming battle, and he felt it strongly now. Tomorrow, these folk would face the *Ahrkun* and needed to witness the undaunted confidence of a king on the cusp of victory.

When his duties were done, he sat with Sygna outside their tent. It was a cloudless night, revealing the great sweep of the stars in fascinating glory. "A learned man I met in Assyrna once imparted his theory as to the stars," he told Sygna.

"That they're not truly guiding lanterns cast into the sky by the Altvar?" she asked, smothering a yawn and pressing herself closer to his side. "But far-away suns? I've heard it."

"Not only suns, but hosts to other worlds, like ours. The scholar slept during the day and spent every night peering at the sky through a giant spyglass. He avowed that this world of ours does not sit at the centre of the Altvar's creation. Instead, we abide upon a small speck in a vast collection of worlds, so vast it defies imagination."

"Then he'd be well advised to keep quiet about it," Sygna murmured, resting her head on his chest. "That kind of talk will get you beheaded or burned alive in many a realm . . ."

She trailed off, interrupted by a low hum. It resembled the buzz of a wasp's wing, but louder, and more constant. Shifting from Felnir's embrace, she looked to the Bow of the Altvar. She had left it strung in expectation of combat, and Felnir could see the string vibrating, even though no hand touched it and the wind was gentle.

"Has it done that before?" he asked.

"Never." Reaching for the bow, Sygna tensed the instant her hand closed on the stave, the thrum of the bowstring immediately falling silent. Seeing her brow crease and jaw tighten, Felnir worried it might be causing her pain, but she made no attempt to release her grip.

"What is it?" he prompted.

"A feeling . . ." Sygna's frown deepened before her gaze fixed on Felnir's. "I think it's a warning. Something is afoot, my love."

Rising, Felnir cast his gaze to either side of the slope. It was a full moon this night, scattering silver specks over heather and grass untrammelled by an approaching force. Yet Sygna's tone was so emphatic he couldn't cast it aside. It was as he turned to the western plateau that he caught it, just a small tinge to the air he might have missed otherwise. Faint as it was, familiarity enabled him to parse it from the competing melange of woodsmoke and camp filth. It was a scent he knew: the mingled sweat and breath of a host on the move.

"Arm yourself," he told Sygna before buckling on the sword of the Altvar and striding towards the neighbouring fire where his captains shared a flask of Vorl Tuhrk brandy.

"Beyorn, Tulvik, ready your companies," Felnir told them without preamble, keeping his voice low. "And keep it quiet," he added when Tulvik began to ask a question. "No raised voices. Beyorn, arrange your shield wall along the north facing slope. Tulvik, muster your people in the centre with me. Tyrheld, find Gyrwald Baldyr and tell him the Sea King requests he align his *menda* along the crest of the southern slope, and remind him of what I said about stealth."

To his veteran ear, the subsequent convulsions of the camp sounded appallingly loud. He doubted their approaching foe would have missed the clatter of shields and spears punctuated by the occasional raised voice. Yet, when he moved to Tulvik's side and took hold of Bolt's reins, a quick glance at the shoulder of the western plateau confirmed that the *Ahrkun* were coming on undaunted. Either they had missed the tumult or the *Sindra* was determined to seek battle regardless of caution.

He guessed the number of horsemen at around two hundred, riding in a formation that any captain of Ishtan cavalry would have termed shambolic. Behind the riders came a dark mob of warriors on foot, far larger in number, but still less than he expected. Climbing onto Bolt's back, he turned the horse about. The sight of another force advancing from behind the eastern plateau confirmed his suspicion that the cultists were intent upon a two-pronged attack. As the dark multitude drew nearer, he concluded that they were aiming for the centre of his line. *Trying to cut us in two*, he decided with a grunt of annoyance. It was what he would have done.

"Sygna," he said, seeing her standing close by among her company of archers. "I'll be very disappointed if a single rider reaches our shield wall."

Replying with a grin, she snapped an order to her archers, sending them running for the northern slope. Felnir watched the leading horsemen gallop within three hundred paces of the rise, whereupon the foremost rider toppled from the saddle. It was an impressive shot, even for his queen, made more so by the fact that she repeated it twice before the remaining riders came within range of her archers. The first volley claimed only a dozen, the second more, and the third thinned their number to half.

As was typical with horses poorly trained for war, the mounts began to shy as they reached the base of the slope. Beset by a continual rain of arrows and alarmed by the scent of massed humans, many reared and turned away, some tipping their riders from the saddle as they fled. A group of stalwarts braved the arrows and exerted sufficient command of their horses to continue the charge. Numbering barely thirty, they withered under the steady barrage of arrows until barely half-a-dozen remained. Mostly wounded and spent, they made little impression on the southern shield wall before being speared or hacked down.

Shifting his attention between the *Ahrkun* cohorts approaching across the open ground to the south and north, Felnir's respect for his enemy's plan diminished at the sight of their loose formation. His estimation of their chances was further eroded by the fact that they were running. With near three hundred paces to cover before reaching his lines, it would have been far wiser for them to form ranks and approach at a steady walk. Thus, strength and speed would be saved for a rush during the last dozen or so yards. As the running mobs drew nearer, he could hear their cries. The words were lost but the clamour of raised voices conveyed a sense of unbridled ferocity. The *Ahrkun*'s bloodlust had been stoked to an unreasoning pitch, but Felnir knew well that, in the exhausting fury of battle, it was always a finite commodity.

Judging the group approaching from the north to be about a third larger than its southern counterpart, Felnir kept Sygna's archers in place. Their arrows extracted a suitably hefty toll as the cultists came within range, although their pace never slowed despite the many warriors falling on all sides. They swept up the slope in a dark tide, Felnir hearing Beyorn shouting exhortations to his company, his strident commands to hold echoing along the line. The same chorus rang out from the southern slope where the charging force faced a marginally less steep incline, meaning their attack struck Baldyr's shield wall a few heartbeats before the northern assault slammed against Beyorn's line.

As the song of combat filled the air, Felnir saw Tulvik tense in the saddle, instinctively drawn to Beyorn's aid. "Hold fast," Felnir told him. "You'll get your chance soon enough."

He was thankful for the full moon and absence of clouds, which enabled a clear view of both sides of the unfolding battle. As Felnir expected, they quickly became mirrors of one another. The *Ahrkun*'s initial charge, thanks to sheer momentum, succeeded in bowing but not breaking Beyorn's line. The cultists following the vanguard, faced with an impassible press of bodies, had little option but to veer around it and attack a different portion of the shield wall. Consequently, both the north and south cohorts soon spread out along the length of the defending ranks, dissipating the effect of their assault. Still, the battle raged with greater violence in the centre of each line, becoming a dark knot of struggling combatants. The cultists' war cries merged with the screams of the maimed or dying, while the warriors of the Sea King's host answered with their own defiant shouts.

It soon became apparent to Felnir that Baldyr's *menda* had quickly gained ascendancy over their foes. The bowed shield wall soon straightened and the attacking *Ahrkun* began to resemble waves beating upon an unyielding shore. The northern assault was more concerning, even though the resolve of his novice warriors had exceeded expectations. The bulge in the line grew as the cultists continued their frenzied attack, falling by the dozen but still managing to advance.

"There," Felnir said, gripping Tulvik's shoulder and pointing just to the left of the expanding bulge. "Kill me those filth, and be known hereafter as Tulvik *Ahrkun Nyra*, the Raven Scourge." He tightened his grip, meeting the young warrior's eye. "Earn your name this night!"

Trembling with battle lust, Tulvik was incapable of speech. Baring his teeth in a snarl, he raised his sword above his head, calling out a wordless command to his company before spurring his horse forward. The constricted space atop the rise meant he could only canter into the fray, which had the benefit of allowing his warriors to follow close when he plunged into the chaos of the melee. Felnir watched him force his way into the thickest cluster of cultists, sword raising a dark fountain as he hacked down foe after foe. When his horse was unable to push deeper, Tulvik leaped from the saddle, disappearing into the swirling throng of thrashing bodies. However, it was clear his charge had done enough. The northern shield wall steadied then straightened. Although no order had been given to advance, the right and left flanks began to edge forward as the enemies they faced thinned in number.

Looking to the south, Felnir was surprised by the advanced state of the unfolding rout. Baldyr's *menda*, having repulsed the *Ahrkun* charge, had nearly completed an encirclement of the survivors. Although a gap remained which would have allowed some cultists to flee, none did, choosing to fight on to the death. A quick survey of the northern flank confirmed the same result would soon unfold there, both wings of the shield wall now arcing round in a clumsily executed but effective envelopment.

All too soon, Felnir mused, drawing the Sword of the Altvar. *For the Sea King must spill his share of blood this night. All will know this as his victory, so the tale will be told.*

Jerking his head at Falk, he kicked Bolt into motion. With the outlaw following, Felnir galloped around the right wing of his northern company, aiming for the battling knot of cultists still attempting to stave off impending destruction. He hoped to find the *Sindra*, Dyssha having assured him the Ahrkun leader's presence would be marked by a tall banner. But, as he sped towards the melee, no standard waved above the fight, which raised the prospect of the cult leader having already met his end. "Annoying," Felnir grunted before plunging into the fray, sword whirling. The tale of the Sea King's ascendancy would have been greatly enhanced had his arch foe fallen to the Sword of the Altvar. *Still,* Felnir reflected while hacking open the skull of an *Ahrkun* warrior, *who's to say he didn't?*

Come the morning, a thorough search of the piled dead revealed neither the *Sindra's* corpse nor his banner. "I'm sorry, my king," Dyssha said, having completed the unsavoury task of inspecting every body with intact features. "He's not here."

"Does it matter that much?" Sygna asked. Her count of the fallen made it plain that the *Sindra's* possible survival didn't change the fact that his power was broken. The entire *menda* of the *Ahrkun Krayl* lay dead upon this field. Most had fought on despite stark evidence of their defeat, refusing to run and continuing to hack at their foes regardless of wounds until claimed by a killing blow. The few who succumbed to panic in the battle's dying moments had been chased down by Tyrheld and the mounted scouts. Returning at midday, she stated, with notable pride, that not a soul had escaped. Still irked by the *Sindra's* absence, Felnir curtly ordered all his mounted warriors to undertake a thorough reconnaissance of the surrounding country. It was Falk who found the cult leader, galloping into the camp at twilight to report sighting the *Ahrkun* banner atop a plateau some miles north.

"It flies from one of those odd places carved into the rock, my lord," the outlaw said. "Couldn't see any sign of fortifications, nor any warriors at all, truth be told. The banner stands tall, though."

Despite the encroaching darkness, Felnir ordered camp broken and put the host on the march to the plateau. They reached it when night had fully fallen, a taller promontory than most with sheer cliffs all around save for a steep track ascending its southern flank. The structures carved into its cliffs were far more extensive than the settlement further south. They featured a uniform tallness, walls interrupted by windows that were too broad to be arrow slits. Also, the roofs were slanted and lacked the crenellations of a battlement. This was a place where people had lived without fear of attack.

The banner of the *Ahrkun Krayl* fluttered atop a pole rising from the top of the track, the billowing raven silhouette illuminated by a large fire. A tall figure stood beneath it, alone and unmoving. As Felnir drew Bolt to a halt, he heard a voice bellowing above. He expected some form of challenge, but it was not his own name that echoed from the plateau's heights.

"ANGMUND!" the lone figure called, Felnir hearing the note of peerless demand in his voice. This was a soul that had known only servile obedience from others for decades. "SEND ME ANGMUND!"

Felnir turned a raised eyebrow to Wohtin. The old man slumped atop the back of his pony, features set in an even more morose mask than usual. "Why should he call for you, I wonder?" Felnir said.

Wohtin gave a weary sigh as he climbed down from the saddle. "Probably because he greatly desires to kill me," he said, starting up the slope. "Perhaps you should accompany me, my king."

"Stay here," Felnir told the others as he dismounted from Bolt's back.

"My king," Tulvik said, groaning with the effort of dismounting to sink to one knee before Felnir. The young warrior had been dragged near sense-less from beneath a mound of corpses that morning, still miraculously alive, albeit with some new scars and a few busted ribs to show for his selfless courage. "With all . . . humility," Tulvik said, forcing the words through a veil of pain, "do I beg the honour of dispatching the *Sindra*."

"Fuck off, boy!" Baldyr said, slipping nimbly from the back of his horse. "You promised me his head, brother," he said, approaching Felnir with a purposeful stride. "And I intend to collect."

"You'll have it," Felnir said, holding up his hand. "But first, I'll crave your indulgence, brother. Just for a short time." Scanning the harsh incline of the slope, he added, "Save your strength for the celebration to come, eh?"

Baldyr's scowl deepened, but he raised no argument. Felnir might call him brother, but only a fool would have claimed equal standing now. And the Gyrwald of the Vorl Tuhrk was no fool. "Make it a clean cut," he muttered, stalking back to his horse.

"An hour," Sygna said. She held the Bow of the Altvar, but appeared to find no reassurance in the string's failure to thrum. "Then I'm coming to get you."

"I've a sense you won't have to," Felnir said, following Wohtin's plodding form. "Still, double the picket line around the camp. There's a chance some cultists are still lurking about."

Wohtin said nothing as they climbed together, his hooded eyes fixed upon the blazing fire at the crest of the slope. His reticence did nothing to stem Felnir's questions. "You've known who this bastard is from the start, haven't you?" he demanded. "Ever since that ship attacked us on the Red

Waves. Which means he knew of our coming. How?" When his questions elicited no reaction from Wohtin, he went on, "If he's minded to kill you this night, know well that I'm minded to let him."

This finally provoked a response, albeit one spoken in a gruff mutter. "Then that sword you carry will remain just a sword, my king."

After that, Felnir was content to continue the climb in silence, suspecting any further exchange would stoke his anger to a killing rage, regardless of any consequence.

Knowing the *Sindra* to be one of the *Ehilkun*, Felnir anticipated finding a far more wizened and age-marked soul than the man of impressive stature waiting at the top of the slope. His identity couldn't be doubted, not just in the raven silhouette tattoo that covered the lean muscle of his bare chest, but in his bearing. He was unarmed but exhibited no fear at all at the sight of Felnir, merely affording his rival an imperious, dismissive glance before fixing all his attention upon Wohtin.

"So you've come, Angmund," the *Sindra* grunted, a tone coloured by a note of surprised admiration. "I could never call you a coward. At least that still holds true."

"Halgard," Wohtin said, offering a nod of greeting. Felnir read no fear in his bearing, but for the first time saw a genuine measure of guilt in the tension of the old man's face.

"I knew sending one ship wouldn't be enough," the *Sindra* continued. "Not to drown a rat of such renown."

"Then why not send two?" Wohtin asked.

To Felnir's surprise, this provoked the cult leader to laughter rather than rage. The timbre of his mirth was strange, at first hearty and full throated, before trailing off into a shrill giggle. This, and the animation of the man's features, twitching one second and composed the next, told Felnir much. The *Sindra* was insane.

"Because I had no more to send," the cult leader told Wohtin. "The *Ahrkun* commanded only one port worthy of the name. A strategic error you would have surely warned me against, had you been here."

"No." Wohtin formed a smile that was more of a grimace. "No, Halgard, I doubt I would have warned you of anything were I to have remained at your side. In truth, I should have killed you before I departed these shores. That was *my* error."

This produced another laugh, but far shorter than the first. "So ashamed of your creation, are you?" Noticing Felnir's puzzled frown, he grinned. "Didn't he tell you, *Uhra Vorun*? The *Ahrkun Krayl* are his creation. As am I, in any way that matters."

"I accept no blame for your fate, Halgard," Wohtin said. "What you have become is entirely of your own making." He closed his eyes, head lowered in sorrow. "What shames me most is the thought that, should I face your uncle again, I will have to account for how badly I failed in fulfilling his command to me."

Noting the weight the old man put on the word "uncle", Felnir looked again at the *Sindra*'s face. The spasming madness was distracting, but still he found an echo of the noble features he had seen captured in bronze in the fallen city of Ostan Hardta. "Velgard," he murmured. He spoke softly, but the *Sindra* caught his words.

"Oh yes, puppet," he said, turning to Felnir with a new, manic gleam in his eye. "The blood of the greatest king runs in my veins. I, son to his beloved sister Ilevna. Strange that he should cherish her, but ever despise me."

"He loved you," Wohtin said. "When your father was lost to a storm, he took on the role of parent, and allotted me the role of tutor. Velgard had no sons, and sought to make you walk the path to greatness, as he had. When the kingdom fell and we came here, I sought to fulfil the promise I made to him. 'Make of him a king, Angmund,' he had commanded me. And so, between my bouts of madness, I tried. But you were never meant for kingship, Halgard. The *Ahrkun Krayl* was supposed to unite Vorunvahl in worship of the Altvar. They were to stand apart from feud and discord, to raise up this kingdom of lost souls. But you perverted it, steeped it in so much blood it could never be cleansed."

"It always was steeped in blood," Halgard returned. "Or did your madness take your memory as well as your wits?" His gaze swung back to Felnir. "What has this liar told you? What did he promise? You are a fool, as I once was. There is no greatness to be had in this land. The heirs of Velgard are cursed. His great crime lives in our blood and nothing will wash it away."

"What crime?" Felnir asked, but the *Sindra*'s twitch returned then and he began to ramble.

"Crime?" he asked, letting out another shrill giggle, his next words emerging in a rapid torrent. "Crimes and punishments. Punishments and crimes. My uncle did both, and so many suffered for it. Reach into the darkest shadows and you'll find more than dust. And he found it. Oh yes, he found it." Another giggle, one that quickly turned into a distressed, plaintive sob. Halgard put his hand to his mouth, biting the knuckle of his thumb as if to stem a sudden upswell of terror. When he spoke again, it was in a hushed whisper. "And not content with his crime, he set his creature to make me like him. Made me reach too, didn't you?" Drool dripped from the *Sindra*'s lips as he lowered his hand, gaze now fixed upon Wohtin, his large frame hunching in predatory anticipation. "Be careful he doesn't do the same to you, puppet. The things you'll see. The roads not yet travelled. The threats that might or might not come. Like detestable old men returning from far away when they should have stayed dead."

He crouched lower, taking a short, tentative step towards Wohtin. "But there's more, puppet. More to see. More than you ever want to see. And—" he slapped his hands to his chest "—it keeps you young so you'll never stop seeing it. An unceasing plague of possibility. Centuries of lost sleep, Angmund." Halgard's lips slid back from his teeth in a snarl. "That's what you owe me. All the nights and days uncounted I have known only nightmares. Let me show you . . ."

Felnir had seen panthers move with less speed than the *Sindra* in that moment. Halgard covered the distance to Wohtin in a single leap, bearing him down, meaty fists clamped upon the old man's neck. "See them, Angmund!" the *Sindra* raged, staring into Wohtin's bulging eyes. "See the nightmares you made for m—"

Halgard possessed a thick neck, tendons and muscles swollen with murderous intent, but the Sword of the Altvar sliced through it all with ease. The headless torso slumped onto Wohtin, blood pulsing from the stump to bathe the old man as he squirmed and fought from under the corpse. Once free, he crawled on his hands and knees, retching, coming to an abrupt halt when Felnir touched his sword point to Wohtin's chin.

"Now," he said, "it's time you fulfilled your promise to me, old man."

Chapter Thirty-Seven

Thera

"You know I watched your brother kill mine, I suppose?" Veilwald Torlund Speldorr, the Dark Eye, phrased his question in a languid tone. He was young for his rank, appointed to governance of the Turon Geld after the previous incumbent had perished without siring a suitable heir. Thera recalled he had been Sister Silver's choice, promoted due to his prowess in commerce rather than battle. He certainly didn't appear a warrior, being of slender build and clad in a manner akin to foreign fashion. Wearing a black sable-trimmed cloak and finely tailored doublet, his only concession to martial adornment was the narrow-bladed sword dangling from his belt like an afterthought.

"I do, Veilwald," Thera replied. "A dark deed for which he was justly exiled."

"And recently allowed to return, I hear." Veilwald Torlund smiled, a practised expression that managed to convey as much judgement as it did solicitation. "Welcomed back by the Traitor Queen only to sail off and get himself killed in the Fire Isles. From what I gather, this wouldn't have occasioned much grief on your part."

She saw how well named he was then, his eyes so lacking in colour the pupils were lost in twin discs of black. It made it hard for her to read the intent behind his words. Was he taunting her, or merely expressing satisfaction at Felnir's end? Doubt kindled a yearning for Lynnea's presence. But she had decided her Tielwald would remain absent from meetings with those of high status. Her role was best performed beyond the sight of one such as this. Inscrutable or not, Thera felt certain these eyes saw a great deal.

"You are well informed, Veilwald." Thera inclined her head. They spoke on the Vorun Hardta wharf where she had come to welcome the arrival of the forces from the northern Gelds. Kahlvik and her other emissaries had been swift in delivering the formal letters of introduction penned by the new Queen of the Isles. In the three weeks since the shared dream with her great-grandfather, a steady stream of ships had arrived from various corners of northern Ascarlia. Some came in large numbers, crammed with the *menda* of Uhlwalds keen to demonstrate either allegiance or detestation of the invaders. Others were smaller, contingents formed from those who chose to answer her muster of their own volition. Torlund was the first Veilwald to arrive, sailing no less than ten ships into the harbour via the north-eastern channel. They all sat low in the water thanks to the many warriors they carried. It was an impressive display of commitment to their shared cause, but his words gave her pause.

"In truth, I know not my brother's fate," she said. "Nor will I pretend there was any great affection between us." *But, whatever his countless faults,* she added inwardly, *I would very much welcome his sword just now.* "Regardless, his fate has no bearing on the current crisis," she went on briskly. "One, I trust you'll agree, requires us to set aside prior grievance."

"Grievance?" Torlund laughed. "Hardly that. In fact, I owe your brother a great debt. With Vorlund dead, I no longer had to suffer his endless spite, nor shiver in his shadow. Father grieved, of course. Never quite got over it, sentimental old sot that he was. Spent his last few years mired in drink and left the governance of the mines in my hands. In time, Sister Silver took note of the increased taxes we were paying, all down to some simple efficiencies I instituted. And thus, the path to the Veilwald's chair was open."

Torlund came to a halt, his notice drawn to the largest Nihlvarian warship captured in the strait. She was anchored beyond the marble reef, made impressive by virtue of her sheer size despite a hull blackened by flames. "Oh my," the Veilwald said. "She's quite something, I must say."

While Torlund's gaze continued to betray nothing, Thera did detect the raised brows and softened tones that told of an avaricious soul seeing something he wanted. "The only one we've yet to name, or find sufficient crew for," she said. "Perhaps you would like to do so, Veilwald?"

He turned to her, lips pursed in surprise. "Truly?"

"Yes. A gift from the Queen of the Isles to the Veilwald of the Turon Geld. I noticed your *menda* appeared somewhat constricted aboard your own ships."

"A fine gesture. And happily accepted. However, I would remind you that the terms of a formal alliance between us have yet to be agreed."

"Then let us do so now."

Inclining his head, Torlund reached into the folds of his cloak to extract a scroll. "I think these are reasonable in the circumstances."

Scanning the document, Thera was unable to contain a grimace of surprise. "You wish to swear fealty to me?"

"In return for generous concessions as regards the current crown levies on copper exports, yes, it appears I am."

"I am but Queen of the Isles—"

"Forgive my interruption, but you are not." Any sense of flippancy was gone from his features now, replaced by the serious frown of an intelligent and calculating young man. "This realm finds itself with a deficit of queens. A state of affairs that cannot continue if we are to deal with this current difficulty." Stepping back, he drew his narrow sword, keeping his movements slow so as not to agitate her guards. "It is custom in Albermaine for a lord to pledge his loyalty to a sovereign upon his sword. A practice we would do well to mirror." Lowering his head, he offered her the blade. "Most humbly, I beg you to accept, my queen."

Thera hesitated. Should she touch a hand to this sword, it would signal her intent to rule all of Ascarlia. While the folk of the Isles had been enthusiastic in hailing her ascendancy, she doubted that would hold true in those parts of the realm as yet untouched by war. "And will the Uhlwalds of your geld follow you in this?" she asked.

Torlund glanced up at her, lips thinned in a smile. "They will if they know what's good for them. As will my fellow Veilwalds. I shall be happy to act as your ambassador to any reluctant souls."

"It is my hope that won't be necessary," she said, placing a finger on the hilt of his sword. "Your service is accepted and your geld hereby welcomed into my care, Veilwald. As for the copper tax, I shall agree to one-third of the reduction you request. Even when this war is won, our realm will require funds for rebuilding, for so much has been lost."

Torlund straightened, sheathing his sword. "And yet I feel certain we have a great deal more to win, my queen. Now, if I may be excused. I should very much like to tour my new ship."

Since naming Lynnea her Tielwald, it had become Thera's habit for them to meet atop the merchant's house roof every few days. Lynnea's reports on the mood of the port and its greatly swollen populace were valuable, as were the shared visions of her winged spy.

Barely four days from Olversahl, Lynnea commented as Thera watched the Nihlvarian fleet round the smaller islands marking the main seaway into the Fjord Geld. As before, seeing the world through a gull's eyes brought jarring clarity and a sharp pain in the forefront of her skull. *You were right.*

Gesturing for her to withdraw the vision, Thera asked, "And Veilwald Torlund?"

I've found no evidence of Volkrath allegiance, but plenty that points to greed and duplicity. A good man to have as a friend, and a very bad one to have as an enemy. He sees you as something he's been waiting for since boyhood.

"And what's that?"

Lynnea's mouth quirked in a suppressed smirk. *A suitable mate.*

Thera let out an amused sigh. "Then it will be a shame to disappoint him."

Something best left unsaid until victory is secure. I've a sense he doesn't respond well to rejection.

Grimacing in acknowledgement, Thera turned to other matters. "The new arrivals. Any Volkrath among them?"

Just one. A slave rescued from that Nihlvarian hulk. Veltta's crew took him in. He lacks a tongue, a common punishment they inflict upon the more vocal and troublesome slaves. A clever tactic, since it prevents him betraying himself with an ill-chosen word. But they would have been wise to choose a soul with less hate in his heart. Murder, rape and destruction are all that he dreams of, and dreams cannot be guarded by a missing tongue.

Thera could feel the repugnance in Lynnea's thoughts, and was grateful she hadn't chosen to share any of the dreams she had garnered. "He has a knot?" she asked.

Lynnea nodded. *He keeps it well hidden, but Mohlnir has a keen eye for shiny things. I don't believe he's used it yet.*

"Good." An upsurge of hearty cheers drew Thera's notice to the blackened Nihlvarian ship she had gifted Torlund. He had renamed her the *Golden Hawk* and convened a ship-borne feast to celebrate his good fortune, one Thera had politely declined to attend. From the sound of things, those who had were enjoying themselves full well. She hoped their heads wouldn't be too clouded on the morrow.

"In the morning, I'll give you orders for the *Chainbreaker*," she told Lynnea. "Veltta is to sail her within sight of Linsker Fjord to gauge the number of Nihlvarian ships guarding Skar Magnol. You will go with her, and so will Snaryk. When you're sure this tongue-less spy has informed his masters of your course, kill him. The *Chainbreaker* will then sail south to rendezvous with our fleet off Aeric's Fjord."

Lynnea's face clouded. *So it's time, then?*

"The Nihlvarians will already have begun their assault on Olversahl by the time we arrive. We can only trust to the Altvar that we won't be too late."

CHAPTER THIRTY-EIGHT

Elvine

The wall was completed barely a day before the warship appeared through the morning mist off the dockside. Ahlgrun stood at her prow, calling out his warning and pointing to the occluded waters to his rear. He was too distant to fully discern the words, but Elvine knew the meaning: the Nihlvarian fleet had arrived.

Gruinskard ordered the warship scuttled close to the eastern extremity of the wharf, where it met the jagged rocks covering the brief stretch of shoreline to the Gate Wall guarding the coastal approach. A small forest of masts already sprouted from the same stretch of water since the few merchant craft remaining in port couldn't be allowed to linger at anchor. "That's where we're weakest," the Tielwald said. "Put a bunch of sunken hulls between them and the wall, and hopefully they'll think twice about attacking there."

Once ashore, Ahlgrun and his crew were swiftly recruited into Elvine's personal guard. From the fisherman's flushed urgency, she expected the enemy to appear at any second, but it wasn't until the midday sun had banished the mist that the leading vessels hove into view. These were the swifter, smaller ships of the Nihlvarian vanguard. Near forty in all, they described a surprisingly slow course as they took up position in the middle of the fjord, shipped their oars and dropped anchor. The larger vessels that followed displayed the same curious lack of energy, steering to an anchorage south of the smaller ships.

"Waiting for the evening tide," Gruinskard judged. He and Elvine stood atop the harbour master's domicile. A thick-walled building separated from the quayside by less than twenty yards, it was a natural choice for both vantage point and command post.

"You're certain they'll attack right away?" Elvine asked. The steadiness of her voice was the result of stern control and practice, rather than inner fortitude. Her guts roiled at the sight of the Nihlvarian fleet and she nurtured hopes of a delay before battle inevitably dawned.

"They can't afford not to," Gruinskard said. "Only so much in the way of victuals you can carry aboard ship. If it came to a siege, they'd starve before we did."

Elvine searched the enemy fleet until she found the flagship, marked by the huge banner fluttering from its mainmast, black fabric emblazoned with a white sigil: the scroll of the goddess Vysestra. Lore's sigil. *Yes, she's there, child*, the spear informed Elvine. The spirit's tone was one of regretful sympathy, albeit tinged with a faintly amused lilt. *I can feel her passion burning even from here. She tells herself it's hatred, but we know it's something else, don't we?*

Forcing her gaze from the banner, Elvine scanned the wall. With time pressing, Gruinskard had eschewed employing stone for the upper sections, instead creating a wooden barricade twelve feet high atop the foundation blocks. Built on two levels, the lower walkway featured a series of narrowed shuttered windows, enabling archers and spearmen to assail any attackers. The upper level, where she knew most of the fighting would take place, was formed of a broad parapet and crenellated barrier. At first she had expressed concern that the Nihlvarians would use fire to breach the upper wall, but her fears had been allayed by Gruinskard ordering the seaward side covered in sheep hides. These were kept continually damp by the snow and drizzle of winter. While the bulk of Olversahl's defenders were stationed at the harbour, strong companies also guarded the Gate Wall. Another smaller contingent had been secreted in the Rent to prevent the Nihlvarians making use of the tunnels that honeycombed the mountain.

"You should rest," Gruinskard advised. "Nothing is likely to happen for a good while yet."

Elvine shook her head. "They need to see me."

"As you wish." Resting himself on the roof's edge, the Tielwald began running a whetstone over the blade of his axe. His legendary stone-bladed weapon having been seized by Ilvar, he had been obliged to source a replacement from a local smith. Formed of a single, two-foot-long cleaver affixed to a plain oaken haft, it was an unadorned but impressive instrument. Elvine marvelled at the old man's ability to carry the thing with apparent ease. His mangled hand was now concealed in a tight leather binding, and, although he betrayed no pain when using it, she knew it must ache terribly.

"Still practising, I hear," he said, affording the Spear of the Altvar a brief glance. "Are you actually any good with it?"

The fact that he knew of her training sessions with Colvyn didn't surprise her. It was in his interests to keep a close watch on everything she did. Whether he knew of the spear's latest gift to her was another matter. "My brother tells me I've made significant improvement," she said. Swallowing, she added, "As you'll see when they come against the wall."

The whetstone halted its scrape along his axe blade, Gruinskard fixing his eye upon her. "That won't be necessary."

"I cannot stand idly by while . . ."

"You die and this place falls." He spoke softly, but the sincerity in his tone was clear. She also heard a note of reluctance, too. *Doesn't like admitting he needs me,* she concluded. "Besides," he added, resuming his task, "your mother hates me sufficiently already. Should you fall in battle under my command, I've little doubt she'd find a way to kill me. And she's one of the few living souls who might actually be capable of doing it."

The comment brought a question to Elvine's lips. She required a moment's fortitude before forcing it out, for the answer frightened her. "My mother spied for you for years. Did she also kill for you?"

"She did what was necessary to unite the Ascarlian people. In her own way, she is one of the great heroes of our recent history."

"And yet she despises what she did. As she despises you."

"I know. But, even after everything that happened, after the library burned and so much blood ran in the gutters of these streets, did you ever ask her if she regrets it?" His beard bunched in a smile when Elvine said nothing. "She can't, can she? For, if she had never served me, she would never have had you."

A sudden blaring of horns from the wall forestalled further conversation, Elvine seeing a boat approaching the harbour. Standing beneath a banner flying a truce pennant was a figure she recognised despite the distance. "She sends Ilvar to threaten," she observed.

Gruinskard grunted in agreement. "Could let him come within bowshot then kill the bastard."

"No. That would signal that we fear allowing the people to hear his words." Turning, she made for the stairs. "And at least it'll be a distraction from all this endless waiting."

Ilvar, much to his ill-concealed fury, was obliged to order his oarsmen to halt the boat close to the impaled heads of his slaughtered warriors. When he spoke, it was with reddened features, the anger ringing loud in his voice: "The High Queen of Ascarlia wishes it known that she cherishes your lives as she cherishes her own!"

Only those occupying the portion of the wall directly to his front could hear what he had to say. As he spoke on, Elvine heard his words being repeated to left and right, spreading along the fortification in a rapid mutter. She experienced a brief spasm of amusement when it occurred to her that, once this speech had been conveyed to both ends of the wharf, its meaning may have been completely transformed.

"But," Ilvar continued, "as queen, she must place the needs of all her people above the compassion of her heart. This city is therefore judged to have risen in bloody rebellion against the Altvar-ordained ruler of this realm and thus stands condemned to destruction. However, in deference to her love for you, the High Queen offers this one chance to wipe away the stain of treachery. The heretic and traitor Elvine Jurest must be surrendered to my custody along with the property she has stolen. If this is done before nightfall, this city will be spared. If it is not, no quarter shall be shown to any inhabitant regardless of whether they bear arms against the queen. Every building will be rendered to rubble and all vestige of your history extinguished forever. It will be a crime to even utter the name of this city. Think on this and know that my queen never speaks false. The choice before you is clear: one life for many."

The collective murmur of Olversahl's defenders began as soon as he fell silent. Initially, Elvine heard only angry defiance. But, with the stakes so high, would every soul be so resolute? As she looked to either side, the spear's gift revealed the combined auras of nigh eight thousand souls. Of resolve, she saw plenty. It was an unwavering hue of grey, solid like granite, but here and there she saw reddish cracks that told of fear and doubt. These people had families, children huddling in their homes at this moment, awaiting the storm to come. She couldn't begrudge them their uncertainty, but nor could she allow it to fester.

Spying an oil barrel nearby, she climbed atop it. The sight of her quelled the nearest voices and birthed another cascade of whispers along the wall, heralding a thick, expectant silence.

"I know this man," she said, pointing the spear at Ilvar. "I know him to be a murderer and a liar. With my own eyes did I see him spill innocent blood upon the sacred stones of Nerlfeya's Hall. He is the creature of the false queen, a queen he says utters no falsehoods. But we know that another lie, for did she not plot the Sister Queens' downfall in secret for years? Did she not deceive and scheme, winning the trust of all so that she might betray this realm to the most vile enemy? An enemy that will steal all you own and render your children into slavery. Are the words of this man to be trusted by any but the worst of fools?"

The auras flanking her darkened, blossoming into a rage-filled storm cloud. Seeing an archer nearby put an arrow to his bow, features set in deadly intent, Elvine raised a hand. "No. I wish this dog to carry my words back to his mistress." Fixing her gaze upon Ilvar, she felt a pulse of sadistic glee at the miasma of impotent rage that enclosed him. *Not just anger, child, the spear informed her. Jealousy too. He has loved and lusted for his queen for many years. It's how she bent him to her will. Years of unconsummated longing burn within him, so fiercely they have unseated his mind. In you, he sees a rival as well as a foe. It would be prudent to kill him now.*

"Not while I still have use of him," Elvine whispered before drawing breath to call out once again. "But, though I have no doubt of his falsity," she proclaimed, casting her voice as far as she could, "unlike his liar queen, my love for this city and its people is true. If there is a chance you will be spared by my surrender, I shall take it. If it is your will, I give myself into the hands of our enemies, then so be it . . ."

Anything else she might have spoken was swallowed by the shouts of her personal guard, led by Colvyn and quickly taken up by Halkyr and the others. "We stand with the Spear Maiden!" they cried out, brandishing their weapons. "We stand with the Spear Maiden!"

Within seconds the same call was being repeated along the entire wall, men and women thumping sword hilts to their shields to create a rhythmic chant. As it continued, it shortened to simply: "Spear Maiden! Spear Maiden! SPEAR MAIDEN!"

Looking at their combined auras, Elvine could still see a few islands of doubt among the elongated sea of enraged defiance, but they soon dwindled as the will of the crowd buttressed even the faintest hearts. With so many inflamed passions, it was impossible to prevent some venting their fury with more than words. Arrows began to ripple the water around Ilvar's boat, forcing him to order his oarsmen to pull clear. Elvine took a great deal of satisfaction in seeing how the flaming hatred of his aura burned bright all the way back to the Nihlvarian flagship.

"A bit too much of a risk for my liking," Colvyn murmured in Elvine's ear as he helped her down from the barrel. "Calculated though it was."

"War is all risk, dear brother," she told him. It was a quote from the Aphorismus. That copious collection of Ishtan wit had much to say regarding war, although she would later reproach herself for not paying more heed to its second line: *But scant reward.*

True to Gruinskard's prediction, Tuhlvyr Vahlak lost no time in mounting his first assault. With the sky beginning to dim and the late evening tide at its height, twenty of the smaller ships raised anchor and rowed for the centre of the wall. They were followed by a dense throng of smaller boats launched from the great warships beyond the vanguard. Elvine watched events unfold from the roof of the harbour master's building, where Gruinskard insisted she remain until he called for her. To an eye uneducated in warlike matters, the Nihlvarian attack seemed unstoppable. She couldn't credit how a hastily raised confection of stone and wood could contest the mass of warriors carried by the approaching armada. It was only when the first volleys of arrows flew from the wall that she began to understand the scale of the task faced by their enemies.

Throughout his preparations, Gruinskard had set every fletcher in Olversahl to work crafting arrows, drafting in additional labour from the elderly and the young to ensure sufficient stocks. So, when the leading Nihlvarian ships drew within bowshot, the archers along the wall felt no need of restraint. A dark blizzard of arcing shafts filled the air between wall and ships. The sound of them striking home resembled a hailstorm, punctuated by the occasional scream as a barbed warhead found flesh. Fire arrows joined the torrent when the attacking vessels came within a hundred paces of the wall. Smoke soon blossomed on the deck of the foremost ship, followed by a yellow orange flare as fire took hold in her innards. Within moments, the craft was fully ablaze from bow to stern, sailors and warriors diving clear of her deck as she drifted out of formation. The ship behind suffered the same fate, but the third in line, despite the flames licking at her hull and mast, managed to reach the harbour wall. She rebounded from the quay while a salvo of grappling lines sailed out from her deck. Those that managed to latch onto the wall were quickly cut away by the defenders before the Nihlvarian crew could secure her in place and allow ladders raised. While she floundered, an avalanche of rocks descended from the top of the wall, shattering the deck and the hull below. The harbour waters swallowed her in the space of a few heartbeats.

Three more ships attempted the same feat without success. One was sunk, her deck liberally drenched in flaming oil before the torrent of boulders sent her under. The other two drew away wreathed in smoke, their sailors scrambling to cast buckets of water at the spreading flames. By then a horn had begun to sound from the Nihlvarian flagship, recalling the survivors and sparing them a similar fate.

"He's just testing us," Gruinskard concluded in the aftermath. Elvine had come to tour the wall and pay homage to the fallen. In all, the attack had cost them three killed and a half-dozen wounded, all victims of Nihlvarian archers. Paltry losses in comparison to those inflicted. But still Elvine felt a lurch of her heart at the sight of the bodies being carried away.

"Also letting us know he's not afraid of spilling a good deal of blood to win," Gruinskard added, fingers tracing through his beard as he contemplated the enemy fleet. With night coming on, it was shrouded in darkness, save for the torches flickering along the warships' rails. "Don't like it." The Tielwald's voice slipped into a mutter. "Tells me he knows his business far too well."

"I did warn you he was clever," Elvine pointed out. Once again, she failed to add that Vahlak also benefited from her excellent summary of the port's history and defences. "Don't expect him to repeat a mistake."

"That's the point. This wasn't a mistake. Now it's just a question of what the bastard will do next."

She didn't expect to sleep that night, yet it transpired her body had other ideas. Hemund had insisted on giving up his quarters for her. Having charge of the wall's western flank, he spent all his time with his warriors in any case. Nyhlssa, his wife, busied herself cooking copious amounts of broth and stew to sustain the defenders. Consequently, Elvine was able to enjoy some true moments of solitude in between making her presence known. The gaggle of worshippers was an irksome distraction, their cries for attention sometimes growing loud enough to be heard through the thick walls of the harbour master's house. Halkyr and his guards did their best to keep them at bay, the young captain haranguing them for failing to add their number to the fighters on the wall. However, it appeared their devotion to the Spear Maiden overrode any desire to defend their city. Although she tried not to, Elvine detested them. Their preference for the nebulous comforts of divine favour in the face of destruction felt blasphemous in itself. If the Altvar were real, would they not have wanted them to fight for their lives?

Even with a mind beset by such questions, she still managed to slip into sleep within seconds of settling onto the bed. She kept the spear at her side, one hand resting on the haft in case the spirit within felt obliged to issue a warning. None came, but her slumber was filled with dreams she couldn't properly recall upon waking, except as a vague melange of contesting forms, as if the clouds in the sky had gone to war with one another. It left her with a headache that grew worse when Colvyn briefly pounded a fist on the door before flinging it open.

"They've come again," he told her. "Better get dressed. That old bastard thinks the Gate Wall will benefit from your presence."

Gruinskard had ordered the construction of a stout wooden tower overlooking both the eastern extremity of the harbour defences and the Gate

Wall. Elvine found him perched atop it, his face grim as he surveyed the battle already raging along the battlement of the thick stone barrier forming the terminus of the coast road.

"Vahlak must've sent at least a third of his ships further east during the night," he said when Elvine climbed to his side. "No torches, so we didn't spot them." He nodded at the Gate Wall. "This lot came charging along the road at first light with a battering ram. Didn't make much of an impression on the gate, but they also brought plenty of ladders."

Surveying the fierce struggle, Elvine beheld a scene of remorseless, seemingly pointless slaughter. The Nihlvarians had propped ladders along the length of the Gate Wall. Yet, the width of the barrier was such that only a few dozen warriors could climb to the battlement at any one time. Gruinskard had been astute in placing his more experienced fighters here, three hundred in all, working in relays to hack down their assailants. The fight appeared so one-sided Elvine wondered at the grimness of the old man's demeanour.

"It's a diversion," he said, jerking his head at the docks. "The more he occupies us here, the less care we have for the harbour." His words took on clear meaning when Elvine saw another seaward assault approaching the wall. This time, Vahlak had sent three contingents rather than just one, all angling towards different sections of the barrier. Each was at least the same strength as the attack the day before.

Seeing the way Gruinskard's gaze shifted from the Gate Wall to the harbour, Elvine said, "Go. I'll remain here. If need be, my guard can be added to the fight."

After a moment's further indecision, he nodded and began to descend the tower. "Make sure it's just your guard," he grunted. Watching him run towards the wall with a dozen warriors in tow, she wondered how so aged a soul, one who had recently suffered torture, could remain so vital.

Because, as you must know, he is more than he seems, child, the spear informed her. *There's a power in him I find . . . distasteful, for I am not entirely sure whence it comes.*

"He's afraid of you," Elvine told her. "So it appears your sentiments are shared."

As morning gave way to noon, it transpired, much to her relief, that ordering Colvyn and her guard into the struggle atop the Gate Wall wouldn't be necessary. Having lost close to a hundred warriors in a futile attempt to overcome the ancient barricade, the Nihlvarians abruptly gave up. They retreated along the coast road, covered by a strong contingent of archers. Watching their withdrawal to the eastern flank of the mountain, Elvine found it odd that their flight should be far more orderly than their attack.

The seaborne assault on the harbour had been even more costly for the Nihlvarians. Only one of the three flotillas managed to secure enough ships to the wall long enough to raise ladders and attempt an assault. Half-a-dozen red-faced warriors even succeeded in gaining the parapet for a short time. But, without reinforcements, they were soon cut down and their bodies cast into the fjord. By late afternoon, the waters off Olversahl were littered with the husks of burned ships and drifting wreckage, the sight making Elvine question both her own and Gruinskard's estimation of Vahlak's cunning.

The enemy mounted another sally with the evening tide. This time, they contented themselves with running their swiftest ships along the length of the wall. Rowing at fast stroke, each was crammed with archers casting out a torrent of fire arrows. This attempt to burn the wooden barrier succeeded in birthing a few small fires, all quickly extinguished by the simple expedient of tipping buckets of water over the parapet. Most of the flaming shafts that lodged onto the timbers failed to spread their fire to the dampened sheep hides and all soon guttered out.

Convinced the Nihlvarians weren't yet done, Gruinskard insisted the defenders sleep in shifts and remain at their posts throughout the night. Yet, it wasn't until the following dawn that they came again. A thousand-strong contingent hurled themselves at the Gate Wall, while the strongest attack yet came against the harbour. Events unfolded in a grim, if enlarged, repeat of the previous day. Nihlvarians died by the dozen attempting to breach the gate, this time focusing their efforts on their battering ram rather than scaling the wall.

The great iron and oak gate had been heavily reinforced with additional timber over the preceding weeks, rendering the ram's pounding a pointless exercise. It was an interesting contrivance formed of a massive tree trunk upon wheels, the business end of the ram featuring a great steel head in the shape of a hawk. In the aftermath of its first abortive foray, a canopy had been added along the length of the ram to afford overhead protection to those charged with bringing it to bear on the gate. However, it proved to be of flimsy construction, easily dislodged with a barrage of thrown boulders, whereupon the warriors working the ram became easy targets for the archers above. After gouging a few splintered gashes in the gate, the Nihlvarians once again abandoned the attempt and fled, this time leaving the ram behind. At Colvyn's suggestion, Elvine ordered a party over the wall to heave the thing down the southern bank of the coast road. It tumbled end over end with satisfying volume before coming to rest at the water's edge.

The Nihlvarians had more success in the harbour, albeit short-lived. Suffering grievous losses, they were able to gain two lodgements on the parapet. One was swiftly overrun, but the second, located at the western extremity of the defences, successfully fended off repeated counter-attacks until Gruinskard personally led a twenty-strong contingent into the fray. Elvine didn't see what transpired, but the tales told later spoke of the old man's ferocity, his crude axe cleaving skulls and limbs in a bloody rampage as he cut his way through the red-faced throng.

Visiting the scene of the worst fighting at nightfall, she found Hemund among the wounded. The harbour master had suffered a hefty blow to the shoulder, leaving his arm useless for the time being. Still, he refused to shift from his post, haranguing his surviving warriors back into order with his benumbed limb in a sling.

"How many did you lose?" Elvine asked him.

"One is enough," he replied, and for a moment his stern resolution slipped. His heavy features bunched in grief as his gaze went to the row of covered bodies nearby. Elvine counted fourteen in all. Hemund's company consisted mostly of stevedores and others who had made their living on the docks. Many of those now lying under canvas had been known to him all their lives. She wanted to tell Hemund that things would be easier on the morrow, make some allusion to the Nihlvarians' far more serious casualties. But it felt like an empty and dishonest gesture. She had no notion of how long this struggle would continue.

"I'll stand with you tomorrow," she said instead. "My guards will make good your losses."

Hemund shook his head, using his free hand to wipe moisture from his eyes. "You shouldn't risk yourself, Elvine. Don't worry. We'll bear up well enough when they come again."

She began to argue, but stopped at the sound of a polite cough to her rear. Turning, she felt a tightening of the gut at the sight of Aldunna. Elvine hadn't seen this woman since that first day in Olversahl and had begun to entertain the appealing prospect she might never set eyes on the poisoner again.

"Spear Maiden," Aldunna said, inclining her head. "The Tielwald requests your presence at the Elderman's House."

Elvine squinted at her in bafflement. Why would the old man call her away at a time like this? "I'm busy," she said, waving a hand in dismissal. "Tell him I'll be there later . . ."

"Your pardon, Spear Maiden," Aldunna said, stepping closer. She halted at a warning growl from Colvyn, forcing a smile and speaking in a near murmur. "You insisted that your permission was needed for a particular task. That task is now at hand."

Elvine's stomach clenched further as Aldunna's meaning sank home. Gruinskard had finally found a spy, and it fell to her to pronounce sentence of death.

Her first sight of the captive brought a relieved sigh to her lips. She didn't know him, although there was a vague familiarity in the narrow cast of his features, now pale and rigid with fear. Gruinskard had him chained hand and foot in the cellar of the Elderman's House. The dank space was empty save for a small table upon which sat a number of sharp implements. When Elvine entered the cellar, she found Coelnyr arranging them in neat order, each one sharpened to a gleam.

"There's no doubt?" she asked Gruinskard, containing a wince when the captive shuddered at the sound of her voice.

"I wouldn't have called for you if there was," the Tielwald said, holding up a small silver knot on a cord. "He had this hidden in his house, and he lives alone. He caught Coelnyr's eye when skulking about the Rent. Not an overly suspicious act, considering this one is often called there on account of his work. He's a locksmith. But Coelnyr is very skilled in spotting the combination of gesture and expression that tells of a spy at work. When not engaged in reconnaissance, this man was often seen among that mob of fanatics who are so fond of following you around. Very vocal he was too in his adoration of the Spear Maiden. A somewhat clumsy effort to allay suspicion."

That's where she had seen him: one of those shouters at Dehny's side. The realisation led to a worrisome suspicion, one Gruinskard evidently saw register on her face. "Your friend isn't part of his scheme," he said. "Nor any of her deluded cohort, so far as we can tell. But they'll bear close watching in the days to come, depending on what this one tells us."

The spy cast an involuntary glance at the table, convulsed and vomited onto the cellar floor. He trembled for a time, drawing in deep draughts of air before righting himself, whereupon Elvine was surprised to find his features composed in a mask of defiance. His aura flickered into view then, granite grey like the resolute souls along the harbour wall, but without any cracks.

"He's not going to tell you anything," she said.

"Not at first," Gruinskard agreed. "But they always break eventually. You just have to find the right place to cut." He turned to Elvine with brows raised in expectation. "I trust our evidence meets your standards, Spear Maiden?"

"He's not going to tell you anything," she repeated, moving closer to the prisoner. His aura changed as she neared, the stone-like firmness shimmering. *This one tries to hide his thoughts,* the spear mused. *And hopes fervently for his own death lest he reveal something . . . something important.*

What is it? Elvine asked her.

He's skilled at building walls around his mind. Simply plucking it from him won't work. I need to touch him.

The prisoner shrank from her as she reversed her grip on the spear, extending the iron point towards his head.

"I need him alive," Gruinskard warned. "Much as I applaud your commitment to justice."

Elvine ignored him and continued to push the spearpoint towards the prisoner. He cowered against the damp wall of the cellar, teeth clenched and nostrils flaring. Spittle flew from his mouth when she laid the leaf-shaped blade upon the crown of his head. *Ah,* the spear said. *There it is. Would you like to see?*

The images flooded Elvine's head before she had time to answer, a confused, rapid jumble she failed to parse into meaning. She realised she was seeing the workings of a panicked mind, one determined not to reveal what it knew. She saw a confused parade of faces, rooms, buildings, skies and the mountain. As the stream of visions calmed, the mountain began to dominate, focused mainly on its slopes and summit. It faded when the captive convulsed again, not in fear this time, but in pain. Foam covered his mouth as he writhed, chains scraping stone, his eyes bulging.

"Ulthnir's eyes, girl, he's no use dead!" Gruinskard growled, pushing her aside. The spy's convulsions ceased when the spearpoint separated from his skin, leaving him gasping, staring vacantly with drool spilling from his gaping mouth.

"You say he worked in the Rent?" Elvine asked.

"And elsewhere. A locksmith has many opportunities for rummaging around places he shouldn't." Gruinskard's ire softened as he straightened from the insensate prisoner and noted the deep frown upon Elvine's brow. "What of it?"

"The mountain," she said. "That's where they'll attack next."

"Impossible. Every tunnel has either been sealed or is so well guarded an ant couldn't crawl through. It would be madness for them to even think it."

"They're not coming through it," she said, hefting the spear and hurrying towards the door. "They're coming over it."

Chapter Thirty-Nine

Ruhlin

"We call it the *Ochra-mah*, the Hot Pools," Olchar explained. "A place where the soul fire of the earth rises to heat the water, discolouring and reforming the very rocks. Only there do the spirits of plain, mountain, wind and river come together. To receive the favour of them all, that is where you must go."

"The clans have already hailed the *Telchak's* coming," Velkar pointed out. "Why should more favour be sought?"

Olchar's expression tightened into an embarrassed wince. "Hail him the elders did, but when they returned to their clans, not all were swayed by their tale of what occurred in the *Vikra-sah*. Many refused to believe it, fearful of the consequences of war with the *Rulchakin*. But should the *Telchak* win the spirits' favour at the *Ochra-mah*, most sacred of all places, all doubts will fade."

"How far is it from here?" Ruhlin asked.

"A dozen days' journey south, where the mountains meet the river lands that flow into the sea."

Nigh a month gone from the mountain, Ruhlin mused inwardly, disliking the prospect. But a confirming nod from Velkar made it clear the old man's summons couldn't simply be ignored. "Very well," he said. "Guthnyr, lead them back—"

"You're not going alone," Guthnyr cut in, the flatness of his tone brooking no argument.

"You'll be needed at Tahrim Kyrn," Ruhlin told him. "If it'll ease your mind, Tuhlan and Julette will come with me." He spared a glance for Deyna. "Be sure the Tuhlvyr receives all the comfort and respect she deserves."

"The shed next to the shit-house is free," Guthnyr grunted.

Grinning, Ruhlin clasped his hand. "Keep the iron flowing and the forge working. Tirohk assured me more help will arrive soon."

"More worried about having to explain to Aleida why you're not with us." Guthnyr clapped him on the shoulder before turning to harangue the others into motion.

"I would ask that you go with them," Ruhlin said when Velkar lingered. "My people will benefit from your wolves' protection."

She tarried a moment longer, making him wonder if she nurtured a hankering to see so sacred a place as the *Ochra-mah* with her own eyes. Yet, he read more doubt in her face than resentment when she gave a reluctant nod. "Two of my children will go with you," she said. A pair of wolves promptly trotted to Ruhlin's side. They were the largest of the pack, and, judging by the old scars upon their muzzles, also the oldest. "To ensure your safe return, *Telchak.*" Affording Olchar a brief but respectful nod, she turned to follow Guthnyr's party.

Looking up at the old man perched on the *altahnk's* back, Ruhlin saw him frown as he regarded the two wolves, the great beast shifting uneasily beneath him. "Calm now," the elder said, patting a hand to the creature's shaggy head. "They won't hurt you. We'd best get on while daylight remains, *Telchak.*"

During the journey, Olchar proved to be a far more reticent companion than he had been in the forest. Remaining mounted throughout the day, he kept to the head of their small party, silently guiding them along the trail south. Come nightfall, he would dismount, with a chorus of muted groans, and settle wordlessly by the fire until sleep claimed him. Ruhlin suspected he resented the presence of the wolves, who never ventured more than a few feet from their charge. He knew there to be some form of communication between the pair and their mistress, but he had no knowledge of how much Velkar saw or heard. It occurred to him that Olchar might see them as an affront, as if Velkar had impugned the old man's ability to offer sufficient protection to the *Telchak.*

"Velkar is diligent," Ruhlin ventured when they encamped on the second night. The larger of the two wolves lay at his side with its head resting upon his lap. The other sat peering into the darkened landscape beyond the fire's reach. Julette and Tuhlan were equally attentive, positioning themselves at opposite sides of the camp, gazes cast outward. Ruhlin disliked the fact that they now resembled warriors in his service rather than friends, but supposed it to be inevitable.

"Perhaps overly cautious too," he added, when Olchar failed to respond.

"In a time such as this, there is no such thing as too much caution," the old man replied. He sat with his back resting against the bulk of his mount, warmed as much by the *altahnk*'s body as the campfire. "Long has it been since outright war between Morvek and *Rulchakin*. We skirmish with them often, but I was still a child when last we fought a full battle, and that was just a small echo of the great struggles of the past."

Olchar lapsed into silence, seemingly lost in contemplation of the fire, but then he spoke again. "The tale is passed from elder to elder so that it is never forgotten. Even so, too much was lost. The names of clans that had walked this land for generations uncounted, wiped away as if they had never existed. Their stories, their songs and their wisdom lost forever. This is the true responsibility of an elder, Ruhlin ehs Kestryg, the terrible burden of ensuring that such a crime against all that is good and right in the world never happens again."

"And it won't," Ruhlin assured him. "With the weapons we forge, and the strength of the clans united, the *Rulchakin* will be defeated. Their king has stretched his arm too far in seeking to conquer my homeland. My people are fierce and will not fall easily. He has begun a war he can't win, and in doing so, laid his back open for a killing blow."

Olchar's gaze flickered from the fire, and for a brief moment, Ruhlin caught the gleam of a tear before the old man wiped it away. "Spoken like the *Telchak* I know you to be. Soon to receive the favour of the spirits. Witnessing that shall be the pinnacle of my life, and I thank you for it."

A week later, steep slopes and deep gulleys had given way to a rolling blanket of snow-covered hills and forested valleys. Ruhlin expected to find Morvek clans residing in such fertile land, but saw no evidence of any settlements. Wildlife was plentiful. Herds of deer and elk ranged across distant hills and the woodland they camped among was rich in all manner of bird and scurrying creature.

"Wild place this is, dear boy," Julette commented. She tended to move in a perpetual crouch when they ventured into the trees, as if poised to respond to any threats. "Plenty of things out there keen to eat you."

"Isn't that also true of the sea?" Ruhlin asked.

She shot him a peeved scowl before resuming her narrow-eyed vigil of the surrounding foliage. "Only if you're daft enough to swim in it."

By contrast, Tuhlan proved far more enlivened by his surroundings than at any point in their acquaintance. Smiles were rare from the Caerith, but now there was a faint curve to his lips. His gaze was brighter, and he often paused to take a deep breath. Ruhlin didn't need to ask to know that Tuhlan was finding an echo of his homeland in this unsettled region.

"The Morvek call it the *Sehra Chak*," Olchar explained. "The Forsaken

Land. No clan has settled here since the coming of the *Rulchakin*. It's said that the invaders once ventured here, but instead of steel and fire, their slaughter was achieved through a great sickness they carried with them. The ill humours are said to linger, and also the unquiet souls of the dead. My people think the land cursed, despite its richness, and do not come here unless in dire need."

Although he saw no ghosts during the four days it took to traverse this land, Ruhlin felt a definite weight to the air whenever he settled down to sleep. The sense of hidden eyes lurking in the forest was strong, evidenced by the agitation of Velkar's wolves. Several times he saw them tense, low growls emanating from their quivering lips as they peered into hollows or impassible thickets. He had taken to calling the larger male "Frost", and the smaller female "Ice" due to her slightly paler fur. They seemed happy to respond to these names until the aggression came upon them, whereupon they were deaf to any entreaties. So far, these interludes lasted only moments and they would soon return to padding along at Ruhlin's side, yet his unease lingered.

"You sense no threat here?" he asked Tuhlan as they made their way through an especially dense stretch of woodland. The canopy was so thick as to bar all but the thinnest streams of daylight. Ruhlin thought himself accustomed to forest these days, despite a lifetime spent on a mostly treeless island. But the enclosing gloom put him on edge, stirring memories of the *Vikra-sah* and what had lurked within its darkness.

"All wild places contain threats," the Caerith replied. "I saw bear tracks this morning. Yesterday, I found the claw marks of a large cat upon a tree."

"But nothing . . . else?"

Tuhlan regarded him with a quizzical squint for a moment before letting out a rare laugh. "You imagine all my people have what your kind calls by many names, be it a blessing or a curse?" He laughed again, shaking his head. "This land pleases me because of its lack of people, that is all. In my homeland there are vast tracts of plain and forest where people had rarely walked in many years, if ever. But I have no . . ." Tuhlan fumbled for the right word ". . . special insight. That I leave to the likes of the *Eithlisch*."

This was a name Ruhlin remembered from their days in that subterranean prison. Tuhlan had spoken it after first witnessing the monster's emergence, something he appeared deeply reluctant to discuss. Julette had recognised the term. *A Caerith holy man of immense power*, she said, going on to describe how this *Eithlisch* had played a key role in the downfall of the Albermaine-ish tyrant Evadyn Blackheart. *A man grown to monstrous size*

and strength by arcane means. He rampaged through the Blackheart's army,
leaving bloody ruin in his wake . . .

"The *Eithlisch*," Ruhlin said. "He's like me, isn't he? He becomes a
monster."

"A foolish word," Tuhlan said, his features far more serious now. "For it
does not fit the *Eithlisch*, or you. But yes, he changes, and I have seen it.
Unlike you, he changes when the need arises, not when beset by the storms
of rage. And he remains the *Eithlisch* when changed. His wisdom is as great
as his strength. Never did I dream I would see another like him. It was . . .
troubling to me."

"Do you know how he does it? Remains himself?"

"A question only he could answer. Though I feel sure he would do so if
you were to ask it. One day we will travel together to my homeland, and I
will present you to the *Eithlisch*. That will be a day of great renown."

"I would like that," Ruhlin said, although he doubted Aleida would be
so amenable to such a long and difficult journey. But, if he could learn from
this *Eithlisch*, find a way to master the monster, he knew it was a sojourn
he would have to make. "But first, we'll need to win this war."

As Olchar had promised, they emerged from the forests and hills of the *Sehra*
Chak twelve days after setting out, Ruhlin looking out on a broad grassy
plain interrupted by a matrix of winding streams. In the distance, he saw
plumes of steam rising into the chill morning air.

"The *Ochra-mah* awaits," Olchar said, pointing one of his gnarled walking
sticks at the drifting clouds of vapour.

The intervening terrain seemed to forbid any approach, but the elder
had been here before and set his mount to lead the way. The *altahnk* traced
an irregular course through the grass-covered spits of land, leading them
to shallow crossings through the streams.

"How long will this take?" Ruhlin asked Olchar, as the billowing clouds
grew larger. The closer they came to this sacred place, the more disconcerting
he found it. A faint acrid smell tainted air made uncomfortable by increasing
heat. The steam rose from a long stretch of water surrounded by banks of
what he took to be red and yellow clay. To his eyes, it appeared an unsightly
wound upon the landscape.

"Not long," the old man assured him. Despite his cheerful tone, Ruhlin
saw a pained tension in the elder's aged features, regarding the *Ochra-mah*
with an unwavering gaze. "See," he said after a short interval, pointing his
stick at the steaming pool, "the guardian of the sacred waters awaits us."

It required a good deal of squinting before Ruhlin made out the cloaked figure through the drifting banks of steam. They were tall, features and garb concealed by the cloak. "Another elder?" he asked.

"Yes, but they have no clan," Olchar replied. "The *Ochra-mah* is their sole charge. Only they decide who is worthy of bathing in its waters."

"Bathing?" Ruhlin eyed the befogged pool, finding little appeal in the prospect of submerging himself in it.

"Fear not, *Telchak*. The waters are cool around the edge. But only by bathing can the spirits gauge the measure of your soul."

The elder called a halt when they came within fifty paces of the pool. The sulphurous tinge to the air had grown more potent, and the steam intermittently obscured much of their surroundings. "From here the *Telchak* must proceed alone," Olchar announced, climbing down from the *altahnk*'s back. "Not even these most faithful friends can follow," he added, crouching to run his hands through the neck fur of Frost and Ice. They whined a little when Ruhlin started forward, but the elder's touch calmed them.

"You sure about this?" Julette asked, she and Tuhlan moving to flank Ruhlin. "Doesn't look like a place I'd ever want to go for a swim."

"Nor I," Ruhlin admitted. He scanned the rippled surface of the pool, recalling the shadowed depths of the *Vikra-sah*. The thought that some other nightmarish entity might exist beneath these waters had him pondering the necessity of this ritual. But Olchar had been so insistent, and travelled so far to accomplish this task. Turning back now would surely be seen as a terrible insult to the Morvek's most respected elder.

"It's not supposed to take long," he said, starting forward. "But stay and keep a close watch."

The tall figure beside the pool remained so still Ruhlin wondered if it might be a statue of some kind, a symbolic guardian rather than a living soul. But, when he closed to within a dozen yards, the elder raised a hand. Coming to a halt, Ruhlin peered into the figure's cowl, hoping to catch a glimpse of his face, but seeing only shadow.

"Disrobe," the figure said, the words emerging from the cowl in harshly spoken Ascarlian. When Ruhlin hesitated, the elder went on, "None can enter the sacred waters clothed. The spirits demand it."

Grimacing, Ruhlin set down his maul and sloughed off his jerkin. It was as he pulled his shirt over his head that the elder finally drew back their cowl. The face Ruhlin beheld was not Morvek. It was the face of a hollow-cheeked man, the pallor of his skin made pale in contrast to the many scarlet tattoos covering his visage from forehead to neck. This was a Nihlvarian, his eyes fixed upon a particular feature of Ruhlin's bare chest.

The stagna!

The realisation came too late. The all-encompassing flare of freezing agony spread through him in an instant, sending him onto his back. He felt the monster's fire swell, then dwindle in the face of the dominating chill. His back arched, eyes widening so that he saw in full what befell his companions.

The first salvo of arrows pierced both Julette and Tuhlan through the neck and chest. They fell instantly, with no time to fight or struggle. More arrows followed, Ruhlin seeing archers rise from the surrounding banks, throwing off the grass capes they had used to conceal themselves.

An alarmed, high-pitched whine snapped his gaze to the wolves in time to see Olchar drawing a knife across Ice's throat. Frost already lay twitching at the old man's side, silver fur staining crimson as his lifeblood leaked from the gaping wound in his neck.

"Awake!" Ruhlin grunted through teeth clenched so tight he wondered they didn't shatter. He fed the monster all the rage and hate he could summon, forced his gaze to the lifeless, skewered bodies of his friends to stoke yet more. The only response was a brief flicker of warmth, which died almost as soon as it blossomed. Despite the searing pain, Ruhlin managed to move his arms, dragging them under him in an effort to push himself upright.

"No, don't do that," a harsh Nihlvarian voice said. A booted foot stamped into his back, forcing him into the dirt. "Stronger than you should be, aren't you?" The voice enquired, Ruhlin seeing the tattooed face looming into view. *Not an elder!* Ruhlin seethed, self-recrimination joining the storm of impotent emotion raging within.

"Just a little jab," the Nihlvarian said, Ruhlin catching the gleam of the needle in his hand before he felt a sharp pain in his mouth. The needle sank deep, its wielder keen to ensure its coating made its way into his captive's veins. Ruhlin's flailing slowed, then halted as he felt the drug do its work, robbing him of all strength and rendering his vision into a confusion of blurred shadows.

"Ruhlin ehs Kestryg?" The softly spoken sound of his name banished the fog for a moment, the swirling mess resolving into Olchar's face. The old man appeared bereft, eyes dark with both sympathy and guilt. Yet his voice held no note of uncertainty as he said, "I said this would be the pinnacle of my life, and spoke no falsehood. Ensuring the peace of centuries. That is my charge. Although—" Ruhlin tried to flinch away as the elder put a hand to his forehead but lacked the strength "—high is the price I pay. If any soul could ever have truly been the *Telchak*, it would have been you."

The confusion closed in again as Olchar removed his hand, Ruhlin feeling the scrape of iron on his wrists and the jangling of chains. Dim voices kept him anchored in the world a moment longer, despite the beckoning tug of oblivion.

"On your way, you Morvek wretch," the Nihlvarian said. "He belongs to the Vortigurn now . . ."

CHAPTER FORTY

Felnir

Hahl-Trova burned bright against the waning sky, the tall flames fed by the barrels of oil and stacked kindling Felnir had ordered placed within. Even at a quarter-mile distance, the roar of the inferno was loud, but not so much as to smother the sound of Dyssha weeping. The Sea King's host had come upon the Great Nest of the *Ahrkun Krayl* the day before, finding the conical stone structure utterly silent. No arrows flew from the walls as Felnir led his mounted vanguard towards the gate, nor was any voice raised in defiant challenge. The gate stood open, allowing a familiar, sickly stench to seep out. The stink told the tale of what had occurred here, but it is the nature of the human heart to cling to hope until the last despairing second. So it was with Dyssha.

"Taynvar!" she called, dismounting from the back of her stout pony and rushing into the Hahl-Trova. The sound of her son's name echoed continually until, inevitably, it became a shriek. Felnir found her in the circular hall where the *Sindra* had once convened his perverted court. She sat slumped amid a mound of bodies, dead for days judging by the state of decay, cradling the corpse of a boy no more than ten in her arms, flies buzzing about the gaping wound in his neck.

Sygna counted over three hundred bodies in the stronghold, old and young, but no warriors. They had all died in the Craggens while those cultists left behind orchestrated a slaughter. Some had plainly fallen to their own hand, lying with desiccated hands still clutching the daggers they had plunged into their chests. But the children had been murdered, and not all had gone willingly to their fate. Deep in the cellars, Falk found a group of youngsters burned alive in a storeroom.

"Looks like they barricaded themselves in, my lord," the outlaw reported. He spoke with his usual uncoloured gruffness, but tears leaked from his eyes. "So the *Ahrkun* doused the place in oil and set it alight. Hard to tell how many were in here."

Hahl-Trova was undeniably a well-built fortress. Its thick, high walls would have made it a fine seat for the Sea King's reign, but Felnir doubted any amount of scrubbing would ever get rid of the smell. "Burn it," he told Beyorn. "Then tear down what's left."

"The bastard knew he was going to lose," Baldyr said as they watched the stronghold burn. Reaching for the stained canvas bag tied to his saddle, he held it up to deliver a hefty punch to the contents. "Didn't yer, yer mad fucker? Pity we can't kill yer twice and take our time over it, eh?"

He delivered a few more punches to the bag before tiring of the amusement and once again hitching it to his saddle. "Only fair to tell yer," he said, turning to Felnir, "I'll be taking my lot home on the morrow. Since our arrangement is fulfilled and all." His tone remained affable, but his gaze was hard, as if he expected some last-minute betrayal of their pact.

"Then bear my good wishes with you, brother," Felnir said. "And my regrets that this place didn't yield more reward for your efforts."

"The *Ahrkun* are gone. That's reward enough. Besides, there were enough pickings in the Craggens to keep my *menda* happy. And I got a prize above all, don't forget." He patted the bag, then grimaced at the sticky substance on his fingers. "It'll only get harder from here, y'know? Some Gyrwalds will be happy to swear fealty to the Sea King after this, but by no means all, especially in the north where the Silver Dove holds sway."

"Silver Dove?"

"A pretty name for an ugly soul. Her given name is Jorhyld. She's the last *Ehilkun* to draw breath on the northern shore. No Gyrwald in Vorunvahl holds more lands or commands more spears. Further south there's the Mahra Isles where the Black Gull rules, a pirate in all but name, and with a vicious streak to match his greed. Sorry, brother, but ye've fought one war only to face several more, and that sits outside our bargain." Gripping his reins, he turned his horse about. "But there's a hundred or so of my lot keen to stay with yer and see how it all turns out. I suspect it's more loot they're after, but they're yers if yer want 'em."

"I do." Felnir offered his hand. "Fare you well, brother."

"Yer too." Baldyr paused after they shook, offering a smile that was more of a wince as he added, "My king."

Watching the Gyrwald of the Vorl Tuhrk ride away, Felnir hoped he wouldn't have to kill him in the years to come.

* * *

The following day he sent Sygna back to the lake lands, despite her objections. "I should stay with you." She cast a dark glare at Wohtin waiting nearby atop his pony. "That one can't be trusted. You know that."

"I do. But a kingdom so recently won is like a fragile vessel. Handle it too roughly and it'll shatter. We need to establish sound governance over the lands already taken. Beyorn has not the stature to rule alone and I've already sent Tulvik back to his great-grandfather demanding obeisance. Politely, of course. Our subjects must see their queen and know she rules in my name. Also, most of our *menda* will be keen to go home. Baldyr has agreed to keep supplying food throughout the winter, but preparations must be made for the following year's harvest. Besides, I'm keen to complete the building of our holdfast. A worthy stronghold where the Sea King and Queen will raise their heirs."

As usual, the mention of the children she hungered for served to overcome any argument. "As my king and husband wishes it," she muttered. Casting another baleful glance at Wohtin, she said, "At least take Falk. I'll rest easier."

"He says it must be only the two of us." Seeing her doubtful frown, he pulled her close, speaking softly. "He claims he can awaken the power that resides in this sword. If he speaks true, then no Gyrwald in this land will stand against us. It's worth the risk, my love."

Nodding, she returned his embrace before stepping back. "If any harm befalls him, old man," she grated, rounding on Wohtin, "know that anything you've suffered in the course of centuries will be nothing compared to what I'll do to you."

Wohtin, as had become his habit, said nothing. Turning his mount north, he kicked his heels and set off at a steady canter. Pressing a kiss to Sygna's forehead, Felnir mounted Bolt and followed in the old man's wake. Not for the first time, he began to ponder how differently everything would have been if he had just left this aged troublemaker in that cell.

The country north of the Hahl-Trova was mostly heather-clad hills interspersed with stretches of pine forest. Recurrent snowfall and vicious winds prevented conversation for much of the journey, not that Wohtin was minded to provide any answers to Felnir's questions. The knowledge that the balance between them had shifted again chafed on him. Until he awakened the power of the sword, the old man could maintain his insulting silence as much as he liked. Consequently, Felnir's resentment stirred a rare taunting impulse.

"It must be strange," he mused when they made camp the first night. "To have lived so long and known so much failure." They had found a sheltered nook of granite boulders in the lee of a forested slope where the wind was gentle enough to light a fire. Felnir paused in his jibes to blow air on a smoking handful of kindling before gently settling it into the cone of neatly arranged sticks.

"I mean to say," he went on as the flames caught and the fire began to build, "Velgard entrusted you with his great mission to reach between the worlds. Yet your response was to bring back a treacherous pupil who contrived to destroy his kingdom. Then you come to this land and attempt to turn his crazed nephew into a king, and we know how that turned out. Not content, you then set out on a sojourn across the world and find yourself slung into an Albermaine-ish prison. So far—" Felnir tossed the last few branches onto the fire before settling back "—I appear to be your only success."

He didn't expect an answer, but this time the old man consented to reply, a soft, bitter mutter in Ishtan. The words were poorly accented, but Felnir was equal to the task of translating: "All success is relative. A beggar considers himself rich if he has one coin in his bowl instead of none."

Felnir had killed men for lesser insults, but found this one failed to stir his anger. Perhaps because his detestation of Wohtin had already reached its peak and there was little he could say to worsen it. "Wherever we're going," he said, leaning forward to fix the old man with a steady, purposeful eye, "and whatever you intend when we get there, it had better work."

"It will," Wohtin stated, shrugging his spindly shoulders. "Though I make no promises as to your liking of the result."

"Like Halgard? You took him to the same place, did you not?"

"I did. His fate taught me that the circle does not truly transform, it merely accentuates what is already there. Halgard was both weak of mind and avaricious of spirit, and so became a monstrous embodiment of his soul. You may be different. But know it will be a gamble, my king."

"You keep calling me that, but I hear no respect in your voice, nor see any evidence of true loyalty. Why did you bring me to this land if I am so unworthy of Velgard's legacy?"

"Because, after many years of searching, I couldn't find anyone else." Wohtin's brow crinkled as he paused to think. "Save perhaps Elvine. What a queen she would have made. So rare to see both compassion and wisdom in a ruler."

"Except Velgard, I assume?"

The old man's gaze settled on Felnir for a time, no doubt comparing him to a long-vanished king and finding him wanting. "Yes," he said, turning away to settle down on his blankets. "Except Velgard."

* * *

The circle Wohtin spoke of came into view a week after setting out from Hahl-Trova, another arrangement of standing stones, although it was smaller than those in the forest. The ancient, weathered slabs of granite sat upon a windswept promontory overlooking a broad river. They were arranged around a small rectangular plinth, overgrown with grass and mostly concealed by piled snow.

Wohtin halted his pony and dismounted a dozen yards from the circle, Felnir noting the fearful tension of the old man's features. "Now what?" Felnir asked, climbing down from Bolt's back.

"Go inside the circle," Wohtin said. "Touch the stone in the centre. And wait."

"For what?"

"For whatever it wants to show you." The knuckles of Wohtin's bony hands were white as they clutched his reins, his eyes continually flicking towards and away from the stones, as if he worried what he might see.

Felnir tethered Bolt to a suitably large rock and spent a moment in contemplation of the circle. Moving closer, he peered at the base of the nearest stone, sighing in satisfaction at the sight of a faint spiral carved into the rough surface.

"Who built this place?" he said. "It seems too old to be the work of Velgard's exiled subjects."

Wohtin said nothing, his throat constricting and gaze growing yet more fearful.

"Like the stones in the forest," Felnir continued, moving towards him. "Or the buildings carved into the Craggens. They were not the work of Ascarlian hands, were they?"

The old man stared at him, face quivering now, but with more than just fear. Felnir could almost smell it on him, as thick a pall of guilt as he had ever witnessed. "There were people here," he said, grasping Wohtin's jerkin and hauling him close. "When the exiles arrived, this land was already settled. What became of them?"

"I was in the throes of my first madness," Wohtin rasped, his voice near a babble. "I had no part in it . . ."

"You killed them. Velgard's noble subjects, the greatest of Ascarls, came to this land and wrought bloody murder upon its people."

"They attacked us. Refused to trade. Refused to treat with our emissaries. We would have starved . . ."

"How do you know this if you were in the throes of madness?"

"They told me. Arnhilt and the others. They said they had no choice. The *Kearling* were savages, they said. Eaters of human flesh, barely more than beasts."

Felnir recalled the meagre feast Arnhilt had convened in his honour, the shadow on the *Ehilkun's* face when he spoke of those distant days. *Much was different then, and not all the prey so easily hunted.* "Prey," he said, "that's what Arnhilt called them. You must have known their tales were lies. The folk who built the settlements in the Craggens were not bestial. That's what drove you, wasn't it? Your great mission to redeem these blood-soaked murderers by creating the *Ahrkun.* When that failed, you fled, unable to stomach what they had become. For, without Velgard, what were they? Just a beggared and desperate band of thieves and killers."

He thrust Wohtin away and turned to confront the circle. Snow was blowing thick across the river, rendering the stones into dark sentinels in a shifting white haze. "You don't truly know what this place is, do you?" he said. "Only that it changes those who venture inside. For good or ill, there is no way to know. Or do I miscalculate?" He cast a final, disgusted glance at the huddled old man, brows raised in faint expectation of an answer.

"I . . . feel it," Wohtin faltered. "It is a place where the veil between worlds has thinned. When first I came here, there were bones in the circle, a great many skulls. The *Kearling* had come here in their final days, perhaps to beseech whatever power lies here for succour. Or perhaps they hoped for a peaceful death rather than face the fury of the invaders from across the sea. I . . . I was too scared to venture inside, but Halgard was not. He was already half-mad by then, driven so by the horrors he had taken part in. It's easy to see him as a monster now, but then he was merely a man. Flawed and desperate for anything that would silence the screams of his victims. That is what he asked for when he stepped inside, and that is what he was given. But the price . . ." Wohtin slumped lower, his face softened in misery. "Know that there will be a price, my king. And it will be steep."

Groaning, he got to his feet, inclining his head at the horses. "Come. Let us depart this place. If you'll allow me, I'll counsel you as best I can in the days ahead. You will have your kingdom. It will not be Velgard's realm reborn, but I know now that can never be . . ."

He trailed off, interrupted by Felnir's harsh laughter. "You think I came all this way to turn my back on greatness? You brought a guilt-ridden madman here and wondered at his failure. But I am not mad and this—" he drew the Sword of the Altvar and started towards the circle "—is my due."

He heard Wohtin call his name, voice frail and faltering in the mounting blizzard, but paid him no heed. The wind battered Felnir as he stepped through the ring of stones, his sight stolen momentarily by a stinging blast of icy needles. When it cleared, he fixed his gaze upon the snow-covered mound in the centre and forged a path towards it, fighting the gale. For a time he wondered if the elements conspired to keep him from his goal, the storm's fury having grown so violent. Finally, his fingers touched the chill surface of the mound, pushing deeper through frosted grass to find the stone beneath. Felnir drew in a painful breath of freezing air and waited, tensed but eager for what came next.

Several heartbeats later, he was still waiting and the invading cold had reached his nethers. Looking around, he beheld only the vague shapes of the stones amid the raging blizzard. "Nothing," he said, breath steaming as ice began to form on his beard. "There's nothing here."

Grunting in anger, he removed his hand and struggled back towards the gap in the stones. Before he managed a step, a hammer blow of wind bore down, sending him sprawling. For an instant, the sword was jarred from his grip. When Felnir gripped the handle once again he felt a new warmth too potent, and growing, to be the result of his imagination. The heat spread through his palm and into his wrist before flooding his body, banishing the chill and fortifying him enough to stand. As he raised the sword, he saw the blade was glowing, emitting a bright silver luminescence from tip to hilt. Shifting to and fro, he realised the wind had lessened, then saw that the snow appeared to be curving around him.

"What is this?" he murmured, his gaze torn between the mesmerising glow of the sword and the impossible actions of the storm. The fact of what he was seeing became inescapable when he moved, the roiling hail of flakes shifting to avoid him as if he were encased in an invisible cocoon.

"Well, that's certainly useful," he said, twirling the sword so that the blade described a brilliant arc. *A light to mark the path of the Sea King's march to glory*, Felnir mused to himself. *Better than any banner.* Who could doubt that he possessed the Altvar's favour now?

He began to ponder how to stop the thing's glow when he felt it change. The heated handle flared in his grip, blossoming into something painful. As his fingers reflexively opened, Felnir found they wouldn't obey the instinctive command. The sword, it seemed, refused to be released. Wincing at the growing discomfort, Felnir tried to shake it free. As he did so, the light emitted by the wavering blade appeared to seep into the blizzard. His sense that it was merely an illusion born of mounting alarm faded when he saw the light spread, tendrils snaking out to ensnare the snow. Moving with blinding swiftness, it gathered myriad swirling flakes into a form. What began as a shimmering blur swiftly resolved into a face. As the snow coalesced into cheekbone, lips, nose and forehead, Felnir gaped in recognition. It was the face of a young man, fully bearded and strong, but with a worried cast to his eyes.

"Guthnyr!" Felnir breathed.

He saw his brother's lips moving and wondered if his spectre was attempting to convey some message from the Halls of Aevnir. Then the wind stalled and shifted, the howling gale forming itself into a facsimile of Guthnyr's voice: "Why would you think I would ever trust you?"

Felnir staggered, struck by the accusation he heard in that voice. His brother's soul was clearly unquiet in death, beset by a sense of betrayal, for had Felnir's ambition not been the author of his demise? "I . . ." Felnir stammered. "There was nothing I could do . . ."

"I'm not asking for your trust." A second voice. Female and unfamiliar. The light seeping from the sword swirled anew, forming a new face. Felnir had never seen the woman it conjured. Her features were austere but beautiful, decorated with some form of tattooing around her eyes. "Merely for you to think," she continued. "Face it. Your leader has been betrayed. The Vortigurn has him and the Morvek move against us. We cannot stay here!"

The urgency in her tone and the conflict he saw play over his brother's features brought a jarring realisation. These were not ghosts. "Guthnyr!" Felnir shouted, hoping his brother might hear him, but the faces began to fade then, dissolving back into swirling snow. "No!" Felnir lurched forward, stumbling to his knees. "Where?" he demanded, holding the sword up to his eyes, staring into the glowing blade. "Where is he!"

The response was immediate, and shocking in the pain it conjured. The tendrils emitted by the sword coiled and lashed at him, sending pulses of agony through his being. His vision was flooded with the purest flare of white, then slowly shifted into drifting clouds, parting to reveal a snow-covered landscape seen from above. A dark circle marked a rise alongside a winding river. Within the circle knelt a man holding a sword with a blazing white blade. Abruptly, the man and the circle shrank, Felnir feeling himself ascend into the sky. Beneath him, river, hill and forest tilted as he flew north, flung by an unseen hand. The land below blurred, its wintry green soon giving way to the grey of a choppy sea. Felnir swept over miles of waves, passing through a dense miasma of foul-scented smoke above a long chain of islands. Beyond, more water until he came upon a procession of cliffs beaten by tall waves. Further inland, he saw fjords cutting through broad, cultivated fields. North of this settled land were more mountains, the tallest he had seen so far, granite giants topped by white summits. It was here that he finally slowed, plummeting down to behold a small cluster of huts clinging to the side of one of the lesser peaks. He saw no people, but knew without the slightest shred of doubt that this is where his brother now lived.

It all vanished in an instant, the vision evaporating and the sword's glow blinking out to leave him face down in the snow. The numbness of his flesh made it plain he had lain there too long, but the pain of reawakened muscle felt distant, smothered by the flame of exultant certainty. As Felnir climbed to his feet and stumbled from the circle, there was but one thought in his head: *Guthnyr is alive!*

CHAPTER FORTY-ONE

Thera

"Sails to the south, my queen!" the lookout atop the *Great Wolf*'s mast called out, pointing at the southern horizon. "Counting a dozen with more behind!" he added, his stance relaxing a little. "No red among them!"

Thera was able to make out the leading ships a short while later, concealing a sigh of relief at finding the lookout's judgment true: these were allies. Since leaving Vorun Hardta, she had known there was a possibility the Nihlvarian battle fleet might abandon its attack on Olversahl and come against her instead. Battle upon the open sea was not something to relish, but so far at least, the approach of the Queen's Fleet had remained undetected by their enemies.

"Signal the fleet to trim sails," she told Ragnalt. "We need to join with our friends."

The subsequent waving of flags to nearby ships, the signal then passed on from vessel to vessel, brought about the required reduction in speed. Soon, the approaching craft drew close enough for Thera to recognise the sleek lines of the *Silver Hawk* ploughing through the waves at the head of the loose formation. Behind her came the larger but still swift flagship of Veilwald Hakkyn Rohnlank. The Aiken Geld had evidently received her summons and responded in fulsome manner. The many vessels spread out to the rear of Hakkyn's ship varied in size, but all sat low in the water, laden as they were with the warriors of the Outer Isles.

They began to cheer when Hakkyn's warship drew level with the *Great Wolf*. The cry rose from every deck, each thick with warriors acclaiming their queen. The wind robbed the words of meaning, but the collective expression of fierce loyalty rang out as clear as any clarion. Thera tried to remain as regally inexpressive as possible while the Outer Isles fleet joined with their Inner brethren. But she couldn't quell the rising sense of nauseous unease overwhelming any small kindling of pride or gratitude. Within days, this entire fleet would be pitched into the fiercest contest yet seen in this war, and many of those throats now calling her name would be filled with seawater.

"Full sail," she instructed Ragnalt, managing to keep the catch from her voice. "Best speed to Olversahl."

The *Chainbreaker* appeared the evening they anchored off Aeric's Fjord, the gateway to Olversahl. The waters were too treacherous for so many vessels to proceed without the benefit of full daylight. This meant a further delay since they would have to wait for the sun to burn away the inevitable morning fog. The nimble warship came swiftly towards the *Great Wolf*, her helmsman angling the tiller to bring her alongside. Lynnea stood at the starboard rail, Mohlnir a small smudge upon her shoulder. Despite the distance, Thera heard her Tielwald's thoughts with the usual clarity when their minds touched.

It's done, Lynnea told her. As with the spying barmaid in Vorun Hardta, Thera could sense the discomfited ache that arose from a recent killing. Though it wasn't as potent as before. Her former apprentice was growing accustomed to her role.

You're sure he sent the message first? Thera asked, receiving a pulse of confirmation in response. With luck, the Nihlvarians in Skar Magnol would be engaged in panicked preparations for an assault. If any knot-bearers among them felt compelled to send word to their fleet off Olversahl then all to the good. Their commander might decide to dispatch ships to Skar Magnol's aid, or abandon the attack on Olversahl completely. Either way, they wouldn't be expecting the Queen of the Isles to appear with all her strength.

Good, she told Lynnea with warm approval. *Tell Veltta to place her ship to our stern and expect battle on the morrow.*

Fortune smiled the next day with a cloudless sky and a bright sun that banished the fog with welcome alacrity. Before setting out from Vorun Hardta, Thera had made it clear to her captains that the *Great Wolf* would lead the fleet to Olversahl. Some had argued, Veilwalds Ossgrym and Torlund chief among them, that she should place herself in the heart of the force, both for protection and to buttress the courage of her warriors. She had refused to be swayed, stating: "You made me queen. I'll thank you to allow me the choice of my place in battle."

In truth, her decision owed more to a desire to exert at least some control over coming events. Once battle was joined, it would be next to impossible to maintain command in the unfolding chaos. Sea battles, she had learned, were often decided in the first few moments of action, and she wanted to reserve those vital decisions for herself.

An excess of prideful arrogance? she wondered. Like most of her more self-critical thoughts, the question was phrased in Sister Iron's voice. Would that most jaded of veteran warriors have approved her plan? *Perhaps not. She would have thought it overly reliant on chance.* Thera's gaze shifted to the party of carpenters busily readying the contraption set upon the *Great Wolf's* foredeck. *But I do have something to make the dice roll in my favour.*

"How goes it, Engine Master?" she enquired, moving to Teylhar's side as he applied a mallet to a bolt in the device's locking mechanism.

"She's about as ready as she's going to be, my queen," he said, straightening from his work. His eyes were hollowed from lack of sleep, he and his crew having worked through each turn of the glass since they put to sea. The finished engine was very different from the stone slingers that had wreaked havoc in the Crusher Strait. Her initial instructions to Teylhar had been to construct a smaller version of those devices for use at sea. Yet, after a few days pondering, he had come to her with an alternative design. Set down on parchment, it had appeared an outlandish, possibly absurd notion. Still, her Master of Engines insisted it could be done and she opted to trust his judgement.

"One hundred paces, you said?" she asked, smoothing a hand over the engine's recently shaped rear stock. Now fully assembled, the whole contraption resembled a greatly enlarged version of the crossbows beloved by Albermaine-ish soldiery. The main body consisted of three conjoined blocks of oak while the crossbeam was a single bar of tempered steel three yards long. More impressive still was the great iron bolt now being manoeuvred onto the stock by four of Teylhar's crew.

"With a favourable wind, yes, my queen," he replied. "Though it might be best to try for eighty in practice." He paused to let out a cough. "And stand well back when we loose her."

"That I shall, so long as you do the same. I've no appetite for returning your headless corpse to your mother."

She clapped a hand to his shoulder and proceeded to the prow. She had ordered the oarsmen to steady stroke upon entering the fjord. Any faster risked outrunning her slower ships and tiring her *menda* for the fight to come. She had sailed these waters only infrequently during her time as Vellihr of Justice. Olversahl, despite a few malcontents' lingering attachments to the twin nonsense of Covenant belief and Albermaine-ish rule, had been a mostly law-abiding city. Its people were largely unencumbered by the feuding and generational grievance that had underpinned so many of her missions for the Sister Queens.

She smelled the smoke when they swept around the first bend in the fjord, even though they were still several miles from their goal. It grew thicker by the mile until she saw the tall black columns of roiling ash rising above the headland to the east. The height and colour of the smoke told the tale with awful clarity and had her calling out an order to the oarsmen to increase the pace of their stroke.

Olversahl was burning.

CHAPTER FORTY-TWO

Elvine

The struggle at the Rent was already raging when she emerged from the narrow streets bordering the approach to the ruined statues of the Altvar. Nigh a hundred warriors battled at the broken feet of Ulthnir's monument, with more descending the huge stone edifice by rope. As Elvine pelted towards the scene with Colvyn at her side and her guard close behind, one thought raged in her mind, laced with a sickening thread of guilt: *I told him! I told him how to do this!*

Her report on Olversahl had included a detailed description of the mountain, and the many, often abortive attempts to climb it. Of the few that succeeded, the least hazardous had involved scaling a spiral course around the peak from the eastern flank to the steeper western cliffs. Despite their sheerness, they sported a fissure extending not only to barely a hundred feet below the summit but also all the way down to the crown of Ulthnir's head. A perilous climb to be sure, but she knew Vahlak well enough by now to know that he regarded risk as a gift rather than an obstacle.

Nearing the scene of combat, she saw several bodies on the ground and a growing knot of combatants at the base of the Rent. The outnumbered town recruits stationed here were fighting a losing battle to prevent the Nihlvarian force entering the mountain's matrix of tunnels. She had expected Vahlak to send this force against the Gate Wall but realised now he had a different intent.

"Hurry!" she called to her guards. "We have to stop them getting inside!"

Colvyn sped past her as they closed on the melee, Halkyr and the other guards quickly following behind. "Stay here, Spear Maiden!" the young captain implored before entering the fray, hacking left and right. With night coming on, the scene was lit only by a few scattered torches, denying her a clear view of the unfolding struggle. She heard shouts of alarm as the

Nihlvarians found themselves attacked from behind, though the resultant clamour indicated they were fighting back with swift ferocity.

Pounding feet to her rear caused her to turn, finding Gruinskard leading another contingent of warriors to the scene. Before turning back to the struggle, she once again paused to marvel at the old man's ability to stay at the head of the charge. The ongoing tumult of clashing weapons made it plain that the Nihlvarians were successfully holding off her guards. Then a wayward flicker of torchlight revealed a score of them plunging into the narrow dark of the Rent. Unwilling to stand witness to impending disaster, Elvine hefted the spear and plunged into the throng of battling warriors.

The spear's gift took hold with welcome immediacy, the thrashing figures slowing, enabling her to slip unmolested through a chaos of flailing swords and axes. She ducked blades and sidestepped men and women locked in deadly combat. Only once did she use the spear. A lithe Nihlvarian warrior leapt into her path, hatchet whirling and moving too fast to avoid. Still, the spear's gift made slamming the butt of the haft into the warrior's unprotected head an easy task. It rendered the sound of a cracked skull into a dull echoing thud, the Nihlvarian dropping like a stone. As Elvine leaped her inert form, the spear's gift faded. With the Rent lying open before her, she hurtled into the gloom.

Although there were many passages through the mountain, she knew Vahlak would have sent his warriors against but one: the tunnel leading all the way through to the eastern foothills. It was this channel that had allowed Gruinskard's stratagem to succeed. She supposed it was inevitable that Vahlak would seek to exploit it if he could. Finding the trail of his warriors wasn't difficult. She simply followed the dead and wounded left in their wake.

Elvine deafened herself to the cries of the maimed, calling out for succour as she pushed deeper into the Rent. She soon came to the sturdy door to the corridor of cells where she had once been caged, finding it open. The gaoler was slumped upon the floor, his blood pooling on the stone and his keys stolen. As she hurried on, she wondered why she had never learned his name. Beyond the cells lay another door, also open, and a steep stairwell. She found no more bodies upon descending the steps, emerging into a broad chamber where a group of Nihlvarians were clustered at the locked and chained entrance to the tunnel through the mountain. She heard a good deal of cursing as she slowed to a walk, the chains rattling as the gaoler's keys were repeatedly tried in the locks.

"They were changed recently," Elvine said. "The keys are kept elsewhere."

The rattling stopped as the group, half-a-dozen strong, all turned to face her. Their instant aggression froze when a voice barked out a harsh command: "Stop!"

The Nihlvarians moved aside to allow a tall figure to come forth. Like his comrades, he was lightly armoured, she assumed, to ease the perilous climb they had endured. He wore no helm, his handsome features marred by a bruise on the side of his head. Halting a few strides short of her, he offered a courteous nod of greeting. "Scholar Elvine," said Vahlak. "Such a pleasure to see you again."

Elvine found it hard to speak, a combination of fear and fury clenching her jaw as she crouched, raising the spear in readiness. "You shouldn't have come yourself, Tuhlvyr," she told him, the words emerging as a barely intelligible hiss.

"And you should not be here," he said, eyes flicking to the untarnished head of the spear. "Battle is not your province, and it would pain me to see you hurt."

"But not your sister, I'd guess."

This summoned a smile to his lips and a reflective arch of his brows. "I suppose not. But don't worry. I've always had a gift for leavening her temper. Now, if you'll excuse me." Inclining his head, he turned back to the sealed door. "I have pressing business to attend to. Restrain her," he added, flicking a hand to his warriors. "Without harm. If I find a single bruise, you all die by my hand."

The spear's gift surged as they came for her, revealing the shadow forms of their intended lines of attack. If there had been but one or two, she might have found a way to spare them. But with so many flailing arms to avoid, she knew mercy to be a perilous indulgence now. She killed the Nihlvarian closest to her with an upward thrust to the chin, the spearpoint crunching through bone, vessel and brain to emerge from the rear of his skull in a ponderous red cloud. She drew the weapon free and swung the point across the throat of the warrior lunging from her left. She was forced to drop to her hands and knees to evade the next two, scrambling under their entangled forms, then reversing her grip on the spear to deliver two swift thrusts. The point pierced their light leather breastplates with ease, Elvine finding herself briefly mesmerised by the twin expressions of shocked surprise on their faces as they fell.

Tearing her gaze away, she whirled to face Vahlak. He stood with a good deal more wariness now, placing himself between her and the sole surviving warrior pounding a hammer to one of the chain locks. "It truly is a weapon of the gods, then?" he asked, face grim as he regarded the bloody spear in her hands.

"I don't know what it is," she replied, seeing little reason for dishonesty now. "But I know if you stand against me, I will kill you."

Vahlak's features tightened in regret, a resigned sigh issuing from his lips as he raised his gold-hilted sword. "And I will try not to—" he began, but Elvine was already moving.

Surging into a lunge, she thrust the spear directly at Vahlak's chest. Her form was good, the swift precision of the strike a tribute to Colvyn's many hours of tutelage. Yet the Tuhlvyr batted it away with ease. As he stepped to the side, drawing his sword back, time slowed once again. The spear revealed his intention, the shadowy facsimile of his form delivering a blow with the flat of the blade to Elvine's temple. Even now, he was trying to spare her. The echoing clang and clatter of a hammer shattering one of the locks convinced her to eschew any defensive moves in favour of another attack. Leaping high, she stabbed the spear at Vahlak's throat. Her sheer speed forced him to pivot clear, leaving the path open to his hammer-wielding companion. Elvine let out a yell as she threw the spear, a skill Colvyn hadn't taught her, but she seemed to know instinctively. It took the warrior in the back as he raised his hammer to shatter the remaining lock, the iron head piercing him through to pin his body to the great barrier's timbers.

Shorn of the spear's gift, time immediately resumed its normal course, leaving her naked before Vahlak's sword. She sprinted for the door, intending to reclaim her weapon, but a kick from the Tuhlvyr sent her sprawling. Breath rushed from her lungs as she collided with the rough stone floor. Gasping, Elvine rolled onto her back, trying to stand, then stopping at the sight of Vahlak looming above. She expected rage, but saw only amused admiration on his face.

"He told me it would be like this," the Tuhlvyr said, shaking his head. "'The one you have longed for awaits you across the great ocean,' he told me. 'But there is no claiming her.'" His brows knitted together in a sorrowful frown as he crouched at Elvine's side. "He said I would have to kill you. To claim the glory that is my due, that was the sacrifice he demanded." She flinched as he traced a finger across her cheek. "But I can't, Elvine. Though it may condemn me to the Vortigurn's wrath, I ca—"

The sword point emitted a tearing grind as it emerged from his nose, sending a spatter of hot gore onto Elvine's face. Vahlak didn't die instantly. Elvine watched his eyes flare in shock and panic, then roll up into his skull. Before he slumped into a lifeless huddle, he made a curious sound that resembled a cat choking on a fishbone.

"Bastard!" Colvyn grunted, putting a boot to Vahlak's head to drag the sword free. Elvine hadn't seen her brother so riven with anger before. Besmirched by blood from the battle at the Rent, the ugly mask of his fury was hard to look upon, even more so when he proceeded to deliver a series of blows to Vahlak's corpse.

"Enough!" Elvine rasped, struggling to rise. "The door!"

Colvyn helped her to her feet, and they rushed to the barrier, now shuddering under the weight of bodies pressing from the other side. Elvine could hear their voices, all raised in an urgent clamour that soon took on a rhythmic quality. The door began to heave anew, this time with repeated, concerted shoves. Even steel chains and heavy timbers would buckle under such pressure.

"They're going to break through," she said, gripping the spear and pulling it free of the Nihlvarian warrior's corpse.

"Then," a low, gravelly voice said, "let us prepare a welcome for them."

Gruinskard came stomping from the gloom with his axe trailing gore. His blood-matted brows bunched as he considered the shuddering door. "Back," he said, jerking his head to the passage behind. "I've brought a gift for our visitors and it would be best if you weren't here when they received it."

"Wait," Elvine said, crouching at Vahlak's body. "Help me with him," she told Colvyn, drawing a baffled squint in response.

"What for?"

Elvine didn't reply, waving an impatient hand until Colvyn consented to take hold of Vahlak's legs. Together they dragged him to the stairwell then up to the next chamber, where they met a score of men pushing oil barrels.

"My gift," the Tielwald explained. He ordered one of the barrels positioned at the top of the stairs, then slammed his axe into the lid, sending the contents gushing down the narrow passageway. "Tip out all of it," he told the barrel pushers. "And someone bring me a torch."

Gruinskard insisted Elvine leave before he set light to the pool of oil. She assumed he waited until the Nihlvarians had forced the door before throwing the torch and beating a hasty retreat. Once clear of the Rent, Elvine watched a thick pall of smoke seep from the great crack in the mountain, growing thicker by the minute as the spreading blaze found more barrels the Tielwald had ordered stacked within. He appeared when the first flames began to blossom in the gloom, a large slouching figure silhouetted against an orange curtain. For the first time since this battle began, Elvine saw tiredness in him. His shoulders were slumped, and he walked stiffly, leaning on his axe for support.

Even the brightest flame will gutter eventually, the spear said, Elvine detecting a note of satisfaction in the observation. *Useful as he is, child, you already know there will come a time when he has to fall.*

They stood watching the massive tongue of flame lick from the vertical maw of the Rent until a messenger came running to tell of the Nihlvarians preparing another seaborne attack on the harbour. "This bugger's timing was impeccable," the Tielwald grunted, nudging a toe to Vahlak's corpse. "Launching two assaults simultaneously, one from within, the other without. Come on then." Hefting his axe, he turned towards the docks. "Seems there's still work to do this night."

In contrast to previous attacks, the Nihlvarian assault came against just one section of the harbour wall. A strong force of their smaller ships, each towing boats crammed with warriors, attacked the eastern portion of the defences. It was a point opposite the most direct approach to the mountain, confirming that Vahlak had made careful study of the maps Elvine provided. The enemy clearly expected at least part of the wall to have been taken by the time their attack struck home. Elvine fancied she heard a chorus of collective dismay rise from the leading ships when they were met by the now typical blizzard of arrows.

The two ships at the forefront of the formation were sunk by a combination of fire arrows and falling boulders. The remainder milled about for a time, their archers exchanging volleys with those on the parapet above, without particular effect. A handful of the boats made it to the wall, the occupants casting out their grappling lines and attempting to climb. All were swept away by tumbled stone and burning oil. Within an hour it was over, the survivors trailing smoke as they limped back towards the safety of their fleet.

When the last ship had faded from view, to the puzzlement of both Colvyn and Gruinskard, Elvine convened funeral rites for Tuhlvyr Vahlak Tahrimsturm. Ordering a small boat brought to the wall, she instructed that the blood be wiped from Vahlak's body before he was laid in it, along with his possessions.

"The price I could've gotten for this in Leynkora," Colvyn sighed, fingers lingering on the golden hilt and engraved handle of Vahlak's sword as he placed it on his chest. His face showed a measure of chagrin at Elvine's disapproving frown before he stepped back. "Given your object," he said, "returning Lore's brother in relatively unmolested condition might have the opposite effect."

"It won't," she assured him. Whatever the state of Vahlak's corpse when Lore beheld him, Elvine was certain of the queen's response. *As far as I know, Lore has loved only two people in her entire life*, she thought, choosing not to share the insight. *One is now her most implacable enemy, and the other is dead. Hate and rage are all she has left.*

She had the boat lowered over the wall before dawn, ensuring the changing tides would carry it to the Nihlvarian fleet. Colvyn tried to persuade her to withdraw to the harbour master's house for a rest, but Elvine refused, waiting upon the parapet throughout the remaining hours of darkness. She thought perhaps she would hear Lore's plaintive, grief-stricken screams echoing across the water, but none came. Instead, the fjord echoed with the sound of ropes being worked through tackle and the thud and grind of many hands at work. It wore on for hours, any clue as to what the Nihlvarians might be preparing concealed by the gloom and then the morning fog. When the mist began to thin, the results of the enemy's labour became plain.

All but one of the great red-sailed warships had been repositioned so that their prows pointed towards the harbour wall. Their banks of oars started sweeping before the last of the fog had been burned away. As a consequence, they had covered near half the distance to the wall before Elvine made out the ramps fitted to their bows. The warriors they carried all cried out a hungry song of impending vengeance. Vahlak had evidently been a popular commander. Elvine stared at the approaching monsters with a thudding heart, her mounting panic competing with a potent flare of guilt. She had known sending Lore her brother's body would provoke a reaction, hopefully another reckless and hopeless assault. She hadn't expected the queen to expend near all her strength in such dramatic fashion.

"Madness," Gruinskard growled, Elvine turning to see him studying the oncoming ships with a contemptuous scowl.

"It is?" she asked. Appalled at the quavering whisper of her voice, she coughed and repeated the question.

"She must have stripped every other ship of warriors," the Tielwald said. "Even if they make it over the wall, the fight will cost them too many lives. They won't have the strength to take the city. Still—" he took up his axe with a businesslike sniff "—gives us plenty to be getting on with in the meantime. Best if you retire to the harbour master's house, Spear Maiden. Our lot will take heart from seeing you there. Just until they break through somewhere," he added when she began to object. "I'll need you to lead your guards forward to contain it." He cast a reluctant eye at the spear, the point wiped clean but the haft still stained by her exertions in the mountain. "Now I know what you can do with that thing it would be foolish not to use it."

Persuaded of the wisdom of his counsel by Colvyn and Halkyr, she hurried to her rooftop perch to watch events unfold. Thanks to their many oars and a favourable tide, the huge warships made a rapid approach to the wall despite the weight of warriors crowding their decks. The hulking vessels spread out to form three wings, those to the east and west moving at a faster stroke than the trio of ships in the centre. These appeared content to wallow beyond bowshot while their comrades came on. All the while, the Nihlvarian flagship waited at anchor among a flotilla of smaller craft. Elvine found her gaze returning to that unmoving giant, knowing that Lore would be staring back.

Do you weep for him? Elvine wondered, surprised at the savage twist of enjoyment the notion provoked. She hadn't fully realised before just how much she hated the woman on that ship. Memories crowded in of the massacre in Nerlfeya's Hall, the utter shock and terror of the queens and their servants as blood flowed and screams echoed through the sacred chamber. She remembered all those hours discussing history and literature with a woman who had wrought such horror. The perverse normality of it was made worse by the knowledge that Elvine had actually found worth in many of Lore's insights. It raised the unwelcome notion that the connection between them had not been one-sided.

A more deceitful and murderous a soul could not be found in all the world, Elvine decided, seeking to buttress her hatred in the face of worrisome conjecture. *I hope your tears were bitter. I hope your grief hurts like the worst poison . . .*

Her inner diatribe faded when the spear spoke up. The chiding note Elvine had heard before now blossomed into a dark and ominous warning: *Beware your passions, child. Lest one day you too find yourself intent on burning a city just to snuff out a single life.*

The eastern wing struck the wall first, the ships suffering a hail of projectiles in order to draw close enough to release the ramps on their foredecks. They swung down to clamp iron hooks onto the upper edge of the wall with a splintering crash. One ramp had been released a fraction too early, scraping the top of the timber barricade but failing to gain purchase. Still, the warriors aboard the great ship attempted to charge across it. A few leaped onto the parapet to be cut down in swift order, while the rest tumbled into the water as the vessel edged back from the harbour. The ships to either side fared better, managing to secure their ramps, although the subsequent rush of yelling warriors met with intersecting arcs of arrows and a torrent of stones. Dozens were sent plunging into the fjord before a few succeeded in hurling themselves at the defenders. Furious combat erupted where the ramps met the wall, the chaotic scene soon becoming hard to follow. However, Elvine gained the impression of a steady stream of outnumbered Nihlvarians being systematically hacked down.

A similar story played out to the west, although the attackers appeared to be paying an even higher price for their efforts. Fire arrows and flaming oil set one warship alight before it could even drop its ramp. The smoking hulk collided with the ship on its port side, dislodging it from the wall just as it began to disgorge its cargo of fighters. Screaming men and women cascaded into the harbour waters as the fjord's current carried the entangled vessels away. Only two ramps remained and, so far, Hemund's company of dock workers seemed capable of containing their attacks.

"The old man was right," Elvine mused. "This is madness."

"I'm not so sure," Colvyn said. Following his gaze, she saw that it was fixed upon the three ships still wallowing opposite the centre of the wall. Except now they had begun to move. Oars sweeping, all three angled their bows towards the wall, but the one in the middle remained in place while the other two started forward at fast stroke. As they drew nearer, Elvine realised that neither of the flanking ships had a ramp fitted to their prow. Nor were their decks crammed with warriors. Instead, each were laden with numerous barrels and bundles of kindling. She counted only a few sailors on their decks, all of them holding torches. Before the defending archers could bring them down, they began to kick over the barrels, soaking the decks in viscous fluid. All of them then ran to climb up onto the rails, casting their torches behind them before diving into the fjord. The upper works of both ships exploded in a blaze of igniting oil that swiftly consumed the rigging before spreading to the lower decks. The rapid sweep of the oars became a confused jumble of clashing blades as the slaves chained below realised their impending doom. Elvine could hear their screams even above the roaring flames and cacophony of battle.

The fire ships both lost their heading before colliding with the wall, each striking a portion of the wooden palisade some thirty yards apart. The fire was so intense that even the soaked sheep hides couldn't prevent it taking hold as burning debris descended in a fiery rain. Men and women ran, some beating at the flames licking their hair and garb. The resulting smoke blocked Elvine's view of what came next, but she heard the thud of the middle ship's prow impacting the wall before the now familiar clatter of its falling ramp. A gust of wind dispelled the roiling grey haze to reveal a score of Nihlvarian warriors on the upper parapet, swiftly cutting their way through minimal opposition. The continuing blaze prevented reinforcements rushing to the aid of the overwhelmed defenders in the centre. Ropes flew from the walkway and soon red-faced warriors were descending to assail the few shocked Ascarlians on the wharf. Heart pounding, Elvine squinted through the acrid miasma to see more warriors crowding the deck of the great ship between the two blazing hulks. A forest of masts swayed in the smoke beyond the central vessel's stern, ever more Nihlvarians climbing up from the smaller ships to join the breakthrough.

Spying a growing number on the wharf forming a battle line, Elvine took up the spear, then paused when she saw a dense cluster of defenders charging towards the incomplete Nihlvarian formation. They were led by a hulking figure with an overlarge, single-bladed axe. The smoke closed in again when the Tielwald's charge struck home, obscuring the subsequent chaos of furious combat.

He'll die if you don't save him, the spear informed Elvine. As she had acknowledged her hatred of Lore, Elvine now found herself reliving her encounters with Gruinskard. Each memory was underlined by her mother's service to the ancient intriguer, the guilt that had plagued her ever since the burning of King Aeric's library. Would it be so terrible if the old man died? A heroic end worthy of a tale or two. After all, did the people of Olversahl really need him when they had the Spear Maiden?

How sharp your thinking has become, the spear observed. *And so many bright edges to it too. Careful you don't cut yourself, child. And while you're so busy pondering, ponder this: There will come a time when he has to fall. But it's foolish to cast away an axe when it still has a keen blade.*

"I do believe, dear, esteemed brother," Elvine said, slipping into Ishtan and turning to Colvyn, "it's time we joined this fight. Don't you?"

For once he didn't argue, his face showing a resigned grimness as he drew his sword. "Don't get too far ahead this time."

CHAPTER FORTY-THREE

Thera

"Steady!" Teylhar called out, crouched on the foredeck with one hand on the release lever of his contraption. Frequent gusts of smoke repeatedly obscured the waters to the *Great Wolf*'s front, making the aiming of his device a difficult business. Upon rounding the final bend in the fjord and beholding the sight of Olversahl, Thera had been faced with the stark dilemma of how to proceed with a battle plan without a clear picture of what lay ahead. A few salient facts were obvious: the fortifications her great-grandfather had constructed along the harbour were beset by a fulsome attack, its central portion ablaze and fighting raging atop the wooden palisade. She assumed the bulk of the Nihlvarian fleet had been committed to this assault, but the ever thickening smoke made it impossible to gauge how many ships they held in reserve. Should she commit her entire force against the Nihlvarians on the wall, she may well be leaving her starboard flank open for a deadly riposte.

You came here to save a city, she reminded herself, grimacing as a great blossom of flame erupted from the centre of the defensive wall. The haze was still maddeningly thick, but she could make out the vague silhouettes of dozens of Nihlvarian warriors rushing over the parapet via a ramp fixed to the prow of one of their hulking warships. To the giant's rear lay a broad cluster of smaller ships and boats, all feeding a continual stream of reinforcements into the larger vessel by means of a matrix of ropes and ladders tracing over her hull.

With no other clear targets, and knowing that swift decision in battle was preferable to a single moment of dithering, she ordered Ragnalt to steer the *Great Wolf* for the centre of the defensive wall. She also had flag signals made to the Outer Isles vessels off her starboard bow, instructing them to sweep on to the eastern side of the harbour, hopefully guarding against a counter-attack from the Nihlvarian reserve. However, whether these were noticed in the smoke was impossible to say.

"Steady!" Teylhar called again, then, "Two points to port! Steady . . ."

His voice faded as he concentrated all his efforts on aiming the engine. Although too heavy for one man to lift, it had been placed atop an ingenious ball and socket contrivance that enabled the whole contraption to be pivoted about without undue exertion. As the dark mass of the Nihlvarian great ship loomed out of the haze, barely sixty yards off by Thera's reckoning, Teylhar raised the rear end of the engine up a few inches and pulled the release lever. The device shuddered as its steel crossbeam straightened in a blur, the iron bolt transformed into a black streak. It birthed a twenty-foot spout of water as it struck the great ship's hull just below the waterline.

"Reload!" Teylhar called out, his crew of fellow artisans hurrying to ready the engine for another launch while Thera tried to gauge the damage already inflicted. At first she thought it minimal, but then noticed the mass of bubbles rising to the surface that told of water rushing into a sundered hull. She could also hear the alarmed shouts of those manning the oars on the vessel's lower decks. *Slaves*, she knew, quelling the sickening lurch in her gut at the thought of those imperilled souls chained to their benches while the sea began to flood in.

Turning, she exchanged a glance with Achier standing on the mid-deck with a small group of freed slaves. Each carried chisels and hammers in addition to their weapons. Since the grievous loss of innocent life at the Crusher Strait, Thera had allotted them the role of rescuing those they could in the coming battle. From the grim comprehension on Achier's face, she knew they faced a near impossible task this day.

Every victory exacts a cost, she thought, pushing the guilt away and returning her focus to the engine. Readying the contraption for a second shot required two full minutes of well-practised labour. A pair of craftsmen worked the great windlass that drew back the crossbeam, while three others manhandled a bolt onto the stock. By the time it was done, the *Great Wolf* was less than thirty yards from the great ship and had attracted the aggressive notice of the Nihlvarians on the cluster of smaller vessels. Arrows flew with increasing rapidity, forcing Thera to crouch as they whistled overhead. Her own archers replied in kind, though not before she heard the grunts and pained exclamations from her crew that told of barbs finding flesh.

Teylhar appeared not to notice the deadly hail, barely flinching as an arrow skittered from the release mechanism an inch from his hand. Raising the engine yet higher, he loosed again. This time the damage was more evident, the bolt striking a little to the left of the first, the shortened range ensuring a larger hole. The muted yells of the slaves within became screams as the hulking vessel began to list, water frothing as her stern subsided. Thera had seen many a ship founder by now and reckoned this one had perhaps a quarter turn of the glass before she sank completely.

"Ramming stroke!" she called out, raising the dreadaxe high, then pointing it at the clustered vessels to the great ship's rear. "Althsten! Put us among them!"

The storm of arrows briefly intensified as the *Great Wolf* charged towards the close-packed craft. Thera crouched at the prow, waiting for the thudding crunch that told of the warship colliding with the enemy. When it came, she raised the dreadaxe once more and stood, climbing up onto the rail to survey the scene before her. The *Great Wolf* had sundered the hull of a far smaller ship, the prow jammed into the opposing deck amid a forest of splintered timbers. The force of the impact had dislodged many others from their formation. Some were attempting to row clear, while others were keen to bring their new foe to battle. Their attempts were frustrated first by the disarrayed mass of bobbing vessels, then by the appearance of several more Isles ships, all coming on at ramming stroke. Thera watched the *Chainbreaker* smash into a wallowing Nihlvarian warship of equal size less than twenty paces away. Beyond her, the *Ohlira* swept in to plunge even deeper into the unfolding chaos.

Thera issued no orders for her *menda* to follow as she leaped from the prow. The words would have been lost in the overall din, and she knew they would already be scrambling to gather their weapons and hurry in her wake. She found the sundered deck she landed on free of enemies. Also, she noted with relief upon peering through the shattered boards, no slaves chained below. However, the screams still echoing from the sinking hull of the great ship made it clear there were plenty of souls nearby in need of salvation. Turning to confirm that Achier and his group were among those now pouring onto the wrecked Nihlvarian ship, she beckoned him on and ran for the adjoining vessel.

She was met this time by a hastily organised shield wall, only half a dozen strong and easily broken at the first rush. However, the subsequent melee quickly grew in size as Nihlvarians from neighbouring craft swarmed towards the scene of combat. Impatient to reach the great ship, Thera didn't restrain herself. Charging towards a trio of red-faced warriors, she ducked at the last instant to sweep the dreadaxe at their legs, leaving one clutching a stump and another reeling back so swiftly he tumbled into the sea. Undaunted, the third came at Thera, heaving a large two-handed broad sword with impressive speed, if not skill. Feeling the press of her own warriors at her back, Thera sidestepped the Nihlvarian's overhead swing, feinted a jab at his face then allowed Ragnalt to hack him down.

Glancing up, Thera realised they were under the great ship's stern now. It dipped lower with each passing moment, but they were still obliged to grab the ropes dangling from her rails in order to ascend to the deck. Once there, she engaged in a brief fight with a mixed group of sailors and warriors. The former mostly opted to leap over the side when she hacked down two of the latter. The arrival of Ragnalt and the bulk of her *menda* swept aside any further opposition, and the tilting upper deck was soon cleared of Nihlvarians.

"Save as many as you can," Thera told Achier, pointing to the nearest hatch. "Ragnalt, give him ten warriors to help."

Making for the ramp at the ship's prow, she shrank from the heat of the tall fires blazing to either side. She had hoped to turn and take measure of the state of the battle, but the smoke was a thick black fog here, forcing her to move on. Once upon the wall, a fortuitous breeze dispelled the haze enough for her to make out the struggle raging on the wharf below. A hundred or more Nihlvarians were engaged in ferocious combat with a far smaller contingent of Ascarlians. They were being gradually pushed back despite their desperate, near frenzied courage. One figure caught her eye, a large-bearded man wielding a crude, single-bladed axe with deadly skill. It occurred to Thera that she had never seen her great-grandfather fight before, and she found it a fascinating spectacle. He whirled the axe back and forth as if it weighed no more than a broom handle, cleaving skulls and limbs with every sweep. The bodies, maimed or dying, of those who had fought him lay in an untidy circle.

If this is him as an old man, Thera wondered, *what was he when young?*

It was his age that undid him, the axe moving fractionally too slow to parry the sword stroke of a tall Nihlvarian. The blade scored a cut on Gruinskard's face, creating a moment of distraction, enabling the swordsman to strike again, this time delivering a precise cut to the old man's wrist. Thera let out an involuntary shout at the sight of both axe and hand tumbling to the ground. Her great-grandfather, teeth clenched in pain and fury, collapsed to his knees, clutching the gushing stump while the swordsman drew his blade back for a killing blow.

Casting about, Thera spied a grappling rope nearby and lunged for it, knowing she would be too late. Yet, as she prepared to descend, she saw a dark streak part the smoke below and strike the swordsman full in the chest. The impact sent him flying back to land several yards away from Gruinskard. As Thera stared in surprise, she saw a slender shape sprinting through the smoke, flaxen hair trailing. Rushing to the fallen Nihlvarian, the figure wrenched the spear from his body and turned to confront the red-faced warriors rushing to encircle her. There were too many, Thera expecting her great-grandfather's saviour to die within seconds. But she didn't.

What came next happened so quickly, and seemed so utterly impossible, Thera wondered if she had momentarily slipped into a dream. The flaxen-haired woman made only a few movements, swaying low then angling her body while ducking her head, yet in doing so she evaded every blow aimed at her. Then she moved again, a fluid dance through and around her assail-ants, her spearpoint jabbing. When she had whirled beyond reach of their weapons, she paused and watched them all wither, each falling with blood leaking from a single, fatal wound.

"What in Ulthnir's name was that?" Ragnalt said, his breathless exclama-tion shocking Thera from immobility.

"Still plenty more down there," she said, taking up the grappling rope and launching herself from the parapet. She reached the wharf in a few swings, then ran for the slumped form of Margnus Gruinskard. The spear wielder stood close to his side, levelling her weapon at Thera, then relaxing when she made out a face free of red ink. Fighting raged around them, a score of Ascarlians charging from the smoke to battle the surviving Nihlvarians. The combat was fierce at first, but put beyond doubt when Ragnalt led her *menda* into the fray.

Hearing a guttural exclamation from her great-grandfather, Thera crouched at his side. Pulling a clean muslin cloth from her breastplate, she wrapped it around his stump. "There's a man in my crew who can seal this," she said. "It'll hurt though."

Gruinskard replied with another wordless sound that might have been an attempt at a laugh. He coughed and spat something dark onto the ground before putting his remaining hand on her shoulder and levering himself upright. "At least it was my bad hand," he groaned. "It seems I'm cursed to lose a bit of myself every time I fight for this fucking city!"

"They're done, my queen," Ragnalt said, striding from the haze. Thera was pleased to see he had once again avoided acquiring any more scars. "Sounds like there's still fighting to east and west."

"Best send them towards the Gate Wall," Gruinskard grated as the woman with the spear placed his stricken arm in a sling. "If they take that, we can still lose this day."

"Not without a fleet, they won't," Thera said, but nodded to Ragnalt. After quickly assembling the *menda* into rough order, he led them towards the eastern end of the harbour.

"This is Elvine Jurest," her great-grandfather said, nodding to the young woman at his side. "Renowned scholar and Spear Maiden of Olversahl. I think I told you about her."

"She doesn't look much like a scholar," Thera said, looking over the maiden's besmirched and bloodied form. She realised the scholar was far younger than she had first thought, barely more than a girl. Yet, for those few impossible seconds, she had seemed a demi-goddess from some ancient tale of the Uhltvar.

"But you look very much like a queen," Elvine said. Her voice was strained and her gaze had the overly bright, unblinking quality of one unaccustomed to killing. Her fingers twitched continually on the haft of her spear, as if she greatly desired to put it down. *The Spear of the Altvar*, Thera recalled. *So it's real.*

"Lore," the scholar said, stepping towards Thera, gaze lit by a near desperate plea. "Did you kill her?" The spear clattered from her grasp as she clutched the vambraces on Thera's arms. All strength seemed to seep from her then, Thera catching her when her legs gave way. She saw a great weariness overtake the maiden, her eyes dulling and the tension leaching from her body. Thera worried she might have suffered a wound but could see no blood upon her skin or garb.

"You see . . ." Elvine Jurest, Spear Maiden of Olversahl, murmured before Thera saw the light in her eyes flicker into something far deeper than sleep. "If you do it . . ." she went on, voice diminishing into the faintest whisper, "I won't have to. And . . . I don't want to hate this much . . ."

CHAPTER FORTY-FOUR

Ruhlin

The bear came to him as he slept, for which he was grateful. Until it appeared he had been lost in a welter of nightmares. These were worse than the dreadful conjunction of terror and memory that had plagued him during the voyage from Ayl-Ah-Swahl all those months ago. The sadistic dream smith lurking in his mind now had even more fuel for its terrible forge. So he was subjected to repeated scenarios in which he was forced to watch Aleida inflict various tortures on Ryma's small, screaming form before subjecting herself to inventive mutilation.

"You left us," she told him at one point, her eyes dangling from her sockets by tendrils of gristle. "Walked willingly into the old man's trap. What other choice did I have?"

Tuhlan and Julette were, of course, especially prominent in this cavalcade of horrors. "Why'd you kill me, dear boy?" the pirate asked him, grunting in pain while Tuhlan dragged the wet ropes of her intestines from the hole he had carved in her gut. "Not that I mind," she went on, bloody froth staining her teeth as she afforded him one of her signature grins, "just curious is all."

His tormentors all fled when the bear came lumbering out of the swirling fog. Bellowing a roar of dismissal, it chased the nightmares away before coming to Ruhlin's side. He sat shivering and naked beside the smoking remains of a campfire, awaiting the moment when Julette and Tuhlan would take turns cutting strips of flesh from his limbs. The bear's proximity warmed him, its steaming breaths banishing his chills. Although he suspected this would soon transform into yet another farce of suffering, Ruhlin welcomed the warmth, even as he eyed the wicked barbs of the beast's claws.

He experienced only faint surprise when it spoke, the words flowing from its mouth in Achela's voice. "You recall what I told you?" it asked.

"What must happen will happen," Ruhlin replied in a quavering croak. Her words from that day in the *wuhltra* of Turihmvek, when she had revealed her long-laid plan to free her niece and the man he now understood she had come to see as the promised *Telchak*.

"Yes." The bear let out a sorrowful huff as it settled back on its haunches. "When I said those words, I didn't fully understand their meaning, nor the cost that would be required of both of us. Me, my life. You, something worse." The bear turned to him, the sparse fur of its brow furrowed in contrition. "I am sorry, husband to my niece. For all you have suffered, and all you will suffer."

"You saved me before," Ruhlin said. "Can you not do so again?" The plaintive desperation in his voice shamed him, but he was past such trivial concerns as pride now.

"I am dead." She rolled her massive shoulders in a shrug. "And the influence of the dead upon the living is far less potent than you would believe."

"What . . ." Ruhlin swallowed, forcing the words past his fear-clenched teeth, for he feared the answer more than he feared the return of his nightmares. "What will happen now?"

"I told you once that a spark cannot birth a fire without kindling. The spark caught, now you must endure the fire." The bear leaned closer, breath hot upon his skin. "And though your pains will be great, endure it you will. What must happen will happen."

When the beast opened its mouth, he expected it to sink those massive teeth into his flesh, but instead, its long tongue emerged to lick his face. The chilly wetness of it was shocking, leaving him gasping, his breath coming in ragged heaves until he heard a fresh voice.

"You still able to think?" it asked.

Squinting, Ruhlin realised the bear had vanished, replaced by a blurred outline of a face. Blinking to clear his vision, he beheld the red-inked, angular face of the Nihlvarian from the *Ochra-mah*. An instant bout of fury set a fire in his core, his muscles swelling until the chill of the *stagna* blossomed in his chest.

"You remember me," the Nihlvarian said with a grin, his eyes locked on the band of metal embedded in Ruhlin's flesh. "Good. Quite a potent mix I shoved into your veins. Not everyone survives it with their wits intact." His face took on a far more serious cast. "You going to settle down, or do I have to administer another dose? We're close to our destination and I'd rather not present the Vortigurn with a drooling half-wit. Your choice, though."

Face quivering, Ruhlin forced himself to nod.

"Very wise." The Nihlvarian smiled again, and the chill vanished, leaving Ruhlin slumped and gasping. He realised his cheek was pressed into rough planking and smelled the signature combination of brine and lamp oil that told of a ship. A glance at his surroundings revealed the bars of a cell, not unlike the one he had found himself consigned to when this journey began. *The river lands leading to the sea*, he remembered. *They had a ship waiting. This was carefully planned.*

"I'm Silvahk, incidentally," the Nihlvarian said. "Ventra to the Vortigurn. Thought it best to introduce myself since we're likely to be spending so much time together."

Glaring up at his affable visage, Ruhlin was reminded of Radylf, Aerling Eldryk's whip-man. Another cheerfully cruel soul who had died a fitting death during the escape from the *wuhltra*. Ruhlin made a silent oath that this one's demise would be equally appropriate.

"Tell me something, for I find myself curious," Silvahk said, unperturbed by the stark hate shining from Ruhlin's gaze. "Did you give Deyna a quick death or make it last?"

Doesn't know she's alive, Ruhlin decided. Which meant Olchar hadn't felt obliged to enlighten his Nihlvarian masters as to the Tuhlvyr's survival. It also made him reconsider the defeat of Deyna's small army. Had it all been a sacrificial ruse? An easy victory to buttress his confidence before Olchar's betrayal. If so, such a plan bespoke a subtle mind.

"Slow," Ruhlin grunted. "And I made her beg first, like I'll do with you."

He expected either scornful laughter or anger, perhaps a punishing flare of icy agony from the *stagna*. Instead, Silvahk's face remained carefully impassive. "I'm not one for offering unasked for advice," he said, "but know this, my fire-blooded friend, anything you do from here on will only happen with the Vortigurn's consent. You're his prisoner, his property, not mine. So—" his lips formed an amused grimace "—if you ask him to let you kill me, there won't be much I can do if he says yes. But you will have to ask *very* nicely."

The Nihlvarian drew a dagger from his belt and rapped the pommel against the bars, birthing a loud clang. "Bring water!" he barked. "And fresh clothes. Time we made him presentable."

Night had fallen when they took him ashore. Having warned Ruhlin that a single step in the wrong direction would cause him to ignite the *stagna*, Silvahk led him down the gangway to a carriage flanked by an escort of torch-bearing guards. Looking around, Ruhlin saw that the harbour was free of other ships for a distance of a hundred yards in each direction. Also, there were no stevedores on the quayside. His gaze was soon drawn to the ascending lights of the city beyond the harbour. It was too dark to discern much detail, but he quickly recognised this as a far larger conurbation than any he had seen before, dwarfing Turihmvek and the other towns in the north.

"Welcome to the Citadel," Silvahk said. "Capital of the Vortigurn's domain." He gestured for Ruhlin to enter the carriage, a box-like contrivance, all black save for the inverted version of Ulthnir's sigil painted in red upon its sides.

Ruhlin saw little through the small window in the carriage's door as a team of four horses drew it from the docks and into the city. He caught glimpses of lantern-lit windows and narrow streets, but no sign of people. *The curfew*, he remembered, thinking back to that abortive foray in Speltsaer. *The Vortigurn prefers his people remain indoors at night.*

He did gain an impression of ascending successive inclines as the carriage wound its way along several switchback avenues. This Citadel had apparently been constructed on the slope of a broad and tall hill. Given the status of his captor, Ruhlin assumed, correctly, that their journey would end at the top.

Upon being told by Silvahk to exit the carriage, he looked out at a port that was even larger than he first thought. Lanterns and torches flickered all along the slope of a curved ridge line overlooking a broad bay where several dozen ships lay at anchor. Although he had never seen them, Ruhlin felt that this would rival even the fabled cities of the southern seas for sheer size.

"Don't dawdle, my friend," Silvahk said. "He's expecting delivery of his prize."

Turning, Ruhlin's eyes tracked up the tall stone walls of the largest free-standing structure he had ever seen. The *wuhltra* he had been forced to fight in were dwarfed by this gigantically enlarged version of an Uhlwald's hall. As his gaze roamed the numerous shuttered windows and high, buttressed walls, he realised it was not one hall, but many, all conjoined in a near chaotic sprawl that covered a good portion of the ridge's summit.

"The Unfinished Hall," Silvahk said, gesturing for Ruhlin to precede him as they made for the tall oaken gate. "So called because it's still being built after Ulthnir knows how many centuries. The Vortigurn has many whims when it comes to his hall. There are whole galleries and towers designed to his very exacting specifications that he's never once set foot in. Although, that may be just the idle gossip of servants with scant regard for their own lives. Unlike me, I assure you."

A small door set into the gate opened at their approach, Ruhlin stepping through to find another armed escort waiting. Numbering twenty in all, they all wore uniform armour emblazoned with the Vortigurn's sigil. The faces beneath each iron helm were also similar in their hardened hostility.

"Don't mind them," Silvahk said, motioning for Ruhlin to move on. "As his personal guard, they don't have much else to do save regard anyone who comes within a mile of the Vortigurn's hall as a bloodthirsty assassin."

The guards fell in on either side as they made their way up a broad set of stairs to the large structure beyond. The doors were flung open at their approach and Ruhlin found himself marching along a corridor of marble floors and tall oaken pillars. The guards' boots echoed louder when they came to a broad chamber. Here, the beams ascended to a ceiling lost to shadow, for it was lit with only a few torches. Ruhlin could see nothing of particular interest apart from the scale and emptiness of the space, yet he detected a palpable agitation in his escort. It wasn't just Silvahk whose eyes began to rove the shadows. The guards were equally unsettled, their skin beading with sweat, as if they feared what might come lurching from the gloom.

They stood in tense silence for a time until the faint tap of wood upon stone began to echo. Soon, a hunched figure stepped from the shadows, leaning heavily on a stick as he hobbled towards them. When he came fully into the light, Ruhlin looked upon the most ravaged face he could remember seeing. This man wasn't just old, he was ruined by time. His skin sagged upon the bones of his skull, discoloured and flaking. His neck appeared to be covered in boils, some of them leaking pus onto his already stained clothing. The stench he gave off caught the throat with its sickly melange of decay and unwashed flesh.

This is the Vortigurn? Ruhlin wondered, finding it scarcely believable that a figure who might die from a hefty slap could command the fearful loyalty of so many.

"Fire-blooded, eh?" the figure enquired in a throat wheeze, coming closer to Ruhlin. His nostrils twitched as he sniffed, Ruhlin marvelling that he could smell anything through his own stink. "You sure?" he demanded, swivelling towards Silvahk. Unlike the rest of him, his eyes appeared untouched by illness, dark and gleaming as they fixed the Nihlvarian with a demanding glare.

"Saw it with my own eyes," Silvahk replied, Ruhlin finding the absence of respect in his voice curious. *Is this how he addresses his king?*

The hunched figure made a wet, dismissive sound with his tongue. Hobbling yet closer to Ruhlin, he flicked a hand that resembled a malformed spider at Silvahk and the guards. "Get you gone, then," he said. "I'll present him . . ."

"No," Silvahk stated, tone flat but also very precise. "You will not. As Ventra, I was instructed by the Vortigurn to bring this one to him, and I will do so."

Watching the ancient man reveal yellow black teeth in a sneer, Ruhlin remembered what Deyna had said about her audience with the Vortigurn. *No actual courtiers, save one. The vilest, most grasping soul you could ever meet.*

"I know how to tweak a *stagna* as well as you, boy," the malformed man said. "And much besides. Don't presume to test me . . ."

His words died when a fresh sound echoed through the chamber. It wasn't especially loud or remarkable, simply the opening and closing of a door so far as Ruhlin could tell, yet it sent every other soul present into rigid silence. Deeper into the chamber, a circle of torches created a dim pool of yellow light, to which all eyes now swung. The man who stepped into view was a stark contrast to the wretched, ill-humoured servant, standing tall and unbowed. He was of impressive build, broad of shoulder and long of limb, and clad in simple dark-hued trews and jerkin. Ruhlin noticed after a moment of frozen silence that he was the only one returning the newcomer's scrutiny. The bent-backed servant, Silvahk and the guards all stood with their eyes averted.

"Only Silvahk," the tall man said, voice mild but still carrying to all corners of this vast space.

He said nothing else, but the response of the guards was immediate, all turning smartly about and marching from the hall. The bent-back took longer to leave. Casting a hate-filled glare at Silvahk, he afforded Ruhlin a longer look of fierce, near desperate scrutiny, before hobbling away into the gloom.

"Come," the tall man said, raising a hand to beckon them forth. As he approached, Ruhlin made out his features, seeing a man who might have been called handsome but for the austere leanness of his face. A short beard, peppered in grey, covered his chin and a mane of black hair swept back from his head to his shoulders. The expression with which he greeted Ruhlin was one of focused curiosity, a man studying something of importance but not danger.

When they had come within a dozen feet of the tall man, Silvahk put a hand on Ruhlin's shoulder, bringing him to a halt. "As you ordered, so I obey, Vortigurn," the Ventra said, lowering his head.

The tall man didn't appear to hear him, angling his head and stepping closer to Ruhlin, he asked, "Have you a name, young man?"

Ruhlin saw little point in silence, or deceit. "Ruhlin ehs Kestryg," he said. "Of Ayl-Ah-Swahl."

"Ah." The Vortigurn's brows rose in faint interest. "A wild place, as I remember it. Barely a few hovels clinging to a hostile shore. Do the white whales still come every year?"

"They do," Ruhlin said. "And there are no hovels there."

The Vortigurn's lips thinned in a smile, faint and quickly gone. "Your name is ill fitting," he said. "We shall have to provide you with a better one. A title fit for the Vortigurn's champion."

"I am not your champion," Ruhlin stated. Silvahk instantly tensed at his side, a sudden chill spreading from the *stagna*.

"No," the Vortigurn said, holding up a hand to forestall the punishment. "A fire-blood does not respond to pain the way a mortal does. They can be restrained but not conditioned. That requires . . ." a distant cast crept into the Vortigurn's eyes ". . . something more. Besides." He smiled his faint smile again. "I will not begrudge my champion his attachment to a name he has borne for years. We grow fond of them, do we not, like an old scar that tells a story? I have had many names, and find they are more easily cast aside with each passing year. For I've come to understand that, ultimately, they mean nothing. But that first one, the one I carried through war and besmirched with murder, that was the hardest to throw away. For they would call it out with such ardour, such devotion, my lost, forgotten people. It pained me to think of them, and so I decided upon a new name. But still, in the darker hours, I hear their voices echoing through the ages, from those days when they called me Velgard."

The story continues in...

Book Three of the Age of Wrath

ACKNOWLEDGEMENTS

Thanks to Paul Field for once again proofing the first draft. Also, thanks to my agent Paul Lucas, my editors James Long and Bradley Englert, and everyone at Orbit books on both sides of the pond for their efforts in bringing this book to fruition.

MEET THE AUTHOR

Ellie Grace Photography

ANTHONY RYAN lives in London and is the *New York Times* bestselling author of the Raven's Shadow and Draconis Memoria series. He previously worked in a variety of roles for the UK government, but now writes full time. His interests include art, science and the unending quest for the perfect pint of real ale.

Find out more about Anthony Ryan and other Orbit authors by registering for the Orbit newsletter at orbitbooks.net.

Follow us:

f **/orbitbooksUS**

𝕏 /orbitbooks

▶ /orbitbooks

Join our mailing list
to receive alerts on our
latest releases and deals.

orbitbooks.net

Enter our monthly
giveaway for the chance
to win some epic prizes.

orbitloot.com